ERIN'S CHILD

Sheelagh Kelly was born in York in 1948, but now lives with her husband in subtropical Queensland. She attended Knavesmire Secondary School for Girls, left at the age of 15 and went to work as a book-keeper. She has written for pleasure since she was a small child but not until 1980 were the seeds for her first novel, *A Long Way from Heaven*, sown when she developed an interest in genealology and local history and decided to trace her ancestors' story, thereby acquiring an abiding fascination with the quirks of human nature. *A Long Way from Heaven* was followed by *For My Brother's Sins*, *Erin's Child*, *My Father, My Son*, *Dickie*, *Shoddy Prince* and *A Complicated Woman*.

ALSO BY SHEELAGH KELLY

SHEELAGH KELLY

Erin's Child

HarperCollins*Publishers*

For my aunt
Beatrice Wilcox

HarperCollins*Publishers*
77–85 Fulham Palace Road,
Hammersmith, London W6 8JB

This paperback edition 1999

3 5 7 9 8 6 4 2

First published in Great Britain by
Century Hutchinson Limited 1987

ISBN 0 00 651158 9

Set in Ehrhardt

Printed and bound in Great Britain by
Omnia Books Limited, Glasgow

PART ONE

℘

1875–1878

CHAPTER ONE

The pain was excruciating. Her peaceful existence had come to this abrupt end when she had suddenly found herself grasped by two constrictive hands and had jumped with the unexpectedness of it. After a moment the squeezing had subsided and she had nestled back down into the dark warmth, the fingers of one hand splayed over her cheek as she slept. But then the manipulation had begun again, continuing at regular intervals until now she was forced head downwards into a dark, narrow tunnel of pain, pushed and pummelled unmercifully. Each time the squeezing passed so she would slip back a little, reluctant to leave her snug haven; but just as peace was about to reclaim her the arms of pain would wrap themselves around her once more, compressing, hurting. With each spasm her mouth puckered into a tight circle of protest.

How long this endured she could not gauge. Time was unknown to her. She only knew that her head felt about to be crushed. Inside her skull she could hear the bones groaning at the onslaught. She could no longer move her limbs. Her whole being was consumed by agony. For the first time in her existence she knew fear; fear that it might never end.

Then, without warning, she was ejected from the tunnel with one violent thrust, spluttering and choking, into a world of blinding light and chaos. Lungs, until now superfluous, ballooned on either side of her thumping heart. The deafening noise which had accompanied her liberation now subsided into two levels – one, an anxious

5

questioning tone, the other, a low answering murmur. Trying to move her head she could only make out vague, blurry shapes amid the gleam, before feeling herself being grasped by the two hands again – were they the same? – lifted from the warm dampness and transferred to a place so icy cold that her arms and legs shot out at the shock of it against her nakedness. Slowly her body warmth began to ebb away as she lay there, helpless.

One of the shapes appeared over her again, mouthing unintelligible sounds. Then everything was obscured as a suffocating mass came down on her and covered her face, cutting off the life-giving air. She tried to struggle but was too weak, too small. Life would soon be over before it had begun.

'In heaven's name what're you trying to do?' Sam Teale burst into the room, his eager anticipation turning to shock at the scene he now witnessed. Snatching the pillow from the midwife's hands he hurled it to the far side of the room, then stared down at his newborn daughter in consternation.

'It's the best way, Mr Teale.' The midwife defended her action, voice furtive. She had seen many such babes go the same merciful way. 'Kinder for everyone. She won't have much of a life, you know.'

Sam's questioning face looked down on the child – his child – still daubed with her mother's blood, caked in the black substance that her bowels had secreted in that safe place; cast aside like some piece of offal. There was nothing wrong with her. She was beautiful, beautiful.

The midwife, seeing his incomprehension, picked up the babe and turned it over on her big red palm, revealing the crooked spine that rose up like an obscene question mark under the translucent skin. Tentatively, the father reached out to touch the offending slur.

'She's so cold,' he whispered. Then his pity turned to anger – anger at God, anger at the midwife. The same gentle hand that had touched the baby grabbed a blanket from the basinette and wrapped it around the child, finally tucking the little bundle inside his baggy shirt to transmit some of his body heat to her. He fought to hang onto his manliness, but lost. Bending his head he cried into his chest, the tears spilling onto the child's face. Her cheek encountered his nipple and reflex opened her mouth. Her father laughed then through his tears and cradled her to him, sobbing quietly, half-proud, half-cheated.

'Sam?' Erin's weak query jolted his preoccupation and he went slowly through the dancing shadows of the candle towards the bed. The birth had been long and difficult. She was very tired, too tired to question the midwife who had informed her that the long-awaited child was stillborn. She looked up at him with hooded eyes, eyes that could not cry. Her ebony hair flowed over the pillow in long, damp tendrils. Sam could not dispute the midwife's competence when dealing with the mother – his wife had been washed and made comfortable, clean sheets had been put on the bed and all the covers tucked in neatly – but still he was angry, incensed that this woman should have the audacity to kill his child with nary a word of consultation nor compassion.

'I'm sorry about the baby, Sam.' The tone of her soft Irish lilt begged his forgiveness before drowsiness closed her eyes. Her piquant face was drawn, pallid from the agony she had endured. Purple hollows registered her lassitude.

He wondered whether to tell her now, then decided that it would wait; she might accept it better after she had slept a while. 'Don't worry about anything, love. It's going to be fine. Just let yourself rest. We'll talk later.'

A snuffling noise from within the folds of his shirt showed that the baby was regaining some of its warmth. Erin forced open puzzled eyes. 'What was that, Sam?' When he did not answer immediately she dragged herself up on one elbow and repeated the question. Hesitantly, he pulled the minute bundle from his shirt and laid it gently in the crook of her arm. 'But . . . you said she was dead,' Erin weakly accused the midwife, who flung a scathing, purse-lipped glare at Sam.

7

'It's better dead she would be,' she muttered darkly, brawny arms hugging the pillow that Sam had tossed aside.

'What does she mean?' Puzzlement at first, then, 'Oh, my baby! My baby!' Erin, suddenly awake, prised the blanket away from the tiny, crumpled face. Her eyes pored over it as she touched every perfect feature with an exploratory finger. 'Why, Sam, why?' She looked up at him, frowning. 'I don't understand.'

He told her, as gently as possible, that this exquisite child, their beautiful, lovely daughter who had taken so long to conceive would never be like other children. Erin turned her perplexity back to the child. 'She's deformed, Erin,' blurted Sam, unable to think of words to couch the tragedy.

There was brief silence. Then the tears that had hitherto refused to come now flowed in torrents. 'Oh, my poor baby! The poor little soul,' wept the young mother as Sam folded both her and the child into his arms and cried with her. The newborn watched them with grave, unfocusing eyes, while the midwife pretended to busy herself. 'What have I done that God should punish my baby?'

'Erin, Erin.' He pressed his wet face to hers. 'It's nowt you've done. You could never be bad . . .'

'It must be! God's sent this to punish me.'

'No! I was angry at Him at first, but God wouldn't do a thing like that. You're not to blame Him or yourself. It's just one o' the things that get thrown at us from time to time.'

'But why us, Sam?' begged Erin tearfully. 'We've waited so long for her. It's not fair. Why does it never happen to people like Mrs Johnson? Oh, God forgive my wickedness, but she's got eight perfect children and doesn't give a fig about any of them. If they didn't beg and scavenge their food from neighbours they'd get nothing. Why isn't our child perfect, Sam? What harm have we ever done anyone? Why, why, why?'

Each repetition brought her nearer to the brink of hysteria. The midwife intervened. 'Men! Look at the state you've got her into with your meddling.' She elbowed Sam out of the way and made to take the baby. 'If you hadn't poked your neb in there'd be no need for any o' this.'

Erin hugged the baby protectively to her breast and glared up at the intruder. 'Get out! Get out! You were going to kill my baby. Murderer, murderer, get out!'

'Calm down, love.' Sam attempted to soothe his wife as the midwife stepped out of the line of fire. 'Don't go upsetting yourself. She's safe now.' As he spoke he motioned violently for the nurse to leave the room. 'Please, Erin love, do calm yourself – look, you're makin' the babby cry.'

His wife's hysteria waned as the baby's howl rose above her sobbing, and though her grief continued her emotions were now under control. 'I'm sorry, Sam. I'm sorry.'

'You've nowt to be sorry about, lass.' Sam kissed the tear-drenched cheek and wiped her running nose with his own handkerchief. 'An' nowt to worry about neither, your mam's downstairs, she'll take us all in hand.'

'Aye, Mam'll look after us,' sniffed Erin to the baby who was quiet once more. 'She won't let anyone harm ye. May God forgive that woman for her terrible thought – ye won't let her in Sam, will ye?' Her eyes were round with alarm. 'Don't let her near the baby, she might . . .'

He shook his head. 'No, the baby's safe now.'

'But ye won't let her in? Promise?' At his firm promise she regained her calm and all was silent for a while. Her attention became so riveted on the child that Sam felt a wave of loneliness wash over him, as if he were not part of all this. Turning from the bed he slowly made his way over to the window, leaned his blond head against the curtained wall and watched the evening shower sluice down the pane.

It had been this way since Erin's own waters had broken in the early hours of the day. In fact there had barely been a week he could recall this year when it had not rained. The exceptionally wet summer would make for a poor harvest. That was not of personal concern to Sam – apart from the sympathy he felt for his neighbours – for his money was in cattle. Oh, for the sight of those lush green

9

meadows speckled with red and white milkers instead of these dreary, rain-lashed streets. They had arrived at Erin's parents' home in York a week ago. Their own home had few facilities and with young Ralph Dobbins to take care of Sam's herd of Shorthorns it had been decided that Erin should give birth to her firstborn here where it was safer, where the love and support of her family would be at close hand. Safe! He issued a silent snort of irony. As for love and support, well . . . he hoped they would still be forthcoming, for she would need both of them desperately now.

His mind went again to his herd – his pride and joy. He thought of all the healthy calves that he had raised. Yet, when it came to his own child . . . That he was in possession of the herd plus the sixty acres of grazing land was thanks to his mother-in-law's generous settlement on her daughter's marriage. As the son of a poor farm labourer Sam would never have aspired to such grand ideas, but he was not too proud to accept this gift from Thomasin Feeney, seeing it not as charity as his father might have done, but merely commonsense. He loved his wife dearly, so why inflict hardship on her if it was unnecessary? He was glad now that he had taken the decision to go into dairy farming instead of growing crops. Sam had grown to love those cows – he liked the company of all animals. Some people might have considered this as rather an anomaly for an ex-butcher, but not anyone who knew Sam, who was a soft-hearted chap.

He rubbed a hand around his unshaven jaw. There was barely a rasp as the hand travelled over a face much younger than its thirty-one years. He could have been taken for a lad with his ruddy complexion and cheeky grin – when it was in evidence. The reflection in the darkened window showed a man suddenly burdened with responsibility, one he found difficult to accept.

The combined glare of oil lamp and candle on the windowpane turned the rain to liquid gold. He stood there watching its slithering journey to the sill. It made him feel lonelier than ever. How was he going to tell them? They were all waiting downstairs to hear the news – his parents-in-law, Grandmother Fenton, Erin's brother . . . how could he go down there and say, 'Your grandchild is a cripple.'

With a sigh he turned back to the bed; the canopied bed with its pillars and headboard of polished yew, its expensive counterpane, its heavily-tasselled drapes, the embossed wallpaper . . . a far cry from his own modest accommodation. But the thought was not a resentful one. He was well-acquainted with the Feeneys' humble beginnings – more humble than his own, truth to tell – and Erin's parents deserved everything in their fine house. God knows they had met with some bad luck in their time – and now the young couple had landed them with some more.

Erin pushed a stray lock of hair behind her ear and tore her face away from the child's to watch his approach. Giving birth had made her more beautiful than ever, thought Sam, if that were at all possible. Though her eyes had always been the kind that rotated one's belly just to gaze into them, maternity had added a glowing depth. She was like something unearthly.

His wife was speaking. 'Forgive me,' he said, stretching and then sitting down on the edge of the bed. 'I was miles away.'

Erin repeated her question. 'What are we going to do?'

He ran a finger over her cheek, then dropped his hand and shrugged hopelessly as he stared at the baby. 'I don't know . . . just love her, I suppose.'

The tiredness had been miraculously displaced by her concern for the child, and this showed in the irritability of her response. She had expected something more constructive. 'Well, of course we'll love her! Everyone will – how could they fail to? Just look at her, Sam. She's so gorgeous. But we must be more positive. She isn't going to be able to live the rest of her days on our love. We won't always be here. For one thing we must make sure we protect her from all the terrible things that people will say about her – the cruel names.'

11

He cupped her face with his square hands and smiled into her hair as he embraced her. 'You're ahead o' yourself. She's nobbut ten minutes old.'

But she reiterated her intent. 'I'm serious, Sam. As the person who's to blame for her condition 'tis up to me to make things right for her.'

'Erin, don't take this upon yourself. How can you be to blame? I had a hand in her creation too, y'know – more than a hand.' His eyes twinkled but the smile that his wife returned was full of sadness. She covered his tanned fingers with her own cool ones and was silent.

Then, 'You're not thinking she's damaged because . . .' The question trailed off, unfinished, but they both knew its content. Erin and Sam had been married in name for more than four years, but the marriage had only been a physical actuality for the past nine months. A blissful nine months admittedly, but that was only just reward for the torment of the three previous years; a torment born from Erin's sheer terror of the act of love. It was those remembered nights – the screams, the accusations, the revulsion – that now caused Erin to assume guilt for the child's deformity.

'That's rubbish!' he vociferated. 'You're not to blame, d'you hear?'

'I can't help it, Sam.'

'No! It's too bloody stupid.' His blunt Yorkshire manner percolated his concern. 'I won't have you talkin' that way. First you blame God, then you blame yourself . . .'

'Somebody's responsible, Sam, and it certainly isn't you.' Sam had been so good and kind even at the height of her childish fear. It had never crossed his decent God-fearing mind to force her.

'For pity's sake, why does someone have to be to blame? It's just an accident of birth. Like I said, one of those things. Will pinning the blame on someone make our daughter any better? You're not to feel guilty. I forbid it. You'll only make yourself poorly, an' then where will our little girl be?'

12

They both looked down on her. She had fallen asleep, the tiny pink mouth working unconsciously.

'She's like a little fairy, isn't she?' whispered Erin who, behind her smile, could not banish the self-indictment. Whatever Sam might say it was all her fault. But she wouldn't allow that to spoil her daughter's life. The child would have what Erin had planned for a normal, healthy daughter: a first-class education, the thing which she herself had coveted above all else; the prize she had never managed to win. Of course it was not so important to Erin now, she had Sam and a good life, but this little one would never be denied the things her mother had. 'You'll not scrub floors like your mammy did, my pretty colleen,' murmured Erin to the baby. 'No one is ever going to look down on you.'

Sam, feeling left out again, raised the question of names. They had chosen two before the birth – Dominic, after Sam's father if the child had been male, and Thomasin, after Erin's stepmother. Secretly, Erin would have liked to name the child Mary after her own dead mother, but knowing how this would hurt Thomasin had kept the thought to herself. Now it seemed to Erin that neither name was suitable for this baby. This ill-formed child with its exquisite face.

'We'll call her Belle,' she decided on impulse. 'She'll be named for her beauty an' be damned to anyone who cares to argue.'

And so, as his wife's fatigue overcame her desire to nurse the child, Sam gently picked up his sleeping daughter and, swallowing his trepidation, carried her downstairs to introduce her to the family.

However, it was not left to Sam to dampen their expectations. The midwife, whilst not specific, had made it plain that there was something drastically wrong upstairs. When Sam appeared on the threshold of the drawing room bearing his daughter there was no rush of congratulation but a show of apprehensive faces.

It was a spacious room, untrammelled with the usual

13

fashionable clutter. All the Feeneys' assets had been lost in a terrible fire. Though it was not lack of cash that was responsible for the sparse furnishings – everything had been covered by insurance – it was simply that to fill a house of this size took time and that was one commodity which Thomasin Feeney could not spare. What few decorations there were gave a pleasing effect, however – deep blue velvet drapes drawn against the night's downpour, the walls covered in silver-grey paper and edged with dove-grey architraving. Above, the crystal lighting arrangement was topped by an expansive and intricate ceiling rose. Sam wavered on the perimeter of the Persian carpet, unwilling to answer the collective question that was on their faces.

Erin's father was the first to rise from a brocade-upholstered sofa on which he had been seated with his wife. Patrick Feeney, at fifty-five still as straight and tall as he had been at thirty, if perhaps a little more solid these days, came hesitantly towards his son-in-law, the query in his pale-blue eyes manifesting itself with difficulty. 'It's Erin, isn't it?' The Mayo accent was still detectable even after almost thirty years on English soil. 'Something's happened to her?'

Sam was quick to right the assumption as the others rose, too. 'No, no she's fine. She's sleeping now.'

Patrick indicated the bundle in Sam's arms. 'We thought it was the baby at first . . . the midwife wouldn't tell us – please, Sam, if it's Erin I'd rather know.'

Sam came further into the room and moved through the network of chairs to the hearth where the log fire added false cheer to the gas-lit room.

'Please, Sam, don't keep us in purgatory.' Thomasin ached to hold her grandchild, but could not touch it till she knew the fate of her step-daughter.

'It's not Erin,' repeated Sam, staring into the flickering fire. 'You can see her when she wakes up.' He turned to face them. 'It's the baby. She's . . .' He examined each waiting face. 'She's deformed.' What a bloody ugly word.

14

Thomasin put her hand to her mouth and exchanged looks with her husband and son.

'Well, can I take it none of you want to hold her now?' asked Sam defensively when the silence grew too much for him.

They were around him instantly. 'Oh, Sam! Sam dear, of course we do.' Thomasin lifted the baby gingerly while Patrick clamped a supportive hand to Sam's shoulder. The deformity must be very slight, there was no evidence of it on her face at least. 'Oh, she's beautiful! Look, Mother.' She held the child in the direction of Hannah Fenton who made a sound which no amount of charity could have construed as anything other than distaste and shuffled back to the circle of chairs, leaning heavily on her walking stick.

John Feeney, Erin's brother, came forward. Still encumbered by the childhood nickname of Sonny he had now matured enough for it to be of no concern to him. He bent his auburn head over the slumbering baby. There was a sensitivity to his eye that was not evident in his build – Sonny looked more like a navvy than the artist he was. 'She's like her mother,' he tendered, to which Patrick agreed.

'Beautiful, Sonny,' he murmured in his soft Irish brogue.

Sam was aware of three pairs of eyes flitting involuntarily over the concealed body, searching for the imperfection. 'It's her back,' he provided quietly. 'Her legs, too.' And taking possession of his daughter he gently pulled aside the blanket to reveal just a portion of her twisted body.

Tears welled instantly in Thomasin's grey eyes. Sam expected her to take the baby from him again, but instead she turned her back and moved away muttering, 'The poor bairn.'

It was Patrick who held out his arms and said, as Sam laid the child in them, 'We'll call in the doctor first thing tomorrow. She'll have the best attention money can buy. Sure, ye never know, it may not be as bad as it looks.' He

15

cringed as he realised he'd said the wrong thing, adding, 'They can do all sorts these days.'

Unconvinced, Sam enquired after the midwife and was informed by his brother-in-law that she had left. 'That's just as well I suppose,' sighed Sam. 'I've orders from Erin not to let her back in.'

'She didn't look too pleased when she came down,' said Patrick, cradling his new grand-daughter fondly. 'I've seen more amiable gargoyles.' Sam revealed what had taken place upstairs. 'God dammit!' stormed the older man. 'It's as well I didn't know about that before else she'd've gone out feet first, the filthy bitch.'

'Maybe she was just doing what she thought was right.' The comment was Thomasin's. Surprise and accusation met her when she turned back to the circle.

'How can ye say such a thing, Tommy! Didn't ye hear what Sam said? She was going to kill your grandchild. I'd've thought you'd've been the first to reach for the rope.' Patrick knew his wife had been going through hell since the death of their eldest son Dickie several months ago. She had thrown herself into the running of her two general stores, dividing her time equally between them and leaving none for her husband. He saw less and less of her these days. It was only the fact that Erin's child had chosen the Sabbath to make her début that commanded Thomasin's presence now. Any other day and Patrick doubted that the event would take precedence over such vital matters as her stocking, invoicing and planning. The business was her life nowadays; he accepted that, albeit unwillingly – but to go and voice a statement like the one of twenty seconds ago . . . he shook his head. The death of their son must have affected her more than anyone had imagined.

'Take that look off your face,' she muttered, coming back to take charge of the baby, rocking it tenderly. 'I've not lost me marbles.' Thomasin, like Sam, was a product of Yorkshire – though her broad accent was reserved for the family circle. The business world saw a more refined Thomasin, as did their neighbours. Years ago it had not

16

mattered one jot what they thought of her, but she had learned quickly that the way one spoke could be either asset or hindrance to one's financial success and had adapted accordingly. Respect had been a long time coming. The main cause of this delay was standing in front of her with condemnation in his piercing blue eyes. The Irish had always attracted a great deal of dislike and suspicion and naturally enough this rubbed off on one's marriage partner. Like her own origins this hadn't mattered in the old days, when there was just the five of them in the little courtyard hovel – Patrick and Thomasin, Erin, Sonny . . . and Dickie. She wished she could fix him in her memory as a bonny, twinkling-eyed child of five, when they were perhaps at their happiest despite the poverty, but the Dickie she saw every night when she closed her eyes was an immaculately-tailored twenty-one-year-old dashing into the burning house to rescue his sister-in-law . . . only to be killed by a huge fireball that had caused the roof to collapse on top of him. She assumed full blame. That was why she would not allow herself to be happy, saw less and less of her husband. The close relationship they had shared seemed to burn out with the gutting of the house. They still slept in the same bed – twenty-three years of marriage added to working-class upbringing made such habits hard to break – but their infrequent love-making was due to more than just advancing years.

Now, Thomasin appraised her spouse, a tall, distingui-shed-looking man with greying hair, trying to picture him as he had been on the day they had met. She had thought him incredibly handsome – as he still was. The greatest difference between then and now – age apart – was his clothes. Then, there could be no other name for them but rags. Patrick was one of the few Irish immigrants, flocking to the city in their thousands, who had made good. The filth, the cholera and typhus of those terrible, ramshackle hovels had all been left behind. Only his sing-song lilt served as a reminder of his heritage. Standing there in his well-cut apparel with neatly-trimmed hair and gold watch

17

dangling from his waistcoat he would have been instantly accepted by society, had it not been for his name and his accent. Some years ago he had remarked that one of the reasons Thomasin's business had enjoyed so much success was because when she had inherited the store she had not placed her husband's name over the door but had left it as it was – *Penny's*. She had denied the fact, but secretly recognised that he was probably correct; anti-Irish feeling was still as rife as ever. It was only respect for her business prowess that brought their new neighbours to associate with the Feeneys. They had moved here to Peasholme Green shortly after the destruction of their home in Monkgate. The house itself was very grand and stood among a select cluster of mansions, but not a stone's throw away one could find the most appalling slums; it seemed the Feeneys could not escape from their origins.

Thomasin smiled down at the puckered face. Sonny was right, she was like Erin. She made an attempt to justify the extraordinary statement that had shocked them. 'You see ... I believe it's wrong to tamper with nature, Sam. When animals are born like this they don't normally survive more than a few days. The mother either abandons her offspring or it's ...'

'Jazers!' burst in Patrick. ''Tis not an animal we're on about – 'tis our grandchild.'

'I know that, Patrick,' she returned calmly before he jumped in again.

'Your comparison isn't valid! Belle wouldn't've died naturally, that woman was going to kill her.'

'But you must see it from the child's point of view, dear. What sort of life is she going to lead? She's not going to be able to run or jump or play like other children. People are going to treat her with suspicion.'

'Well, that's nothing new,' Patrick laughed bitterly. 'She's half-Irish isn't she? She had it coming anyway.'

'Then in a way she'll be doubly damned,' responded Thomasin with what she saw as logic. 'Isn't it bad enough that the poor scrap will have to defend her parentage without the physical disability, too?'

'What d'ye suggest we do then?' snapped Patrick. 'Call the midwife back an' say we've changed our minds – here's a pillow an' get on with it?'

Thomasin argued on. Sam couldn't believe that this was the same woman who had championed her husband's cause as long as he had known her. 'So, as Dad says, you think I should've stood by an' let the midwife smother her, is that it?' When she took her time in answering he gave a bitter exclamation and looked at Patrick. 'Blazes, she's not even bothering to deny it! You think that woman was right to try and murder my daughter.' He seized the child from Thomasin, his cheery face disfigured with betrayal and outrage.

'Sam, it sounds so callous when you put it that way.' She watched the tragic figure pace the carpet, his thick forearms curled under the child, awkwardly protective.

'I can't think of any other way to put it! What gives you or anyone else the right to take this child's life?'

'I'm thinking of her, Sam,' she pleaded. 'It would've been in her best interests.'

'Oh, I'll bet that's what King Herod said.'

'That's not fair. I *am* thinking of her.'

'Are ye, Tommy?' Patrick broke in. 'Or is it that ye think this child is going to mess up your nice ordered life?'

'That's despicable, Patrick,' came the wounded reply, even though she knew there was some truth to his accusation. People had just started to accept her, look up to her even – and now this. But she denied it strenuously. 'What difference will this make to my life?'

'None whatsoever.' Sam beat Patrick to the reply. 'But she will to ours, to mine and Erin's – that's your daughter if you hadn't forgotten, the one who's probably lying upstairs listening to all this. I can't deny that I'd have preferred to have her whole and healthy, but I'm damned if anyone will tell me to discard her like the runt of the litter.'

Thomasin encompassed both him and Patrick with a look of helpless compassion, then flapped her arms and said evenly, 'So, you've saved her life – what now? What'll be the quality of that life, Sam? Who'll be there to pick her up every time she falls – always considering that she will learn to walk in the first place with her gimpy little legs. Who'll chase away the boys when they tease her and make cruel sport of her? I'll tell you: Erin. It's all very well for you to play the outraged father, but it isn't Father who'll be in the house with her twenty-four hours a day, is it?'

'Both Erin and I will protect her,' vouched Sam firmly. 'You needn't worry yourself on that score. I know my responsibility and none of it'll fall on you.' What had he said to Erin before – your mam'll look after us?

'Confound it, Sam!' Thomasin grew angry. 'I couldn't give a toss about responsibility. I'm worried about Erin and how she'll cope. How that bairn will manage when she's ready for school – if she ever reaches that age. Eh, lad, you've landed yourself with a right load of problems. No one can be there every second of the day to see she comes to no harm.'

'I don't intend to,' announced Sam. 'Everyone, whole or otherwise, has to learn how to take knocks from the time they learn to walk. Belle will be no different. Molly-coddling would make it all the harder for her. I'm going to raise her as if she were – for want of a better word – normal. And why shouldn't I? After all, it's only her body that's malformed, not her brain.'

How tempting for her to utter, 'How can you know that? It's too soon to tell.' But the look of determination on Sam's face dissuaded the remark which would have been an added cruelty, and her words had not been motivated by sadism. She just wanted him to have a taste of what his and Belle's future would be like. 'Belle.' She smiled sadly at the baby and nodded. 'It suits her.' Then she clasped her hands in a businesslike gesture. 'Considering that the midwife's done a vanishing trick, hadn't one of us better bath her and make her comfy?'

Sam, still hurt by her apparent rejection of his daughter, needed further prompting before giving up the child. 'Well, if you'll excuse me I think I'll go snatch a bit o' sleep.'

'Aye, you do, lad,' said Thomasin as she rang for the maid to order water and towels. 'You look fair whacked – and Sam,' he paused at the door, 'I didn't really mean all those things I said. I'm sure we're all going to love this baby very much.'

He searched her eyes and, finding no duplicity, nodded his understanding and quietly closed the door. Before glancing back at the baby Thomasin caught her husband's dubious expression and looked away swiftly. If Patrick had guessed the insincerity of her last comment she could only hope that he would keep it to himself.

The extent of the child's deformity was rather worse than the fleeting glimpse had first informed them. When Belle, wide awake now and screaming with indignation, was lowered into the bathwater they were able to see that, presumably because of the twisted spine, one of her under-developed legs was considerably shorter than the other. Patrick, Sonny and Hannah sat in their separate chairs watching the red-faced child squirm about in her grand-mother's slippery hands as the streaks of dried blood and meconium were washed away.

'Eh, it's a long time since I've done this.' Thomasin knelt beside the marble fireplace with no regard for her blue silk dress, not allowing her disagreement with Sam to overcome her strong maternal qualities. 'Come here, you little devil, you're wrigglier than a pint o'maggots.' That she undertook this task personally was another give-away of her lower-class origins.

Sonny watched the scene and thought of his own perfectly-formed children asleep upstairs; motherless, but not for long if his plan went ahead. Their mother had been burnt to death along with Sonny's brother. The children were aware of this. They themselves had only just been rescued from the fire before the house caved in. What they were not aware of – and Sonny had no intention that they ever would be – was that the man they called Father was actually their uncle. It would have been a very complicated relationship to explain to them even if he had wanted to. Both children had been sired by Sonny's brother on different women – one of them Sonny's wife. Both had been adopted by their uncle and raised as his own, and that was the way it would stay. After a decent interval he could marry Josie and they would be a proper family again.

'The fire's getting low,' provided Patrick. 'Shall I ask Abi to fetch some more coal? We don't want the little'n to catch a chill.' He rose, intending to ring for the maid but Thomasin replied that it was nearly bedtime and the baby was almost done.

'If you ask me, catching a chill would be the best thing for her.' It was Hannah who spoke, sitting like a wizened old dragon, one trembling, arthritic hand curled round the knob of her walking-cane, wearing the black dress that had become uniform to her widowhood. She had been invited to live with her daughter and son-in-law last year when her husband had died and not a day went by without either one of them having cause to regret it. If her eyesight and hearing were not as they used to be her outspokenness was still intact. 'I agree with Thomasin, it would have been better all round if Samuel hadn't interfered.'

'Better for whom, Hannah?' Patrick's hand which had been about to pull the bell-rope moved to take up his pipe. 'Seems to me there's too many people around here trying to take on God's responsibility. It's His right to take life an' no one else's. Anyway, I can't see what all the fuss is about.' He gestured at the baby who had been bound up and was now being thrust, protesting, into a nightgown. 'Once she's dressed ye can hardly tell she's anything amiss with her.'

'Flapdoodle,' delivered Hannah testily. 'Anyone can see that the child is going to grow up an idiot.'

'If ye can see that, Hannah, then ye've got better eyes than me,' retorted Patrick. 'All I can see is a bonny wee girl who just missed having the finishing touches put to her, that's all. How anyone can possibly forecast her intelligence at this stage is beyond me.'

'Well, it would be,' sniffed Hannah, her prim lip

displaying a downy moustache. 'There are many things that are beyond your comprehension, Patrick. And if one gave closer examination to your statement it would take little reckoning to trace the root of the child's deformity.'

'What exactly are you implying, Mother?' Thomasin had looked up sharply, her grey eyes flint-like.

'I think she's trying to tell me in her own diplomatic way,' said Patrick, 'that Belle has me to blame for her imperfection. See, Hannah,' he winked exaggeratedly, 'I'm not as thick-skulled as ye thought.'

'Mother, that's insulting.' Thomasin struggled to her knees, holding the baby in one arm while her other hand hoisted her skirts. Seeking the aid of a chair she rose fully. 'I think you owe Pat an apology.'

'Thomasin, it's only logical. There was never any question of imbecility in our family. It is obvious where it comes from.'

'It is not logical at all!' shouted Thomasin. 'It is most illogical, wholly ridiculous.' Instead of gaining greater patience with age she seemed to be losing her temper more and more nowadays, especially with her intransigent mother. 'You seem to be quite forgetting that this child has no connection of blood with our side of the family at all. I'm not Erin's natural mother.'

This made the old lady crow delightedly. 'Why, yes of course. I'm becoming quite forgetful. Oh well, there you are then.'

'And where is that?' snapped Thomasin, hushing the mewing baby.

'Why, Thomasin, you really are getting quite dilatory,' said her mother. 'Samuel, though far from being an academic, is from good Yorkshire stock. It is as I told you in the first place – the child most definitely owes her imbecility to her Celtic forebears.'

There were gasps of impatience from all, Thomasin muttering, 'I'm going to swing for her one o' these days.'

Hannah cupped her hand to her ear. 'What was that?'

'I said isn't it about time you were in your bed, Mother?' Thomasin shared a grimace with Patrick. 'The hour's late. Abigail's had your sheets warmed for the past thirty minutes or so.'

'Oh, I know,' replied the old lady tetchily. 'But I wanted to be here to welcome the new baby. I wish I hadn't bothered now. Hmph! Belle, what a name.'

'I think it's pretty,' said Patrick, drawing on his pipe.

'It's ridiculous. She'll sound like an actress. I refuse to call her such a name. I shall call her Isabelle.' She flapped her arms for assistance in rising from her chair. Patrick and Sonny came forward to hoist her as was their usual contribution. They had often joked about having a pulley connected to the ceiling with a cord attached to Hannah's waist – in uncharitable moments Patrick had even suggested the neck might be more appropriate. 'I'm going to bed, will someone carry a candle for me?'

'I doubt there'll be many volunteers,' murmured Patrick to his son who smiled and went to select a candle from the hall table. On lighting it he offered the loop of his arm to his grandmother. 'I think I'll turn in too. Goodnight, everyone.'

'Goodnight, Son,' replied Patrick. 'I think maybe it's time we all put our heads down, it's been a hectic day.' The sounds of his daughter's labour pain still echoed round his head.

'I'll just look in on Erin first, poor lass,' said his wife, ringing to inform the domestic help they could retire, too. 'Would you like to join me?' He nodded as she added, 'I may have to wake her to suckle the babe else none of us'll get any sleep. There's nothing wrong with her lungs, is there?'

Patrick concurred, tapping his pipe against the fireback and placing it in the rack. 'I think we've been worrying about the wrong person. If her voice is anything to go by this little minx will be well able to look after herself.'

They came through the shadowy hall. Abigail, the maid, stepped aside for them to mount the staircase first, brown eyes lowered in respect. News of the child had filtered to the servants' quarters. Abi thought it a very dirty blow for such a nice family.

24

Thomasin paused to issue orders. 'Abigail, tomorrow morning could you slip round to the Harrisons and inform them that Mrs Feeney is indisposed so will have to postpone our dinner arrangements until some future date.'

The girl inclined her brunette head, frizzy from the over-use of hot tongs, and bobbed a curtsey. She waited until her master and mistress had retired before proceeding to her own attic room.

'Now what did ye tell her that for?' asked Patrick when they had distanced themselves from the maid.

'Do you have to ask?' She sauntered along the corridor to Erin's bedroom.

'Because of the baby?' said Patrick, frowning.

'They're bound to ask after Erin, as I'm bound to tell them she's given birth. I just couldn't cope with all the questions at the moment. They look down on us enough as it is. If they knew about this . . .'

'But ye can't go on saying you're indisposed forever.'

'Of course not, but I need time to think of what I'm going to say.' She opened the door of Erin's room, leaving him no further time to voice his disgust. But that didn't stop him feeling it.

CHAPTER TWO

Erin and Sam were to remain at the house in York for the next two weeks. At any other time Erin would have enjoyed the break, but being in bed all day with nothing else to do but feed the baby made it hard to sleep at night, and the noise from revellers at the Black Swan made her all the more irritable. That, added to the immense worry about Belle, was the reason why Thomasin received an earful of abuse on catching her daughter in the garden at two o'clock in the morning.

'God's stockings!' Thomasin stood in her nightgown on

the terrace, holding a candle at eye-level, her once auburn hair dangling over her breast in a pure white plait. 'I thought we had burglars. What on earth are you doing out here in the middle of the night? You'll catch your death.'

'And who would care if I did?' returned Erin sourly, her back to the older woman, staring out into the night garden.

'Oh dear, violin time is it?' Thomasin, hugging a long shawl around her nightdress, came to stand beside her. 'Come on, tell Mother all about it.'

Erin looked at her now, but the response was not pleasant. 'Oh, so that's who the strange woman is. I'm sorry, I found it hard to recognise ye, not having seen much of ye while I've been here. Doubtless I'd not have had the pleasure of your company now if ye hadn't thought it was somebody creepin' round pinchin' all your fancy doodahs.'

Thomasin, though she knew the comment to be justified, was hurt. 'If it's sympathy you're after, lass, I don't regard sarcasm as a fair swap.'

'Call it sarcasm if ye wish, I see it as the truth. I've been virtually imprisoned in my room for the past ten days and in that time ye've deigned to visit me twice.'

'Oh dear, Erin, I've been that busy at the store I didn't realise I'd neglected you so ... But surely you've had plenty of other company without listening to your boring old mam? You've had Sam there and Sonny tells me he's been popping in, and I know your father spends most evenings with you.'

'Yes, I'm pleased to say Father at least has shown some interest in his grandchild. I'd like to think his visits were solely for that purpose but we both know that's not the case. He comes 'cause he's lonely too, 'cause his wife is never there. I dare say if I hadn't been stuck up there he'd have no one to keep him company at all.'

'Erin, it's not like that. You know how the store takes up most of my time ...'

'Oh yes, I'm well aware that it's more important than any of us!' shot back Erin. 'So is Father. But don't worry,

26

we know how to take second place. Unfortunately Belle is too young to understand why her grandmother chooses to neglect her.'

'Erin, it isn't because she's . . .' Thomasin paused.

'A cripple? Yes, do go on, Mother.'

'Oh, for pity's sake!' Thomasin swished back towards the house. 'I'm not standing here nithered to the bone to have a load of insults flung at me. I'm off back to bed. If you're in a better frame of mind tomorrow we'll discuss it then.'

'I'll make an appointment.'

'Do that! And you can get yourself back to bed as well, else we'll be forking out for funeral fees.' She marched through the open french windows, then stopped exasperatedly and turned back to watch the figure on the terrace. Erin's head slowly lowered and both hands came up to her face. There followed the faint sound of weeping.

Thomasin sighed and wandered back out into the cool night, the white linen flapping round her legs. 'Come on, bairn. Come inside.' Putting her arm round her daughter, who was taller than herself, she drew her into the house, snapping shut the french doors after them. 'There.' She rammed a poker into the glowing coals and rattled it about. Then, going across to a cabinet, she brought back a decanter and two glasses. Filling each with sherry she handed one to Erin.

'I don't know that I should,' sniffed her daughter, wiping her face with the sleeve of her nightgown. 'It mightn't be good for the milk.'

'It'll not harm. Babby'll enjoy a little bevvy same as the rest of us. Go on, get it down you and plant yourself by this fire, such as it is. By God, it's colder than an Eskimo's bum – and they call this summer!' Scorning the chairs she dragged a footstool up to the resurrected fire and hunched herself over its weak flame.

Erin sank quietly to her knees on the rug and sipped the sherry, the flickering light of the coals playing over her troubled face. 'I'm sorry I said all those nasty things to ye, Mam. I didn't mean them.'

'I know you didn't, love.' Thomasin smiled and reached out for her daughter's free hand. 'Ee, these hands feel as if they've been in t'ice house for a week. Give us 'em here.' She put down the glass and rubbed Erin's cold fingers briskly between her own, breathing warmth onto them between bursts. 'How long had you been standing out there?'

Erin shrugged and put down her glass as Thomasin gestured for the other hand. She felt like a child again, coming in from building a snowman and having her hands brought back to life, and for a moment the image of the half-formed babe upstairs was put aside as she dwelt in childhood memories.

The brisk movement stopped but Thomasin did not release the hand, entwining comforting, motherly fingers with those of the younger woman. 'It's quite natural, the way you're feeling, Erin,' she intoned supportively. 'Most of us go through some sort of upheaval after giving birth.'

'Most of us give birth to normal babies, Mam,' sighed Erin, retrieving the glass of sherry and pressing her lips to the rim. 'An' is it natural to want to die?' The eyes welled up.

'Oh, love.' Thomasin put both arms round her weeping daughter. 'You don't really feel like that. It's the birth that's taken it out of you, making you talk this way.'

'I do, I wish I was dead!' sobbed Erin. 'I wish Sam hadn't stopped the midwife when she tried to smother Belle. It would've been the best thing. I wish somebody would put a pillow over my face, I feel so wretched.'

Thomasin patted her heaving back as she rocked her to and fro. 'Cry, love. Get rid of it. You'll soon feel better.' She kept this position for many minutes until Erin could cry no more, then prised her gently from her shoulder. 'Eh, I shan't have to worry about having this nightgown washed this week, it's already been done.' She tugged at the saturated patch where Erin had shed her unhappiness. Her accent during the exchange had regressed into the blunt Yorkshire dialect with which Erin had been familiar as a child. It was strangely comforting.

The young woman ran the flat of her palm over her eyes. 'Have ye got a hanky, Mam? My nose is running all over the place.'

Thomasin felt up her sleeve. 'No, love, I haven't. Never mind, use the bottom of your nightie like you did when you were a bairn.'

Erin gave a soft laugh as she hoisted the hem of the garment and trumpeted into it. 'Ye weren't supposed to know about that.'

'And what was I supposed to think all those little stiff patches were – broderie anglaise? Mucky little cat. You were nearly as bad as your brothers. It's a wonder they never wore their noses away the amount of fingers they had shoved up 'em. Lying in bed, rake, rake, rake. They must've thought I couldn't count all those extra patterns on the wallpaper in the mornin'.' Having succeeded in making Erin giggle she forged on. 'Still, I suppose I was as bad when I were a lass. Course, we didn't have wallpaper. Luckily the patchwork quilt had a lot of green squares on it.'

'Oh, Mam, stop it! You're making me feel sick!' Erin's shoulders shook and they fell against each other, laughing heartily.

The following minutes were given to reminiscence; what good fun they used to have in the old days, when Erin and the boys were children. Naturally enough, the subject of children brought the conversation back to its original course.

'What plans have you got for Belle?' asked Thomasin casually, reaching for the decanter and refilling both glasses.

The other smiled sadly, hugging her arms over her swollen breasts and clutching them to her sides. 'I can't bring myself to plan even as far ahead as tomorrow.' She took the sherry from Thomasin. 'Every morning I wake up and pray that a miracle has happened. Isn't that soft? I actually believe that in the time it takes me to cross the room to Belle's crib when I pull away the covers I'm going to find a flawless, healthy child. I meant it before, ye know, when I said I wished Sam had been just a few seconds later in coming. Oh yes,' she nodded at Thomasin's sceptical face, 'I love her deeply of course, an' I know it's a terrible sin, me feeling that way, but I keep thinking of her future. Every time she fails in some task because of her disability or each time she comes home crying 'cause someone's called her crookback, I'm going to wonder at the wisdom of Sam's intervention. What if she hates us for it, Mam? I don't think I could bear that. D'ye think his choice was the right one?'

Thomasin tipped the sherry into her mouth before answering. Erin took the silence for disapproval. 'Sam was evasive when I asked him for your reaction to Belle, but I get the impression that ye thought he'd made a mistake. I can tell when he's angry, even when he thinks he's hiding it.'

'Yes, he was angry,' said Thomasin softly. 'And he had every right to be. I said some unpleasant things. I didn't mean them; it was just the shock.'

'Then, do I assume ye thought we'd made a mistake?' came the tentative cue.

Thomasin turned to look her full in the face. The apprehension in the large blue eyes betrayed the fact that Erin did not want her mother's true opinion. She wanted reassurance that the decision to let Belle live had been the right one. 'If there was a mistake made it wasn't of your doing, Erin. No mother could lay back and allow another to dispose of her child, however badly crippled. It was Sam's decision ... and to be honest ... I took him to task over it. But,' the apprehension in her daughter's eyes intensified, 'I've had a week or so to consider my view, and I've come to the conclusion that if I'd been in Sam's shoes I'd have done the selfsame thing. However difficult life is going to be for her I'm sure he couldn't've done anything else. Belle will have good parents in you and Sam. I'm certain she'll never grow to hate you, Erin.'

The uncertainty was deposed by relief and Erin allowed her head to drop to her mother's shoulder. 'It makes me feel so much better, knowing you're behind me, Mam.'

I know it does, love, came the bleak thought. I only hope the lie turns to prophecy. Oh God, I wish I could find some feeling for that twisted little creature. *Real* feeling, the type I have for Nick and Rosie, not just pity. Perhaps it's because the child was conceived at the time of Dickie's death that I find it so hard to love her – though some might consider it a bond. Perhaps when time has healed the terrible hole in my life that his death made, maybe then I'll come to care.

She patted Erin's arm and gestured at the moribund fire. 'Away, I've got to be up at six to go to the warehouse, and it'll do you no good being out of bed for so long.' As they rose together she said something else. 'About putting the store before my family . . .'

'I've apologised for that.'

'I know, but I wouldn't want you thinking that it's because Belle's the way she is that I haven't been up to see you much. I find this very difficult to explain.' Erin brushed away the need for explanation. 'No,' said her mother, 'I owe you that at least. If I haven't been very attentive, it's not because I consider my job more important, it's just that . . . since Dickie's . . . since he went, I've had to throw myself into my work, because that's the only time I can manage to forget about him, when I'm working flat out. The moment I stop, the moment I come home and see your father . . . I just can't shut out the sight of that burning roof caving in on my lad.' Her voice broke. 'I can't stand to be in the house with nowt to do. The store keeps me occupied. I need to work for my sanity.'

'But why can't ye share this with Dad?' pleaded Erin. 'He wouldn't feel so bad if he understood why you're doing it. He thinks you blame *him* for Dickie's death.'

'He said that?' Thomasin was cynical.

'No,' admitted Erin. 'But sometimes he sits there deep in himself an' I get the feeling that in these silences he's his own prosecuting counsel.'

'Perhaps he is to blame. Perhaps we both are.'

'Now ye know that's utter nonsense. Dickie was a womaniser, a cheat an' a liar.'

'You're not to speak so of the dead! Especially your brother.'

'Mam, I didn't mean to be cruel, I just want ye to see that everything that happened to him was of his own making. You're not to blame.'

'We brought him up, didn't we?'

'Ye brought me up, too. D'ye hold yourself responsible for Belle's misfortune?'

'No, but you do, don't you, love? That's what's really behind your sadness.'

'We weren't talking about me. Don't change the subject. Please, Mam, talk to Father. I hate to see a good marriage being spoilt by misunderstanding.'

Thomasin chuckled. ''S funny, I remember saying exactly the same thing to you last year.' She sighed. 'Your father understands more than you think, Erin. He and I know each other very well. He's a wise man, he understands that I need to lose myself in my work. He's allowing me to do this because he knows that I'll get over it in the end.'

'Isn't there a danger that ye'll come to depend on your work permanently? Mightn't it push ye both farther apart? Hurt's better if it's shared. Me an' Sam know that if anyone does.'

'Listen.' Thomasin ended the subject firmly. 'You've got your own problems to worry about. Don't be taking ours on your shoulders as well. Your father and me'll be all right.'

Just then the door opened and a tousled Sam stood yawning in the doorway, a candle in his hand to light his path down the staircase. His bleary eyes followed Thomasin's passage to the sideboard with the half-empty decanter and glasses. 'When the Temperance Committee has finished holding its general meeting d'you think it would be possible for one of its Right Honourable members to see to the human bellows upstairs? I think she's tryin' to tell us summat.' Now that the door was open the sound of Belle's angry howls floated into the room.

Erin pressed one hand to the damp patch that had sprung from her tingling breast at the baby's cry, the other to her mouth. 'I'm sorry, love, I clean lost track of time. I'll come right away. I hope she's not woken everyone else.'

'The whole house,' yawned Sam, running his fingers through the corn-coloured thatch. 'Come see for yourself.'

When Erin and Thomasin went to the crib, it was empty. Sam crooked a finger over his shoulder from the doorway and summoned them to the master bedroom.

In the centre of the room were three ghostly figures, their candlelit shadows gyrating around the walls. Patrick, clad only in his underwear and clutching a shrieking Belle to his chest, danced round in a circle with Rosanna and Nick, chanting an Irish ditty. Catching sight of the others he broke away from the circle, 'God be praised, the absconder's been nabbed!' and panting, he thrust the crimson-faced child at Erin. 'Woman, do your duty before we're all rendered deaf. Faith, we're definitely going to have to hire another nurse for these brats.' This job had previously been given to Judith, one of their former maids, but she had found Rosanna's spirited behaviour too much of a trial and had given notice.

'Is anyone allowed to ask just what's going on here?' requested Thomasin amazedly. 'It is three o'clock in the morning, you know, rather early for a ceilidh – even for the mad Irish.'

'Sure, will ye tell that to her ladyship?' asked Patrick, pointing at the cavern-mouthed baby before Erin spirited her away. 'An' where were all you womenfolk while the men were getting their ears blasted?' A grinning Sam provided the answer. 'Oh, suppin', was it? Isn't that a fine thing for a mother to be doin' while the poor fellas are left to tend the livestock!'

'Did you really have to get Nick and Rosie up, too?' chastised Thomasin, frowning at the two bright-eyed children swinging on the ends of Patrick's arms. 'We'll not get them back to bed now.'

'*I* didn't get them up,' retorted Patrick. 'Ye can direct your tongue at Clamorous Clara. She must've been laughing up her little lace cuff at us lot, going on about, "Aw, the poor little bairn, ain't it a shame!" 'Tis us who're going to need the pity. I tell ye, that child is going to rule the roost.'

'Aye, well she's certainly got you where she wants you,' said Thomasin, advancing on the trio. 'Like two more I could mention. Come on, you little articles, let's be having you back in the pit.'

Rosanna and her brother tried the charm that had worked on Patrick, with little hope of success. Grandmother was not so easy to manipulate.

'I'll give you five seconds to get back to those beds and then it's the wooden spoon for both of you,' warned Thomasin and began counting. 'Yan, tan, tethera . . .' Before she had reached methera Patrick had whisked the children into his arms and hurriedly spirited them off to bed.

Thomasin shook her head at Sam as he made his exit too. 'To listen to him sometimes you'd think he was the master at the workhouse. But just let those bairns get their hands on him – especially Rosie – and he's like a big daft lump o' putty. Your lass'll be just the same when she's old enough to get his measure. He'll spoil her rotten like the other two. Still,' she smiled before closing the door on Sam, 'I daresay a bit of spoiling won't go amiss in Belle's case. Goodnight, Sam.'

''Night, Mam,' returned her son-in-law and went to join his wife with the thought that it was just as well they did not live here permanently. Belle was not going to be spoilt just because she was crippled. He wouldn't have them all feeling sorry for her. No, as he had told Thomasin on the night Belle was born, she would be brought up like any other child – Sam would see to that. It would be hard going, granted, and he would have to protect her from the harsher elements. But spoil her? Swaddle her in cottonwool? No, if Sam spoilt Belle it would be purely because she was his little girl and not out of pity for her deformity. Belle was going to have as normal a life as her father could make it.

It was arranged that the baptism should take place on the Sunday before Erin and Sam returned to their own home. Belle, exactly a fortnight old, was dressed in the long christening robe that had been hastily purchased when Patrick had brought Rosanna into the house three years ago. No family heirlooms for this child; Patrick and Thomasin had been too poor to afford such luxuries for their own offspring. But this tiny creation of lace and silk would ensure that subsequent generations would never go to their baptism in pauper rags. Father Kelly would be officiating as he had at every one of the Feeney baptisms, an old and respected friend as well as confessor. It was his patient constancy that had drawn Patrick back to the faith he had denied during the Great Hunger, and Feeney had a great love for his fellow Irishman.

The ageing priest shambled down the aisle to meet them as they entered. He seemed to have shrunk with the years. His skin didn't fit him any more but hung on his brittle bones like an oversized jacket and fell into deep pleats over his smiling face. Like an understuffed sausage, Liam would remark when looking down upon his naked self. But the eyes that had marked him from that first meeting as a strong and compassionate man were as vividly green as ever.

'Faith, will ye ever look at her,' exclaimed Liam when the parents, grandparents and sponsors gathered round the font and Erin gingerly placed the babe in the old priest's arms. 'The spitting image of her mother. To be hoped she doesn't harbour the same devious habits and perform in the disrespectful manner her mother did at her own baptism.'

Erin held her face at a puzzled angle.

'Ye piddled on me,' supplied Liam with dancing eyes.

35

'I never did!' Erin laughed blushingly, and elbowed Sonny for his loud appreciation.

'As true as there's no snakes in Ireland,' confirmed the priest. 'Piddled all the way through to me unmentionables, didn't she, Pat?'

A smiling Patrick confirmed this, then was momentarily distracted by a black-clad figure drifting up and down before the altar. On encountering Patrick's interest he turned his back and pretended to busy himself.

Liam followed his friend's gaze. 'Ah, we've got the spies in again, I see. Father Gilchrist and his little black book.'

Patrick asked what the man was doing.

'He's registering all my sins,' replied the priest lightly, pulling the shawl away from the sleeping baby's face.

'Sure, he'd need a ledger for that,' joked Patrick.

'I do not cod. I can tell ye the exact words he's writing at the moment: "Sunday – caught Father Kelly in the blasphemous act of laughing in church." By next week I should say he'll have tallied enough evidence to have me either excommunicated or committed to an asylum. Whichever way he'll not be bothered as long as I'm off the stage.' Patrick's bemused face prompted Liam into fuller explanation. 'Ye see, some of our more devout parishioners have been complaining about my sermons. My bluntness, apparently, isn't to their taste. So, Bishop French has sent his lackeys to see if I'm still up to the job. They take it in shifts, Father Gilchrist an' his accomplice, vying to see who can fill his little book first. Presumably the winner gets my job.'

Patrick enquired how long this had been going on. He had heard no mention of it before.

'About a fortnight,' replied Liam. 'Did ye not notice all the "help" I've been getting at Mass lately?'

Patrick shook his head. 'I noticed the new faces o' course but never put any significance on them. Ye didn't think to introduce us?'

'If ye knew the man ye'd not be wondering why I kept ye apart.' Liam glanced over his shoulder. 'I think we'd best proceed else Father Gilchrist will have something else to write in his black book: "Father Kelly appeared to forget the words of the ceremony of baptism." Dear God, ye'd think they could allow a poor old fella to retire gracefully without hounding him to it. I'm almost eighty-five. Ye'd never've guessed that, would ye? Another year an' I'll probably pop me clogs voluntarily without their help. Ah, she's a good wee bairn an' no mistake.' He cradled Belle in his arms, feeling the bony deformity, about which his old friend had informed him on his last visit to Mass. It was a great tragedy at any time, but particularly when it was Erin's first child. Still, it was Liam's opinion that God was not indiscriminate in His placing of such children. They were delivered to the families who could be relied upon to provide the extra love the babes would need. Erin and Sam, he knew, would give of their best.

Hobbling closer to the font he asked who were to act as sponsors and the chosen came forward. 'As ungodly a bunch as ever I've seen,' commented Liam. 'If the Devil cast his net . . . tut, tut, tut.'

The family, knowing Liam so well, shared a smile. Josie, the Feeneys' ex-housekeeper and the girl whom Sonny planned to marry, was a little unsure how to take the priest's observation. He was a strange one and no mistake. Her religious upbringing had been much more staid and respectful. This priest seemed to treat everything as a joke. However, she had been very honoured when Miss – oh, would she ever be able to rid herself of that habit? Calling them all Master and Mistress – when *Erin* had asked her to be godmother, even if, she presumed, it was only done out of politeness because soon she would be a member of the family.

There Josie was wrong. Her inclusion at today's ceremony was not simply because she was Sonny's future wife, but that Erin's instincts told her Josie would care for Belle as one of her own should anything befall the child's parents. If further commendation were necessary it was illustrated by Sonny's children who had made it plain they would accept Josie as their mother when the time came. If looks were any indication of worth then poor Josie would have little going for her, being plain of feature and wide of girth. But the ex-housekeeper had more lasting qualities. Josie was the sort who wore her colours on her face, who would never commit an unkind act nor mutter dark intent behind a person's back. And it was obvious to all that she doted on Erin's brother – it wasn't simply the church's coolness that had her pressed to his side.

In that fact Erin pitied her, for she knew – as did Josie at heart – that for Sonny, love the second time around was not a thing of passion. There was only one great love in his life. That he had decided to spend the remainder of the year in the arms of that love by the River Seine was a source of lament to Josie, but she knew the separation must be endured – it was far too soon after the death of his first wife to marry again. Besides, it was not as if he were going to another woman; no female could capture Sonny as did his painting. All this said, they were both well aware that in Josie he had what he needed – a mother for his children, a wife to come home to and, above all, a friend. When he felt able to return Josie would be waiting. She watched the priest trickle holy water over the tiny head and felt her stomach tighten with joy and anticipation at the child's wail. How long before her own child's cry echoed round these walls? Please God, not too long. She gripped Sonny's hand and he smiled down at her. She adored Rosie and Nick, yes, but that didn't stop her wanting a child of her own.

'Wait for it, 'tis coming,' muttered Liam after a string of Latin. Then almost triumphant, 'There! Didn't I tell ye? They're all alike; as soon as they feel the water on their heads they can't wait to match it at the other end. That's another batch of laundry for Mrs Lucas.'

Erin laughingly apologised as she took the damp infant from the priest. 'Will ye come back to the house, Father, an' take a bite with us as way of making amends?'

'I will,' said Liam immediately, then glanced at the furtive shadow by the sacristy. 'Er, on second thoughts perhaps Father Gilchrist has enough on me for one day without me dashing off to a party. Ye can save me a piece o' the cake – an' will ye please all take the smiles off your faces? Don't ye know you're not supposed to be happy in church?'

'Aw, come on, Liam,' urged Patrick, clamping a large hand to his friend's shoulder. 'Surely he can't take exception to an old friend coming to wet the baby's head.'

'We-ell, maybe for a wee . . .'

'Father Kelly!' Liam groaned as the voice rang out and the sound of footsteps resounded through the otherwise quiet church. 'Father Kelly, if you've conducted the baptism I wonder if I might have a word with you about this evening's sermon?' Father Gilchrist was a young man, in his late twenties perhaps. His face was narrow – narrow face, narrow mind, thought Liam distastefully as the man came alongside. This lack of breadth meant that the eyes were perforce closely-set; green – not the sparkling green of the older priest, but pale, the irises like two pinpoints of emptiness; the eyes of a fanatic. The lips were but a sanguine gash in the austere face. The nose, in keeping with the rest of his features, was pinched, its nostrils mere slits.

'Ah, Father Gilchrist.' Liam forced himself to be cheerful. 'Allow me to introduce you to more of our faithful parishioners. Patrick Feeney, friend of long standing,' the young priest inclined his head with a half-smile, 'his wife, Thomasin, their son . . .' Liam went through the entourage.

'Delighted to make your acquaintance, Father,' lied Patrick who had taken an instant and virulent dislike to the man. Which was wrong of him, he told himself. One shouldn't judge by appearances. I still don't bloody like him, said his other self.

'Likewise, Mr Feeney.' The young priest turned off his obsequious smile as swiftly as he had manufactured it and made it plain he was not interested in prolonging the conversation. 'Father Kelly, if you are all done . . . ?'

'I'd be obliged if ye'd allow me to take proper leave of my friends, Father,' reproved the senior man.

'Of course, please excuse me, Father,' said Father

Gilchrist contritely. 'But you will remember we have other duties to perform?'

'Oh, I'm sure if it did slip my mind you'd be the first to remind me, Father,' replied Liam, ushering the Feeneys to the exit.

'Goodbye, Father Gilchrist,' said Patrick over his shoulder. 'If ever you're passing Peasholme Green...' Don't come in, came the private addition.

The young priest pricked up his ears. 'But I understood Father Kelly to say you were parishioners, Mr Feeney. Surely your residence would come within the boundary of St George's parish?'

'Oh, God,' mouthed Liam through a fixed smile. 'As soon as I close the door it'll be out with the boundary maps an' the ruler.'

Patrick quietly apologised for his unintended slip, then paused to respond to Father Gilchrist. 'Ye may be right, Father,' the answer was delivered lightly but its content showed his dislike of the way this young upstart was treating Liam. 'But ye see, Father McNaughlty and I didn't see things eye to eye. In fact he was the one who excommunicated me twenty years ago.'

'Oh, Patrick, Patrick,' sighed Liam as the younger priest spun on his heel, 'what did I ever do to you?'

'We-ell, the jumped-up snoteen, speaking to you like that,' returned Patrick in a dismissive tone of voice as they slipped into the open air.

'Indeed, he is,' agreed Liam. 'But if ever there was a comment destined to fit Father G.'s intent it was the one about excommunication. Will ye look at him now, earning himself writer's cramp.' The young priest retreated down the aisle, hunched assiduously over his chronicle, pencil eating up the blank pages. 'Ah well, I suppose I'd best go face the music.'

'There'd be sweeter balm for the savage breast at the Feeney residence,' pressed his friend. 'Erin's promised to give us a few rounds on the harp and Tommy's had the piano specially tuned. It'll be a grand do.'

'I'd love to,' said Liam, nudging Belle's soft cheek with

a horny-nailed finger. 'But Father Gilchrist keeps lining jobs up for me. Says he, I've put ye down to call on Mrs Fitzgerald this afternoon. Why for, says I? To give her the last rites, says he, her brother sent word that the poor woman's near to death.'

'Did ye tell him ye've been reading her the last rites every Sunday for the last fifteen years?' smiled Patrick.

'And have himself put an end to one o' life's little pleasures? Sure, I did not. She serves a great class o' brew does Mrs Fitzgerald. 'Tis not her fault that the Lord keeps sending her false alarms.' He shared a laugh with Patrick. 'I tell ye, Pat, that woman's had so many Extreme Unctions she's got her own oil-bottling plant out the back.' He accompanied the family to the waiting carriages and watched each climb aboard. 'God bless ye, Erin, ye've a beautiful child there. Take special care o' her.'

'I will, Father, an' God bless you, too.'

'Poor Liam,' said Thomasin as the carriage transported them home. 'He's got his hands full with that one.'

'He has,' replied her husband grimly. 'An' if Father Gilchrist gets his way I'm thinking it'll not just be poor Liam, but poor all of us.'

Sonny was in his studio, packing his brushes and paints ready for his journey to Paris. With Erin and Sam's departure from York he had decided it was time for him to leave, too. It might seem a bit back-to-front to some people, him spending time in the haunts of starving artists when he already had a successful career, but he felt the visit might provide him with new concepts and even more importantly, would give him time to be alone. Much as he loved his family and Josie he desperately needed solitude. Like his parents, Sonny's grief over his brother's death was still strong. He paused in his leisurely packing to sink into memories.

Dickie had been so colourful, had made such an impact on the folk around him, that even months after his death he still filled their minds . . . though now they all seemed to find it difficult to talk about him. A couple of months

41

after his death there had been a surprise visit from Dickie's solicitor. Bogged down by misery as they were, no one had given a thought to Dickie's assets, but it transpired that he had made a will. At the time Sonny had been struck by the thought that this was rather out of character for his normally irresponsible brother, but had been too upset to bother questioning the man. His emotion was heightened on learning that Dickie had left him the house and its entire contents, his liquid assets to be shared equally between Erin, her parents and Sonny's children – though this was hardly a generous bequest for it turned out that Dickie hadn't been as rich as he had led them to believe.

Sonny hadn't wanted the house. When he had gone to look round it, he had found two maidservants dining in luxury and had immediately given them notice. But there had been a third person there – his brother's ghost. Sonny couldn't live with that. He had put the house and its contents up for sale, keeping nothing; he needed no memento to remind him.

He thumbed the bristles of hog's-hair and pondered on the subject of houses for he was in rather a quandary. He knew that when he and Josie married they should buy a house of their own – the bad experience of his first marriage had taught him that – but what of Rosie and Nick? They looked on their grandfather's house as home and doted on Patrick as he did on them. It would be too big a wrench for either to move – even down the street. Sonny and Josie could hardly leave them, so they must stay too . . . but Sonny knew it was going to be very hard for his new wife to live amongst people to whom she had been a servant. All these considerations needed serious thought, that was why he was going away. He tore himself from his daydreaming and packed the last of his brushes. After this he took a lingering look around his studio then locked up and went home.

Josie came round that same evening. Since leaving the Feeneys' employ she had taken a cook/housekeeper's post with another family. Sonny had seen the sense in this –

she still needed to live while he was making up his mind and she wasn't prepared to accept financial help from him until they were married. Apart from this, the household for which she worked was small and the work light. She had plenty of time to visit Rosie and Nick on an evening and on Sundays – though tonight her visit was mainly for Sonny whom she would not see again until Christmas. Hence the meeting was not exactly a carefree one.

She and Sonny were seated close together on a sofa, a child on each lap. The four had the room to themselves. 'Will you still come to see us when Father goes away?' asked Rosanna. The conversation so far had been about little else but Father's trip.

The woman's arms were laced more tightly around the little body. 'Of course I will.' She kissed the child noisily.

'Every night?'

'Well . . . not every night – but as often as I can and definitely on Sundays.'

Rosanna and Nick spoke their gladness, causing the man and woman to share a fond smile over the children's heads. 'When Father gets back will you get married?' enquired Nick.

Josie laughed softly, her eyes full of love for the man and his children. 'That's not a question a little boy should be asking.'

'But will you?'

'Why so nosey?' Josie reached a hand up to smooth the fair hair from his brow.

'I just want to know when I'm getting a proper mother,' stated Nick.

'Don't you think it's time you were in bed?' smiled his father.

Rosie cuddled her cheek against the woman's softness. 'Not yet.'

'Well, I do.' Sonny rose, lifting the boy onto his shoulders. 'You've commandeered Josie enough. It's my turn now – I won't see her till Christmas.' He had promised faithfully to come home then.

'You won't see us either,' Rosanna pointed out, trying

to press Josie back into her seat. 'What d'you have to go for anyway?'

'I've told you, it's for my work.'

'Gramps and Nan have work too but they come home every night.'

'Eh, you always have an answer, don't you?' Sonny jabbed a finger into his daughter's ribs making her squirm and giggle. 'I'm not going for that long. I'll be back before you've even missed me. I need to talk to Josie and give her instructions on how to keep you two in order while I'm gone. Away now! We'll go find your Gramps and get him to tell you one of his tales, then maybe if you get ready for bed without a fuss you can spend a little more time with me later. Shall I ring for Abi or will you find Gramps yourselves?' They said they could do the latter and he set Nick on his feet, waiting for the children to kiss Josie goodbye before telling them to run along.

When he and Josie were alone he sat down again, putting his arm around her and chuckling over his children. She laid her head on his shoulder and nothing was said for a while.

'I might be mistaken,' Josie said finally, 'but I thought I heard you tell the children you wanted to speak to me?'

He clutched her fondly. 'That was just to get rid of them. What I really want is this.' He craned his head round to kiss her.

She gave a long sigh with the parting of their lips. 'Oh, I don't know how I'm going to last till Christmas – you promise you will write?'

'Promise. I don't want to be away from you, you know. I wouldn't want you to think I was trying to escape . . .'

She smiled and touched a hand to his cheek. 'I understand why you're going . . . I'll just miss you, that's all.'

They shared a long amorous embrace until Josie broke loose and panted laughingly, 'I think it's just as well you are going away!'

With a rueful grin Sonny changed his position on the sofa. Josie wasn't the sort to yield to passion before the wedding. He wished he could give her a definite date . . . but he must have time.

She sensed his dilemma and turned the conversation to less personal matters. 'Oh, I tell you who I saw today!' She sat up and smoothed her clothes. 'You know Dusty Miller who your Dickie was going to wed? Well no, not her,' she forestalled his question, 'but a girl I used to know who worked for the Millers. Well, I was in the butcher's for a piece of beef – didn't get it, mind, ended up with lamb,' – she caught his amusement and said, 'aye well, that's beside the point. This girl, Betty, she was telling me that Dusty Miller has gone to live in America. Fancy that!'

Sonny showed interest. He had liked Dusty. 'Has she sold the wholesale business, then?'

'Apparently not. She just did a flit and left somebody in charge, didn't say how long she'd be gone or anything. Well, I'm telling you backwards way on, really. How I got to know about it was that Betty was grumbling about the fella she left in charge, then it led on to her telling me about Dusty.'

Sonny used her well-fleshed shoulder as a pillow, closing his eyes and making himself more comfortable. 'How long's she been gone?'

Josie laid her head against the flaming-red one and stroked the hand that gripped hers. 'Since late last year. She must've been having a good time. I wonder if she'll ever come back?'

Late last year. Sonny thought of the events that had been affecting this family late last year. The image of his brother's roguish, laughing face stirred remembrance of their last conversation: Dickie had been going to America too . . . if he hadn't been burnt to death. He mouthed this softly to his partner who stroked him comfortingly. 'S'funny how things turn out, isn't it?' sighed Sonny. 'I mean, Dusty going to America. Did she ever get married, d'you know?'

'Don't think so.' Josie smiled then and nudged him gently. 'You've gone and done it, haven't you?'

'Done what?' Puzzled grey eyes met her grin.

45

'Brought the subject around to marriage again when you don't really want to talk about it.'

He shuffled round and pinioned her arms. 'Who says I don't want to talk about it?'

Her face was kind as she shook her head. 'I'm not pressing you for a proposal, love. You go away if you have to and think about it for as long as you like.'

He became serious then, breathing the earnest words against her cheek. 'It's not that I need to think about marrying you, Jos. I *know* I want you for my wife. I want you and me and Rosie and Nick to be a family . . . I just have to be sure I'm grown up enough to offer you the life you deserve. There's things I have to sluice from my mind.'

She knew well what these things were and put a hand to his lips. 'John,' she always used his proper name, 'I don't expect you to have got over everything already — even after a year, two years, who knows how long it'll take? Last year was terrible, you lost your brother, your wife . . .'

'I had stopped loving her, Jos.'

'And no wonder after what she did . . . but it was still a dreadful thing to happen to her, and I'm not going to push you into anything. Take all the time you want.'

And it was this generous offering that served to comfort Sonny in the months of solitary evenings that followed.

CHAPTER THREE

The farmhouse kitchen was well defended against the cool evening. An ample fire crackled in the inglenook, the logs which formed it shooting red sparks up the chimney. At the foot of each door was a length of material, rolled up and stuffed with rags to form a sausage. Pretty chintz curtains deterred any cold air from sneaking through a loose windowpane, and if the stone floor of the cottage did reflect the cold, the effect was muted by brightly-coloured rugs strewn about its surface.

The couple seated on either side of the well-scrubbed table were picked out in the spotlight from the lantern that flickered from the beam over their bent heads. They said little as they consumed their evening meal. Only the snapping of the fire and the clink of cutlery on china broke the silence.

Erin's head came up suddenly from the meal she had been making a pretence of eating, instantly alert. 'Is that Belle crying?'

'I didn't hear nowt,' said Sam, enjoying his mutton. 'Get on wi' your meal, lass.'

'I'd better just go . . .' She began to rise.

'Sit down. 'S probably only t'pup wanting to be where it's warm. He'll have to learn his place.' The bitch had recently had a litter. Sam had kept one dog for himself to help its mother with the herd. 'Come on, get your tea afore it's cold.' He watched her push the pieces of meat aimlessly around her plate. She was still listening. 'Erin, for Heaven's sake! You're gonna waste away if you go on like this.' Not once since leaving her parents' house had she enjoyed a proper meal, always preoccupied, waiting for Belle to cry so she could jump up and answer the summons. God only knew how she performed when he wasn't here to keep her in check. 'Doesn't she cry enough without you imagining it?'

'But I'm sure it was her. Let me go up and see, Sam. I couldn't sit here and eat knowing she was crying with hunger.'

Sam shook his head wearily, but allowed her to go. Hunger indeed. Belle would never know real hunger, not like her grandparents had. The minute her mouth opened in a demanding squall Erin was there to shove herself into it. That was all she seemed to live for nowadays, to see to Belle's constant needs. The thought was not without resentment. It had taken Sam years to win his wife's whole-hearted attention, and now Belle had arrived the nights of abstinence had begun again.

She returned from her sortie, slipping wordlessly back into her seat.

'Didn't I tell you it was the dog?' he said peevishly. 'Now sit down an' don't budge till you've eaten that meal.'

'It's cold.' She pushed away the plate.

He pushed it back. 'Cold or no, you'll eat it. I'm damned sick of all this, Erin.'

His strict tone pierced her befogged state. 'All what?'

'You know bloody-well all what. All this toing an' froing, never sitting still for five minutes. A man expects his wife's attention when he comes in after a hard day's work. All I get is Belle this, Belle that . . .'

'Sam!' she cried accusingly. 'She's your daughter.'

'An' I'm your husband, Erin. Oh, don't give me those eyes. Just because I say these things doesn't mean I love her any less. I'm just getting damned sick of her getting all the treatment.'

'Of all the selfish . . . she's a helpless little child, Sam. You're a man, easily capable of taking care of yourself.'

'That's just as well, isn't it? 'Cause that's what I've been forced to do these past months.'

'Don't exaggerate,' reproved Erin. 'I'm always here when you get in, aren't I?'

'Are you?' he demanded. 'You're sat at the table, yes, but your mind is miles away. If I get as much as half a dozen words from you before we go to bed I count meself lucky. It's as if I'm not here. Your whole world is focused on Belle. Instead of her fitting into our lives we have to fit into hers. She rules us, night and day. Look at the state she's got you into. Just look at yourself! I've seen more flesh on a pauper's dog. You must stop allowin' her to interrupt your meals. I won't stand by an' see you waste away, watch you treating her like . . . like . . .'

'Like a baby?' enquired Erin hotly.

'Erin, I wouldn't mind if you did treat her like a baby, but you don't. You wouldn't allow a normal baby to dictate to you like she does. You'd simply put it to your breast when it needed feedin' then tuck it up in its cradle an' that would be that.'

'I thought you'd noticed, Sam, Belle isn't a normal baby.' Her fork stabbed pettishly at bits of meat.

'An' scant chance she has of becoming a normal adult the way you treat her. You're moulding yourself a tyrant. She can't be allowed to go through life thinking all she has to do is ask an' whatever she wants will be given.'

Erin tried to draw on his sympathy, her voice wheedling. 'I can't deny her, Sam. She's such a helpless little scrap. I'm responsible for her.'

'An' so am I – as I'm responsible for you, an' I won't allow this to continue. Now, you'll sit there until that plate is clean an' if Belle cries then she must learn to wait her turn.'

Defeated, Erin closed her eyes to the congealing fat and forced a morsel of mutton between her lips. She didn't seem to have any appetite lately, which was surprising for she was run off her feet for most of the day. Night too, sometimes, for Belle still demanded a midnight feast. That wouldn't be for much longer, though. Erin's breasts no longer tingled with milk at the baby's first whimper. She knew she was going dry. Sam was right, she must eat for Belle's sake. She gagged on the half-chewed meat as her gullet unwillingly accepted it, then scraped up a forkful of mashed potato.

'Don't look at it – eat it,' commanded her husband.

It could have been a mouthful of cottonwool for all Erin tasted of it. The fork paused again. 'I'm sorry I've been neglecting you, Sam,' she mumbled. 'I'll try to be more dutiful when you come home tomorrow.'

There was indignation. 'I don't want you doing owt out o' duty, but because you want to do it.' He reached across the table for her hand. 'I'm not just sayin' it outa selfishness, love. You do understand that I'm saying it for all our sakes? You won't be no good to neither me nor Belle if you wear yourself away worryin'.'

'Oh, I know you aren't a selfish man, Sam, but . . . I can't help myself . . . whenever she cries I have to go to her. I just can't sit here stuffing food into myself knowing she's crying her heart out upstairs.'

'But she can't be hungry all the time, Erin. Mostly she's just crying for attention.' Going back to his meal he was thoughtful for a while, ploughing through the heaped plate. Then he paused again to voice his idea. 'I don't suppose she's bothered whose attention it is she gets. Tell you what, I'll take her out wi' me tomorrow, that ought to give thee a rest.'

Erin's face showed doubt. 'It's too cold – an' what if she should need changing? What if she's hungry? Still,' she mulled it over, 'I suppose I could meet you at feeding time . . .'

He thumped his fist on the table, rattling the cutlery on the plates. 'There you go again! You're reducing yourself to nowt more than a feeding trough, a milking parlour. You're a human being, Erin, you've got a life to live outside your baby. Now, I'm telling you, tomorrow morn after you've fed her you can rig up some sort o' sling that I can wear on me back an' I'll take her wi' me when I go fetch cows in for milking. Wrapped up warm she'll come to no harm. If nowt else it'll give you a couple of hours' respite from her bawlin'. Give you chance to get your feet up.'

She had to smile then. 'Get my feet up? I don't know what you think I get up to while you're out all day but it certainly isn't getting my feet up. Look at this place. It hasn't had a good bottoming since before I had Belle. There's the baking to do, the hens an' geese to feed, the washing, the butter, the cheese . . .'

'Erin Teale, here I am giving you the opportunity to put some colour back into those washed-out cheeks o' yours an' all you can do is look for work.'

'It doesn't take much looking for – besides I can't just do nothing.'

'Whyever not? Where's t'rule that says a woman must slave from morn till night? I'll help you wi' the butter later.'

'But what will people think if someone should pop in an' see me sat down amid all this mess?'

'An' what would your mam an' dad think if they called to find you looking like summat outta the cemetery?' asked

50

her husband. 'I'm not having nobody call me a slavedriver. Anyroad, what's it got to do with anyone else? Nosey buggers. It's what I think that counts an' I'm not having my wife looking like a worn-out frazzle. Leave all this an' get some rest.'

'Oh, and I'd like to hear what you'd have to say when you came in and found no bread on the table,' retorted Erin playfully, watching Sam collect the plates. 'And just what d'ye think you're doing with those?'

He poured some water from the singing kettle into a bucket and dropped in the plates. 'I'm washing them, that's what I'm doing.'

'You most certainly are not!' She leapt from her seat and tried to push him aside. 'I've still got sufficient energy to do that, thank ye very much. The very idea!'

But Sam grabbed her, picked her up bodily and transported her to the fireside chair. 'If you so much as move a muscle you're for it.'

'Oh, Sam, what will Dobby say if he catches you doing woman's work?'

'He can say what he likes. I'm not above dunking Ralph Dobbins in the hoss trough if I get any truck from him. God, anyone'd think a drop o' dishwater was going to turn me into some nancy-boy.' A twinkle came to his eye. 'Though the amount I've been getting since Belle arrived I might have to resort to that.' With dripping hands he came to lean on the arms of her chair, addressing himself to her blushing face. 'Nay, I'm only joking, lass – but can't you see I'm worried about you, Erin? Between Belle an' the housework you're just wearing yourself away. I don't want to sound cruel, but you're a far cry from the girl I married.' He tugged at a sprig of lank hair. 'What the hell's this? I've tied up stooks of straw with better stuff. You used to have such lovely hair, Erin. Here, look.' He reached for a mirror from among the willow-patterned plates on the dresser and held it to her face. 'Just take a look at yourself an' then tell me you're fit to do the housework.'

Erin stared at the mawkish reflection and put a hand to

her cheek, genuinely shocked. There had simply been no time lately to look in a mirror. 'Oh, Sam, no wonder you're cross with me. I didn't realise what a state I looked.'

'There's nothing you see in there that a decent night's rest an' a bit o' cossetting won't put right.' Taking away the mirror he bent to kiss her. 'That's why you're gonna do as I say an' sit there while I wash these. Then you're gonna drink the cocoa I'm off to make for us. Then you're off to come wi' me up to our bed an' act like a good wife should.'

'That's all you ever think about.' But it was said with a smile.

'Aye well, I reckon I've done enough thinking for the time being.' He went to start on the pans. 'Tonight I'd like some action, if you please.'

Erin watched him work his way through the dirty crocks. Some still had gravy trickles on them when he had done but she said nothing. Her silence caused him to turn and look at her. 'I promise I'll be careful. T'last thing I want right now is another bairn.'

She smiled and lowered her lashes in affirmation.

Later, they sat side by side drinking the cocoa that Sam had made for them, staring into the glowing logs, each with different thoughts. Sam opened his mouth to speak, then changed his mind. Erin noticed the motion.

'What were ye going to say?'

He closed the book that rested on his lap – *Coates' Herd Book* – and moved his face to watch her as she raised the cup to her lips. It was difficult to phrase. 'You . . . oh, it's nowt.'

'No, go on,' said his wife.

A long deliberation, then, 'You do still feel the same about me, don't you, Erin?'

Immediately she put the cup on the hearth and gave him her full attention. 'Why, of course I do! What a question.'

'Is it? What with you not having much time for me lately . . . well, a bloke gets to wondering.' He took a swift sip from his cup to mask his anxiety.

'Aw, Sam! Here, put that down.' She took the cup from him, also the book, placing both on the hearth, then leaned over to put her arms round him. 'If I'd known you were entertaining such mad fancies . . . pfff! Of course I feel the same way about you. I always will. 'Tis just that I never seem to get the time to show it these days, what with the baby. I know it must seem like I'm concentrating all my love on her, but it's not so. I love you as much as ever, Sam – more. But I can't help the way I feel about Belle. God knows, if a mother can't lavish attention on her there's no one else will.'

'You're still feeling guilty, aren't you?' Sam smoothed back the wisps of greasy hair from her pale face.

After a pause she nodded. 'I've tried not to, but 'tis no use. If only I could talk to somebody who was in the same position as me . . . but everyone I seem to look at has a healthy child.'

'Aye well, it's no use my going over old ground. What you need is someone who's not involved to convince you. What about Father Kelly? Next time we go to Mass you could have a chat with him. If anybody can put your mind at ease it's him.'

'Yes, I must make an effort . . . I've never been to Confession in ages.' There was no Roman Catholic church nearer than York, but this wasn't what had stopped her going to Confession – she had in fact attended church several times since Belle's birth, but her feet always stopped short of the confessional. She was afraid to admit her thoughts.

'Erin, I said a chat. There's no need for purging, just a private little talk with the Father.'

'No, I'd feel better if I got it off my chest the proper way.'

Sam sighed. His wife still saw Belle's disablement as some sin on her part. 'As you like. We'll go on Sunday.' He reached down for his cup, drained it and stood to bank the fire up for the night. 'Well, my lady, ist thou coming to my bed?'

She smiled and, standing, linked her arm with his,

pressing her face to his shoulder. Like this they climbed the creaking oak staircase, Sam bearing a candle aloft to light their way. Taking her nightgown from beneath the pillow she stole a peep into the silent cot before undressing. Sam sat on the bed to pull his stockings off, privately cursing the groaning bedstead. Stripping off the rest of his clothes he inserted himself gingerly between the cold sheets to watch his wife brush her hair – probably for the first time that day. 'Hurry up, lass,' he whispered eagerly.

Erin put the brush down, padded to the bed and slipped in beside him. Whence, he enclosed her in an enthusiastic hug, burying his face in the hollow of her neck, pressing fevered lips to her moist skin. She accepted his overtures willingly, if not with mutual passion, stroking his hair and clasping him affectionately. His calloused hands found the hem of her nightgown and tugged at it until the feel of linen against his body was replaced by that of warm flesh. His lips found her breast. There was the familiar hardness pressed between their two bodies, the urgency, 'Oh, Erin, I do love you,' . . . and then came the snuffling from the cot – a truculent whine which, however hard Sam tried to ignore it, soon rose to a full-blooded yell.

Erin immediately stiffened and Sam's hands paused in their frenzied caress. The hardness shrivelled to nothing. With a great sigh, inaudible above the child's wail, he rolled off her and grasped the iron bedrails above his head in frustration. 'Damn!'

Erin was already up and tucking her hands into the crib to lift the tearful infant. 'I'll take her down and feed her by the fire so's she won't disturb you,' she told her husband. 'Go to sleep if you're tired.' With this unpromising suggestion she was gone. Only the soft musk of her body remained on the sheets to drive him almost senseless.

And not one word of apology had she spoken, thought Sam emptily, not one crumb of regret; leaping up and seeing to the babe, belying all she had said that evening about loving him the same as ever. It was as if she had been waiting for the child's cry to save her from some repugnant act. He slammed his fist against the mattress and flung himself over onto his side. He loved Belle – she was his child, part of him – but so help him, he was not going to let her ruin all their lives.

Erin's anxious face bobbed at his shoulder as he made his way up the garden path, Belle strapped securely to his back. 'Ye promise ye'll have her back on time, love?'

'Never fear, I'll have her back half an hour before breakfast. That'll give you time to feed her then sit down at the table wi' me.' One way or the other he was going to fettle this child. 'An' I'll bet you five bob she comes back a different person. We'll not hear a peep out of her all morning.'

'You're not thinking to let her cry an' cry?'

'No, I shan't let her cry herself daft – but I'll not be at her every whim neither. Now, get back into that house and sit your body down.'

Opening the gate she saw him through it. 'I'll sit down later. I want to wash my hair and have a bath.'

'Lord a'mercy! A bath in t'middle o' the week. Whatever next?' He kissed her and marched off down the lane. Erin stood on tiptoe watching him until he disappeared then, feeling at a loose end, wheeled to survey the lie of the garden.

The gate by which she paused opened onto a path which veered away from the tree-shaded road and sloped down to meet the small stone cottage, built a century ago. Its length was bordered, at differing seasons, by the great bobbing heads of crimson paeonies, violent swathes of Sweet William, foxgloves, larkspur, hollyhock. The upper leaded lights of the cottage were in danger of being obscured by the creeping fingers of wisteria that had invaded the front wall over the years. Beneath the lower windows were beds of lavender whose fragrance crept over the sill to perfume every room. Here and there, terracotta urns spilled over with herbs . . . as if you've time to stand looking, Erin told herself and, hugging her arms about her body, ran down the slope and into the cottage.

Sam strode down the lane that led to the field where he kept his herd, the dog at his heels. Glancing down, he smiled at her as she snapped at the pup that had been linked to her with a piece of rope, in order for it to learn its trade – only a good idea if the parent had no faults. 'That's right, Nip, you keep that lad o' yourn in line an' we'll have him bringing t'cows in on his own in no time. He'll soon learn t'game if you keep givin' him plenty o' that – like this'n o' mine. We can't have the young'ns running the show, can we? Hold on.' He stopped and bent to extricate the yapping pup's leg which had become entangled with the rope. 'By, he makes good company for my lass. Shut your whining an' get on wi' yer.' He strode on.

It was very early. The hedgerows still glistened and the air was heavy with that silent quality that only occurs at this hour. It was mornings such as this that lightened one's mood and made the troubles of the previous night seem less significant. He'd been a bit of a dog to his wife over the babe. He decided to pick her some flowers on his way home to make up for his badness.

When he reached the field Dobby was already waiting for him, perched astride a stile and devouring a crust of bread. Seeing Sam he jumped down, pushed the last of the crust into his smiling mouth and dusted off his hands, tugging his curly forelock as he came up to the other man. 'Mornin', Maister Teale, tha's late. These ladies've been complainin' summat awful.' He retraced his steps and prodded the herd of cows away from the gate in order to open it.

'Don't talk to me about moaning women,' grumbled Sam goodnaturedly. 'I've enough o' that at home.'

The young man, solid of build and friendly of face, laughed and slapped Sam on the back, then jumped back in alarm as a squawk pierced the quietude. 'Jesus save us! What the 'ell you got in your sack, Mr Teale?'

Sam rolled his eyes as Belle shrieked her annoyance at the rude awakening. 'That there, Dobby, is what you might call a noise-box. A very noisy noise-box.' He bobbed up and down, shushing the infant.

Dobby cocked a worried face at the other man's odd stance. 'Has summat happened to Mrs Teale?' he asked concernedly, having great liking for Erin. She always gave him sup when he visited her kitchen. It had not passed Dobby's notice that she hadn't looked too well lately. He would be most upset if she were seriously ill.

'Why do you ask that?' Sam continued to jig up and down.

'Well . . . you bringing the babby out, like. I thought summat must be up wi' the missus.'

'There's nowt wrong wi' my wife, thank you, Dobby,' replied Sam firmly. 'Now let's be having that gate open. We're behind enough already as it is.'

Dobby grinned as he unlatched the gate and hitched a ride on the lower bar as it swung open. Nip dived through, dragging her yapping offspring. She dashed around the rear of the herd, barking orders, taking an occasional hold on a dawdler's heel. Sam watched the cows jostle their way through, then followed the swaying red and white rumps back along the lane.

'What're you grinning at, Ralph Dobbins?' he challenged the younger man without looking at him, though his severity did not ring true.

Dobby knew this easygoing chap too well. He shrugged and brought his stick down on a straggler. 'Oh, nowt, nowt, Mr Teale.' He started to whistle nonchalantly.

Belle had stopped crying now. She eyed him from the warm cocoon on her father's back.

'Come on, if you've got summat to say spit it out,' ordered Sam. 'I'm not puttin' up wi' sly looks all morning.'

'Well . . .' Dobby forced back a laugh. 'I'm just a bit worried about that growth you're developing on your back, Maister.' He could hold back his amusement no longer and let loose a guffaw.

'I can't see what's so funny about a man bringin' his child to work with him,' replied Sam evenly. 'If she were a few years older an' a lad I doubt the sight'd spur your hilarity.'

'Aye – but a babby, Maister!' laughed Dobby. 'I reckon you'll get some pretty queer looks when we go past the Johnsons' place.'

'Johnson couldn't look owt but queer if he tried,' answered Sam, but shrank as the herd neared the said residence and hoped Johnson would still be in bed. The man was not a favourite of Sam's who had no time for a person that spent more money on drink than food for his family. Though Sam had little benevolence for Mrs Johnson, either. She was a slattern who left her children to fend for themselves and if truth be known, was as big a drunkard as her spouse if she could filch a florin from the insensible Johnson's breeches.

His heart sank as Belle set up her caterwauling just as they drew level with the Johnsons' house. The man was sat on his front step, idly sharpening a knife. Slitting his eyes against the sun he watched the lowing herd pass, then his eyes fell on Sam with the bellowing infant on his back, and his unshaven jaw twisted into a grin. Coming out of his squat he stepped up to the gate and leant on it to watch the procession.

'Somebody got out o' the wrong side o' bed an' put her husband's clothes on by mistake. Mornin', Mrs Teale!' He uttered a coeliac laugh and beckoned his wife. 'Ey, Sadie, away an' look at this.'

Mrs Johnson stepped into the fresh morning, wiping her hands on a grubby towel. Catching sight of Sam before he passed she cackled appreciatively and, along with her spouse, began to hurl jokes by the score. Their ill-tended brood wandered out into the lane to see what had caused the merriment. Sam ignored them all and carried on past, but the Johnsons, with nothing better to do, came beyond their boundary and tagged onto the procession.

'Eh! I don't think you heard me. I said, good mornin', Mrs Teale.'

'Hop it, Johnson,' said Dobby, glancing at Sam's determined face. The lack of title from the younger man showed that he had no respect for Johnson, either.

'Ah, you're her bodyguard, are yer?' smirked Johnson, keeping step with them while his wife pirouetted alongside Sam. 'What's she doin' for you, then?'

Sam stopped dead, causing Mrs Johnson to bump into him. 'Just leave it, will you, an' allow us that choose to work to get on with it.'

Johnson threw up his hands and observed amazedly to his wife, 'Goodness gracious! It isn't Mrs Teale at all. Well, well, well. I allus knew he were a bit of an odd sort, that Sam Teale, but I didn't think he had the equipment to be a wet nurse.' He reached out to feel Sam's chest. 'Nay, I don't know how I could've mistaken him for his missus. Fine pair she's got.'

Sam knocked the hand away. 'It's a good job for you I have more respect for a woman than you have, Johnson. You can thank your wife's presence that you're not flat on your back.' Pivoting, he strode to rejoin Dobby who had kept up with the herd.

But the pair would not be deterred from their baiting, and between this barrage of insults and Belle's incessant crying Sam's temper burgeoned.

'Er, if you've taken on t'job o' feedin' bairn,' persisted Johnson, 'd'yer reckon t'wife'll be able to accommodate me if I just nip round?'

'Aye, it'd gimme a nice rest,' shrieked Sadie.

'I've allus fancied her,' continued the man. 'Right tasty, she is. An' if her old man's gone molly on her she'll no doubt be glad of a proper bit o' tuppin'.'

Sam stopped again, this time wriggling out of the sling on his back, his eyes mirroring his intent.

Dobby watched in alarm. 'Take no notice, Mr Teale. Yer know he's talkin' through his arse. Mrs Teale wouldn't touch him with a clarty pole.'

Sam, free of his screaming daughter, passed the sling to his labourer. 'Here hold that!' and was off back down the lane before Dobby could say more. The young man's hands, fumbling with the tiny body, brought an uncomfortable awareness of its crooked proportions, and his kind heart turned over, wishing he could retract his jocular comment about the growth on Sam's back. Feeling sick at his conduct he watched as Sam approached the other man. The grimy children formed a ring around them.

'Eh, now I wouldn't want thee to exert thissen,' mocked Johnson. 'Tha's got to keep up all tha strength when tha's a nursing mother.'

Sam's fist shot out and upwards, lifting the man off his feet and planting him on his back at the roadside. The children scattered. Mrs Johnson, far from being upset, laughed loudly as Sam departed, rubbing his knuckles with grim satisfaction. He returned to where Dobby stood holding the baby and, with the young man's assistance, refitted the sling.

'I'm sorry, Mr Teale. I didn't know. I'd never seen the babby but in her crib. I wouldn't've joked . . .' Sam frowned his incomprehension. 'About her bein' crooked, like,' Dobby provided. 'I wouldn't've said that about you havin' a growth on yer back. I could cut me tongue off, honest. I hope you didn't take offence.'

Sam set off as the herd passed out of sight round the curve of the hedgerow. 'If I had you'd be lyin' there alongside that pile o' muck. Now him I find extremely offensive.'

Dobby tapped his stick against his boot as he walked. 'Yer'll find a lot more like him, Maister. Tha's got to admit it's a strange sight, a man carryin' his bairn around on his back.'

'I know, Dobby and . . . oh, look at that blasted pup! I'll have to fettle him.' Whistling for the bitch, who dragged her wayward son with her, Sam bent and shoved one of the pup's front paws through its collar. 'There, run on three for a while. Happen that'll slow you up. He's over-keen, is t'lad,' he explained to Dobby as they moved again, then took up his original theme. 'I know I look daft like this, an' I don't mind folk taking a laugh at my expense if that gives 'em pleasure – though they must have small minds. But Johnson . . . well, I won't have no foul-mouthed bugger spoutin' about my Erin. An' that wife of his is no better.' He turned a grim face on Dobby.

There was a delay, then Dobby said, 'Happen you'll be in for more pezzle when he finds out about your young'n being crockity. There'll be a few more folk round here won't take to her, neither.'

'Are them your feelings, Dobby?' came the soft query.

The youth gave a mirthful bark. 'Lord no! Pardon my laughin', Maister, but I've no cause to look down on other folks' misfortune. Our Freddy's as barmy as Bedlam's bull. That's him what got shut in t'stocks last week for frightening the vicar's wife.'

Sam remembered now. He had gone to the village and had seen poor Freddy fettered there on the green being pelted with mud and rotten eggs. Even though the archaic custom was supposed to be done away with the law was hard to enforce out here where people were far behind the times. 'That was your brother?' he said to Dobby as they followed the herd across to the cowhouse. 'Nobody said owt.'

'No, well . . .' Dobby ran an embarrassed hand over his neck. 'I try not to let on about it – I don't mind you knowin' o' course, though.' He saw Sam's expression change. 'Yer think I'm rotten, don't yer? S'pose I am, but . . . I just couldn't bear for folk to start tormentin' me about him, an' they would if they knew.'

'But surely they know already?' Sam threw over his shoulder as he stepped into the dimness of the shippen. This was a small village. Everyone knew everyone else's business.

'Some o' them, mebbe. But I reckon most are ignorant,' Dobby shouted over the bawling of the calves separated from their mothers in another part of the shippen. Taking a cloth and pail he started to work his way down the row of swollen udders, sluicing and rubbing the teats – the master's idea, not his. Everyone he knew made do with a quick wipe. Sam had probably got the idea of all this cleanliness from that book he was always reading. 'He doesn't live with us, yer see. He lives in the poorhouse.'

Sam frowned. 'Why's that, Dobby?'

'Well, me mam couldn't manage him, y'see. She had enough wi' me dad dying on her. I know it doesn't sound like motherly love, but she knew t'poorhouse'd take him in an' he'd get fed an' bed. So she left him on t'doorstep when he were a babby, pretended to folk that the child she'd been expecting was born dead. Well, she couldn't afford to keep somebody who wouldn't be bringin' no money home, could she?'

'No, I suppose not,' answered Sam, deep in himself. The lash of a cow's tail brought him back to consciousness. 'Ow, that was my eye, madam!'

'There we are, Maister, all done.' Dobby straightened and stepped back to admire the row of sleek, red rumps. 'By, you're building up a crackin' herd o' coos there. Look at them udders, full to bustin'. Couldn't fancy walkin' round wi' that lot between my legs, could you?'

'No,' replied Sam. 'An' I don't suppose it's all that comfy for them neither, so let's get crackin'.'

The bitch, Nip, still tethered to her son, lay down in a corner to survey the workings of the byre. Her master and his boy worked silently for a time, the only sound being the chomping of the cows as they snatched mouthfuls of hay from the manger and the spray of milk into the wooden pails. It was Dobby who broke the silence first as he emptied one udder and moved on to the next.

'Is the missus comin' down later?' Previously Erin had stood by in the dairy attached to the shippen, waiting to pour the milk into the flat earthenware separating pans. The process would take a lot longer with just the two of them.

'I told her thee an' me'd see to the skimming for a while.' Sam upturned a pail of warm, frothy milk into another container. 'She's got her hands full at the moment. I'm trying to lighten her workload.' He caught Dobby's grin. 'You think I'm soft, I can tell. Well, I'm not bothered. I'm not a man who'll work his wife into the ground. She's not her usual self, Dobby. Needs to build up her strength before she gets back to turning heavy butter churns. That's why I brought Belle along wi' me. She's allus howling summat wicked an' I thought it might do Erin a bit o' good if I got her out o' the road. It'll not harm me for a while.'

The reference to Belle caused them both to realise that she was no longer howling and now slept contentedly, her fluffy head lolling on her father's back as he worked.

'Well, it looks like you've got 'em both knocked into shape, Maister,' grinned Dobby, grasping two more teats. 'Her an' t'pup.'

Sam grinned back. 'Aye, females an' dogs, lad, it's just a question o' showing 'em who's t'boss – now all we have to do is convince the wife o' that.'

CHAPTER FOUR

'Now then, can milady tell us if she's feeling any better?' Sam placed a cup of tea in front of his wife and joined her at the table.

'Much, much better, thank ye, kind sir.' That was obviously no lie. The hitherto lank hair was now brushed neatly into a chignon, the eyes had begun to regain their vitality and the crumpled apron had been exchanged for her Sunday dress. Sam's burden-sharing scheme had only been in motion for a few days but it was certainly showing results. 'And I shall feel better still when we've been to church.'

'Come on then, sup up else we'll not get there.' He dropped two sugar lumps into his lukewarm tea, stirred it briskly and swallowed it at one lifting. 'I'll get Belle ready.'

'No, *I'll* get Belle ready,' she replied firmly. 'I'm beginning to feel like a spare part what with all this spoiling. An' it's going to stop as from today. I only needed a few days' rest to put me back on my feet and now I'm fine again.'

63

'It's good to tell that, bossy-breeches.'

'Never mind bossy-breeches, just put down that cup and – Sam Teale, what d'ye think you're doing?'

'I'm only taking me cup to rinse.'

'Give it here!' She took the cup from him. 'Now, go get your jacket on and harness Bluebell while I get on with *my* work.'

Sam spoke to Belle who lay gurgling on the rug. 'See what thanks we get for our servitude?'

'Sure, did I forget to thank ye?' asked Erin lightly. 'Well, thank ye very much for your kind assistance an' I'll admit it was very welcome at the time, but 'tis not right you should be doing women's work at all, let alone on top of your own job, so we'll have no more – understood?'

'Does Belle still go to work with her dad of a mornin', or what?'

'There's hardly the need now, is there?'

'There's isn't, no, but . . .' He pulled at his ear, 'Well . . . I've grown quite used to having her wi' me of a morning. If nowt else she keeps me back warm – an' Dobby's grown fond of her company too.'

'What funny creatures you men are,' said Erin, smiling. 'Well, I don't see any harm in her going with you while ye do the milking. It gives me time to get straightened out here I must confess – though I can't say I don't worry about her when she's away.'

Sam picked Belle up. 'Eh, I don't know what your mother thinks thee an' me get up to when we're on us own.' He pretended to whisper. 'Don't let on about them games o' pitch an' toss we have while we're supposed to be milkin' t'coos.'

'Less of your blarney an' go get ready!' Erin took Belle from him and wrapped her tightly in a shawl, whereupon the baby immediately began to wail.

'Oy, I've warned you about that!' Her father wagged a finger. 'Doest want me to take bullwhip to thee like I did t'other day? Did you see the way she started the minute you looked at her? She knows when she's onto a soft touch.'

'Soft touch, is it?' Erin advanced on him, hand upraised. 'Ye'll be feeling my soft touch round your ear if ye don't go – and – get – ready – for – church!'

Leaving Dobby and the dogs to look after his herd, Sam harnessed the pony and very shortly he and Erin set off. It was an enjoyable ride along those twisting country lanes, with the soft rush of air against one's face, the melodious accompaniment of the birds. Erin was feeling happier than she had done for a long time. She imagined how much better she would feel on her way home, unburdened of all the things she had been bottling up over the past months.

On reaching York they made their way through the streetfuls of other worshippers to be met by Patrick and Thomasin at their own church, sitting as usual six rows from the front. Only their grandchildren, Nick and Rosanna, accompanied them today. Sonny was now in France.

'Hello, strangers,' whispered Patrick from the side of his mouth as Erin came out of her introductory prayer. 'How's my wee angel?' He put his face close to Belle who patted his mouth with pudgy, splayed fingers. Patrick nibbled one of the tiny digits tenderly.

Thomasin watched forlornly, wishing she could find the same enthusiasm for Belle. The conversation ceased with the arrival of the priest. Sam and Erin swapped confused glances when they saw that their old friend was not to take Mass, but Father Gilchrist.

Patrick saw the look. 'It's been going on for a few weeks,' he informed them in a low voice. 'Father Gilchrist started by taking one Mass per week, now he's doing most of them. Liam's being slowly edged out. He doesn't crack much but I know it's breaking his heart.' He settled back as Mass commenced.

Later, clutching Belle, Erin joined the line of sinners who waited outside the confessional. Sam, not as devout, said he'd wait near the door with her parents. His wife ran a rosary through the fingers of one hand, biting her lip nervously as Father Gilchrist stepped into the confessional and shut himself off from the rest of the world. Erin hoped the baby would not aggravate matters by crying. Being fifth in line she had time to study the doleful faces as each transgressor emerged to do his penance, and her fingers worked more fitfully along the tiny spheres. It would have been preferable to talk to Father Kelly. She wished she had taken Sam's advice and arranged to have an informal chat with the old priest. But it was too late now; it was her turn.

She perched on the edge of her seat in the confessional and whispered to the grille, 'Bless me, Father, for I have sinned. It is three months since I made my last confession . . .'

The smooth voice filtered through the mesh. 'Such a long absence. You must be a truly virtuous person – or is it that you had better things to do than beg the forgiveness of your Maker?'

'I'm truly sorry, Father.'

'Apart from indifference to your faith, what else have you to confess?' The voice was cool, impersonal.

'I don't quite know how to begin.' There was a long pause. Liam would have given kindly prompting, but not Father Gilchrist.

'Is it the magnitude of your transgression that procures this speechlessness, or have you sinned so often you are unable to enumerate the times?'

There would be no forgiveness here, but the realisation had come too late.

She must go through with the purge. 'It's my child, Father,' she whispered falteringly. 'She . . . she was born with a crooked spine. We'd waited so long . . .'

'Woman, I am not a doctor. If you have a sin to confess please do so.'

Confusion. 'I haven't any sin to confess, as such. 'Tis just that . . . well, Father, I hold myself responsible for her deformity. I feel it must be something I did, some bad thing I committed when I was carrying her.'

'If you did not confess this bad thing at the time then you are right to hold yourself responsible,' nodded Father Gilchrist on the other side of the grille. 'Had you cleansed your heart to Our Lord you would have found Him merciful . . . but our sins cannot go unpunished. God has obviously seen fit to avenge Himself through your child. He has put His mark upon it and you will watch it struggle through life knowing that it was your unconfessed sin that made it so. You say you have no sin "as such" to confess. I find that statement incredible and extremely arrogant.'

Erin's mind was in turmoil. 'Well, I have committed sins, yes, Father . . . but anything I can think of would be of such little import against my baby's deformity . . .'

'After an absence of three months you blithely set aside your sins as of "little import" and expect Absolution as simply as that . . .'

'I didn't intend it to sound arrogant, Father,' pleaded Erin tearfully, clutching the baby more tightly. 'I'm truly repentant for all me wrongdoings, believe me.'

'Very well, I shall pray to Our Lord that you be forgiven . . . Now, will you complete your confession?'

Erin tried to remember all the things she should have done, but hadn't, and vice versa, but all her mind saw was her poor baby, marked by her mother's sin.

'Is that the full extent of your misdeeds?' asked the priest when she had finished. Erin whispered that it was. 'And that is the list of crimes which a minute ago you wrote off as insignificant?'

'It wasn't my intention to say that, Father!'

'But that was your inference – nothing on that list was quite so important as the maiming of your offspring.'

He's twisting everything I've said, thought Erin.

'And what of the sin that brought about this malformed child? The gravity of it has apparently made enough impact on you for you to think that it was the cause of the child's deformity, yet you have made no mention of it.'

I can't tell him. I *won't* tell him what I think it was. She inhaled. 'No, I can't think of anything I've done that would warrant such harsh punishment, Father.'

'You really cannot imagine anything? That is very strange, for a perfectly sound reason immediately springs to my mind, one which has already been mentioned several times. It is the sin of extreme arrogance that has visited this scar upon your child.'

'Oh no, Father! I can't believe Our Lord would be so cruel . . .'

'You see! Even this you are too self-centred to accept. It is a common failing of women. I see you all, sitting before me on a Sunday, none of you concerned with the warning from the pulpit but more interested in the size of your neighbour's hat. That is all the church has become to many of you – a social gathering, a place where you can brag and preen in your fashionable clothes, thinking that nothing can touch you, that Our Lord will sit idly by and watch His house reduced to the level of a public meeting hall.' Each word was coated with rime. 'And when He chooses to register His disgust by putting His mark upon your child you still arrogantly maintain that it couldn't possibly be anything you have done.' Erin's sobs woke the baby who joined in. 'Go now, woman, and every time you look upon your hapless child remember that it was you who brought her such misery.' He ended by giving her an extremely stiff penance.

Blinded by shame and humiliation she stumbled from the confessional.

Though her tears were dried before she rejoined her husband and parents, Sam at once sensed the regression in Erin's mood. Half an hour ago she had been quite perky, now she was the same nervous creature of a week ago.

Liam, who had seen Patrick and Thomasin from his study window and had come to join them on the church steps, remarked on her doleful expression. 'I see Father Gilchrist has had the old whip cracking again. What did he give ye, a hundred rosaries?'

'Nothing so steep,' replied Erin, hushing the baby.

'But steep enough, judging by the change in your disposition,' said her father. 'Are ye feeling all right, muirnin? Ye're not sick, are ye?'

'No, no, I'm perfectly well.' Erin began to get testy with

the child. 'Oh, do shut up, Belle, will ye!' Instantly she burst into tears.

'What the devil has the man been saying to ye?' demanded Liam as they all crowded round her. 'Here, fetch her over to the house, Pat. We'll get to the bottom o' this.'

With Sam and Patrick's support Erin steered her feet to Liam's house, Thomasin bringing up the rear carrying Belle. Father Kelly ushered them into the drawing room where a raging fire crackled and ordered his housekeeper to fetch a tray of tea.

'Now then, we'll be knowing what all this is about.'

''Tis nothing. I cry at the drop of a hat these days. I'm all right now.' The combination of cool weather, hot fire and tears had produced a stream from Erin's nose. She blew it noisily then put away her handkerchief and started to rise.

Liam put a hand to her shoulder. 'You're forgetting, this is the man who gave ye your first set o' rosary beads. I can tell there's more to it than you're letting on. An' if I didn't know you I *do* know Father Gilchrist. Now, what did he say that's upset ye so?'

'Nothing really . . . he only supported the view that I held when I went into the confessional . . . that I'm responsible for Belle's affliction.'

There was chorused outrage. 'Eh, I've never heard owt so daft!' exclaimed Thomasin. 'And just how are you supposed to be responsible?'

'Father Gilchrist agrees with me that it's some sin I've committed that's brought this about.'

'God, the man wants locking up,' breathed Liam, then sat himself next to Erin and took hold of both her hands. 'Child, child! If I believed all he told me about meself I'd be dancing with Old Nick by now. The man's a fanatic. He's never happy but when he's telling someone how wicked they are. It makes him feel the holier, d'ye see?' What a terrible shock for a poor girl who had gone into the confessional for comfort and Absolution to come across a woman-hater like Gilchrist. 'Erin, would ye agree that I've

69

been in the business longer than Father Gilchrist?' She nodded, sniffing. 'An' wouldn't ye say that I've more experience in interpreting Our Lord's teachings – if that doesn't sound too arrogant?'

'That's what he said about me.' Erin drew in a shaky breath, tasting salt. 'That I was too arrogant.'

'God, the man's an eejit,' said Pat, thinking of all the things Erin had done for both her parents as a young girl; the sacrifices she had made. 'There's no one more selfless than you. He's bloody mad.'

'I'll endorse that,' said Liam. 'At least where dealing with my parishioners is concerned. He's not such an eejit when it comes to ousting a fellow from his post. 'Tis a pretty good job he's made of blackening my character with the Bishop. Erin, I'd have ye know what sort o' fella we're dealing with before ye give credence to his homily. Far be it from me to cast the first stone – but I will, since he's been in the habit of slinging half bricks in my direction. There's not a week gone by without that man upsetting one o' my people. Poor Mrs Cahill – I'm not breaking any confidence now, poor soul – she came to him 'cause she'd fallen for another bairn an' her with twelve already. She wanted him to tell her husband to curb his appetite for a while – I'd've stuck my boot up the man's backside – but did he? He did not. He told her that it was woman's lot in life, that it was her fault for leading her old man on with the temptation that was Eve's. Damned fool. It happened while I was away, summoned before the Bishop and told to be a good boy or else. I didn't know anything about it till I picked up the paper the following week. The poor woman took her own life. Jumped off the top o' the Minster. Six lines, that's all she was worth. Six lines in a newspaper and instantly forgettable. And when I confronted him with the article, "Oh, yes," says he, calmly as ye please. "I knew the woman. Told her only last week that her sinful ways would bring about her downfall and I was right, wasn't I?" God forgive me, I could've cheerfully chucked *him* off the top o' the Minster. Only conscience made me suffice with a few harsh words. And was he repentant? Not he! Quite ruffled, in fact. He trotted straight back to the Bishop an' told him all I'd said, adding a bit of his unique kind of embroidery for luck. Once again I was hauled over the coals to explain my inexcusable behaviour.'

'An' that's why he was taking Mass this morning while you're not,' said Patrick.

'Correct. At first it'd be, "Oh, Father Kelly, I think it would be a good idea if Father Gilchrist took Mass today, just so's he can gain a little experience". I'm lucky if I'm allowed to take Mass once a week now, and definitely not on Sundays when all the nobs are there – all the money. The Bish doesn't mind losing one or two of his flock as long as they're not the paying kind.' He shook his head. 'God, I'm getting an uncharitable devil in me old age. It might be true o' Father Gilchrist but my Lord Bishop is a good man really. He just listens to too much gossip. So, most of the time I'm sat here twiddling my thumbs, unless Father Gilchrist has any dirty jobs he wants doing. That's the sort o' man he is, Erin. Oh, I wish ye'd've come to your old friend instead o' him. I could've put your mind at ease right away.' He stroked her hand. 'Never mind, 'tis not too late to put things right. Ah, here's Mrs Lucas with the tea. Thank ye, Mrs Lucas, I'll ring if we need anything else.' He waited for the woman to leave, raising and lowering his cup before speaking again. 'Now, Mrs Teale, ye won't be surprised to hear that I hold an entirely different point of view on Belle's condition. Unlike Father G. I see her arrival not as a sign of God's disapproval but as a blessing, an act of His confidence in your faith. From time to time He sets tests for us who see ourselves as true Christians. Some of us turn out to be not so righteous after all, while some win through with flying colours. I'll endorse His confidence in you, Erin, an' say that I think you're one o' the latter. Despite what's been said to ye today, you're not the type to sit moping and wondering why this terrible thing has happened to you. If perhaps ye feel that way at the moment 'tis only because ye've not been a mother for very long. It takes time to get back to

71

your old vitality – sure look at me after I'd had the twins.' He joined Erin's chuckle. 'There, that's better. I'm sure you're going to prove Father Gilchrist wrong an' God right. You're going to make something out of this child, Erin. Nobody expects ye to do it alone. Ye've a good man in Sam, an' all of us here today are going to help ye, aren't we?' There were murmurs of confirmation. 'So forget whatever the man told ye and listen to an old hand. Stop holding yourself responsible for something ye had no say in. If there's guilt to be apportioned it should be attached to people like Father G.'

After his friends had gone home to breakfast, Liam put on a determined face and went over to the church. Confession was still in progress. Another sinner was about to slip into the box, but Liam placed a delaying hand on his shoulder and, motioning the man back to his seat, took his place in the confessional. His lips enunciated into the grill. 'Father Gilchrist, I have a message from your Employer.'

'Who is this?' A dissected face tried to guess the identity of the speaker but Liam pressed himself into a corner.

'He says, are ye trying to do Him out of a job, too?'

'If this is some sort of joke . . .'

'Oh, 'tis no joke. He's awful miffed about it. He doesn't care for these impersonations ye've been doing of Him. Says ye've not captured Him at all.'

'Who is this?' demanded Father Gilchrist.

'Oh, 'tis just one of His humble messengers come to give ye a few pointers on your act.'

'This is outrageous!' Father Gilchrist stormed out of his half of the confessional to confront his tormentor and found Liam sitting there calmly, arms crossed and a dangerous glint in his eye. 'Father Kelly!' came the amazed hiss. 'What is the meaning of this?'

'I'll tell ye what the meaning is.' Liam rose to his feet. 'I've just spent fifteen heartrending minutes trying to convince a dear friend o' mine that what ye told her was a load of horsemuck.'

'I beg your pardon?'

''Tis her pardon ye should be begging,' said Liam. 'Heartbroken, she was. As if she hasn't a big enough cross to bear with her half-formed child without you driving the nails in deeper.'

'Ah, you refer to the woman to whom I have just given penance.'

'A totally unjust penance in my view.'

'Father Kelly, if you insist on taking umbrage every time one of your parishioners dislikes the penance I've meted out then I shall . . .'

'You'll what? Leave the job to me? Good, I'd be most gratified.'

'I was going to say I shall have to have a word with the Bishop about our disagreement.'

'Another one? Sure, you're not one to use words sparingly, are ye, Father? Nor kindly neither, judging by what ye just said to my friend.'

'Father, the woman had not been to Confession in three months. You surely do not expect me to condone that? It's my duty as a priest to uphold the teachings of the church.'

'Is it also your duty to tell a woman that she's responsible for the malformation of her baby?' demanded Liam.

'Father, kindly lower your voice. This is neither the time nor the place to discuss this matter.' He glanced uneasily at the row of people waiting to confess, then began to move away. 'We shall talk about this later.'

'What's wrong?' Liam's hand shot out. 'Annoyed that I've foiled another suicide bid from the top o' the Minster? A spectacular thought, isn't it?'

'That is unforgivable!' accused Gilchrist.

'Yes, it is,' nodded Liam. 'I apologise – but tell me, Father, why did ye say the wicked things ye did? There's no knowing what the poor girl would've done if I hadn't been there to talk her out of it.'

'Wicked?' There was genuine disbelief. 'I didn't consider them wicked but totally justified. I told her but the truth.'

'The truth? Whose truth, Father?'

Father Gilchrist grew impatient with the game. 'I am simply a vessel for God's ruling, as are you.'

'So, it was God who told ye to say those things? Ye don't think ye could've interpreted Him wrongly?'

'I do not.'

'Then 'tis a very different God that speaks to you from the one that instructs me, Father. The God I'm familiar with is one of love and forgiveness, support. Yours is one of vengeance.'

'You verge on the blasphemous, Father Kelly. I would warn you, be very careful.'

Liam ignored him. 'Ye know what I think?'

'What you think does not particularly interest me.' But Father Gilchrist's anger was not without its tinge of delight. The senile priest had finally stepped over the edge. Bishop French must surely have him replaced now.

'No, I don't suppose it does. You're far too engrossed in yourself to heed anyone else's opinion – including Our Lord's. See, I don't think it's God who tells ye to say these things – you enjoy playing at God too much yourself to listen to what He has to say. Which brings us back to the original message I have for ye.' Liam locked his hands behind his back and thrust out his chest. 'Your impersonations of Him, impressive though they are, will never work. See, there's one point where you and He vastly differ – you're just too bloody holy.'

Father Gilchrist's legs almost buckled. The man was not only senile – he was insane. But Liam had not finished.

'An' let me tell ye another little thing before ye go running off to the Bishop. If ye don't moderate your approach and treat my – or should I say *your* – parishioners like human beings instead of whipping boys, I am personally going to kick your holier than holy arse from here to Kingdom Come.' With that he marched away, leaving a furious Father Gilchrist to vent his frustration on the row of penitents.

CHAPTER FIVE

By the time Belle attained her second year people had grown used to the sight of her accompanying her father to milking and the rude remarks which had plagued them for those first weeks had long since worn themselves into redundancy. Now, instead of sitting in the sling on his back she would travel on Sam's shoulders, grasping two tight handfuls of his blond hair to steady herself. Possessed of the strikingly-blue eyes that ran through the family she would watch everything and everyone who passed, seemingly filing all this away in her pretty head. Folk would say, 'Eh, she's a canny lahl thing' as she craned her neck to follow them past, and then, would invariably add, 'Such a shame she's crooked.'

Erin would wave them off on a morning and welcome the couple of hours' grace which enabled her to get the bulk of her work done before Belle's demands recommenced. Although she was long past breast-feeding, the child still managed to run her mother off her feet. If anything, Belle was even more of a handful than she had been in babyhood. Despite the fact that she could not walk, just shuffle along in an ungainly, toadlike fashion on her bottom, she succeeded in getting into everything and anything. Erin's nerves were constantly ajangle for fear of what the child might get up to next.

An extra worry was Belle's inability to talk. Even the simplest words escaped her. Erin would plant herself in front of the child and say, 'Dada' and 'Mama' and hold a biscuit tantalisingly out of reach. But no amount of bribery could coax one word from the obstinate Belle. At least she didn't cry so much now. Erin supposed that was because she had discovered how to get about on her own and, prising open cupboard doors, could gorge herself on whatever she came across, so there was no need to cry for mama unless she particularly sought Erin's attention. This wasn't very often; as is sometimes the way of girls she preferred the company of her father.

Erin was better in herself. Liam's words of comfort that day had obviously sunk home. She was still more nervously disposed than she had formerly been, but that was to be expected with a child like Belle. Surprisingly, after what she had suffered at the hands of Father Gilchrist, she was still a regular attender at Mass. Less surprisingly, she had never visited the confessional since that day.

Sam's herd was doing marvellously. With excellent service from Judson's pedigree bull there had been no stillbirths this year, and his expanding herd of Shorthorns had become the envy of many a neighbouring farmer. 'That's 'cause I treat 'em like ladies,' Sam would tell them quite seriously.

'He's right there,' Dobby would add. 'He's more in love wi' them coos than that bonny wife of his. I'll bet if I should peek in his bedchamber I'd find owd Daisy tucked up alongside him an' his missus tethered out in t'barn.'

If only they could be left to their own devices they would have the idyllic life Sam had always dreamt of, but unfortunately the short stays which they often enjoyed with Erin's parents also took them into the company of Grandmother Fenton. Much as he liked to see Pat and Thomasin Sam always dreaded these visits for he knew they set Erin back to the post-natal days of melancholy. Hannah Fenton had always been this way, of course. But knowing this did not lift the veil of depression if it were your child she was pulling to pieces. The period from Friday afternoon when they usually arrived to the hour they left on Sunday was the most exacting test Sam's patience had ever had to face.

'I suppose I do have to go?' he asked Erin hopefully, watching her make the kitchen tidy for her leave of absence. How quickly these ordeals came around.

'Sure, isn't that a fine thing to be asking?' She used a

cloth to scoop crumbs from the table into her cupped palm. 'I thought ye liked my mother and father.'

'It weren't them I were thinking about.'

Erin showed her understanding. 'Sure, I know well enough. I'd put a gag on Grandmother myself sometimes. But ye'll not leave me to suffer it alone – Oh, s'truth, who's that?' Someone had knocked at the door. She opened it to four of the Johnson children, who were regular visitors – and what a pinched and poverty-stricken collection they were. Admitting them, she entreated Sam to go and get ready and resumed her hurried chore. When she turned, the children had moved to the fireside rug and Vicky was cuddling Belle. 'Careful now. I wouldn't really pick her up, she's only small.'

'I won't drop her,' replied the girl.

'I'm sure ye wouldn't, but best not.' Erin rinsed the cloth and hung it out to dry.

'Me mam's gone out,' Vicky informed her as she rushed back into the kitchen.

'Has she? And Vicky – didn't I say for you to put Belle down?'

'Why?'

''Cause I told ye to an' don't be so cheeky.'

'Aye, she's gone off to t'Bull,' sighed Vicky, placing Belle on the rug.

Erin knew from experience what these long sighs meant: there would be no lunch, probably no tea and possibly no supper either. Erin was quite willing to do her share of charity work, but wouldn't you know they'd make their appearance just when she was wanting to be off. But one exasperated look at those undernourished faces told her she would get no peace if she slung them out. So, snatching up a loaf and a breadknife she hacked off four thick slices and threw them across the table to Vicky. 'Here, put some butter on those – but then ye must be off or between you an' Mr Teale I'll not get to York by next Christmas.'

'Haven't you got any jam today then?' asked one of the boys, watching her race back and forth. She paused only to glare at him. With a resigned air he accepted the bread-and-butter from his sister. After a moment his hand moved to the sticky purple stain which marked his trouser pocket and withdrawing a handful of crushed blackberries spread them over his bread.

Erin happened to turn as he was about to clean his fingers with Belle's tongue. 'God love us, are ye trying to bring a curse on this house?' She cast down the cloth she had just that minute folded. 'D'ye not know what day it was yesterday?'

'Thursday,' replied Freddie, licking his own fingers.

'It was Michaelmas Day!' came the stern retort. 'The very day Lucifer fell out of Heaven an' landed on a bramble bush. Has your mother never told ye not to eat brambles after Michaelmas Day?'

Freddie shook his head, teeth clamped on the crust.

'No, I don't suppose she would, the Godless creature,' muttered Erin, then flared again as Belle, who was trying to haul herself up Freddie's leg to reach the forbidden brambles, was shoved roughly away by that same knee and fell bawling to the rug. She swooped forth and took Freddie by the ear. 'If I catch you doing anything like that again, young man, I'll skin ye alive. You're not to push the baby that way. Go on now, away home with ye, the lotta yese. Didn't ye get what ye came for?' She shoved them towards the door as Sam came down the stairs.

'Did somebody shove her before?' asked Freddie. 'Is that why she's crooked?'

'No, it's not. She was born that way.' Erin tried to push the children out.

'He knows that very well,' said Vicky, her expression chafing. 'He's heard me mam talking about it often enough.'

'Oh, an' what has your mother been saying?' demanded Erin, poised to cast them out.

'She says if that babby'd been a kitten it woulda been drowned,' provided seven-year-old Horace.

With an exclamation of disgust Erin ejected them from the house and slammed the door. 'I don't know why I put 'myself out, I really don't,' she stormed at Sam. 'There's me keeping her children from starving while she sits in the pub making horrible remarks like that. I've a good mind to stop them coming in.'

'Now you know you wouldn't get any satisfaction by turning hungry bairns away from our door.' Her husband calmly adjusted his starched collar. 'An' you won't alter people like Mrs Johnson by pulling your hair out.'

'I like that! You'll be sat there at Mam an' Dad's fuming over what Grandma has to say about Belle – never hear the last of it, I won't, till it's time for our next visit – but when I have anything to say about the Johnsons . . .'

'Oh shurrup wittering, woman.' He grabbed her teasingly and swung her off her feet. 'An' let's be off.'

'Oh, all eager now, are we?' She pushed against his chest.

'The sooner we're there the sooner we get it over with.'

'What a way of looking at a visit to my parents,' declared Erin with a laugh.

'It amazes me how they put up with her, too,' said Sam, putting his wife down. 'I often wonder if she goes on about Belle after we've gone home, do you?'

'I do not. I've enough catty remarks to contend with without worrying about hypothetical ones. What I do wonder is are we ever going to get there? Go get that pony round or I'll sit ye next to Grandma for the rest of the afternoon.' She clicked her tongue at her own remark as she picked up Belle and followed him out. 'We shouldn't talk about an old lady so. Sure, ye never know, she might be a little sweeter this week. Well, she might!' she exclaimed at Sam who had given her a doubting look.

Unfortunately, no sooner had they arrived than it began. A brief escape on Friday evening when Erin's parents took her and Sam to the theatre was punished by an hour-long diatribe about the inclemencies of staying out late when they came home for supper. Most of Saturday morning was taken up with Hannah's complaint that no one had thought to ask if *she* would care to go to the theatre. When invited to come shopping for clothes with Thomasin and

Erin in the afternoon she had snapped, 'On these legs?' and had stayed at home to make life as miserable as possible for Sam and Pat.

Now, at Sunday tea with just an hour or two left of what should have been an enjoyable break from work but was more like hard labour, Sam rolled his eyes over his teacup as his wife's grandmother harped on.

'I see the child has made little improvement since your last visit, Erin.' Hannah raised her teacup with trembling fingers. 'Has she made no attempt to speak at all?' The old lady, her memory failing, had asked this at least three times during their stay.

Bearing with her, Erin shook her head and watched Belle sitting on the carpet while Rosanna ran shrieking round and round the chairs. The comparison carved a hollow in her stomach.

'It certainly looks as if my prophecy at her birth was well-founded,' sighed the old lady. 'The child is an idiot.'

'I don't know how you can bring yourself to say such a heartless thing about your own great-grandchild, Hannah,' said Patrick. 'Just look at the expression in those bright little eyes. That's not the face of an imbecile. Anyway, I'm sure we've heard enough debate on her shortcomings for one day.' He, too, was sick of the repetitive slander visited on the child by his mother-in-law.

'Please! Will somebody deter that child from running amok?' cried Hannah.

'She's only excited because her dad and Josie are coming home tonight,' said Thomasin. Sonny had been home from Paris for well over a year now but his painting commitments had delayed the couple's marriage plans. Recently, he had been granted an exhibition at the Royal Academy – a great honour which made them all very proud.

This weekend, he had taken Josie down to London to share in his glory. They would be returning tonight.

'I don't care! Her manners are atrocious. It's time someone took her in hand.' Collecting her decorum, Hannah went on, 'I'm sure I didn't wish to cause Erin and

Samuel further distress than they already bear, Patrick, but it seems to me that I am the only person in this room who is not afraid to voice the patently obvious. Isabelle makes no effort to talk or even walk. Not a sign. She just sits there, looking. Isabelle! Isabelle, come to Grandmama. See? Not a glimmer.'

'Perhaps it'd help if you used her proper name,' muttered Sam.

'What's that, Samuel?'

'I said she'll do both in her own good time, Grandmother.' Sam spoke impatiently. '*If* people would only give her a chance.'

'Sometimes I'm rather glad she can't walk,' confided Erin distantly. 'I have a hard enough time keeping track of her as it is. She's into everything.'

Sam confirmed this. 'Yes, if you want proof of her intelligence, Grandmother, you only have to come and see the way she tackles the cupboards. She can worm her way into anything.'

'I never know what she's likely to get into next,' added Erin.

'You must forbid it,' announced Hannah to Sam. 'You mustn't allow her to tax your wife's health. Erin is looking decidedly peaky.'

'Oh? I was just about to comment on how much better she's looking,' interceded Thomasin, holding out her hand. 'More tea, Mother?'

'Well, I claim that her life of stagnation in the country is beginning to reflect in her looks,' insisted the old woman. 'It is ridiculous to permit the child to add to her drudgery. I can't think why she doesn't employ a maid. Besides which, children should be taught their place in life – and that applies to another ill-behaved brat I could mention.' She glared as Rosanna came rather too close to her painful legs. 'Do take care, child! Remember my rheumatics.'

Rosanna, almost six now, continued to dance, skirts twirling, hair wrapped around her pert face.

'Such a naughty child,' opined Hannah. 'At least, Erin,

you can be grateful you will never have to put up with this. As for Isabelle's expeditions to the cupboard, I suggest you secure her in a chair where you can keep an eye on her.'

'But she has to explore, Grandmother,' argued Sam. 'How else is she to gain knowledge?'

'That's as ridiculous a statement as I've heard,' replied Hannah. 'That child has not the tiniest capacity to learn. She has proved that by her unresponsiveness. Her reasons for rifling the cupboards are of no more significance than that she is hungry. You must try giving her more to eat to curb her adventurous spirit.'

'But the very fact that she goes to the cupboard when she's hungry displays her intelligence!' Sam's voice was rising. Erin wished Grandmother would shut up. 'She knows that she'll find food there.'

'Just as a dog knows he'll find crumbs under the table,' snapped Hannah. 'It is nothing more than habit which drives her.' The lined face softened. 'Samuel, by allowing your daughter to go unrestrained you are placing a greater burden on your wife, not to mention the danger to the child herself. She could crawl into the fire or anywhere. One envisages a hundred possible areas of harm.' She shivered.

'There's danger everywhere if you came to view life that way,' contradicted Sam. 'Normal children have to face it some time or other. Their mothers can't protect them forever. Why should it be different for Belle?'

'Do I have to repeat the obvious, Samuel?' retorted Hannah, then sighed with despair. 'Samuel, Erin dear, is it not time you faced up to the fact that you're never going to be able to make anything of Isabelle? Don't imagine that I don't admire your perseverance but instead of directing all your energies on her why do you not have another child? It has, after all, been two years. It would take your mind off things.'

'I don't want my mind taken off Belle, thank you, Grandmother,' replied Erin. 'I love her, whatever her limitations. I can't say we wouldn't like to add to our family,' she glanced at Sam, 'but sometimes things don't happen the way ye plan.'

'Well, I'm sure we don't want to go into too much detail with all these little ears wagging,' murmured Hannah. 'It would be most unseemly. But have you seen a doctor? You're not getting any younger.'

'There's nothing the matter with me, Grandmother. When God wills that we should have another child I dare say He'll send us one.' She passed her cup to Thomasin for refilling.

'Then let us hope He is more discerning this time, dear,' said Hannah and turned to Rosanna who was sniffing noisily. 'Go and blow your nose properly, child.'

'But my nose doesn't need blowing, Grandmama,' answered Rosanna, still sniffing. She said it politely, calling the woman Grandmama and not Grandma which would have earned a rebuke – though she often used the latter in private.

'Rosie, be a good girl and come sit by me like your brother,' commanded Thomasin who appeared to be having trouble with her new Langtry bustle. It was meant to fold up when one sat, but a rib had come astray and was threatening to pierce her bottom.

Rosanna obeyed, seating herself primly on a footstool, and was quietly observant for a moment before announcing in a loud whisper, 'I think Grandmama needs to go to the nessy, Nan.'

'Thomasin, I demand that you instil some manners into that child!' Hannah's arms shot out for assistance from the chair and with Pat and Sam's compliance she limped stiffly from the room, trying to hang onto her shattered authority.

There was clandestine laughter which Rosanna noted but could not comprehend; weren't they quick to tell her when she needed to go?

'Well, that's the last we'll hear of Mother for today.' Thomasin wheeled on Patrick in a flash, adding, 'Did I hear you say thank God?'

'Sure I never said a word,' chuckled her husband and

reaching for Rosanna swung her onto his lap. 'Oh, Rosie, ye do have a knack of saying just what's needed. 'S a pity it didn't come a wee bit sooner.' She didn't understand him, but snuggled into his tobacco-scented embrace, enjoying the feel of his scratchy chin on her cheek. Patrick released her and nodded at Nick, who now had his face buried in a book. 'Now why do we never see you like that, Rosanna?'

She screwed up her nose. 'Boring old Nick, he's always reading.'

'No, I'm not,' murmured her brother, possessing the cuteness that enabled him not to miss anything in the conversation whilst seemingly immersed in something else.

'Yes, you are. You never want to play with me.' She looked down as Belle started to complain at the lack of attention. 'Will she play with me when she's bigger?'

'Well, she's not as strong as you,' explained Patrick. 'She might get hurt in your rough an' tumble.'

'Why doesn't she walk?'

'Because one of her legs is shorter than the other an' if she stood up she'd keep tipping over,' he answered honestly.

Rosanna digested this, then said thoughtfully, 'I once saw a man with one little shoe and one big shoe. Was that 'cause he had one leg shorter than the other?' Patrick nodded. 'Then we could buy her some of those shoes, couldn't we?'

'Ye're right, we could. She's a bit young yet, but next year when she's a bit stronger we could have a pair o' special little boots made to help her to walk.'

Sam praised the child's perception. 'I must be getting addled in me old age. It takes a six-year-old to suggest the obvious. Belle's hardly going to attempt to walk if she keeps cockling over, is she?'

This thought cheered him as he drove his wife and child home on that still-light evening. Added to the jollity over Rosie's faux pas, it made the journey happier than it had been on many previous occasions.

'Out of the mouths of babes,' quoted Sam, leaning on his knees and watching the horse's round hindquarters roll slowly towards home. 'It never even entered my head about shoes. By, that Rosanna, she's wick all right. Always good for a laugh.' He chuckled for emphasis. 'I can still see your grandmother's face. Oh, but what a load o' tripe she does spout.'

Erin laughed with him, then said more seriously, ''Tis not all rubbish though. It would be nice for us to have another child. I'm getting a bit concerned about that.'

Sam brushed this off. 'Nay, what's to worry about? It's as you said yourself: God'll send us one when He's ready. Your hands are full enough at the moment, don't be wishin' any more on yersen. Besides,' he shuffled closer to her, 'I'm enjoying my bit of unrestricted lovin'.'

She laid her head on his shoulder. 'Men, you're all alike.'

He arched his brows. 'Oh aye, an' how would you be knowin'? I hope that Ralph Dobbins hasn't been sniffing round while I'm out tending me cows.'

She laughed and wrapped her free arm around his back. 'He'd be within his rights if he did. Sure, he pays me more attention than you ever do. Didn't he bring me a fine bunch o' flowers on Friday morning?'

'Oh, he did, did he? I can see I shall have to have words wi' Mr Dobbins.' He steered the horse into the final stretch of lane, then became alert, spotting a figure further ahead. 'Why, I'll go to Pudsey if it isn't the very bloke I want to see. Oy!' he shouted to the youth sitting at the roadside. 'I know I said I'd pay thee when I got back but I'd be grateful if you'd let me get in me gate afore I get me hand down. By God, there's not much chance o' me escaping, is there?' This to Erin. 'I hope you haven't been slackin' here all day, Ralph Dobbins. I don't want to get home an' find that scabby beast that Robson has the neck to call a bull making a nuisance of himself wi' my young ladies.' This was said jokingly; had Sam thought the young man incapable of looking after his prize cattle he would never have entrusted them to him for three seconds, let alone three days.

Dobby had, on hearing the initial shout, scrambled to his feet and now came to meet the cart as Sam hauled in the reins. His face was unusually serious.

'What's up, lad? I know I'm a few minutes later than normal but you don't have to have a seizure, tha'll get thi brass.'

'Maister, Missus.' Dobby pulled off his billycock hat and screwed it through anxious fingers. 'It's not my wage I'm bothered about . . .'

Sam made the sign of the Cross. 'Erin, will you get down an' feel this fella's head?'

'Please, don't joke, Mr Teale.'

'Nay, I'm sorry lad, I'm full o' the devil tonight. Away then, hop into the back an' tell us what's made your face like this horse's backside.'

'Maister, it's coos.' Dobby tortured the hat. 'I'm worried on 'em.'

The older man sobered instantly. 'What's amiss, Ralph?'

'I don't rightly know, but one or two on 'em 'aven't been right since I went to milk 'em on Friday eve, 'aven't been eatin' nor didn't seem in very good mettle all round.'

'Jump up, Dobby,' ordered Sam immediately, and urged the horse on towards his field.

'I split 'em up, Mr Teale,' shouted Dobby over the rumble of the cartwheels.

'Good lad, Dobby. You did right.'

Nothing more was said until they reached the pasture. The scene they came upon had the deceptive appearance of tranquillity. A shimmering disc of sun hung low in the sky, spraying the verdant acreage with its warm light. Clouds of midges performed their evening dance above the hedgerow. All calm. Too calm. Sam jerked on the reins and jumped down, a spot of acid beginning to gnaw at his stomach.

'Who's that?' He pointed to the figure silhouetted by the sun, who moved from one recumbent cow to the other.

'It's the vet'nary, sir. I thought it best to go for him

when they didn't get no better.' Dobby knew Sam would never trust his herd to a primitive cow doctor. He followed Sam who was now moving across the field, leaving Erin to cuddle the child, her eyes misted with apprehension.

The veterinary surgeon stood as Sam drew alongside to stare down at the stricken cow. The hair beneath its apathetic eyes was stained with discharge, the muzzle slimy and sore-looking.

Sam squatted and ran a hand over the roan hide, his face disbelieving. 'Poor old Sukie,' he crooned to the cow, rubbing the poll between her horns. Her breath came in laboured puffs. 'Poor old girl.'

Dobby hurt for his master, knowing more than anyone what these creatures meant to the man. Squinting up at the vet Sam finally posed the question to which he dreaded hearing the response. 'What is it, sir?'

The vet bobbed down again and unclamped the cow's jaws. The gums were pasty and inflamed by ulcers. The sight of these sores jolted Sam upright like a jack-in-the-box.

'Oh Christ, it's foot an' mouth!'

'Not necessarily,' came the muttered reply. 'I was about to test these ulcers when you arrived.' Sam urged him to go ahead. The vet took an instrument from his bag and rubbed it over the cow's gums. When the tool came away there were bran-like scales adhering to it and the ulcers were left with a ragged appearance. 'Mmm.' He showed the result to Sam. 'Well, that tells me it isn't foot and mouth.'

For one precious, cruel moment Sam was given hope. Until the vet looked up, grim-visaged. 'It's rinderpest,' he said. 'I'm afraid we're going to have to slaughter the entire herd.'

CHAPTER SIX

He would never, ever, see anything that would devastate him quite so much as that empty shippen. Even the grotesque pile of red and white corpses with horns tilted at an unnatural angle, the same milk-laden udders that he had once followed as they swayed heavily down the lane, now shrivelled, empty bags, none of this brought tears to his eyes. But when he had gone that morning after the slaughter to his empty shippen . . . oh! how he had wept. The echoes of their healthy cries wished him good morning for a long time after they had gone. He would walk slowly along the line of vacant stalls, seeing each face swing round to look at him as he passed: Sukie, the timid one, Rachel, who would nuzzle his pocket in the hope of a tit-bit, little Mousie who had not grown as he had expected and was not as pretty as her sisters but had turned out to be as good a producer as any cow he had owned . . . All gone.

Oh, he had been offered compensation – the princely sum of ten pounds per cow. Some might have been thankful for it – twenty years earlier and there would have been nothing – but not Sam. How could money compensate for such a loss? They weren't just cows, they had been his friends. Years, it had taken him, years of toil, of painstaking breeding and selection to bring them up to their enviable standard. Years wasted. Sam didn't know if he'd ever get over it.

Each morning when he looked down at Belle's expectant little face the anger and helplessness would well up in his throat to choke him. But he would swing her onto his shoulders just the same, even though there was no herd to follow. He varied his days between taking Belle for long strolls down wooded paths, pouring out his feelings to someone who would merely listen and not try to provide him with answers, or lazing by the river, deep in self-examination. What could he turn his hand to now? There seemed no point in anything. Why slave your life away when all your gains could be stolen from you in one lightning blow?

Erin ached for him, but there was nothing she could do. The healing of such a bereavement could only be found within oneself. She finished tying the bunch of goose wings onto a stick and tested the feather duster against her hand, studying her husband out of her eye-corner. He was trying to conjure up enough enthusiasm to bring himself out of the chair, absently clasping the small hands that tugged at his trousers.

'There's no need for you to keep taking her out, ye know,' she told him, fearing that Belle would only add to his burden. 'I can cope well enough now.'

Dispirited eyes pursued her as she flicked the feather duster over the furniture. 'It's not just to help you that I take her, love,' confessed Sam. 'How else would I fill my days?'

She put down the duster to grip his hand comfortingly. 'Ye'll get another herd, darlin'. The disease will burn itself out an' ye can start again.'

He laughed bitterly. 'As simply as that? I'm not sure I want to rebuild only to risk losing them again.' His knuckles were white as his fingers kneaded his thighs. 'All I've worked for, all I ever dreamed of, gone overnight. I don't know that I could face that again.'

'There's no reason why ye should,' soothed Erin. 'Didn't the vet tell us the disease was becoming rarer nowadays? I can understand your chariness but this is a once in a lifetime disaster, Sam. It's not the kind of thing that happens every day.'

'Isn't it? Poor Sutherland's lost two herds to foot and mouth.' He imagined what it would be like to watch that horrifying slaughter all over again.

She saw he wasn't going to be coaxed out of it. 'Ye've not lost everything, ye know; ye've still got us.'

He reached for her and hugged her, a spark of his old self coming to the fore. 'Yes, I have, an' here's me mopin' about as though it was the end o' the world to lose a few cows. I want my backside kickin'.'

'If ye want to bend over I'll oblige,' offered his wife, then laughed softly, kissed him on the nose and ruffled his blond hair before she pulled away. 'Oh, Belle!' She clapped a hand to her mouth and dashed across the kitchen to snatch up her daughter who was struggling to gain position on a high stool. Her little knees scrabbled for a hold while the rest of her clung on like a leech. 'How on earth did ye get up there?' she scolded. 'Naughty girl, mustn't do that.'

'Leave t'lass be,' said Sam, coming to chuck Belle under the chin. 'She got fed up o' waitin' for her old dad, didn't you? It'll do her good to exercise her inquisitive nature.'

'An' I'm to stand by while she breaks her neck?' asked Erin hotly.

'She'll not do any harm even if she did fall,' answered her husband. 'It's hardly a long drop, is it, an' there's a soft rug underneath.'

'If we allow her to climb on the stool it might lead to higher ambitions.'

'Then good luck to her, I say.'

'You would! Ye don't seem to worry about anything that happens to her, all you're concerned about is those bloody cows.'

'Now, that's nonsense . . .'

'Yes, I know it is. I'm sorry, Sam . . .'

' . . . I look after her as any good father would – but we must give her some sort of independence, love. She can't stay on the carpet all her life. She must move on to higher stations. We really must make an effort to get her them shoes an' all. Put her back on t'stool an' see what she does.'

Erin studied him defiantly, then, tutting, sat the wriggling child on the oak seat. Belle assumed her frog-like posture to return their scrutiny for a few seconds, then, reaching out, grasped the handle of a cupboard and stretched upwards.

'Why, she's after that,' exclaimed Erin, reaching for the shiny copper pan which hung on the wall and reflected all that was going on in the kitchen.

But Sam clamped a firm grasp on her wrist, drawing it back. 'Let her get it. Look at her. As soon as she saw you reach for the pan she sat back waiting for it to come to her. She's never going to make any effort if things come to her as easy as that.'

'Eejit! How's she going to lift down a heavy pan like that?'

'She can allus ask for it, can't she? Most bairns have some sort of vocabulary at her age, why doesn't she? It's because you see her making a move towards summat an' immediately leap to her assistance, put everything right there in front of her. Why waste words when you've got a lackey at yer beck an' call?' Bending his knees he addressed his daughter. 'Now then, Belle, if you want that pan you must get it. Go on!' He pointed to the pan. 'Belle take it.'

The child grinned and shuffled to her knees again, the little fingers stretching up, reaching, but falling just inches short.

Erin clasped her hands to her chest. 'Sam, 'tis too high. Let me . . .'

'No!' Sam remained adamant. 'You get it, Belle.'

'Oh, don't be so mean! Look, she's given up.' Belle had flopped back to her bottom, wide blue eyes gazing up at the unattainable.

'No, she hasn't, she's just thinkin' what to do,' said Sam. 'Look now.'

Belle had spotted a toasting fork which was within her reach and, taking it from its hook, pointed it at the target, trying to insert it through the hole in the pan handle that sat on the peg.

Erin was fascinated as the child jiggled the fork about, attempting to dislodge the pan. Suddenly it fell.

Sam's hands were there to catch it. 'There y'are!

There's your prize, madam.' He placed the shiny pan in Belle's outstretched arms. She patted the base, smiling delightedly at her reflection. 'It's nowt more than I'd expect from a daughter o' mine,' issued Sam. 'I wish Grandma could've seen it. She'd not call you a dunce then, would she, Belle?' He lifted her onto the rug where she continued to play happily for a while, her proud parents looking on and remarking on her cleverness.

'What're ye going to do today, then?' asked Erin finally, setting about her baking. Flour, fat and rolling pin were dumped onto the pine table. 'I hope ye're not going to be under my feet.'

Sam stooped to pull on his boots. 'Well, if me wife doesn't want my company 'appen I'd better go find somebody who does. I think I'll just nip down to Scott's an' ask if they want a labourer.'

It was sufficient to stop her measuring the flour. 'A labourer?'

Sam spread his hands, 'We've got to get some brass from somewhere. We've no butter or cheese to sell.'

'What about the compensation money?'

'I'm reluctant to break into that, you never know when we might be really desperate. All I need is a few bob to tide us over till I get on me feet an' decide which way I'm headin'.'

'I understand that – but a labourer, Sam! 'Tis a bit of a comedown, isn't it? After ye've enjoyed so much standing.'

'Aye well, that's all over an' done wi' now,' replied Sam. 'Coos've gone.'

'Maybe Mam would . . .' she began.

But, 'No,' he said firmly. 'Your mother's done enough for us. You mustn't take away all a man's pride, Erin. Anyway, it's not just the money, it's . . . well, you know how much I put into them cows. I don't seem able to motivate meself to owt o' me own. No, labourin'll do me for a month or so, keep me mind off things. Anyroad, I'm off. I'll take Belle wi' me. Don't know when we'll be back.'

She hurried after him with floury hands. 'Ye will watch

her Sam, won't ye? I'm not suggesting ye'll do anything silly, but . . . I just keep getting this feeling that something dreadful's going to happen.'

He laughed. 'You an' your feelings.'

'It's been with me for days.'

'Aye, well, your feeling's come a bit late this time, lass.' He was grave once more.

'No, 'tis something else. I don't know what, but I know something horrible's going to happen.'

He kissed her. 'Erin, you're never happy lest yer've summat to worry about. Things can't get any worse.'

She watched them through the door then dropped the latch and moved to the window. Poor Sam. She had never seen anything affect him like the death of those cows. As she watched, Belle decided to let go of Sam's hair, nearly falling backwards had Sam not caught her and made her refasten her grip. The action made Erin catch her breath. She understood that Sam thought he was doing her a good turn by taking Belle out of her way for a spell, but oh, if he only knew how she worried while they were gone in case Sam let her do anything dangerous.

And there was still that feeling.

The enquiry at Scott's farm turned up nothing. The farmer was sorry but he had no need of another labourer at the moment. 'Try Wood's!' he shouted after Sam as the blond man loped back down the drive, Belle rocking on his shoulders. 'He's getting his crop in tomorrow, he might need a lad.'

A lad, thought Sam dully, but nevertheless shouted his thanks and proceeded to Wood's farm. Here, temporary employment was offered and, after gratefully accepting, Sam told the farmer he would be there in the morning, then made his way to the river for a last spot of relaxation.

Once there, he unhooked Belle from his neck, swung her down onto the river bank and flopped beside her, lying back to gaze at the sky. Tearing up a blade of grass he nibbled it pensively, sucking on the juices from its pink root. It was surprisingly mild for the time of year. The brightness of the day closed his eyes, squeezing trickles of moisture from them that deltaed into the laughter lines on his cheeks. 'Oh, Belle, what're we gonna do about our moo-cows? I bet if you could talk you'd tell me you miss 'em as much as I do, wouldn't yer? I don't know, I can't seem to do owt right, can I? Look what happened wi' you. Still . . . you love your dad, don't yer?' He turned his head, opening his eyes. Belle had gone. He rolled his head in the other direction. Not there either. Sitting upright, he was just in time to see her shuffling into the water.

'Oh blazes, tha'll get me hung, lass!' Leaping to his feet he made the three strides to the water's edge and plucked her dripping to safety. 'What will yer ma say when she see your wet clothes? She'll say, "I told yer so, my feelings're allus right". Oh well, I suppose we'll have to stop out till they're dry – good job for you it's warm.' An idea struck him as Belle screeched to get to the water. 'Like it, doesta? Well, 'appen we'll have to do summat about that. Can't have you playin' in water an' not be able to swim, can we? Away, let's have them wet togs off an' we'll see how you take to it.'

Despite its coolness Belle took to it like a young duck-ling, splashing all four limbs in an ungainly but effective paddle and crowing with delight.

'Good lass!' called Sam, stripping off his own clothes. 'That'll strengthen your legs for when we get them shoes. By, won't yer mam be surprised!' He hobbled over the stones on the gently sloping bank and waded up to his waist, then striking out with practised, even strokes circled around her. He flicked the hair out of his eyes, laughed at her obvious enjoyment and hurled himself into a back-stroke. The action of the water rushing over his lithe body seemed to cleanse away some of his depression. He rolled over and over in the lapping waves joyfully. With each stroke his optimism was reborn. Erin was right, he could and would start again.

Erin wandered round the garden bending her face over a bush of pink roses as she passed. Sam had been gone longer than usual. It wasn't like him to be late for his dinner. The feeling still nibbled at her mind. Leaning on the gate she peered up and down the lane for a sighting. After a moment's indecision she stepped into it and fled off in the direction Sam had taken that morning.

Mrs Scott answered the impatient rapping on her farmhouse door. 'Good Lord, I thought we must have deathwatch beetle wi' all that tappin'.' She came out into the sunshine to join her worried-looking neighbour, and was asked it Sam was here.

'No, love, I heard Mr Scott send him along to Wood's – why, what's the pother?'

Erin answered only with her thanks and rushed off in Sam's tracks, the feeling of disaster taking firm hold now.

At Wood's farm she was told Sam had been there but that was three hours ago. 'Did he say where he was going?' Erin, the sense of foreboding rising every second, anxiously awaited new directions.

But the farmer's wife shook her head. 'I never saw him, love. Mr Wood just happened to tell me your Sam'd called. Why, is it owt urgent?'

'He's late home for his dinner,' replied Erin distractedly.

The woman burst into laughter. 'Eh, is that what's got thee all worked up? I thought it were summat drastic.'

'No, no, ye don't understand! I feel something's happened to him an' Belle.'

Just then, the farmer appeared and when asked about Sam pointed a black finger over his fields. 'He were going over to coppice when I last saw him. But that were hours ago.' He had no sooner finished than Erin was off across the fields like a panicked mare. The farmer and his wife stood watching her fleeing figure. 'Eh, she's an odd sorta lass is that,' muttered Mrs Wood. 'Doest know what got her all het up? Her man's late home for his dinner. Fancy.'

'I could just see thee getting worked up an' coming to look for me if I were late home,' returned Wood. 'More likely I'd get me dinner chucked at me when I did get in.'

'Happen it's 'cause she's Irish,' replied his wife with a knowing nod, then went indoors.

Erin reached the coppice and plunged down the wooded path, her breath coming in rapid gasps. The branches seemed to reach out for her as she dashed past, clawing at her hair and skirts to hinder her flight. She pulled up sharply as a particularly spiky branch caught in her locks. The more she struggled the more entwined her ebony tresses became. She twisted and writhed, emitting little cries of frustration. Her struggles to free herself drew moisture from her eyes as the delicate hair at her temples became more and more tangled. In desperation she snapped off the ensnarled branch and, with it still dangling from her hair, ran blindly on. There was a brief terrifying interlude when an equally startled grouse flew right from under her feet. She screamed once, then ran on.

She was nearing the edge of the wood now. Where were they? Where were they? She emerged from the tangle of trees with breast heaving, eyes round, scanning the beautiful open countryside that swept down towards the river.

The river! Grabbing her skirts she hurled herself onwards, her feet moving rapidly over the meadow, trampling the banks of wild flowers, seeking, calling.

Then, at last she spotted Belle. To her horror she saw her child floundering alone in the brown water – drowning.

With a scream, Erin galloped towards the river, heart and feet thudding as she flew. She hurled herself in, fully dressed, lashing hysterically at the water, her skirts dragging her down. The child, seeing her mother's terrified face became infected by the panic and inevitably started to sink.

'Belle!' screamed Erin. 'Mammy's coming!' Her lungs were screaming also, like two pieces of raw flesh banging against the wall of her chest. Belle went under. With flailing arms Erin clutched at handfuls of water, trying to find her child. The little head buoyed back up, spluttering and coughing. Erin grasped it and hauled the child to her bosom as she herself went under, the weight of her many skirts dragging her towards the pebbled bed. She lashed furiously, forcing her head up, reaching with her chin for the blue sky, gulping down mouthfuls of minute riverlife, coughing, retching.

Something became anchored around her neck, threatening to drag her back under. She struggled. 'Erin!' Sam shouted in her ear. 'Keep calm! I'm here, it's all right.'

But the panic had made her deaf and she continued to writhe in his grip, still clutching Belle, frenzied of eye and jaw. There was nothing else he could do. Making the punch as merciful as possible he lashed out, made contact, then towed his semi-conscious wife and their screaming baby to the bank. Depositing Erin on the bank he comforted the distraught baby, pressing her bare skin to his and very soon overcoming her distress. The child calmer, he sat astride Erin to pummel the water from her until she started to gag and vomit. Finally she turned onto her back to look at her rescuer. Recognition brought back her anger and she flew at him, nails gouging at his face, pinching and slapping wildly at his bare chest.

'Whoah, Erin! It's all right, it's me!'

'You left her! Ye wanted her to drown!'

'No!' He shook her dripping shoulders. 'I was only a few feet away, hidden by that shelf o' grass. She was quite safe.'

She didn't hear. 'That water's freezing! She could've caught her death.'

'Rubbish! It's lovely an' warm if you're moving about, splashin' an' that.'

'I hate you! You left her to die!'

'You don't think I'd leave a little child in t'water alone, d'yer?' he threw at her. 'I were there all the time I tell yer, teachin' her to swim.'

'She wasn't swimming,' sobbed Erin, clawing handfuls of his skin. 'She was drowning. Couldn't ye see she was terrified?'

'Of course she was! But not o' the bloody water – of you. She was perfectly happy before you came along screamin' at her. It's seein' you like this that made her cry. Look, she's started again. Come on, woman, pull

97

yourself together.' Releasing his wife he went to pick up Belle, but Erin leapt to her feet and knocked him aside.

'Get off her! I won't let ye touch her. Ye wanted her to die!'

Sam's fingers curled around her arm, spun her to face him while his other hand descended like a whiplash, catching her full on the cheek and nearly taking her head off with it. 'Don't you ever say a thing like that to me again. Ever! I was the one who stopped her from being smothered at birth like a runt puppy – remember?' He shook her savagely, not the gentle, easygoing Sam she knew. 'Remember? *Remember?*'

'Yes, yes!' she shrieked, then fell against his chest and sobbed unrestrainedly.

Sam pressed her gently from him only to pick up Belle and held both his women while they shed their pain and terror, kissing each alternately, whispering endearments. They stood there, dripping, for quite some time until a cool breeze made Sam shiver. 'Come on, we'd best get home an' get you two in front of the fire before yer catch yer death.' He helped to dress Belle, then clothed himself, laid one arm over his wife's shoulders, his child in the other, and walked them home.

Erin curled her hands round the mug of tea and let forth a sharp laugh of embarrassment. 'I'll bet Mrs Wood takes me for a right pratie, getting into a panic just 'cause you were late for your dinner. It'll be all over the village tomorrow. God, I feel so stupid! I get these notions in my head – I thought something had happened to you an' Belle. I really believed it. When I saw her in the water . . .' She shivered.

Sam noticed the wild look still in her eye. 'There's no call to go over it again. She's safe. She was never in any danger.'

'I know that, Sam. I know ye'd never really let her come to any harm, an' I'm sorry I said the things I did. It's just . . . I get so worried when she's out o' my sight . . . even when she's with you. I can't help it. I've been this way since I had her. Sometimes, like today, it gets out of all proportion.'

He patted her hand. 'Aye well, happen you'll grow out of it when you've got another bairn to occupy yer mind. Pass us one o' them biscuits, will yer please?'

Erin handed him the plate, then gave a biscuit to Belle who crouched in her little corner by the fire. 'Well, if one good thing's come out of today it's to show me what I'm gonna do,' munched Sam. 'I'm gonna start again like you suggested. Build another herd.'

She was delighted. 'Oh, Sam, I'm so pleased. I know how much the cows meant to you an' how badly their loss affected ye. Tell me, what changed your mind?'

He grinned. 'Belle. I watched her swimmin' about this morning, having a whale of a time, not a care in the world, an' I thought what a hypocritical bugger I am, telling you we mustn't let Belle give in then doing exactly that meself. If that wee lass can bear her burden cheerfully then surely I can stand the loss of a few cows. So, I'm gonna dib into that compensation money and I'm off to market. It'll take a damn sight longer than last time to build up a good herd – but I'm ready to try.'

'I'm sure however long it takes you'll manage it, dear,' said Erin.

'Aye well, it's all thanks to . . . oh hell, look at her!'

'Belle, come out of that coal bucket!' Erin put down her cup and, sighing, rose to deter Belle from her new game. 'Just look at ye.' She tried to wipe off the coaldust with a cloth but made no impression. 'Oh, 'tis no good, ye'll have to go in the tub. Sam, will ye fetch it in for me? I daren't let her go else there'll be black fingermarks all over my clean covers. Grrr!' She shook Belle playfully. 'I'm going to call in the nuisance inspector for you, child.'

Sam filled the bath with water from the kettle and, topping it up with cold, swished it around while Erin stripped Belle.

'Let's see how ye like your swim this time.' Erin held the child over the bath and began to lower her.

The moment Belle felt the water lap around her

buttocks her small body went rigid and her eyes rolled with terror. She set up such a screaming that Erin was forced to take the infant on her knee and leave the task for a while.

'It's just the memory of this morning,' Sam comforted his wife. 'She'll be right as rain tomorrow. She really loved it, yer know.'

But the following day the performance was the same. It took days of coaxing before Belle would allow as much as a wet rag near her face without yelling. Indeed, the fear of water that Erin had instilled in her daughter that day was to remain with her for the best part of her life.

CHAPTER SEVEN

Sam decided it was more sensible to postpone the rebuilding of his herd until the spring came round again. Hence, Christmas was spent in more leisurely vein than usual – a week with Erin's parents, a week with his, for once the really bad weather arrived, it might be a couple of months before they met up again. While they were away Dobby was given the task of caring for the remaining livestock – the fowls and the dogs. Sam felt guilty at having nothing more for the fellow to do, but Dobby seemed to be getting by on odd jobs in the village.

After the prolonged festive season the couple seemed to spend the next two months in isolation. For Erin, being indoors all day made little difference – there was always some chore or another to be done. But Sam grew itchy. Waiting for the spring was always a bad time, but it was more than that; his current idleness meant that he had more time to study his wife and what he saw concerned him. The improved health she had been enjoying of late was gone. Just what had caused this neither of them knew. It could be the adverse weather or simply the strain of looking after Belle, now more adventurous than ever. Whatever the source, it had stripped the weight from Erin, rendered the roses and cream complexion the colour of whey. Sam, on being presented with her waxen face on yet another morning when he came down to breakfast, told her she must go and see the doctor. 'You can't keep soldierin' on like this.'

'I'll be all right tomorrow,' came the pat answer as she moved dreamlike round the kitchen, getting his meal.

But Sam had heard that too many times. 'Yer keep tellin' me that but you never are. If yer won't go to t'doctor I'm off to bring him here.'

'Oh, he'll be most grateful for that, I'm sure.' Erin sagged down into one of the chairs at the table, hand over mouth. 'Ye're meant to be dying before Doctor Wrigglesworth makes a call. God, I feel so wambly.' She flattened her forearms to the table and laid her weary head on them.

'That settles it!' Sam spoke through a mouthful of bread. 'Directly I finish this I'm hitching t'hoss an' taking you down to the village.' He waited for another objection but none came. That in itself showed how ill she was.

But on the return journey from the village there was little sign of their previous mood. 'A babby!' Sam roared with laughter as he drove them home through a snowstorm, blinking away the flakes that settled on his eyelashes. 'Oh, Erin – aren't we a pair? I never gave it a thought, did you?'

She hunched up to him, happy face held in defiance of the swirling flakes. 'Sure, you had an excuse for your naivety, you're a man. I should've known better. What a dimwit!' The feeling of lethargy had been overridden by joyous anticipation.

'D'yer still feel terrible?' he asked solicitously.

'Yes.' She clutched her stomach. 'But wonderful terrible.'

After a couple of weeks the 'terrible' bit faded, leaving her just 'wonderful'. Sam, too. Now he had something to salve the indignity of labouring for someone else.

By the spring of 'seventy-eight he felt able to implement

his plan of rebuilding his herd. One crisp morning in April, his thirty-fourth birthday, he set off for market with Belle as usual perched on his shoulders.

Five hours later Erin heard his voice calling her name as she knelt tidying her herb garden. Dusting the soil from her hands she heaved her thickening body up and made her way up the steps to the gate where Sam's smiling face proclaimed his success.

'How d'you like her, then?' His sparkling eyes held her face as she came into the lane to inspect his purchase. 'I thought I'd just do a bit o' swankin' before I put her in t'shippen. All right, eh?'

'She's really pretty!' Erin appraised the Jersey cow smilingly whilst stroking the attractive dished face with its dark muzzle. 'Thought ye'd have a change this time, did ye?' He told her his reason – he couldn't even bear to look at a Shorthorn nowadays. Her hand moved over the fawn, convex belly. 'Oh, an' in the same condition as myself if I make no mistake.'

He gave a pleased nod. 'I reckon she's two months further on than you. Come summer an' we'll have two instead o' one. Keep your fingers crossed for a girl.'

'A girl?' Erin raised her eyebrows. 'I thought your heart was set on a little boy?'

'For me, aye,' grinned Sam. 'I've already got my little girl.' He gestured at Belle astride the cow's back. 'She's definitely taken to her new form of transport. It gives my poor old shoulders a rest anyroad. Tell Dad what you're riding on, Belle. Moo cow. Belle, say it.' The only response was a row of milk teeth. 'Tsk! Not a peep. Ah dear, I wonder if she'll ever be able to talk, Erin.'

'Maybe when the new baby comes it'll make her feel more inclined.'

Sam had ideas of his own about that. How would Belle, a spoilt child – he recognised this fact even though he did his best to curtail his wife's overindulgence – how would she react to the young interloper? There would be no Ma at her beck and call then. Erin just wouldn't have the time. He could picture the awful tantrums . . . But then, happen it could go the other way, too. It might just allow Belle to unleash the independent spirit that Sam knew was there if Erin would only recognise it.

'Right then, I'll just take Hannah down to t'shippen.'

'Hannah?' queried Erin.

Sam winked. 'The truck I've had from this crusty old cow on t'way home I thought it were a suitable title.' Erin laughed as he set off, then waddled back down the path to check on the contents of the oven.

In the time it took Sam to drive the new cow to the byre and return with Belle, the table had been laid with new bread, bowls of steaming potatoes, vegetables from Erin's garden, a joint of mutton and a pungent sauce. After devouring all on his plate Sam took a deep breath and showed his appreciation by patting his stomach. 'Well, that were smashing, lass – I don't think I'll bother to sell you after all. Belle's enjoying it too, aren't you? Look at her trenching away there.'

The mother smiled fondly at her child. 'Yes, nobody can fault her appetite, an' she's a lovely little eater, isn't she? She's never thrown her food about like ordinary babies.'

'She's got more sense than that, haven't you, Belle? Her mam's cooking's too good for chuckin' at walls.'

Erin waited for Belle to finish, then stacked the plates and took them away. Shortly she took something from the cupboard, her back hiding whatever it might be from Sam's view.

'Yer mam's up to summat,' the man whispered to his daughter.

Erin cast a secret glance in his direction, then went on with her task. The smell of melted candlewax wafted around the kitchen.

'Happy Birthday, Sam!' When she turned she bore before her a rich fruitcake, in the middle of which burnt one candle. Placing the cake on the table she bent over and kissed him heartily.

'Where's all t'other candles then?' he asked playfully.

'Belle, tell your daddy if I'd got sufficient candles to match his age the cake would never've taken the strain.'

'She's got a talent for flattery, has your mother, Belle.' Sam blew out the candle and screwed his eyes shut. 'I wish . . . I wish for us all to be as happy as we are today.'

'Ye're not meant to tell,' accused Erin, slapping him. ''Twon't come true now.'

'Oh, yes it will.' He pulled her arms around his neck and stroked them. 'I don't need such a fragile thing as a birthday wish to make sure I'm gonna be happy wi' you, Erin Teale. I *know*, 'cause I'm gonna make it happen.'

'I do love ye, Sam.' She tightened her embrace and looked fondly at Belle over his shoulder. 'You an' Belle, an' your son when he comes. This is all I ever wanted.'

'Me, too,' answered Sam, kissing her. 'I don't think I could ever be happier than I am today.'

It was commonplace at haymaking time for all the villagers to take part – mainly because, from the poorly-paid farm-workers' point of view it meant the chance of a few rabbits. Erin and Sam were no exception. Indeed, neither of them would miss it, even though, this year, it occurred at the time the cow was due to calf.

'I don't think she'll have any trouble,' Sam told Dobby when the question of their attendance at haymaking arose. 'The calf's lyin' normal. Even if she gives birth while we're away she'll get by without any help. She's an independent madam, I can tell thee, not like the old Shorthorns.'

'I could sit with her till you come back if you like,' offered Dobby.

'Nay, lad, I'm anxious about her but not so worried I'd rob thee of a good day's work. I feel responsible for you being poorly off at the moment, cows dyin' on us, like.'

'Nay, you're not to blame! Anyroad, I've been earnin' a few bob with Old Harry. We've not been starvin'.'

'Nevertheless, the minute I've any work for thee yer'll be back here where you belong. Now then, est comin' up to house an' see my missus for some breakfast before we join t'others? She's missed your smilin' face she tells me, though I can't see no beauty in it missen.'

Dobby followed Sam home. 'How's Mrs Teale feelin' now?'

'Oh, champion, Dobby, thanks. She's gettin' quite plump. I haven't made me mind up yet whether to keep her on as a wife or auction her off for Christmas fare.'

Erin had just finished packing the hamper when they entered the kitchen. 'Ah, there you are! I thought I was going to have to eat breakfast alone. Hello Dobby, nice to see ye. Will ye be coming to haymaking with us? I've packed plenty of food.'

'That's very kind o' yer, Missus.' Dobby took off his hat and flapped it against his thigh.

'Kind, my foot,' said Sam. 'She simply wants yer to carry t'hamper.'

'Well, I don't suppose there'll be any offers from anyone else,' chided Erin amicably. 'Now hurry up, both of yese. Eat your eggs an' we'll be away. 'Tis a lovely morning.'

When the clock that stood on the oak mantel chimed six they were not there to hear it, already two miles away and setting up in the sun-kissed hayfield with the others.

'Right, everybody!' The owner of the field, Tom Cartwright, issued instructions. 'I hope them scythes are nice'n sharp. I want a good acre out of each of thee afore it rains.'

'Nay, there's not a cloud in t'sky!' scoffed one of the mowers.

'I remember t'last time you said that, George Hawksby. You'd no sooner opened yer gob then it siled down. Away, yer've spent enough time jawin'. I want to see t'sun glitterin' on them blades.'

'Bit o' sun makes him go all poetical,' said Dobby, then lined up with Sam and the other mowers. They began to work their way through the ripe grass, swinging their scythes in harmony. The women gave them a few yards' leeway, then slowly followed, shaking out the mown grass for drying. One of the men broke into song and after the first line everyone joined in. There was a great sense of community, everyone working together. Even the Johnsons had dragged themselves from their beds to assist. Erin wondered what it was that produced this feeling, for every other day of the year, Christmas and Harvest apart, most of the participants were at each other's throats.

She cast a nervous eye to where she had left Belle in the care of Vicky Johnson – Sam couldn't possibly carry her while he was scything – but she seemed to be playing happily. Erin turned her energies back to her work, breathing in the sweet smell of the newly-mown hay.

After approximately three and a half hours' toil the mowers, with sweat-dampened hair and florid faces, straightened their backs to survey their progress. 'Not bad. Not bad,' said Cartwright, nodding. 'I might just let thee have a bit o' snap if tha's nifty about it.'

'What a generous old bugger you are, Tom,' said Sam, laying down his scythe. 'Now, yer sure yer wouldn't want us to work right through? We'd get it done quicker.'

'Eh, Maister, don't make jests like that wi' Tom Cartwright. He'll take thee at tha word.'

'Away then, Dobby, let's go see what the women've got for us.' Sam walked back along the channel he had shaved in the field to where Erin had spread a cloth and was lifting food from the hamper. 'Ah, just what I need!' He sloughed the moisture that dripped from his brow as she brought out a flagon of ale. This was the only alcohol Sam allowed himself. Taking out the bung he put the neck to his lips and drank long and deep.

'What about Dobby?' Erin reminded him. 'His tongue's hanging out to his boots, thinking you're going to drain the jug.'

Sam gasped and wiped his hand across his mouth. 'God, that's better! There thoo ist, Dobby lad.' He passed over the flagon and the younger man slaked his thirst.

'Where's Belle?' Sam sat down and sank his teeth into a meat pastie.

Erin tossed a right-handed gesture. 'She's over the . . .' The hand came up to her mouth. 'Oh Lord, Sam, she's gone!' As quickly as her extra burden would allow she got to her feet, scouring the pastoral scene with shaded eyes. 'God, if she's crawled anywhere near those scythes!' She had started to run towards Vicky who was stretched prostrate on the grass, when Dobby shouted, "S all right, Missus! She's there, look.' Stopping to follow his pointing finger Erin saw her daughter playing happily only yards away from where her mother had been sitting, partially hidden in the unmown grass.

Watching her obvious relief, as she collected the child then rebuked Vicky for her laxity, Dobby observed, 'T'missus is awful jumpy about that bairn, isn't she? I mean, Belle were only over there.'

Sam sighed. 'Try tellin' her she's worrying for nowt, though. I've run out o' words to explain to her that even though Belle's crippled she can take care of herself. I'm surprised she left her in that little lass's care, though I don't suppose she would've done if I hadn't suggested it. God knows what she'll be like when we get round to buying the youngster these special shoes.' He savoured another hunk of Erin's light pastry. 'She keeps puttin' that off, too – "I've got this feelin'," she'll say.' He shook his head, smiling.

They fell silent as a flustered Erin returned with the crowing infant under her arm. 'Honestly, that child!' and after taking fifteen minutes or so to consume their victuals they sharpened the scythes on the whetstones that hung from their belts and returned to their positions in the cutting ranks. This time Erin gave a stern lecture to Belle's young minder and told her to be more vigilant.

Throughout the day the sun beat down on the workers as they sweated and scythed, bronzing forearms, causing the women to rip off their wide-brimmed hats to fan their brows. At Sam's instruction Erin did not return to her task after the midday break, dismissing Vicky from her post and watching, idly happy, from the edge of the field beneath the expansive shade of a horse chestnut.

She propped herself on one elbow, surveying the toilers with a slitted eye, the other marking Belle's progress as she shuffled within the confines of the shaded area. Her free hand ran over the mound of her belly as the child within protested at her position, giving the impression that he was thrusting his heels under her lower ribs and levering with all his might. She moved her gaze to watch in fascination as her belly undulated beneath the thin cotton gown, sucked in her breath as little elbows and knees shoved the hummock out of true. The moment was marred by a tiny thrill of alarm; would these limbs be strong and healthy, or would she bear another child like Belle? This fear had never been far from her mind since she had learnt of her condition. What if she gave birth to another deformed baby? People would say she was possessed of the devil.

Her thoughts were diverted as Belle started to stray. Erin sat up and called to her daughter who dutifully shuffled back into the shade and continued to play there until teatime when the womenfolk lit a fire to boil the first brewing of the day. Erin investigated the contents of the hamper as her husband collapsed in the shade and used his hat to chase the flies from his face.

'It's times like this I wish I was a smoker,' he complained as the flies insisted on resettling. 'Dobby, fetch your stinkin' owd pipe over by me an' get rid o' these damned flies.'

'I'd let him stew, Dobby,' said Erin, leaving just enough in the hamper for suppertime and spreading the rest on the cloth. 'All the unflattering things he's called your pipe but 'tis fine enough when it suits him. Sit by me, I like the smell o' baccy.' It reminded her of her father's house.

Dobby settled himself next to the woman.

'I wonder how Hannah's gettin' on. It'd be a right surprise if we got back an' we had two coos instead o' one, wouldn't it?'

'I'd rather she waited for me,' said Sam, giving up wafting the flies to reach for a thick slice of brown bread. 'Apart from wanting to make sure she gives birth safely I should like to be present at the start o' my new dynasty. At the risk o' being classed a sentimental old bugger I must confess it's a real big thing in my life.'

'I trust ye could display the same sentiment when it's time for your human dynasty to expand,' stated Erin wryly, with a wink at Dobby. 'An' give me the same consideration as ye show that blessed cow.'

'Oh, I might be there to rub you down wi' a handful of hay an' bring thee a bucket o' water if yer behave yerself.'

Erin laughed. 'You'll get the bucket o' water over your head for your cheek. Come on now, eat your tea. The sooner ye finish the sooner ye can get back to the love of your life.'

'Well, away, Dobby.' Sam washed down the meal with his pot of tea some twenty minutes later. 'I'm sick o' sat here, being bitten to hell while you're sat there flyless.' He scratched his neck as he clambered to his feet. 'By God, some o'these thunderbugs must have jaws like crocodiles.'

'By, he doesn't like to see anybody sat doin' nowt, does he?' Dobby complained, then rose and prepared to attack the last quarter of the field.

Shortly after seven the work was completed, save for a few square yards in the centre of the field which had been saved for a special custom. There began a great clamour with women banging sticks on empty kettles and pans, the children squealing with anticipation, the deep baritone exhortations of the tired men, all urging the wildlife that had taken sanctuary in that shivering remnant to come out and take their chance.

'A bunny for yer supper, Maister!' shouted Dobby and dived in a headlong tackle as a wide-eyed rabbit shot from its hiding place and bounded away across the mown field.

'Sam Teale's already had his bunny by the look of his wife's belly,' shouted Bert Johnson, bringing forth ribald laughter, blushes from Erin and looks of reproach from the women for such coarse humour.

Sam was about to let the comment pass with a good-humoured jibe, when some creature shot up his trouser leg and lodged in the most inconvenient place. All participants began to roar with laughter at Sam's frantic efforts to dislodge the culprit.

'That'll teach thee to fasten yer breeches proper!' bawled a mower, whose own garment had been secured with string at the ankles to prevent such predicaments.

'Nay, he's freetened it'll tek too long to unfasten 'em when he wants to jump on his missus!' yelled Johnson.

Sam, still hopping, took it all in good sport, but after several such comments from Johnson drew a halt to spare Erin. 'Now then, lads, less o' this indecent talk. I don't want my missus upsetting.'

The men apologised – even Johnson – and Erin accepted goodhumouredly, even attempting a little risqué humour of her own to show she could give as good as she got. 'The looks your good wife is giving you, Mr Johnson, I don't think ye should even bother to untie the string on your breeches tonight.'

The men gave noisy appreciation and Johnson, more affable without a gallon of liquor inside him, replied with a sigh, 'Aye, lass, yer reet – 'twas missus who tied 'em up in t'first place.'

They all took supper in the mown field, now appearing much larger after its haircut. Had Sonny been present his brush and palette would have found much to capture: the sky, a glorious sunburst of pink and orange, the shorn field bathed in late sunlight, a company of weary mowers beneath the great leafy arms of the chestnut tree. For Sam, wanting to be home to check on Hannah, a brief gaze while he polished off his sandwich was sufficient. He was soon urging Erin to pack up.

At the fork in the lane they took leave of Dobby, continuing homewards. Erin nursed her side and made a pained face. 'Sam, love, are your boots on fire? Don't walk so fast, I've got a stitch.'

'Sorry, love.' He put his arm round her, fingers curling onto her distended stomach. 'Dobby's right, I do give more consideration to the cow than me wife.'

Erin looked at Belle cradled in his other arm. 'Poor babe, she's dog-tired. So am I, come to that. I'm glad there's no meal to cook when we get in; we can go straight up.'

'Eh, an' that from somebody who's been sat on her bum half o' day.'

'I'll crown you!' Erin tapped him on the head. 'A woman in my condition can't be expected to slave all day in the burning heat.'

'I'm only having you on. Ah, home sweet home!' Sam unlatched the gate and escorted his wife and child into the house. 'D'you mind if I just nip over to t'shed an' see how Hannah is? I don't suppose owt's happened but I'll never sleep for wonderin'.'

The bitch who had greeted them at the gate now yapped excitedly. 'Shush!' said Erin, then to Sam, 'she thought when you said "nip" you meant her. Thinks you're off to the field.'

'She can come wi' me.' Sam lit a lantern. There was no need for one outside but the shed where Hannah had been confined for the imminent birth would be in darkness.

'Don't be long,' yawned his wife, taking Belle off to bed. 'And don't be fetching any cowclap into my kitchen. I'm not scrubbing floors at this time o' night.'

Sam stepped outside, the lantern swinging at his side, the bitch and her son at his heels, and made for the small outbuilding. 'Well, I'll go to . . . Hannah, my little beauty. Out, dogs, out!' Shooing the bewildered dogs from the byre he hung the lantern on a hook, its soft beam illuminating the mother and child. Hannah lowed and held a protective head over the wobbly creature who tottered and beheld Sam with mild surprise. 'Don't fret, little lady, I won't harm her,' muttered the man, feeling the surge of achievement rise in his breast. He must fetch Erin to share this moment. Pulling the door to, he left the cow to lick her still-damp offspring, reappearing with a sleepy but curious Erin.

'Oh, Sam!' was all she could utter, gazing at the spindly, doe-eyed creature.

'See! I said our bad luck would come to an end, didn't I?' Sam's arm supported her. She felt his energy. 'This little lady's brought us back the good times.'

Erin's hand went automatically to her child-filled abdomen as the mother's rough tongue moved over the damp curls. Standing there, she felt such empathy with this animal. There was hope. There was.

'Oh, mercy, I ache all over!' Sam groaned as he rolled from the bed and put his feet to the floor.

'Lack of work.' Erin, already dressed, had come to tell him his breakfast was on the table.

He took a casual swipe at her and stood to dress. 'Aye well, with a bit o' luck my idleness has ended. I shall have milkin' to do of a morning, even if it is just the one cow.'

'You're not going to take that poor child away from its mother already, are ye?' demanded his wife, leading the way downstairs.

'I've not gone to all this expense to have her suppin' all t'milk that could be earning me brass.'

'Ye'd not be so cruel for the sake of a few coppers?' Erin spun to confront him at the foot of the stairs, hands on hips. 'I'll not let ye.'

'Well, you can have your way today an' two more days, then I'll have to separate 'em. Yer don't make money by being soft-hearted; yer mother'll tell yer that.'

Erin smiled knowingly as he took his seat at the table. 'Listen to him, Belle, making out he's hard. Wait till his precious cow keeps him awake all night bawling for her baby. Your nature won't allow ye to do it, Sam Teale. I'll put money on it. Look at all the other times.'

Masticating his bacon he shook his head. 'It might've been that way with the last lot, but I'm gettin' to learn that sentiment doesn't mix well wi' farming. If the calf's bawlin' worries yer there's plenty of rags to stuff in yer lugs.'

'Ye callous monkey!' Erin picked up a knife to add weight to her argument.

'Well, 'appen she can have four days,' relented Sam, then wagged his own knife. 'Don't think you frighten me, mind.'

'Terrified he is, Belle.' Erin, victorious, went about her work.

Immediately he rose from breakfast Belle's arms stretched out to be picked up. 'Aw, I'm sorry, Tuppence.' Her father picked her up but only to kiss her. 'I can't take you wi' me just now. I've a whole load o' shishamagrawdy to move. Your mam really will take the knife to me if yer come in stinkin' o' violets.' He put her back in her chair and had not reached the door before the tears started. 'Belle, I promise I'll come back in half an hour. Watch that clock . . . eh, Erin, did yer see how she looked straight at that clock? She knows every word I say. Right, Belle, shush now, watch that clock an' when t'big hand gets round to there,' he touched it, 'that's when I'll have finished. All right?' It wasn't all right as far as Belle was concerned but Sam left anyway.

Belle wouldn't be pacified and her screams continued to grate on Erin's nerves for a long time after Sam had departed.

Outside, Sam called to the dogs then went off to clean out the cowshed, marvelling at the perky creature that greeted him, a seemingly different beast from the previous night. 'You two'll have to stop out there,' he told the dogs, whose presence made the calf skittish and the mother uneasy. 'There's not enough room in here an' I can't have this little lass breaking her leg. She's gonna be a champion, isn't she, Mother?'

After hanging the lighted lantern on the hook he bolted the doors against the dogs, grabbed a pitchfork and sang his way over to the cow. 'Now you two'll have to shift yerselves over there while I gi' thee a new bed.' He untied the cow from the iron ring and left the halter rope to trail. 'Away, lest yer want pitchfork up yer arse.' The cow gave a moo of protest then ambled out of his way, the calf hugging her side. Sam hummed as he tossed the straw about. The place seemed alive again. That big empty shippen would soon have all its stalls occupied. He'd maybe take another trip to market today and see what was for sale.

'Right, is that to madam's satisfaction?' he asked the cow on completion. 'Fine. Then we'll have you tethered an' see to them moaning dogs.' He leaned the pitchfork against the wall and surveyed his work. 'Mebbe just a bit more straw over there.' Taking another bale he began to shake it over the floor. 'Come out!' he told the calf. 'You're in the way. Come out, I said.'

It could have been high spirits that persuaded him to make the error, or maybe he was simply daydreaming. But as he worked his way round with the straw he suddenly found himself between the cow and her calf and his back against the wall. 'Easy, girl,' he coaxed in an even voice as he realised his idiotic mistake. 'Away now, gimme room.' The cow sensed his apprehension and, fearing for her calf, began to lean on him. 'Hannah, back!' He slapped at the warm flank. The calf slipped from behind him and ran to join her mother. Sam tried to squeeze past too, but the cow had him completely imprisoned now. The fingers of his only free hand crept along the wall, groping for the handle of the pitchfork, so stupidly discarded. He reached over the cow's finely-skinned rump, stretching, stretching. She moved in closer. It was beginning to hurt. 'Oh, Christ!' His ribs started to bend under the assault. 'Hannah!' The urgency in his voice transmitted itself to the dogs outside. Another mistake, he thought dazedly; the dogs could have saved him. Now his only hope was in that pitchfork. His arm tortured itself to its full reach, fingers curling, grasping, their tips inching out his agony along the wall, almost making contact, just a little further . . . stretching, yearning . . . another half inch and it would be in his grasp. Once more his fingers reached, tickled the wood . . . the pitchfork fell. 'Oh, Jesus!' Sam began to scream at the pain from his crushed ribcage. The cow pressed her body against his in a deadly caress, grinding him into the ancient brickwork. Something snapped in his body; he heard it, felt it. Pure agony. Never had he experienced anything like this. He couldn't get his breath. His mouth gaped, trying to suck at the air, but his lungs refused to expand. There came a terrific explosion of pain in his chest. He tasted blood on his lips. He wanted to shout to her: *Erin! Erin, I love you!* but there was nothing left. A warm curtain was descending across his brain. His ears began to ring. The last sound . . .

'Belle, will ye stop your wailing!' scolded her mother. 'I've enough on with listening to that yapping dog. What the devil's wrong with all of yese?' She tutted exasperatedly and waddled to the door to admit a frantic Nip. On entry the dog went wild, leaping in the air and snapping at her. 'Goodness, the dog's off its head! Nip, stoppit, stoppit!' But the dog leapt at her relentlessly, catching her apron in its teeth, running back and forth in front of the door, imploring her to follow.

'Get out!' She took a broom, struck the dog on the back and forced it to the door. When she had finally barred its re-entry she turned on Belle, hands over ears. 'Belle, will ye please, please stop!' She hunched there, trying to repel the noise from dog and child. Eventually she was forced to open the door again to the bitch who was hurling herself frenziedly at the timber, setting the latch a-rattle.

Seeing Erin on the threshold she dashed away up the path, tail held banner-like.

'I'm not playing silly bloody games!' cried Erin, preparing to use the broom again. 'Where's that master o' yours? Go find him.' Suddenly the reason for the dog's agitation struck home. Some nerve inside her leapt with the shock of realisation: the bitch wouldn't want Erin if Sam were there – something had happened to him.

Ignoring, for once, her daughter's screams, she ran all the way to the outhouse where the other dog sniffed and pawed excitedly. The door was bolted from the inside. At once Erin set up a hammering. 'Sam! Sam, are ye there?' Her only answer was the snorting of the cow.

There was a knothole in the wood. Erin pressed her eye to it, squinting. Despite the light from the lantern she could see nothing, but the dogs' incessant barking confirmed that there was something terribly wrong in there. She banged on the door again, then looked round wildly for something with which to prise it open. There was nothing.

She ran back to the house, supporting her large belly with her hands, skirts tangling around her flying legs, almost tripping her. Searching the bucket of tools which Sam kept in the house for indoor jobs she rejected everything her scrabbling fingers came across, damning them as useless and dropping them onto her spotless kitchen floor. Her heart was leaping into every crevice of her ribcage. She could barely breathe. Then her eyes fell on the axe by the fireside. Grabbing it she tore from the house, forgetting all about Belle who still screamed from her special chair, and returned to the shed where she wielded it against the door, time after time. Hardly able to see in her fury whether the axe was doing any damage she continued to bring it down with all her strength, sobbing with the effort, crying his name with each blow. 'Sam! Sam! Sam!'

Eventually she had chipped a big enough hole in the door to insert her small hand. She shoved it through, not feeling the splintered edges puncturing her skin. With difficulty she extracted the bolt from its casing, then withdrew her hand and paused. The door was open to her but she dare not go in, dreading what she might find.

The dogs took the decision for her, Nip thrusting her nose between door and jamb and barging in, the younger dog, tail wagging, in pursuit. They entered with such force that the door flew wide open, banging against its other jamb. Erin uttered a low moan and clutched her stomach, falling against the doorpost for support.

It didn't look like Sam at all, that crumpled heap at the cow's feet. His beautiful, cheery features were hidden under a mess of blood and bruises, streaks of dung, the blue eyes staring, the mouth sagging open in a last silent cry for help.

She wanted to move, to go to him, but she couldn't. She could only stand there, imprisoned by the horrific sight, watching the dogs dance round the cow, barking, weaving out of reach of those threatening horns, watching those great clumsy feet, cloven devil's feet, stamp on Sam's hands, his warm, loving hands. Oh, don't, she begged the

116

cow, shaking her head hypnotisedly. Don't stand on him, don't, don't, then aloud, '*Don't!*' It came as a scream as the volcanic surge of pain shot up her spine to inhabit every nerve of her body. It grasped her stomach with indescribable ferocity, trying to wrench the life from her body. Her belly was like a solid lump of concrete, the child within crushed. No, it's too early! her mind screamed as her arms hugged the ravaged body, recoil throwing her back against the hard doorpost where she whimpered in terror. 'Somebody, help me please.' Louder: 'Help! Help me!'

Nip came to her, licking at her face, only to dash back to the body of her master, nipping at the cow's heels. Erin, clutching her screaming bulk, lurched back in the direction of the house, her skirts bogged down with the water that had cushioned the baby. White-hot pokers tore and shredded her innards. She staggered to the gate, fell, rolled over from side to side in her torment, then reached out and used the gate to haul herself up. Stumbling through it she made her way down the steps, tripped over her skirt and fell again, tumbling over and over like a pace-egg at Easter, bouncing off the cottage wall and coming to rest in the fragrant bed of lavender beneath the kitchen window.

It was here, his poor, semi-conscious mother able to go no further, that Sam Teale's perfect, but too-small son was born. He never drew breath.

PART TWO

1878—1881

CHAPTER EIGHT

I must just be one of those people to whom bad things happen, came Erin's bleak thought as she stared fixedly at the Rossetti print opposite her bed. There were people like that, their lives filled with one tragedy after the other. That was the trouble with lying in bed; it gave one time to think. By rights she should be up and helping at the store or around the house, anything to take her mind off her double loss. The first few days after the miscarriage it had been deemed unwise to move her so she had been forced to lie there in the big double bed; the bed where she had learned to love Sam with her body as well as her mind; the bed in which they had snuggled together on cold winter nights, making plans for the future. What future was there for her now? The cottage and its land had been put up for auction, the furniture with it. Here she was back where she had started with nothing to show for her marriage but a bewildered, cock-eyed child and her memories.

After that crucial first week when, unbeknown to Erin, it was feared she might die, they had carried her out to the waiting carriage and brought her directly here to her parents' home. The transition seemed so unreal. Given time she would have liked to wander through the rooms of the cottage, remembering the events that had taken place in each. Instead she had to visit the rooms in her mind: through that door she had returned to Sam after a brief parting to yield the physical love she had denied him for so long; through that open window he had presented her with a late-flowering rosebud when she had bashfully informed him that she carried their first child.

But one place she didn't want to revisit was the byre. Instantly her brain took her there, recaptured the image of Sam crushed to a pathetic shell, devoid of all the things Sam had been – kind, fun-loving, human. She wanted the cow to die, would have wielded the knife herself had she the strength to pull this wretched body from the bed. But first she would have wanted to kill the calf before its mother's eyes, wanted the cow to know how it felt to be robbed of one's child, to have it torn from one's body and not be able to do a thing about it. The anger surged through her as she lay here, now. Under the crisp linen her fingers clenched into trembling fists. Her teeth clamped together. Her whole body was filled with a tension so overwhelming that she wanted to scream and scream, fill their nice, orderly house with her anguish, have them know what it felt like to listen to their stupid, well-meant comments of, 'Time's a great healer' and 'You mustn't upset yourself'. Why mustn't she? She *was* bloody upset. She was devastated. But no one would let her show it. If she started to throw things, rant and rave like she had done once when the silence of her room grew too much to bear, they would dose her with laudanum. Didn't they know that she had to work the sense of injustice from her system?

Pain registered in her hand. Withdrawing it from beneath the bedclothes she stared at it dumbly. The action of clenching her fists so hard had drawn blood, her fingernails digging into her palms. Apathetically, she shoved the hand back under the covers. What was pain? She had grown used to it.

Poor Dobby. Apparently he had been the one to discover the tragedy and raise the alarm. She pictured the look on his face as the carriage rolled past him in the lane, the imploring eyes that had met hers fleetingly then had dropped to the hands clutching the billycock hat. What about the funeral, had he been there? She didn't know, not having been there herself. That was what made the whole thing unreal, incomplete. Standing round a grave in a windy churchyard, watching your man being lowered into the ground, it all gave the situation credence. As it was there were too many loose ends. She had wanted to

122

visit his grave before they had brought her here but Mother wouldn't let her. It had probably been Thomasin who had organised everything – the sale of the house, the disposal of Sam's clothes. Erin supposed she should be grateful that she hadn't this heartrending task to do herself, but she saw it as one more comfort that had been denied her. To sift through Sam's meagre wardrobe, to press his jacket to her face and breathe in his familiar smell. . . . some might decry it as morbid but it would have comforted her, made her feel as though he was still here, instead of in Purgatory.

I must stop dwelling on it all, she told herself, trying to concentrate on the Rossetti print. If I lie here much longer I'll go mad.

'The doctor's here, ma'am.' Abigail stood before Thomasin and awaited the command. Patrick was there, too. It suddenly struck Abigail as odd that it was always the mistress whom one addressed first – probably because she was the more forceful of the two. The master didn't seem to mind, he was an easygoing soul. Abigail felt sorry for him sometimes. Since the fire he and the mistress had not appeared so pally as they used to be. But of course that was no concern of Abi's.

'Oh good, bring him in, Abigail,' replied Thomasin, rustling forward to meet the physician. 'Then after we've spoken you can show him up to Mrs Teale. Good day, Doctor, I hope you'll be able to give us some better news about our patient today.'

'My sentiments too, Mrs Feeney.' The doctor exchanged a perfunctory tilt of the head with Patrick. 'Mr Feeney. Has there been any improvement since my last visit?'

'That's for you to say, I think.' Thomasin gestured for the doctor to sit down.

Hitching up his trousers the man sat on the sofa. 'Actually I was not referring to her medical condition but her state of mind. Has there been any lessening of the violent outbursts?'

123

Thomasin raised an eyebrow at her husband. 'Well, I don't think there's been quite so many in the past few days, d'you, Patrick?'

Her husband shook his head. 'I don't know which is worse, the mad rages or the doldrums that follow them. How much longer before she's well enough to be on her feet, Doctor?'

'Well, the miscarriage was of a very violent nature. It takes time and rest to repair damage like Mrs Teale has suffered.'

'Will she be able to bear other children should she wish to remarry, Doctor?' cut in Thomasin who, after her own miscarriage, had been left incapable of producing further children.

'I believe so, Mrs Feeney,' he responded. 'As to your query, Mr Feeney, I should be able to give you the answer when I have made my examination.' He rose and picked up his bag.

Thomasin rang a handbell and Abigail entered from the hall where she had been waiting for the summons. 'Take the doctor up, Abigail, then inform Mrs Howgego that we'll take some tea in fifteen minutes.'

Abigail bobbed and showed the doctor up to Erin's room. While he was away making his examination there was another visitor. Thomasin answered the door herself. 'Ah, hello, Liam! Come in, dear. Have you called to see Erin?'

'I have.' Father Kelly stepped into the spacious, oak-panelled hall and gave her his hat. 'D'ye think she's taking visitors today?' He had tried several times to see Erin, never getting beyond the wrong side of her bedroom door. Her improving physical condition had brought with it a hostility towards those who loved her most. There had been some terrible language through that door. But it would take more than that to make Liam give up on her.

'Eh, I don't know I'm sure.' Thomasin helped him off with his coat, then piloted him through to the drawing room. 'She doesn't seem to want to know anybody. Pat, Liam's here.'

'Hello to your good self.' Liam clasped the proffered hand, then sank onto the middle seat of the sofa. 'How's the body?'

Patrick went to the sideboard and took out a decanter 'Pretty much the same – d'you want one, Tommy?' She declined saying it was too early. He filled just the two glasses, handing one to Liam. ''Tis not too early for this fella.'

The priest inclined his grizzled head. 'May your still never run dry.'

'Sláinte,' said Patrick, then repositioned himself in his chair. 'She may not see ye, Liam. I hope ye don't take all this personal? 'Tis the way she's been with all of us.'

Father Kelly sighed. 'Ah, the poor, poor child. Nothing seems to be smooth-going for her, does it?' He sampled the whiskey again. 'If I could only speak to her, if she'd only see me, I'm sure I could offer her some comfort.'

'Well, ye may – just may, mind you – get a chance today. The doc's up there seeing if she's well enough to come down. If she is, then ye could catch her at the lunch-table. She'll not escape so easily then.'

'That makes me feel like a bailiff serving an eviction order,' answered Liam. 'I'd not corner her if she truly doesn't want me poking my nose in.' He saluted with his glass. 'But I will accept your kind invitation to luncheon, if that's what it was.'

'You're always welcome here, Liam, you know that,' said Thomasin. 'I'll get Cook to serve an extra portion of tripe.'

His face became uneasy. 'Oh dear, I've just remembered Father Gilchrist has a job lined up for me – thank ye all the same.'

'By God, that speaks volumes for how much he hates tripe,' laughed Thomasin to her husband. 'Oh, Liam, I was only teasing. I just wanted to see your face. I know tripe's not your favourite meal.'

''Tis a terrible woman ye married, Pat,' said Liam. 'But I'm glad she can still joke with so much trouble on her mind.'

'Well, it's as I always say, Liam,' sighed Thomasin. 'You have to laugh else you'd cry.'

'Ye would, Tommy, oh, ye would indeed.' There seemed to be something else worrying the priest.

Patrick thought he knew its source. 'As you were the one to raise that unmentionable name,' he said to his friend, 'how is Father Gilchrist treatin' ye?'

'He doesn't go in for treats,' replied Liam, holding out his glass for a refill which was duly supplied. 'In fact I hardly dare tell ye, knowing your hot temper.'

'What's he done now?' demanded the other heavily.

'He's taken over my entire duties,' replied Liam, then dropped his gaze to his whiskey and swilled it around the crystal tumbler.

'He's what?' blasted Patrick. 'D'ye mean to tell me ye've been given the sack?'

'Oh, nothing so inhuman,' responded Liam. 'Retired is the word that was used.'

Thomasin leaned forward. 'But what about your house and everything?'

'Father Gilchrist's house,' corrected Liam.

'Oh, Liam.' She put a hand to her mouth.

'Why, the devious, black-hearted spatchcock!' stormed Patrick, crossing the room in great strides and returning with the decanter to fill Liam's glass almost to the brim. 'I'm off round there an' fix his teeth for him. D'ye think they'd suit, growing out of his forehead?'

'And have me thrown out of my lodgings?' asked Liam.

Patrick digested this, then flew into more invective. 'That pious prick of a poltroon.'

'Patrick, if you're going to use bad language I wish you'd lower your voice,' scolded his wife.

'I like that!' Patrick directed himself to the priest. 'Since I've been married to her I've had more Anglo-Saxon thrown at me than William the Conqueror.'

'Not for some years,' objected Thomasin. 'And certainly not in the same house as my grandchildren. What if the doctor should walk in?'

His temper ebbed. 'Aye, ye're right, I didn't give it a thought. I'm sorry – I'm just so bloody mad.'

'As I am,' she answered. 'But swearing's not going to help Liam, is it?'

Patrick seated himself once more. 'So, ye mean to tell us, Liam, that you're a lodger in your own house?'

'As I said, 'tis Father Gilchrist's house now. It goes with the job ye see, an' not being the resident priest any more I'm not entitled to it.'

'Not entitled, pfff!' Whiskey hit Patrick's tonsils again.

'However, Father G. very kindly said he'd not see me thrown out after so many years' loyal service an' me with no family to go to . . .'

'Too kind.'

' . . . he said I could stay on as his guest for he'd not need all that room for himself.'

'Most noble of him,' spat the other man. 'God, Liam, 'tis criminal. How long have ye been in York – forty years?'

'Forty-one.'

'An' all that time at the same church?'

'Virtually,' nodded Liam. 'First the chapel, then the new church.' Liam still called it the new church though it had been built fifteen years ago. 'But that's how things go.' He sighed defeatedly. 'I speak lightly of it but you being an old pal I must admit it came as a terrible shock. Oh, I knew he fancied my job all right. But . . .' he groped for reason, 'couldn't he wait for me to die? I mean, look at me, Pat. Have y'ever seen a body nearer death? I can't have more than a year or two to go. Though,' he accomplished a chuckle, 'I've been saying that since I reached my three score years and ten an' here I still am almost a score later.' The seriousness returned. 'But I never envisaged retirement. I thought I'd be preaching till I dropped, that they'd have to scrape me up from the altar steps an' drop me in the box there an' then. I don't know what to do with meself, Pat, an' that's a fact.'

After listening to the contents of Liam's heart, Patrick spread his hands. 'Liam, I wish there was some way we could help ye. Might ye be wiser to get away from it altogether an' live somewhere else? We could help financially, couldn't we, Tommy?' His wife endorsed this.

'Ah, your kindness is much appreciated, but no, I wouldn't know where to go.'

'But surely you can't want to stay in the same house as the man who robbed you of your job,' said Thomasin.

'Ah, if t'were just a job, Tommy,' Liam answered forlornly. ''Tis my life he's taken. I couldn't feel much worse if he'd plunged a knife between me shoulderblades. Ah, but no, I think I'll take him up on his offer, genuine though it isn't, if only so's I can be a nuisance to him for the rest o' me days. An' o' course I have Mrs Lucas my housekeeper – if he keeps her on, which I think he will. He might be a rogue but he's no fool and she's the finest cook in York, barring your own, of course.'

'So we can't persuade ye to come an' live with us?' enquired Patrick.

'God love ye, no! Though your generosity touches me. You're a good friend, Pat, but I think ye've enough problems without a liability like me. I'll remember your kindness, though.'

'Aye well, when you're writing your will my name is spelt with one em,' Thomasin smiled, then looked up as Abigail showed the doctor back in. 'Oh, how is she, Doctor?'

'Bodily, everything appears to be healing nicely.' The physician put his bag on the carpet. 'However, I'm not at all happy with her mental state. I suggest that she be watched carefully.'

Patrick showed his alarm. 'Ye mean she could try to kill herself?'

The doctor was uncomfortable; families were usually reticent when it came to discussing madness. Then he nodded, supposing it was better to call a spade a spade in order for them to be on their guard. 'Mrs Teale is much deranged by her tragic loss. She seems unable to communicate. May I suggest that a member of the family try to get her into conversation, to speak of her loss?'

128

'It's not as if we haven't tried,' Thomasin told him. 'She doesn't want any of us.'

'Nevertheless I beg you to persist. She mustn't be allowed to meditate on her grief, otherwise . . .' He shook his head.

'God,' breathed Patrick.

'Can't you keep sedating her until she becomes more stable in her mind?' asked Thomasin anxiously.

'I can of course,' answered the doctor. 'But still she should be watched.'

'Naturally we'll all be most diligent,' said Thomasin. 'Doctor, have you decided when she'll be able to leave her bed?'

Patrick read her thoughts instantly – she's worried that she'll have to sit with the girl and not be able to get out to that blasted store, he thought angrily. But he kept his voice unaccusing. 'We don't want to get the lass up before she's fit, Tommy. I'll sit with her if ye like.'

'I wasn't suggesting dragging her out of her sickbed, Patrick. I was simply going to suggest that she be given some light occupation to take her mind off things.' She turned questioning eyes to the doctor.

'That may be a sensible course of action, Mrs Feeney,' nodded the man. 'She is, I feel, quite well enough physically to leave her bed and take on some light work – nothing too strenuous of course. But what she really needs is someone to whom she can confide.'

Patrick looked at his wife. 'You've lost a child, Tommy. Knowing that you understand the way she's feeling might help her.'

'She hasn't just lost a baby, Pat. She's lost a husband she adored, a home . . . my fault, I know, but I simply thought to take some of her worries off her shoulders. All that on top of bearing a crippled child.' No wonder the girl was in danger of losing her mind.

'God forgive me,' broke in Liam. 'I never thought to ask how all this is affecting Belle.' All these visits to Erin and never once had he enquired after the child. They had obviously been keeping Belle out of the way in case the

129

sight of her upset her mother. Out of sight, out of mind . . . but that was no excuse for him. 'She and Sam were very close, weren't they?'

Thomasin looked even more solemn and nodded. 'The odd thing is, she doesn't seem to be affected by this in the least. All this upheaval hasn't produced any response whatsoever. She's upstairs with Rosie and Nick playing quite happily – as much as she's able. Of course, she can't tell us what she's feeling, can she? Oh, here's Abigail with the tea. You will join us, Doctor?'

The physician accepted, but declined the further invitation of lunch and twenty minutes later went on his way. Towards midday Erin came down. Immediately, everyone rose and fussed about her as she selected a chair.

'Is there anything I can get you, dear?' asked Thomasin. 'Would you like an appetiser before lunch?'

'Nothing, thank you – an' don't expect too much of me at lunch either.'

'Oh, but you must eat!' cried Thomasin.

Erin held her with lifeless eyes. 'Why must I?'

'Because there's people here who love ye an' don't want to see ye going the way of your dear husband,' put in Liam.

'And you've been appointed Job's Comforter, have you, Father?'

Liam held her gaze, thinking how awful she looked, her sparrow-like body hardly filling a corner of the chair. Erin was the first to look away. 'I'm sorry,' she mumbled. 'I have no right to take it out on you.'

Patrick and Thomasin watched helplessly, not knowing what to say. The latter wished that she and Erin were alone. It was hard to voice one's feelings before an audience. 'Can't I get you anything?' she asked lamely.

Erin moved her head, staring at the wall.

'D'ye fancy a walk round the garden before lunch?' asked the priest.

'For God's sake, you don't have to make conversation,' she flung at them all. 'Treating me as if I'm some oddity . . . I wish ye'd all bloody leave me alone.'

'I asked if ye'd fancy a walk round the garden,' persevered Liam. 'I wasn't thinking to regale ye with yarns of idle palliatives. A little fresh air might just help to sharpen your appetite.' She didn't respond. 'Well?' he pressed.

'Oh, all right,' she returned apathetically and rose to link her arm with that of the old priest.

They wandered over the terrace and stood for a while by a bed of lavender to admire the vista. The garden was in full colour. Designed to meet the previous occupant's taste it also suited the Feeneys, who had added nothing. The scent of lavender was so strong it stung one's nostrils. Liam filled his lungs deep. 'God, that's beautiful.'

'I hate it,' said Erin feelingly, and with her insistent pressure on his arm caused him to move on down the winding path that bisected the lawn.

'Why?' asked the priest after a while.

A scarlet fuchsia bled over a crumbling brick wall. Erin pulled off one of the delicate blooms as she passed, fingering it thoughtfully. 'I always think fuchsias look like little ballerinas in their pretty red dresses, with the stamens like legs,' she said evasively. They had turned down another shaded walkway before she answered his question, showing no emotion. 'My baby was born in a lavender patch. He was dead.'

'Had he lived, what would you have called him?'

Erin frowned at the strange question. 'Why d'ye ask? He's dead, isn't he?'

'But when ye remember Sam ye think of him by name. How d'ye recall the baby?'

'I recall the blueness of his face . . . the blood . . . the smell of lavender.' There was a pause, then she added decisively, 'Luke,' and turned great, pain-filled eyes to him. 'We were going to name him Luke, Father.'

'A fine name,' Liam nodded, diverting his step around a clump of yellow flowers that had sprung from a crack in the paving. 'He would've made a fine man, like his father.'

'It didn't do him any good though, did it?' said Erin, not bitterly, just stating a fact. 'Being a fine man.'

'That depends on your viewpoint.' Liam steered her in and out of rosed cloisters. They came upon a sun-warmed bower where a garden seat offered hospice; they took it. 'If ye believe in the Catholic teaching – an' I know you do, being a faithful and devout follower – then ye know that death is not the end of everything, only the beginning.'

The same old clichés, thought Erin dully; the reasons she had been keeping him at bay until today. 'An' where are my beginnings, Father?'

'I know ye can't see them now but give it time, you'll make them.'

Time! As someone who was going nowhere that's something she had plenty of.

'Father,' she turned her body round to face him, 'there's no need for ye to tell me that Sam an' Luke have gone to a better place; I know that. I've always believed in the Hereafter and losing them doesn't suddenly change that.'

'But 'tis a comfort to ye?'

'No!' she shouted. 'It should be, but it's not. I don't want to know that they're happy with God, I want them here, with me, they're my husband, my child. Oh, Father, what am I ever going to do without them?' She broke down and sobbed against the shoulder that had given comfort to her father before her. 'I want to be with them.'

He pressed her back so he could study her face, saying gravely, 'Ye'll not be doing anything foolish?'

She pulled away, eyes swimming. 'Don't worry, I'll not kill myself. Your teachings are too strongly embossed on my conscience.' He doesn't understand either, she thought dejectedly. He's only concerned with my soul.

'I'm not,' said Liam as if he had read her mind. She looked up sharply. 'Ye think I'm only here to see ye don't commit an unpardonable offence against the church, but I'm not. If my priestly role can give ye solace then gladly I'll give it, but Erin, I'm here as your old friend. Talk to me, get rid of your anger, hit me if I talk rubbish, use me to punish God. Yes!' he shook her gently. 'I can feel it. Ye do want to punish Him. You're askin' yourself how God can be so cruel after all the devotion ye've shown

Him. Why does it have to happen to me, you're saying. I can hear your mind screaming with the question. Let it out, shout it at me. Come on, child!'

She denied it strenuously. 'No! I don't feel that way, I don't.' Then, after repeated, harsh promptings she yelled, 'Yes! All right I do, I do! Damn God. I hate what He's done to me. I can't bear it, Father. Help me. Oh God, please help me!'

The garden fell silent again. A bumblebee hummed dizzily around her ebony head as she wept into Liam's shoulder. He brushed it away. ''Tis a sorry thing for a priest to confess, Erin, but I don't know how to help ye. 'Tis no good me saying I know how ye feel. How could I know? I do know, though, what it's like to have your whole life taken away from ye. Sam an' your children were your life, the church was mine. When something like that happens it brings an emptiness that no amount of well-meaning talk from friends can bridge. I know my loss will seem very meagre compared to your own plight . . .'

'Oh no, Father,' she moved her face against him, 'I know how much the church means to ye . . . but,' puzzlement showed through the tears.

Liam explained the situation.

'Oh, God, how hurt ye must be,' sniffed the young woman.

He nodded. 'I expect it will heal in time or so they'd have us believe. I'm like you at the moment – can't foresee anything replacing what I've lost. I was as miserable as sin for ages after the Bishop broke the news, couldn't see any point in anything. But, I'm a rational sort o' fella and pretty soon I got to seeing that I hadn't quite lost everything. I still had my faith, an' there were still some folk who needed me.'

'There's plenty of us need ye, Father.' Erin squeezed his hand, tearfully.

'Thank ye. The same goes for you, Erin. Apart from your parents, your brother, me, ye've still a small daughter who needs ye.'

'Belle.' It was as if she had completely forgotten, thought

133

Liam, watching her, trying to guess at her thoughts. They finally emerged. 'She was never as fond o' me as of Sam.'

'I'm sure ye do her wrong.'

'No, I accepted it. I was the same myself when I was a child, followed my dad like a puppy. I just hope she can make do with me now. Sam was so good with her.'

'I'm sure she'll get all the love she needs from you, dear,' whispered Liam, patting her.

Then she put voice to the statement she had kept repeating to herself whilst lying in her sickbed. 'It's not fair, so many bad things happening to one person.'

'I can understand ye thinking of it in that light,' said Liam carefully. 'But half the answer lies not in counting the bad things but all the good times you and Sam shared. Ye'd seven good years with each other for a start . . .'

And four of those years I wasted, came the negative thought.

' . . . ye've parents who love ye deeply. When I think o' some o' the poor children I see . . . an' ye have your daughter . . . she's a part of Sam ye still have left.'

'All true of course.' Erin managed a weak smile. 'I know I should be thankful for what bit I have of Sam . . .' – But oh, Father, her mind sighed. 'Tis not enough. 'Tis not enough.

CHAPTER NINE

'What's your second name, Abigail?' asked Rosanna, elbows on the kitchen table, watching Cook's sinewy arm beat at the cake mixture.

'Nancy,' replied Abigail, running a tea-cloth briskly over a stack of plates. She was a good-natured girl who had been with the Feeneys for about four years. Quick to make friends she had soon become a favourite with the children, especially when she sneaked biscuits from Cook's private store.

'No, I mean your last name,' said Rosie, wagging her bottom from side to side.

'Bickerdike.' Abigail positioned the dried plates on the huge dresser that ran almost the length of one wall. 'And don't kneel on that chair, sit down properly, the way you've been taught.'

'Bickerdike.' Rosanna savoured it, still moving her bottom, now in rhythm. 'Abigail Bickerdike.' She grinned and repeated the tongue-twister rapidly. 'Abigail Bickerdike, Abigail Dipperbike, Agibail Kipperdike.'

'You mind your manners, Miss Rosie, else I sh'll ask Cook to let Master Nick clean t'bowl out on his own — and sit down, will you?'

Undeterred, Rosie asked, 'What about Belle, doesn't she get a turn?'

'I shouldn't think she'll notice,' muttered Cook under her breath, glancing at Abigail as she whipped up the mixture with a wooden spoon. Here was none of the plumpness that one usually visualised when provided with the word 'cook'. A woman of dour countenance, her fore-head was wrinkled in a perpetual state of apprehension, the lips pale and turned down at the edges. 'God knows why the master's asked me to make this here birthday cake for her. T'poor child doesn't know whether she's three or thirty-three.' Her currant-brown eyes took in briefly the little girl seated with the others, chewing on a carrot that Cook had given her that they might enjoy some quiet. She stopped mixing to examine Belle. 'Just look at her, Abigail,' she said in furtive voice. 'I mean, what point was there in bringing that into the world?'

'Careful, Mrs Howgego,' muttered Abigail between her teeth. 'I can see little lugs flappin'.'

'It's all right, I won't tell, Abi,' said Rosanna as Mrs Howgego resumed her mixing. The words brought work to yet another standstill.

'Eh, listen to that!' declared Cook to the maid, then to

Rosanna, 'You've been in t'knife box again, Miss Rosie; too sharp for your own good.'

'Why don't you like Belle?' asked the child, throwing a profusion of dark curls off her face.

'Eh, you do ask some questions! Doesn't she, Abigail?' Cook scraped the mixture into a baking tin and moved briskly towards the oven.

'But why?'

Cook tutted and looked uncomfortably at Belle. 'Well . . . I don't dislike her, Miss Rosie . . .'

'It's because she doesn't speak,' contributed Nicholas. 'She frightens people when she just looks at them.'

'S'truth, I think he's been in t'knife box with her.' Cook nudged the maid. 'Honestly, them two. They certainly make up for t'other one, don't they?' She rounded on Nick. 'Now then, Master Nicholas, what would you be knowing about all that?'

'I heard Nan saying it to Grandad,' provided the small boy, unaware of the breach of etiquette. 'She said it made her feel creepy when Belle just stared at her.' He found it hard to understand grown-ups. One minute they were complaining that you were making too much noise, the next they were saying Belle didn't make enough noise.

'An' what did the master have to say to that?' Abigail flashed a barely perceptible wink at Cook.

'He told Nan off.' Nick drew a pattern in the flour that had been spilt on the table.

'I'll bet he did,' muttered Cook as she turned her back. 'He won't have no wrong said about any of them bairns. I'll say that for him, he treats 'em all equal.' She pushed the mixing bowl at Nick. 'There you are then, children. Miss Rosie, fetch yourself a spoon. Master Nick, get the wooden one to lick.'

'Master Nick get the wooden one to lick,' sang Rosie, jumping from the chair. 'Master Nick get the wooden one to lick! Shall I fetch one for Belle?'

'I suppose so,' sighed the cook. She started on another task. 'Isn't it funny how them bairns never notice anything up with her? She's just another playmate to them.'

'I should've thought that was a good thing,' replied Abigail. 'Poor little tyke, it'd be rotten if the kids were agen her an' all. I think she's a lovely little thing meself.'

'Granted she's got an angelic little face,' said Mrs Howgego. 'But I mean, look at rest of her. It looks as if somebody's used her for a squeeze-box. An' it makes it worse her not talkin'. I must say I have to agree with the mistress; she makes you feel uncomfortable the way she looks at you. I've never seen eyes as blue as that on a bairn. They don't look human.'

'Rubbish!' countered the maid bravely. Cook could be quite a formidable opponent, especially down here in her own domain and normally Abigail toed the line, but she wasn't having that said about Miss Belle.

'I beg your pardon?' Cook's eyes widened. The children's spoons halted at the tone of voice.

'I said rubbish, Mrs Howgego. She gets her lovely eyes from the master, like a lot of other people in the family, an' I think she's got enough against her without you implying that she's some child o' the devil.'

'I never said anything of the kind! An' I think you're getting a bit above yourself, my girl.'

'Well, I might be, but someone's got to stick up for her, haven't they?'

'At the expense of your job? I don't want no back-chatters working for me, thank you very much.'

'Oh, an' you're going to have the mistress sack me, are you?' retorted Abigail.

'I might do.' Cook stalked over to the range to check on a simmering pan.

'An' I might just tell her what you've been saying about her grandbairn!' was Abigail's broadside.

'Eh!' exclaimed Cook frustratedly. 'No wonder they call you Bickerdike – just go wash them pots an' less of your cheek!' She made herself look busy to cover up for lost pride.

Abigail winked at Belle, receiving an instant smile. – There you are! said the maid to herself. You have got all your marbles, haven't you? It's just taking you a while to put them in order, that's all. 'I think t'master's right in giving her a birthday party what wi' poor little mite losin' her dad an' that.'

'I still say she won't know whether it's her birthday or Christmas,' emphasised Cook when the golden cake was brought out of the oven. 'Still, who am I to argue wi' them that knows better.' A scathing look for Abigail. 'Can you be trusted to mix the icing while I visit my store cupboard?'

'I dare say it wouldn't be too taxing. Would you like to help me, Miss Rosie?'

'Can Belle help too?' came the reply.

''Course!' Abigail smiled fondly. 'It's good that you look after your cousin.'

'Why?'

'Well, it just is, that's all. Get yourselves a couple o' spoons – not the ones you've just licked, thank you very much.' Abigail emptied some icing sugar into a bowl.

'May I do that?' asked Nick.

'No, 'cause you'll get it all over the floor – oh, bother-ation!' A bell jangled on the rail. Abigail began to swap her apron for an 'upstairs' one. 'Now, you three don't touch owt while I come back. You hear?'

'I'll stand guard,' promised Nick, the moment she had disappeared licking his finger and dipping it into the icing sugar. Rosie was about to do the same. Nick plucked the finger from his mouth with a pop. 'Hands off!'

'You're mean – isn't he, Belle?' Rosie leaned sulkily on her elbows and watched him dib in again. 'We shall tell.'

'Tell-tale-tit.' The boy sucked his finger noisily, then grinned. 'Go on, then. We can always say Belle did it if there's any trouble.'

Abigail bustled up the stone steps, then across the hall to the drawing room. It was Erin who had rung. Her physical health was much improved but there was about her a constant state of edginess. When the maid entered she spun round anxiously.

'Is my daughter with you, Abigail?'

'Yes, Mrs Teale, you know she is.'

'If I knew I wouldn't be asking!' At the look of shock

138

on the maid's face Erin was immediately contrite. 'I'm sorry, Abigail, I was just worried when I couldn't find her, that's all.'

'But you were here when I took Miss Belle down to the kitchen wi' the others, ma'am,' Abigail reminded her.

'I know, but I thought ye might've got fed up with her and sent her back upstairs.' She worried her finger ends.

'I wouldn't've done that, ma'am. Anyway, how would she get upstairs by herself?'

'You'd be surprised,' sighed Erin, moving her twitching fingers to her temple. 'Just because she can't walk doesn't mean to say she isn't mobile. You will watch her carefully, won't ye?'

'O'course, Mrs Teale. I'll give her the same attention I give the others.'

'No! Ye must give her extra attention, Abigail. She's so adventurous. She has only to put her fingers on the hot oven . . .' Erin's fingers went to her mouth. It didn't bear thinking about.

'Honestly, there's no need to worry, Mrs Teale . . .'

'Who're you to tell me I needn't worry?'

Abigail accepted the rebuke. 'I'm sorry, ma'am, I didn't mean to be impertinent . . . but Miss Belle is quite safe wi' me, I promise.'

The sharp expression remained. 'Then who's with her now? Ye've not left her on her own?'

She's going off her head, thought Abigail, but not without sympathy. Miss Erin hadn't had a great deal of happiness out of life. 'She's safe, ma'am. Cook's with her.'

Erin let out the breath she had been holding. 'Oh.'

'Did you want anything else, Mrs Teale?'

'What?' Erin felt as if she were not involved in this conversation, but hearing it through a thick curtain. Her feet seemed two inches above the ground. She sat down before she fell. There had been a lot of these feelings lately. She had tried to keep them to herself but she knew by the way people stared at her – like the maid was staring now – that she had not succeeded.

'You rang, Mrs Teale, was it for anything in particular?'

Erin tried to chase the muzziness from her brain. 'No, no, I only wanted to make sure Belle was all right. Thank you, Abigail.' When the maid left she slipped back into her forlorn trance.

'Oh, Jesus!' exclaimed Abigail on entering the kitchen, empty save for Cook. 'Where the bloody hell are they?'

'D'you have to use such language, girl?' Mrs Howgego added another plate of pastries to the table of birthday goodies. 'You'll notice I've iced the cake by the way – seeing as how you sloped off.'

'I didn't slope off. I got rung for. Where are they?'

'Miss Fancydrawers came down to fetch 'em.' She referred to the governess.

'What, all on 'em?'

'Just Rosie an' Nick. T'other one's over there.' She nodded to a far corner where Belle was investigating the contents of a bread bin.

Abigail clutched her chest. 'Oh, thank God! I thought summat had happened to her an' me just tellin' her mother she's as safe as houses.' She went to pick Belle up. 'How on earth did she get that heavy lid off by herself?' She stroked the cow-lick of hair from the child's forehead.

'If there's food inside that one'll find it,' opined Cook, tutting as Belle waded through a half-loaf.

'Well, what did you let her do it for?' Abigail took the loaf from the child.

'What a cheek! I can't be expected to watch her every second, I have my work to do. Oh, cut her a slice off where she's had her teeth in!' she exclaimed as Belle began to wail. 'I can't abide all that row. She's never happy but that she's got summat in her mouth. It's a wonder she isn't like a house end. I don't know where she puts it all. I shall have to have a discreet word with the mistress about havin' her wormed.'

Abigail repositioned Belle at the table to eat the bread, leaning on the still floury surface to watch her. 'I wonder what she makes of all us lot, Mrs Howgego.'

'Not much, judging from her expression,' decided Cook. 'And haven't you any work to do?'

The maid set her mouth. 'Aye, I suppose I'd best go lay table for t'party.'

'Well, I trust you're taking that with you.' Cook flapped a hand at Belle. 'Left to her own devices down here she'd work her way through t'larder before teatime.'

At four o'clock Miss Piggott – 'Piggy' to her charges – brought Rosanna and Nicholas to the drawing room. The birthday guest of honour was already there with her mother, grandparents and great-grandmother, playing with the building bricks Erin had bought her. Thomasin asked if the governess would care to stay for some cake.

'Oh, yes, Piggy, do!' Rosanna in her excitable fashion ran to the woman and seized her hand, hauling her to a chair.

'I'm sorry, Rosanna, but I have someone to meet this afternoon. Your grandmama has kindly given me time off.' Rosanna whined in protest.

'Rosanna, if Miss Piggott has declined I think we should accept her decision,' said Hannah, sitting in the most comfortable chair like a shrivelled, moth-eaten crow. 'After all, this is supposed to be a family gathering.'

'But Piggy is family, aren't you?' objected Rosanna.

'*Miss* Piggott is an employee of the family, Rosanna – and kindly desist from your acrobatics and sit down like a young lady.'

The governess lost her smile and levelled her voice at Thomasin. 'If that will be all, Mrs Feeney, I should like to keep my appointment.'

'I trust you are not going to meet a young man,' cut in Hannah.

'Thank you, Miss Piggott.' Thomasin watched the gliding exit of the governess before scolding Hannah. 'Really, Mother, I think you might show a little more sensitivity. It was quite plain you hurt Miss Piggott's feelings.'

'I can't imagine why. I only asked what you should have done. You don't want her bringing her followers to the house, do you?'

Patrick, helping Belle to build her bricks, changed the subject. 'Liam should be here by now. I wonder if Father Gilchrist has found something for him to do.'

'We'll wait on him awhile,' said his wife. 'There's nothing to go cold. Well now, Rosanna . . .' She twisted her body in the chair, searching the room. 'Rosanna? Where has that child got to now? She's always disappearing.'

'It's her tinker blood,' announced Hannah to the sound of condemnation.

'Mother, would you kindly keep those sort of opinions to yourself.' Thomasin noticed that the french windows were open, the lace curtains billowing gently. Rising, she went over to them and shouted into the garden. 'Rosanna? Come here at once!' The child appeared as if from thin air. Thomasin caught her hand and led her back inside. 'I do wish you could sit still for five minutes. Now, come and tell us what you've been learning today.' She released the miscreant and settled herself once more.

Rosanna spoke from Patrick's lap where she always took refuge after being rebuked. 'Piggy's been teaching us our tables.'

'Five sixes!' Patrick threw at her instantly, then put a hand down to stroke Belle's head as she ran exploratory fingers up his trouser leg.

After some calculation on her fingers Rosanna came up with, 'Thirty!'

'Very good,' praised her grandfather. 'But that was an easy one. Can ye tell me this: if I have twenty-six sheep an' one dies, how many have I?'

'Easy – twenty-five,' cried Rosanna.

'Nineteen,' contributed Nick who had taken Patrick's place with Belle on the mat.

'Ah, ye can't catch that one out, he's heard it before! Tell your sister, Nick.'

Nick sighed as Belle knocked down the house of bricks he had just spent ten minutes constructing. 'Grandad's trying to trick you. He didn't say twenty-six sheep, it just sounded like it. He really said twenty *sick* sheep.'

'Cheat!' Rosanna raised her hand to her grandfather who laughed.

'There's always some old villain who'll try to cod ye, Rosie – beware.' He cocked an ear. 'Ah, there's the front door – it must be Father Kelly.'

Heads turned as the inner door opened. After a second's puzzlement, 'Daddy!' screeched Rosanna and hurled herself from Patrick's knee at the red-haired man in the doorway.

Swiftly, the man passed his hat to the maid and swung the child up in a froth of petticoats and lace-trimmed drawers. 'Oh, my wee Rosie! You almost didn't recognise me, did you?' He hugged her and she squealed in delight. 'Oh, I've missed you so – and you too, Nick lad.' Sonny put Rosanna down to seize his less-exuberant son. 'How've you been? My, how big you've grown! I can barely lift you.' The boy was lowered to the carpet where he returned Sonny's kiss.

'I'm glad you're back, Father. Did you bring us a present?'

'Well, that's a fine welcome,' said Sonny, arms akimbo. 'I've been away months and all you can ask is have I brought you a present!' He had been back to France to carry out work commissioned on his first trip – he had such a busy schedule that he had only just got around to it. Nick hung his head and said he was sorry. Sonny cuffed him tenderly. 'My trunk's in the hall.' He took a key from his pocket. 'D'you think you can open it?' Nick's eyes lit up and he reached for the key. 'Don't chuck everything all over the place!' Sonny shouted as the boy and his sister sped from the room. 'Yours is the one in the green box! Hello, Father.' He stepped forward to grasp Patrick by the hand, pumping it warmly. 'Mother, what a lovely gown!' Sonny always made a point of noticing things like this.

Thomasin returned his embrace, then held back to study him. 'Well, I wish I could say how lovely you look, but I never have been very adept at lying – talk about gaunt!

Painting isn't a substitute for meals, you know . . . still, we'll soon get you fattened up again.'

Sonny laughed and moved to Hannah's chair. 'And how's Grandmother been in my absence? Enjoying good health, I trust?'

'Oh, much the same as you left me, dear.' Hannah accepted his more restrained peck on the furry cheek. 'My legs grow worse by the hour. It is all I can do to drag myself from my bed on a morning.' Despite Hannah's secret enjoyment of her infirmity this was not an exaggeration; her legs were extremely crippled and the days when she chose to remain in bed were at risk of outnumbering those which saw her vertical.

Sonny moved along to hug his sister, trying to cover his shock at the change in her with a compliment. 'That dress is very becoming, if I may say so.' Less a compliment, more a white lie; the mourning gown drained her complexion of any smudge of colour she might have had. Holding both her hands he whispered sincerely, 'I was really sorry to hear about Sam. I thought he was a smashing chap. I'll miss him.' At her grateful nod he added, 'Judging from the date on Mother's letter it didn't reach me till after the funeral, otherwise I would've been there, naturally . . . I hope you understand.' He would hate his sister to think it was because he would rather be painting.

She pressed her cheek to his, nodding silently. Then, after thanking him for his letter of condolence, said, 'I wasn't there either.' Sam looked at his mother over Erin's shoulder and, catching the slight movement of her head, exclaimed more cheerfully, 'Why, who's this ravishing person?' Moving across to where Belle sat in her frog-like posture on the carpet he hunkered to inspect her. 'I don't believe we've been introduced, madam.'

Patrick took up the pretence, coming to stand near him. 'Would ye believe that this is your niece, Belle?'

'It never is! This big girl can't possibly be that little scrap of a thing I saw last time I was here. Goodness me, I do swear it is!' He held out his hands. 'Aren't you going to greet your Uncle Sonny then?' The child beheld him with round eyes, lips slightly apart. 'Come on, I don't frighten a big girl like you, do I?' He picked her up and spoke in a kind, quiet voice as he straightened her skirts over the useless legs. 'Now then, how's that? Don't be shy. Listen, my eyes might have been deceiving me but I could swear I saw a birthday cake on a trolley out in the hall. That couldn't be yours by any chance, could it?'

'It is,' Patrick answered. 'Our Belle is three years old today.'

'Jesus, Mary an' Joseph!' declared Sonny, still referring himself to Belle, his eyebrows rising to meet his violent splash of hair. 'Well now, I wonder if there might be a present in my bag for my grown-up niece. Would you like to go and see? Come now, you're not too shy to tell me if you want a present, are you?'

'I'm sure she'd tell you if she'd learnt the words,' provided his father softly.

'No different then?' came his son's gentle query.

Pat shook his head, then said optimistically, 'But sure, she's only three, there's plenty of time.' Sonny agreed in bright manner.

Just then the door opened and Abigail admitted Father Kelly. 'God save all here!'

'Liam, whatever have you been doing with yourself?' demanded Thomasin, pointing at the stick that supported his stooped figure. She watched him limp to the nearest chair and flop into it.

'Oh, saints deliver us that's a relief! Tommy, ye may well ask. My poor old leg's swollen up like a balloon. I'd ask ye to take a look but there's ladies present.' He smiled a greeting at Erin and Hannah.

She made her face stern. 'You'd best go out and come in again.'

'Sure I was only codding ye. I wouldn't dream of exposing ye to such a gruesome sight.'

'The leg,' said Patrick. 'What happened?'

'Nothing that I know of. I just woke up this way. If I didn't know better I'd say it was one o' Father Gilchrist's ruses to stop me coming out an' enjoying meself. God, that man gets worse. D'ye know I had to sneak out the back door to get here. Sorry if I'm a bit la . . . why, Sonny!' He tried to rise but Sonny, still holding Belle, motioned him to stay in his seat, coming over to shake his hand.

'I wondered when you'd notice.' His fingers slipped around the priest's shrunken hand.

'Ah well, I spotted the red-haired thing in the corner but I thought it was just another o' your mother's newfangled ornaments. How are ye, boy? An' how long have ye been here?'

Sonny released his hand and looked at the clock. 'About five minutes.'

'God, you're looking great, isn't he, Pat? Ah, sure ye get more like your mother every day.' He waved at the child in the other's arms. 'Well, I tell ye, ye couldn't've chosen a more auspicious time to make your return, could he, Belle? We hope ye've brought us a good present after being absent so long.'

'You're as bad as my son,' laughed the red-haired man. 'Where's he got to anyway? I think we'd better go and find them before he does any damage with his gift.'

'Why, what did you bring?' asked his mother.

'A doll for Rosie and a clasp knife for Nick.'

'A knife! What a bloody silly present to buy a little boy.'

'Do have a care for my delicate senses,' moaned the priest, feigning shock. 'An' you objecting when I didn't class ye with the ladies.'

'I'm sorry about the language, Liam – but I ask you! What sort of person would bring his six-year-old son a knife? Come on, we'd better go and retrieve him before he does any damage. We can go and eat at the same time.'

Patrick and his son gave assistance to the invalids. When they all arrived in the hall it was to find that Nick had made a start on slicing the birthday cake. 'Well, I suppose I should be grateful it isn't my furniture he's carved,' said the boy's grandmother, then held out her hand. 'I'm sorry, Nick, but I think you're just a bit young for knives.'

'Oh, Nan!' His mouth turned down as the gift was confiscated.

'No arguing.' She dropped it into the pocket of her skirt. 'Not if you wish to attend this party.'

Nick looked helplessly at his father, but received only a shrug and a sympathetic expression, whence he spun on Patrick. 'Grandfather . . .' Sonny felt a twinge of annoyance though he didn't show it as Patrick reproved, 'Ye shouldn't've cut Belle's cake before she even had a chance to blow out the candles.'

Dolefully, Nick joined the drift to the dining room, but was soon cheered at the sight of the heavily-laden table. Throughout the meal he and Rosanna bombarded Sonny with questions about Paris. What had he done there? Who had he been with? When she was allowed to slip a word in Thomasin asked when her son was going to see Josie.

He passed Rosanna the water-lily he had made from a napkin. 'I've already seen her – for a flying visit, anyway. I stopped off at her place of work on the way home.' He bit into a scone overflowing with cream and jam, catching a blob with his little finger before it fell to his plate.

'And she let you in? I can't say that I'd be so well-disposed towards someone who'd promised to marry me, then kept leaving the country.' She flicked a crumb from the gathers on her bodice. 'You have kept her dangling for a long time, poor lass.'

'I've had a lot of thinking to do.'

'Or was it that you got so carried away in your painting and forgot about her?'

He frowned reflectively, but took no offence; it was a fair point. 'That was one of the questions that held me back for so long: had I been simply using her as a crutch for my wounded pride when my marriage to Peggy broke down? The other was: could she ever be as important to me as my painting?'

'Well, I know the answer to the second,' said his mother, bringing his face round expectantly. 'I don't think anything – even your children – could be as important as your painting.'

Finishing the scone he dabbed his mouth and took a sip from his glass. 'That's only partly true, Mam. It would be correct to say I could never be complete without my work – but on the other hand, I wouldn't gain half so much fulfilment if I had no one to share it with.' He pondered over what to choose next from the spread. 'That's why Josie is right for me; she's willing to share.' Foregoing another pastry he swivelled to face her, submitting, 'I've finally set the date, Mother. We'll be married on Rosanna's birthday, November the fifth.' Actually, it was mere guesswork that had placed Rosanna's birthday on this date. She had been approximately six months old when Sonny had adopted her, but the family had decided that November the fifth – Firework Night – was the most apt birthdate for a firecracker like Rosie. 'That's why I wanted to see Josie before I came home, wanted to make sure she'd still have me.' He smiled. 'She's coming round later – tells me she's got a birthday present for Belle.'

'You are positive you're doing the right thing?' his mother asked.

'Mam, I know it's going to be awkward for you to accept Josie as your daughter-in-law, her being an ex-employee, but . . .' He had his chin tucked into his chest and Thomasin knew instantly that he was about to add a warning. She jumped in first, covering his hand.

'Don't worry, I won't interfere like I did in your first marriage. I hold myself partly responsible for that unhappy episode.'

'There was no one to blame. Peggy and I were very young . . . anyway, that's all water under the bridge. I know this marriage is going to be a success. I've had ample time to think about it. I've done thinking. Aren't you going to congratulate me?'

'Indeed I will! Listen, Patrick! Everyone!' She banged her glass on the table. 'Rosie, cease that din, this concerns you too.'

'Oh, no!' hissed Sonny and put a hand up to object though it was far too late. 'I didn't mean everyone else to know yet, I wanted to wait for Josie to get here . . .' He looked at his children who were his main concern. It would have been preferable to let them know in private that they were to have their new mother at last – or rather, mother without the prefix, for Peggy had been no mother to them.

'Oh, Son, I've gone and spoilt it for you . . .' Thomasin looked round, all were waiting expectantly.

'I don't suppose it matters that much,' relented Sonny, then blurted out bashfully, 'Well . . . I've decided to get married,' and blushed all the way up to his ears at their congratulations. At twenty-four he still couldn't control that childish trait.

After the 'oohs!' had died away Hannah asked, 'May one know the lady's name?'

'Why, you know it already, Grandmother.'

Hannah exhaled heavily. 'Oh dear . . . I had hoped that these long separations might have changed your views. Still intent on marrying beneath you . . . ah well, it looks as though it will be left to the fourth generation to carry my family's blood on its proper course. Perhaps Nicholas will marry according to his station – though I have grave doubts about Rosanna.'

Sonny ignored the sour note and divulged more of the wedding plans. 'It isn't definite yet, but I think it more than likely that we'll be getting married in the Register Office.' He saw the shadow on Liam's face. 'Josie doesn't want to become a Catholic and I can't get married in her church . . . so we think the best thing would be – if it were possible – for both you and Josie's priest to attend. Just so's we can feel it's been done in the sight of God.'

Liam swapped glances with Patrick, then picked up a stray currant from his plate and nibbled it. 'I'm not sure that'd be possible, Son, much as I'd love to oblige.'

Sonny's frown forced an explanation and Liam told him what Thomasin's letters had not – indeed, why should they have, thought Sonny, his mother's worries never went further than her shop window. Patrick's son lost his good humour. 'Has anyone thought to have words with Father Gilchrist?'

'Aye, an' a few choice ones,' said Liam. 'But it'll take more than words to budge him from his obduracy. You know he'll never recognise your marriage to a Protestant?'

'But, Father, I always thought you blessed Mam and Dad's wedding?'

'An' so I did . . . but then I'm not so holy as Father G.'

'You don't have to tell him, do you? Couldn't you just do it?'

'I'm not sure that'd be above board. I mean, I'm supposed to be retired.'

'Retired my foot!' shot Sonny. 'A priest never retires.'

Liam grinned mischievously. 'I suppose I could manage to sneak past the guard . . . But less of himself! Right now let me be the one to wish you and your bride every health and happiness.' He looked into his glass. 'Even if it is only with a poor substitute. To Sonny and Josie!'

'Sonny and Josie!' All glasses of lemonade were raised.

Rosanna had sidled round to stand at her father's side. When he noticed her he pulled her onto his lap. 'Are you still happy to have Josie as your mother?'

'Ooh, yes! . . . As long as we'll still be able to live here with Nan and Gramps.'

'Oh well, I don't know about that . . .' he glanced at Thomasin. 'It might make things a bit overcrowded now.'

'I don't know why you're being so coy,' returned his mother. 'Unless it's because you like to hear your mother grovel. I've told you a hundred times we'd love to have you.'

'But that was before . . .' Sonny looked at Erin.

'Oh, I see,' nodded his mother. 'No, we've still plenty of room for as long as you want it.' At his thanks she waved a hand. 'Don't flatter me with gratitude. It's a selfishness that spurs the generosity – the house'd seem dead without those cherubs.' She placed an arm around Nick who was sitting beside her, the other around Rosie, and squeezed. 'Oh, they're loved are these two!'

Erin's eyes went to Belle whose unobtrusive nature had caused her to be overlooked. Rosanna, too, examined the child. 'Will Belle stay here as well, Nan?'

Thomasin glanced up abstractedly. 'Oh yes, we can't forget Belle, can we?' Then she returned her energies to the able-bodied.

150

No, but you'd like to, wouldn't you, Mother? thought Erin bitterly.

CHAPTER TEN

'What're you grinning at?'

Sonny looked down at his new bride dressed in oyster satin and pulled her closer. 'I'm just watching Belle – look at her stuffing that cake in her cheeks.' But this was not the true reason for his mirth. It was the amusing thought that this wedding was almost as furtive as his first had been. Then, the reason for it had been his bride's pregnancy, now it was simply to keep it from Father Gilchrist's ears. To be here Liam had given the excuse that he was going to visit the doctor with his leg – this had nearly backfired when Gilchrist had offered to have the doctor called in, but Liam had said that he'd prefer the walk – which was a daft thing to say when one was meant to have a bad leg. Still, it had given the wedding guests a laugh when Liam repeated the story in his speech.

'Rosie's as bad.'

'What? Oh aye!' Sonny laughed at his daughter who was celebrating her seventh birthday as well as the wedding. The ends of her hair had been trailing in the custard which she was eating. 'I don't think I've ever seen her look tidy in her whole life. Maybe you'll be able to make an improvement now you're her mother.'

Josie's face showed how happy she was at the new status, but she raised a pertinent question. 'D'you think I'll be able to? I mean I know they're fond of me and they're so excited at having a new mother . . . but they've been under your parents' rule for so long, it might take a while to alter that.'

'I know exactly what you mean,' Sonny nodded. 'I felt it when I came back from France. They were pleased to

151

see me, yes, but if I ever refused them permission to do a thing they'd always turn to my father for confirmation. Still,' he sighed, 'I suppose I haven't been as much of a father as I could've been.'

Josie objected. 'You've been away a lot, true, but you always sent them letters and when you are home you spend a lot of time with them.'

'Well, I hope we can spend a lot more time together now, all four of us.' He smiled. 'When we come back off our honeymoon, that is – and I promise that for the next two weeks I'll not try to pick up a paintbrush.'

Sonny's promise was fine while it lasted for the fortnight of their honeymoon, but painting was the way he earned his living and once they were home Josie was left to fill her days as best she could. At first this tended to be with the children, when they weren't at their lessons, and the three would spend lovely afternoons going to the swings or on nature walks. Once or twice Josie had taken them to their father's studio but when she realised how much this interrupted his concentration she stopped doing so. Her mornings were mostly spent alone. Josie had hoped to find a friend in Erin, but the other seemed consumed with one worry or another, never listening to what Josie had to say, just sitting there dreamily until Josie had finished speaking then responding with a totally different subject from the one her sister-in-law had been discussing. And then there was Mrs Feeney Senior. Josie couldn't help the deference acquired whilst in the other's service and would let slip the odd 'ma'am' at the end of a sentence. She knew it annoyed Thomasin but she couldn't help it and it made her even more nervous when John's mother snapped at her for doing it. Josie had always assumed that when she and John married it would be happy ever after – she *was* happy when she was with him and his children, but it didn't feel like home. Had it not been for Rosie and Nick she would have asked John to take her away, but she couldn't do that to them and neither could he. So, she just went on having these miserable mornings until it grew too much to bear.

'I'll have to get a job,' she told her husband in their bed that night. 'I just can't go on feeling like this, no use to anybody. If I'm upstairs I irritate your mother, if I'm downstairs Mrs Howgego thinks I'm poking my nose in. I knew it'd be hard, John, but I didn't know it would be this lonely.'

He sympathised, but added, 'I can't have you going out to work, Jos. Maybe we can find you something here that wouldn't put Mrs Howgego's nose out of joint – I'll ask Mother.' He broke off. 'Oh no, she's part of the trouble, isn't she?'

'I'm not going against your mam – she's lovely, really. I think a lot of her . . . but I know I get on her nerves.'

He comforted her. 'I don't think it's really you, Jos. It's worry over Erin that's making her ratty. She's jumped down my throat a dozen times this evening.'

'D'you think . . . well, I'd like to ask her if I could have my old job back – at least part of it, the housekeeping side, I don't want to annoy Mrs Howgego any more than I have done. But I'm scared your mam would laugh at me.'

Sonny didn't seem to think his mother would do that. 'But are you certain it's what you want?'

'I must have something, John.'

He pressed himself against her plump body and mumbled into her throat, 'I could give you something.'

She knew his meaning and smiled as he rolled on top of her. 'There's nothing I'd like more than your baby . . . but until it happens, would you ask your mam if I can keep house?'

'Ooh, anything for you, you lovely squashy creature!'

Josie giggled as his fingertips searched for her ribs through the ample flesh and the question of an occupation suddenly became redundant.

Thomasin agreed to let Josie play the role of housekeeper, though she hoped it wouldn't exacerbate the girl's problem over her identity which was still an irritation – as was Erin, who did nothing but ghost about the house all day as if searching for something. Thomasin had hoped to have a little respite from her mother who was confined to her bed most of the time now, but Hannah was able to make life just as difficult from there, banging on the floor every five minutes with her cane. However, Thomasin had countered this annoyance by having a bell rigged up from the kitchen so it was the maid who took the brunt, but all this added to the bouts of depression she had over her dead son.

And then there was the child. *Why* can't I love her? Thomasin asked herself so many times. Why does she look at me so accusingly? The partition which had existed between herself and Patrick before Belle came, had since acquired another layer of bricks.

In relief, there was the women's committee which had invited her to join when she and her family had first moved here after the fire. It had taken some time to pluck up the courage or the interest: the first because she knew that her marriage to an Irishman was an open topic in the neighbourhood – she didn't know whether the women had merely wanted her presence so that they could insult or ridicule her; but that had not been the case, instead they were full of admiration for the way she had transformed a small shop into a competitive business. Yes, membership of the women's committee had turned out to be quite enjoyable, especially of late when they had elected her chairwoman.

It was one of these meetings she was preparing to chair now. She dabbed a touch of light perfume behind each ear and adjusted the beads at her throat. Though she had little time to spare for these pursuits she had found that the newly-formed connections could be useful to her financially and so her time was not really misspent. Holding her skirts from the floor she hurried downstairs and, on Abigail's information that Mrs Alderson had arrived, rustled across the hall and burst into the drawing room. 'Good afternoon, Clara! I'm so sorry I wasn't here to greet you.'

'You are forgiven, Thomasin,' smiled the visitor, a

dumpy woman wearing a very loud purple dress. 'I have your daughter-in-law to keep me entertained.'

On Thomasin's entrance Josie had risen. Her fingers played with the material of her skirts. 'Well, now that Mrs . . . now that my mother-in-law is here I'll go and leave you in peace.' Feeling ill at ease she made for the door.

'Won't you stay?' enquired Clara. 'I'm sure you'll find our little discussions to your liking.'

'That's most kind of you.' Josie backed away. 'But I've got the household accounts to do, ma'am.' She caught her lip – another blunder! Mother-in-law would probably be furious. Without further comment she rushed from the room.

'Did I say something wrong?' asked Clara perplexedly.

Thomasin came to sit beside her. 'No, no, Clara. It's simply . . .' She dismissed the episode with a flick of her wrist. How did one explain that one's son had married one's former maid? She was saved from any attempt at this by the sudden arrival of the other members of the committee. Thomasin opened the meeting. After the Minutes of the last gathering had been read out by Rosalind, their Chairwoman embarked on the theme which she hoped would fire as great a concern as her own. 'I don't know if you are aware, but there is a plan afoot to demolish yet another stretch of the city walls.' She awaited the indignant exclamations. Silence. She searched the politely-attentive faces, then went on, 'I propose that this committee add its weight to that of the Yorkshire Architectural Society which is already engaged in the battle. Now, it is . . .'

Clara held up a fat little hand and said politely, 'My apologies for interrupting, Thomasin, but I don't quite follow. You wish us to assist with the demolition?' There were peals of laughter as she added, 'I really cannot see myself wielding a pick.'

'Clara, this is serious! Yet another part of our heritage is about to be completely destroyed and all you can do is joke about it.'

Clara controlled her chuckle. 'Pray forgive me if I've offended you, my dear, but I really can't see what it is you expect us to do – join forces with the Yorkshire . . . what is it?'

'To put it briefly, Clara, the Yorkshire Architectural Society has been responsible for halting the council in many of its proposed acts of vandalism. In the past fifty years this council and its predecessors have succeeded in demolishing three of the four Barbicans to the city gates, various postern gates, huge sections of the city's defences, churches . . . don't you care that by the time your grandchildren reach adulthood there may be none of this ancient craftsmanship left in our beautiful city?'

'Surely that is progress, dear?' tendered a meek-looking woman.

Thomasin emitted a sharp laugh. 'A multitude of sins can be committed under the guise of progress, Laura.' Her determined expression embraced them all. 'Don't tell me you're going to sit there and let them get away with it. Where's your spirit?'

'Thomasin, it's only a few old bricks they're getting rid of,' said Clara. 'Insufficient in my opinion to warrant such emotive talk.'

'A few old . . . Clara, where have you been living all your life? Certainly not in the same city as me. Have you never wondered how many horses it took to drag those great slabs of stone from the quarries? How many craftsmen chiselled and set each piece into such an impressive monument?' At their bemused glances she fell back in her chair. 'You really don't care, do you? I'll wager not one of you would shed a tear if the Minster were knocked down tomorrow and its stone used as a foundation for a new fashion house.'

There was indignation then. 'It's ridiculous to compare the Minster with a bit of crumbling wall!' cried Clara. 'I'm sure every citizen would be most put out if . . .'

'But how can you say when these people will stop!' Thomasin fought down the urge to swear. 'Today the walls, tomorrow the Minster!'

'Thomasin, you really are making the most awful fuss over nothing,' accused Clara. 'The Minster is a place of worship, one of the country's most important cathedrals, they'd never knock it down. Now that would be a worthy cause for us to fly our banner, would it not, ladies?' There were murmurs of affirmation.

'I agree it is impressive,' replied Thomasin impatiently. 'But to me the walls are every bit as impressive in their simplicity – and the lack of adornment doesn't make them any the less significant historically. They've survived sieges and wars, surely we can help them withstand a handful of modern assassins?'

At this point Abigail arrived with the tea, which was unfortunate, as it destroyed totally Thomasin's moment of passion. 'Ah, refreshment—' Clara accepted the cup that Abigail handed to her, then, turning away from Thomasin, began to chatter to her neighbour. 'How is your tapestry coming along, Theodora? You mentioned you were having difficulty . . .'

Thomasin's enthusiasm dwindled as she listened to the motiveless twittering, wondering if they would feel the same if it were their own garden walls the council proposed to demolish. Oh well, there was nothing to stop her joining the Society on her own, and it would make a change to enter into pertinent discussions rather than the drivel she had to put up with now. Boredom caused her to think of Erin and what she might be doing. 'Abigail,' she put the cup in its saucer, 'go ask Mrs Teale if she'd like to join us for a while.' She told her companions, 'My daughter's still in such low spirits. It's a lame hope that she'll join us. I've been trying to coax her out of her despondency for weeks, but one can only try.'

She was pleasantly surprised when Abigail returned to say that Erin would join them directly. 'Oh, that's most heartening – she must be feeling better.'

'Is she still possessed by her husband's tragic demise?' asked a concerned Clara, receiving a nod. 'Such a terrible shock . . . and losing one's baby, too.'

'Dreadful,' said Thomasin. 'I've never seen anyone so . . . oh!'

Erin had appeared. She was carrying Belle – Thomasin had not foreseen that. A few awkward seconds passed before she recovered her composure. 'Come in, dear, and sit down. I'm glad you decided to come down, it'll make a nice change for you. Would you like to pass the baby to Abi and take your tea more comfortably?'

'No, that's all right, thank ye.' Erin inclined her head to the ladies as she moved among them. 'I don't want tea, just company.' She had hoped to find this when Josie moved in but the girl seemed ill at ease with her.

'Well, there's plenty of that here.' The women were staring at Belle who had been deposited on the carpet. Thomasin fought for some comment that might distract them. 'Returning to my topic, I was just trying to instil some sort of historical awareness in our. . .'

'Oh, Thomasin, please!' Clara flapped an impatient hand. 'Enough of those dreary walls – leave that to the Society you mentioned. Hello, my dear.' She leaned forward to speak to Belle. 'Such a pretty thing. And what is your name?'

Belle affixed luminescent eyes to the polite face. 'She can't speak,' supplied Erin candidly.

'Oh, how unfortunate,' replied the woman, drawing back to sip at her tea and examine Belle from a safe distance.

As if reading Clara's unspoken hope – that Belle would remain where she was – the child lurched into her grotesque mode of travel, pausing only to study the captive audience and making directly for Clara. Thomasin thought they would never leave. She sat on the very edge of her chair, contributing desultory remarks designed to lure the eyes away, but no one seemed at all interested in her son's exhibition at the newly-opened art gallery. She saw – could hardly miss – the interplayed looks, some of pity, others of a more feline quality. They couldn't wait to get home and tell their husbands: 'Guess what?'

'Will you be joining us at next month's gathering, Mrs

Teale?' asked Clara now, drawing in her legs with alarm as Belle put out a hand to examine the shiny silk.

'I may do,' answered Erin vaguely. – She's in one of her trances again, thought her mother. 'I certainly enjoyed today's company.'

– How can she fail to notice? thought Thomasin with amazement. Their opinions are so obvious.

'Thank you, my dear,' smiled Clara while eyeing the child with distaste. 'I'm sure we have all enjoyed yours. I think however,' she placed her cup on the tray, 'it is time we were taking our leave. Doesn't time fly when one has interesting companions?'

Thomasin watched the others make ready to go. 'May I take it that no one shares my concern about the council's proposal?'

'Dear Thomasin,' Clara replied for them, 'I'm sure you are very sincere in your intentions but I really think it is asking a little too much of our committee to take on the might of the council, even if we shared your views. Our meetings are usually such fun – discussion of social topics, the exchange of receipts – please, could we keep them that way? I cannot speak for the others but if I hear a conversation of a political nature I tend to steer well clear.'

'Very well.' Thomasin's voice was curt as she rang for Abigail. 'Maybe one of you could think of some item for next month's agenda. The subject of my choice is obviously not to your taste.'

'I do hope you are not offended,' said Clara worriedly. 'I wouldn't insult you for the world, Thomasin. Normally your choice of subject is most agreeable. It's just that I feel . . . well, this is a women's group, dear. We should confine our discussions to those feminine topics with which we are more familiar.'

Abigail saw them into the hall, handing out coats.

'Well,' said Clara under her breath, a glint in her eye. 'What did you make of that?'

'About the demolition of the walls?' ventured Laura.

'Goose,' muttered Clara. 'The child! What a tragedy for that poor woman. To be so talented and have such a stain on one's family. Of course, one tends to forget that they are only trade people . . .' She slipped her arms into the coat which Abigail held. 'I hope Mrs Teale won't choose to make a habit of bringing the child to our meetings should she decide to join us. I really couldn't abide being in the same room with that odd little creature looking at me all the time. And I certainly cannot understand Thomasin allowing her daughter to parade it so unashamedly. If it were me I should have it hidden away.'

'Why do you suppose we haven't seen it before today?' asked another impishly. 'Thomasin has obviously been attempting to keep it a secret. Did you see her face when her daughter brought it in? I thought she was going to pass out.' There were soft giggles.

Abigail bit her lip so hard she almost put her teeth through it. If Mrs Teale could hear the things them bitches were saying about poor Miss Belle. And if the master knew – God! he'd kick every one of them up the bustle. Still, Abigail helped the last woman on with her coat, tugging it roughly over the shoulders, he wouldn't hear it from Abigail. It didn't do to repeat what one heard.

Clara's hopes that Erin would come unaccompanied to further committee meetings were in vain. It was simply terrible, she declared afterwards, to sit through a meeting with that misshapen oddity slithering about one's feet. One never knew where it was going to put its grubby little hands. She finally announced that she could not sit through another hour such as the last. Many of the others thought similarly and with each month their numbers began to diminish.

Thomasin was quite aware of the reason for these shrinking attendances. She also knew the remedy and in her bleakest moods often came close to it. But oh, how hurt Erin would be if asked not to bring her daughter to any more meetings. No, there was only one solution; she would simply resign. At least if she did it now she might save a little face. She was damned if she was going to sit by and watch them all drop out. From a personal stance the meetings would not be missed – she had joined the YAS now and what time she did not spend at the store was dedicated to saving buildings of historical importance – but it was a great pity from Erin's point of view because the meetings had clearly done her a lot of good. After first having to be drawn into the conversation by her mother she had now begun to initiate it herself. So sad that it had to finish, but if Erin realised why people no longer came to the meetings it would set her back months.

This month's sparsely-attended gathering was coming to a close. Laura, one of the three loyals, shut the Minute book and was about to tuck it into her bag.

'Before you put that away, Laura,' said Thomasin, rising, 'I have something to add. You are all aware, I'm sure, how busy I am with two stores to supervise. Well, I am finding it increasingly difficult to create any spare time for my family lately, let alone for myself. Much as I love these chats of ours it would not be fair to use what little leisure time I have so selfishly. So, it is with great regret that I must resign my position as Chairwoman.'

Soft murmurs of mock regret met her announcement. 'Should the economy allow you any free time in the future, Thomasin, I'm sure you will be made most welcome at our meetings,' ventured Laura kindly. 'Are you certain you won't change your mind?'

'Quite sure,' said Thomasin with dignity. 'Besides, at the present rate of resignation there will soon be no one left to chair. I must say, there seems to be a great deal of ill-health around lately. But perhaps the contagion will be alleviated when those afflicted come to hear of my own resignation.'

Laura looked at the others uncomfortably. 'Well, I trust we won't lose touch completely, Thomasin.'

Her hostess, ringing for Abigail, assured her they wouldn't. 'Even in my absence I'm quite sure you'll keep me in your conversations, Laura.'

The woman blushed and, after much stuttered leave-taking, went out with the maid.

'I didn't think ye were so busy at the store lately,' said

a puzzled and somewhat disappointed Erin when they had gone.

'I'm not really,' confessed her mother. 'It was just an excuse. I've grown sick of these meetings. We never discuss anything of importance, just knitting, sewing . . . When I try to direct them towards something more meaningful look what happens. Well, they can feed their faces somewhere else, I've had enough.'

'Well, I say it was very self-centred of you to break up the committee without thinking of anyone else.'

'Breaking up the committee? Perhaps you hadn't noticed, Erin, but there was little left to break up. And when you say "anyone else" do you refer to yourself?'

'Yes.' Erin's face showed her displeasure. 'I'd started to look forward to something for a change . . .'

Thomasin showed sympathy, laying a hand on her daughter's shoulder. 'I'm sorry, love . . . but, oh they're such an awfully shallow crowd, Erin. If it's purely the company you'll miss wouldn't you rather join me at the YAS? That would furnish you with a pastime – something more worthwhile. That's how I felt anyway. Would you like me to have a word for someone to propose you as a member? I've not been there long enough myself.'

Erin gave an apathetic shrug. 'Oh . . . I don't care. Do what ye like.' She sank back in her chair.

Thomasin studied her carefully. She looked healthy enough, but there was no sparkle. 'What you need is a holiday, my girl, away from all of us. You're not going to improve while you're stuck in the house all day. What about a couple of weeks at Harrogate to take the waters? It's a marvellous tonic, they say.'

'What're ye on about "improve"? There's nothing wrong with me.'

'Oh, come on, lass . . .'

'I don't know what ye all expect of me,' flared Erin. 'Am I supposed to be throwing parties – after what's happened?'

Thomasin came to sit beside Erin. 'I'm not condemning you for the way you are, all I'm suggesting is that a break

162

might help you to come to terms with it. Harrogate's a lovely place, you know. Come on, a couple of weeks – I can write off today and book you a place.'

'It'd be a bit awkward for Belle.'

'When I said away from all of us I meant all of us, Belle included – especially Belle. I think it's all the time you spend worrying about her that's made you ill.'

'I've told ye, I'm *not* ill.'

'All right,' challenged her mother. 'Tell me you're fine. Look me in the face and tell me. No, you can't, see, because you're not all right. Now, I'm telling you you're taking that holiday.'

'I can't see what enjoyment I'll get from going on my own,' protested Erin. 'I'll be thinking of Belle all the time, wondering if she's being cared for.'

Thomasin pretended to be hurt. 'I have had babies of my own, Erin.'

'Not like her, though.' Erin looked down at the child who seemed to be engrossed in their every word. After a deliberate pause she added, 'Ye don't really like her, do ye, Mam?' There was no accusation there. Erin's brief spark of animation had relapsed.

The hurt was not an affectation this time. 'What an awful thing to say! She's my grand-daughter. I treat her the same as the others.'

'Ye give her the same material things,' granted Erin. 'But it's as if ye're afraid to show her the same affection that ye give to Rosie an' Nick.'

'I was right about you needing a holiday,' declared Thomasin, skilfully evading a truthful response. 'Saying rubbish like that.' She rose and marched up to Belle, sweeping her off the carpet with a noisy kiss. 'There! Doesn't your mother talk nonsense? Come on, we'll go up to the schoolroom to see what your cousins are up to, give your mam five minutes' rest.' She shoved a footstool up to Erin's chair with a toe. 'Get your feet up, lass – and while you're at it rest your brain an' all. Eh, I don't know!' She marched purposefully from the room.

But outside the schoolroom she paused, her vigour

evaporated. The door was slightly ajar; through it she could see the eager alert faces of her other grandchildren, heard the kindly, informative voice of their governess. Her burden was making its weight felt. Thomasin put a timid hand around Belle's back to support her, forced herself to move her fingers over the malformed spine, feeling every groove.

Instead of going into the schoolroom she changed direction and wandered miserably along the landing, coming to her own room. Here, she settled herself on the straight-backed chair beside her washstand, the child on her knee. Everything seemed to be closing in on her. Such despair. She hadn't fooled Erin for one moment; even whilst trying not to notice the look of non-belief as she had left the room she had known that.

'Oh, Belle.' Her voice was weighed down with her problems. 'What's life got in store for you, eh?' A hand came up to stroke the black curls. 'Come to that, what's it got in store for me?' The Lord knew she had no right to complain. Apart from a slight dip in profits last year her business was making her richer by the hour. The Parliament Street store was now composed of two floors with another in the making. She had purchased a warehouse on the Foss and two barges to ferry her wares from the docks; the elimination of yet another middleman. Where finance was concerned she couldn't put a foot wrong. But what of her private life? Her marriage? That it was on very shaky ground was of her own making, she knew. She had shut Pat out after Dickie's death. Oh, she was a hypocrite, telling Erin that time would heal the pain of Sam's death when the lesion of her son's demise had not yet knitted after all this time. Would it ever? Did one ever truly get over the death of one's child? Would she ever be able to look upon Rosie – so like her natural father – and not see Dickie being swallowed up by flames? And what of this poor, crippled child, yet another cause of the widening rift between Pat and herself. Would there ever be a time when she could introduce Belle proudly as she did the others and say, 'This is my grand-daughter', instead of trying to hide her away from her fickle, fair-weather friends; from the world. She felt a hot prickle of shame for the way she had contemplated asking Erin not to bring Belle to those blasted meetings, and all for the sake of keeping a few shallow companions who wanted to be associated with the affluent Mrs Feeney but not with the grandmother of a crippled, mute child.

– Why can't I love you? she asked silently. You've such a bonny little face and it isn't your fault that your body's twisted. I could kill myself for the way I feel. But it was so hard not to equate Belle's conception with the time everything had started to go wrong.

The child had picked up a worn tablet of Pears soap from the washstand and was holding it up to the light. There must be some intelligence there, thought the woman, for her to do that. The sun pierced the wafer of soap and dappled the exquisite skin with amber lights. – God, she's like an angel, thought Thomasin, even more beautiful than her mother and much prettier than Rosanna. That made her deformity all the more cruel. She pictured Belle as a young woman, imagined the youths who would have flocked to court her had it not been for the grotesque detour in her spine. The thought produced a prickling of tears in her grey eyes, blurring the picture. But was it pity for the child or for herself?

'Look at the pretty colours, Nan,' said Belle.

Thomasin stiffened. A shock sliced viciously through her breast. Quickly she dashed the tears from her cheeks and stared at Belle who still held the soap to the window. She opened her mouth, then closed it again. No, the voice must have come from the schoolroom. Nevertheless, 'Pretty,' she said tentatively.

Belle turned stunning blue eyes on her and smiled. 'It's like those.' She put out fingers, still sticky from her last barley-sugar, to grasp one of Thomasin's earrings: amber like the soap.

'Bugger me,' breathed the woman and stared, mouth agape, for many seconds before leaping to her feet and dashing from the room, Belle's head flopping from side to side with the rapid movement. 'Miss Piggott! Rosie! Nick!' She burst into the schoolroom. 'Belle can talk!' Without waiting for a response she hared back along the landing and was about to fling herself at the stairs when she remembered her mother and went scooting back along the corridor to Hannah's room, legs tangling with the bouffant turquoise skirts.

'Thomasin!' Hannah almost threw the book she had been reading up in the air. 'I do wish you wouldn't startle me so!' She pulled herself forward. 'Now you're here you may as well straighten my pillows.'

Thomasin used her free hand to punch and shake the pillows in excitement. 'Mother, Belle can speak! She's not an idiot like you said!'

'Impossible,' snapped Hannah with a bad-tempered scowl, picked up the book and pretended to read it.

'Say something for Great-grandma,' Thomasin urged Belle who remained silent, fixing Hannah with her enormous blue orbs.

Hannah compressed her lips. 'It's just as well she can't speak! I've asked you several times not to address me in such a fashion.'

'But she can! Belle, please.' Thomasin removed the soap from the child's grasp and held it in front of her face. 'Pretty! Say pretty, Belle.' Belle just smiled and reached for the soap.

'Thomasin, I have always maintained that the child is mentally defective and see no reason to change my views just because you have taken to hallucinating.' Hannah put the book directly in front of her face.

Her daughter emitted a small scream of frustration and ran out.

'Kindly close the door!' ordered Hannah, but Thomasin was halfway downstairs.

Josie came running out of the kitchen to see what the noise was about. Thomasin had just begun to give her the news when the door opened. 'Oh, Pat!' She hurled herself across the hall to meet him. 'Oh!'

'Tommy, what is it?' His concerned eyes took in the flushed face – she looked ten years younger.

'But, 'Oh . . . !' was all she could say, her breast rising and falling with exertion and discovery. Moving to the drawing room where she had left Erin she told him, 'In here!' An alarmed Josie scuttled after them.

Erin was still reclining in the same position, propping up a lack-lustre face with her palm. Thomasin ordered her husband and Josie to go and stand beside her daughter, then faced all of them, clutching the child. Erin caught the air of electricity and her fingers gripped the arm of the chair. 'What is it? What's amiss?'

Thomasin found Belle's hand and extricated the sliver of soap, holding it to the light. 'Belle . . .' she gave the cue, nodding encouragement to the child whose face had turned grave – she felt the excitement too.

'Tommy . . .' began Patrick doubtfully.

'Shush, Pat! Belle,' persevered Thomasin, willing the child to speak with all her might. There was a long, painful silence. Defeated, Thomasin dropped the hand holding the soap and heaved a sigh. 'I'm sorry, it was idiotic of me . . .'

'Bugger me, Nan, give it back now.'

There came a gasp from Erin and her hands flew to her cheeks as Thomasin exclaimed triumphantly, 'There!' and rewarded Belle with the remnant of soap, kissing her heartily.

Josie donned an attitude of sheer delight. Patrick moved forward, his astonishment plain. Tenderly, he cupped the child's face in his large rough hands, but could not speak. Belle's eyes went past his to the woman who sat in stunned paralysis. Erin sat rigid, let her lower lip fall, then covered a crumpled face with her hands and wept.

CHAPTER ELEVEN

With the confirmation that Belle was far from being a half-wit the family decided to do everything within its power to enrich her life. The days in the wake of the revelation were crammed with optimism, set-backs, tears and laughter. Though she had undergone a thorough examination by a doctor shortly after birth the recent discovery renewed hope: perhaps there might be some way to ease the enormity of her disablement. Sadly, the physician told them an operation was out of the question. The spine had been pushed too far out of true in the womb and would doubtless appear even more pronounced as the child grew into maturity. His kindly-meant advice, that perhaps with skilfully-tailored clothes the affliction might seem less noticeable, was a dreadful anti-climax after their expectations, but if cosmetic remedies were the only option they would have to suffice.

Thomasin called in her personal dressmaker to seek advice. Having drawn on the woman's skill to hide her own less than perfect statistics she hoped that Miss Arundale's expertise could aid her grand-daughter's predicament. Mere days later a boxful of little dresses arrived and, after tremendous decision on which she should wear first, Belle plumped for the blue one which she said, gazing into the mirror, matched her eyes, and was then taken by her mother to be measured for her first pair of shoes.

The shoemaker told Erin that theirs was not an uncommon request and with great patience chatted to Belle as his tape took precise calculations which resulted, with little waiting, in her first footwear. Made of soft black kid, one shoe was as normal while the other bore a three-inch sole which made Belle giggle when she felt its weight at her first fitting. Today the shoes were finished. Tears came to Erin's eyes as she watched the delighted child totter around the shop, initially stiff-legged, but then, with kind assistance from the shoemaker, becoming more relaxed in her movements.

'May I walk home?' the child begged as Erin helped her towards the cab.

'But it's such a long way,' protested her mother. 'Ye'll be worn out.'

'Oh, please, please!' She pulled at her mother's skirts.

'No, darlin',' replied Erin firmly, then touched the infant's cheek. 'Sure, I know how excited ye are with your shoes – I am too – but 'twon't do to get over-ambitious.'

Even Belle's indignation at being lifted into the carriage went unheeded. To her mother she was still to be babied; a humiliation after the intimations of adulthood that the shoes had brought. Nevertheless Belle did not allow her great day to be entirely spoilt and spent the remainder of it marching through the house, showing off in front of everyone and making herself extremely unpopular with her cousin Rosanna who could not see why everyone was making a fuss over a pair of silly old shoes.

'I'll bet she even wears them to bed,' she complained to Nick, and sure enough her prophecy was realised when the girls were tucked in that same night.

The shoes retained their novelty for at least a week. Belle disported herself from attic to cellar, rolling perilously from side to side as if just setting foot on dry land after weeks at sea. Not everyone, however, found the sight uplifting. Erin, who had been so eager for Belle to walk, paradoxically viewed her daughter's mobility with dread.

'Don't be such a fusspot,' Patrick would tell her on seeing the look of alarm flit across her face whenever Belle disappeared from view. 'Ye're trying to keep her an invalid an' she isn't one.'

'Father, ye know what kind o' tricks Rosie an' Nick get up to. I'll not have them including her in their madcap pranks. Everyone seems to think that now she can walk she can play the same as they do.'

'I thought that was the whole idea of the shoes. Given

a chance she might be able to play like they do. She's got to be treated as normally as possible.'

'Oh, I see. I'm meant to let her break her neck climbing trees and jumping off walls. Faith, she's the only thing I have left, Dad. Ye must understand my position. I can't allow her to risk life an' limb just because she wants to be normal. She's not normal.'

'God, poor Sam'd turn in his grave if he could hear ye now.'

The grave that even now Erin hadn't visited. She still could not face it; seeing his name upon a cold slab of stone.

Patrick shook his head sorrowfully as his daughter stormed out to find Belle. The poor child had just found her feet and Erin was set on knocking them from under her. At least that's where he and Thomasin agreed; Belle should be treated like any other child – though he doubted from his conversations with Thomasin that her reasons were the same as his.

After parting with her father Erin went first to the schoolroom, thinking Belle might have joined her cousins. There was only Miss Piggott, preparing lessons for the following day.

Erin presented an anxious face. 'D'ye know where I might find the children, Miss Piggott?'

The governess's absorption gave way to a smile of greeting. 'If it is your daughter you are specifically looking for you might try Nicholas's room; she was playing there when I peeped in some thirty minutes ago.'

Erin turned to leave and the governess scraped back her chair. 'I've been hoping to have a word with you if you could spare five minutes, Mrs Teale.' She came around her desk and approached Erin, who asked if it was important while flitting nervous glances at the door. 'Well, yes, rather. It's about your daughter. I know you are aware that she has lately been in the habit of visiting the schoolroom . . .'

'If she's been a nuisance . . .'

'Oh, no. Quite the contrary.' The governess put a

170

thoughtful hand to her chin. 'It is quite amazing – I should find it hard to believe if anyone were telling this to me, but Belle has learnt to read and can also write her name and other simple words.'

Erin's anxiety turned to interest. 'How long have ye been teaching her, Miss Piggott?'

'That's just it, Mrs Teale – I haven't. She appears to have gleaned this knowledge from the other children.'

'It's preposterous!' A fortnight ago Belle could neither walk nor speak and now . . .

'I agree that's what it sounds like but I assure you it's perfectly true. Whilst I was pointing out words to Rosanna I noticed Belle watching very closely. I offered no encouragement at the time. It didn't register itself that she could be making a genuine study. Then, when Nicholas came to my table to read aloud for me, Belle came up close beside him – she had been doing this for some days so I found nothing strange about it – but then I noticed that as he read the words Belle's mouth would move as if she were reading them with him. Initially I assumed there must be some fluke to her apparent skill, that she had heard Nicholas read the book aloud before and was simply repeating parrot fashion. But no, I stopped Nicholas and asked Belle to read certain words. Mrs Teale, each word I pointed to the child repeated, it was astounding. All this was three days ago. She can now read every word in that book. I have also taken it upon myself to set simple arithmetical exercises which she has performed with ease and, as I stated before, she has also mastered the pen.'

Erin floated back into the room, feeling for a chair, her mind awhirl. 'But she's not yet four years old.' Through the elation she heard Miss Piggott speak again.

'Although it is rather premature to apply the label of genius, I feel that you have a very gifted child indeed. Her mind is in urgent need of stimulation if it is to realise its full potential.'

Since Sam's death Erin seemed to others – herself too – to have been waiting for something. She had never understood the feeling until now. Now she felt as though

171

someone had lifted the lid of her coffin. There was purpose to her life. Her brain fizzed with exhilaration. There were plans to be made. It had always been her dream as a young girl to be a governess like Miss Piggott, but Father hadn't believed in wasting his money on educating a daughter. Denied this wish she had sworn that should she have a daughter of her own that child would have the chance that her mother had missed. Of course, when Belle was assumed to be backward those hopes had been set aside, but now they could be fulfilled. She jumped to her feet. 'Miss Piggott, would ye be willing to educate my daughter with the others?'

'Why, of course. Such a prospect would be a pleasure.'

Erin thanked her perfunctorily and whizzed off to resume her search. Finding Belle was more pressing than ever now. An investigation of Nick's room turned up only Belle's rag doll. Impatiently Erin barged from room to room before travelling right up to the maid's attic.

Abigail swung round guiltily as her door was flung open, the periodical falling from her lap. 'Oh, I'm sorry, Mrs Teale, I just came up for . . .'

'I'm not here to tick you off, Abigail.' Erin showed unconcern at the magazine. 'I just want to know if ye've seen the children.'

'They were down in the kitchen plaguin' Cook summat awful when I came up,' answered the maid, reaching for a clean apron whilst trying to shove the magazine out of view. When Erin reversed her tracks Abigail followed her down the stairs. 'I were ever so glad to hear the news that Miss Belle can talk, ma'am. I'll bet you were cock-a-hoop, weren't you?'

'I was, Abi.' Erin's rapid leg movement devoured the stairs. 'But there's some even better news now. Miss Piggott's just told me that Belle's very clever. She's going to give her lessons with the others.'

'Oh, that's wonderful, Mrs Teale! I'm ever so glad. I think a lot o' Miss Belle.'

Erin smiled in recognition of the fact as she rustled over the tiled hall and took the steps that led to the kitchen,

Abigail still tailing her. When they descended, however, there was only Cook to greet them. It seemed that Rosie and Belle had been there, but Mrs Howgego had sent them packing.

'Miss Belle's off to take lessons with the other children,' Abigail announced to Cook. 'Isn't that lovely?'

'Oh, my word, things are moving fast!' Cook had never been so surprised as when that child came out with a string of perfectly-composed sentences. Of course, Abigail had been puffing up her chest and rubbing it in about all the things Mrs Howgego had said about Belle in the past, the clever little cat. 'I were only saying the other day what a chatterbox she's become all of a sudden. Has she . . .'

'Forgive me, Mrs Howgego,' Erin sliced in impatiently, 'I really must find my daughter. D'ye happen to know where she and Rosie went?'

'As far as I know they went off to the master's library – they went upstairs anyway.'

Erin was off as if carried by a tornado.

'Eh, she still gets in a flap if she can't find that bairn, doesn't she?' observed Cook, resuming her pounding. 'She'll be wearing her clothes out from the inside if she isn't careful.'

Erin knocked on the library door in case her father was in. He wasn't – neither were the children. The habitual anxiety began to chew at her. With each empty room she became increasingly alarmed. Apart from the garden there was only the drawing room left to investigate.

'Well, unless they're hiding in the flower vase they're not in here,' laughed Josie in answer to her breathless query. 'They won't be far away 'cause they know I'll be taking them out shortly. Don't wo—' The slamming door lopped her sentence. Smile fading, Josie went back to the household bills.

Erin's ears were alert for the sound of childish laughter as she stepped onto the terrace, but all was quiet save for the birdsong and the steady drone from the beehive in the neighbouring garden. Fear settled over her stomach like a mantle of ice. She scanned the whispering borders of lupin, pink daisies, larkspur, all serene, then set off along the outer path of the lawn, running under pergolas of rose and clematis, dipping into every cypress-shaded nook, calling, calling, 'Belle! If ye don't come out now you're for it!' Panting, she finally reached the bottom of the garden and stopped, swivelling her head in desperation. 'Belle! Belle!'

Suddenly, her eyes focused on a dome-shaped construction secreted beneath the dark canopy of a group of trees and her heart jerked. 'Oh, Jesus!' She clamped a hand over her mouth and began to walk slowly towards the brick-built igloo.

The key should have been on the lintel but it wasn't; someone had taken it, but it wasn't in the door. She turned the handle. The door resisted her pull. She hauled more forcefully and it came open in stages, scraping its underside on some pebbles and refusing to budge further. The gap was big enough for her to get through. The cold and fear sent shivers down to her feet. 'Belle!' The sound echoed round and round, causing more tremors. Her toes felt their way through the darkness, towards the pit in the centre of the house where the ice was kept. Placing her hands on the low brick wall that circled it she tried to peer down into the pit, the cold bouncing back at her. 'Belle, Bel-le-elle!' There was no response. Erin straightened slowly and took a step backwards . . .

'Boo!'

The woman almost fell over into the chasm as three shrieking figures danced around her, laughing roisterously at her shock. 'You demons!' she yelled on recovery, supporting herself with the wall. 'Get outside, all of yese! Go on, out!' She shoved the three children into the daylight, face livid. 'Whose idea was this? Rosanna, was it yours?'

The little girl's smile petered out. 'It was only a joke, Aunt Erin.'

'Well, it was a stupid, stupid joke! You're a very silly girl! I could've fallen down the pit an' so could you. Ye know very well 'tis out of bounds.'

Nick squinted through the sunshine at the half-hysterical woman. 'We weren't doing any harm, Aunt Erin.'

'Ye took Belle with ye! She could've toppled over the edge an' been killed an' you would've been responsible for her death. You're very naughty children, both of you!'

'But Belle wanted to come,' attempted Rosanna.

'Don't you dare talk back to your aunt! As if Belle would've known about this place unless you planted the idea in her head. How did ye manage to get in anyway? The door's so stiff.' Nick said they had just pulled it. 'Well, ye could've locked yourself in, stupid boy! Now get back to that house, I'm going to have ye thrashed. I'm sick o' these tricks ye're forever playin'.'

'But it was . . .'

'Nicholas!' Erin's voice cracked. 'Go back to the house this minute an' wait for me to come to you – not you, my girl!' Belle had been about to go with them. Erin snatched her arm and almost pulled her off her feet. 'I'm going to put a stop to this!'

'It's not fair,' grumbled Rosanna as she and her brother wandered back up the garden path. 'It was Belle who wanted to see it.'

Nick returned a dull nod. 'But it's no use saying that to Aunt Erin, she won't believe that Belle can do any wrong.'

'Should we tell Mother?' Rosanna was taking small steps, the later to arrive for her punishment.

Nick shook his head. 'She'll listen to Aunt Erin, grown-ups always stick by each other.' At Rosanna's complaint of unfairness he turned back to see Erin gripping Belle by the arms, reprobation spilling from her lips. 'I think Belle's getting hers now.'

'The minute we go in I'm going to take those shoes from you, Belle Teale!' Erin was saying angrily. 'An' ye'll only get them back when ye learn that ye can't play the same games as Rosie and Nick.'

'But I can!'

'No, ye must get it into your head that if ye try to do

as they do ye'll be hurt. I want ye to promise me that ye'll never come to the ice-house again. 'Tis a very dangerous place. Ye only have to cockle over that low wall an' ye'll be down to the bottom.'

'All right – but please don't take my shoes, Mother!'

Erin yielded at the woebegone face. 'If ye do as you're told I won't have to.'

The fun of the afternoon was completely spoilt. 'Aren't I allowed to play with my cousins at all then?' Belle's voice was plaintive.

'No, Belle, they're far too high-spirited for you ...' Erin softened at her daughter's look of dejection. 'But I tell ye what ye can do with them. If ye promise to be a good girl, Miss Piggott says ye can take lessons with Rosie and Nick. Would ye like that?' It appeared from Erin's tone that she assumed this to be a treat. Belle's eyes held no opinion, but she nodded dutifully. Erin was beginning to calm down. 'But only if you're a very good and obedient daughter an' swear to me that ye won't let Rosie tempt ye into doing naughty things.'

'Why am I different, Mother?' digressed the child.

She was not to get the answer from her mother. 'Belle! I asked for your promise.'

Belle hung her head submissively. 'Yes, Mother, I promise.'

'Right!' Erin set off, dragging the child after her. 'Now I want you to go to your room while I speak to Aunt Josie.'

Aunt Josie was mortified at Erin's vociferous attack and stood there mutely, taking everything that the irate woman threw at her. She did not tell Sonny until they were in bed and it was too late for him to go and remonstrate with Erin. 'Don't blame your sister, John.' She tried to settle him back to the mattress as he made to jump up. 'She's still in a right old state over Sam. It wasn't the real Erin speaking.'

'Nevertheless I can't have her treating you like that, Josie. She has to learn that you're an equal, not a servant.' He abandoned his attempt to leave the bed and lay back.

'I suppose I'm as much to blame there,' she answered

quietly, relaxing on feeling his own tension disperse. 'I've had plenty of time to get used to this life but . . .' her voice trailed away.

For that second he relived his anguish with Peggy, when she had begged him to take her away and he had been unable to. But there was nothing stopping him now – no monetary reason, that was. 'We'll have to move out, Jos,' he said flatly. 'I can't see you unhappy here any longer.'

'What about Rosie and Nick? We can't just uproot them.'

'They'll be given a choice.'

'You know what they'll say, don't you?' He pressed his face into her shoulder and nodded his woe. They would want to stay here. She rubbed his thumb between her fingers, wrapped in indecision. 'I wouldn't want to think I was never going to see much of them – if that were the case I'd stay here and suffer things.'

'We'll see them,' he told her. 'We'll buy somewhere as near as possible, then you can continue more or less as you are doing, taking them out on an afternoon and that.'

'It all sounds very fair, but is it?' said Josie. 'I mean, their mother and father living in a different house however near, won't it confuse them?'

'They've got the choice.' His tone was slightly pettish. 'They can come and live with us if they want.'

She stiffened at the sudden dawning. 'John, you're . . .' She broke off.

'I'm what?' He pulled his head away from her shoulder to look her in the face, though all he saw was shadow.

'You mustn't think . . .'

'What were you going to say?' he demanded.

'You're jealous, aren't you?' came the gentle prompting. 'Jealous of your parents.'

For a moment he resisted. Then he collapsed against her. 'Oh, Jos! You really know me, don't you. Aye, I'm bloody jealous . . . but who have I got to blame? Just me. They're bound to be closest to the people who're around them all the time and I've been away so much . . . I'm sorry.'

'For what?'

'Sorry that my shortcomings as a father are going to make you suffer. I know how much you want to be a mother to them – *are* a mother to them . . . but if we don't make a move now things'll just get worse for us.'

She clasped him to her lovingly, her voice confident. 'No, they'll get better.'

'I wish I was so sure.'

'Ah, well, that's because you don't know what I know.' Her voice had become sly.

'Oh aye? And what little secret is this then?'

A pause. Suddenly it was hard to phrase. 'I was sick this morning . . . and yesterday . . . and the day before.'

It took but a second to sink in. 'Oh, Josie!' He hugged her and they rolled around the bed in gleeful fashion, gasping their gladness and congratulating one another.

Once the celebration had died down he said firmly, 'Well, if we're not going to move out there's one thing I do know. *This* child is going to be in no doubt who its parents are.'

Sonny didn't know why the announcement to his parents should make him feel so embarrassed, him already the father of two children – but then he hadn't actually sired them. It seemed funny just to blurt it out in the normal conversation. However, he was given some help by his observant mother at the dinner table the following day.

Patrick was slicing an apple onto his plate. 'I must say, Josie, that married life certainly seems to agree with you. I've never seen cheeks that pink since your mother-in-law sat on the stove.' Thomasin censured him laughingly. 'Don't you think she's blooming, Tommy?'

Thomasin caught the look that passed between her son and his blushing wife and beamed. 'Aye, I do. She looks really bonny.' She was more tolerant of Josie these days. 'Would I be considered premature in offering congratulations?'

Josie's mouth fell open. 'How did you know?'

'Know what?' asked Patrick innocently.

178

'Eh, men!' scoffed his wife to Erin who smiled back, then to Josie. 'It's the eyes that are the giveaway, dear.' She reached across the table for Josie's hand. 'Oh, I'm so glad for the pair of you. Sonny, it's absolutely lovely.'

Patrick finally grasped the situation. 'Oh . . . I see! Well done!'

With his announcement forestalled, Sonny smiled around the table at his family. 'Well, now my moment of glory's been snatched from my lips I think the children should be acquainted with the news that they're to have a new brother or sister.' Rosie and Nick seemed quite pleased, he thought, though they weren't particularly interested in babies. After the meal they were allowed to go and play while the adults discussed the new arrival.

'Well, there didn't seem to be any jealousy there, I'm glad to say,' commented Thomasin. 'Though you might just find there is when the baby actually arrives. Eh, I remember you,' she was looking at Erin, 'when our Dickie arrived. Your grandmother used to be forever hovering over you in case you poked his eyes out.' Her face reflected poignant memories and her mouth twitched sadly. 'Ah dear . . . if we'd known what lay in store for that little bundle. I was just thinking the other day, what sort of husband would he have made for Dusty Miller? If anyone could've tamed him, she could. I noticed her wholesale business was up for sale recently; brought it all rushing back . . . Oh, now I've gone adrift – what was I saying?'

'Jealousy,' provided Sonny. 'But I don't see why there should be any trouble with Rosie and Nick. They're old enough to understand.'

'But with Josie not being their proper mother . . .' Thomasin broke off at the look on her daughter-in-law's face. 'Oh, I didn't mean it like that, love! You've been as much a mother to those children as anyone. It's just that I know from experience what it's like to be a stepmother. They could view this baby as a threat because it'll be something you and Sonny share.'

'We share Rosie and Nick too,' said Sonny. 'At least we would if we were allowed to get on with it.'

Thomasin gauged from the tone of Sonny's voice that there was going to be an argument. She donned a pained expression. 'Don't tell me I have to start shifting the best china.'

'I'm not going to start a row,' said Sonny firmly. 'But I just think it's high time we made it clear who Rosie and Nick's parents are. Now, I know I've been away a lot and I've ever so much to be grateful to you for and I can't blame the kids for being confused over whom to consult when they need permission to do something – but I *won't* have them in any confusion over who their mother is.' He included Erin with his determined mien. 'Josie is their mother. If there are any orders to be given she will give them. She kindly consented to keep house for us because she wanted to feel useful . . .'

'Oh, whoever said she wasn't . . .'

'Listen, Mam!' warned Sonny, pointing. 'I know how difficult it is for all you womenfolk under the one roof, but we have to get this sorted out. Josie is my wife and now she's the mother of my children and I want her treated with respect. I'm sure that's not impossible, is it?'

All present were quick to mouth their apologies for ever having created the impression that Josie wasn't one of the family. Thomasin came to sit next to Josie. 'I know I'm a bossy old bugger, Josie, but I didn't mean to make you feel unwanted. Eh, dear . . . You're our daughter. Me and Pat love you very much, don't we, Pat? And we're thrilled to bits about the baby. If ever you think we're trying to take things over then all you have to do is speak your mind – after all, your husband does.' She tossed a wry smile at her son.

Josie had been a little uncomfortable while her husband had been airing his opinion but now she was so glad that he had made a stand against his parents, for his own sake as well as hers. She swore to them that if anything was troubling her in future she would make it known.

'Good!' said Patrick loudly. 'Now that's all finished can we wet the baby's head?'

180

CHAPTER TWELVE

With a baby, the housekeeping and two lively children to fill her day Josie had no more time for moping. Now, eighteen months after the birth of her daughter Elizabeth, she was fully integrated with the family and blissfully happy. Sonny and the children were, too. There had been a little jealousy at first, but now Rosie and Nick had grown used to seeing their parents cuddling someone else and anyway the baby didn't seem like a real person to them.

If Sonny's small family was happy, others in the house were definitely less contented. Patrick was among these, his annoyance being put to voice at this moment.

'Well, I say 'tis not right that a child of six should be cooped up in a classroom all day,' he decreed vehemently to his wife. ' I can see what's happening: Erin is trying to live her life through Belle, having the child stuffed with all the education she wanted for herself.'

During the two years which had passed since the discovery of Belle's acute intellect Erin's daughter had not been allowed to waste her talents on playing with her less scholastic cousins but force-fed with knowledge from morn till night. Two special tutors had been engaged to teach her for so many hours per week. For the rest it was left to Miss Piggott to educate her, but the governess felt it would not be many years before her meagre achievements were insufficient to teach this gifted pupil. Certainly it would have been a joy to instruct Belle, had the child's mother not made such heavy weather of it.

'You can't deny it's done wonders for Erin,' countered Thomasin with the thought that it was just as well the days when she and Patrick found themselves in the house at the same time were very few; they always seemed to be at odds. 'I've never seen her looking as radiant since she was carrying Belle. Finding out that the child's so clever seems to have put the purpose back in her life.' It had also seemed to bring her to terms with Sam's death. Shortly after being told by Miss Piggott about Belle's intelligence Erin had summoned the courage to visit her dead husband's grave. Thomasin's fears for her sanity had now diminished.

'That's all very well for Erin,' replied Patrick. 'But her vitality's purchased at the expense of her daughter. Ye can't exactly say Belle's looking radiant.'

Thomasin frowned. 'I'd agree that she isn't happy with the situation and would rather be out at play – but show me a child that knows what's good for it. Erin's discovered that Belle has a chance of making as near normal a life as possible, you can't fault the lass for wanting to take every advantage of that. And Belle must know at heart that her mother is doing it for her own good.'

'I disagree. If she did have the child's benefit at heart she'd see that all this cramming is doing Belle no good at all. She used to be such a pleasant little thing, now it's as if her personality is being squashed. All these facts an' figures are turning her into a walking encyclopaedia. If it isn't arithmetic 'tis music. An' not content with teaching her to play the old harp she's got her playin' the fiddle, the piano – it'll be the blasted bedstead next.' He held up a rigid finger. 'Another thing I notice is that the child only has to ask for something an' she gets it . . .'

'Well, you're a fine one to talk!' broke in his wife. 'Look at the way you spoil all of them.'

He rammed his hands into his pockets, rotating a florin between thumb and forefinger. 'True . . . but Tommy, that's what grandparents are for.' He eyed her speculatively. 'Speaking of which, I notice you haven't spent much time with them lately. Ye used to enjoy their company, or so I thought.'

'I still do. I just haven't had the time recently.'

'Ye haven't had time for a lot o' things,' came the soft answer.

Not wishing to become involved in deep debate she

crossed the carpet to the row of decanters. 'Would you care for a drink?'

'Why not?' It was always like this nowadays – she just wouldn't talk to him about anything personal, real talking, like they used to. He watched her pour a sherry for herself and a whiskey for him. The green dress she was wearing stirred his memory. He remembered Thomasin as she was on the first day he saw her, waltzing around the cake shop, hugging a green silk dress to her diminutive frame. He had thought her a real lady and much too good for the likes of him, but he had set out to win her all the same. She hadn't been exactly beautiful even in her youth but . . . what was the word? . . . handsome. Yes, handsome – as she still was, but in a different way altogether. Then, she had been all vibrant and auburn, laughing mouth, sparkling eyes, a carefree spirit; now, she had adopted the dignified carriage and mannerisms of a lady and only in her unguarded moments did they glimpse the old Tommy. She gave him his drink and sauntered away. Away, always away. 'Ye don't appear to be busy today,' he conjectured, turning the glass in his fingers.

'Mmm?' She had opened her bureau and with one hand began to sift through an untidy sheaf of papers, the other bringing the glass to her lips.

'I said ye can't be too busy if ye found time to come home.'

She gave a sharp laugh. 'I came home because I'd left some papers I needed in here. I would've been gone half an hour ago if you hadn't detoured me about Erin.'

'So busy, yet ye found the time to speak to me about our family. I should be flattered.' He tipped the glass into his mouth, emptying it.

She continued to search for the document she required. 'Sarcasm seems to be a trait of this family lately. Don't think it'll draw me into another argument, I've been longer than I meant to be already. Why aren't you at work, anyway?'

'Work?' He gave a brittle laugh. 'What work? All I am is a wet-nurse these days.' At first Patrick had grown his produce by his own steam with only occasional help from an old molecatcher who had since died. At Thomasin's insistence he had taken on a labourer, and then another, and another . . . Now he had only to supervise while the others dirtied their hands. He supposed some men would be grateful, but it was not what he had intended when he had purchased that first strip of earth. Patrick *liked* to get his hands dirty, liked to feel the sweat trickle between his shoulderblades, the pull on his muscles as he rammed his spade into the earth. It was sexual; a love affair with nature. One would think that with the amount of land he had accumulated the consummation would be frequent, but in fact it was very rare nowadays, as rare as that which took place in his marriage bed. A master wasn't meant to work alongside his men; it was indecent somehow.

'Anyone would think there was some great sin in being an employer.' She put aside the glass to concentrate on the bundle of documents in her hand, straightening them as she worked. 'Besides, you can't expect to be doing a lot of physical work at your age.'

'I'm not that old!'

'Of course you're not, dear.' She threw the tidied papers into a jumble again, rummaging through the bureau. 'But – ah! here's what I'm looking for.' She stuffed the rest of the papers into untidy wads and closed the flap on them. 'I can't think why you're complaining, Pat. Some men would give pounds to be in your position.'

'Well, I like to feel as though I'm doing something useful,' he said emphatically, 'an' being nursemaid to a load o' fellas doesn't fit that. So . . . I thought I might as well come home, the good I was doing. There's a fair on, an' I could take the children.'

'You don't need to tell me there's a fair on,' said his wife cryptically. Her store was in the same thoroughfare in which the festivities were held. 'What a time my delivery wagons have had trying to get through that lot. I don't know whether to give my customers their requirements or hand them hoops and let them lasso their own.' She pulled on her muslin gloves, ready to return to the store.

184

'I was hopin' ye might like to join us.'

'What! You must have a slate loose. I don't have time to go gadding off to the fair. I have to be there to see that those workmen who're putting in the new fittings don't have too many breaks.'

'Is that all that's stopping ye?'

'No, I've got to sort out the staff rota for stock-taking.'

'Look, I didn't intend going to the fair until after lunch. Surely ye can take a little time off – just an hour – to spare for your grandchildren – if not for your husband. It's been ages since we've taken them out together, Tommy.'

She faltered at the accusatory note. Then, 'All right,' she decided impulsively. 'I'll go with you.' His face broke into the old crinkly smile. 'Providing you meet me at the store. I haven't time to be running backwards and forwards.'

'Grand!' He put down the glass and rubbed his hands. 'Listen, d'ye think we should ask Erin to let Belle come with us? The poor child needs a treat.'

'Since when has a father asked his daughter if he can do something? Just tell her to have Belle ready and that will be that.' She left him in good spirits.

But that wasn't that, as far as Erin was concerned. 'Ye want me to instruct Mr Ingleton that his services aren't required this afternoon because his pupil's gone to the fair!' she challenged disbelievingly.

'Erin, 'tis only for a couple of hours,' coaxed her father. 'I can't see what difference that's going to make to her education.'

'No, you wouldn't, Father,' she replied strongly. 'Ye think I'm wasting time an' money by educating a female anyway, don't ye?'

Patrick retained his good nature. 'It's your money and she's your daughter, Erin, 'tis not for me to comment on how ye bring her up – though I do think you're being a wee bit heavy-handed in your enthusiasm. That child hasn't had one day out since all this started. All work an' no play, ye know . . . 'Tis time Belle had a chance to enjoy herself after all her hard work.'

'Ye seem to think it's some sort of enforced labour I'm putting her through. This is for her, Father, for her future. She's got nothing going for her but her brain. It has to be put to full use, which it won't be if you insist on dragging her off to the fair every five minutes.'

Patrick stared at her. He couldn't believe this was his loving, gentle daughter. After great thought he put a strange question to her. 'Have ye ever noticed Father Gilchrist's eyes?'

'What on earth has that scoundrel got to do with anything?' demanded Erin.

'They have this special gleam about them, like someone set fire to his brain.' He took his daughter by the shoulders and turned her to face the wall. 'Look in the mirror, Erin. Look closely. Ye'll see the same gleam there.'

She was shocked that he could liken Father Gilchrist's fanaticism with her own selfless moulding of her child. 'Ye think I'm doing this out of ambition?'

'Erin, muirnin.' He spoke to her reflection in the ormolued glass, his hands still gripping her shoulders, chin resting atop her neat head. 'I'd not cast a stain on your motives. I believe ye when ye say this is all done for Belle's sake. But don't let your self-sacrifice blinker your good sense. Ye're still a young and attractive woman. Ye may want to marry again some day, an' ye give yourself little opportunity by shutting yourself up within your child. This education bit has become an obsession with ye.'

'I shall never marry again,' announced Erin with surety. 'I'm going to dedicate all my energies into ensuring that Belle makes the most of her gift – and the only way she can hope to do that is through hard work.'

'Erin, ye're only concentrating on the one side of her make-up. What about her social life? She's a little child, she should have a chance to play with dolls n' skipping ropes, not cram her brains full o' figures all day long. There's plenty o' time ahead for education. What point is there in it, anyway?'

Erin made a noise of suppressed fury. 'I'll tell ye what point there is! There's the point that she won't have to scrub floors like her mother had to do because she was qualified for nothing higher; there's the point that her learning will take her any place she wants to go and – most valid point of all – with an education such as I intend for her, there's no one in the world will be able to call her dummy.'

Patrick could see that nothing he had to say would shift his daughter from her entrenched views, but he knew that Erin was trying to enact her own ambition through her child; a mistake for which he could hold himself partly responsible. If only he'd allowed Erin a little schooling . . . ah, well, it didn't do to look back all the time. One could see one's mistakes in retrospect but nothing could be done to rectify them now. But how shallow and arrogant he must have seemed to others as a younger man; the thought tickled the corners of his mouth.

'And what d'ye find so amusing?' demanded his daughter.

He started. 'Oh, not you, colleen – at least not directly. I was just thinking how narrow-minded I was at your age, thought I knew it all.'

'You're accusing me of being narrow-minded?'

'Perhaps single-minded is a more apt expression. Still as damaging to the people around ye. 'Tis a mistake to try to live your life through your child. There'll come a day when she'll want to leave home.'

'No!' The response was swift. 'There'll be no need. Belle will never marry.'

'How can ye possibly say that this early?'

''Cause I know what people are.'

'Is that why ye never let her out of the house, because you're afraid of what people will call her?' He received no answer. 'Ye're doing her no favours, Erin. She'll have to go into the big world some time. Best let her have a taste of what's to come while she's still young enough to accept it philosophically. Children are tougher than we give them credit for. Go on, let her come this afternoon, I'll take good care of her – or come yourself if ye like. Your mother will be with me.'

She managed a weak smile. 'That'll be nice for ye. I'll wager y'almost forgot ye had a wife.'

'It will be nice,' he nodded, then touched her cheek pensively. 'Ye know, ye mustn't be too hard on your mother. There's an unholy scrap going on inside of her. I don't know what it's all about but she has to sort it out for herself – as we all do in the end. Now come on, what d'ye say?'

'Oh . . . very well! Ye've talked me round as usual, you unscrupulous charmer. Belle can come.' She levelled a finger. 'But don't think it'll be a regular occurrence. Whatever any of ye say or think of me I'll not waste that child's brain for anyone.'

Patrick's arrival at the store with the children came too early for his wife. 'Oh, damn,' she muttered, seeing their boisterous entrance from her position in the counting house which was cut off from the main store by a glass partition. She had hoped to tie up loose ends before leaving George Ackworth in charge for the afternoon. Well, they would just have to dangle now. Placing a weight on the papers that had not yet been cleared she went into the store to meet them, scolding mildly, 'I wasn't expecting you so soon. I suppose I shall have to leave the outstanding bills till I come back.'

'Sorry. Once the brats knew where I was takin' them it was like trying to control a riot. There's no rush, you finish what ye have to.' Patrick looked around the busy shop. 'No wonder ye can't find any spare time. I didn't realise custom was this good.' The area where he and the children were standing was dedicated mostly to groceries but there was also a bread counter, stocked daily with piping hot loaves, fruit pies and various pastries from the bakery at the rear of the building, though the smell of fresh bread was overpowered at the moment by that of roasting coffee beans.

'Well, business has been a bit slack but it's gradually trickling back to normal after the trade recession,' said Thomasin, sharp eyes wandering, watching her assistants packing customers' baskets and weighing goods. She made a note to give Mary a talking-to for that missing button on her dress. 'There was a period when I contemplated closing one of the shops, I might tell you, during that bad do of the Seventies, but the depression appears to have eased. Now . . . what am I going to do with you four till I'm ready?'

'Ah sure, don't concern yourself about us,' said Patrick lightly. 'We'll just take a stroll round your empire.' He doffed his hat to an exiting customer. 'Right then, away to your lair an' us'll look after ourselves.'

'And have people say I neglect my husband?' She spotted the cryptic gleam in his eye and turned quickly, 'George!' summoning a young man who tugged at his jacket and came hurrying over. 'I want you to show my husband round the store,' Thomasin told him.

'The new extension too, ma'am?'

'Yes, and the new bakery – everywhere. Oh, and before I forget, how many of those new pastilles have we left?' George said there was only what was on the counter. 'Hm, they've been moving like cascara. If the Rowntree man comes in you'd better double our order for that line, it's a real winner.' Smiling, she left Patrick and the children in the care of George who asked if they had seen all they wanted to here.

Patrick looked around quizzically. 'There were some tables here one time where people could take a cup of tea.'

'Ah, we've had a bit of a change round since then, sir. That area's through the archway now. It got a bit cramped in here what with folk queueing for their goods so Mrs Feeney made what used to be a stockroom into the café and put the stock on the third floor. 'Course, now that the missus has made that into a new department she needs somewhere else to shove the stock. That's why she bought that new warehouse on the river – but you'll know that already.'

'Yes, yes,' said Patrick, not knowing it at all; Thomasin rarely discussed her business moves with him. 'It sounds

as though there's little room left for you an' the others.'
George told him the staff didn't live in. Thomasin, something of a revolutionary in this, had decreed that she wasn't
going to waste good floor space on beds if her assistants
could just as well live at home. 'And does that suit them?'
asked Pat.

'Oh, that's not for me to comment,' replied George
hurriedly and moved on to a room where a group of young
women were sticking labels on containers.

Nick asked one of the women if he could have a go.
She smiled and said he could. 'Might the young ladies
want a go, too?'

Patrick caught her anxious eye as Rosanna undid a sack
of currants. 'Rosie, be a good girl an' leave things alone
that don't concern ye.'

'I thought all this belonged to Nan.' She made a
sweeping gesture.

'It does – an' ye know how your Nan shouts if she finds
ye playin' with her things at home. Come try your hand
with the others.'

'I'm hungry.'

George, who liked children, dipped into his pocket and
produced a bag of boiled sweets. 'There y'are, miss. Get
your teeth round one o' them.'

Rosanna delved into the bag. 'May I take two?'

'Rosanna, don't be rude,' scolded Patrick.

''Course you can.' George let her help herself, then
offered the bag to the others, giving a special smile to
Belle. There was something about this little girl that
particularly impressed him but he was damned if he knew
what it was. He allowed her to keep the bag, oblivious to
the look which Rosie passed to her brother. 'Shall we let
the children stick a few more labels on while we go further,
sir?' He made to lift Belle onto a stool but she pushed
him off haughtily. 'I can do it.'

Nick expressed a keen interest in the workings of the
store so, while he went with Patrick and George the girls
dabbed paste onto labels and chatted to the women,

exchanging names. One of them, Susan Mills, made a quiet aside to her neighbour, but Rosanna caught it.

'Like what?'

Susan presented a questioning face to the little girl.

'You said you didn't think Nan would have a grandchild like that,' repeated Rosanna. 'Like what?'

'I just meant she's awfully pretty – as you are yourself,' tendered the woman, then under her breath, 'Lor', we'll have to be careful what we say, this'n's got lugs like an elephant.'

Rosanna smoothed the label with her small palms. Belle, after doing a few, struggled down from the stool and began to wander around. She, too, had heard the woman's comment and knew that it was not her prettiness that caused the attention. People always looked at her in an odd way. Soon bored, Rosanna climbed down, too. Thinking she was out of earshot Susan's partner said, 'Blimey, you wouldn't think the missus would be over-eager to have her paraded about, her being so keen to whip up custom. Put a lot o' people off, seeing that while they were tryin' to do their shoppin'.'

Rosanna tried to untangle the statement. Why didn't the women like Belle? Come to that, why did everyone seem uneasy in her presence? I mean, she told herself, one could understand either me or Nick being mad at her when we get the blame for something she's done, but not people who had never met her before. The answer was to come.

'Eh, we'll have summat to chuck at her the next time she's gobbin' off, moanin' about shoddy work. I'll say, aye, mebbe we can't stick labels on straight but we don't have a bloody hunchback in our family.'

Rosanna sneaked a look at Belle who was patrolling the ranks of produce. There was a sort of mound on one of her shoulders. She had never given it much thought before – but what difference could that make? She listened.

'Maggie, that's rotten,' accused Susan. 'She's such a bonny little thing. I think it's a shame . . .'

'Aye well, mistress's grandbairn or no, she needn't think

191

she's hangin' round here all day. It'll be bringin' bad luck on t'place.'

'You're gonna tell her then, are you?' smirked Susan, then shushed her companion as Belle scrambled back up to the table and casually resumed her pasting. 'Come to do a few more have you, miss? Eh, you're a right help.'

Belle smiled sweetly, pretending to be busy, but when the woman looked away she slipped down from her perch bearing two pasted labels. Very delicately she attached one to each woman's padded bottom, wishing it said something funnier than 'Penny's Homeopathic Cocoa Promotes Glowing Health'.

She pulled her hand away swiftly as Susan turned, smiling. 'Had enough?'

'Yes, thank you,' said Belle politely. 'I'm going to find my grandfather now.'

'What's up with her then?' Susan grinned at Rosanna who had started to giggle. 'Does she come from Giggleswick?'

The girls clasped hands and scurried away. The labels were small revenge for the nasty things the women had said about Belle, but it was a token, and for Rosie the incident had served to make her more aware of her cousin's differences. Taking a flight of linoleum-covered stairs they found Patrick and Nick in the new extension. George was outlining Thomasin's project – this was to be the new hardware and haberdashery department.

'My wife's really branching out,' murmured Patrick, eyes surveying the new fittings that smelt of sawdust. 'How many has she working here now?'

George counted on his fingers. 'There's me an' three apprentices, Cook what works in the back – I'll show you round there next, two lasses to help her, three in the shop an' those two women in the stockroom . . .' A hefty wagebill, thought Patrick. 'An' then o' course there's Mr Farthingale,' added George. Patrick asked what position this man held. 'Oh, he doesn't work here, sir – I thought you'd know him, him being a business colleague o' the missus'. Nice chap. There's talk . . .' he broke off,

192

realising he had gone too far, but Patrick made him go on. 'Tut! The mistress'd kill me if she knew . . . Oh well, I heard talk that the mistress was thinking of taking Mr Farthingale on as a partner.'

Patrick thought aloud, 'Why should she do that if she's doing so well?'

George didn't know. 'You won't let on I've been tittle-tattlin', sir?'

'No . . . no, 'course not.' Patrick was still thinking. As they went down again he continued to question the young man until they reached the counting house where Thomasin had just completed her work. Patrick thanked the young man for the guided tour, nudging Belle who thanked him for the sweets – the sweets she had consumed entirely by herself, Rosanna noticed.

Thomasin agreed with Patrick's observation that George was a nice young chap. 'Yes. It's a pity he hasn't more up top and then I could delegate a little of my responsibility sometimes – that's why I wanted to get this finished before we left, so's he wouldn't have much to do.'

'When I grow up I'm going to help you, Nan,' announced Nick.

'Well, you've obviously enjoyed what you've seen,' smiled Thomasin, threading her arm through the handle of a fringed bag. 'I must say, I look forward to that, Nick. I wondered who was going to take over when I die – nobody else seems that bothered.'

'Oh, I am! I want to sit in a counting house like this and build big piles of money.'

'Oh, with an outlook like that you can come and work for me anytime.'

'Today?' asked the boy hopefully.

'Don't ye want to go to this fair, then?' enquired Patrick.

The children began screaming excitedly. 'Ssh!' ordered their grandmother. 'You'll frighten away all my customers and then where will we find our big piles of money?'

CHAPTER THIRTEEN

'We should take more time off to do things like this,' said
Patrick as they wandered amid the bustle of the fairground,
having to raise his voice above the clamour of hurdy-
gurdy, vendors' cries, yapping dogs and general hullabaloo.

Thomasin smiled at him abstractedly over the heads of
their grandchildren as they edged their way through the
crowd, paying more attention to the window displays of
her competitors. 'What?'

Though piqued at her distant expression he kept his
smile. 'For heaven's sake will ye take your mind from your
work for once.'

'I'm sorry, I genuinely didn't hear what you said,' replied
his wife. He repeated his statement. 'Oh yes, lovely,' she
responded unconvincingly.

'Roll up and see the freaks!' shouted a raucous voice as
they moved into the thick of the festivities.

'What's freaks, Gramps?' asked Rosanna.

Patrick answered with a question. 'How would ye like
a toffee-apple?'

'Oh, yes, please!' chorused the children, jumping up
and down.

'Come on then, let's go get one.' He held out his arm
to slice a passage through the crowd, steering them away
from the offending sideshow.

After the toffee-apples had been consumed, leaving
sticky red rings around mouths: 'I want some silkworms,'
said Belle.

'I want never gets,' reproved Thomasin, pulling aside
her skirts from sticky fingers.

'Oh, let them have some,' said her husband. 'They're
only a penny.'

'Patrick Feeney, if those children asked you to jump in

194

the river I think you'd do it. You don't build reputable characters by giving them everything they ask for.'

She might just as well have saved her breath, for Patrick poured out handfuls of copper. The owner of the stall handed each a jar of silkworms – presumably they were there among the bunches of leaves – and collected the three pennies.

'Mine are going to spin you some material for a dress, Nan,' said Belle.

Thomasin smiled. She had become quite fond of this child now that she was able to talk with her – even if she could be rather precocious. 'They'll have to put in a bit of overtime, there's only half a dozen of them.'

Rosanna was examining her own jar worriedly. 'There's none in mine.'

Patrick reassured her, pointing. 'They're just hiding from ye. Look – there's one.'

'That's not a worm,' reproached his grand-daughter. 'It's a bit of fluff. The man's a cheat.'

'Now, you mustn't say that about people, Rosanna – not without good reason anyway.' Thomasin patted her head. 'We'll have a good look when we get home. If there are none in I'm sure Belle won't mind sharing hers.'

Belle clutched her jar to her chest, saying nothing but making it perfectly clear to her cousin that there would be no sharing.

'Who's Mr Farthingale?' asked Patrick out of the blue as they meandered. There was the slightest stiffening of the arm linked with his but Patrick noticed it immediately. After almost thirty years of marriage he knew when a remark had disturbed Tommy.

'Mr Farthingale?' She repeated the name as though reacquainting herself. 'He's a friend of mine from the YAS. Why do you ask?'

'Ye'd surely think it strange if I didn't take an interest in your friends,' replied Patrick lightly. He kept one eye on the children as they danced ahead of him. 'How long have ye known him?'

'Only since I joined the Society.'

'A short time to establish one's trust in a man who's going to join forces with ye.'

'I can see that George Ackworth has been letting his tongue run away with him,' said Thomasin stiffly. 'I shall have to have words with him when I return about breaches of confidence.'

'Breach of confidence?' He stopped dead and turned to her. 'I'm your husband, not a business rival.'

'That's not the point. You could've been for all George cared. I won't have my employees blabbing their mouths off – especially when they're not supposed to know about it in the first place.' She set off again, he with her. 'Anyway, nothing's definite. Francis and I have been . . .'

'Francis?'

She returned his swift examination. 'Francis Farthingale. We've merely mentioned the possibilities of him joining me as a partner. Nothing's been signed.'

'Ye might've "merely mentioned" it to me. I felt a bit of a fool when young George was spouting away there assuming I knew all that went on in the store.'

'But you've never shown much interest before – why now?' It was a superfluous question; she knew very well why.

He responded to her query with a question of his own. 'Why haven't I met this Mr Farthingale? If you're on first-name terms with him I would've expected ye to have invited him for dinner.' She was always throwing dinner parties, making him feel cloddish with her genteel friends.

Thomasin didn't like where this was leading. 'He's not my lover, if that's what you're suggesting, Patrick!'

He let go of her arm in order that they might pass through a narrow gap, making sure the children were within a safe distance. 'Did I say he was?'

She chose not to take his arm again. 'You didn't have to. I can tell what you're thinking.'

'I doubt it.' The noise of the fair was beginning to aggravate. 'Why haven't I met him, then?'

'Have you met Mr Sledwick?' she threw at him. 'Mr Graves? Mr Castleford? You're surely not implying I bring home all my business associates so my husband can inspect them?'

'I'm sorry if I spoke out of turn. I was just trying to show an interest. I thought maybe that's where I'd been going wrong. If I'd shown more interest in your work then perhaps ye'd be more inclined to tell me things an' wouldn't have to jump down my throat when I ask an innocent question.'

She stopped and faced him, the crowd snaking round them, nudging them. 'But it wasn't innocent, was it? You do think Francis and I are more than just friends.'

'I didn't say it.'

'No, but you damn well thought it!' The old Tommy spirit flared, then just as quickly turned to exasperation. 'Oh, I'm not wasting an afternoon being put through interrogation when I've plenty of work I could be seeing to. You can manage the children on your own – I'm sure they won't miss their stuffy old grandmother. I'll see you this evening.' She began to walk away.

He put out a restraining hand. 'Tommy, this is the first time we've spent together in ages . . .'

She turned on him. 'And you've gone and spoilt it with your childish, jealous probing! Look to the children, they'll get lost.'

He flung a hectic glance at the children who were being enveloped by the crowd. When he turned back she had widened the gap. 'Tommy!' He hailed her with a desperate look at the children, then, 'Oh!' He dashed after them.

'Where's Nan got to?' asked Belle when he caught up.

'She says she's sorry but she got called back to the store. There's a crisis.'

'What's a crisis?' Rosie wanted to know.

'It's . . . oh, it's when something important goes wrong,' said her grandfather. Doesn't it always?

'Who came for her? Was it George?' Rosanna found herself being dragged after her brother.

'Quiet, ninny!' he hissed in her ear. 'They've had a row and Nan's gone off in a huff.'

Patrick, overhearing but pretending not to, marvelled at

197

the observance of his young grandson. Nick never said much but noticed everything. He cleared his throat. 'I don't suppose I could persuade any o' yese to have a ride on them gallopers?'

This was met by a general clamour for money which Patrick supplied and the three rushed off to claim a seat on the carousel, Patrick following. He stood and watched with the crowd as the merry-go-round rotated, thinking of his wife's words, wondering what this Farthingale man was like. He knew it was crazy to be jealous – oh yes, Tommy had been right there – jealous of this one man among all the others his wife met in connection with her work. But it was when she had said his name – Francis. Until then his query had been harmless enough.

The roundabout stopped. Patrick stepped forward to receive his grandchildren. They must have disembarked on the other side. He strolled around the collection of painted horses until he found them.

'May we have a go on the lucky bag, Gramps?' asked Rosanna, leaping off her golden steed into his arms, flying skirts revealing her drawers.

He gasped laughingly as she thudded into him, placing her on her feet. 'Aye, I suppose so. Just let's get Belle down.' He held his arms out to his other grand-daughter.

'I can do it, Gramps!' She swung her right leg over the horse's back and slithered down to the platform.

'Careful now. Good girl.'

'I want to jump off.'

'No!' He snatched her up before she had the chance. 'Your mother'd have me planted alongside the praties.' He put her down beside Nick. 'Now then, what did Rosie say she wanted to do?' He looked around for her. She was nowhere to be seen. 'Nick, where's your sister?'

'She's already gone to the lucky bag,' Nick pointed. 'Over that way.

'Ye oughtn't to have let her go,' reproved Patrick. 'Come on, Belle.' He hurried them through the crush to the nearest lucky bag holder, but when they arrived Rosanna wasn't there. 'Is there another lucky bag besides this?' Patrick asked the man.

'What's up, isn't this'n posh enough for yer?' was the stallholder's reply.

'Don't be stupid, man, I meant no offence.' Patrick was irritable. 'I'm searching for my grand-daughter an' she said she wanted the lucky bag. Is there another besides yours?'

The man tossed his hand to the right. 'I think there's two more over that road.'

Patrick turned to the children and spoke to them seriously. 'Look, you two'd best stay put. I can find her better on me own. Here, take these pennies an' have a go on this stall – but don't budge, d'ye hear?' He pelted off, excusing himself as he jostled people in the crowd.

Rosanna was not at either of the places the man had indicated. Patrick's concern grew. The long street was packed, he could be going round in circles all afternoon and still not find her. He searched about him frantically, then dashed from stall to stall, bombarding the vendors with questions as to her whereabouts. Then he spotted a brief flash of pink bow-ribbon through a parting in the crowd. Straining on tiptoe for a better look he finally saw her – holding the hand of a rough-looking character. The Fallons! The tinkers had come back to claim her!

No excuse-me's this time. He barged roughly through the squash, eyes firmly fixed on the lank head of the tinker whose hand Rosanna held. 'What's yer bleedin' rush? Oy, yer clumsy bastard!' He ignored the abuse at his bad manners and forged on. There she was! He stumbled the last few steps, grabbed her and swung her into a protective embrace. The tinker pivoted swiftly. 'What the bleedin' hell's this, mister?'

Patrick's mouth fell agape as the little girl struggled and kicked in his arms. 'Oh, Mother o'God, I'm sorry!' Rapidly he put the child on her feet where she escaped to her father. The wrong child! The girl who now clung to the tinker, glaring at him, had Rosanna's long hair with the pink bow-ribbon in it but that was the only resemblance.

This child's attire was distinctly more poor. He felt his neck redden and swiftly apologised again. 'I've lost my grand-daughter, ye see. I thought 'twas her . . .'

'And why would I want her?' asked the tinker dangerously.

How could Patrick tell him the truth? That he himself had kidnapped Rosie from her tinker grandparents and brought his son's child to live with him and Thomasin where she might have the best of everything. The crowd pressed the men closer together. He held out a coin to the tinker, apologising profusely. The man played him with challenging eyes for a few worrying seconds, then snatched the sovereign and moved briskly away, dragging the child after him. Patrick ran a palm from his forehead over his hair, wiping the sweat from his brow. He was getting as bad as Erin. Where the hell was that child?

Belle was scowling imperiously at the urchin who openly inspected her. 'What are you staring at, boy? Go away this instant.' It had not taken long for them to dispose of Grandfather's pennies and now they must wait here enduring the unwelcome company of this ragged tyke.

'Free country, I can stand where I like,' replied the snub-nosed offender.

'Not if you're making a nuisance of yourself,' corrected Nick.

'I'm not makin' a nuisance of meself, I'm just looking at her.' The boy scraped a finger round the crease of his ear, eyes adhered to Belle.

'You're staring,' said Nick. 'And it's rude to stare.'

'Why's she gorra bent back, then?' demanded the other, doing a tour around Belle who moved her head to follow him. Long before his observation she had come to understand what her mother had meant when she said 'you're different'. If the experimental hands and the mirror had failed to tell her, the stares had not. What she could not grasp was why this physical disability should draw forth scorn. Wasn't everyone different from everyone else? Then why did Belle come in for all the adverse attention?

'Mind your own business. Take no notice of him, Belle.'

'I was only askin' a civil question.'

'You were being bloody rude.' It made Nick feel older – surer – using the swear word.

'And who're you to call me rude, Lord Muck?' The boy looked him up and down derisively.

'I'm one of your betters,' replied Nick airily. 'And if you don't stop hectoring my cousin I shall have to give you a mashed nose.'

The urchin sized Nick up and, seeing that the boy would most probably be well able to fulfil his threat, decided to concentrate on the girl. Who did these people think they were, calling him names? Just 'cause they had fancy clothes didn't mean they were any better than him. He continued to stroll around Belle, making comments.

'Why're you being so rude?' she questioned. 'What have I done to you?'

'I can look if I want to. I haven't seen nobody like you before.'

'Don't take any notice of him, Belle,' warned Nick. 'Don't let him upset you.'

'Upset, by an upstart like him? Pooh!'

The urchin returned her level stare. – Just look at her, Miss Hoity-Toity. He suddenly wanted very badly to see her cry for looking at him in that superior manner. 'You're ugly,' he told her bluntly.

'No, I'm not,' returned Belle, a pulse in her neck starting to pound.

'He's just being a pig,' said Nick. 'Shall I bunch him for you?'

'I don't need you to stick up for me. I can deal with rubbish like him myself. Besides,' she tilted her nose in the air, trying to look nonchalant, 'he doesn't bother me in the least.'

Annoyed at her calmness the boy humped his shoulders and started to imitate her, prancing up and down and making weird noises.

'I don't know who he thinks he's supposed to be,' said Belle to Nick.

'This is what you look like.' The boy's arms swung low like a gorilla's.

'No, it isn't. Only monkeys look like that.' Belle stared at him dispassionately though inside a furnace raged.

Nick marvelled at how calm she was for a six-year-old when he, three years her senior, was hopping mad. He stepped forward but she caught his sleeve. 'I said I don't need your help, Nicholas. He's just making an ass of himself.'

He stopped cavorting. 'Yer wha'? At least I don't wear big clomping boots like you.'

'No – because you can't afford any.' Belle sneered at his naked, dusty feet.

He crossed his arms and locked his eyes to her special boots. 'Why's one big n' one small? What're they for?'

'This,' replied Belle and dealt him an almighty crack to the shin.

The boy burst into tears. 'I'm gonna tell me dad o' you!' and ran off into the crowd.

'Tell him I'll give him one too!' shouted Belle and her scowl split into a wicked grin at Nick who laughed aloud.

'Wait till I tell Gramps.'

'Don't tell him, ninny!' Belle's heart still palpitated with the exchange. 'If Mother hears what's gone on she'll never let me out again. This is just what she's been afraid of. She thinks I'll be upset when people call me names.'

'Does it truly not affect you?' asked her cousin.

'Pooh! Why should it?' she lied. 'Names never hurt anyone. Besides, one has to put up with these troublesome episodes from one's inferiors.'

Nick wondered where she had heard that little gem. There was no doubt that she meant it, either. Belle did have a superior air about her. He sighed heavily. 'I wonder if Gramp's found Rosie yet. She's such a pest.'

It was as Patrick passed the tent marked 'Curiosities' that he finally found her. She emerged from beneath the canvas wearing a lollipop in her mouth and a frown on her forehead. 'Rosanna, come here at once!' He marched up to her and took her by the shoulder. 'Has the devil got into ye? What's the meaning of your running off like that?'

'Oh hello, Gramps.' She broke out of her vague frown to smile up at him.

'I'll give ye hello, young lady! D'ye realise I thought ye'd been kidnapped? I've been running about all over the place tryin' to find ye.'

She took his hand. 'Sorry, Gramps. I was on my way to the lucky bag when I saw this funny lady and decided to come in here.'

'Ye shouldn't've even gone to the lucky bag without me. Anything could've happened to ye. Come along now, let's go find your brother an' Belle.' He gripped her sticky little hand, 'Gob, what a mess!' and led her through the hubbub. 'What did ye want to go in there for anyway? That's no place for a young lady.'

'I wanted to see what a freak looked like,' she responded after relieving her mouth of the lollipop. 'You never answered me before when I asked.'

'You want to know too much for your own good, miss,' he told her. Then, after a short pause, 'Well, did ye find out what a freak was?'

She pulled the lollipop noisily from her mouth again, smacking her lips. 'I'm not sure. There was a lady with a beard and a great big fat man, some animals with five legs – I didn't like them, they frightened me – a gigantic pig, a man with pins sticking out all over his body – he hardly had any clothes on . . . Then I saw a tiny little man, he was only as big as me but he was a grown-up. I thought he was a little boy at first, but when I spoke to him he said grown-up words.'

Patrick glanced down at her. 'What did ye say to him?'

'I said I was looking for the freak and asked him if he was it.'

Patrick cringed. 'An' what did he say?'

'He said naughty words that Abigail sometimes says to Cook when she thinks no one's listening. The other words he said weren't bad ones, I'm allowed to say those. He said, "Mm-mm off, you little mm-mm".'

Despite himself Patrick couldn't help the short laugh that burst from his lips. Even at her naughtiest Rosanna could always get round him. 'How did ye get in there in the first place? Ye had no money left.'

'I sneaked underneath the tent.' She bit the last of the lollipop from the stick and proceeded to crunch it noisily.

'For Heaven's sake, child, d'ye have to do that? Ye're setting me teeth on edge. So, did ye find your freak, then?'

'I don't know. If I knew what one looked like I'd know if I'd seen one. Don't you know either, Gramps?'

'Ah, Rosie,' he sighed. 'I suppose ye could say that a freak is something or somebody that isn't like other people.'

'So *all* the people in there were freaks?'

'Yes, ye could say – but it's not a nice word to call folk. I wouldn't want to hear you saying it to anyone.'

'That's why the little man was rude?'

He nodded. 'Ye hurt his feelings.'

'I see. But if it upsets him to be called that, why was he in there?'

'Because he gets paid for being insulted, Rosie. 'Tis probably the only way he can earn a living.'

'You mean he couldn't do proper work because he's so small?'

'Well, there are jobs he could do, but ye saw the amount o' people who were queueing to see him an' the others; he probably earns a better living that way.'

'Some of the people were laughing at him,' divulged Rosanna. 'I don't know why.'

'Sometimes folk laugh at things like that because they're stupid an' cruel. Others laugh because they're relieved that they don't look like the little man.'

'Why was he so little?' asked the girl. 'I'm bigger than him and I'm only nine and a half.'

Lost for an answer, Patrick was relieved to spot his other grandchildren. 'Ah, there's Belle and Nick still where I put them.' Reaching them he patted both on the head. 'Good as gold. Everything all right?'

'Yes, Gramps,' said Belle quickly.

Rejoining his hand with Rosanna's he held the other out to Belle. 'You hold Belle's other hand, Nick, so we don't lose each other again.' He happened to glance at Rosanna who was staring at Belle closely. 'Rosanna.' The tone held a warning. She uplifted quizzical blue eyes to meet his face, the question forming on her lips, but when she saw the stern features she merely smiled instead and kept the enquiry to herself. She must never say that word in front of Belle.

CHAPTER FOURTEEN

'Oh, mercy on us, if it isn't the skew-whiff brigade!' cried Patrick as the grandchildren tumbled into the drawing room for the usual story before they went to bed. 'I'm glad to see ye've got all that sticky stuff off your faces before ye come climbing all over me. Right, whose turn is it for the old lap?'

They started to argue. 'Mine! Me-e. No, it was your turn yesterday, I want a go. Grandfather, tell Nick he must sit on the stool!'

'Simmer down! We'll decide this sensibly. I've only the two knees so one of yese will have to sit on the stool. Nick, if I remember rightly you gave my poor leg a right punishing when ye took your place yesterday. I'd hardly forget that in a hurry – even if you're pretending to now. So, 'tis Rosie n' Belle on my lap an' you for the stool, old lad.'

''S not fair,' mumbled Nick. 'They have more goes than I do.'

'Snot fair, where's that? Sounds a filthy place to me. Now sit there on that stool an' do as you're bidden. A gentleman should always let the ladies go before. Right, I believe Rosie chose the story last night an' Nick the day before, so 'tis Belle's turn. What shall we have tonight,

Belle dear? Ah God!' he hugged her impulsively. 'Ye're a bonny wee thing. I love ye.'

'D'you love me too, Grandfather?' asked Rosanna, cupping a small hand to his cheek. The installation of Belle as rival prompted the need to seek assurance that Patrick loved her as much as he ever did.

'Ah, I surely do.' He delivered a resounding kiss on her forehead. 'Nick too. I don't know what I'd be doing without you three.'

Rosie pillowed her head on his chest, snuggling into his maleness. It wasn't as comfortable as sitting on Mother's lap – no soft platform on which to lay one's head – but Grandfather's cuddles were the best of all. Belle, annoyingly, had done likewise. Rosie closed her eyes and tried to pretend she had sole rights on the property.

Patrick assumed a posture of deep concentration. 'Let's see. Ah yes, I think we'll have that one.' He settled himself more comfortably. 'There was once this woman called Sinead who had a baby boy, the most beautiful baby ye ever saw, the fairest in all Ireland. He was so bonny in fact that his mother thought the fairies would come and steal him away in the night – as they sometimes do. Even though she kept him in skirts to confuse them into thinkin' he was a girl – for the little people don't seem so fond o' the colleens – she still couldn't get the fear out of her mind. It became an obsession with her . . .'

'What's an obsession?' cut in Belle.

'Well, 'tis like you thinkin', I wonder if we'll have iced buns for tea and wonderin' an' wonderin' all afternoon till ye can think o' nothing else but them iced buns an' feel ye might die if Abi doesn't serve them up.' He went on with the tale. 'Well, Sinead got to thinkin' what she could do an' pretty soon she hit upon a splendid idea. If the baby was made ugly then the fairies weren't likely to steal him, were they?'

'No.'

'So, she took a great hammer and she bashed him over the nose – three times just for luck an' pretty soon his perky little nose looked as if it'd been stood on by an

elephant. Sinead stood back and looked at him an'
thought, sure that's a big improvement, but what if the
blankets are covering his nose an' the wee folk see those
wonderful eyes? They're sure to take him. So, she plucked
out his eyes an' stuck them back the wrong way round so
that they kinda looked at each other over the smashed-up
nose. An' Sinead stood back to take another look an'
thought, but what if the blankets are right up over his face
so's the wee folk can only see that golden hair? So she
took a razor an' shaved it all off. Well now, ye can imagine
the state o' the poor wee fella.'

'Horrible,' said Rosanna.

'Now, one night the fairies, having heard o' the wondr-
ous-lookin' babe, did come. They snuck up to his crib in
the middle o' the night with one o' them holding up a
candle to light their dirty deed. "Jaze!" cried the one
with the candle, "what a monster! What a horrible lookin'
sight." "What a revolting child," said another. "That's no
baby, somebody's chucked a broken egg on the pillow –
a bad one at that – will ye look at the colour o' the yolk."
Ye see, the fairy was referring to the baby's eyes which
with all the bashing they'd received did look like bad
scrambled egg. Anyway, the wee folk said, sure we can't
take that horrible thing back, the others'll think we've gone
crazy. So they left. Well, the years passed an' the babe
grew into a young man an' started to look for a wife. Well
o' course he was so ugly that none o' the colleens would
even entertain him – ran a mile when he so much as
smiled at them. His poor mother was at her wits' end
tryin' to find someone who'd take him on, for after all
these years she was sick o' the sight of him herself. One
day she was passing a stream with her son an' up pops a
creature who was almost as ugly as himself an' says,
"Jazers, isn't he the wondrous sight, I'd surely like to
take him for me husband." Sinead looked at her son an'
wondered if she an' the creature could be looking at the
same person and said so. The creature replied that
Sinead's son was the only thing she had ever seen who
was even uglier than herself an' if folks were busy taking

their fun out o' him they might be leaving herself in peace. Well, the son didn't want to go, but Sinead pushed him into the stream where he was promptly married to the creature. He hated it down there. He hated his wife, but nevertheless, like most married couples, the two produced a child which if anything was even more ugly than its father. It took such torment from the rest o' the creatures of the stream that it immediately buried itself beneath the mud an' wouldn't come out for nobody. Until . . . one day a shaft of light speared his watery home making him inquisitive as to what might be going on above the surface. Feeling a little afraid he pulled himself from his hole and with the aid of a reed dragged his ugly body towards the dazzling sunlight. Once out there o' course he didn't want to go back, but he wondered just how he would get along with the other beautiful creatures he saw.

'Then all at once he felt his body tighten, the heat of the sun seemed to shrivel him up. He felt as if he was about to burst his skin. And lo and behold that's just what he did. An' wonder upon wonders! he discovered that under that ugly casing had been hidden a huge pair o' wings.

'The dragonfly – for that was what he was – opened and shut these wings, hardly believing the sight of them. Then suddenly, along came another just like him an' she winked her eye an' he thought, "Jaze, surely she can't be winkin' at me", but then he looked at his wings again an' saw that they were the same as hers; they shone like the colours of the rainbow, an' as he flapped them they lifted him up into the air to meet his lady love an' that poor, ugly creature knew that he was ugly no longer, but the most beautiful . . .'

'Creature in all Ireland!' finished Rosanna. 'Oh, Gramps, you do tell such lovely stories. Who told them to you?'

'My father. He was a grand class of a man for the tales.'

'Tell us about him,' ordered Rosanna, making herself more comfortable on his knee.

'Ah, I don't fall for the old coddum that easy! 'Tis just

a ploy to keep ye from your beds a while longer. Ye know all there is to know about my old dad.'

Rosanna swore she had forgotten and Patrick laughed. 'Rosanna Feeney, I know you inside out. Ye're always trying to get round this old duffer.'

'Oh, just another five minutes.' Belle joined her plea to Rosie's. 'It's the only bit of fun I have all day.'

Patrick's smile lost a little of its buoyancy. The child was right there. He hoped Erin would think the end product was worth robbing Belle of her childhood. 'Ah, all right, colleen, but if your mother comes for ye then ye must go.'

'I wish my mother had gone away like Rosie and Nick's,' said Belle petulantly. Sonny had gone to Nottinghamshire to carry out a commission, taking Josie and baby Elizabeth with him. He would be busy for many weeks as the job involved turning the plain ceiling of a mansion into a masterpiece.

'Belle, that's a wicked thing to say!' reproved Patrick. 'After all she's done for you. Ye know ye'd miss your mammy if she wasn't here.'

I wouldn't, thought Belle. I hate all this work she makes me do. But she lowered a remorseful face to her chest. 'I'm sorry, I didn't mean it. Will you tell us about your father and when you were a litle boy? Please.'

Patrick scratched his head. ''Tis hard to remember such a long time back.'

'How old are you, Gramps?' asked Rosanna. 'Nick says you're ninety-three but I said more like seventy-three.'

'Oh, that's enormously kind o' ye,' said an indignant grandfather and diverted their inquisitiveness with another of his Irish tales.

'It must be lovely in Ireland,' said Rosie dreamily. 'Why did you come here?'

He breathed out the old sadness. 'There was a terrible disease came one night and killed all the praties. We were starving.'

'Didn't you have any biscuits to eat?' enquired Nick.

Patrick gazed down at his scrubbed and innocent face.

That was the extent of his grandchildren's knowledge: when you were hungry you ate a biscuit until it was dinner-time. Patrick thanked God it was so, but nevertheless wanted them to know that it hadn't always been thus for this family. 'We didn't have any biscuits, Nick. We didn't have cake, we didn't have bread even. Just the praties. Our livelihood depended on the potato an' when the blight came it killed every pratie in Ireland in the one week. Imagine that.' He looked into each attentive face. 'Think what it would be like if Mrs Howgego suddenly decided to stop cooking and Abigail wouldn't get the groceries in. The larder would soon be empty, would it not? Think of the noises your bellies would make when ye opened the larder door an' saw only empty shelves. What would ye do then?'

'I'd dismiss Cook and Abigail,' said his grandson emphatically, 'and go round to the shop myself.'

'But where would ye get the money?'

'I'd ask you for some,' answered the boy logically.

'But what if I refused to give it to ye – besides, there were no shops where I came from.'

'We could always go and ask one of our neighbours for some food,' donated Belle.

Another obstacle. 'Your neighbours are in the same pickle.'

The children looked to each other for an answer. Patrick provided it. 'I'll tell ye what ye do – ye starve, an' then ye die.'

'But, you're still here, Gramps,' pointed out Rosanna.

'I'm here.' Patrick loosened his grip on her to point a finger at the floor. 'But I'm not where I was born. I'm in a foreign country. The only way I and most of the others who survived did so was to leave our Mother country and go to America or England where we might find work. Many of those who stayed to weather the blight perished; they looked like skeletons.'

'Did your father die?' asked Belle quietly.

Patrick looked at her and his eyelids lowered in affirmation. 'I think so. I never heard no more of him. The last I remember is the old man shoving his harp at me – that's the one your mammy taught ye to play, Belle. Faith, he loved that thing . . . I neither heard nor saw of him again.'

'Will you go back some day?' queried Rosanna.

'Oh, I don't know. I always said I would but sure I'm getting old now an' I seem to've collected so many things around me that I'm not certain I'd want to leave.'

'You could go for a holiday,' suggested Belle brightly. 'And take me. I'd love to see Ireland.'

'Oh, so would I,' issued Rosanna, piqued that Belle had said 'take me' and not 'us' as she would have done. Rosie loved to hear her grandfather speak of the land he so obviously ached for. It appeared to her as some magic land in a fairytale – Paradise, Utopia.

'An' Ireland'd love to see you, I'm sure,' said Patrick, rubbing his cheek to hers.

Just then the door opened and Erin came in. There was the usual chorus of protest. 'Never mind all that,' she told them. 'Bedtime. Come on now, before Nan gets in. She'll be cross if she has to put up with your chattering after a hard day's work.'

'Could I go out with Grandfather tomorrow?' asked Belle hopefully. 'Just for a little while.'

'No, I'm afraid not. Ye'll need to catch up with the work ye missed today. Mr Ingleton wasn't too pleased, I can tell ye, when he found ye'd skipped lessons to go the fair.'

Belle turned to Patrick for support, her eyes pleading, but Patrick merely kissed her. 'Go on now, be a good girl for your mammy. We'll have another outing one o' these days.'

Belle looked up at her mother. 'Is my father dead?'

Erin was startled. This was the first reference Belle had ever made to Sam. True, she herself had not wanted to remind the child of her loss and so had not mentioned him, but once Belle had gained the power of speech Erin had been expecting some query. There had been none.

When her mother did not answer immediately the child added, 'Gramps' father died – did mine die too?'

211

Erin glanced at Patrick, then, after a second, nodded and gave a quiet, 'Yes.'

'Will I get another one?'

'No.' Her mother was quite definite.

Belle was used to getting what she asked for. 'I want one.'

'Well, ye can't have one!' When the little girl demanded to know why, Erin said, 'Some people have fathers an' some don't. That's all there is to it. Now come on to bed.'

Belle didn't appear to be too perturbed at this refusal and wished her grandfather goodnight.

'Goodnight, my pet. Goodnight, Nick. 'Night, Rosie darlin'. Sleep tight.'

Left alone with only his pipe he began to chew over his memories, pretty soon feeling downright maudlin. Where was Tommy? Was she out with that Farthingale fellow? Damn, it was no good sitting here wondering, she'd do as she pleased anyway. He would pay Liam a call. He wasn't due to visit until Sunday but was sure he would receive a warm reception from his old friend.

Poor Father Kelly, bedridden for some time now due to his ulcerated leg, was enormously pleased to have any company, especially Patrick's. He slapped his newspaper on the bed in delight as the housekeeper showed the visitor in.

'Pat, me boy! Ah, God love ye this is a surprise. 'Twasn't till Sunday I was expecting to see anybody. Sit down, sit down.' He watched fondly as Patrick hauled a wicker chair up to the bedside and lowered his bulk into it.

'Ah well, I can't be accused of philanthropy, Liam, I'm afraid,' said his guest, smiling. 'I have an ulterior motive for coming.'

'If it's my money you're after then ye've wasted your shoe leather,' Liam told him. 'I've not seen so much as a half-farthing for weeks. Father Gilchrist sees to all my wants – or so he'd have ye believe. Have ye ever seen a man suffering from unrequited thirst? Well, you're looking at one now. Not a drop have I tasted since last Tuesday.

He's forbidden Mrs Lucas to bring me any liquor, says 'tis bad for the leg and my soul, the hound.'

'It came to my ears that ye're also suffering great pain from colic.' Patrick tugged a flask from his pocket. 'So I brought ye a bottle o' Yellow Mixture. 'Tis very efficacious for the windipops, so they tell me. I never touch the stuff meself.'

Liam crossed himself. 'Oh, chivalry beyond expectation,' and untopped the flask. 'Go have a spy on the landing, Pat, will ye? See if Funny Franks the Laughter Manufacturer is about.'

Patrick opened the door a crack and peered to right and left. 'You're safe, old lad. Oil your tonsils.'

'Sláinte.' Liam gave the flask a brisk upwards tilt, then gasped as the whiskey stung the back of his throat. 'Ah, God, that's wonderful.' He leaned over to his bedside table and took up an empty glass, using that for his next measure and handing the flask back to its owner who employed the tiny silver cup that went with it.

'I'll just take a drop, I'd not deprive a parched man.'

Liam watched over his glass. 'A veritable martyr. Now, ye said ye had an ulterior motive for coming.'

Pat gave a crooked smile. 'Ah, not really. 'Tis just that I was sat there all on me own an' it made me think of you. So, I thought us two old soaks ought to get together.'

'Less o' the "old" business.' Liam held out his glass for a refill. 'Tommy still as busy as ever?'

'Aye.' Pat spoke into his drink, then rolled the whiskey around his tongue, savouring it. 'Ah, hell, Liam, 'tis no good, I'll have to get it off me chest. I think . . . well, I think it may not be just work that's keeping her out late.'

'Another man?'

Patrick nodded glumly and leaned his elbows on his knees. 'We were going to have such a lovely afternoon at the fair. I persuaded Erin to let Belle out of her manacles for an hour an' we all went off to collect Tommy at the store. It was when one o' the boys there mentioned the name . . . I'd never heard Tommy mention it herself.

When I asked her about the man I nearly got me ears chewed off.'

'Did she admit to having a relationship with this man?'

'She'd hardly do that, would she?'

'Was there any hint from the boy who divulged the man's name – what was it by the way?'

'Farthingale, Francis Farthingale. Sounds like somebody out of a bloody nursery rhyme. No, as far as anybody else is concerned – me too at first – he's just a business colleague. But the way she flew at me when I broached the subject made me think there's more to it.'

'What d'ye intend to do?'

'I'm buggered if I know. I'm getting a bit long in the tooth for the bunching stakes.' Patrick stared out of the window at the beautiful summery evening.

Liam syphoned his glass and picked up the flask again, swilling it about to test the volume of its contents. 'It's no good, ye'll have to get a bigger flask than this, Pat. 'Tis a spit on a sponge to one so desiccated. May I?'

Patrick indicated that the priest was welcome to take whatever there was, his own glass barely touched. Liam placed the replenished glass on the bedside table showing, he considered, great restraint.

'I'll have to make that last. It'll probably be the only one I get for a while. Funny how the stuff hits ye when ye've suffered so much enforced abstinence. I feel quite impish. Now then, about this woman o' yours. Ye say ye've not met the man?' Pat shook his head. 'Well, I'm pleased to say I can enlighten ye.'

'You've met him?' Pat was instantly alert.

'I have – though it was two years ago an' only the once. But 'twas enough for me to form an impression. He presented himself as an intelligent and sensible chap, a little older than yourself I'd hazard. I had quite a long confab with him about the state o' the city's churches. I recall his deep concern at the amount of mediaeval architecture that was being indiscriminately razed. Got quite passionate about it.'

'That would follow,' mused Pat. 'She said she'd met him at the Architectural Society.'

'He also spoke briefly about his wife . . .'

'He's married, then?'

'He was at the time, but I doubt he will be now. She was dying, poor woman. I never heard anything afterwards but I should say he's almost certainly a widower. Though I made him to be a man of the utmost integrity, I doubt he'd stoop to stealing another's wife. 'Tis my thinking you're doing them both a dishonour.' Liam's hand shot out in a playful cuff at Patrick's bent head. 'Come on, Pat, ye know where your jealousy landed ye before.'

Patrick remained grim-faced. 'I had just cause to be jealous that time.'

'Perhaps, but I think in this instance 'tis your wild imagination leaping to conclusions – the wrong ones. Why don't ye invite the man to your home? Ye'll soon see if there's anything going on.'

Patrick grinned then. 'That's a novel idea: a man inviting his wife's lover to dinner.'

'He's not her lover an' you know it, otherwise ye'd not be sat there laughing.' Liam used his last drink sparingly.

'D'ye know, I believe I'm getting worse with age,' proclaimed Patrick. 'I sat there at home visualising all sorts o' things. Thank God I've still a friend like you to knock some sense into me. Ah well now, less o' me. How's life treating *you* these days?'

'Diabolical,' replied Liam tartly. 'That man has taken my every pleasure – well almost.' He waved a newspaper at Patrick. 'I still manage to pick a few winners. Mrs Lucas helps in that quarter by taking my slips round to Danny Molloy's. Doesn't realise o' course. Poor soul thinks she's been entrusted with ecclesiastical missives.'

Patrick laughed heartily and consulted the paper. 'Let's see what himself is tipping for tomorrow.'

'Don't waste your eyesight, the fella couldn't tip a bucket o' slops.'

'Have ye had any winners yourself lately?'

Liam replied that he was due to pick up four pounds

ten. 'Listen, if I pass on the benefit of my knowledge of horseflesh for tomorrow would ye crave me a boon, kind sir?' He pulled a piece of paper from beneath his pillow. 'Take this to Danny's an' collect me winnings. I think Father G. is getting suspicious of all Mrs Lucas' comings an' goings.'

'I'll fetch it on Sunday,' promised Patrick, leaving the betting slip where Liam had dropped it on the bedspread.

'Don't bother. Ye can stop off at the King Willie an' exchange it for a month's supply o' gripewater.'

Patrick smiled reflectively. 'My, I haven't been near the place in years. I wonder if it still has the same clientèle.'

'It must've been hard for ye, breaking off with all your old pals,' ventured Liam, referring to the year the Feeneys' inheritance had taken them into a more favourable district. 'D'ye never see Molly Flaherty or any of the old crowd now?'

Patrick shook his head. 'Not since she turned up unexpectedly at Erin's wedding. I daren't show me face after the reception she got. Mother o'Mercy that's ten years ago.' Another shake of head. 'I expect you still see her from time to time though, an' Ghostie an' the others. How are they all?'

Liam's face looked its true age as sadness took over. 'You know as much as I do. I never get the chance to talk with them now. If my leg does allow me to get to Mass Father G. keeps me well out o' the way. Molly's still with us as far as I know. Ghostie passed on, God protect him, and Jimmy Ryan, Michael Flynn, Thomas Grogan . . . the list's endless. Isn't it strange? Here's me nudging ninety and still going, an' none o' them a day over sixty – some much less – all dead an' gone.'

'I wonder if their grandchildren have it any better than they did,' meditated Patrick. 'God, when I think o' some o' the places they lived in . . .'

Liam was grave. ''Tis no better. They're still living in hovels that should have been condemned forty years ago. Ye can imagine what they're like now.'

''Tis time they blew the whole bloody place up,' said

Patrick strenuously. 'Somebody ought to do something about it.' He caught the slight arch to Liam's brow and hung his head sheepishly. 'Aye, you're right, Liam, I've no cause to be shouting the odds. Me, with my big fancy house an' full table, my servants, strong, healthy grandchildren who've never known hunger like we did. If anybody should be doing something about it then 'tis me; me who upped an' left my friends fifteen years ago an' never spared a thought for them since. I blamed that on Tommy wanting to act like a lady, but if I'd really given a damn about them I wouldn't've let that stop me.'

'Your trouble, Pat, was that ye felt ye didn't fit in anywhere. Am I right?' Pat nodded. 'Your old friends saw ye in your smart clothes an' felt awkward with ye, as ye did amongst them. Yet ye've not quite managed to make the same transition as your wife. Her friends intimidate ye with their impeccable manners and conversations about finance, stocks an' shares, things ye have no interest in. So you're left in a state o' limbo with only a poor old priest who's got death-watch beetle, rising damp . . . an' terminal wind.' With these last words he grinned and examined his glass.

Patrick covered the wrinkled hand that lay on the counterpane. 'An' I'm glad I've got you, Liam. You're as dear as a father to me.'

'Stop it, you're making me cry.'

Pat slapped the hand affectionately. 'Ah, didn't we used to have some times? 'Twas hard but it was good. Everybody looked after each other. We might not have had much money but at least we were happy.'

'An' you're not happy now?'

Pat shrugged. 'I'm not exactly unhappy; the children see to that. God, I love those bairns, Liam. I do wish Erin could be more flexible; she's driving that child much too hard. Matter o' fact we had a bit of a set-to over it this morning . . . Sam's death altered her, ye know. I often wonder, if Belle's intelligence hadn't come to light, just how long Erin would've lasted. She seems to live for nothing else but to see that child through her education.'

217

'Education's no bad thing.'

'Thomasin's words, and I'd agree – but in moderation, Liam, not the way Erin's been going about it. Belle never gets a moment to play unless it's on an instrument. No childish pastimes, her mother says.'

'Listen, ye'll have to bring the girl along some time. Tell Erin I've asked to hear the old harp – it'd not be a downright lie, I'd love to hear the girl play like her mother used to, but maybe we'll find time to indulge in a little childish pastime, too.'

The two men sat in silence for a spell, Patrick's lower lip jutting out as he mused. 'Ye know, I think ye got it right when ye said I was in limbo. I can't come to grips with meself lately. Don't know what it is. I can only describe the feeling as restless. I feel as if I'm not doing an honest day's work, just overseeing the men. There should be something more . . . an' then there's this business with Tommy. I see less an' less of her these days, Liam. Ever since the fire when we lost Dickie she's taken to wearing this armour. Ye can't see it but sure as hell the minute ye put out a hand to touch her 'tis there. It's so obvious ye can almost hear it clanking. 'Tis as if she blames me for Dickie's death.' He tossed the remainder of his drink into his mouth. 'Oh come on, don't get me on that one again. I came here to be cheered up.' He snatched up the paper again. 'Are ye going to let me have those winners for tomorrow, then?'

Liam winked and rummaged under his pillow again. 'Get those copied out.' Another slip of paper floated onto the coverlet. 'An' ye can put my money on at the same time, take it out of my winnings.'

Patrick rubbed his hands, then reached into his pocket for pipe and tobacco. 'Will ye join me, Liam? I've a spare one here some place.'

'Patrick Feeney, you're procuring this young fella to evil ways.' Liam accepted the clay pipe, plugged it with his friend's tobacco and lit up. The room was infused with a perfumed haze. 'Ah, heaven indeed.' Liam sighed content-edly, pipe in mouth, glass in hand, and relaxed against his pillow. 'Ye're a good pal, Patrick, I shall miss ye when I go.'

Patrick continued the conversation as he copied Liam's tips into a notebook. 'Is there anything else you're in need of, apart from more medicine?'

'If it's in your power to order a thunderbolt for Father G. I'd be in your eternal debt. My powers of persuasion seem to be failing me lately. God, the man gets worse. He's well-named I can tell ye: Gilchrist – servant of Christ. Sure, I've never met anyone quite so pious. I'll bet he even pees Holy Water, God forgive the blasphemy. 'Tis a real eye-opener to see him working on the Bishop, Pat. I got a visit from himself the other day, just to see if I'd expired or anything. Father G. didn't dare let the man out of his sight, crawling round his ankles like a fawning dog. I tell ye, the Bish wouldn't need his shoes cleaning for a week after he left here. Ah,' he relented slightly, 'he's not such a bad bloke himself, 'tis just this aching leg making me say all these uncharitable things. He brought me some books to read, seemed genuinely concerned about my state of health. No, 'tis Father G. that poisoned his mind, making out he was worried about the job being too taxing for me. The Bishop is an artless soul, he didn't realise he was being manipulated.'

'He'd best watch out,' said Pat. 'Father G. will be having his job next.'

'Well, that's the odd thing about the fella – oh, if it were only the one – he's not ambitious. Well, when I say that you're to take it very loosely. No, I don't believe he has any wish to go further up the ecclesiastical ladder because promotion would detract from his role of humble parish priest, sacrificing his all for the sake of his God. D'ye know the man's never off his knees. There's a great dint in front of the altar where he kneels. Every Mass the hollow gets more worn an' he sinks lower an' lower. Won't be long before he's taking Mass from the crypt. Sure, we'll have to start a fund for the restoration of the church. D'ye know, Pat, he makes me feel like Barabbas he's so bloody good.'

'Nobody's that good, Liam. Ye can be sure he'll come unstuck one o' these days.'

'Aye, that's what I keep telling meself. Ye can cover a pile o' horsemuck with roses but the smell will always creep through to tell ye 'tis still a heap o' shi . . . ah, hello, Father Gilchrist! Weren't we just discussing your good self.' The subject of Liam's discontent had made a sudden entry, nostrils quivering at the clouds of tobacco-smoke that swirled like fog around his head.

'I was unaware that you had visitors, Father.' The younger priest's eyes alighted on the flask and glasses.

Liam saw the look of disapproval. He stuck his pipe between amused lips and crossed his arms over his chest. 'I'm sorry ye didn't come sooner, I'm unable to offer you any sustenance now.'

'You are quite familiar with my views on alcohol, Father,' replied the other sternly, coming further into the room and addressing himself now to Patrick. 'Mr Feeney, if your visits to Father Kelly are to continue might one request that you do not pollute his sickroom with tobacco-smoke?' He crossed to the window and flung it open. 'And I must also protest strongly at my house being turned into a taproom. I specifically asked Father Kelly to discontinue his unworthy penchant for liquor. He is a very ill man. You are, I believe, supposed to be a friend of his? Then you will do him the utmost benefit by restricting your habits to your own home.' He was about to move on when he spied the betting slip on the bed. His face turned white as he picked it up between thumb and forefinger. 'And what, pray, is this?'

'Sure, you're holding it as though I've wiped me arse on it,' slurred Liam, the whiskey coarsening his tongue. ''Tis only a list of horses' names.'

'I can see very well what it is,' replied Father Gilchrist, his face advertising his repugnance of the gutter language employed by the old man.

'Oh, you use Danny Molloy too, d'ye?' asked Liam mischievously. Patrick, biting his lip, sat awkwardly between the two.

'Father Kelly, I regard this as a serious matter! I refuse to allow my house to be used for immoral purposes.'

Liam feigned shock. 'God, don't tell me Mrs Lucas has taken to peddling her body?'

The young priest turned on Patrick. 'Mr Feeney, I must insist that you leave as you are obviously the instigator of Father Kelly's unseemly behaviour.'

'Just a moment, Father . . .' began Patrick.

'Do you deny that it was you who smuggled tobacco and liquor in here?' demanded Father Gilchrist.

'That's an odd choice of word, Father. I merely brought them as gifts for my old friend. He doesn't seem able to obtain them in his own house.'

The priest tucked in his chin. 'Mr Feeney, what sort of a man is it that encourages a sick and ageing priest in these demoralising pastimes?'

Patrick laughed uncomfortably. 'Father Gilchrist, 'tis only a pipe an' a glass o' good whiskey.'

'And what of this?' Father Gilchrist flourished the betting slip. 'Will you deny that this is yours?'

Before Patrick could answer Liam slurred gaily, ''Tis mine, Mr Feeney was simply doing me a good turn by collecting my winnings.'

'The devil's disciple reaping the harvest of vice.' Father Gilchrist's voice was an accusing hiss. 'Are you both not ashamed to admit to such dealings? And you, Father Kelly, a man of the cloth.'

'Not any more,' replied Liam, losing his befuddled smile, becoming hard. ''Twas you who robbed me of my bit o' cloth, Father.'

'That is most unjust of you,' returned the other in a hurt voice. 'You are a sick man, Father. It would be inconceivable that you be expected to carry on with your ministerings in such a condition.'

'I am sick, yes!' spat Liam. 'Sick to bloody death o' you telling me that all this is for me own good. There's only one person gained from me being stuck in this bed – an' that's you.'

'Father Kelly!' The other priest lost his calm and his

voice rose above the normal low disapprobation. 'I would ask you to remember that you remain in this house at my intervention. You would have been at the workhouse, were it not for me. It is my home which you defile with your ungodly pursuits.'

Liam turned to Patrick. 'If this is what we get for having an innocent tête-à-tête we might as well make it worth our while an' have a couple o' women in here next time.'

Father Gilchrist surrendered the last shreds of self-control. He launched himself at Liam, calling him a worthless priest and a disgrace to his vocation. 'I will no longer honour you with the title Father! You will burn in Hell for your defilement of the cloth. I am going to speak to the Bishop about this. My charity does not extend to seeing my house so ill-used.' He turned to go.

'Oh, Father,' called Liam pleasantly. The priest spun round. 'Don't be forgetting to take your hammer and nails.'

'God, you're a terrible man,' said Patrick as the door slammed. 'I hope you're well-stocked with asbestos.'

Liam sighed at his empty glass, then put it aside. 'A few years ago his words might've frightened me but not any more. When I throw myself on Our Lord's mercy I trust He'll be the same person I've been taking orders from for the last seventy years. He'd not commit a man to the eternal flame for enjoying a couple o' glasses o' fine whiskey.' He took his friend's hand. 'Pat . . . I want ye to make me two promises.'

'Anything.' Patrick squeezed.

'After I'm gone . . .'

'Aw, Liam . . .'

'No, listen. After I'm gone I want ye to promise that however much Father Gilchrist annoys ye, ye won't let him drive ye from the church. It took me a long time to coax ye back into the fold after the last upset, I'll not be here to do it again. Please, Pat, promise me ye won't give up on the faith. Change your place of worship if ye like. The priest at St George's now is a lovely man, nothing like McNaughlty. Do this for me, son.'

Patrick inclined his head with a quiet promise.

'Ah, that's good.' Liam slapped the captive hand in gratitude. 'Now the other thing: I've always wanted to go back to my birthplace but the church has commanded my life. The only time I'm likely to get back there now is when I die. The favour I ask of ye is, will ye ship my body home when I'm gone? I've little money, as ye know . . .'

Patrick swiftly waved aside the need for money. 'But ye'll be with us a long time yet, Liam. Sure, I thought ye were trying for the century.'

'Maybe, maybe, but I'd rest easier in my mind if I knew I was going home to the place I love.'

'Sure, I'm more worried about the present situation,' said Patrick. 'The bugger won't jib at throwing ye out. Still, ye won't be short of a place to go, and yes, I'll do what ye ask, Liam.' He shook the liver-spotted hand, then chuckled. 'Has it crossed your mind that I could go first?'

'What, an' you a mere youngster of sixty-one? I don't think.' Liam smiled and kept a grip on Pat's hand, holding him also with a fond eye. 'Have you no itch to see the Old Country again, Pat?'

The other sighed. 'I have – desperately sometimes. But I'll probably be like you an' only go back in a box.' He released the old man's hand and began to rise slowly. 'I'd best make a move, Liam. 'Tis getting late.'

'Aye, your good lady'll likely be there to meet ye when ye get home.'

'Beat me, ye mean. I'll be round on Sunday with the old Yellow Mixture.'

'You do that. This colic o' mine seems to be getting worse by the second.'

Patrick gave the old priest a farewell smile and went downstairs to collect his hat from the hallstand. Father Gilchrist intercepted him before he reached the front exit.

'Mr Feeney.' Patrick turned unsmiling eyes on the priest. 'It is regrettable that I must ask you not to call on Father Kelly any more. I feel that you are an adverse influence.'

Patrick had to laugh, but the sound was not one of

223

amusement. 'Ye can ask all ye like, Father, but I shall still be here on Sunday all the same.'

'The door will be barred to you.'

'Then I'll just have to break it down, won't I?' answered Patrick breezily. 'Goodnight to ye.'

Thomasin was not in the drawing room when he arrived home. At first he thought she was still out and his temper returned, but on his way up to their room he spotted the jacket she had been wearing tossed carelessly over the mahogany stand. His entry to the bedroom brought her sleepy eyes to the door. He closed it gently and moved across the flowered carpet to disrobe.

'I thought you were in bed,' she disclosed. 'That's why I came up. Where've you been?'

He glanced at her but said nothing as he tugged the dark-brown cravat from his neck.

She was quiet for a while, watching him undress, then said, 'I'm sorry about this afternoon, Pat. I had no reason to go for you like that.'

'Didn't ye?' He sat on a chair to pull off his boots which he left where they had fallen. 'Will ye tell me there's nothing between you an' this Farthingale?'

'No, I won't tell you that,' she responded honestly. 'But it's not what you're imagining. Francis is still in love with his wife – she's dead, by the way.'

'I know, Liam told me.' Patrick continued to disrobe.

'Oh, you've been discussing me.' The statement bore a spattering of annoyance.

'I was worried about ye. I needed to discuss it with a friend.'

'That's something we all need; a friend to tell our troubles to. Patrick, I'm fifty-five years old, isn't it time you stopped regarding every male I talk to as if he's going to steal my virtue? Francis is my friend as Liam is yours, nothing more.'

He was naked now. She thought what a marvellous physique he had for a man of his years and wished her own body had weathered so well. There was no loose

224

flesh on his stomach, no pouches of fat to hang over his waistband. His limbs, if not as muscular as they had been at thirty, nevertheless were still firm; when he moved there was no tripe-like wobble. He climbed into bed. Choosing not to lie down he jacked himself on one elbow and looked down at the small face on the pillow. 'There used to be a time when we didn't need anyone else to talk to but each other.'

Her grey eyes remained fixed to the ceiling. 'That seems like a long time ago.'

'It does. Liam an' me were just going over old times tonight.' His fingers selected a piece of ribbon on her nightgown which he used as a plaything as he talked.

'How is Liam?'

'The leg's still troubling him but not as much as Father G. does. I've been warned not to go again.'

She perused him sleepily. 'Why?'

'Oh, 'tis just Father Gilchrist's way o' showing his authority.' He had a sudden urge to cup her cheek in his palm and gave in to it. 'What have you been doing with yourself?'

'I've been at a YAS meeting.' She frowned. 'I hope all this fund-raising we're doing for Saint Crux will put paid to the gossip about pulling it down. Francis is very worried.'

He stroked her cheek with a leather-like thumb. 'Is that why you're so fond o' this Farthingale, because he shares your passion for preserving history?'

'Partly,' she divulged. 'But also because he's a very nice man. He's been a tremendous help to me. You'd like him, I'm sure.'

'Then why don't ye invite him for dinner some evening?' he suggested.

She smiled, grateful and not a little surprised at this softening. 'Why thank you, I will.'

He kissed her then. She folded an arm round his neck and stroked the hair at his nape with a forefinger. His lips became fired and his hands moved under the blankets to wander over her body. They made love then, not with the passion of their youth but with an unhurried languor born

225

of familiarity. Afterwards, listening to Thomasin's soft snores, he experienced the act again in his mind. She had denied him nothing – as loving as ever – but he was troubled.

He might still be in possession of her body, but her mind belonged to someone else.

CHAPTER FIFTEEN

Abigail sighed noisily as one of the bells on the rack jingled for the third time in thirty minutes. 'Don't tell me, Mrs Howgego.' She wiped her hands on her apron. 'I don't have to look to see it's Mrs Fenton's bell. I'm gonna be hearing bells in me sleep if this goes on much longer. I mean, how do they expect to have their luncheon on the table if I'm up and down stairs like a jack-in-the-box? I wouldn't mind if it were a genuine request she had, but when I get there all she'll want is to know what we're having for lunch an' what time it'll be served.'

The tendons on Mrs Howgego's arms stood out as she lifted the goose from the oven to baste it. The mistress had asked for a special luncheon to welcome back Mr Sonny and his wife who had come home for a weekend break. 'I don't know why she's bothered what's on the menu. All she does is push it round her plate and make a mess of it. You watch, this goose'll be too tough for her. A waste o' good food, I say.'

'You have to feel sorry for her though,' relented Abigail. 'Her teeth are that rotten. You can barely tell what she's sayin' what with all those cloves stuck in her mouth. Oh, all right!' Her impatience flared again at the persistent jingle. 'Keep your hair on. But if she asks me once more is the goose ready I swear I'll swing for her.' Puffing and sweating she worked her way up the numerous flights of stairs to Hannah's room, grasped the knob and pushed open the door. 'Yes, Mrs Fenton, what can I do for you this time?'

Hannah squinted shortsightedly. 'Is that goose cooked yet?'

Abigail swore under her breath. 'No, but yours will be if you keep draggin' me up an' down these bloody stairs for nowt.'

'Speak up, girl!' snapped Hannah. 'And come in. How do you expect me to hear you when you dangle about the threshold?'

'It's nearly ready, Mrs Fenton,' shouted Abigail, demurring the invitation, ready for flight. 'Can I get you anything else while you're waiting?'

'I've a raging toothache,' whined Hannah pitifully, her face wrinkled in pain. 'Bring me some fresh cloves.'

'I only brought them fifteen minutes ago, Mrs Fenton. They should still be effective.'

'Well, they're not, you impudent girl! Bring me some more, I tell you. And before you go you may pass me my sewing.' She indicated a half-finished garment on a bedside chair.

Abigail, biting back the sigh, went across the room to obey. 'Making anything nice are we, Mrs Fenton?' she asked pleasantly.

'My shroud,' replied Hannah. 'You may go now and on your way you will kindly ask my great-grandchildren if they will pay me the courtesy of a visit. They are back from church, are they not? Oh! and I should like my sheets to be changed when you bring up the cloves. These haven't been changed for a fortnight.'

– Yesterday, more like. Abigail compressed her lips. They were going to have to do something about that bladder of hers.

'And while you are in the linen cupboard,' added Hannah, 'you may as well fetch me a clean cap and night-gown. I think I shall take a bath before lunch.'

Abigail's heart sank. 'Would you like me to prepare the bathroom, Mrs Fenton?' she asked without optimism.

'Use a bath that every other member of the household

has used? Certainly not. I shall take my bath in here as usual.'

'Well, you may have to wait a while,' said Abigail as she made her escape before there were any more demands, and under her breath, 'I'm not lugging any baths up till I've seen to lunch.'

'I shall expect my bath in fifteen minutes,' said Hannah. 'Now kindly inform my great-grandchildren I require their company.'

Abigail flounced off to the schoolroom, 'Oy! Mrs Fenton wants to see you lot right away,' then disappeared, highly ruffled. As if she hadn't enough to do.

'Oh no, I hope she doesn't know it was us who stole her chocolates,' said Belle, hand over mouth.

Nick shook his blond head. 'No, all she knows about is how to piss the bed.' He had overheard Abigail saying this to Cook yesterday and had been waiting for an outlet for this knowledgeable remark.

'I wonder what she wants then,' said Rosanna, sitting on the window seat, legs bent under her, the Sunday-best dress crumpled from the tree-climbing expedition she had just undergone. They were supposed to be sitting here reading, but that was much too boring for Rosie. 'D'you think if we keep her waiting she'll forget about us?'

'I hope so,' replied Belle, running a thumbnail down the corner of the wall, thereby splitting the flowered paper. 'I can't bear the way she insists on calling me Isabelle, and the smell of her nearly makes me sick.' She reached the top of the skirting board and stood up, her eyes searching for a corner that had hitherto escaped her vandalism. 'Still, we could have some fun.'

'How?' asked Rosanna.

Belle's face was saturnine. 'We've got our silkworms from the fair, remember? We could put them in the box that held the chocolates and slip them back on her table.'

Rosanna was already anticipating the shrieks this would cause and wasted no time in helping put Belle's plan into practice. The dirty deed completed, the trio composed their expressions to that of dutiful angels and made for Great-grandmama's chamber.

'Ah, children!' exclaimed Hannah at their entry. 'How nice of you to come and see Grandmama. I see so little of my family now. There they all sit downstairs enjoying themselves but do they think of poor Hannah in her exile? They do not. Ingrates. Well, no matter when I have you! Come and sit by me and tell me how your schoolwork is progressing.'

Down in the steaming bowels of the house Abigail was giving vent to her outrage. Hannah's bell had sounded yet again. 'Well, I'm not answering it, Cook. She can hang on to her wet sheets for a while. If I don't get this veg. done they'll have no bloody lunch up there and then there will be fireworks.'

'I can't think how the old biddy manages to last so long,' said Cook, slapping away at the Yorkshire pudding mixture. 'She's had chill after chill. She had that bad do with her insides last year. There's been time after time when we all swore she was at death's door and still she comes bouncing back. She must have the constitution of an ox.'

'Perhaps a pole-axe might do the trick,' said Abigail darkly. 'By, if anybody said to me, give us a year's wages an' I'll do away with her for you, I swear it'd be money well-spent.'

'Oh, Abigail, you shouldn't wish anybody dead!'

'Well, God forgive me, but I do her.' Abigail still fumed. 'She's a bloody old nuisance an' for two pins I'd help to fill that bloody shroud she's sewing up there.'

During lunch Abigail was given an opportunity to voice her grievance. Sonny smiled apologetically as the maid reached for his plate on which lay a legion of untouched, rather burnt, peas. 'The rest was beautiful, Abi. A pity about the accident.'

She blushed. 'I'm ever so sorry, sir, but I just got ready to pour them into the tureen when Mrs Fenton rang. I thought I'd turned the gas off and put them back on the stove. When I got down they were nearly alight. Cook went wild. She said I'd spoilt the entire meal.' – Might as well rub it in, thought the maid. She's sure to ask about Mrs F.

Sure enough, 'I hope my mother isn't proving too much of a burden, Abi?'

'Well, ma'am . . . I wouldn't want you to think I'm complaining . . .'

'I wouldn't think that of you, Abigail, you're a very long-suffering soul. Come on, voice your opinion and we'll see what we can do.'

'Well . . . it's just that Mrs Fenton does tend to be a bit heavy on the bell, ma'am. I wouldn't mind if her requests were reasonable, but half the time when I get there she asks me something she asked five minutes before. I don't mind seeing to her, honestly, I'm not moaning, but there is the rest of the family's needs . . . then there's the delicate subject o' the sheets, ma'am.'

Thomasin gave an understanding nod. 'Yes, well we won't prolong that topic at the dinner table, I do know my mother is a fulltime job on her own and we can't expect you to have all that to see to on top of your own work. Don't worry any more, Abigail, I'm going to hire a nurse. I shall also inform my mother that in future she must only ring when it's absolutely necessary. If you go up to her after lunch there's no possible reason why she should disturb you again before afternoon tea. If she does, you have my permission to ignore the bell.'

'Thank you ever so much, ma'am.' Abigail began to serve dessert. 'I shouldn't want Mrs Fenton to distress herself, though.'

'I wouldn't dwell too much on that. My mother has a peculiar capacity for distressing everybody but herself. She's been provided with every comfort in that room, she must learn that this house does not revolve around her.'

'This is nice, Abi,' voiced Rosanna through a mouthful of trifle, and was reprimanded for her action.

The maid smiled and thanked her. 'I'm sure Cook will be very pleased to hear it – will that be all, ma'am?' After being told it would she bobbed and went down to tell Cook about her new instructions.

Josie wiped her tiny daughter's mouth, then settled back with her hands clasped over the dome that bespoke the coming of her second child. 'That was a lovely welcome, Mother. Our lodgings were comfortable but it's not like being at home, is it?'

Her husband voiced his accord and with a fond look at his elder children had the sudden urge to indulge them to make up for the enforced parting. He seized a bowl and spoon. 'Away – who's for more trifle?'

'Me,' replied Belle immediately.

'You would, young lady,' answered Erin and stopped her brother from depositing the spoonful of trifle in Belle's dish. 'I thought ye told me that Grandma had asked to listen to your reading?'

'Jazers, can ye not give the poor child a rest from all that work?' cried Patrick as Sonny transferred the dollop of trifle to another's dish.

'I'd hardly call reading a few lines to her great-grand-mother work,' responded Erin tartly.

'That shows how long it is since you paid her a visit,' put in Thomasin. 'I must remember to tell her to keep her hands off that bell this afternoon . . . though short of tying her arms to the bedposts I'm pressed for a solution.'

'I suppose I should take my turn at visiting her,' said Patrick half-heartedly. 'But sure, all she ever does is to pick holes in my grandchildren, then I get mad an' we end up fallin' out as usual. She's never happy unless she's got something to moan about, the grumbling old groat.'

Thomasin was forced to side with this. 'I did look in on her this morning but she was about as pleasant as a cow's husband – had raging toothache. I don't know about anyone else but I find myself tiptoeing past her door these days – not that it works. Her hearing's supposed to be going but by gum, she could hear ant droppings fall onto cottonwool when it suits her.'

'If Belle and I keep her company for a while that should give everyone else a rest.' Erin's words were reproachful.

'It wouldn't do if we all forgot about the poor soul.' She rose and held out her hand to the reluctant child. Josie asked if she would mind putting little Elizabeth down for a nap on her way to see Hannah. 'Certainly.' Erin plucked the child from her seat and continued on her way.

'See she doesn't keep you all afternoon,' warned Thomasin as Erin was leaving. 'It isn't often this family's all together. I had hoped we could have a nice chinwag before Sonny and Josie have to go back.'

Erin promised she wouldn't be more than half an hour. 'But if a grandchild can't show some compassion for her old grandmother I don't know who will.'

Patrick rose too. 'Don't tell me you're deserting us as well?' exclaimed his wife.

He could have offered sarcasm on her habitual absences but didn't. 'I said I'd go see Liam. But I'll be back well before Sonny leaves – always allowing that Father G. will let me over the threshold in the first place.' After a consultation of his watch he kissed his two remaining grandchildren, pressed a hand to Josie's plump shoulder and left.

Hannah was asleep when Erin and her daughter entered, but Belle's relief didn't last long. 'Ah, Erin dear!' The crackling voice drew the tiptoers back into the room. 'How nice.'

'I'm sorry if we woke ye, Grandmother.' Erin hauled the child up to the old lady's bedside. 'Belle was just coming to read to ye.' She helped Hannah into a sitting position and plumped her pillows.

'Sit down, dears.' Hannah indicated a raffia-seated chair with her spindly hand. 'Who is going to read to me? D'you say it is Rosanna?'

'No, Grandmother, Belle.'

'Who? Oh, you mean Isabelle.' The old lady squinted at the child in the white dress. 'Come and have a chocolate, dear.' Hannah's fingers hovered tremblingly over the box which Belle and the others had laced with silkworms that morning.

The child spoke hurriedly. 'It's very kind of you, Grandmama, but I've just had lunch. I really couldn't eat another thing.' The alarm in her eyes gradually receded as the old woman's hand moved away from the box to rest on the crimson counterpane. It would be dreadful if Grandma had opened the box in front of Mother.

'Why are you sitting all hunched up?' demanded Hannah suddenly. 'Spine straight, girl, knees together, hands in lap. Erin, your daughter will certainly need to improve her carriage.'

Belle tutted and narrowed her eyes. Erin elbowed her, then exchanged long-suffering glances. Hannah's mind did tend to wander lately. 'Grandmother, ye mustn't chastise Belle for what she can't help.'

Hannah looked puzzled for a moment, then her face cleared. 'Ah, yes, I remember now.' Her expression became one of mourning. 'Oh dear, such a tragedy that it should happen to this family – and Isabelle such a pretty girl, too. Much prettier than that tinker child. Does she speak?'

'Grandmother, ye know she does. Ye've just heard her! She's waiting to read ye a story.'

'Then why does she not get on with it?' replied Hannah maddeningly.

'I'm sure if we're both quiet Belle will begin, won't ye, dear?'

Hannah addressed Erin as Belle inserted both thumbs in the book and laid it on her knee. 'I haven't seen Samuel for some time, dear. Will he be coming today?'

Erin sighed. This was going to be a very long half-hour.

Abigail sat nibbling her nails as her eyes pored over the open copy of *Vengeance of the Vampire*. She had just reached a crucial moment in the bloodthirsty tale when Cook's voice encroached: 'Hadn't you better be making that tea?'

'Ooh, God, don't do that to me!' Abigail flopped back into the chair, then studied the clock on the mantel. 'By gum, I didn't realise it was that time.' She tucked the book behind a cushion and went to arrange the teapot and cream jug on a silver tray, pausing to ask, 'Is it me who's gone deaf, Cook, or is it a fact that Mrs Fenton's bell's never rung all afternoon?'

Cook tilted herself backwards in the rocking chair and held her stockinged feet to the fire. 'Aye, your little chat with the mistress seems to have worked. Get us another cup o' tea before you take that tray up, will you?'

Abigail complied. 'By, I'm glad they're eating out this evening. I don't fancy having to wash up after another big meal. Right, that's that.' She finished setting the two trays. 'I'll take Mrs Fenton's up first. We must be due for a tinkle soon.'

'Aren't you taking her any of my fruit loaf?' asked the cook. 'Poor old bird'll be feeling peckish I shouldn't wonder.'

'I certainly am not after what I got lumbered with the last time she had some. It's bad enough having wet sheets to contend with, without a pillowslip full o' tods.'

'Oh, Abigail!' Cook made a face, then laughed deep in her chest.

''S all very well you shouting "Oh, Abigail". You saw what state the wash tub was in after I put her sheets an' pillowcases in to soak. It were like apple-bobbing time. The mucky old bugger, can't she find nowhere else to hide 'em? It's bad enough normally but if she gets her hands on your fruit loaf I reckon it'll be a trowel job.'

The maid departed for Hannah's room, glad to find when she arrived the old lady sleeping peacefully. 'Eh, now shall I wake her?' she asked herself. 'If I take it back down she's sure to wake up in ten minutes, then I shall have to make another pot.' She made her decision and shook Hannah gently. 'Mrs Fenton, it's tea-time.' She rattled the cup in its saucer and clanked the spoon but none of these things succeeded in waking Hannah who lay propped against the lace pillows, jaw slightly agape.

Abigail tutted and shook her more forcefully. 'Mrs Fenton, time to wake u-up!'

Hannah slid sideways, one of her bony arms crashing onto the tray and knocking the cup askew.

'Oh, bloody Nora,' breathed Abigail. ''T'owd bugger's

234

dead.' She gnawed at the knuckle of her index finger, staring at the bed unable to move, then suddenly took control of herself and sped from the room, hurtling down the staircase.

Thomasin's expectant smile faded when a flustered maid burst into the room. 'Oh,' she said half-disappointedly. 'I thought it was my husband. I do hope he gets home before it's time for you to leave, Sonny. He gets talking about old times with Liam and clean forgets about anyone else.'

Abigail hopped from foot to foot. 'Oh, ma'am!'

The air of disaster brought Thomasin to her feet. 'What is it? Something's happened.'

'It's Mrs Fenton, ma'am,' stammered the maid behind her fingers. 'Oh, ma'am – I'm ever so sorry.'

'Sonny.' Thomasin held out her hand to her equally-alarmed son who took it and led her briskly towards the door. The others made to follow. 'No!' Thomasin motioned them back to their seats, then, apprehension putting a brake on her swiftness, she followed her son and the maid up to Hannah's room.

'Oh, Cook! Whatever am I going to do?' wailed Abigail on her return to the kitchen. 'It's all my fault. I wished her dead. How am I goin' to tell the mistress I killed her ma?'

Cook placed a cup of tea in front of the sobbing maid and patted the quaking shoulder. 'Now, now, Abi, don't let your imagination carry you off. Mrs Fenton was an old woman. She was bound to go soon. You had nowt to do with it.'

Abigail was not to be appeased. 'But Cook, I once read a book that said you can do harm to a person just by wishing it. It must've been me. I've been playin' holy-hell about her all week, saying she's a moaning old bugger . . .'

'Abigail Bickerdike, for the last time it wasn't you! By, I always said it were book-learnin' that caused all the troubles in the world an' I were right. You're a housemaid not a bloomin' scholar. You remember your place, stay

235

away from them books in future. Here, where is it?' She tugged Abigail away from the chair-back in order to lift the cushion. Seizing the book which Abigail had been reading earlier she tossed it onto the fire. 'There! An' that's what'll happen to any more I find. Blasted nonsense.'

A more subdued Abigail sipped her tea, but she still blamed herself and knew she would never sleep until she had thrown herself on Thomasin's mercy . . .

She was not alone in her guilt feelings. In the school-room three worried children were debating the issue.

'It was all your fault,' Rosie accused Belle. 'You were the one who had the idea of putting the silkworms in the chocolate box.'

'How was I to know she'd eat them?' protested Belle, then looked to Nick for support. 'Should we own up?'

'Oh, it's all right for you saying that!' snapped Rosanna. 'You're not the one who'll get the blame, even though it was your idea. You *never* get the blame.'

'Might we get sent to prison?' asked Belle fearfully.

'It depends on who we own up to,' said Nick thought-fully. 'I think it should be Grandad. He'd never let us be sent to prison.'

'He's right,' said Rosanna to her cousin. 'And as you're the one who started this you can be the one to tell him. Come on, we'll come with you.'

'He's not back from Father Kelly's yet,' hedged Belle.

'Never mind, that'll give us more time to think of what we're going to say.' Nick stretched and yawned. He of the three of them was the least concerned. 'Don't worry, Belle, Grandad won't be mad. He didn't like Grandma either.'

'Oh, I do wish your father would hurry,' said Thomasin tearfully. She and her son were once more in the drawing room along with Josie. What an awful thing it was to have to tell the children. Still, they had taken it well. She looked at the clock for the tenth time since re-entering. 'It's almost time for you to leave and I've not the slightest idea of what to do about poor mother.'

'You don't think we're going back now, d'you?' asked

236

Sonny. 'We'll stay until after the funeral. Now don't worry, everything's taken care of. The doctor should be here any minute.'

'And much good he'll do her – oh, Sonny!' She clasped his hand. 'It's my fault Mother's dead. I was the one who told Abigail to ignore the bell. What a way to treat your own mother.'

Sonny was in the act of trying to comfort her when Patrick entered, his face drawn. 'Abigail's just told me.' He came straight to Thomasin. 'She's taken the doctor up.'

'Oh, he's here then?'

'Yes . . . Tommy, I'm sorry I wasn't here. How did it happen?' He sat beside her, presenting a stalwart shoulder of which she took advantage.

'It was all my fault,' she wept. 'I told Abigail to take no notice if Mother rang, and I never went to visit her after lunch as I'd promised. The poor woman. She could've been ringing for someone all afternoon and we all ignored her.'

'That's not true, Father,' Sonny told him. 'Abigail definitely said that Grandma hadn't rung since just after lunch. Nobody could've known.'

'They could if they'd taken the trouble to look in on her,' sobbed his mother. 'But I warned everyone to keep away. Let her stew, I said, she's had enough attention for one day. What sort of daughter am I?'

Patrick dotted her shoulder with comforting pats. 'Tommy, Hannah was an old lady. She could've gone at any time. Now confess,' he held her from him and spoke into her tear-stained face, 'ye've been expecting it to happen for a long time.'

She nodded and sniffed. 'I suppose so – but I can't help feeling guilty.' With a hiccuping sigh she wiped her eyes and put away her handkerchief. 'Well, there'll have to be arrangements made. I've not the slightest idea . . .'

Sonny, interrupting, told her not to worry, he would conduct the funeral plans. Thomasin thanked him and sighed again. 'Life must go on, mustn't it? Josie, would you ring for some more tea, please? Patrick, Sonny and Josie are staying on for a while.'

'I'm glad,' he nodded at his son. 'I only wish it could be for a happier reason.' Commenting on Josie's pregnancy he said, ''Tis odd, isn't it, how when one person leaves the world another comes into it.' Quite unexpectedly he covered his face with a hand, his posture one of deep grief.

Thomasin was stunned that Hannah's death had affected him so; he and her mother had never seen eye to eye. 'Sonny, get your father a drink quickly.'

Sonny hurried to pour a tumbler of whiskey whilst his mother tended the stricken Patrick. Racing over, drink in hand, he attempted to comfort his father. 'Here, get this down you, Dad.'

Patrick's hand slid from his racked face and reached out gratefully. His eyes were swimming. Not for a long time had his wife seen him like this. The whiskey consumed in one toss of his wrist he stared into the hollow glass. 'I'm sorry to have to add to your troubles, Tommy, but 'tis best I warn ye now. We could be getting a visit from the police.'

Everyone was obviously taken aback. First to come out of it, Sonny went to refill his father's glass. Patrick thanked him, tossing only half of it down this time. 'I had a bit o' trouble getting in to see Liam,' he told them, then broke off to ask, 'Where's Erin, by the way?' Thomasin told him his daughter, upset at the loss, was in her room. He nodded and went on, 'Mrs Lucas answered the door and informed me that she had orders not to let anybody in. While I was trying to coax a reason from her Father Gilchrist appeared and said that Father Kelly couldn't see me. He became quite abusive. He wasn't the only one, I'm afraid. I threatened to render his celibacy permanent unless he let me in to see my friend.'

'You did get in eventually, I take it?' said Thomasin.

'I did,' he answered. 'After the initial charade Father G. became unaccountably affable and showed me into the parlour. "He's in here today," he told me.'

'And was he?'

'Oh aye, he was in there,' said Patrick, then took a deep breath and held her with red-rimmed eyes. 'In a bloody coffin.'

CHAPTER SIXTEEN

Though the anticipated police visit did not materialise it came very close to doing so after Patrick and Father Gilchrist crossed swords at the church service for Father Kelly. The Irishman still attended the same church, determined not to be driven out and equally determined to carry out his friend's final wish that he be taken home for his burial. After much violent abuse and several visits to higher clergy from both parties, Patrick was granted permission and today had gone to Liverpool to see his old pal's earthly body safely onto the ferry. Liam had no relatives to meet him at the other end but all that had been carefully organised by Patrick, who had sent a letter to the priest of the parish where Liam was to be interred.

'Poor Gramps,' said Rosanna, twirling a pen between inky fingers as she and the others sat awaiting their tutor. 'He looked so sad when he left this morning. I wish there was something we could do to cheer him up.'

Patrick had put their minds at ease over the silkworm incident, revealing that the box containing them was still as they had left it on Hannah's bedside table. She had not been poisoned, after all. 'But it was very naughty to play such tricks on an old lady,' he had chastised gently. 'Ye must never do anything like it again.' When they had solemnly promised he had given his guarantee that no one else would hear of their mischievous deed. The box of suffocated silkworms had been committed to the dustbin.

'He must be awfully lonely without Father Kelly to talk

to,' said Belle. 'He hasn't any other friends besides us, has he?'

'It's not just Father Kelly's death that's upset him,' put in Nick knowingly. The others eyed him with interest. 'It's that friend of Nan's who's coming to dinner on Saturday – Fartingale or whatever they call him.'

The girls giggled, Rosanna rolling on her back in a most unladylike posture.

'Don't go calling him that to his face,' warned the boy. 'I just made that up because I don't like him. His real name is Farthingale. It's him that's making Grandfather such a misery. That's what he and Nan were arguing about at the fair when Nan went off in a huff.'

'But I don't understand,' complained his sister.

'Oh, you really are a dunce! Grandad's frightened that this Fartingale fellow is going to steal Nan from him.'

This gave rise to uproarious ridicule. 'But Nan's old! Old people don't elope.'

'Don't believe me, then,' replied Nick airily. 'I'm only repeating what I heard.' He turned his back and began to leaf through an atlas.

Rosanna chewed her lip and glanced at Belle. 'D'you think he could be right? It'd be awful if Nan left us.'

Nick spun round in his seat. 'Of course I'm right! It isn't just because of what I heard Nan say to Grandad, I heard this fellow's name mentioned at the store, too.'

'Who by?' asked Belle.

'George whatsisname.'

'Oh, I liked him, didn't you?'

'You like anyone who feeds your face,' scoffed Rosie, then adamantly, 'We've got to do something; help Gramps get rid of this man.'

'Leave it to me,' said Belle with a calculating smile. 'I'll think of something good.'

They grinned with intent, then stood to attention as their tutor came in.

Saturday arrived.

'Mr Farthingale's here, ma'am.' Abigail took the visitor's hat and cane as he stepped past her into the drawing room.

'Francis, do come and meet my husband.' Thomasin took the guest's hand and introduced him to Patrick, who sized him up warily before accepting the handshake. There was nothing here to suggest any physical attraction on Thomasin's part. Farthingale was an extremely thin man, emaciated one might even say, and his face held great cavernous hollows beneath the jutting cheekbones. The mouth was weak, the chin shallow. Yet the glowing sherry-coloured eyes belied all the other features; they mirrored an inner strength, reflecting Patrick's scrutiny with never a waver. The handshake was firm but brief. When it broke the two men continued to inspect each other for so long that Thomasin grew embarrassed and felt the warmth spread upwards from the low-cut neck of her dress.

'And this is my son John.' She directed Francis towards Sonny, acquainting him with the family nickname to save confusion during later exchanges. 'His wife, Josie.'

Farthingale smiled politely and inclined his head over Josie's hand, doing the same with Erin when introduced to her. Following this appetisers were passed around and Francis offered his condolences on the death of Thomasin's mother. 'I should not have taken offence, Thomasin, you know, had you sent word to cancel our dinner engagement. I hope my presence is no intrusion on your grief.'

Thomasin shook her head and spread out the skirts of her black dress. 'My mother was an old lady, Francis. Her death, though a shock, was not unexpected. One has one's own life to lead. Besides, it isn't as if this is a roisterous occasion, merely a quiet evening among friends and family.'

Francis inclined his head sympathetically, then trained his still warm eyes sharply on Patrick, who had been watching the couple closely. 'Your wife tells me that you are responsible for her store's supply of fruit and vegetables, Mr Feeney – or may I call you Patrick?'

Patrick was unshaken at being caught in his open inspection. 'Please do. Yes, that's correct, fruit, vegetables and oats.'

'You raise cereal too?' Francis sipped his drink.

'Only in a modest way. I did try growing wheat at one time. Trouble was I chose the wettest year I can ever remember to embark on my experiment. Lost the lot. But I have to say that oats've been pretty successful, even though I've only had the one harvest so far.'

'And what of your other crops?' asked the guest.

'Apples – cookers and eaters – currants, gooseberries, potatoes, carrots . . .'

'A wide variety, then. I expect it keeps you extremely busy. How many men do you employ?'

'Five – and seasonal extras. I don't know about it keeping me busy. They're the ones who do all the work.'

'But they require supervision,' said Francis. 'There's the administration, the rotation of crops to be worked out, fertilisation . . .'

'I don't regard lookin' after a bunch o' men as work,' corrected Patrick. 'Work is when you're holding a shovel in your hands.'

'You underrate yourself, Patrick. I should find your responsibility terribly exacting. All that worry about whether the elements were going to be kind this year, waiting for signs of leaf-rot and whatever. Oh no, I think you are too hard on yourself.'

Patrick slanted an eye at Thomasin whose face gave nothing away. It was as if she had said to her guest before his arrival, 'Butter him up, he's feeling sorry for himself.' He said aloud, 'What exactly do you do for a living, Francis? Thomasin mentioned you were a business colleague.'

'Of sorts – but not in the same league as your dear wife.'

'She also mentioned some sort of merger,' began Patrick, but the conversation was aborted by Abigail's entry. Dinner was served.

'Francis.' Thomasin gestured that she wished him to escort her to the dining room, which he did. Sonny and

Josie followed with Erin and her father bringing up the rear.

'He's very charming, isn't he?' said Erin as they passed through the hall.

'Yes, he is,' murmured Patrick, frowning, and meant it. He hadn't intended to like Farthingale but dammit the man was so very nice it had happened without Patrick being aware of it.

Francis assisted his hostess into her chair, then took his own, to her right. 'I must confess it is very pleasant to sit down at a family table after so long dining alone. Thank you so much for inviting me.' This mainly to Patrick.

'My wife's friends are always welcome at my table,' answered Pat. 'Have ye no family at all, Francis?'

'Oh, yes.' Francis arranged his napkin. 'I have four grown-up children with families of their own. Unfortunately, they all live some distance away and our meetings are not as regular as I would wish.' He looked around the table. 'You're most fortunate to have your family under one roof.'

'I doubt Abigail would agree with you there.' Thomasin smiled at the maid who hared round the large table. 'I really must get around to hiring another maid. It's ridiculous to employ all those assistants at the store and keep the house understaffed.'

'God love us an' save us!' Everyone's eyes were drawn to Patrick whose hand was wafting furiously at his mouth. 'I think 'tis a new cook we need, not a maid.' He snatched up his wine glass in an effort to douse the appalling taste of the soup he had been the first to sample.

'Patrick, whatever . . .'

'Don't eat the soup!' Patrick held up his hands warningly. 'Don't anybody touch it.'

Contrarily, Thomasin sipped a little from the edge of her spoon and immediately made a face. 'Oh, good heavens, that's appalling!'

'I told ye not to touch it.' The twist of Patrick's lips showed he had still not rid himself of the taste.

Abigail looked from one to the other in consternation

until Patrick ordered the bowls to be taken away, whence she hurriedly came to life.

'Let's have the next course, Abigail, and forget all about it,' said her mistress, then turned to a bemused Francis. 'I'm so terribly sorry, Francis. Cook's so good normally. I can't understand it.'

He asked her to think nothing of it and commented upon the meal which Abigail laid before him. 'This looks absolutely delicious.'

Unfortunately Francis, the first to taste this course, found that it was quite the opposite. The piece of succulent-looking beef in gravy tasted absolutely revolting. He gagged, unable to help himself and covered his face with his napkin, eyes streaming.

The others muttered solicitously over their untouched plates whilst Thomasin rose from the table to pour some water for her guest. Abigail stood there, mesmerised.

'Abigail,' Thomasin's voice made the servant tremble. 'Inform Cook that I wish to see her here immediately.'

The maid scuttled off to the basement, reappearing minutes later with a puzzled and apprehensive Cook.

'Ah, Mrs Howgego!' said Thomasin tartly. 'I wonder – would you care to sample the roast beef? It appears it is not up to your usual standard.'

'It was fresh this morning, ma'am,' said Cook. 'Lest that butcher's boy was lying to me.' She took a sliver of beef from Francis's plate. Instantly her bemused expression changed to one of disgust and, lacking her superiors' manners, spat it straight out into her cupped palm. 'Bloody Hell! Ooh, begging your pardon, ma'am, but it's revolting.'

'I quite agree, Cook, and I'm sure our guest does, too.'

'But, ma'am, I can't understand it!' bewailed the poor woman. 'It smelt lovely while it were roasting an' it was a good colour. I'm sure it wasn't off.' She dipped her fingertip into the gravy and licked it masochistically. 'Why, it's not the meat! It's that there what's the trouble – but I swear, ma'am, I don't know how it got to taste like that.'

'It wasn't only the gravy, Cook,' said Thomasin sternly. 'The soup was not up to your usual standard, either. I'm

244

very annoyed to say the least. For this to happen at any time would be off-putting but when we have a guest it is unforgivable.'

'Please don't concern yourself about me,' Francis managed to say through his discomfort.

'I'm so sorry, ma'am,' offered Mrs Howgego.

'So am I, Cook. I trust there'll be no more disasters like this?'

'Indeed no, ma'am.'

'Very well. Oh, and before you go,' she pointed to the lemon soufflé, 'can you put our minds at ease by testing a little dessert.'

Cook did so, informing her mistress that it was untainted, then left the room with Abigail.

'You haven't been messin' about with that food, have you?' she demanded as she marched across the hall. Abigail denied it strenuously. 'Well, summat funny's going on here an' I'm off to find out what it is an' when I do . . .' Her voice tailed off as she and Abigail took the stairs to the kitchen, but the children peering through the banisters caught the gist of it.

'Now look what you've done!' hissed Rosie to Belle. 'Cook'll never let us in her kitchen again if she finds out.'

Belle gripped a banister in each hand and peered concernedly through the gap. 'It's not working. He should've been going home by now.'

'Maybe he didn't even get to taste it,' suggested Nick. 'Maybe it was one of the others.' It would be awful if it were Grandad who had got the mouthful of Belle's concoction. 'I told you not to put it in everything, just his portion.'

'Don't be stupid,' snapped Belle. 'How could I do that when it was all in the same bowl? Anyway, it hasn't worked and we'll just have to think of some other way to get rid of him. Something more drastic.'

'I can't imagine what you must think of us, Francis,' said Thomasin when the unappetising meal was over. 'I really can't apologise enough.'

'Thomasin, Thomasin, do stop,' laughed Francis. 'The company alone is such a welcome change that the meal was purely incidental. I'm not about to break off our friendship just because of a little spoilt beef.'

'You're so understanding,' replied his hostess, then began to rise. 'Erin, Josie, shall we go and take coffee in the drawing room and leave the men to puff off their smoke?'

When the men were left alone Patrick poured out three glasses of port and produced a box of cigars. 'Can't say I normally use these, Francis. I'm a pipe and whiskey man myself, but Tommy likes me to do things properly.'

Francis took one, rolled it between thumb and forefinger and smiled at the man's lack of artifice. Thomasin could be a little pretentious at times, which was a shame for she was at heart a very kind, warm person and he liked her immensely – as he was warming to her husband.

Patrick leaned back in the dining chair, sipped and puffed alternately, then said, 'So, about you joining forces with Tommy . . . what can you offer that's so attractive it makes my wife consider sharing an already flourishing business with ye?'

'A question I've asked myself,' smiled Francis and tasted his port rather apprehensively, the terrible meal still adhering to his palate. 'But Thomasin seems to think we'll do well together and who am I to argue with such a shrewd, far-thinking lady as your wife?'

'She was the one to broach the proposition?'

'She was, though I must admit to putting a few idle hints on the efficacy of such a venture. You see, our aim would be to continue on your wife's theme and delete more and more middlemen. You don't need me to tell you that much of the produce in the store comes from your own efforts, the fruit and vegetables from you, all the bread and cakes are manufactured at the store, the coffee beans are roasted there. We want to spread production to, say, preserves, biscuits, as much as possible so we can pass on the benefit to the customer – and of course make more profit for ourselves. Naturally there are still many items that by reason of their nature cannot be home-produced, like tea and the more exotic fruits for instance, but it seems stupid to pay high prices for goods which we could just as easily produce ourselves given the space. So, if we do go ahead with the proposal, which is more than likely, our first step would be to obtain some building, a warehouse or whatever, that could be used for such a purpose.'

Thomasin Feeney, factory owner, thought Patrick. What next? Does she never stop? Despite his own abhorrence of risk he had to admire her. She'd even maintain her firm footing on quicksand. 'More port, Francis?' He held up the decanter but the other covered his glass. 'Well, ye seem to have it all in hand, the pair o' ye.'

Francis sensed the tiniest hint of jealousy but made no reply, merely shrugging modestly. Sonny caught it too and, feeling that his presence checked their willingness to speak plainly, diplomatically finished his port and excused himself.

Again Patrick offered the decanter to Francis and again it was refused. 'I will, if ye don't mind.'

Francis gave unspoken permission and watched the man carefully. He was plucking up the courage to say something, Francis could tell. He also knew what that something was and thought it expedient to offer assurance before Patrick was forced into a corner. 'You are so very lucky, Patrick, in Thomasin. I envy you, and I want to thank you for permitting her to befriend a pathetic widower like myself. Many men, I know, would be extremely incommoded by the friendship, unlike you who wisely see it for what it is: a kind woman's pity for a lonely man. I don't know if Thomasin has told you anything of my wife?' Patrick moved his head and Francis proceeded. 'The manner of her death was painfully drawn out. It was as agonising for me to watch as for her to endure. Even though we knew she could not get well the end still came as a blow. We were so very close. I could never feel that way about another woman. My senses tell me that you are of a similar disposition.'

Patrick ground out the cigar in an ashtray. 'I take your

meaning, Francis,' came the quiet response. 'Thank you.'
It should have eased his concern, knowing that Farthingale
had no designs on his wife, yet it didn't. There was so
much she shared with this man that she could not share
with her husband: her love of ancient architecture and the
will to keep the city's heritage intact; the excitement of a
business deal. Patrick was unable to converse with her on
either of these levels, at least not out of genuine interest.
But this man could.

He finished his port. 'Shall we join the ladies?'

Francis rose with him and the two men went for the
door.

'He'll have to go for a piddle soon,' yawned Belle, still
in her hiding place on the landing. 'He's had all that wine
at dinner and he'll have had some port with Gramps. He
must be bursting. I would be.'

'God, I wish he'd hurry up,' complained Rosanna. 'I'm
nearly falling asleep and my back's killing me.'

'Shush, you two!' hissed Nick. 'They're coming out.'

The children became alert as the two men paused in
the hall to undergo a brief exchange. Patrick pointed up
the stairs and the children ducked out of sight as the guest
parted company with his host and began to ascend the
stairs. They remained hidden until he had passed and
disappeared into the lavatory further down the landing.

'Right, hurry,' said Belle. 'We've only a few minutes.'

By the time the cistern sounded the children were safely
tucked up in their beds. Francis emerged from the bathroom tugging at his jacket and adjusting his collar. Try as
he might he could not recall what happened next, but his
hosts, alerted by the series of dull thuds, the brief cry of
surprise and the sound of breaking crockery, rushed from
the drawing room to find their unconscious guest at the
foot of the stairs amid a pile of broken plant-pot, blood
on his temple and soil all over the tiled floor.

'Oh, my God, what now?' Thomasin picked up her
skirts and pattered swiftly to the spreadeagled figure,
kneeling over him and tapping his white face. 'Francis!
Francis! Pat, it looks like he's dead.'

There was a groan to indicate otherwise. 'No, he's just unconscious,' said Patrick. 'Sonny, give us a hand to lift him into the drawing room.'

Between them they half-carried, half-dragged their guest into the drawing room and deposited him on the sofa. Thomasin poured out a glass of brandy and pressed it to his lips. Francis coughed and gasped as the sharp liquid went down the wrong channel and, pushing it away, tried to sit up.

'Oh dear, my head.' Tenderly he held his throbbing skull and just as quickly brought the hand away, sucking in his breath.

'Erin, go fetch a bowl of water and bandages,' ordered Thomasin. 'Francis, whatever happened?'

He groaned and lay back. 'I don't know. One minute I was coming down the stairs and the next I'm at the bottom with all of you around me.'

'There might be a loose stair-rod,' said Patrick and went off to check. When he returned his face was noncommittal.

'Was it the stair-rod?' Thomasin was forced to ask. – Please God, don't let it be, she begged. I couldn't stand another disaster. Francis will get the impression we're trying to kill him off.

'No, it wasn't,' answered her husband. 'But I think ye should come look for yourself.'

Thomasin affixed her eyes to the loop of black twine on the banister to which her husband was pointing. His finger then moved to indicate the banister at the opposite side of the stair which wore a similar loop. 'Somebody set a trip-wire,' he informed her unnecessarily. 'They've removed the main of it but they didn't have time to untie the whole evidence.'

'But who'd do a thing like that?' breathed Thomasin disbelievingly. 'Good God, they could've killed the man!'

'I don't know why, but I think I could hazard a guess as to who,' said Patrick and jabbed his thumb towards the children's rooms.

'The children?' she mouthed inaudibly.

'When I came up to investigate, Rosie's head was poking

out of her door. When she saw me she ducked in very sharp.'

'But why?'

"Tis no use conjecturin', we'd best just come right out an' ask them.' He strode off in the direction of the children's bedrooms, Thomasin in pursuit.

'It'll do no good to pretend ye're asleep,' Patrick told the two lumps beneath the bedcovers. 'Come on, out with yese.'

Slowly the lumps materialised into two tousle-headed girls who bit their lips and stared at him speechlessly.

'Downstairs. I want to speak to ye.' He watched their ponderous exit, then went to insert his head into Nick's room. 'Nicholas, you too. Don't act as though ye don't know what I'm talking about, I know ye've been listening. Now downstairs all of ye.'

The assembly in the drawing room showed surprise as the nightgowned children were herded reluctantly in to join them. Francis, having had his head attended to, was now sitting upright, the beginnings of a purple bruise on his right cheekbone.

'I believe these children have something to say to ye,' prompted Patrick sternly. 'Come along, who's going to be your spokesman?' There was silence.

'Do you mean the children are responsible?' asked an amazed Sonny.

'I do. They tied a trip-wire across the top o' the stairs. Francis was fortunate to escape with bruises, I can tell ye. He could've broken his neck.'

'I'm sure they didn't know . . .' began Francis, but was curtailed by Sonny's bark.

'Nicholas! Rosanna! Explain yourselves at once.'

'We were only trying to help,' proffered Rosanna, waiting for Belle to own up as the instigator but knowing that was too optimistic.

'Help?' blurted her father. 'For heaven's sake, you almost killed the gentleman!'

'We didn't mean to,' said Nick. 'We only wanted to get rid of him so he wouldn't come again.' There were gasps.

Nick looked at each uncomprehending face, then at Patrick. 'We were doing it for you, Gramps.'

The elderly man stared at his grandson. 'For me? But why?'

'We knew you were afraid that Mr Far... Mr Farthingale was going to take Nan away. We were only trying to put him off coming again. That's why we put the mixture on the dinner.'

His grandmother clapped a hand to her brow. 'And I went and blamed Cook. I might've known.'

'It was only because we didn't want you to run away, Nan,' said Rosie, looking through a veil of dark lashes.

Thomasin spread her hands. 'Francis, what can I say? How very embarrassing this must be for you.'

The man accomplished a shaky laugh. 'On the contrary I'm rather flattered that anyone could think me capable of abduction.'

Nick compared the two men openly. 'Yes, it was rather stupid of us to think Nan would run off with you, wasn't it?'

Thomasin gave an explosive breath at this candour but Francis forestalled any further chastisement. 'I'm certain they were simply being loyal – that's to be admired.'

'Not if it almost kills my guests,' she replied firmly. 'Sonny, Erin, I trust you'll deal with your children accordingly?'

Her son and daughter said they would. Josie began to rise but Erin told her to sit where she was. 'Save your strength. I may as well deal with both girls. I suppose it's rather irrelevant to ask,' she turned to Belle, 'but who masterminded this dangerous prank?'

Belle looked at the pattern on the carpet. 'Don't think you're being loyal,' said her mother. 'Come on, speak up.'

Belle altered her weight to the other leg, then, after appearing to deliberate for some moments, divulged, 'Rosie said we should do something to help Grandfather. I don't suppose she thought it would end like this.'

Rosanna opened her mouth in indignation but Erin was already bundling the children from the room. 'You're a very wicked girl, Rosanna Feeney, and it was especially bad of you to lure Belle into your dangerous antics.'

Sonny objected, a hand on each of his children's heads as they climbed the stairs. 'I'm not condoning their behaviour, but don't you think it's a wee bit unjust to lump all the blame on Rosie?'

'Ye heard what Belle said! It was Rosanna's idea – as usual. Belle would hardly be able to accomplish such a feat on her own. Besides which the idea would never have entered her head. Ye know how Rosie's always at the centre of any mischief, Sonny. It really is time you took her in hand. I'm terrified that one day she'll lead Belle into something really dangerous.'

'Well, I'll leave you to see to the girls' punishment,' sighed her brother as they parted company outside the adjacent bedrooms. 'I'll tend to this rascal.'

Nick spun round immediately the door was closed. 'Father, you mustn't let Aunt Erin beat Rosie, it wasn't her fault.'

'Whose was it, then – yours?' Nick looked down at his bare toes, undulating them. 'Come on, Nick, tell the truth.'

'Dad, I'm not trying to wriggle out of it. I mean I don't mind taking my medicine, but you mustn't allow Aunt Erin to think that it was all Rosie's fault. It was Belle's idea . . .'

'Now, Nick.' Sonny looked extremely stern.

'It's the truth, honestly! I'm not trying to pin it all on Belle so that she gets all the punishment. I've told you I don't mind taking what's coming like a man, but you must believe that it was truly Belle's idea. It always is, but Rosie is the one who gets the blame. It's because she giggles. I know you've taught us not to tell tales but you should know what Belle's really like. Everybody thinks she's nice but sometimes she can be really obnoxious.'

Sonny halted the flow of defence. 'How often has this happened – Rosie getting the blame for something her cousin's done?'

'Hundreds of times. Rosie's never complained because she felt sorry for Belle being made to take all those extra lessons and for the way her mother won't allow her to play like us. But I don't think it's right that she should get Belle's share of the punishment.'

'No, indeed it's not,' agreed his father gravely. 'Hold there a moment.' He left the room and went to intercept his sister before the injustice was meted out. After knocking he opened the door and looked around it. 'Ah, there's no blood – I must be in time.' Erin regarded him impatiently, a hairbrush in her hand. 'I think maybe it'd be better if you left Rosanna's punishment to her mother, Erin – right? I'll see you downstairs.' With no further offering he returned to his son's room to lift the child into bed, tucking him in and sitting at his bedside. 'I'll explain to your Aunt Erin.' A sigh broke in. 'Not that I think she'll believe us. Y'see, Nick, she feels very protective of Belle. The child is all she has and she doesn't want to see her hurt. She sincerely believes that Belle can do no wrong, that she's always bound, by her situation, to be the victim. Even though we know that's untrue we have to be charitable. Aunt Erin has suffered a lot.'

'I understand that, Father.' His son was growing sleepy.

'Good man.' Sonny smoothed the fair hair. 'And don't worry about your sister. She'll never be punished again for something she didn't do – but don't think I regard you as totally innocent in this! You're quite old enough to know how stupid and dangerous it was, and if there's any repetition there will be serious trouble.' After a kiss he left. Meeting Erin on the stairs he told her what Nick had said.

'Well, that was predictable, wasn't it?' Erin lifted her skirts as she trod the stairs. 'As you're bound to take Rosanna's side. You're too protective of her, Sonny. I understand why, of course, it's because of her hard beginnings, but ye really must see what a little minx she is.'

Sonny was amused despite his concern; she had taken the words out of his mouth. No matter, Erin would be made to realise some day just what she was bent on protecting. 'I respect your opinion, Erin.' They had reached the door of the drawing room. 'But if ever you feel that Rosie is in need of chatisement in future I'd be obliged if you'd send her to Josie.' He opened the door for her.

'Tsk! Josie's softer than you are with them.' She saw his face and made a gesture of compliance. 'All right – but I warn you, Sonny, if ye don't handle her more firmly you're going to have trouble on your hands.'

As they arrived Patrick was scratching his head. 'Well . . . I suppose 'tis all out in the open now. I'll not deny there was more than a grain o' truth to their supposition. I did have doubts about ye, Francis.'

The guest nodded understandingly. 'Naturally, with such an attractive wife I too should be cautious of those I invited into my home. I hope, though, that I've allayed your suspicions to some extent. Thomasin is a dear friend I must admit, but I would never stoop so low . . .'

'I believe that,' interrupted Patrick. 'Otherwise I'd never've invited ye in the first place. Besides, a dear friend o' mine endorsed your credentials.' Francis creased his brow and Patrick explained, 'Father Liam Kelly. I believe ye met about two years ago.' Francis had little need to search his memory even though the meeting had been brief; Father Kelly had made a strong impression, as he told Patrick now.

'Aye, he was left with a similar impression of your good self,' replied Patrick. ''Tis thanks to him you're here.'

'Then you must relay my gratitude,' smiled Francis.

Patrick looked at his wife, then back at the guest. 'I'm afraid I can't do that, Francis. Liam died on the same day as Tommy's mother. He was my oldest and dearest friend. I don't have to tell you how much I miss him.'

Francis offered condolences for the second time that evening. 'I know it sounds silly to say this of a priest . . . but he struck me as a very Christian man.'

'Not silly at all,' answered Patrick with Father Gilchrist in mind. 'I know exactly what you mean. Often I'd feel put to shame by his goodness. As a matter of fact we were discussing the other day . . .' The other day – how long ago it seemed. 'Well, I think he believed I should be

254

makin' more use of my fortunate position by helping my less-fortunate brothers.'

Thomasin reminded him of all the men he employed, men who might otherwise be hard-pressed to find work. 'That's hardly something to be ashamed of.'

'But 'tis such a paltry concession,' said Patrick. 'Think of the hovels we used to live in ourselves, then think of those still confined to them. There must be something we could do.'

'It must be the weather,' donated Sonny who had been listening with quiet interest. 'I've been experiencing the same feelings lately. Here I am with a thriving career, a well-fed family, a lovely home . . . what right have I to all this? There's some who'd consider just a hundredth of what I have as wealth. It's so unjust.'

'But we didn't just draw our fortune from a lucky dip,' protested Thomasin. 'We've all worked damned hard to get where we are.'

'I'd be the first to agree with that, Mother, but don't you think that point of view a wee bit selfish? I've made my money, now bugger the others – sorry, Francis,' he apologised for his language.

Francis waved this aside. 'But you can't accuse your mother of selfishness, John. To use her own illustration, look at the number of people to whom she gives employ-ment – and at far above the going rate for wages.'

'Again, I agree with that, Francis,' replied Sonny. 'It's not really Mother I'm speaking of but myself. You see, all I ever wanted to do was paint – I admit it's an addiction with me. The money I received for my pleasure hardly registered. I'd just take the cheques and shove them in my bank account. I didn't even realise the amount I'd accrued until a few months ago. It was rather daunting to find myself so rich . . . that's what's so disgusting, really – not knowing, or caring what you are worth, while others are starving. It brought me to some serious thinking . . .' Here he glanced at his mother.

'I hope you're not intending to arm yourself with bags of sovs and visit the ghettoes,' said Thomasin.

'Credit me with a little savvy, Mother.' Sonny divulged his intention to buy a mill where he would design and produce his own fabric. 'I'd still be doing something I liked while helping those less well-off – and of course I could still undertake the odd commission when it suited.'

Thomasin was enthusiastic. 'We could have the fabric made up into clothes to sell at the store.'

'Actually, what I had in mind was household textiles, and maybe later I might apply my designs to wallpaper. I do so hate all this heavy stuff that's around at the moment.' He embraced his father in his smile. 'And that would mean you could have a whole new department, Mam. What d'you think to that?'

Thomasin said she thought it was splendid. 'And so do I,' endorsed Patrick. 'Where and when d'ye intend to begin?'

'There's a mill near Leeds up for auction in a couple of . . .'

'Oh, he doesn't waste much time, does he?' remarked Patrick to the others.

Sonny met his smile. 'It's not as impulsive as it sounds. Josie and I have talked about this a lot but we wanted to discuss it with you before we decided.'

'Discuss nothing,' scoffed his mother to laughter. 'You had it all worked out.' She asked him what he knew about the textile industry, his choice having surprised her.

'Nothing much,' he confessed. 'But this fellow I know – who was actually the one to put the idea into my head, he's going to be in charge of the weaving side. I'll be concentrating solely on the designs – when I've finished at Nottingham, of course.'

'Will this chap be contributing any finance?' enquired his cautious mother.

'No, he'll be working as an employee. Don't worry, Mam, I am grown up now you know, I won't let anyone fleece me.'

'I'm not bothered about anyone fleecing you, I was just wondering whether or not I might be allowed to buy shares!'

After the flippancy came a moment of seriousness. 'It isn't so much the mill we wanted to discuss with you . . . it's the children.' Sonny looked at his wife whose face had grown clouded. 'You see, with the mill being at Leeds we're going to have to move there.'

'An' ye'll be taking Rosie an' Nick.' Patrick's face was downcast. 'It never occurred to me that they'd ever leave . . . still, I suppose when they grow up they'll go anyway.'

'We don't know if we will be taking them,' replied his son awkwardly, adding quickly, 'Naturally we want them with us . . . but we don't want to tear them away from their home and you and Mam. We've been in a right pickle about it . . . but we think we may've reached a compromise. Rosie and Nick could live here through the week, take their lessons as normal, have their friends to play with, and then at the weekend they can come to us – or we'll come here, one or the other. When you think about it, a lot of children their age would be away at boarding school, anyway.'

'Aren't you overlooking something?' asked his mother, making him cock his head. 'What makes you think I want two budding executioners living with me?' She grinned at Francis who rubbed his bruises woefully.

Sonny laughed. 'Of course I could always ship them off to a penal colony,' and took hold of the hand that his mother reached out to him.

'You know we'd love to have them stay – if you're sure you won't miss them too much?' Thomasin had turned to Josie when saying this and took her hand from Sonny's to grip her daughter-in-law's fingers.

'We'll miss them dreadfully,' confessed Josie. 'But I think John's scheme is a fair one for all concerned. We haven't put it to them yet,' she added hastily.

'I won't say anything,' promised Thomasin.

Josie gave a little laugh. 'They might even want to come with us.' But it was said without conviction.

Sonny tried to shrug off his real feelings, joking,

'Anyway, Nick tells me he's going to work for you when he's older, Mother.'

'Is he indeed?' said Thomasin. 'I'm glad everyone is so certain of their plans, aren't you, Pat? I think you and I might just as well enlist for the workhouse, considering that none of them seems to think it necessary to consult us any more.'

Patrick, with one eye on his guest, replied, 'I can see Francis thinks he's got himself a good deal. Since he made his proposition the store's acquired itself an extra department, another contributor and a new manager.'

'Yes, I can see it all now,' said Thomasin grandly. 'Another decade and our store will take up the length of Parliament Street – *Penny and Co.*'

Francis caught the brief flash in Patrick's eye and felt for him. 'Are you to keep the old name on, Thomasin? Why not your own name now? Take credit for your endeavours.'

'Nonsense,' dismissed Thomasin. 'Haven't you noticed the allusion? Feeney and Co. Fenian Co. That would certainly bring us lots of custom, I don't think. Anyway, people know it as *Penny's* now. Even if I did put my own name up they'd still call it *Penny's*. No, we'll keep it as it is – maybe even make it a limited company in a few years. Who knows?' She intercepted the look of sympathy that travelled from Francis to her husband. 'Oh, I see! You're worried about Pat's opinion. Eh,' she touched him affectionately, 'you're a soft-hearted soul. Pat, tell him he's no need for concern. You're not bothered one way or the other, are you?'

'Of course not,' answered Patrick. 'Ye can call the place what the devil ye like.'

His voice was light but Francis interpreted the lie. The man was deeply hurt that his wife denied his name. He tried to inject a little genuine lightness. 'Might it be presumptuous of me to propose a toast to the new partnership?'

Thomasin rapidly twinned the motion and soon everyone was holding a glass of either sherry or whiskey.

'May I?' Francis rose. 'Ladies and gentlemen, it gives me such great pleasure to be counted as part of this family business. I shall do my utmost to fulfil your expectations of me. To *Penny and Co.*, prosperity, longevity, harmony.'

The others echoed and raised their drinks to smiling faces. Patrick applied his lips to the rim of his glass. – To Mrs Penny and Mr Farthingale, he thought emptily – but what of Mr Feeney?

PART THREE

❧

1883–1889

CHAPTER SEVENTEEN

Patrick frequently relived his last conversation with his old friend Liam. Even two years after the priest's death his own words returned to mock him – what had he done to credit them with sincerity? Nothing. It was all too easy stating that he wanted to help those less fortunate, a different matter actually to do it. Sonny had made the effort. He and Josie had secured the mill at Leeds and a house to go with it and now employed dozens of people. As Sonny had predicted, the children were happy to stay with their grandparents. Patrick knew what a wrench it had been for his son and Josie, but he couldn't say that he was unhappy with their decision; his grandchildren's presence was about the only thing that cheered him these days. When they went off at the weekend or, even worse, for a holiday with their parents he felt bored and useless. Thomasin's continued involvement with the YAS left him in need of some pastime to fill his lonely evenings.

In fact, it took the chill of autumn and the current political by-election to provide one – and indirectly, a means to help the people in the slums. Patrick had never really been interested in politics before, but he *was* concerned over anything to do with his homeland. The current bickering for Home Rule was the item that acted as tinder to his stale imagination. Having tasted repression at first hand he had for years been appalled at the injustices to the Irish meted out by press and politician. Hitherto, as he had told Liam, he had done little more than complain within his family circle, but now he felt the need for more positive action. Without a mention to his family he went tentatively along to a meeting chaired by the Liberal candidate, Frank Lockwood. By the time the meeting broke up Patrick felt as if someone had stuck a spoon in his vitals and given them a good stir, so uplifted did he feel. And for those few weeks leading up to the November by-election his involvement marked a period of renewed self-esteem.

'Gramps seems very cheerful these days, doesn't he?' remarked Nick. Now eleven, he was almost as tall as his grandmother and a constant headache to those who had to clothe him. 'I bring him new trousers,' Thomasin would say, 'I blink my eyes and they're at half-mast. I think somebody's putting fertiliser in his boots.'

'Mmm,' said Rosanna, lying on her stomach. She was engrossed in her drawing. Lost in concentration, one foot rose to meet her back, then was lowered to the carpet; up, down, up, down, displaying petticoats and drawers.

'I wonder if he'll buy me that train I've been wanting.'

'Hmm?' Rosanna's tongue curled onto her cheek as she pencilled in her grandfather's eyes. Gramps was going to like this. It was the best picture she had ever done.

'You're not listening, are you?'

'Hmm?'

'Oink, oink, pig-face, stinky old baggy drawers,' chanted Nick.

'Camel-face,' retorted his sister. 'Anyway, I was listening.'

'What did I say, then?'

'What you usually say whenever you speak about Gramps – you want him to buy you something. You don't want him for himself, you want him for his money.'

'That's stupid – anyway, Gramps doesn't mind. He's got plenty of cash.' Nick watched his sister impatiently. 'Are you going to lie there all day drawing?'

'What else is there to do? It's raining.'

Nick mused, 'We could go ask Abi to call for Cecilia and ask if she wants to come and play.' Lessons were over for today – except for Belle. This was agreed upon and Cecilia – who lived in the house next door and was a regular playmate – was brought in, all of them enjoying a boisterous game until an irate tutor poked his head from the schoolroom. 'Some people have to work, you know!' and slammed the door.

'Poor Belle,' panted Rosie after she had finished giggling. 'It's not fair, is it?' The episode with Farthingale was long-forgotten. 'There must be some way we can rescue her.' Hence, a new game commenced. Making as much din as she could – which was considerable – Rosie poised outside the schoolroom door waiting for the tutor to come out, which was not long. Off she fled in the hope that he would pursue. He did, granting Nick and Cecilia the chance to rush in and abduct a not-unwilling victim.

Rosanna, having outpaced the tutor and rejoined them, decided that they had all better hide or Belle's freedom would be short-lived. Grabbing her picture, she fled. Down in the potting shed with hair lank from the rain, Cecilia made an announcement. 'I'm having a birthday party.' She sat on a dusty workbench, swinging her legs, an expression of importance on her heart-shaped face.

'Who're you inviting?' asked Rosanna nonchalantly.

'Mm.' Cecilia dimpled her chin with a finger and rolled her eyes upwards. 'I haven't decided yet.' Then she grinned. 'Who d'you think, silly?'

'All of us?' said Rosanna delightedly. 'Belle too?'

'Why of course Belle.' Cecilia linked arms with the girl sitting next to her. 'She's my best friend, aren't you?'

A little of Rosanna's pleasure evaporated. 'I thought I was your best friend, Cec.'

'Well . . . you are, you both are. I can have more than one best friend, can't I?'

Best friend, thought Belle dazedly, feeling the warmth of Cecilia's arm; something she had always wanted. All the other children who came to play at the house gravitated towards Rosie, her being so gushy and pushy – but now she had a best friend. She snuggled up to Cecilia, feeling all fizzy inside.

Rosanna unbuttoned her bodice and slipped her hand inside, withdrawing the portrait. She had placed it there to prevent it getting soggy. Now, she sat and stared at it, waiting for someone to ask what it was. Recognising the pose, Belle said nothing – she could tell that Rosie was jealous and was revelling in the idea – but Cecilia complied innocently. 'Oh, may I see? Who's it a portrait of?'

'Gramps,' supplied Rosanna, at which Belle burst into rude laughter.

'I hope you're not going to show it to him!'

When Rosie asked why not Belle pointed to Patrick's eyes and guffawed. 'Oh look, Cec, he's cross-eyed!'

'He is not!' Rosanna snatched the portrait back.

Despite the fact that she personally thought the picture was very good, Cecilia was infected by Belle's laughter and pretty soon there were tears streaming down her cheeks as she bumped heads with Belle. They continued giggling as Rosie stormed out of the shed followed by Nick – which is what Belle had hoped for. Now she had Cecilia all to herself. She could still hardly believe that this was happening to her. When the laughter eventually died she asked what Cecilia would like for a present. 'Choose anything you like. I want it to be the best present you receive. I'm going to be your friend forever.'

A child's antagonism being notoriously short-lived, the afternoon found the three together again, purchasing presents in a city toy store. Belle took an age to find the right article. 'It must be exactly the right thing.' This turned out to be the most expensive doll in the shop.

'Miss Belle, I can't let you buy that,' objected Abi as the shopkeeper took it from the shelf. 'Wouldn't you sooner have something like Miss Rosie's chosen?'

'That wouldn't be right for Cecilia.' Belle was scornful. 'You can't be stingy when you're buying for a best friend, Abigail.'

Rosie put the toy monkey back on the counter. 'I hadn't decided yet.'

In grand manner Belle instructed the man to wrap up the doll. Defeated, Abigail sighed and turned away. 'Right, Master Nick, is that what you've chosen – come on, Miss Rosie, we haven't got all day!' Rosanna reluctantly handed over the toy monkey, pursing her lips at Belle's snigger.

The invitation came on Tuesday. Abi was the one who, with leaden heart, handed it to one of the recipients.

'To Master N. and Miss R. Feeney,' read Rosanna, then ripped it open. Belle waited.

'Maybe yours'll come later, dear,' said Abi at the crest-fallen face.

Rosie's soft heart came to the fore. 'Perhaps they ran out of invitations and're having some more printed,' she suggested, then bit her lip at Belle's icy stare.

Belle, still hopeful, waited all afternoon for the special sound that the letterbox made, but never once did it speak. Towards evening her optimism was forced to capitulate; there would be no invitation now. Down in the kitchen Abigail pounded crossly at the dishwater, splashing her apron front. 'No bloody invite yet, I see.'

'Happen it's as well she didn't want to go, then,' replied Mrs Howgego.

The maid turned on her. 'Course she wanted to go!'

'Abigail, didn't I hear her myself not five minutes ago saying she wasn't bothered, she was only going to suit Miss Cecilia anyway.'

'I was there when that invitation came, I saw her face! She was heartbroken – heartbroken! I'd bloody lock 'em up, I would. When I think of all the trouble she took choosin' that present . . . "it's for my best friend", she tells the bloke, "wrap it up very carefully". Ooh!'

'Aye well, I don't reckon it would be Miss Cecilia's fault,' sighed Cook. 'She seems a nice enough young lady. But from what Cook-Next-Door tells me, Miss Cecilia's parents aren't too keen on the friendship.'

'Happen they think it's catchin',' snapped Abigail. 'Who do folk think they are? Eh, I don't know, Cook.' She wiped her hands on a towel. 'That poor little soul . . . if this is what she's got to put up with for the rest of her life then it won't be worth much, will it? S'pect we'll be in for a right spell o' naughtiness after this an' all.'

'Doesn't take a disappointment to give her an excuse for naughtiness,' sniffed Cook. 'Tricky little demon.'

'I'll agree she can be a monkey – well, I should know

267

after all the tricks she's played on me – but *real* naughtiness is what I'm on about . . . it always seems to come after she's had one o' these upsets, as though she has to take it out on somebody.'

'That's all well and good if she takes it out on them as is responsible, Abigail. But I hope she doesn't think I'm putting up with a load of argey-bargey just 'cause she couldn't go to a party, 'cause I'm not!'

'Ooh, you are hard, Mrs Howgego.'

'Aye, well I'm not one o' them as feels sorry for her just 'cause she's not normal, like some I could mention.' She was still smarting over the way Belle had raided her larder two weeks ago and made off with the piece of pie Cook was saving for her own lunch. Abi saw no virtue in prolonging the topic, for Cook had always had a down on the child. She continued with the washing up, while upstairs the question of Belle was carried forth into the next twenty-four hours by the child's grandparents.

'Are we to let them go, then?' demanded Thomasin impatiently.

'It'd be a shame to spoil their fun just 'cause we're mad with our neighbours,' answered her husband.

'But it's the principle of the thing! They've deliberately snubbed her, Patrick, because she's . . . the way she is. Erin's furious! If we permit Nick and Rosie to go then it looks as though we're letting them get away with it.'

'If it's revenge you're after surely it can wait till after the party? I understand your argument – I side with it meself – but they're only children.'

'Nonsense, they're eleven and twelve years old,' persisted Thomasin. 'They have to learn about principles some time.'

'Does it have to be this way? For God's sake let them go, then tomorrow when Mrs Ridley comes to call ye can send Abi out with your not-at-home card, or Erin with a mallet, or whatever.'

'And are we to let Belle sit in her room all alone thinking of the fun her cousins are having?'

'I'll see to Belle, just you see to your own affairs. Ring

for Abi. When the others have gone to this blessed party we'll have Belle down.'

After giving Abigail instructions Thomasin enquired what result Patrick foresaw of tomorrow's by-election. 'Do you think your fellow will get in?'

'If enthusiasm's what's needed to get that seat then he will,' stated her husband.

'And all these votes you've been promised, will they follow through with the genuine thing?'

'Listen,' he told her, 'I'll see Frank Lockwood elected even if I have to drag those idle so an' so's to the polls by their – ah, here's Belle.' He gestured to the child who had interrupted his speech. 'Ah, come on to your old grandad an' give him a cuddle.'

Thomasin, with a tight smile for Belle, made for the door. 'I'll leave you two to it.'

'Aye, we'll leave you to it, too,' said Patrick, making Belle laugh despite her hurt as she came to stand between his legs. 'Ah, I'm glad ye can still do that, darlin'. 'Tis the most powerful weapon ye have, laughter. A laugh in the face of your enemy can be as effective as a slap.' He sighed. 'I'm sorry ye didn't get an invitation to the party, love . . . but maybe Cecilia's mother felt she could only cope with so many.' He saw the disbelief in her expression and actually blushed. That child knew well enough why she hadn't been invited.

'Well, as it happens, Gramps,' she told him lightly, 'it's quite fortunate that I didn't receive one. I couldn't've gone anyway as I've such a lot of work to do.'

'Ah well,' Patrick nodded, then his eyes fell on the enormous parcel tied with pink ribbons, abandoned by the piano. 'Ye can keep the doll by the way. I don't see why Cecilia should have it, d'you?'

She shook her head and stared down at the large boot that protruded from the hem of her dress. For some time she had been wearing her skirts longer, her mother deeming it a kindness. Hidden or not, the boot was still there.

'Well,' he finished awkwardly, 'I'd love to spend some

time with ye but I have to go out. 'Tis the by-election tomorrow an' Mr Lockwood's making his final speech. I have to go, Belle.' She nodded, not raising her eyes. 'Aw, Jaze.' He sat her on his lap. 'Ye're making me feel terrible.'

She brightened. 'It's not your fault that Cecilia's so stupid, Gramps.'

'I know, I know . . . but someone should be here to cheer ye up. Listen,' he added thoughtfully, ''tis scant consolation, I know, but ye wouldn't like to come with me, would ye? It'll be awful noisy an' perhaps there'll be a bit o' bad language but no more than ye'd hear when your Gramps has had too much whiskey, an' at least 'twould get ye out o' the house. I hate to think of ye listening to the sound of the party next door.'

'I told you I'm not bothered,' she laughed, and hugged him. 'And I'd love to come with you.' How she loved this man. He was the only person whom she would never dream of upsetting.

'Right!' He slapped her knee. 'Get your togs an' we'll be off.'

'May I just put this in a safe place?' She had picked up the birthday present.

At his smile of assent she clomped upstairs and sought the privacy of her room. Ripping off the paper she dragged the huge doll from its box and, grasping the body between her knees, began to twist the head round and round, wrenching and contorting until, with a dying snap, it came away. Snatching a piece of paper from Rosie's sketchpad she scrawled 'Cecilia Ridley' in bold letters and attached it to the decapitated torso. The head she kicked around the bedroom, dashing her boot into its prim face until it split open. Tossing it into the chamberpot under the bed she returned to join her grandfather with a serene smile.

Grandfather was right, there were a lot of rude words flying around and plenty of noise. But what he had omitted to mention was that the excitement which Lockwood generated among his supporters was highly infectious. Belle had never seen anything like this. When Lockwood appeared in the hall the place erupted. Hats were thrown into the air and wild huzzas almost shattered the windows. For the child it was frightening, the power that emanated from this assembly. Imagine he were *not* their hero; imagine that this mob was out to lynch him . . . but no, that was silly. Look at the admiration on their faces – on Grandfather's face, as Lockwood took the rostrum.

While he made his address Belle sat on her grandfather's lap and studied the listeners' faces. What it must be to inspire such a following! She was not really interested in the content of Lockwood's speech, more in the effect it was having on the crowd and in particular, on her grandfather. At the moment, the candidate's talk centred upon the unsporting antics of a man called Sir Frederick Milner. Belle asked who he was.

'He's our opponent – a Tory,' whispered Patrick. 'Not only our main obstacle against Home Rule for Ireland but also the enemy of the Irish in this city – curs, he called us in a speech the other week!'

This was sufficient to damn the man in Belle's eyes but there were other things she wanted to know. What was so important about Home Rule? 'You live here,' she pointed out. 'What does it matter who rules Ireland?'

'Belle, I live in England but I'm still an Irishman. It concerns me a great deal what happens to the folk left behind. Shush now, I want to hear Mr Lockwood – I'll explain to ye later.'

Lockwood went on to suggest what the Conservatives would do if they got into power, reminding the crowd of a speech made by Sir Frederick Milner labelling Gladstone a murderer and a robber and asking who in their right mind would vote for such a slanderer.

'And who in their right mind would support a bunch of Irish barbarians?' called a Tory infiltrator to the rear of the Irishman and his grand-daughter. Patrick spun on him, but before he could voice a protest the man had added, 'What about Phoenix Park last year? How can we permit those murderers to run part of the British Empire?'

'Don't tar us all with the same brush!' called Patrick

amid growls of annoyance. 'The ordinary people don't want violence, they just want to be able to run their own affairs without interference from absentee landlords and their extortionate rents.'

'Hah!' The heckler was struggling to keep his feet as Lockwood's supporters dragged him towards the exit. 'I doubt *ordinary* would apply to you! How did you manage to get your wealth? How many fellow Irishmen have broken their backs to put those fancy clothes on yours?'

Patrick set his mouth to offer an expletive, but remembering his grand-daughter's presence shouted, 'Won't you give my regards to your mother? A fine woman . . . such a shame she never married.' And the man was ejected to cheers.

Belle's hands worked frantically with those around her who issued their appreciation of the taunt. Though she did not understand it, it was obvious these people held her grandfather in high regard – and she was sharing his moment of pride. Rosie would be so jealous!

Rosanna and Nick returned from the party bearing consolation parcels of sweets they had sneaked from the table. Rosanna, primed to award her hapless cousin her own pink balloon, looked around the empty drawing room disappointedly. 'Oh, she's not here.'

Nick threw himself down on the sofa, propping his boots on the arm. 'Probably off sulking somewhere.'

But the triumphant entry of Belle some minutes later told otherwise. As Nick, thinking it was his grandmother, hurriedly swung his feet off the sofa, she came across the room in her tittupy gait and plonked herself next to him.

Rosanna furrowed her brow at the bright eyes and cheeks pink from the cold night air. 'Where've you been? I must say you look awfully pleased considering you missed the party. Nick and I thought you'd be miserable.' She came to sit on the sofa arm.

'Gramps took me to a political meeting,' said Belle airily.

Rosie snorted. 'If he was just feeling sorry for you he could've taken you somewhere a bit more interesting.'

'Hah! You're only jealous because he didn't take you,' said Belle perceptively.

'No, I'm not. You're just being clever to make Nick and me feel sorry we went to the party without you – and after we've brought you these, too.' She threw the sweets onto Belle's lap. 'I was going to give you my balloon too but I can see you don't need cheering up; I think I'll keep it.'

Belle hit out at the balloon, banging it against Rosie's face until it burst. Tears formed in Rosanna's eyes – not for the balloon, it was after all only a balloon – but for Belle's spite in the face of her friendship. 'I don't know why you're being so horrid to me. Just because you had to go to a boring political meeting instead of a party...'

'It wasn't boring, actually,' replied Belle haughtily. 'It was very informative – of course, *you* wouldn't have been able to follow it because there were too many big words. It was all about Ireland and how the Irish people are repressed because of their faith and customs.'

'What's repressed?' asked Rosanna.

'Oh there you are, you see! What would've been the point of you going, you're so stupid. You ought to pay attention to your lessons. It means, dummy, they get put upon and made to do all the dirty jobs and have low wages...'

'Like me,' said Abigail, who had entered bearing a tray of milk and biscuits – though it wasn't really true, the mistress had hired another maid as she had promised. It was Helen who got all the dirty jobs now. 'Now don't be takin' all night over that. I've orders you've to be changed for bed in fifteen minutes.' She went out.

Belle continued whilst munching a biscuit, 'And it doesn't just happen in Ireland, they're downtrodden here too, because the British rule them, see? Mr Lockwood – he's our man, Gramps has been helping him to campaign – he's in favour of Home Rule, which means the Irish running their own country. I must say it seems fairer than the way it is at present.' The biscuit finished, she cuddled her knees and carried on talking, Rosanna listening jealously. 'You ought to have heard Gramps telling the men

273

to use their votes correctly – he got quite excited.' She saw Rosanna pretend to yawn. 'Naturally *you* wouldn't be very interested. People always call things boring if they can't quite grasp them.'

'I do understand it,' retorted her cousin. 'In fact I shall ask Gramps to take me to the next meeting.'

Belle laughed scornfully. 'That shows how ignorant you are of politics. There won't *be* another meeting; the by-election takes place tomorrow and Mr Lockwood's going to win.' She yawned herself. 'Oh dear, it's so wearying the amount one has to do at election time. I think I'll go up now. Do try not to wake me when you come up, won't you?'

'Goodnight, Belladonna,' commented Nick as the door closed.

'I wish we hadn't bothered to bring her anything.' Rosie slid from the sofa arm into the seat Belle had warmed. In the quiet that followed she pictured her dear Gramps with Belle at the meeting. He knew how Rosie loved to hear about Ireland, so why hadn't he offered to take her instead of making her go to that silly old party? She'd much rather have gone with him – but instead Belle had monopolised his affections – Oh she'd love that, thought Rosie acidly. She's always trying to make out he loves her more than me. But he doesn't, I know he doesn't.

CHAPTER EIGHTEEN

One slight triumph in Rosanna's eyes – bad though it was for the Irish – was that York was robbed of its Liberal MP. This meant that Belle's knowledgable predictions were made to look extremely foolish.

'Twenty-one votes,' breathed Patrick over the breakfast table. 'Twenty-one bloody votes, that's all there was between us. Dammit, after all I told them – use your vote, have a say in your own future – and look at the number that turned out. Sure, it wasn't worth spoiling a good box by putting a slit in it. What a poor bloody show.' He crumpled the newspaper and tossed it over his shoulder, drawing a sound of reproach from his wife who sat opposite.

'Patrick, do try and constrain your language at the table.' She glanced at the children. 'And don't be too disappointed, there's always next time. It takes a while to hammer your point into a thick skull – I should know after putting up with the ambidextrous dealings of the council all these years.'

'I mean, ye'd think they'd see it, wouldn't ye?' he persisted. 'But no, all we get for our efforts is another dose of Sir Frederick bloody Milner.'

'Belle said the Liberal was going to win,' announced Rosanna brightly to a display of compressed lips from Belle.

The comment seemed to compound Patrick's embarrassment. 'Ah, that's with listening to her old fool of a grandfather, I suppose.' He sighed and continued with his breakfast. 'But, 'tis nothing for you children to go worrying your heads about.' What a let-down, though.

'Next time there's an election will you take me?' asked Rosanna.

'I'm not so sure I'll concern meself any more.'

'Never mind, Father,' comforted Erin. 'Ye've still got your Liberal Government.'

'I suppose we should be grateful,' responded Patrick miserably.

'There must be some way we could help though, Gramps.' Rosie wouldn't let go. 'At the next election . . .'

'Rosanna, your grandfather has made it plain he doesn't want to talk about politics any more,' said a stern-faced Thomasin. 'If you've finished your breakfast you'd better go and prepare for your lessons.'

Erin left with the children. When Abigail and Helen had taken the plates away, Thomasin leaned over the table to cover Patrick's hand. 'Don't get too despondent, love. As I said, there's always next time.'

He shook his head. 'I can't see the point . . . the only thing that gets my backing in future will have four legs.'

She sighed at his defeatism. 'Ah well, you will put your money on the wrong nag.'

He flared unexpectedly. 'Oh, 'tis easy to see where your alliance would sit if ye were allowed to vote! Good customers are they, the Milners?'

'As a matter of fact they are. I see no value in antagonising the man even if I do disagree with his politics – he's made some abominable claims against your countrymen.'

'Oh, ye surprise me! Ye've never shown much affinity for the Irish – especially the ones in this house.'

'Do you know you get more childish with age?' She rose stiffly and glared at him before making for the door.

'Ah well, ye needn't worry that I'll be upsetting your customers,' he shouted after her. 'I've made a big enough fool o' meself an' that's going to take some living down.'

Demoralised, disgusted and true to his promise this was Patrick's only dalliance in the fickle world of politics, except to utter a month later when told that York's MP was suffering an attack of neuralgia, 'I hope 'tis a bloody bad one.'

For a long time Sir Frederick 'bloody' Milner continued to be the grain of sand which crept under the Irishman's shell and formed a pearl of bitterness. He would read extracts from the press to his long-suffering wife: 'Just listen to this! That bloody Milner is only trying to put the kibosh on Sunday boozing now!' Occasionally his interest in politics was restirred as when the elections of 'eighty-five and 'eighty-six increased the number of Irish seats in the House. It began to look as if Home Rule was about to become a reality. Sadly, Gladstone's Bill of the latter year proved too much of a concession to many of his party and this forced the great man to go to the country. Perhaps with the echoes of the latest bomb outrage still deafening their ears, the people chose the Tories. Besides angering

Patrick, this had the effect of whipping up more trouble in Ireland. The extracts he read out now to his family were of evictions and trial without jury. The children – especially Rosanna – would see his face contort with helpless fury when reading of the treatment of his fellow countrymen, though his outbursts were usually staunched by their grandmother who did not want the children to be alarmed.

Four new calendars were in turn pinned up and taken down since the Irishman's first political involvement. During that time, apart from the odd angry outburst, the Feeney household was relatively peaceful. In Belle's thirteenth year a decision was reached to send her and Rosie to a young ladies' college where they would receive a wider education. She was not certain she wanted to go. Rosanna, at sixteen, was more decisive – she *definitely* did not want to go. It was bad enough having to take lessons at home but at least here she could escape from time to time. For her, school would be like imprisonment. One small point for which she could be grateful was that she and Belle were not being sent to a convent. For this they had their grandmother to thank. Thomasin wanted her granddaughters to be accepted readily by society – and this would hardly come about by putting them in the company of nuns. Despite her staunch Catholicism, Erin agreed with this. She too wanted her daughter, above all, to be accepted. It was no betrayal, she told herself, Belle would still practise her religion at home.

The reasons for sending the two girls were totally different. Belle having outgrown her tutors, should go on to win a place at university from her new school. On assessing her outstanding talents the college had readily accepted the girl, noting that she would probably be ready to take the university examination well before the usual age. Sonny's reason for sending Rosanna was not so much to benefit her education – though she was not unintelligent and would, with self-discipline, have had little trouble in getting to university – it was the simple hope that a smidgeon of the breeding held by her peers might rub off on her, showing her the way young ladies were supposed to behave. Sonny loved her dearly but oh, she was a tomboy. Naturally, her going away to college meant that he and Josie would see less of her than they did now – but then both she and Nick were approaching adulthood and their weekend visits to Leeds were becoming less frequent anyway. They preferred to spend any free time in the company of their young neighbourhood friends.

'I hope you realise you're to blame for all this,' Rosanna was telling her cousin as they sat dolefully on their trunks with Nick, waiting to be packed off. 'If you weren't such a swot the idea of sending me to school would never have entered Father's mind.'

Belle snapped back, 'And do you imagine I enjoy being sent to live with a bunch of stupid girls, away from Gramps? If you can't say anything sensible keep your mouth shut!'

'No, don't blame Belle,' Nick interceded. 'It's Aunt Erin who says she must go. She's hardly any choice in the matter.'

'It's easy for you to be charitable,' said his sister waspishly. Nick was about to be apprenticed at Thomasin's store. It had been deemed unnecessary to educate him further; much better for him to gain experience in the field. 'Oh God, I'm sure I shall absolutely hate it!' She leapt from the trunk and ripped off her straw bonnet to lash irritably at anything in her way, prowling up and down the schoolroom like an ensnared vixen. The college was so far away, too – down south. Father, after an investigation, had said it was the best of its kind. 'I'll bet they never let us out of their sight – and what's the point of sending me now? I'm almost seventeen, I could be married by next year.' She paused to examine her ripening frame in the cheval mirror.

'That, I believe, is their reasoning,' replied her brother, winking at Belle. 'They're hoping to turn you into a young lady to improve your chances of matrimony. Personally I think they've as much chance of that as getting a navvy into a frock.'

She threw her hat at him, not caring when some of the decoration parted company with the beribboned crown. 'You swine!'

Calm as ever, Nick retrieved the battered hat and remoulded the dent in its crown. 'See what I mean?' he asked Belle.

'I'm sure I'll hate it just as much,' said their cousin, to which Rosanna replied, 'But at least you're able to do the things they'll give you. I'm hopeless at arithmetic.'

'I'll help you,' promised Belle in an unaccustomed burst of good nature.

'Oh, it's not just the work,' moaned Rosie. 'I shall feel so . . . hemmed in.'

Any further complaint was curtailed by the arrival of Erin who would be travelling with the girls. 'Oh, Rosanna, I despair of you!' She whisked the hat from Nick's hands and set it back in position, briskly tying the ribbons and tugging at Rosanna's clothes. 'I leave ye for five minutes an' ye look like ye've been caught up in a tornado.' She turned to Belle. 'Come along, dear, the cab is waiting. Nick, you can take Belle's trunk. Your grandfather is . . . ah, thank ye, Father,' she said as Patrick came in and swung the other trunk onto his shoulder, then hustled them along the landing. 'Mind the stairs, Belle. Hang on to the banister – Rosie, do hurry or we'll miss the train!'

On the pavement Rosanna and Belle swapped tearful goodbyes with their grandparents. 'Oh, Gramps.' Rosanna flung her arms round him. 'I'm going to miss you.'

He hugged her slim body, patting her back comfortingly. The heat of her small breasts pierced his waistcoat. He wondered why the onset of womanhood should cause him embarrassment, but it did. They grew up so quickly these days. He prised her gently from him. 'Come on now, dry your tears, the cab's waiting. 'Twon't be long before you're home again.' But it would seem like it to Pat. The house would be like a mausoleum without those girls. He hugged Belle, then helped them both into the cab and closed the

279

door while the cabbie loaded the trunks. 'An' no mischief remember, either of yese. Ye must do what your mistresses tell ye.'

'If I absolutely loathe it can I come home?' begged Rosie, hanging from the window.

'Rosanna, that's no way to face a new adventure,' said Thomasin. 'You must try and make an effort. When you come back your grandfather and I expect to see two young ladies and not the tearaways you are at present. You're almost a woman, time you were behaving with a little decorum.'

Patrick leaned forward to kiss her. 'Try not to be too unhappy, for my sake,' he whispered.

'I'll try, Gramps. Oh, goodbye! Goodbye!' The cab was pulling away, Rosie still draped across the window ledge, waving and crying.

Belle's striking eyes shone above her cousin's as she strained for a last sighting, holding onto her grandfather and dragging part of him with them.

The elderly couple watched until the carriage was round the corner, then Thomasin planted a hand on Nick's shoulder. 'Right, my lad – to work!'

The first time Nicholas had visited his grandmother's store he had known what he wanted to do with his life. The child had seen the man, ensconced in that leather chair in the counting house. So, for him the feeling today was one of exhilaration. The cab bearing him and his grandmother drew up outside the large store in Parliament Street, already open for custom with a display of shiny pots and pans marking the front entrance. In the beginning it had merely been a grocery, but now the shop windows displayed all manner of things, from copper kettles to currants. The one thing each item had in common was quality and a reasonable price. It was all rather grand when compared to the poky little shop which Thomasin had inherited.

The driver alighted to open the door for Thomasin. Nick scanned his future while his grandmother pulled the fare from a beaded purse. It was very impressive, but Nick considered it would be even more inspiring with a uniformed man on the door to bow and scrape to all those important customers. He put this to Thomasin as they went inside.

She took it as a hint and smiled. 'And when shall you be measured for your uniform, Nick?'

'Oh, I didn't mean I wanted the job, Nan,' he replied hastily. 'I have greater aspirations than to open and shut doors.'

They reached the counting house where Thomasin unlocked the door. 'Do you indeed? And what form might this ambition take?' She divested herself of her jacket and handed it to Nick to hang up.

'Didn't I tell you?' he asked lightly. 'I want your job, Nan.'

She laughed and seated herself behind the desk. 'From anyone else I'd treat that as a joke but not from you, Nick. I hope you don't expect me to move over and retire so that you can fill the slot?'

'I'm prepared to wait.' Nick wandered around the office, flicking through stacks of papers, leafing through books.

'Oh, I'm so glad to hear that I can look forward to a few more years' employment. I trust also that you're prepared to work to attain your aim? I certainly don't intend to hand it over on a platter.'

'I'm not averse to work.'

'Good – and naturally you realise, Nick, that you'll be expected to start at the bottom. There'll be no short cuts. Before you're fit to fill my shoes you'll need to learn every task in the store from sweeping the floor to serving behind the counter.' She paused. 'Do I detect a slackening of enthusiasm?'

Nick fondled his earlobe. 'I had rather hoped to concentrate on the accounts, the financial side. I was always good at mathematics.'

'Well, I dare say we'll be able to put your brain to good use in two or three years' time . . .'

'Two years!' He couldn't gag the exclamation.

'At the very least. A normal apprenticeship would be much longer. Running a business begins on the shop floor, Nick. You must learn how to treat your customers, for they're the ones who will carry you on to the counting house – without them there'd be no counting house. But before we let you loose on the public you must acquaint yourself with every commodity on those shelves; find out their country of origin, how to weigh them, everything about them so that should anyone enquire you will be able to supply the answer with confidence. Normally after this an apprentice would move on to provisions where he'd learn how to roll and cut bacon. Moving on in this fashion he'd cover every aspect of the store. However, I think we'll start you off with the roasting of the coffee this morning.' He groaned.

'Look, Nicholas, if I were to put you in a position of responsibility from the outset how would you cope if, say, the coffee roaster should break down?'

He nodded, seeing the wisdom in her question but inwardly determined to be finished with the monotonous jobs long before his two years were up.

'Very well, we'll have George in and make a start on your career. Before you go and fetch him though, will you straighten your tie? My workers must be as neat and presentable at the close of business as they were at the outset; if your tie's crooked now, what will it be like after twelve hours? Also, each morning you must sign your name and time of arrival in this ledger and take it to George for his initial. After this you will line up in the main store for inspection.'

Any hopes Nick had entertained that his apprenticeship would be swift and that his grandmother would whisk him up the ladder without his feet even brushing the rungs had been brutally quashed.

'George, my grandson Nick is about to commence his apprenticeship,' said Thomasin when the man entered. 'I want you to leave aside the groceries until this afternoon and concentrate on teaching him how to use the coffee roaster. Take no cheek from him and let him be under no illusion as to who is in charge. He is to expect no favours just because he's my grandson.'

A mischievous thought came to Nick as he followed George. Making his face innocent he enquired, 'If George happened to be ill at any time, Nan, should I come to you to learn how to use the coffee roaster?'

'I'm afraid . . .' began Thomasin, then broke off quickly.

'I suppose you do know how to use it?' added Nick. 'The owner of the store must be able to turn her hand to all aspects of the running of her business.'

Thomasin presented a shrewd smile. 'Just one more lesson before you go, Nicholas – the most important one. One must never try to make an ass of one's employer – unless of course one feels that egg is good for one's complexion.' She waved them away.

'Right, what do we do first then?' asked Nick when he and George stood beside the coffee roaster.

'Keen, aren't you?' replied the other, taking off his jacket and covering his clothes with an apron.

'Not particularly. I just want to get it over with as quickly as possible so I can get on with more important things.'

'Begging your pardon, Master Nick, but this is a very important job,' objected George. 'Here, put this apron on.'

'It might be to you who has no more brains than to work this infernal contraption,' said Nick haughtily, taking off his jacket and donning the apron. 'But I certainly don't class it as such. So, if you'll just kindly show me what I must do.'

George's mouth tightened at the lack of manners from this young upstart but he clung onto his patience; this was after all the boss's grandson, for all her instructions about making him know who was master. 'Look here, then. First thing when you come in you've got to stoke the old roaster up wi' plenty of kindling. Get it burning good before you stick t'beans on. You'll need to come in earlier than anybody else so's to have it going for when they arrive, 'specially on cold mornings.'

Nick yawned and nodded impatiently as George went through the stages, showing little interest.

'Are you listenin' to what I'm tellin' yer?' prodded George. 'Bloomin' 'eck, you used to be such a keen little thing . . . if you haven't grasped it by the end o' the week the missus'll blame me. Now pay attention.'

'I am keen and I don't have to pay attention as I got it the first time.'

'Right then, you're so clever you just show me what I showed you.'

With a bored face Nick enacted each stage precisely as he had been shown.

George delivered grudging credit. 'Oh well, you've picked it up very quick – mindst I'd already got it lighted for you – but well done, Master Nicholas.'

'Well, it's not exactly a strain on the intellect, is it?' replied Nick. 'Is that all there is to it?'

'S'truth, no. Once you've tackled this we've got to get you onto tastin' and blendin'. That can take years to learn. Some folk never get the hang of it, you've got to acquire a sharp palate. Right now, we'll just have to wait till the beans are done before we reach the next step.'

Nick tapped his foot impatiently and gave a weary sigh, looking about him for something more entertaining. 'Surely there's something more pressing I could be seeing to?'

'We-ell, there is,' said George dubiously. 'But I don't know if you're up to it. If there are any slip-ups I'll get the blame. There's this special order wants collectin' from the market.'

'Come on, I can do it,' pressed Nick.

George appeared to be struggling with a decision. 'It's for one o' the missus's special customers. You have to ask for it precisely.'

'Shall I write it down?'

'Aye, you'd better,' nodded George. 'There's a pad and pencil over there. Yer'll need to take a trolley an' all.'

'Right, fire away,' said Nick, pencil poised.

'Six crates o' cod's eyelids – Danish ones,' said George,

watching the pencil move rapidly over the pad. 'They must be Danish. The customer won't have any other sort. I'm relyin' on you to get it right, otherwise I'm for the chop.'

'Don't worry, you can depend on me.' Nick finished scribbling.

'Good,' said George. 'It needs somebody wi' brains.' He kept his straight face until Nick had departed to find a trolley, then his mouth turned up like a slice of melon.

It wasn't until Nick had made his request to the woman on the fish stall that he realised he'd been taken for a dupe. 'Yes, my dear, would that be the one-eyed variety you'd be requiring?' His face burnt crimson as her cackles followed his rapid retreat, his mouth set in a determined line. – Oh, very funny, George Ackworth. That's one up to you, I believe. Well, let's just see how funny you think it is when I've got your job.

His return to the store was met by sniggers from those whom George had told – which was almost everyone, but Nick put on an uncaring smile, even though he was seething at being made the centre of their ridicule. Instead of going straight up to George he hid for a time behind one of the pillars that supported the roof of the stockroom, waiting to get his own back. George was dishing out instructions to a youth. After he had marched off Nick heard the youth grumbling to a girl, 'I'll bet he's gone for a bleedin' smoke in the closet while I'm slavin' me guts out.'

The lavatory was situated outside at the far end of a dingy passage. Luckily for Nick his adversary had gone first to the staffroom to collect his pipe and tobacco, giving Nick time to get to the closet before him. Lifting the latch he stepped inside and waited in the pitch darkness.

George glanced over his shoulder before sticking his pipe between his teeth and wandering down the murky passageway. He was in the act of applying a match, not taking a great deal of notice of his surroundings as he placed a foot into the dark interior. Suddenly he became aware of a presence – felt it rather than saw it, and peered into the cobwebby shadows of the rear wall.

His jaw fell, along with the pipe which clattered to the floor as a pair of disembodied hands floated out from the darkness, reaching for his throat. His eyes bulged, he took a step back, spluttering with terror as the hands loomed nearer, shimmering translucently like something from another world. Then a ghastly wailing rent the air. With a scream George tore back up the passage, stumbled and fell into a pallet containing the day's delivery of eggs which came crashing down around him, splattering the yard with yolk. Regardless of the mess he was in, George picked himself up and ran back into the store bawling for help as he took the steps to the stockroom four at a time. He did not look back. Only when he made human contact did he stop running to relate breathlessly his ghastly experience.

Nick grinned to himself, scraped the silvery fishscales from his hands into the lavatory pan and watched the evidence disappear. He had Belle to thank for that trick. Discovering, by accident, that fishscales shine in the dark, she had dipped her hands into the herring barrel and waited in the pantry for Abi to finish her tale of the supernatural. Seeing those fish barrels in the market had brought the memory back. It was a wonder poor Abi's hair wasn't as silver as the scales with all the terrible tricks they had played on her. But unlike George she had seen the figure behind the ghostly hands and had issued swift punishment. Nick wondered if owning up to George would bring him the same – still it would be worth it to have made the man look a fool. He stepped out into the daylight, face smug as he tugged at his cuffs.

Poor George was still stuttering the tale to his work-mates when Nick arrived. He caught hold of the apprentice's sleeve. 'Eh, you'll never guess what happened . . .'

Nick waited until the man had finished, then said, 'Sounds very fishy to me. I didn't see anything when I was down there – apart from you, that is. Made a right mess of those eggs, didn't you?' At George's gormless look he laughed and told the others what he had done, causing wild hilarity. His moment of revenge was cut short, though, for a furious George made him go and clean up the mess of broken eggs. The moment he was back, he ordered him to go and help two women who were weighing sugar into bags, telling them that he was leaving the young master in their care and hoping they knew how to treat him. 'Leave him to us, Mr Ackworth,' said Martha with a wink at her partner. 'We'll look after him.'

Nick soon found out that being looked after involved being sat on by the portly Martha while Millie scooped tons of sugar down his trousers. His squirming embarrassment was met with giggles and served only to add gusto to Millie's shovellings as she wrestled beneath his waistband. Such impropriety! At his release, his first umbraged act was to march straight to his grandmother and demand if she knew what sordid games were going on in her own storeroom.

Leaning back in her chair she arched her back stiffly. 'Oh dear, I'm sorry I didn't warn you about the ragging, Nick. I'm afraid it happens to every newcomer.'

'It was more than a ragging, Nan,' complained Nick, hot-eyed and shuffling his hips inside the gritty trousers. 'If you could see the amount of sugar that's ended up on the floor . . .'

'Ah well, it's only the once,' said Thomasin amiably. 'They have to let off a bit of steam now and again. But I think you're safe now; they've had their sport.'

Nick was unappeased. 'If you're not going to do anything, I'd better go back to George!' He tried to dislodge the rough substance from the tender insides of his thighs. When she merely nodded he made a peevish return to the storeroom where he was taunted for another hour until it was time for tea – which Nick was given the task of making. He asked what to do.

'Don't tell me you don't know how to make a pot o' tea – an' you with all them brains.' This from George.

Nick sighed and mooched off to the staffroom, reappearing some twenty minutes later with the news that the tea was brewed.

'Did you enjoy your trip?' asked George, and at Nick's frown added, 'Well, the amount o' time it took you I thought you'd gone to pick your own tea-leaves. Right, dumbcluck, you'd best pour a cup for the missus and take it down on a tray.'

'I don't know about pour.' Millie grimaced at her own cup. 'I should say hack yourself a piece off. I can hardly stir a spoon through mine.'

No sooner had Nick returned from his trip to the counting house and poured himself a cup, it seemed that George had him on his feet again. So tired was Nick when the store closed at seven that the action of the carriage which transported him and his grandmother home all but rocked him to sleep.

It was Thomasin's voice that stopped him from going over completely. 'Well, Nick, and how d'you enjoy working for your grandmother?'

He opened one glassy eye in the dimness of the cab, head lolling. 'Ask me again in a fortnight, Nan, when I've recovered from the shock.' Apparently it was going to take more than a few fishscales to fettle George Ackworth.

By Friday, Nick had learnt how to use the coffee roaster by himself, had undergone sampling techniques, had taken a spell in the bakery, knew what work in the stockroom entailed, had filled shelves, swept floors and was now taking his turn behind the counter. At least being busy made the time go faster but oh God, how could he last another two years of this? It was all so hopelessly boring. When he had envisaged helping his grandmother it had been as a sort of junior partner, designing better ways for them to make money, going to the docks to shop for bargains as that man Farthingale was now doing, the swine. Nick still did not particularly like him; it was nothing personal, just that Nick envied him his position. He must find a way to achieve his goal more quickly.

At ten-thirty George came down and informed Nick he could take his tea. After a ten-minute break he was running down the steps back to the front store when, realising he had left his jacket in the staffroom, he was forced to go back. As he did so he caught George

Ackworth's back view disappearing around a corner. What it was that made him follow he could not say – perhaps it was the furtive crouch of George's shoulders. Treading carefully, Nick peeped around the edge of the wall and watched as, one by one, George removed a stack of crates from before a doorway.

At one point George's head spun round, causing Nick to duck swiftly out of sight. But after listening for a few seconds the man relaxed and, taking a key from his pocket, opened the cupboard door which had been exposed by the removal of the stack of crates. Nick craned his neck as George vanished into the cupboard, then bobbed down once again as the man re-emerged. George's next step was to lift one of the boxes from the stack and carry it into the cupboard. This done he locked the door and replaced the stack in its former position.

Nick was forced to dash, making a mental note to investigate the cupboard at the first opportunity. This, however, did not come until the afternoon.

After lunch Thomasin, pleased with her grandson's progress, told him he would be working with her on the books that afternoon. 'If we get you acquainted with them you'll be a great help to me when it comes to rounding up tomorrow night.'

He was grateful for this chance to display his true talents and, indeed, showed no tardiness in grasping the system, though she had given him little tutoring. The bills of sale accumulated at the end of each day were entered into a ledger, the totals of each day's sales were in turn transferred to a weekly account book, as were any invoices. This in its turn was entered into a monthly ledger, and finally a quarterly tome, at which point a stockcheck was performed, the theoretical figures supposedly tallying with the actual items in stock.

'Could I leave you to sort out those bills, Nick?' asked Thomasin halfway through the afternoon. 'I've a meeting with the accountant at four. I shan't be long. Perhaps, though, you might care to come with me?'

'I'd sooner get the measure of these books if it's all the same to you, Nan,' replied Nick.

This answer gladdened her, though her face showed nothing. It didn't do to praise Nicholas – he had a tendency towards egotism that would have to be dealt with before he made a satisfactory shop manager. However, her following concession showed that she was not displeased with his progress. 'I shall leave my keys in your safekeeping so that you're able to lock up the counting house every time you step out. Don't forget now, every time – even if it's within your view, never leave it unlocked. Understand?' She left him gazing pensively at the keys.

Allowing her time to get well out of the way Nick strode to the door, stepped outside and locked it, then went in search of George. By a stroke of luck, the man was having his afternoon tea. Flitting past the open staffroom door Nick made for the stockroom and began to dismantle the stack of crates one by one. Once the cupboard was accessible he withdrew Thomasin's bunch of keys, testing each before finally coming up with the one that fitted. Slipping inside, he closed the door behind him. It was very dim, but a tiny skylight enabled him to see just what George had been up to.

The place was piled high with boxes, crates and packages, bottles, seemingly in no particular order. Nick quickly totted up how much stock was in here and whistled quietly. Then he exited, relocked the door and hurriedly replaced the stack.

On returning to the counting house he experienced a prickling of his vitals on finding the door ajar; that he had locked it he was certain. Going inside he encountered George who straightened abruptly and snapped down the front cover of the ledger over which he had been stooped. Both showed their relief, with an 'Oh, it's you!' then laughed.

'I thought I'd left the door open,' smiled Nick. 'Nan left me the keys. I had to go out the back.'

'Oh, I see. No, it were me.' George passed him, making

his way out. 'I have a spare set o' keys. I just wanted to check up on a few figures. Right, have you had yer tea?'

'Yes,' lied Nick. There were more pressing matters than tea at this moment. 'I'm going to sit down and practise my book-keeping.'

The minute George had gone Nick moved to the ledger and opened it, skimming through the great pages, each covered in a mass of numbers. It was useless trying to unravel anything significant when one didn't know quite what one was looking for. But he continued to leaf methodically through the ledger until the pages turned up blank, then flipped back to the last completed page and ran his index finger down each column. There seemed to be nothing amiss. Defeated, he was about to close the book when he caught something. It was this he was studying avidly when Thomasin returned.

'Have you got it mastered then, Nick?'

'Not quite.' He uncurved his spine and smiled, then returned to the ledger. 'Nan . . . if somebody wanted to steal from you how would they go about it without you finding out?'

'I don't care for the sound of that.' It was delivered in jocular manner.

Nick half-smiled but persevered. 'I should know if I'm to make anything of the job. How might they do it?'

'Impossible,' replied his grandmother, scrabbling in her bag for the spectacles she had taken to wearing. 'They could get away with it for a while but come stock-taking the deception would be revealed in the figures. Why?'

He smiled and closed the book. 'I just wondered, that's all.'

'Well, stop wondering and go fetch your grandmother a pot of tea. I'm parched.' She pushed him aside to reclaim her seat.

He decided not to tell her about the altered figures yet – the nines changed to eights, the hundred and ten changed deftly into a forty – not until he was sure; knew how George was disposing of his pilfered goods.

On Saturday he found out. Apparently Thomasin's

week followed a set pattern; she did the same things at the same time every day, almost without fail. Late on Saturday afternoon, after the day's takings had been totalled and all the surplus notes and cash taken from the till, she would absent herself from the shop for half an hour in order to take the money to the bank. Whilst there she would enjoy a weekly chat with her bank manager.

George Ackworth, Nick discovered, also had his Saturday ritual. As soon as Thomasin departed a man who had been waiting out of sight for this eventuality would steer his horse and cart into the kerb, pass over money to his friend George, who would help him load the contents of the cupboard onto his cart, and be safely away before Thomasin's return.

Watching them now from an upstairs window, Nick wondered how he could get to the bank to warn his grandmother without George spotting him. It was not enough to inform her of the deception; he had to have proof.

George finished his task, slapped the horse on the rump and saw the cart safely away with ten minutes to spare before Thomasin's return. Nick bristled at the self-congratulatory smirk, the smug dusting of palms and thought – you saucy blighter, robbing my grandmother, in broad daylight too, but I'll have you! He pulled away from the window as George stepped back into the store and went about his business, racking his brain for some remedy. The idea came quickly, but it took another week before it could be implemented.

Thomasin cashed up as normal, packed her money into the leather satchel and was about to call for a youth to accompany her to the bank until Nick made his suggestion.

'Wouldn't it be a good idea if I were to come with you, Nan? After all, you said I should learn every aspect of the trade and I should've thought that banking was a pretty vital aspect.'

'Splendid idea, Nick.' She handed him a receipt book. 'You can total that up and fill in the date while I get my coat. Here's my key, lock the door when you're ready.' Exercising her habit Thomasin went to the bank accompanied by Nick, paid the money over the counter and was about to pop her head into the manager's outer office when Nick clapped a hand to his mouth.

'Oh, Nan! I can't recall whether I locked the door.' He needed an excuse to lure her back to the store. By giving him the keys she herself had provided it.

'Oh, Nicholas, how careless of you! Well, that's that, then.' She started away from the manager's door. 'I can't sit drinking tea with Mr Sims, wondering if someone is creeping about in my counting house. Come along.' Her legs moved rapidly under the rustling skirts. There was no hint of age in her step. 'You really must take more care, you know. You're very competent in some matters but I should be able to rely on you completely.'

She chivvied him all the way back along the street, then, as they neared the store, she stopped dead. 'That's odd. We shouldn't be getting a delivery today.' She proceeded on her way, a grimly apprehensive Nicholas marching alongside. 'George!'

What a picture his face was, thought Nick as the man swivelled in shock, almost toppling under his load of boxes. 'Mrs Feeney!'

Thomasin stared hard for a few moments at the contents of the cart, before coming to the realisation that this was not a delivery but a despatch. 'Would you step into the office, George?' she said icily, then to the man who was about to climb onto his cart, 'My invitation extends to you also. After you.' A sweep of the hand. 'Nicholas, would you accompany us, please?'

In the counting house Thomasin seated herself in the big leather chair and glared regally at the two recalcitrants before her. 'Now, would one of you kindly explain what was going on out there?'

George snatched a look at his accomplice, at Nick, at Thomasin, then hung his head. No one seemed eager to voice the obvious. Unable to stand the fecund atmosphere Nick decided to act as midwife.

'As there are no explanations forthcoming, Grand-mother, might I put forward my solution?' At Thomasin's curt nod he brought forth the ledger and placed it before her. Opening it he pointed out one of the altered figures, telling her also about the secret cache upstairs.

When he had done she asked, 'How long has this been going on?'

Nick twitched his shoulders. 'I've only been here a fortnight.'

'If you knew before today then why . . . ?' she spread her hands.

'I was taught not to tell tales,' replied Nick, causing his grandmother to crumple despairingly. 'That's why I decided it best you should see for yourself.'

'And now I've seen,' answered Thomasin in a low tone. 'To think I trusted . . .' She shook her head. 'Why, George, for God's sake? You've worked your way up from apprentice to a position of responsibility. All those years thrown away in a moment of greed. Didn't you think I paid you enough? Was that your reason for stealing from me?'

He could not face her. 'No, ma'am, you paid very well.'

'Then why? Tell me so I can understand, 'cause I'm damned if I do at the moment. Was it the excitement? Was it a game, or what?'

'I don't know, ma'am.' Shame oozed from every pore.

'Well, if you don't, George, I'm sure I don't.' She sighed again. 'I'm sorry but there's nothing else for it. Nicholas, would you step down to the police station and fetch assistance.'

George's eyes came up like unloosed arrows. 'But, missis, yer can't do that, yer can't! I'll be sent to prison. Mrs Feeney, I've worked for you for fifteen years . . .'

'You didn't appear to give that much relevance when you stole from me, George, so why should I?'

'Please, oh please, missus,' begged Ackworth. 'Don't tell the police. I'll pay back every penny I took.'

'And just how much would that entail, George?'

He was awkward again. 'I don't rightly know.'

'Then how do you propose to pay it back if you don't know the exact amount?'

'I don't know . . . but pay it I will.' His hands pleaded. 'Have pity, ma'am. I've got a family that's relyin' on me.'

'I was relying on you, George. I placed my trust in you and see how you've repaid it.'

'I'll work for nowt, Mrs Feeney! How's my family gonna survive if I'm in jail?'

Nick watched the changing expressions on his grandmother's face, his stomach taut at the fight taking place there – she's going to let him off, he thought. Dammit, he's getting round her.

But no, Thomasin's compassion was overruled by cool authority. 'And tell me, how is your family to survive if you work for no wage, George?'

There was no response. He hung his head again, beaten.

'And how would *my* family survive if I permitted every person in my employ a free hand with my property? We would pretty soon be destitute, wouldn't we? No, I'm deeply regretful, George, but you and your partner knew what the consequences would be if you were caught. You chose that path and must follow it through. Nicholas, go fetch a policeman.'

When the felons had been removed Thomasin went over the event in her mind, wondering if she had been too hard. She posed the question to Nick and he endorsed her action. Her finger and thumb worked at her wedding ring while she issued her disbelief that this had been going on under her very nose. 'And we still don't know how much is missing.'

'A busy woman like you can't be expected to know everything that's going on, Nan. That's what you need me for.'

For once she gave a hint of acknowledgment. 'Fair dues, Nick, I have to agree you've been most vigilant. What would you like for your reward?'

'George's job,' replied Nick with no hesitation, and at her sharp laugh asked, 'Why not? I've learnt how to roast the coffee, keep the shelves stocked, cash the tills, entrance the customers, do the books – that's apparently more than George was capable of,' came the mordant addition. She protested that he had only been at the store for a fortnight. 'What's that got to do with anything, Nan? The important question is: can I do the job and the answer is: yes, I can.'

'You never were short on confidence.' – Like your real father, she thought. You have his deviousness too, but judging by the example you've just given you'll put it to better use than Dickie ever did. After a moment of lip-biting indecision she capitulated. He had, after all, picked things up amazingly quickly. 'Very well, I shall give you a month's trial, the same I'd allow any other person applying for the job. Will that be acceptable to His Highness?'

He cocked his head and answered impudently, 'Mm, for the time being.'

'You're a cheeky young monkey,' she breathed, then studied him carefully. 'You *told* me to wait a fortnight before asking if you enjoyed working for me. Have you decided yet?'

He pulled his cuffs down, adjusted his tie and produced a grin which gave her another painful reminder of the boy's natural father. 'Oh yes, Nan. I think this young man is going to like working for you very much indeed.'

CHAPTER NINETEEN

On Sunday the sky ripped apart, emptying its wet, noisy load on the streets of York. Just the few steps from the carriage to the door of the church turned their crisp Sunday best into soggy dishrags. All day it continued, making any Sabbath outing impossible, so most of the time was given to chatting with Sonny and Josie who had come over for the day with their youngsters. They returned to Leeds after the evening meal and shortly afterwards everyone else went to their beds. The noise of the storm kept Nick awake; he was a light sleeper at the best of times. There was a tree directly outside his bedroom window whose branches slapped and clawed at the wet pane. Instead of lying there trying to sleep Nick lit a paraffin lamp and selected a book from the pile on his bedside table, settling back against his pillow with a yawn.

The wind roared down the chimney, making him shiver and pull the blankets up further. It also had the effect of making the tree tap more forcefully on the pane. He had turned over two pages before he realised the tapping was not performed solely by the tree. Frowning, he screwed up his eyes and peered at the opaque glass. All he could see was his own reflection and the yellow glare of the lamp. 'Nick, Nick!' howled the wind. 'Let me in!' And rap, rap, rap! went the branch. Curious, Nick laid the open book on its pages and padded across to the window. Through the effulgence a face loomed – Rosanna's. 'Let me in for God's sake!'

Quickly, he shoved up the sash, lashing at the curtains which billowed in with the gust. 'What the bloody hell . . .'

'Shut up and get out of the way!' Rosanna slung her knee over the sill and hauled the rest of her body after it, falling in a saturated heap on the bedroom floor.

Nick, hair and nightshirt adrift in the blast, pulled the window down, shutting out the deluge, then turned to stare down at his sister. 'Is it the cheese I had for supper giving me nightmares? What're you doing here?'

'I've run away,' She was pulling off her wet shoes and stockings and massaging her toes. 'I couldn't stand it any longer.'

'But why the window – and why mine?'

'Because,' she stripped off more wet clothes, 'the front door was locked as was the window of my room. I had to crawl along the ledge to yours.'

'But it's four inches wide, you could've been blown off!'

'Well, I wasn't. Oh, Nick, do stop going on like Aunt Erin and get me something to dry my hair with. Just look at me.' She shook her head, spraying him with droplets.

He found a towel with which she wiped her pink face, then rubbed briskly over her hair. 'Oh, that's better. God, I could do with a hot drink, though. I'm absolutely frozen.

Oh, Nick!' She launched herself at him, the tears flowing. 'It was ghastly, terrible. I hated it.'

'So you ran away.' It was said half-accusingly.

'I had to,' she wept. 'I tried writing to Gramps about it but one of the mistresses discovered the letter and tore it up. She said I was being a goose, that I'd soon settle down, but I didn't, it got worse. They kept us in all the time, wouldn't let us out for walks unsupervised.' To Rosie who loved to go wandering off on her own whenever the fancy took her this was the worst possible torture.

'Well, you chose a fine night to make your escape, I must say. How did you get here?' She told him she had had sufficient money saved to cover the train fare. 'And you came on your own? Good Christ, girl, you could've been murdered.' Her shivering had transferred itself to him. 'Look, take off your things and get into bed.'

She sniffed and pulled away to look into his face. 'In your bed, you mean?'

'Well, yours won't have any sheets, will it? They weren't expecting anybody to drop in like this.'

'But I've no nightgown or anything. I had to leave all my clothes behind when I climbed out of the window.'

He suddenly remembered. 'What about Belle?'

'She hates it too, but she said her mother would go hairless and only send her back.'

'I'm glad one of you had some sense. Here.' Nick pulled one of his own nightshirts from a drawer. 'Put that on.'

'In front of you?'

He waved his hand flippantly. 'You're nothing much to see.' He had viewed both his sister and his cousin naked – though they didn't know it – and compared them, not lustfully, just with clinical interest.

'You slug!'

'Oh, very well, I'll turn my back. But do hurry – I'm getting cold now.' He listened to the swish of soggy clothes being ripped from an equally drenched body, then, at the silence, turned to find she was ready. 'Get in.'

'It isn't right.' Her white teeth gnawed at her lip. She knew that this was how babies came about. Nick, who knew everything, had informed both her and Belle some time ago.

'Don't be stupid, I'm your brother. Get in.'

Smiling gratefully Rosie climbed into the still-warm bed whose sheets wafted of her brother, and looked at him as he rolled in beside her, pulling the blankets round them both and snuggling his body up to hers.

'Oo, cuddle me, I'm freezing.' She wriggled.

Nick put his arms round her and hugged her body into his. He experienced an acute awareness, of soft mounds thrusting their erect tips into his chest, burning skin through his nightgown at breast and thigh, the smell of warm, damp feminine flesh, the whisper of breath against his cheek.

'Goodnight, Nick.' She kissed him and snuggled her head into the hollow twixt neck and shoulder.

'Goodnight.' While she shivered he lay with eyes open and thought for a while. It was odd, he had attached so much importance to carving himself a niche at the store that his growing body's needs had passed almost unrecorded until now when the warmth of femininity curling into him stirred a note of wonder – and other things. Rosanna had stopped shivering. Her breathing had taken on the regularity of sleep. His own eyelids became heavy. However, before he dropped off Nick had decided with the same businesslike detachment he had used to gain his foothold at the store that tomorrow he must set about another, equally important task. He must find himself a woman.

'I think your most advantageous position would be to stay in bed until Nan and I go out to work.' Nick stuck his legs out from under the blankets to test the air, then pulled them in quickly. 'Fooh, it's the best place to be as well.' He directed his face towards the tangled head beside him. 'Nan's more likely to send you back than Grandad. If you catch him on his own before he sets off for his fields you should be able to get round him.' A yawn. 'Oh well, I suppose I'd better depart.' He leapt out quickly and without embarrassment ripped off his nightshirt to stand naked by the washstand.

Rosie pretended to hide her face but, as he sloshed water on himself, peeped over the bedclothes. He knew she was looking and grinned to himself, turning quickly to catch her. She snapped her eyes tightly shut. 'Enjoy your geg?'

'I don't know what you're talking about,' she mumbled through the sheet. 'Are you decent yet?'

Still grinning he pulled on his clothes, dancing about unsteadily as he stepped into his trousers. 'All right, you can come out now.' He finished dressing as her puffy face emerged.

'Will you bring me some breakfast?' Muzzy eyes blinked at him over white linen.

'Oh yes, what would madam like?' he asked sarcastically. 'Milk in one pocket and porridge in the other?'

'A bit of dried toast would do.' She pretended to be hurt at his callousness. 'I haven't eaten since yesterday lunchtime.'

'All right, if I can sneak anything from the table I will, but stay where you are and don't make a sound.'

Thirty minutes later Rosanna sat up in his bed devouring a piece of buttered toast.

'And dispose of the crumbs when you've finished,' he warned. 'They can get in the most uncomfortable places. Right, I'm off. I'll see you tonight – if you're still around.'

'I will be,' she grinned with certainty.

The toast made her thirsty. Unfortunately Nick had been unable to bring up anything to drink. Clambering from the bed she went to the door, opened it and peeped round the edge. The landing was empty. She pelted lightly along the Axminster runner to the bathroom where she filled a glass with water. It was tempting to use the closet, but if she pulled the chain they would wonder who it was. She had better use Nick's chamberpot instead.

This she did and had just climbed back into bed when the door opened and Abigail came in. 'God a'mercy on us!' She seized her chest in fright, but on seeing the identity of the intruder relaxed and shut the door hastily, scuttling up to confront Rosanna, who had been equally alarmed.

'Miss Rosie ... You nearly frightened the life outta me!'

'Ssh, Abi!' Rosie put a finger to her lips. 'I don't want anyone to know I'm here. Have Nick and my grandmother left the house yet?'

'Yes, just this minute – Miss Rosie, whatever've you been up to? And what are you doin' in Master Nick's bed?' At Rosie's explanation she asked, 'But where did poor Master Nick sleep?'

'Oh, there's plenty of room in here for two little bums. I didn't deprive him of his comfort.'

'Oh, Lord preserve us!' The maid's hands went to her face. 'You slept all night wi' Master Nick?'

'Yes, what's wrong with that?'

'It's ... it's just wrong, that's all, very wrong. The master an' mistress'd go off their heads if they knew.'

'But why? I mean I've learnt enough to know it would be wrong to sleep with someone who wasn't my husband ... but for goodness' sake, Nick's only my brother! Surely there's no wrong in that?'

Abi studied the innocent face. Her response was awkward. 'Well, it's not my place to tell you ... it's just wrong, take my word for it. An' I shouldn't tell anyone else about it. If the mistress asks tell her you slept in your own room, say you sneaked some sheets from the linen cupboard. I'll take some to your room right now an' make 'em look as though they've been slept in.' She sighed. 'Oh, Miss Rosie, you don't half get up to some tricks. You shouldn't be knowing half o' what you know ... oh well, now you're here what are you going to do? You can't stay up here all the time.'

'Is my grandfather still down there?' Abigail said he was. 'Well, I shall go down and throw myself on his mercy. Oh,' she looked at the pile of clothes on the floor, 'my things'll still be wet. D'you think you could slip and find me something from my wardrobe? I left all my stuff at school.'

Abigail tutted but did as she was asked and helped Rosanna to dress, then brushed out her tangled hair. 'There, you look a bit more presentable now. Well, go on then, you'd better go before the master sets off for his work. Your Aunt Erin is downstairs, too.'

'Oh, damn! I'll have a harder job of it than I thought,' sighed Rosie and gritting her teeth went to meet her fate.

Patrick and Erin were as surprised as the maid had been, the former rising from his seat where he had been enjoying his newspaper until the whirlwind hurled itself at him. 'Rosanna, darlin'! Whatever's happened?'

'Oh, Gramps, please, please don't send me back to that horrid school! I can't bear it. Everyone hates me. The lessons are impossible. If you send me back I know I'll die!'

Patrick made her sit beside him, putting a comforting arm around her and dabbing at her wet cheeks. Erin looked on cynically. 'Ye've hardly given school a fair chance to say if ye like it or not; you've only been there a fortnight.'

Rosie ignored her aunt and directed her plea at Patrick. 'Oh, Grandfather, please let me stay. I swear I'll be no bother. Don't send me back. Please, please.'

'Rosie-posie,' he hugged her slim, shaking body. 'Whatever am I going to do with you?' He was brought upright by a loud ringing. 'Oh, Jazers, that bloody telephone will be the death o' me! I'll never get used to it.' He deserted his grand-daughter and went to the hall where he beat Abi to picking up the receiver. 'Hello! Hello! Yes, this is Patrick Feeney. Who? Oh, Sonny! Yes, yes she's here, hang on.' He craned his neck to take in the occupants of the dining room. 'The school has been on to your father. Ye've had him worried out of his mind.' He applied his mouth to the appliance again. 'She's all right, Sonny! We haven't heard the full story yet but no doubt we ... yes, yes. Oh, no, it's no inconvenience. Oh, yes, I agree, it would be pointless. She says she hates the place. So, will

I . . . ? Very well. Yes, I'll rip the skin from her back . . . all right, Son. Goodbye, then. God go with ye. Yes. 'Bye!' He replaced the receiver on its hook and returned to give Rosanna the news. 'Well, your father wasn't too pleased I can tell ye.' Reseating himself at the table he dragged up the teapot and poured himself a cup. 'But . . .' he turned to her, 'ye don't have to go back if ye truly hate it.'

'Oh, Gramps!' She flung her arms round his neck and kissed him gratefully.

'Careful now, ye'll spill me tea.'

'You and Sonny are as soft as each other,' Erin told him. 'I know what I'd do if it were my child who'd behaved so. I'd give her a good whipping and send her back. Ye get far too much of your own way, young lady. Ye must learn to curb that wilful streak – and what about Belle, might I ask? I bet ye didn't spare a thought for her feelings when ye ran away an' left her all alone.'

'I asked if she wanted to come,' replied the girl. 'But she said no.'

'No, she's more sense, I'm glad to say. Well, and what are ye going to do with yourself now? Ye can't sit around the house all day getting under the servants' feet.'

Rosanna thought for a while, then said, 'Could I go with you, Gramps?'

'And do what – dig praties?'

'Oh, please, I won't get in your way. And it would keep me out of mischief if you're there to keep an eye on me, wouldn't it?' came the sly addition.

'It can get awful cold standing round doing nothing,' said Patrick doubtfully. He wasn't certain he wanted to take his grand-daughter among a bunch of rough labourers.

'Oh, Grandad, I've had a splendid idea! Aren't you always saying how you detest paperwork? Well, I could do it all for you. Oh, go on,' she saw him weaken. 'Just for today at least.'

'Oh, all right then.' He gave in as he always did to his grandchildren. 'But wrap up warm, mind.'

She kissed him again and, grabbing another slice of toast, pelted off to get her coat.

'Ye shouldn't let her take advantage, Dad,' reproved Erin. ''Tis the same with all o' them, they wrap ye round their little fingers. Ye should've made her go back. She'll have to learn some day there are things we all dislike doing but we must do them all the same.'

'Erin, what good would it do if I sent her back? She'd only run away again.'

'Then ye should send her back again till she gets the idea. I'd like to have seen myself get away with it when I was her age.' What angered Erin most was the opportunity of a good education which Rosanna so blithely tossed aside. Erin would have cut off her legs and crawled there on bleeding stumps to be granted the same opening.

'Well, things are different these days. 'Tis obvious that Rosie isn't cut out for learnin'. The best thing I can do for her is to keep her safe till it's time to hand her over to her husband, whoever he may be. She'll he happier being with me than at school. And, as she said herself, at least I'll be able to keep an eye on her, won't I?'

Patrick's land was approximately two miles from the city. Here he not only grew produce for Thomasin's store but supplied other retailers as well, his growing area having expanded considerably since the early days. Once there he steered Rosanna towards a large wooden building where the crates of fruit and vegetables were stored.

She stepped past him into the barn, rubbing her arms to counteract the cold. 'Where's your office, Gramps?'

He nodded to a hook on which was impaled an untidy selection of dockets and a notebook dangling from a string. 'That's it.'

Her jaw dropped, then knowing that to complain might get her sent back to school she snapped it into a resolute grimace and strode across to seize a fistful of dockets. 'Is there a table I can rest on?'

Patrick handed her a piece of board and pointed to a

crate. 'Ye'll have to sit on that an' balance the board on your knee.'

'So modern,' she tendered sarcastically.

'I do apologise. If I'd known I was to get a secretary I would've ordered a bureau and a leather chair. 'Twas your suggestion, Rosie, remember.'

'Oh, I'm not complaining, Gramps.' She pulled out a handkerchief and dusted off the crate before sitting on it. 'Right then, you go ahead, I'll make a start.'

He tugged his forelock. 'Oh, 'tis all right with milady if I go see to me men, then?'

'Quite satisfactory. Run along, young man.'

When the door had closed Rosanna heaved a sigh and stared around her at the crates of cabbages and turnips. Still, anything was better than school. She followed the piece of string that was attached to the notebook and captured the pencil at its other end. Opening the book she glanced back over previous pages then settled down to enter the dockets. It seemed simple enough and didn't take long. With nothing more to do she became bored. Slipping from her seat she went to the door and peeped outside. It looked quite pleasant now that the sun was out. The impulse that was a frequent visitor to Rosanna took hold of her feet again, luring them first over the threshold, then – all thought of work dispersing on the chill air – propelling her towards the sunlit fields.

The path that led from the storehouse took her along the perimeter of the growing area. She wandered unhurriedly down its bumpy route, consuming the sights and sounds. Her grandfather's figure was as a midget's way across the far side of the field where he doled out orders to his men. Holding her face to the sun she smiled and stretched her arms joyfully. Ah, freedom! How lovely to be away from that school.

Adjacent to the path was a hawthorn hedge. Periodically she would stop and delve into its folds, seeking out the small creatures that might be waiting, quivering, for her to pass. Coming across a deserted nest she inserted two fingers into the elongated funnel – which signified to her that it belonged to a long-tailed tit – feeling the interior for an unhatched egg; it was empty. She wandered on.

Where the hedge finally stopped there was a small but dense clump of woodland which looked interesting. She drifted amongst the group of trees scuffling her shoes through the carpet of rotting leaves. A sudden crack brought her head up. She stared as a young man emerged from behind a tree, his hands at his breeches.

Instantly aware that he was not alone the youth started, then swiftly turned his back on her, fingers scrabbling busily at his clothes. When he turned back his weathered face had even more colour than usual. They held each other's eyes for a split second, then abruptly the young man swivelled and would have gone had Rosanna not called to him, 'Hello! What's your name?'

He faltered, then performed a half-revolution, evidently greatly discomforted. 'Rabb, miss.'

'Your first name.' She pushed herself from the tree trunk on which she had been leaning and sashayed up to him.

'Timothy, miss.' He was not as tall as her grandfather. Their eyes were almost on a level – but then Rosanna was not short.

'How do you do? I'm Rosanna Feeney.' She extended her hand.

The youth darted suspicious eyes at it, then, wiping his own down his breeches, slowly accepted the handshake, nodding. Rosanna couldn't take her eyes from him. He had the loveliest face she had ever seen on a man. In fact it wasn't a man's face at all – soft and gentle, timid even – it was the face of a deer, brown eyes wary, poised for flight. Yet the hand she still clasped was very masculine with squared fingers, the bared forearms that led away from it taut and sinewy, powerful. His shoulders would be that way too, thought Rosanna, looking at them. Under that shabby workman's coat was a body like one of those statues in the park that Piggy had always steered her away from. She experienced a sudden hotness. Sometimes, whilst lying in bed she had pulled up her nightgown to roam her hands over her naked body. Closer examination had divined a brown line that travelled from her navel to disappear into soft curls, and when she brushed her fingers lightly over it all sorts of shivers ran through her body. She felt it now, although no one had touched her.

Her voice did not betray her, remaining conversational. 'I'm Mr Feeney's grand-daughter.'

'Yes, I know.' Earlier he had pulled down his sleeves, unsettled by her scrutiny, but now the embarrassment seemed to have been overcome. His eyes held her face. 'At least I guessed.' He stared at her for a good while longer, then bluntly terminated the meeting. 'I have to go,' and he moved off.

'Oh, please!' She took a step after him. 'Won't you stay and talk a while? I'm so bored.'

'I can't.' Though he stopped walking. 'The master doesn't pay to have men stood idle. Besides, he wouldn't like me talkin' to you.'

She detected the barest hint of Irish accent. 'Why?'

'Because I'm a labourer and you're a lady.'

She laughed then. It was apparent from the way his eyes glittered that he found the sight entrancing. 'You're the first person who's ever called me that. That's why they sent me away to school; to be a lady.'

'Then what're you doin' here?'

'I didn't like it and ran away,' Rosie informed him.

'Oh.' He moved again. 'Look, I must go.'

'Will you come and talk to me again?' she called eagerly.

'Yes.' He gave a sudden smile. The sun exploded in her mind. Then he walked away.

'When?' she cried, but he didn't answer. She watched him march across the fields, a cloud of lapwings rising in chorused protest. Wrapping her arms about herself she squeezed joyfully. Squeezed her thighs together, too. *Timothy. Tim.*

She continued her walk and when she eventually made her way back to the barn it was to find her grandfather there. He was none too pleased. 'Rosanna, can ye not bide in one place for more than five seconds? Where've ye been to?'

She threaded her arm through his. 'Sorry, Gramps. It only took a short while to do the paperwork and I got bored with nothing to do. I didn't think you'd mind if I took a walk.'

'Well, I do mind. I like to know where you are. A young lady doesn't go for walks unchaperoned.'

'Oh, Gramps, you're not going to start being stuffy too, are you? I won't come to any harm, you know. I never set foot off your land.'

'Nevertheless, ye don't know who ye might bump into out there. There might be gypsies creeping around . . .'

'And what would they want with me? Oh, come on, Gramps, can we have a drink of tea or something? My stomach's rumbling.'

'An' how d'ye propose we boil a kettle out here in the middle o' nowhere?'

'Don't try to fool me.' She tapped him playfully. 'I saw the men brewing up on a fire as I came back.'

He smiled. 'Aye, well, I usually have my tea with the lads – but I'm not having you sipping tea round a fire like a labourer. I'll go fetch us a cup an' we'll take ours in here. Ye may have to make do with a tin mug, though.'

'Gramps, there's no need,' protested Rosie, eager for another meeting with Tim.

'Rosanna, get this clear,' he was serious now. 'You are not to fraternise with my workers. Understand? I don't mind ye being polite to them but that's the limit.' He went outside, returning with two pewter mugs. 'Here, 'tis a bit strong but it'll warm y'up.'

She accepted the mug, wondering who it belonged to. Making believe it was Tim she placed her mouth to the rim, imagining she could feel the imprint of his own lips.

After the tea was drunk Patrick asked how she intended to fill her morning if there was no more paperwork.

'What about that?' Rosanna pointed to a crate stuffed with papers.

'Ah, that's all old stuff.'

308

'It's a bit of a mess,' said Rosanna. 'What we need is a filing system. Perhaps I could tidy them up for you. We could have some cupboards put in and a desk.'

He laughingly agreed with her enthusiasm. 'Anything ye want, darlin',' and left her to go on with it while he went off to supervise the men.

Instead of sorting the papers Rosanna looked thoughtfully at the mug, running the tip of her finger round its rim. Going to the door she scanned the field trying to pick out Timothy. There he was. She leaned against the wood, watching him covetously. A lock of hair fell over his forehead as he toiled. His hand came up constantly to push it from his eyes, but still it followed its unruly course.

With a wicked grin Rosanna searched for her grandfather, eyes gleaming. Oh, damn! he was there. Regretfully she took a last look at Timothy, then closed the door and made a start on the paperwork.

But nothing could hold Rosanna's attention for very long. The paperwork became exceedingly tedious. Expelling a heavy breath she ceased grouping the documents and turned her mind to Tim, thoughts of whom soon coaxed her back to the door. Her lips parted in surprise and she took a step back. Timothy Rabb stood there, hand raised to push open the door when it had opened for him.

'I . . .' his eyes flicked the length of her body, 'came for the mug, miss.'

'Oh, it *was* yours.' She smiled delightedly. 'Come in, Tim.'

He looked to right and left, behind him, then stepped in after her, closing the door.

'Did my grandfather send you?' She picked up the mug she had used.

He shook his head. 'The master's away up the field.'

She felt greatly encouraged that he had not been sent but had come of his own volition. He must like her then. The hand clasping the mug offered it to him. He looked at it. 'That's Tom's, miss. Mine is the one with the dent in it.' He gestured at the one Pat had used.

Her disappointment was acute. 'Oh.'

'But I'll take them both.' He took the mug she was holding and waited for the other. She went for it and held onto it for a moment, wanting to put her lips to this one, but that would only attract his ridicule. Reluctantly she handed it back. Seeing he was about to go she once again surrendered to impulse and slipping around him placed herself between him and the exit – now I have you, her expression said.

'The master'll be back in a minute.' His eyes dropped to her breasts, then back to her face.

She was blushing. 'Do you like me, Tim?'

'It doesn't matter if I do or don't. You're the master's grand-daughter.'

'It does matter. Tell me.'

His lips twitched. 'Yes, I like you.'

'Do you think I'm pretty?' A nod. 'Would you like to kiss me?'

'Miss Feeney . . .'

'Rosanna. Call me Rosanna.'

'Rosanna, your grandfather wouldn't like it.'

'I'm not asking you to kiss him.' She pressed herself against the door. 'I shan't let you out till you've kissed me.' She pouted.

He took a step towards her, bringing his body inches away. She closed her eyes and awaited the soft touch of his lips, totally unprepared for the hand that grasped the back of her skull and pulled her into a kiss of such savagery that she felt she was under assault from Abi's sink plunger.

She pulled away, panting, heart racing.

'Wasn't it to your liking, madam?' he asked sarkily. 'Oh, I'm so sorry. I'm sorry 'tis 'cause I'm only a poor, rough labouring man.' His face hardened. 'Go take your games somewhere else, miss.' Pushing her sideways he opened the door and went out.

Slamming the wood behind him she burst into tears. She didn't know what she had expected but it certainly wasn't that. It had deeply disturbed her. He was like an animal – and not a deer, either.

When the door opened some time later she was still

310

weeping and, thinking it was Timothy, hurriedly wiped her face with her palms.

'Rosie, what on earth's upset ye so?' Patrick stepped up quickly and took hold of her.

'Oh, I'm so silly,' she sniffed. 'I've gone and got your papers in an awful muddle. I'll never be able to sort them out before it's time to go home.'

'Oh, is that all? Why, that's nothing to excite about. Tell ye what, we'll sort them out in one fell swoop; have a bonfire.'

'No, I feel responsible for getting them into such a mess. I must put them to rights.'

'Rosie,' he laughed, 'they're of no importance, really.'

'No, Gramps, I insist. I shall come with you tomorrow and make things right.'

'I thought ye said this was just for today?' he reminded her, smilingly suspicious.

'Grandfather, you shouldn't permit me to walk away from the problems I've created every time,' replied Rosie firmly. 'It's not good for me. Now, I shall come tomorrow – every day if necessary, until I've put them in order.'

'I don't know why I bother to argue with you,' sighed Pat. 'Y'always get your own way in the end.'

She smiled sweetly. – Tell that to Timothy Rabb, Grandfather, said her inner voice.

Chapter Twenty

It took Rosanna the best part of summer to bring those papers in order. Patrick knew it was only an excuse to get out of the house and into the freedom of the fields, but he didn't really mind. She was a child who needed her freedom and, besides, she would come to no harm under his eye.

Rosanna was growing more and more frustrated. Every

attempt to corner Timothy Rabb had been repulsed. She had tried to understand his words to her on the day of the kiss and had come to the conclusion that he thought she was simply playing with him; that he saw her as the lady she wasn't. She was just an ordinary girl swept off her feet by a handsome young man. The first young man she had ever really noticed. She had wanted to explain this to him, but had never been granted the opening.

The fruit-picking season came around. Rosanna saw this as her big chance to get together with Tim and asked her grandfather if she might be allowed to be one of the pickers.

Interpreting this as a joke at first he soon came to realise she was serious. 'Rosie,' he said impatiently, 'as I keep tryin' to tell ye, young ladies just don't do those sort o' things.'

'Why?' she demanded, chin at an obstinate angle.

'Well, for a start, 'tis no soft job . . .'

'Did I say I wanted one?'

'An' ye'll end up getting your clothes all torn on the branches.'

'It won't take much trouble to mend them.'

''Twon't for you, that's certain.'

'Oh, go on, Gramps.' Her nose wrinkled in persuasion. 'You know how I love being out in the open. Please, please.' She leaned against him like a cat trying to ingratiate itself, cocking her face pleadingly and tickling him under the chin with a finger.

'Jazers, you're a temptress. I suppose ye know Belle will be coming home for the holidays? Wouldn't ye rather spend your time with her?'

Damn, she'd forgotten that. Oh well, Belle could come too she supposed, putting this to her grandfather.

'Oh, her mother'd be delighted I'm sure,' nodded Pat.

'Oh, come on, Gramps. You could get round Aunt Erin, I'm certain.'

'You're the expert when it comes to circumnavigating people.'

312

'Say, Belle's been doing all that hard work at school, she deserves a break.'

'An' a break involves forty-eight solid hours o' fruit-picking, does it?'

'Grandfather!' she threatened.

'Oh, all right, you demon. Have it your way – but don't come running to me with blisters an' sunstroke. God save us, I'm beginning to wonder who runs my house.'

Belle arrived home from college on Tuesday evening, her mother travelling all the way to collect her. After Patrick and Thomasin had agreed how their grandchild had blossomed in her absence Erin produced an envelope, her face alight. 'This is a report on Belle's progress. Oh, it's so encouraging! Listen: "Miss Teale is a young lady of exemplary conduct whose intellect far surpasses that of her peers. Despite her short duration here she is already widely-read in the Classics, can read and speak French and German fluently. She shows great application in the Humanities, though her strongest subjects are political economy, English and mathematics, at which she particularly excels. It is felt that Miss Teale would benefit greatly from a university education and, if it can be arranged, recommend that this be carefully considered at a not too distant date" . . . There! Isn't that wonderful?'

'Magnificent!' Patrick held out his hand for the report, offering congratulations to Belle, as did Thomasin.

'Have you settled into your new school, Belle?' asked the latter, patting the sofa for her grand-daughter to come and sit beside her. 'I must say, it certainly appears that way.'

'Yes, thank you, Nan.' Belle sat down. There was always that certain reserve between the two.

'And what are your views on attending university – I must say you're exceedingly privileged to be thinking of taking the examinations at so tender an age.'

'If that's what Mother wishes,' answered Belle obediently. 'And if I'm clever enough.'

Pat laughed. 'I don't think there's much doubt about that. My, the child could lose an' find me with all her

313

knowledge. Still, she's worked hard an' I think she deserves a rest, don't you, Erin? How about letting her take a trip out to the fields to watch the fruit-pickin'? She an' Rosie could take a picnic or something.'

To Belle's surprise her mother agreed and the following day she and Rosanna dressed in their oldest garments to accompany their grandfather to the fruit-picking.

'Right, what d'ye want us to do, Gramps?' asked Rosie, keeping an eye on Timothy Rabb as she spoke.

He passed them each a basket. 'Ye can go down that row there.' He was pointing to the one parallel to that on which Tim laboured. 'Just strip the fruit off and drop it in the basket.'

'Righto. Come on, Belle.' Rosanna set off purposefully and made herself appear very industrious while her grandfather was nearby. As soon as he moved out of earshot she embarked on her true intention. 'Psst, Tim!'

Timothy heard her but didn't look up, his hands moving deftly over the bushes.

'What're you doing?' asked Belle, peering over the fruit bush at the young man.

'I'm trying to get that fool to talk to me but he's far too pig-headed,' explained her cousin.

'Fool is it?' Tim raked her with a scornful eye. 'At least I don't use people.' Hefting his basket he moved on to the next bush.

'Who is he?' asked Belle as Rosanna moved with him.

'Shut up. I'm not using you, you ass! Please Tim, I've got to talk to you.'

'Don't tell me to shut up,' retorted Belle. 'And aren't you supposed to pick all the fruit on the bush?' She gestured at the still-laden bush which Rosanna was intent on leaving behind.

Ignoring Rosanna, Timothy looked at the other girl. 'Good morning, miss. Would you be another o' the master's grand-daughters?'

Belle felt her cheeks go hot and it wasn't just the effect of the sun. 'Yes,' she responded, unusually civil. 'How do you do?'

'Tim,' Rosanna tried to intervene.

'An' why haven't I seen you before today, if that's not too impertinent?' enquired Timothy.

'I've been at school,' answered Belle, and was suddenly painfully conscious of her shape in front of this young man as his sun-lit eyes examined her. Oh, he was lovely.

'On holiday now, eh?'

'Yes.' She scraped a wisp of hair from her face, tucked it under her bonnet.

'An' will you be with us for long?' She told him she didn't know. 'Makes a change to have a pretty young lady brighten our day.' He hoisted the basket onto his shoulder, grinning down at her.

Rosanna was furious. She began to rip the fruit from the bushes, squashing most of it in her temper and nudging her cousin roughly as Belle resumed her task. 'You're not supposed to talk to the labourers. Grandfather wouldn't like it.'

Belle looked at her amazedly. 'Well, you just did.'

'That's different.' Rip, rip, rip went her fingers, sticky with juice. 'Tim and I know each other.'

'That's funny, he didn't seem to want to talk to you as much as he did to me.'

Hearing Belle's comment Timothy flashed her a smile. Rosanna worked faster, anxious to get Belle away from him. 'Get a move on or we'll never get finished.'

'Less haste more speed,' replied Belle maddeningly.

Rosanna continued to pick frantically, alternating the handfuls of fruit between basket and mouth and widening the gap between herself and Tim but also, unintentionally, leaving Belle behind. She snatched angry glances back along the row, watching them talking and laughing over the leafy barrier. Damn him. Damn Belle. Damn everybody!

Halfway through the morning, work stopped. Rosanna flounced off to the barn where she had left the picnic hamper. Shortly afterwards Belle joined her to be greeted with cutting remarks.

'Oh, decided to tear yourself away, have we?'

'I don't know why you're so uppity,' replied Belle,

315

poking about in the basket. 'He's ever such a nice person is Timothy.' She found a sandwich and bit into it. 'He's been telling me all about his family and the part of Ireland they come from.'

Has he indeed? fumed Rosie to herself, but vented her frustration on the apple in her hand.

'Aren't you going to take something out for Gramps?' asked Belle.

'I'm sure you're quite capable of doing that, seeing as you're always trying to ingratiate yourself.' Rosie ceased champing at the sight of Tim grinning at her and striding to the door slammed it shut.

'What did you do that for? It's beautiful out there.'

'Well, bloody-well go then!' shot Rosanna. Bitch, bitch.

'All right, I will!' Belle snatched a cloth from the hamper and filled it with food. Leaving the door wide open to annoy Rosanna she limped out to her grandfather. Then, to Rosie's burgeoning fury, she brazenly went to sit right beside Timothy, offering him a sandwich which he ate with relish. From time to time she would cast sly eyes in Rosanna's direction, much amused by the black looks she received.

Look at her, thought Rosanna crossly. The pair of them flaunting themselves. What on earth have they got in common?

Moments later her grandfather came to look for her. 'Rosie, what're ye hiding in here for?'

'I'm not hiding,' was her retort.

'Come out into the sunshine.'

'It's bad for my complexion.'

He laughed and was about to go when she stopped him with her pompous enquiry. 'I don't know if you're aware, Grandfather, but Belle is talking to one of the workmen.'

'What? Oh, that's all right. Tim won't do her any harm, he's a sister Belle's age. Come on, lass, fetch those sandwiches out into the sun. 'Tis lovely.' He was waiting for her to obey – she had to.

What torture to sit and watch Timothy focus his engaging smile on her cousin. – Damn Gramps, she bristled. I'd like to hear what he'd have to say if it were me behaving all lovey-dovey to Tim. Belle always got her own way.

That night, lying in her bed, she had to relive the humiliating experience when Belle insisted on waxing for hours over Timothy; what good company he was and oh, how attentive. 'Don't you think so?' pressed Belle when her commendation met with no response.

'He's all right, I suppose.' Rosie yawned. 'If you find his sort attractive.' She flung herself onto her side and punched her pillow viciously. 'Now shut up, will you? I've had a hard day and I'd like to get to sleep.'

But she didn't sleep, she lay awake for ages with a lump in her throat and murder in her heart. – I hate you, Timothy Rabb. I hate you.

Throughout the school holidays the girls visited the fruit fields, when the crop was all picked helping to count and invoice the baskets. As he had done on that first day Timothy continued to make a fuss of Belle, helping her to carry her baskets of fruit, she feeding him from the hamper. Rosanna became increasingly sullen, staying well apart from both of them. She asked herself why she came here every day; was it simply to torture herself? And to think that she was the one responsible for Belle being there in the first place. She could kick herself.

On Friday she was sitting in the barn trying to close her senses to Belle's enlivened chatter about Tim, when the subject of her cousin's monologue entered. She started, her cheeks flushed, and for one fleeting moment his eyes locked with hers and she knew, she just knew that all this attention he had paid Belle, all this stupid fandango had merely been done to make her jealous. He felt the same way as she did; she was sure of it. Then his eyes left her and trained their smiling depths on Belle.

'Well, miss, we shan't be seeing much more of each other after today. I s'pose you'll be going back to school shortly?'

Belle's smile faded. It was quite apparent she was as

taken with Timothy Rabb as her cousin. 'I go back on Monday – at least I'm meant to.'

The inference did not escape Rosanna who looked at her sharply. 'I shouldn't entertain any thoughts about copying my escape,' came her spiteful warning. 'Your dear mother would never countenance it.'

Belle set her mouth, but made no comment. She understood why Rosie was being so hostile; it was because Tim was paying all this attention to her. Rosie was accustomed to being flattered and didn't take kindly to people who bypassed her. Truth to tell, it had come as rather a surprise to Belle who had always been used to being the butt of people's curiosity rather than their admiration, but Tim wasn't like the rest.

'I'll be sorry to see you go, Miss Belle,' he now told her sincerely. 'I enjoyed having such a pretty companion to work with.' He stole a quick look over his shoulder to check on the master's whereabouts, then to Belle's overwhelming delight and Rosie's horror pressed swift lips to Belle's cheek. 'Goodbye. I hope we meet again next holiday.' Then he was gone.

Belle's hand came up wonderingly to protect the spot, her face aglow as she watched his retreating figure stride away across the fields. – He loves me!

For Rosanna this had gone too far. With a mouth that looked as if it had partaken of bitter aloes she flounced from the barn and started to run. She didn't care where to, only that her feet took her as far away from Belle as was possible. For if she stayed she knew she could not stop her hands from closing round that squat neck.

Naturally, there was no escaping her forever – the fact that they shared a room saw to that – but Rosanna postponed the confrontation for as long as she was able by always having a third party present so that she would not be forced to listen to Belle's rambling. After the family had dined that evening Belle, well aware of Rosanna's feelings towards her, gleefully asked her cousin if she'd care to take a walk round the garden before bedtime. 'I

318

noticed the marigolds need dead-heading,' she said artlessly. 'Would you care to help me?'

'That's the gardener's job.' Rosanna chose not to look at her. 'Anyway, I'm tired, I thought I might have an early night.' She excused herself from the table and began to rise.

'You're right,' said Belle. 'We've worked very hard lately. I think I'll take an early night, too.' She began to rise also.

Cornered, Rosanna addressed her brother. 'Nick, why don't you come and tell us how you're getting on at the store before we retire?' Giving him no option she grasped his hand and hauled him from his seat to follow her.

'I must say you're not usually so keen to have my company,' he told her as they arrived on the first landing. 'And you didn't appear to be very interested when I tried telling you about the store last week.'

'Oh, I find it riveting,' enthused Rosanna and pulled her brother into her bedroom.

Always quick to sense an atmosphere, Nick looked with amusement at his cousin who had trailed in after them and now sat brushing her hair at the dressing table. 'Perhaps our coz would rather tell us about the glowing school report?'

'Oh, pooh.' Belle flapped her hand disgustedly and laid down the brush. 'Do you think I have so little of school that I want to keep talking about it when I get home? No,' a smile formed, 'I have more important things to ponder on.'

'Really?' Nick became alert. 'Is there something I don't know about?'

'I'm not certain it would be right to discuss it,' said Belle coyly. 'Besides, I should hate to make Rosanna jealous.'

'Hah!' scoffed Rosie. 'I'd like to see the day when I'd ever be jealous of you.'

'Then why has your face turned green?' countered Belle, swivelling on the stool.

'It's not!'

'It is.'

319

'Not!'

Nick made a cutting motion with his arm. 'Look, if you've simply coerced me up here to act as a punchbag while you two argue over some man . . .'

'Who mentioned a man?' demanded his sister, eyes burning.

Belle was surprised, too. 'How did you know?'

'Well, it doesn't take much working out,' replied Nick. 'There's Rosie been mooning about the house like a love-sick sheep ever since you came home and you, Belle, looking like a cat that's been locked in a dairy overnight. There has to be a man in there somewhere, it's pure logic.' Though the thought of this made him want to laugh. He had never imagined that a cold fish like Belle would harbour romantic feelings – besides she was only a kid.

'Everything's logic to you, isn't it?' answered Rosanna scathingly. 'You never get emotional about anything.'

'A waste of energy, my dear.'

'I'll bet you won't think that when you fall in love,' retorted his sister, immediately wanting to kick herself for giving Belle this bit of ammunition.

'If being in love involves all this bad blood I don't think I'll bother,' said Nick calmly, and looked upon them both with pity. Rosie, though a little older in months than himself, was much younger in worldly matters. However, it was Belle who deserved most of his pity. Nick had never regarded her as anything other than a member of his family – and a rather detestable one sometimes. He could not imagine that anyone could find her attractive. Oh, she was pretty enough, but that wasn't adequate compensation for her nature. She was going to be hurt. That wouldn't happen to Nick. He had found himself a woman – a young widow who, in return for modest financial assistance, provided for his bodily needs – what use had he for love?

'So, let me guess,' he went on, stretching himself on his sister's bed. 'You both fancy the same fellow?'

Belle affirmed this. 'Unfortunately, Rosanna doesn't find her sentiments returned whereas I do. That is the reason for her bad grace.'

'You cat!' Rosie flew at her, but Nick leapt from the bed and held them apart while she spat her invective. 'He was perfectly happy with me until you came along and spoilt it!'

Belle addressed herself to Nick. 'She's going to be even more jealous when I decide not to go back to school. I think I could coax Gramps to get round Mother . . .'

'You couldn't!' Rosie answered the provocation. 'God knows your bloody mother makes me mad sometimes but for once I'm thankful she thinks so much of her namby-pamby daughter. She's so damned obsessed with all this education of yours you've not a cat in hell's chance of being allowed to stay. Anyway, even if you were you don't think this thing with Tim would last for long, d'you? I mean, you're supposed to be some sort of genius but to me you're just plain stupid if you imagine his court is genuine, that anyone as handsome as Tim could possibly contemplate affection for a screwed-up cripple like you. Call yourself pretty? You've obviously never looked at yourself in a full-length mirror.'

In the acute silence Belle's face drained of colour, her nostrils pinched and white. 'You bastard,' she breathed. 'You wicked, horrible bastard – and I mean that in the most literal sense . . .'

'Belle.' Nick tried to put an arm round her but she thrust it away.

'Do you understand that? Have I put it in simple enough terms for a ninny like you to grasp? You dare go on about my mother . . . well, she may be guilty of a lot of sins but at least she could register my birth as legitimate – which is more than your mother ever could. So when I call you bastard you can be very sure it is not just an empty insult but deadly accurate.'

Rosie was less sure of herself. 'You're just baiting me.'

'I can assure you it's true,' replied Belle nastily. 'My mother told me all about it. You're the daughter of some dirty tinkerwoman and Grandfather rescued you. Your father isn't your real father at all.'

'No!' Rosanna covered her ears, gave one agonised look at Nick, then flew from the room, sobbing, 'You freak!'

'You shouldn't've done that to her, Belle,' accused Nick, losing any sympathy he might have had for her.

'Why not?' Belle spun on him. 'After what she said to me?'

'That doesn't make it right. It was stupid and cruel, and you shouldn't use words like bastard so freely.'

'Well, while you're being so pompous and siding with her,' was Belle's splenetic reply, 'here's something else for you to be clever about – you're one, too!' She rushed out and slammed the door.

Rosanna hurtled down the staircase, across the hall and out of the house. Her grandparents in the drawing room heard the door slam, tutted, but were unaware of the crisis until a sombre Nick entered and asked if he might talk to them.

''Course ye can, boyo.' Patrick pulled in his long legs to make room, though there was plenty already. 'Sit ye down. How's work at the store progressing? Does your grandmother find enough for ye to do?'

'Thank you, yes, but it's not about the store, Grandfather,' said Nick seriously. 'It's Rosie and Belle.'

'Ah, been having a little difference of opinion, have they?' replied Pat. 'I thought I heard raised voices.'

Nick had no use for prevarication. 'Belle's gone and told her about Father not being our real father – if you see what I mean.'

Patrick and Thomasin exchanged taken-aback glances, then the former said to Nick, 'Ye don't sound too surprised yourself.'

'No.' Nick leaned on his knees and stared at the floor between them. 'I've known since I was seven. I picked up snippets from what Grandma Fenton used to say . . .'

'Damn that woman!' exclaimed Patrick, before remembering she was dead and looking chastened. 'An' ye've never told anybody, son?'

Nick shrugged. 'I saw no reason to.'

'Ye don't seem unduly concerned if I might say so,' said his grandfather.

'I'm not. I can't see that it matters a great deal. Father's always been Father and always will be. I would be interested to know the full story sometime, though. Belle and Grandma mentioned something about a tinker.'

'Erin had no right to tell that child,' cut in Thomasin annoyedly. 'It was no concern of hers – and what brought Belle to tell Rosie?'

'Oh, you know how they argue,' evaded Nick, not wishing to worsen matters by mentioning Tim. 'Was the tinker my mother too?'

Patrick looked at his wife. Her expression agreed that it was time the boy knew the truth. He shook his head. 'No, the woman who you knew as your mother, the one who died in the fire – remember?' Nick nodded, though the memory was vague; perhaps because she had not visited the nursery often enough to imprint herself on the young mind. His earliest memory saw only Josie. 'Well,' continued Pat, 'she *was* your real mother, but Sonny isn't your natural father. Our other son, he was your father. 'Tis very complicated . . .'

'What abour Rosanna? Isn't she my real sister, then?'

'Oh, yes,' answered Pat. 'The same man – our son – fathered you both. But Belle was right about the tinker. Ye see Dickie – that's our other son, the one who died saving ye – he tended to go a bit overboard where women were concerned. The tinker girl he seduced died giving birth to Rosie. Me and your father – I mean Sonny – we kidnapped her an' brought her home. I didn't want my grandchild being raised in that fashion.' Thinking of the bonny little thing brought his mind back to Rosanna's dilemma. 'How did she take the news?'

'Like someone hit her behind the knees with the edge of a spade,' replied Nick.

'Ah, I'd best speak to her,' decided Patrick, rising. 'Where is she?'

'I don't know. She's nowhere in the house, that's for sure, and I've searched the garden.'

323

Patrick sighed. 'Oh Jazers, then she could be anywhere. Nick, we'll have to go look for her. Tommy, will you telephone Sonny? He'll have to know.'

Thomasin said she would. 'And I'll also have a few words to share with our daughter about that child of hers.'

Exhausted from her non-stop dash, Rosanna reached the barn and hurled herself at the door. It was locked. She thumped out her frustration on it, then broke down and sobbed her heart out. She cried until the tears ran dry and her throat felt scoured, then sank down in a heap to lean her back against the unresponsive wood. What was she going to do? How could she go back there? Belle would be gloating. The worst thing in all this was not the slur of illegitimacy, nor the fact that her father was not her real father – though this was terrible enough. Strangely, most of her concern was centred on Patrick, dear Grandfather – and now he wasn't – wasn't her grandfather at all. That's why, she realised now, he'd always seemed fonder of Belle; she was his real grand-daughter. It didn't seem to matter that there were three other little girls who came into this category; Rosie loved her sisters . . . oh God! they weren't her sisters. Just when she had assumed she could cry no more the thought produced a fresh batch of tears. This time she was not racked by sobs, but simply lounged there propped against the door, staring into the distance through a blur of desolation. A shadow descended to cut out the light. Overwhelmed by the density of her unhappiness she imagined the presence to be just an extension of her mood, until it spoke her name. Alarmed, she dashed her reddened eyes with a sleeve to stare up at the culprit. 'Tim! What're you doing here?'

'There's a fine welcome,' he answered casually. 'I left something behind.' Then more carefully, 'What's amiss?'

She became surly. 'What do you care?'

'I don't. I was only enquiring because I thought you might be in some sort o' trouble. I'll just get what I came for an' be on my way.' Yet he still stood there.

'Yes, that's right, you go!' she snapped. 'I realise my

unhappiness means nothing to you, you're more concerned with my cousin.'

'She's a very pretty girl.' He put his weight on one leg, hands in pockets, still watching her misery.

'She's also spiteful and wicked.'

'I can't believe that.'

'No! No one can,' she declared loudly. It was obvious he was waiting for more. She sniffed and glared up at him, looking for that spark in his eye, the one that had misled her into thinking he cared. There was nothing. If she had seen any warmth before it was because she wanted to see it. He interrupted her thoughts.

'If you're going to make accusations about folk you'd best be able to back them up.'

She hesitated, then decided it couldn't matter to tell him, he didn't want her anyway and it might help to voice her hurt. 'She's just informed me I'm a bastard.'

He laughed. 'People're calling me that every day.'

She showed that his amusement was not shared. 'In my case, apparently, it's not just a groundless insult.'

His expression altered. He stared down at her momentarily, then came to squat beside her. She could smell him; it smelt good. 'D'you want to talk about it?'

'That's just it,' she said helplessly. 'I don't know any more, just that I am one.'

'How did all this come out?'

'We were angry with each other. People think Belle is all sweetness and light but she can be really horrid. I . . .' she felt a hot flush of shame, twisting the material of her skirts through her fingers, 'I suppose it was my own fault. I said some cruel things to her. Some might say I deserved all I got. Oh but, Tim!' She couldn't help herself and turned to him passionately. 'She gets me so angry, going on about you and how she wasn't going back to school. I was so afraid . . .'

'Of what?'

'Afraid . . . you liked her more than me.'

'I do like her,' he said, causing her to drop her eyes, then he put up a hand to stroke the hair from her damp, miserable face. 'Ah dear, if there's a villain in this piece I guess it's me. I was using her like I thought you wanted to use me. I thought ye were just playing games; the lady looking for her bit of rough.'

'That's insulting!' she accused.

'Well, ye must admit ye gave a very fine performance on our first meeting, asking me to kiss you. I didn't like the way you took it all for granted. I'm sorry I got a bit wild.'

'Oh, Tim.' She bit her lip. 'You frightened me. I've never . . . You do care for me, after all?'

'I do, an' I'm sorry you've had to go through all this to find out. Would it be all right if I made amends for my ungentlemanly behaviour?' She nodded dumbly. With the tenderest contact he touched his lips to hers, then pulled away, leaving Rosanna feeling that she must be in a dream. 'Won't they be wonderin' where you are? Be dark shortly.'

She gazed at him. 'Yes, but I don't care.'

'That's no way to show respect for the people who love you.' He got to his feet, pulling her after him. 'They'll be worried. Get along home with you now. D'ye want me to walk a bit of the way with you?'

'Yes, please.' She let him take her hand and it was lovely just to walk side by side with him, just being with each other.

Before they reached the city boundary Tim's keen eyes spotted Patrick and his grandson searching the lanes for Rosanna. Quickly he pulled her into the cleft of a cottage wall. She felt dizzy at the feel of his body against hers. 'I'll have to leave you now . . . the master'll have my hide.' He kissed her, almost as fiercely as that first time but there was no loveless savagery to it now. Then he was gone, leaving Rosanna to touch her bruised lips and wander trance-like to meet her searchers.

'Here she is, Gramps!' Nick pointed, then came dashing up to his sister. 'You ass!' he said and hugged her.

'Oh, Rosie, you really are intent on seeing me into an early grave, aren't ye?' puffed her grandfather, then hugged her, too. 'I thought I'd lost ye.'

326

She allowed him to lead her home. 'Are you on foot?'

'What's it look like? Sure we didn't realise ye'd lead us such a merry dance.'

'I'm sorry.'

'Ah, no need.' He clutched her upper arm. 'Ye shouldn't've let Belle spike ye, though.'

'It's not true, then?' she asked hopefully, then saw the look he gave her brother. 'Is it true – you're *not* my grandfather.'

He stopped dead. 'Not your gran . . . listen, if I weren't your grandfather would I be haring about the country looking high an' low for ye? Sure, there's times when I wish to God I wasn't lumbered with the lotta yese, you're nothing but trouble . . .' he broke off and cuffed her cheek lightly. 'Aw, Rosie, ye soft wee bitch. Did ye never use a mirror? Don't ye see ye've inherited my beautiful features?' She laughed. 'Come on,' he swept her homewards again. 'Home with us an' we'll tell ye all about it. It may not be as bad as ye thought.'

'Now I know you're really my grandfather, Gramps,' smiled Rosanna, 'I don't care about anything else.'

CHAPTER TWENTY-ONE

Erin, at first disbelieving that Belle could be guilty of such badness, was forced to agree that there was no other way Rosanna could have found out about her parentage. Furiously she searched the house for her daughter, finding her in the kitchen with Cook and Abigail. 'Belle, would you kindly go to your room, there's a matter I wish to discuss with ye.'

Belle rose. 'Of course, Mother,' and limped obediently up the stairs, Erin taking up the rear.

Once in private Erin posed the question: 'Have you just told Rosanna who her true mother was?'

Belle donned a pained expression. 'Of course I didn't.'
'Someone did.'

Belle looked her mother full in the face. 'Well, I don't
want to get anybody into trouble, but Rosie and Nick were
arguing and I overheard him call her a . . . these are his
words, you understand? . . . a tinker bastard. Rosie was
ever so upset.'

Erin's face contorted with disgust. 'I can well imagine.
But it wasn't her brother who upset her, Belle, it was you.'

'Nick's lying if he said it was me.'

'How could Nicholas tell his sister something he didn't
know himself?'

'Nick knows everything.'

'Belle, ye've been found out – have the decency to own
up!' Erin moved her head wearily. 'I'd never've believed
you capable of such cruelty, Belle. I conveyed that information in confidence.' Belle had once asked why Rosie
and Nick did not resemble either of their parents and Erin
had answered her honestly. 'I didn't expect ye to fling it
at the poor girl the first moment ye fell out.'

'Mother, if you'd heard the things she called me,'
returned Belle.

'Whatever she called ye it can't've warranted such a
vicious response.'

'She called me a cripple . . . and a freak.' Belle hung
her head and Erin's heart went out to her, but she would
say what she had meant to say. 'Then Rosie was cruel,
too – but d'ye realise, Belle, that ye've wrecked that girl's
entire life? Who knows what it might do to her? Are
y'aware she's run away?'

'That's one of Rosie's traits,' said Belle. 'She's always
running away.'

'Can you imagine what it's like to be told that the man
ye've called Father for sixteen years isn't your father at
all?' demanded Erin.

'And can you imagine what it's like to be called a
screwed-up cripple, Mother?' defended Belle.

Erin stared at her daughter's defiant stance, seeing her

perhaps for the first time as she really was. 'What was it all about anyway?' she asked. 'This bad feeling.'

'It was about Tim. Rosie thought he . . .'

'Tim?' Erin volleyed. 'Who's Tim?'

'He's one of Grandfather's labourers. Rosie thought he was sweet on her before I came along but . . .'

'Just hold on a moment.' Erin put up her hands to stem the flow. 'I want to know more about this fellow. How old is he for a start?'

'He's eighteen and I'm going to marry him,' replied Belle assertively.

'Oh, you are, are ye? An' just when is all this supposed to be taking place, if I might make so bold as to ask? Y' only have two more days before ye go back to school.'

'Please don't treat me like a child, Mother, I'm thirteen.'

'God, I'm beginning to think I'm the child! I couldn't see what was going on right under me nose. As if the lies weren't bad enough, now this. Wait till I see your grandfather, he should never've allowed ye to speak to the boy let alone get this far. 'Tis just as well you're going back to school, young lady.'

'I'm not,' said Belle flatly. 'If I go Rosanna will be in like a flash.' She stepped forward and touched her mother's arm. 'I love him, Mother.'

'Love? You're only a child, don't talk such rubbish. Ye've got years ahead of ye before ye start thinking about love and marriage – an' we'll have no more talk about not going back to school, thank ye very much.'

The girl broke contact immediately. 'I'll refuse to go.'

'Ye've got away with a great deal of cheek, young lady, don't overstep the mark.'

'If you make me go I'll run away,' replied Belle obstinately.

'Then you'll be sent back. If ye think I'm wasting your brain on some soft flirtation . . .'

'It's not a flirtation! I love him. No one sent Rosie back when she ran away.'

'Rosie hasn't your gift, besides the fact that she hated it.'

329

'Haven't you ever given a thought to the fact that *I* might hate it, Mother?' Belle's salvo was like an uncapped geyser. 'Detest all those girls who call me names, be bored to tears with Latin, sick to the teeth of maths, English, maths, English, maths – I hate it! I hate it, I hate it!'

'Stoppit!' yelled Erin. 'If you think I'm going to sit by an' watch you wasting your life just because ye'd rather be in the company of an ignorant lout then you're very wrong. How can ye even consider tossing aside such God-given talent so glibly?'

'Mother, please, can't you remember the way you felt about father . . . ?'

'Don't you dare bring your father into this,' breathed Erin. 'What can a chit of your age know of that kind of love?'

'But I can! I do!'

'Then 'tis obvious this must stop right away. I'm going to ask your grandfather to sack the boy, then we'll hear no more about it.'

'You can't! It would be disastrous. His mother has no husband to support her. Tim's is her main income.'

'Well . . . I wouldn't want anyone else to suffer through it,' said Erin, half-appeased. 'If you promise you'll go back to school sensibly without any fuss I shan't tell your grandfather any of this.'

'Very well, if you're so callous as to force me to it,' replied Belle sullenly.

'My God, you make it sound like I'm sending you to Purgatory!'

'But you are! I've told you I hate it, yet I've never been given any choice in the matter. I think what I heard about you is right.'

'What is it? What have ye heard?'

'That you're trying to live your life through me, that you were robbed of an education and now you think that by pushing me through it you'll somehow make everything right!'

Erin raised an arm as if she were about to strike her daughter, then her face returned to a grim mask. 'Get

330

your cape.' Belle did not move. 'I said get your cape! I'm going to show ye why I'm putting ye through this "hell" as you see fit to call it.'

Belle buttoned her cape disquietedly. 'Where are we going? It's almost dark.'

'Don't worry, it won't take long,' said Erin, adding gravely, 'where we're off to people don't care to tarry after dusk. I'm going to show ye what Hell is really like.'

The cabbie felt unable to hide his incredulity when Erin tapped on the roof of the vehicle and shouted for him to drop them at this end of Walmgate. 'Thank ye driver, we'll walk the rest of the way.' The cab's suspension sprang back into place as the woman assisted her daughter off, then paid the man his fare. 'Would ye be so kind as to wait here for us?'

'That's a joke! I'm not hanging round here for love nor money.'

'I wasn't thinking to offer ye the former,' replied Erin tartly. 'However, I should hate to incommode ye. Come along, Belle.'

Belle could not contain her curiosity at the sights which met her eyes. To start with, the whole thoroughfare was dilapidated, with crumbling architecture and a road which appeared to have been liberally coated with brown sauce, but it was the creatures which populated it who most drew her attention. Only rarely in her life had she seen persons dressed like this and that was on the occasions when her grandparents had taken her into town to visit the fair. There had been the pestilential beggar of whom she had taken little notice then, and of course the urchin who had insulted her, but here there were scores of them lounging about the dirty street wearing what could only be described as rags. A snot-nosed child caught her staring and stuck out his tongue. Undeterred, she poked out her own, then, at her mother's glare, lowered her head, though was unable to maintain that position for very long due to an itchy inquisitiveness. To what possible end had her mother brought her to this place?

Shortly, Erin turned off the thoroughfare and pulled her daughter down a covered alleyway. Belle was quick to clamp a hand over her mouth and nose at the sharp smell of stale urine, and began to be afraid: her mother had gone mad. What she saw when they emerged from the tunnel made her more convinced than ever that this was so. The alley opened onto a courtyard in which were a dozen or so houses – if one could call them that; hovels would be more descriptive. The two windows in each dwelling – blinded with grime, and not an unbroken pane in sight – indicated that these were two-roomed dwellings, one up, one down. The brickwork was caked with the soot that constantly fluttered down from numerous iron foundry chimneys. One of the houses boasted curtains, a pathetic tatter of filthy lace hung from a single nail. Belle became aware of grunting and turned disbelieving eyes to the far end of the yard where two pigs rooted outside what was clearly a slaughterhouse. The yard was spattered with their droppings, not just theirs but human effluent too, which spilled from the tumbledown privies that served the area. The unpaved yard was a quagmire of blood and offal, dung and kitchen refuse. The smell was vile. And to Belle's horror among these piles of filth babies played, sailed their paper boats along the channels of contaminated liquid, their faces smudged with filth, sores round mouths, ugly scabs in close-cropped hair. Ragged, crumpled shifts barely covered their nudity. But the most striking thing of all was that the unwashed adults who squatted and lounged outside their splintered doors, watching their offspring at play, appeared to think this was the most natural environment in the world. They seemed more put out by Erin and her daughter's presence, than by the state of their children's health.

Belle grew extremely uncomfortable as more and more of the residents' heads started to turn. 'Mother . . .'she pulled in towards Erin.

'What's the matter, Belle?' asked Erin cuttingly. 'Haven't ye always pestered to know the place where I was born?'

Belle was aghast. 'You . . . you were born here?' She looked again at the filth, smelt the corruption, saw the people.

'Ye see that child over there?' Erin lifted her hand to indicate a pretty but extremely undernourished child with long black hair, knotted and snarled. 'That could've been me when I was her age.'

'But how . . . I never knew . . .' stammered Belle.

Erin turned on her then, not the angry woman who had confronted her earlier but still gently forceful. 'No, ye didn't. Ye've never known anything but comfort and good food, taken it for granted that ye only have to ask and it'll be given, suddenly decided that ye don't want to go to school, thank ye very much. Don't ye understand, child? This!' She stabbed violently at her surroundings. '*This* is why I see it as so important for you to go back to school. Look at these people. Look at the squalor they have to live in purely because they're uneducated, because no one cares about them. You expect me who came from this to sit by and let you squander your gift because of some childish infatuation? What right have ye to waste such a talent? There's hundreds of these children will never get through so much as one year's schooling – if that – because their parents desperately need the few shillings a week that they can earn. You accused me of trying to live my life through you, well . . . I admit I'd've given anything to have even half the education you're receiving. But the true reason I'm doing this, Belle, is through fear! When someone has lived a good part of their life in poverty they learn never to take things for granted. When ye close your eyes on a night the fear comes creeping back that when ye wake up in the morning all that comfort will be gone. The Feeneys began here, Belle. They've risen above it through perseverance and luck. You'll never have to scour out chamberpots for a trumped-up lady like I did. You've got a gift an' I've no intention of letting ye waste it.'

'Oh, Mother, forgive me,' replied Belle contritely. 'It was selfish and shallow of me. I'm sorry I accused you . . . if you'd only told me . . .'

'I didn't want ye to have to see it, Belle, but now ye have I'm glad. It's proper that a person should be aware of her beginnings.'

– I'm glad too, thought Belle, looking round at the waxen-cheeked babies, some of whom would never reach adulthood. I'm a damned fool sometimes. To think that I almost wasted it all . . . If someone loved you they would surely wait until you'd finished your education, wouldn't they? And Tim did love her, she was positive. He would wait for her to grow.

'So ye'll go back to school with no fuss?' asked her mother hopefully. At Belle's nod Erin squeezed her hand. 'Good girl – an' we'll say no more about Tim, eh?'

'And you won't get Grandfather to sack him?' prompted Belle.

Her mother promised, then frowned thoughtfully. 'Before we go I'd like to look up an old friend. She may not still be here of course, but it won't take a minute an' we'll be home before it gets really dark.' Heading for the nearest woman who pulled upright with apprehension, she said, 'Excuse me, could ye tell me if Mrs Flaherty still lives here?'

The woman curtsied and wrung her hands. 'I'm sorry, ma'am, I never heard o' no one that name.'

'Is that the Widow Flaherty ye'd be after, your highness?'

Erin turned to regard the man who had spoken, seeking mockery but finding none; his face held genuine respect. 'Yes, Molly Flaherty. She used to live at that house there.'

'Ah, she's long gone, ma'am,' returned the man.

Erin crossed herself. 'God be good to her.'

'Ah no, ma'am,' he corrected. ''Twas not my meaning to say she was dead. She's just moved from this yard. The last I heard she'd moved to Rosemary Place, but that's years ago, she could be anywhere now.'

'Thank ye for your help. We'll try there.' Erin's fingers twitched at her purse, wondering whether or not he'd be insulted, then suddenly decided and took out a shilling. 'I'm very grateful.'

The man came alive again. 'Oh, thank ye, ma'am. God go with ye.' He flipped the coin gleefully as the woman and her daughter hurried from the yard.

'It's getting rather late,' said Belle nervously as a drunken man staggered down the street towards them. 'Oughtn't we better be going home?'

But Erin's blood was stirred. 'I'd not like to go before saying hello to Molly if it's possible. Come on, Rosemary Place isn't far.' She set off and Belle was forced to follow.

The route was lined with the oddest characters Belle had ever seen. Most peculiar of all were the wizened old women who sat like men at the kerb, puffing on their clay pipes. Long shadows were beginning to form. It was all very eerie.

At Rosemary Place Erin was disappointed again after knocking on every single door, but luckily one of the residents directed her to Clancy's Yard where Molly had gone to live some two years ago.

But, yet again, she was rerouted from Clancy's Yard to Duke of York Passage and another series of doors to knock upon.

'Mother Flaherty?' said the woman who answered Erin's first knock. 'Aye, she lives over there with her daughter Norah. Yer'll not find her in though, she'll've gone for a bevvy.'

Erin, issuing effusive thanks, told her she would call and say hello to Norah. 'Though she'll probably not recognise me.'

Tentatively she tapped on the door the woman had indicated. A child of about ten answered. 'Hello, is your mammy in?'

'Mammy, there's a lady at the door,' called the child.

'Tell her to leave her calling card, I'm not receivin' visitors today.' The voice was shortly followed by a middle-aged woman who wiped her hands on her apron and offered hasty apologies. 'Oh, Lord, I'm sorry, ma'am! I thought the child was having me on. What can I be doing for ye? Have ye taken a wrong turning?'

'Norah, don't ye recognise me?' asked Erin.

The woman still smiled, but paused in wiping her hands and cocked her head. 'I'm sorry, I don't think . . .'

'It's Erin, Erin Feeney.'

The smile evaporated. 'Oh, come slumming have yese? An' what might ye be wanting here?' Erin's face fell. 'Come to flaunt your fancy clothes, have ye? Come to show us what 'tis like to be well off?' She leaned forward, baring her teeth. 'I don't know how you've got the nerve to come here after the way ye treated my mother.'

'Norah, it wasn't . . .'

'Saved up for ages for that wedding gift she did an' y'all looked down your noses at her, couldn't wait for her to stop embarrassing ye.'

'Norah, please give me a chance to explain.'

'Oh aye, just bide there while I fetch me children an' let ye explain to them why your daughter's all poshed up in fancy clothes while they have to go to bed wi' no supper. Explain to them why the likes o' your people saw fit to sack my Joseph while your husband probably drives round in a fancy gig, smoking a fat cigar which cost more than I spend on a day's food . . .'

'If I'd thought my visit would upset ye so much . . .' began Erin, then spoke to Belle. 'Come on, dear, we'll go now.'

'Aye, go on! Back to your bloody house with a hundred rooms an' your piles o' food. Don't spare a thought that I'm going to have to feed eight bairns with no man in work. Go on! Back to your own kind, we don't want ye here.' She slammed the door.

Belle gripped Erin's hand comfortingly as they hurried through the dim passageway. 'Why didn't you tell her? About Father, I mean.'

'Would it have done any good? No, 'twas a mistake to think I could just stop in an' say hello after all this time. They think we deserted them an' they'd probably be right.' But it had been a painful reunion and Erin remained tight-lipped for some time.

On their way back along Walmgate a fight spilled over

from a public house and a pack of writhing, punching, swearing Irishmen tussled on the footway.

'We'll cross over,' decided Erin, and was about to do so when one of the combatants was pushed and stumbled into Belle, knocking her into the road. 'You scoundrel!' Erin sprang to her child's defence, plucking her from the path of a carriage then beating the culprit about the head and shoulders.

This caused aggression to turn to hilarity. The man's companions roared with laughter at the sight of the big oaf cowering under Erin's bad-tempered blows. Belle marvelled at how one moment these people seemed intent on murder and the next bosom pals, arms draped round each other's shoulders as they shared the joke. One old woman found it particularly enjoyable, dancing about in nimble fashion, rolling up her sleeves and making swift jabs in the air. 'Go on, mash his brains, lady!'

Erin recognised the voice at once and ceased pummelling the man to stare at the ancient crone. 'Molly! I've been looking all over for ye. Oh, Molly!' She grabbed Belle's hand and hauled her up to stand in front of the old woman. The crowd had gone quiet. 'Molly, please hear me out. I've just been to see Norah an' she told me about your troubles. If there's some way I can help I'd desperately like to.'

'Is it knowing the lady y'are?' asked the grey-faced man swaying beside Molly Flaherty.

'Sure, I do not,' replied the woman, whose skin looked like a section of withered bark. 'Never seen her before in me life.'

'Molly, 'tis Erin,' pleaded the other. 'Don't ye know me?'

The wizened old face, seamed with years of dirt, squinted at her closely. Belle received a noseful of liquor fumes though she was well-distanced. 'Erin? Erin who?'

Belle felt her mother hesitate, afraid of the reception, then boldly stated her surname.

'Erin Feeney!' Recognition lit the woman's face. 'Aw,

Erin me little darlin', me baby!' She drew Erin into a bony embrace, her slitty eyes filling with tears.

Vastly relieved, Erin allowed the contact to be prolonged, even though her friend smelt terrible. 'Oh, Molly, I'm so glad you're pleased to see me. Norah threw me out.'

'She did, did she?' Molly stopped hugging to roll up her sleeves yet again. 'We'll see about that.'

'No, Molly, I don't want to bring trouble between ye. I just brought my daughter to see the place where I was born an' I thought I'd look ye up. Belle, this is Mrs Flaherty who looked after me when I was a baby.'

'How do you do?' Belle extended a genteel hand which Molly employed to haul the girl to her bosom. 'Aw, such a bonny child ye have, Erin – but don't tell me just the one?'

'Aye, just the one, Molly. My husband died when Belle was a baby.'

'Aw, that's tragic.' Molly let go of a thankful Belle to claw at Erin's arm. 'But ye should marry again, a good-lookin' girl like yourself.'

'Hardly a girl,' smiled Erin and changed the subject. 'Well, and how is yourself, Molly?'

'Oh, terrible,' replied Molly, clutching her own shoulder. 'The ould rheumatatics, ye know.'

'Norah tells me her husband lost his job.'

'Aye, this is Joseph.' She touched the grey-faced man who, trying to take stock of the proceedings, screwed his cap through his hands. 'We came for a wee drink just to get us from under Norah's feet, y'understand. She's an evil temper on her of late.'

'I can understand that,' answered Erin. 'It must be very hard. What about the rest of the family?'

'Oh, they're hereabouts somewhere. I don't see much of them these days. They have their own families to see to without looking after me. Ah,' she gave a motion of surrender, 'what am I defending them for? If 'twasn't for Norah I'd be in the poorhouse. 'Tis coming to something when a woman's own children throw her out on the streets.' She dabbed at her eyes.

'Is there any way I can help?' enquired Erin, and opened her purse. 'I've not brought much out with me . . .' She offered a halfcrown to Joseph but he waved it aside.

'Ah, 'tis not necessary, ma'am, thank ye all the same.'

But Molly was quick to snatch it. 'Such generosity! Erin, you're a fine girl, I always said so,' and she hung on to the money grimly.

'I'm sorry 'tis not more.' Erin snapped the purse shut. 'And is there nothing else I can do for either of ye?' She looked at Joseph.

'Well now, ma'am,' began Joseph. 'As ye said I lost me job . . . I'm badly in need o' work, if ye could see your way to helping me in that direction.'

'What sort o' work d'ye do?' asked the other immediately.

'I'll do anything, ma'am.'

'Perhaps my father has a place for ye,' said Erin thoughtfully. 'Come back with me now an' we'll ask him. You too, Molly. I'm sure Father'll be delighted to see ye again.'

'I'd love to see himself an' all,' answered a wistful Molly. 'But I'm doubting your mother would want me clutterin' up her fine home.'

Erin, knowing there would be no guests in the house, thought it safe to say, 'I'm certain Mother would welcome your company after such a long absence, Molly. After all ye were very good to her, good to all of us.'

'I'm not so sure. The trouble with Tommy is she's so inconsistent. Ye never know how ye're going to be treated. I'd not care to think she'd be behaving the same way as my last visit.'

'Please, Molly, forgive her that,' begged Erin. 'Forgive us all. 'Twas just the upset o' the wedding caused the misunderstanding. We really were pleased to see ye again.'

'So pleased it took ye fifteen years to stage a reunion,' said Molly wryly, then grinned and tucked her dirty arm through Erin's as the latter confessed it was seventeen actually. 'Ah, sure we'll come with ye, pet. We can only get thrown out the once, can't we?'

Before going home Erin went with Molly and her son-in-law to tell Norah where they were going. Joseph had barely been in the house two seconds when they heard Norah erupt. 'Ye lazy, nogood drunken wretch! Here's your children going with empty bellies an' you an' that woman I have the misfortune to call Mother boozing away our last few pence. Get your filthy hide out o' my sight!' She came to push him from the house, which was when she saw Erin who had waited outside. 'What's she doing back here?'

'Ah, daughter, don't get such a paddy on ye,' said Molly. 'Erin's going to help us.'

'We don't want her help. And you!' She stuck her finger in Molly's chest. 'You're as bad as he is. Ye've taken sixpence from the bloody rent money, haven't yese? Don't bother to lie, I know 'twasn't Joseph, he'd never dare. Well, 'tis the last time. Ye can get your backside down to the workhouse an' see if they'll put up with your drinking 'cause I've had enough.'

'Aw, Norah, me darlint.' Molly stepped towards her.

'Don't darlin' me, you're out! An' he's out. You're all bloody out!' She slammed the door.

'Why did ye not give her the halfcrown, Molly?' asked Erin as the procession tramped back along the passage. 'It might've made her a bit sweeter.'

'Her sweet? Sure, she'd make a lemon screw its face up.'

'She's a right to be mad, I think.'

'An' for what? Sure we only had the one. We've got to have somethin' to make life bearable, haven't we, Joe?'

Erin piloted her daughter around a pile of refuse. 'I trust ye'll not spend the money I gave ye on drink. I meant it for the children.'

'Spend it on drink? Why, no indeed. We won't, will we, Joseph? No, I'll just look after it for a wee while. It might help to buy our way in when we get back.'

340

'She said she didn't want ye back. Said she'd had enough o' ye.'

'Ah, isn't she always tellin' us that? Friday wouldn't be Friday if we didn't find ourselves locked out.'

'But what will ye do?'

'Same as we always do, colleen. Young Joseph here will kick the door in.'

When they arrived at Peasholme Green Erin sent Belle upstairs then went to the drawing room to prepare her mother. Molly and Joseph remained in the hall, gazing in awe at their palatial surroundings.

'Ah, so there y'are!' Patrick pulled himself out of his chair. 'We've been wondering where ye'd got to.'

'I've been out with Belle. I'll explain later.' Erin turned to Thomasin. 'Mother . . .'

'Ah, t-t-t-t, not so fast,' interrupted Patrick. 'Did ye have words with that young madam o' yours?'

'I did. Do I gather ye found Rosie?' With his nod Erin asked if she was still as upset.

'She's over it a little now. I packed her off to bed with a glass of milk an' nutmeg. She was sorely wounded, though. Sonny and Josie are coming over to reassure her. I can't think what possessed Belle to be so . . . Erin, what is it? Ye're leppin' about like a flea doin' overtime.'

Erin hardly dared look at her mother, unsure how she'd take the rash invitation. 'While I was out I bumped into an old friend. I thought ye might like to see her so I brought her back. Will I bring her in?'

'Well, unless ye want us to play Guess the Visitor,' replied her father.

When Molly and Joseph were brought from the hall Patrick gave an exclamation of delight and went straight to his old friend to plant a kiss on her withered cheek. 'God love ye, 'tis wonderful to see ye, Molly!' He hugged her.

'Oh, Pat, me darlin' boy,' cried Molly, observing Thomasin warily with one eye as she returned his embrace. 'Ye've never altered, never.'

To her credit Thomasin belied the extreme shock she

had suffered by coming forward readily, hands outstretched. 'Molly, how are you? Do come and sit down. Will you have a cup of tea?'

'That's mighty gracious of ye, Tommy.' Molly's coming-together with her hostess was a little more inhibited than it had been with Patrick. 'Er, would ye be after having anything a bit stronger?'

Thomasin, still battling with her unpreparedness, smiled. 'Of course. Sherry, whiskey?'

'A drop o' the hard stuff if it isn't too much trouble.' Molly wrung her hands.

'No trouble at all, Molly.' Thomasin looked at Joseph.

'Oh, this here is Norah's husband.' Molly introduced them. 'Joseph, these are two great friends o' mine, Tommy an' Pat.'

'How do you do, Joseph? Won't you take a seat?' Thomasin swept her hand towards the sofa where her visitors perched themselves awkwardly, afraid of transferring the dirt from their clothes to the upholstery. 'Joseph, what can we offer you?'

'Oh sure, tea would be fine, ma'am, if ye please. I'm a very abstemious person meself.' If there was work to be had it wouldn't do for them to get the impression he was a drunkard.

Thomasin motioned for her husband to fetch Molly a drink. 'I believe I could do with a cup of tea myself. Erin, ring for Abi, would you?' She placed her palms together, treading air whilst they awaited the maid. 'Well now, this is Norah's husband, is it?'

'It is. He's a good boy, is Joseph.'

'Joseph is partly the reason they're here,' explained Erin. 'Ye see he's just lost his job, an' we were wondering . . . could ye find a space for him, Dad?'

Patrick didn't really need another labourer but was so eager to rescind the dreadful way his old friend had been treated the last time she came to his house that he immediately voiced an affirmation.

Molly's apprehensive face cracked. 'Oh, that's decent

of ye, Pat!' And to Joseph, 'Didn't I tell ye he was a real pal?'

'Oh, she did, sir – an' thank ye very much.' Joseph rose to perform a series of bows. 'I'm in your eternal debt.'

'My pleasure, son. An' tell me, Molly, are ye still living in the same place?'

'Ah, no,' she told him. 'I'm in Duke of York Passage now.'

He nodded. 'An' is it any better there?' She told him it wasn't.

Abigail came in, stopping dead in her tracks when she saw the unlikely visitors. Thomasin's calm request for tea was met in record time, Abi eager for another sighting of the guests. The conversation was clumsy but amiable. Joseph, a garrulous soul, told them how pleased he was to meet them at last. 'Indeed if we hadn't been introduced just now I could've picked ye out of a crowd.' He looked fondly at Thomasin who was in the act of pouring tea. 'Ah, she was forever tellin' us about your good wife, sir. Oh, yes. I bet ye were a fine-looking woman when ye were younger, ma'am.'

Thomasin gave a lop-sided smile to her husband. 'Would that be one lump of arsenic or two, Joseph?'

'Begging your pardon, ma'am?' Joseph's expression was without guile.

'Just my little joke.' Thomasin passed him a cup of tea, muttering aside to Pat, 'It's good to tell who he lives with, isn't it?' Nevertheless, she was finding it enjoyable to mull over old times with Molly and her son-in-law, if only to prove to herself just how far she had risen.

'Ye know, Pat,' said Molly wistfully, 'ye ought ta come back an' spend an evening down the old place. Ye'd be made to feel at home. Nothing's changed.'

'I might just do that one o' these days, Molly,' replied the man fondly, not divulging that when he had been campaigning for Lockwood his itinerary had taken him within feet of her door. Naturally he had not known she was there . . . but he hadn't bothered to look her up, had he? Oh, times *have* changed, Molly.

'Did ye hear about Father Kelly?' asked his friend, rotating her empty glass to draw attention to this fact.

'I did.' Patrick smiled sadly and reached for the decanter. 'We'll all miss him.'

Molly's glass was immediately at the ready. 'Aye, God rest him. He was one of us. Sure, 'tis a great class o' whiskey ye serve, Patrick.'

The ultimate epitaph, thought Patrick: 'He was one of us.' What more could any man hope to have carved on his tombstone?

After leaving her mother Belle had gone to the room she shared with her cousin. Why this should be so when there were so many vacant rooms was a question she had often asked herself, never more so than now. She didn't want to talk to Rosanna. She didn't even want to see her.

It turned out she didn't have to. Rosanna, mutually hostile, was pretending to be asleep, her face secreted neath the covers. Without lighting a lamp Belle undressed then put on her nightgown and climbed into bed. The curve of her spine always prevented her from lying directly facing the ceiling. She lounged to one side gazing into the darkness, pondering what had been said tonight, and about Tim. Concentrating on the latter she felt the longing burn within her childish breast. It wasn't true, what Rosanna had said. Tim's endearments were no fabrication. Oh, if only she were older.

Thoughts of Tim were rife in the other bed too, though of a more fulsome nature. Picturing him in her mind Rosanna placed the flat of her palm on her body, ran it up over the developing mounds of her breasts, down to the hot, jutting bone that burnt through her nightgown. She heard Belle's sigh and knew that the girl's thoughts were also with Tim – but it doesn't matter, thought Rosie elatedly. He loves me. Tim loves me.

CHAPTER TWENTY-TWO

There'll doubtless be questions, his father had said, and you should be the one to answer them. Sonny looked at his almost grown-up children and tried to anticipate those questions. Rosanna seemed the most concerned – which was understandable after the nasty things Belle had said to her. He had already had words with his sister over that.

Though his wife had travelled with him he was facing the children alone. Josie had thought it best – Nick might want to enquire about his real mother and Josie's presence could make that uncomfortable for all of them. Sonny began with, 'I know your grandfather's explained the fundamentals . . . but if there's anything you don't understand – however intimate a question it might be – I'm here to answer you. Don't think you'll hurt me by asking.'

It was a few moments before either of them responded. Then it was Rosanna who whispered, 'I'd like to know a little bit about . . . your brother.'

Sonny detected the hesitation. 'Your real father.' He smiled at her and reached for her hand, squeezing it. 'I've told you, don't be afraid of hurting my feelings, yours are the ones that're important.'

She swapped chairs to sit close beside him on the sofa. 'I don't feel any different about you – you're still my father . . . I'd just like to know what *he* was like.'

Sonny told her then and from the way he spoke she knew that he had loved his brother very much. His expression was fond as he relived some of the adventures he and Dickie had had as children, how good-looking his brother had been. Before today, Sonny had spoken little of the fire in which the other had died – apart from not wanting to think about those good looks burnt beyond recognition, he had not cared to remind his children of the horror. But he did so now. 'You know he was the one who saved you when the old house burnt down?' They both nodded.

'But I can't really remember him,' said Rosanna. 'I just recall a man carrying me and Nick down the stairs, and the flames and smoke.'

'No, well, you were only three . . . When he'd rescued you,' went on Sonny, 'Dickie ran back into the house to try and save your mother – sorry, I mean Nick's mother, Peggy. He never came out . . .'

'How did the fire start?' asked Nick.

Trust Nick to ask a technical question, thought Sonny, but was rather glad of his son's ability to be cool-headed. All this had affected him very little. 'No one is certain. There was an explosion and the roof fell in.'

Nick asked how the rest of the family managed to escape.

'Oh, they weren't inside,' replied his father. 'Your grandparents had taken Great-grandma to the solicitor's, I was out looking for Dickie and the maids had been given the afternoon off . . .' He paused as if something had just struck him, then went on, 'When Dickie and I got there everyone was out in the street. The house was locked up, we had to break in.' Again a pause for reflection. He had never understood why all the doors had been locked and even less so why Peggy had given the staff the afternoon off; she had never been that charitable.

Rosanna tried to picture the man who had saved her, but failed. 'I remember seeing my mother – well, I know she wasn't my mother now . . . but I seem to remember a man talking to her. I can't see his face, though.'

Sonny knew his daughter's memory was fooling her. He himself could clearly remember Dickie charging from the house with the two children, shouting, 'Peggy's still in there! She's unconscious!' and barging back in before anyone could stop him. It was all so vivid. He patted Rosanna. 'You were only little, you can't be expected to remember. I'm glad you can't in a way. It was terrible . . .'

Nick then asked about his mother. What could his father

say? That she was a harlot and a scold and a poor mother? 'She was very pretty,' he told Nick. 'I loved her very much once . . . but things went sour.' At Nick's cue he told of how he had been set to marry Peggy, then had found she was pregnant with his brother's child. Loving her as he did he had married her anyway, but things had not worked out. 'She wanted a life I couldn't give her, Nick. I don't want to speak ill of the dead, but neither would I want you to hold her in your memory as an angel. Josie's been much more of a mother to both of you than Peggy ever was.'

Both children concurred heartily. 'I remember lots of things about Mother from when I was little.' Rosanna was referring to Josie now. 'In fact even though she wasn't my mother then I regarded her as such. The only thing I really remember about my real mother – I mean Nick's mother,' she laughed almost gaily. 'Oh, it's so confusing! I'll bet no one else could refer to three different women as Mother! I'll call her Peggy, then you'll know who I'm talking about . . . The only thing I definitely recall is that horrible stuff she used to dose us with – d'you remember it, Nick?'

'Do I? It was disgusting. I don't know what it was for but by Heaven I'll always remember the taste.'

Sonny knew what it had been for – to put them to sleep while their mother went off to meet her men-friends. Again something niggled at his mind . . . the doors had been locked, the maids off-duty, only Peggy and the children in the house – there was *something*.

'I remember her smelling nice,' mused Nick. 'It annoys me that I can't picture her face – even though I was always fonder of Josie. I only recall a man carrying us downstairs that day.' He wrinkled his brow. 'I seem to think there was somebody else there, too, but I can't say if it was a man or a woman.' Rosanna was of this impression, too.

'No, there was only Dickie and my wife,' said his father, and envisioning those two distorted shells that had once been human beings steered the conversation to other matters. 'I can't tell you anything about your natural mother, Rosie. I'm sorry, but I didn't know her.'

'That's all right. I'm not really interested.' But Rosanna did wonder if she looked like her real mother at all.

'Anyway,' Sonny answered the unspoken query, 'you're more of a Feeney in looks.' At her smile he rubbed his knees and asked, 'Well . . . is there anything else you need to know?'

Rosie fell against him in her impulsive fashion. 'Only that you love us.'

Bright of eye, he laughed and squeezed her tightly, cementing his paternity, saying that he loved them both very much indeed. Much unburdened, Sonny sought out his wife who had been waiting alone in the drawing room and told her of the children's reactions. But from time to time she couldn't help noticing that his mind would stray and his face would become puzzled. Finally, she commented on this.

'There's just something . . .' he murmured confusedly. 'Don't ask me what . . . just something that isn't quite right. God knows I've relived that fire a thousand times in my mind, but still . . .' He turned his baffled face to hers. 'They both seemed to think that there was another person in the house when Dickie rescued them.'

'They were only little . . .'

'True, and they don't remember much . . . but Josie, why would they both say the same thing?'

'Well, one of them probably heard the other saying it and they've thought about it so much that it's become real. Just because they haven't discussed the fire with us doesn't mean they haven't talked to each other about it.'

'But even taking that to be true, aren't there things that you can summon up from babyhood – silly, insignificant memories?'

'I can recall getting my head stuck in the banisters when I was two but I don't see what that's got to do with it.'

'We both know Peggy had other men.'

Her face rebuked him for introducing Peggy's name and stirring up bad memories, but he wasn't really paying attention. 'I've been going over and over all the things that seemed out of place . . . the house being locked up, the maids being given the afternoon off . . . and I can only come up with one reason why she'd do that.' His grey eyes lost their vagueness. 'She had a man in there.'

Josie gasped at this theory. 'No, there would've been another body.'

'Not necessarily. He could've escaped through a back window before the fire took hold or . . .' Excitement was beginning to flutter in his breast. 'I daren't say it, Jos.'

'Oh, John, dear,' she said worriedly. 'Don't raise your hopes on a flimsy idea like this. Why, after all this time . . .'

'But it's possible, Jos!' He hitched his body round, speaking animatedly now. 'The body found with Peggy's could've belonged to the other man! Dickie could've got out some way! He was going to escape to America anyway, what better way than to have people think you're dead?'

She begged him not to become carried away on the strength of two small children's memories, knowing how devastated he would be to find it had all been fancy. 'And you've no way of proving it one way or the other.'

'Even so, isn't it much better to think that's what could've happened? That Dickie is alive somewhere?'

'John, love, your brother's dead. That solicitor . . .'

He cut her off with a yell. 'Yes! The solicitor – I might get something out of him!' He sprang up.

'What – now?'

'What's the point in waiting? Oh, Christ! What was his name?' He racked his brain. 'Can you remember?' She shook her head. 'Never mind, Dad'll know . . . oh, no, I can't ask him, can I?' He swore and stumped about in frustration. At his wife's suggestion that there might be something in the bureau at home he beckoned to her. 'Right, let's go!'

She tried to dissuade him. 'Your mam and dad'll think it funny us rushing off like this, John.'

He saw that she was right, but could barely contain his eagerness, feeling sure he had hit on something vital.

'Aye . . . we'll have to stay for a bit longer – but directly we're home I'm gonna rip that bureau apart!'

Sonny found a letter bearing the name of his brother's solicitor and wasted no time in journeying back to York. But once seated in the man's office he didn't know how to make his claim without appearing a fool. However, he was given a moment's leeway by the solicitor enquiring if he would care for coffee, and a brief discussion on the weather. Once the smalltalk was used up he was forced to come to the point.

'Mr Sutcliffe, I won't prolong this by hedging; I have reason to believe my brother is still alive.'

There was the slightest alteration in Sutcliffe's features. He took a sip of his coffee. 'Mr Feeney, I take no pleasure in assuring you that you are totally misled. May one ask why you should suddenly believe after – what is it, fourteen years? – that your brother did not die in that fire?'

Faced with such surety, Sonny was hesitant in putting forward his theory, but nevertheless that was what he was here to do. He told Sutcliffe about his late wife's adultery. 'So, you see it's quite feasible that there was another person in the house that day – the bodies were too charred to be identifiable.' He spread his arms in a helpless gesture.

'Mr Feeney,' Sutcliffe toyed with the handle of his cup. 'I don't think you fully realise that by telling me this you are suggesting that I know something which you do not – in effect, that your brother has made me party to deception. Were that true then I should be guilty of unethical behaviour. I trust you're not accusing . . .'

'Oh, no, no!' Sonny was quick to put matters right. 'I just sort of hoped that you might know something – I mean, Dickie could have fooled you too, couldn't he?'

'But if he'd fooled me then how could I know something? Forgive me, but I think that your eagerness to believe your brother is alive has robbed you of your reasoning power. Your theory has no foundation, it is based merely on emotion.'

Sonny's spirits flagged. To the solicitor he seemed to wither. 'My wife was right. She said I was raising false hopes . . . I'm sorry to have given the impression that I was holding your ethics in question, Mr Sutcliffe – that never entered my mind. As you say, I wanted so desperately to hear that he was still alive that I'd almost convinced myself . . .'

Sutcliffe felt very sorry for the man who was obviously stricken. 'You must have been very close, Mr Feeney? I say that not only because of the impression you have given me today, but because – if I recall correctly – your brother left the bulk of his estate to you.'

Sonny gave a dull nod and sighed. 'Ah, dear . . . you'd think fourteen years would have made the memory less painful, wouldn't you? I feel such a fool for coming here. It was idiotic, thinking he could have got out of that inferno. I suppose it's just that I needed something to cling onto, so that I wouldn't have to spend the rest of my life remembering my brother as a piece of charred debris. Not being able to identify him . . . well, I just couldn't truly believe he was dead. It could have been another man in that fire or it could have been Dickie. I wish to hell I just knew one way or another. I'd forgive any deception just to know he was still alive.'

'Mr Feeney,' Sutcliffe's voice was sympathetic. 'I wish I could help, but all I can do is to repeat what I've already said. Your brother made a will, you were a beneficiary. Here,' he got up to rummage in a filing cabinet and after a while laid a document before Sonny – it was the will. 'That contains all the evidence you are seeking.' Seeing the disappointment that clouded Sonny's eyes the solicitor excused himself diplomatically into an outer office until the man felt more composed.

Sonny made no move to go. Josie had been right. It had been stupid to try and resurrect Dickie after fourteen years. All he had resurrected was the heartache. But he had felt so *sure*. He fingered the will apathetically, flicking a corner of it as his weary eyes read the words that the solicitor had recited fourteen years ago. '*I, Richard William*

Feeney, being of sound mind and body, do hereby declare that this is my last will and testament, made this twentieth day of September, eighteen hundred and seventy-four. To my dearly loved brother, John Patrick Feeney, I bequeath my house on The Mount and all its contents . . . ' Even now Sonny could feel the pain as acutely as if it were the day of the first reading.

He lowered the will to the desk and heaved his body from the chair, had almost reached the door . . . when he froze. There *was* something. Lurching back to the desk he snatched up the document, scouring it with desperate eyes. Twentieth of September . . . no, nothing telling there, Dickie hadn't died until November . . . '*My house on The Mount and all its contents. To my dear father . . .*' Sonny's eyes shot back to the previous line – *my house on The Mount!* 'You bastard!' came the involuntary shout. Then Sonny bit his lip hard and made a sound that was a mixture of grief and laughter. Dickie . . . you little old bastard! He spun round to see if anyone had heard his shout. The solicitor had vanished. Wasting no further time Sonny dashed from the building.

Sutcliffe heard the slam and wandered back into his office. The will was still on the desk . . . but he knew it had had the intended effect – had heard the man's cry. With a quirk of his lips he watched from his window as Sonny clambered into a carriage and drove away, hoping that his sentimental gesture would have no backlash.

Sonny was framed in the doorway, his face as red as his hair. 'He's alive, Jos!' He strode forward and lifted her off her feet.

Josie tried to calm him. 'Just sit down and tell me what you've found!'

He gripped her arms, face throbbing with repressed excitement. 'Oh, I can't!' He marched up and down, clasping his hands. She begged him to simmer down and he brought his emotions under tight enough rein to stutter his findings. 'The date on the will, twentieth September . . . it said, "To my beloved brother" . . .' his

voice tremored, ' "I leave my house on The Mount" ' . . .
Josie, he didn't have that house in September!'

'But . . .' She hoisted her hands in confusion.

'In September Dickie still had his . . . house of a thousand delights!'

'The brothel?'

'Yes!' He stormed forward and clasped her again. 'Don't you see? He made that will *after* he died!'

'Oh, John . . .' Her face was dubious. 'Don't go raising . . .'

'Josie! I know he's still alive.'

'You don't *know* anything! And you're going to be hurt . . .'

'Woman!' he roared at her and imprisoned her on a chair while he expanded his notion. 'Just listen! I know that Dickie only purchased that house on The Mount a few weeks before he died. Christ, what am I saying – he's not dead! On the way home, the day the house burnt down, we talked about a lot of things – and he told me himself that he'd sold the brothel and bought a new place.' His face became more intent as he squatted before his wife's chair, speaking directly into her face. 'He could only have written that will *after* he died.'

'But why would he do that, John? If he wanted to pretend he was dead that would only have helped to give the game away – and surely the solicitor wouldn't have gone along with such deception?'

'Josie, you know what Dickie is – he can twist anybody round his finger. Lord knows why he made the will . . . but does that matter?'

'So . . . if he isn't dead . . . what did happen to him?'

His face was triumphant. 'He's in America! I told you he was heading there before the fire, he was in some sort of bother again . . . He went there and *then* he wrote that bloody will and sent it to his solicitor – that's why we didn't get the reading until a few months after his death!' He exhaled loudly. 'God, all these years and I never twigged . . .' A seriousness came over him and he conveyed his fears to Josie. 'I want to find him, Jos, but I don't know how to start . . . an' I'm scared what'll happen if I do. The shock could kill Mam and Dad – if they don't kill him first . . . I just want to see for myself that he's alive.' He stiffened as though his brother's ghost had come swaggering in. His wife saw the action and asked, 'What is it?'

His answer came slowly. 'All the way home I've been racking my brain . . . the little . . . !' He gave a sudden roar of laughter at the audacity of his brother and threw himself back on the carpet, belly trembling with mirth.

Josie fell to her knees beside him. 'John!'

He grabbed her and pulled her on top of him, still laughing. Her body shuddered up and down with his. 'Oh, Jos! Remember what you told me all those years ago about Dusty Miller doing a moonlight flit to America?'

'Aw . . . she wouldn't?' Josie was beginning to take him seriously.

'Wouldn't she? Well, we can soon find out, can't we?' She asked how. 'If we find Dusty Miller we find Mr Richard William Feeney.' He studied the gawping face above his. 'Well, come on, woman! What're you lying there for like a trollop?' He pressed her from him. 'Trying to get your wicked way with me – there's work to be done!'

Laughingly, she smacked him for the insult as both got up from the carpet. 'What're you going to do now, then?'

'Not me – you.' He straightened his tie, then embraced her again. 'I want you to go and see that girl who gave you the information about Dusty.'

'Betty? Why, it's years since I've seen her . . .'

'D'you know where she lives?'

'Yes, but . . .'

'And d'you think she might still work at Miller's wholesalers?'

'More than likely. She's a widow, she wouldn't chuck a regular job up.'

'Then she'd probably welcome a few quid for doing us a favour.'

His wife asked what favour. 'Don't forget that Dusty doesn't own the warehouse any more – don't you remember your mam telling us it was up for sale, ooh . . . it must be all of ten years ago.'

'I know Dusty's sold up but it's just possible that her American address may still be on the files.' He was asked if the warehouse would keep such old files, and puffed out his lips. 'God . . . I hope so. It's the only way we're going to find him, Jos.'

She held him close and put her lips to his cheek in an affectionate gesture. 'Go put that poor blinking horse back in the shafts then – I'll go see what I can do.'

When Josie returned from her visit to York it was growing late. The children had been put to bed and Sonny was reading them a story when he heard the jingle of the harness beneath the bedroom window. Kissing his daughters he pelted downstairs to hurl himself at his wife the minute she entered. 'Does she still work there?'

Josie said she did as she handed her coat to the maid and set off for the sitting room.

'And will she do it?' Sonny shadowed her to the sofa where both sat down.

'She would've done – but they only keep files for the last three years. Ooh, ring for Sadie, love, will you? I forgot to tell her to make a pot of tea an' I'm gasping.' Deflated, Sonny moved to a strip of hanging tapestry and gave it a yank. 'Anyway, it wouldn't have done any good if we had found it – Dusty moved house after the sale of the warehouse.'

Something in her expression alerted him. He narrowed his eyes. 'And how did Betty know that?'

'It seems,' she said lightly, 'that Betty had cause to search the files of her own accord. She tells me she got so fed up with the man that Dusty left in charge that she decided to write to her and complain . . .' She laughed delightedly and held up her hand as Sonny ran forward, 'Whoa!' then fumbled in her pocket and brought out a piece of paper. 'Dusty wrote back to say that she was selling up but that she had made sure Betty would keep .

her job, and if anything else went wrong she should write back to Dusty at her new address . . .'

Sonny grabbed the piece of paper and held it to his face. 'Oh, Josie, we've found him!' He clamped his arms around her and rocked her from side to side in his rapture.

'Not yet.' The face that squashed against his reflected his joy. 'But we will do.'

CHAPTER TWENTY-THREE

He loved New York. It suited his character down to the ground – brash, colourful, ostentatious. His position in the shoe-shine's chair lent him time to relax, set himself apart from the rumbustious city life and view the teeming streets as for the first time when he had set foot here, fourteen years ago. Whoever had named this city had never seen the old York, for there could be no two places so different – although, a wry smile creased his handsome features, he had managed to lift the more ancient city from its sedateness while he had lived there. But he would never go back now. He had found his place. This was home. He was an American . . . well, another grin, an Irish-Yorkshire-American.

He wallowed for the moment in memories of his old haunts. A long, long time ago. Then he had been a boy – now he was a man of thirty-six whose looks and body were at their peak. He felt virile, magnetic . . . and bloody frightened. For a minute, the seething traffic disappeared as he saw himself as an old man. How much longer before he plummeted towards the trough, before the sap ran dry? It had begun to niggle at him more and more lately – four years and he would be forty. As yet the mirror didn't betray him – apart from reflecting the wisp of silver hair at his temples which he quite liked – his jaw was still tight, his hair abundant. A large, square hand searched involuntarily for the paunch that wasn't there, running over the pale-grey suit for signs of flab. But the thigh under his hand was still rock-hard. His eyes focused again as the hand divined a blonde hair clinging to his trouser leg, reinstating his grin. A very reassuring sight. He picked it off and watched it float away on the breeze. An attractive woman caught his eye. Her obvious admiration raised both his spirits and his hat. He winked at her, feeling good again.

'They's done, sir.'

Dickie looked down at the shoe-shine boy who sat back on his heels. 'Ah, God bless you, my son!' Reaching down, he used a thumb to trace the sign of the Cross on the black forehead, then jumped from the chair and began to stride away. There was a cry of objection from the shoe-shine and Dickie looked back, feigning surprise. 'Sure, ye don't want payin' as well, d'you? God love us!' The Irish-Yorkshire accent had almost disappeared, but the phrasing of the words was the same. He tossed a coin which was whipped from the air by the shoe-shine, then, grinning, he adopted his characteristic swagger, hailed a cab and made for home.

Home was a secluded colonial-style building set well back from the road behind a cluster of trees – Dusty's choice, not his. But he had to agree with her that it made a welcome bolt-hole from the manic streets of the city. They had not lived here for the entire fourteen years – their first lodgings had been quite primitive, but Dickie was rather good at making money one way or another and with the sale of Dusty's business the hardship hadn't lasted long. Yet their prosperity was vulnerable, for Dickie could not settle to a regular occupation; his income came from gambling on the Stock Market, buying and selling property and other more dubious activities – a streak of bad luck and it could all be gone overnight. He quite liked it that way, but he understood why Dusty got mad at him sometimes. She needed security. He would have to settle down one day . . . but that could wait until he was an old man.

As the cab wheels crunched to a halt on the gravel

outside his front porch he alighted, paid the fare and went towards the house. Before his hand could grasp the knob the door was flung open by a maid, making him laugh as he stepped over the threshold. 'I'll manage to do it one o' these days, Mary!'

The girl grinned at the tall, good-looking man and took possession of his hat and cane. It was a kind of game between the master and herself – he would try his best to creep into the house without alerting her, but somehow her intuition always got her to the door before him. He ran a hand over his crisp black hair and made his way across the hall. 'Is Mrs Feeney in here?' He gave a flourishing gesture at the door towards which he was headed. At the maid's, 'Yessir!' he applied the flat of his palm to the brass fingerplate and made a theatrical entrance.

A petite woman was sitting by the window, light shining through the frizzy chestnut hair which obscured her face. At his cheery greeting she turned slanting green eyes on him, but didn't reply and duly turned back to stare pensively at the lawn. There was a letter on the lap of her blue silk gown. Instinctively, Dickie knew he was in trouble again. Over which female he wasn't certain, but he knew from his wife's face that he needed an alibi. While his mind grasped for one he lit a cigar and babbled on about some shares he had just purchased, waiting for her to lay into him.

But she adopted a different tack this evening. Still sombre, she told him to sit down and stop jigging about, which he did. It was another few seconds before she swivelled from the window to study him. Dusty's insides flipped over at the sight. Fourteen years of marriage and he still had that same impact on her – the impact he had on just about every woman. She could have left him twenty times over for the pain he had inflicted on her – had tried to once but he'd come after her. Time had taught her that he would never change. If she wanted him she would have to accept his failings – as he accepted hers. Dusty was unable to give him a child, a child they both wanted desperately. So, in spite of the fights and the tears and the betrayals they stayed together, not the least reason being that the only family they had now was each other. And finally she had come to accept the other women – providing he didn't flaunt them – knowing that he didn't love them and that what he told her was true: she was his only love.

She noticed the flicker of apprehension at the corner of his bright blue eye and knew that he had been up to his old tricks again. But she fought the pang of treachery, saying only, 'I don't know how to tell you this . . .' and held up the letter.

He wrinkled his brow. 'Er, bad news, is it?'

'Bad and good . . . it's from your brother.'

'Christ!' The adopted nonchalance was discarded. He shot from his chair and raced over to snatch the letter which turned out to be addressed to his wife in her maiden name. After reading it avidly, he stumped back to the sofa and flopped onto it, cheek cradled in palm.

She left her seat to take one by him, rubbing a hand up and down his thigh. Dickie gave a groan and let his head sag over the ormolued back of the sofa. The will – he had feared at the time it had been a mistake, but his need for money had overcome his caution. When he had written to his solicitor on his arrival here it had, initially, been to ask him to sell the house and transfer as many of Dickie's assets to America as was possible. But on consideration this would have been risky; his parents would want to know what had happened to their dead son's belongings and would find out that he was not dead, after all. He couldn't have that happen. He had been 'dead' once before and his rebirth had caused great upheaval for all of them. He didn't want to put them through it again . . . though the thought was not entirely noble: he had escaped serious charges in England, he could never go back. So, what was he to do? He could simply ask his lawyer to send what money he could lay his hands on and abandon the rest to his family. But there were two things wrong with that: firstly, his parents' solicitor might delve too deeply into his financial accounts; secondly, his parents would be the natural inheritors. A will would settle both points. If Dickie's belongings were allocated there would be no need for investigation and Sonny – who deserved it most – could be a rich man. So, after tearing up that first letter Dickie had instructed his solicitor to act upon the will. Sutcliffe had spouted off about it all being very unethical, but a bit of the old blarney and a fat cheque had soothed his conscience ... until now.

He lifted his head, stared first at the letter then at Dusty. 'I'm gonna have to tell him, aren't I?'

'That's up to you.' Her lynx eyes held his. 'I could always write and say I've no idea of your whereabouts.'

'Give over, Dusty, he damn-well knows I'm here ...' He summoned up one of his devastating smiles and pictured his brother as the boy he had last seen in eighteen seventy-four. 'Good old Son ... Ye know, I'm rather glad he's found me out – I wonder what set it off after all this time ... an' I wonder what he'll say when he gets my letter.'

'That's rather naïve, if you don't mind my saying so.' Dusty rose and glided away across the room.

He laughed, smacked his leg and rose too, tucking the letter into a rack. 'Aye, he'll probably send me a gobful in his next letter.'

'If he replies.' She turned to him. 'He just might feel like not corresponding after what you've done.'

'Ah, he'll forgive me.' The old Dickie grin manifested itself again as he thought of all the occasions he had temporarily fallen from his brother's affection.

'Good! I'm glad about that,' said Dusty in bright manner – then coming towards him delivered a hefty slap round his head.

The big man was transformed into a chastised infant, his pained eyes holding hers bemusedly. 'Dusty! What was that for?'

'That was for whatever you were looking guilty about

when you came in here!' She flounced from the room and slammed the door.

Dickie rubbed the point of contact ruefully, then directed his eyes once more to the letter in the rack and out slipped a laugh. Marching to a bureau he withdrew pen and paper and sat down to form a reply. 'Oh, Son . . . I sure hope you're in a good mood.'

Sonny had been unable to settle, waiting for that reply from Dusty. When he spotted the American postmark he waved the letter in frenzied manner at his wife, 'It's come!' and immediately slit it open, reading out loud to her.

Dear Sonny, If you haven't recognised the handwriting yet you had better sit down before you flip over and look for the signature . . . Sonny donned a frown and automatically turned the page to look at the sender's scrawl. It took his breath away and he shot upright. 'It's from him!' He met his wife's cry with a face that oozed exultation, then proceeded to devour the rest of the letter, picking out the odd line to fling at Josie in excitement. 'He's doing very well for himself! . . . Oh, he and Dusty haven't got any kids yet – they're still hoping . . .'

I often think how bloody ironic it is, Son – me having sown so many wild oats all over the place and now everything's legal I can't manage the one. God's judgment, our Dad would say. Still we're happy with each other. She's a grand wife is Dusty – though she can be a right bruiser when she has a mind. I'm sorry you had to find out about me like you did, Son. I had no wish to upskell things, that's why I stayed dead this time. I thought maybe you wouldn't forgive me for this one. I note from your address that you didn't want to live at my place. Don't suppose I can blame you, you wouldn't want a constant reminder of this rogue. But I hope the money did you some good and you don't hold me in too much contempt . . .

'Oh, no,' breathed Sonny, still in a whirl.

I'm glad you found me. It's nice to have someone in the family know I'm not dead and I'm glad it's you. You know, I often think about the times we had as lads and wish we could share them again. If you ever feel like coming to New York me and Dusty would give you a real American welcome. I guess it's best you don't tell anyone else about this, don't you?

Sonny nodded, mesmerised by the letter.

It's all very well being disinterred once, but I don't think Mam and Dad would be so resilyent this time . . .

Sonny chuckled at the spelling.

They must be getting on a bit now — aren't we all? If you can stop your pen from dipping into poison I would love to hear how they are, and yourself of course. I know I don't deserve it, but now I am alive again I'd like to keep in touch with how everyone is, especially Rosanna and Nicholas. Don't take that the wrong way, Son. They're yours and they'll stay yours and it's because of that I want to hear about them, not because I regard them as mine. It's just that it'll make me feel that my family is a bit nearer. I'd like to hear of any other kids you might have as well — did you marry Josie? I hope you are as happy as me. Well, you know I'm not a very good writer, that's all I can think of to say.

Your loving brother
Dick

Sonny stood there for what seemed like an age. Then he crumpled the letter in his fist, swore loudly and threw it to the carpet.

'I thought this was what you wanted?' proffered Josie in soft confusion.

He moaned and swung round to put his arms round her. 'It is! It is, Jos. I'm so thrilled he's still alive . . . but he's landed me with a hell of a problem, hasn't he? As he says himself I can't tell my parents. They're getting on, one of them might have a seizure or something . . .'

She agreed that he must never tell them. 'Can I read

the letter?' After doing this she looked anxious. 'Are you going to give him the progress report on Rosie and Nick?'

'I don't know that I should even bother to acknowledge his blasted letter! The bloody little wretch!' He screwed his hands into his red hair and scratched furiously to illustrate his indecision. 'Tell me what to do, Jos!'

'I think you know what you're going to do.'

He gave a resigned nod. 'Oh . . . I wish I could see him.'

Josie smiled reminiscently. 'I wonder if he's changed much?'

'I'm not bothered about his appearance, I just want to throttle him!' Sonny paced the room, thumping a fist into his other palm. Then with a gasp of surrender he grabbed writing implements from a desk and planted himself resolutely on a chair. 'I may as well scribble off a few lines now just to let him know . . .' After forming, '*Dear Dickie*' he paused and looked up at his wife. His grey eyes were full of torment. 'D'you think we're right to keep it from them, Jos?'

'Your mam and dad? I don't see as there's anything else you can do.' She came to place supportive hands on both his shoulders. 'As you said, the shock would be tremendous.'

'But Dickie's death seemed to put a sort of barrier between them. If they knew he was still alive they could both stop blaming themselves and be as close as they once were.'

She shook her head. 'They might, but I don't think you should risk it. Oh, I wish you hadn't seen that will! It isn't fair that you should be the only one to bear the burden. This is just like your brother!'

Sonny agreed despairingly. 'But it's done now – and I can't say I'm not happy he's alive. Anyway, I'm not bearing it alone, am I? I've got you.' He patted her hand cheerfully, then set his pen at the paper, so beginning a course of secret correspondence that was to last for another ten years.

CHAPTER TWENTY-FOUR

Eighteen eighty-nine would be remembered as a very significant year by everyone. For Thomasin it was the year of the great business coup in which she succeeded in purchasing the property that backed onto hers and had its entrance in Pavement, knocking the whole lot into one and creating a large walk-through store with two entrances. The building which she had selected for her biscuit factory now bore little resemblance to the crumbling warehouse of three years ago. Directly after purchase both the interior and exterior had been renovated and given a new coat of paint, ovens and work tables moved in and ten people set to work. Now there were fifty working full-time. The bakery which had formerly been at the back of the store was now amalgamated with the factory and turned out not only biscuits, bread and pastries but a wider selection of goods. Each day Thomasin's delivery vans would bring fresh supplies to her store. The new products were also added to the mobile grocery vans that delivered to folk's doors. Not only this, but Thomasin had started supplying other retailers, as had Sonny, whose materials and wallpapers were providing a splendid turnover.

The profits rocketed. Thomasin had the good sense to recognise that Nick had played no small part in these improvements. The lad had considerable flair – though he still had much to learn about customer relationships. Perhaps by the time he was of age he would be reliable enough to be made a partner.

Thomasin found herself more and more in demand at social functions. Patrick, no socialite, persuaded Francis that he would be doing the Irishman a favour if he would partner her. Many nights he found himself alone in their bed with nothing to do but think. At the age of sixty-nine, when one usually settled down into a comfortable rut with one's partner, the reverse was true for Pat. He and Thomasin seemed to have grown even further apart. He saw more of his grand-daughter than his wife. This might once have been some comfort but now even Rosie seemed distanced and aloof. Maybe it was just her age – she was after all a young woman. The times when he could take her on his knee and cuddle her were long past. No more ringlets and ribbons, but nipped-in waists and coiffeured topknots. Of course they had all changed physically. Patrick himself looked like the old man he was, and though he held onto his hair it was not as thick as it used to be, the colour silver-grey. The years of manual work had helped on the one hand to keep his body supple but, conversely, had left a legacy of clicking joints and muscular spasms when there was rain to come. Nonetheless, he was a sprightly sixty-nine-year-old, with barely a stoop to his shoulders . . . even if he did get the impression he was shrinking every time he stood beside his strapping grandson.

Sonny and Josie had bred four children – all female. It was doubtful whether there would be any more as Josie was no longer a girl. Neither was Erin. At almost forty-two her slim figure had given way to a not-unattractive roundness. With Belle away at school her days had seemed a little empty and so, when Thomasin had offered her a supervisory post at the factory, she had been pleased to accept. All these things Sonny included in his letters to his brother . . . yet there were things he couldn't write, things that were going on about which he knew nothing.

To Rosanna, the year eighteen eighty-nine would bring many things, but as yet, barely into its second month, it had not fulfilled the urgent plea she had made when pulling the Christmas wishbone – to give her Tim. Oh, he had pledged himself to her and she saw him every single day except Sundays – how she hated Sundays – but never alone, at least not for more than five minutes, those precious minutes when Grandfather was away up the other end of the cabbage field and Tim would sneak in to share a brief but enthusiastic embrace. But it couldn't go on like this. She ached for him, literally ached. When he had gone she would press her hands to her belly in an effort to massage away the cramp-like response to his overtures.

Tim felt the same way. She did things to him. He had never met anyone as intense as Rosanna. Truth to tell he had never known any girl before Rosie. When it happened it would be the first time for both of them . . . and it would happen. He could tell by the way she pressed her whole body against his, the way she didn't push his hand away when it clutched her breast, that Rosanna would make it happen. Rosie was that kind of girl – she got what she wanted . . . and she wanted him. It made him feel great.

The thing that had prevented it happening so far was her grandfather. Not only because he hardly let Rosie out of his sight, but because he was the master, and if Mr Feeney knew the way his labourer felt about his grand-daughter he would boot him out with no hesitation. So their love-making remained imprisoned in their minds.

It was this which was the main theme of Rosanna's thoughts as she leaned on her elbows, palms propping up her chin, staring at the wall. Instead of having to sit in the cold barn she now had her own little office with a stove for added comfort, both thanks to her doting grandfather. On the table before her was a pile of paperwork waiting for attention but she just could not concentrate. She wondered if Tim had found the envelope that she had tucked into the bush at the place he always visited to relieve himself. Rather an unromantic place for a Valentine she knew, but it was the only way she could think of to get it to him. How very disappointing it had been to arrive this morning and not find his own, anticipated Valentine on her desk. Last night, before falling asleep, she had lain imagining what his card would be like. He would send her one, she was positive. To find he hadn't was shattering both for heart and ego. She had looked between all the sheets of invoices to see if he had hidden it. He hadn't. She had cried bitterly.

With a heartfelt sigh she now began to make a start on her work. If hope had any sway in the matter he would bring her one later in the day. He didn't. In fact, she saw neither hide nor hair of him all day. Horrible thoughts began to go through her mind – what if I've offended him by sending the Valentine? Perhaps – God forbid – someone else had found it first and had teased him about it.

The working day was growing to a close and still he had not been. Rosie hated this time of year – the darkness came early which meant work finished early too; so she had less time with Tim. Dejectedly she tidied up her pile of papers, put on her hat and coat, then flopped back on the stool to wait for Patrick. She held out her gloved hands to the stove. Why, why hadn't he been?

Shortly, Patrick entered. 'Gosh, 'tis all right for the likes o' some!' He too held his hands to the warmth, dancing from one foot to the other. 'The ground's like concrete. 'S going to be a hard night.' He noticed her despondency. 'Whyfor the look of despair, colleen? Is the cold getting to ye?'

'No, no. I'm quite warm enough in here, thank you.' Her eyes were still vacant.

'I should think you are, an' all. Come on then, we'd best not linger.' Pat banked up the stove. 'Wrap your muffler under your sneck,' and made to go. He had just stepped outside the office when he lifted his foot and looked down. 'What the devil's this I'm stepping on?'

Rosanna bent swiftly, her face radiating quiet joy as she gathered up the scattering of wilted snowdrops. Oh, Tim! She caught her grandfather looking at her strangely as she pressed the simple, exquisite blooms to her face. 'Oh!' She blushed. 'I picked them earlier and put them aside so I could open the door of the office, you know how stiff it is to do with one hand, anyway I must've left them there by mistake. How silly. They've been there all day.' The sad little stems drooped between her fingers but to Rosanna they were the most beautiful flowers in the world.

'An' where did ye find them?' asked Patrick, hoisting his collar.

'I went for a stroll down the lane. They were just by the hedgerow.'

'Aye, well, just don't wander too far off, colleen,' he warned. 'Ye don't know who ye might bump into.' Chance would be a fine thing, thought Rosie, and gazed wistfully at the sight of her would-be lover far away across the field as the carriage transported her even further from his side.

He was unable to visit her the following morning either; the master seemed to be forever at his side. When at last he did come close enough to talk to her he was with another man and might as well have been a hundred miles away for the good his closeness did her.

Rosanna left open the door of her office just so, by hearing the sound of his voice, she could feel closer to him. How she loved the sound of that soft lilt.

'Have you given any thought to the matter we were discussing?' she heard him ask his workmate, Joseph, as they stacked their load.

'About me joining the Brotherhood?' grunted Joseph, humping another crate onto his shoulder.

Timothy threw down the one he was holding. 'For Christ's sake, Joseph, are ye bloody puddled? Ye could get me locked up.'

'Sure, there's nobody listening,' replied Joseph nonchalantly.

'Isn't there?' Rosanna caught Tim's inference and was deeply hurt at his lack of trust. She had no idea what they were discussing but if Tim had secrets they were safe with her. 'Ah, forget I ever asked. I'm thinking you'd be more of a liability than an asset. Besides,' he carried on working, 'you're not much of a patriot, are you?'

'I'm as much a patriot as you are,' objected the other. 'Don't I go to Mass every Sunday?'

Tim scoffed. 'What the hell has that got to do with it? Listen, we need men we can trust, men who aren't afraid to put their country before their lives.'

'Ah, well now.' Joseph scratched his head. 'I don't know that I want to get involved in nuthin' dangerous. I've a wife an' seven children relying on me.' He had forgotten about the latest addition.

'There's plenty that could hide behind their woman's skirts,' said Tim softly but making his point felt. 'Lucky for Ireland they're not all like you. Look, Joseph, we've got to rid ourselves o' these chains once an' for all, put down our English masters.'

'But the master's not English.'

'Mother o' God! I'm not talkin' literally. I'm on about politics, man.'

'Oh Jaze, I don't have no truck with any o' that bunch.' Joseph shook his head. 'Can't understand a word of it.'

'I'm not askin' you to put yourself up for election,' said Tim exasperatedly. 'I'm just asking you if you'd be willing to support us. Don't worry, I shouldn't think ye'd be asked to do anything of strategic importance.' He saw Joseph's indecision and drove his point deeper. 'I mean, look at the place you live in, Joe . . .'

'What's up with it? 'S all right to me.'

'All right? An Englishman wouldn't keep a bloody pig in it. 'Tis time y' opened your eyes, man. Look at all the injustices that're going on around you an' in Ireland. They rule us here an' they rule us there – but not for long. That's why we need men like you, Joseph.'

'An' what specifically would ye be needing Joseph for?'

The two men spun at Patrick's question. He came further into the storehouse and, as the two rapidly resumed their task, said, 'Ye wouldn't be trying to indoctrinate Joseph with your Fenian rubbish would ye, Timothy?'

'No, sir.' Tim continued to work.

'No, sir. Then what was all that about the bloody English this an' the bloody English that I heard when I came in? Look at me, Rabb!' Timothy was forced to put down the crate and face his employer. 'Haven't I warned you about bringing this political nonsense to work? Didn't I tell ye the last time that if it happened again I'd dismiss ye?'

369

Rosanna caught her breath as Tim answered, 'You did, sir.'

'Then ye know what's coming, don't ye, son?'

No, no, whispered Rosanna to herself.

'Am I to go right away then?' asked Tim, facing Pat squarely now, no cowedness in his stance.

'I see no reason why not. With the weather bad I've no need of ye. But,' Patrick added charitably, 'I'd not bring extra hardship on your family. Your mother has a hard enough time as it is trying to keep an eejit like you in tow. Ye can finish what you're doing then go, an' take a month's wages with ye. I'll not have ye on my land a moment longer than is necessary. You're a dangerous influence. An' ye'd do well to heed my views when ye set about finding another job. Now get on about your work.' He saw them both out of the barn and was about to follow when a white-faced Rosanna waylaid him. 'Ah, hello, muirneen.' A smile. 'Sorry if we disturbed your concentration. Had a bit o' trouble with one o' the lads.'

'I heard.' She clasped her hands. 'Please, Grandfather, don't dismiss him.'

'Ah, I'm sorry to offend your soft heart but 'tis all sorted. The man's been warned before.'

'But, Gramps, I don't understand. What has he done wrong? Aren't you always singing and telling tales about Ireland? You've always encouraged us to take a pride in our heritage. That's what Tim is doing.'

'Rosanna, dear,' he said, rather condescendingly she thought, as if speaking to a child, 'ye've no idea what the man's about. This isn't about heritage. That boy has been trying to enlist my men in his dangerous activities for months now. He's been warned about it more than once. God knows patience is not one o' my virtues so he can consider himself lucky the axe didn't fall till now.'

'But, Grandfather, he can't afford to leave his job. He has no father and his poor mother is ill.'

Patrick laid his head to one side. 'How come you know so much about him, Rosanna?'

She sought for an excuse. 'Oh . . . I just heard the men talking amongst themselves.'

'Ye wouldn't be trying to cod me now?'

'Why should I do that?' she asked unconvincingly. 'I'm simply concerned that this poor boy is about to lose his job. He's a good worker, Gramps, it'd be a shame to lose him. You mightn't get anyone else so industrious.'

'He's a good worker, aye,' concurred Patrick. 'But so are the others, an' I'd like them to stay that way. Timothy Rabb is of the stuff that makes a mutineer. I'm sorry, Rosie, but he goes.' With that blunt riposte he left her.

Rosanna broke down in tears.

When the realisation that he would soon be lost to her crept through her heartbreak she damned herself for wasting time blubbering and went to seek him out, but by then he had already departed. Feeling sick, Rosanna went back inside for her coat, then wandered aimlessly along the path – please make it all a dream, she begged. I'll wake up in a moment and everything will have righted itself. What optimism.

On reaching the thicket where yesterday she had left the Valentine she stopped to lean her head against a lichen-covered tree trunk. Between the snarled roots of the tree grew a single snowdrop. Stooping, she picked it and cupped it in her hands. It served to make her more aware of her loss.

'Rosanna, over here!'

She looked up, immediately alert at the sound of Tim's hiss, saw him beckoning from the cover of a tangle of elderberry branches and ran to him. 'Oh, Tim, Tim! I thought I'd never see you again.' Their bodies clashed in a passionate kiss.

He held her triumphantly. 'I've been waiting ages, I thought you might come,' then delivered another abrasive kiss.

She thought she was going to burst. 'Did you get my Valentine?' she managed to ask breathlessly between contact.

He nodded smilingly and pulled the crumpled card from his inside pocket. 'I kept it next to my heart.'

'Tim, how romantic you are.'

'Will ye tell me what it says?'

Surprised, she stared at his eager face, then suddenly understood why she hadn't received the expected Valentine. 'Oh . . . you can't read?'

'Only my name,' he answered awkwardly. 'I could read what was on the envelope but not what was inside.'

She felt embarrassed at reading her thoughts aloud, but nevertheless did so. 'It says: I love you, Tim, never leave me.' Her face lost its sheen. 'And now you're going to.'

'No,' he told her confidently. 'We'll find a way.' She asked him how. After some thought he replied with a question. 'Is there any time you're alone? An hour when you could get away to meet me without anyone missing ye?'

'Oh, Lord . . . I don't know.' She searched her numbed brain frantically. 'Er, yes, yes, wait a minute. If we don't go to visit Father and Mother on Sunday I always go for a walk down the garden after lunch. We're at home this week.'

'Won't they think it's funny, you taking a walk in this weather?'

'No, they're used to me wandering off for an hour or so,' replied Rosanna, remembering. 'It's her tinker blood,' Great-grandma would say – she understood now. 'There's an old shed right at the bottom of the garden where the tools are kept. No one goes there on a Sunday. If you could climb over the wall . . .'

'Rosanna, I don't even know where you live,' he interrupted. 'Besides, if someone should see me climbing over the wall they'd think I'm up to stealin' something.'

'Oh, I hadn't thought about that.' She nibbled a fingernail.

'Look, d'ye think you could climb over the wall yourself and make your way out here? There'll be no one around on Sunday.'

'But the storehouse will be locked.'

'Surely you could manage to get the key when your grandfather's asleep or something?'

'Yes . . . yes, of course I could.' She flung her arms round his neck. 'Oh, Tim, won't it be wonderful? We'll be on our own at last.' They both knew what that meant.

There was a darkening of his eye as his hands ran up under her jacket. 'D'ye really and truly love me, Rosanna?'

'Of course I do. Haven't I said so?' She allowed the hands to do as they willed. Everything seemed to have turned to jelly.

'Did you get my flowers?' he said out of the blue. 'I'm sorry they were the only ones I could find.'

'Oh, they were lovely. I've never had such a beautiful gift.'

'That's a lie,' replied Tim. 'I'll bet your other beaux bring ye much more exotic presents.'

'I haven't any other beaux, Tim. I don't want any.'

'There may be a time when ye have no choice.'

'What does that mean?'

'Well, they're hardly going to let ye marry me, are they?'

'Why not?'

'Rosie, just look at the difference between us. They'll be expecting someone better than me.'

'There could never be anyone better than you, Tim.'

'Ye might change your mind.'

'Never! Never, never, never. I'm going to marry you.' She pressed herself to him.

'I don't remember askin' ye.'

She broke away. 'But you . . . ,' then saw the amused twinkle. 'Oh, Timothy Rabb, I'll kill you!'

A slight chuckle. 'I'm thinking that's what your grandfather will say when he finds out.'

'Oh, please don't keep putting obstacles in our way,' begged Rosanna. 'I love you, Timothy. I want you.' She laid her face against his drab jacket. It carried the smell of his damp little hovel but she didn't care. 'Say you want me.'

'You know I do.' He cleaved her to him and kissed her fervently.

She came up for breath. 'And you do love me, Tim, don't you?'

'Of course I do.'

'Say it.'

'I love you, Rosanna.'

'How much do you love me?'

'Be here on Sunday,' he murmured thickly. 'I'll show you how much.'

They locked once more, then he made to pull away.

'Don't leave me yet!'

'I must, there's somebody coming. Look.' He kept hold of her but nodded towards the field where a distant figure approached. Looking back into the flushed face he said, 'You'll come, won't ye?'

She tried to keep hold of his hands as he moved away. 'Oh yes! What time?'

'Three?'

'I'll be here. I love you, Tim.' It was like an amputation watching him go – I'll never see him again, thought Rosanna, straining her eyes as he hared away over the dormant fields. He won't be here on Sunday. I know he won't.

CHAPTER TWENTY-FIVE

A million lovers before her had experienced the same doubt: will Sunday never come? How Rosanna got through the week she would never know. But the hour that dragged the most was that of Sunday lunch. An hour of mixed feelings – excitement, fear, love, despair.

'Are you sickening for something, Rosanna?' asked her grandmother, watching the girl's fork nudge her food around the plate. 'I think we shall have to call in Abi with her brimstone and treacle.'

Rosanna awoke from her introspection. 'Oh, no, I'm

perfectly fit and well, thank you, Nan.' She caught Nick's subtle expression and wondered how on earth he knew. But then her brother always knew everyone else's business – sometimes even before oneself. 'Though I must admit I'm not very hungry today. It's because I've had no fresh air, I suppose.'

'Nonsense, you've had the same as everyone else,' said Thomasin. 'I thought the ride home from church was very bracing. Come on, eat up, I won't have good food wasted at my table.'

'We didn't get much of a breather this morning, Tommy,' put in her husband. 'Fifteen minutes of the elements might suffice two old dodderers like us but sure, I always say Rosie needs ten times as much.'

To Rosanna's gratitude her grandmother agreed. 'Well, a breath of fresh air is as good a tonic as from any bottle – but do try to eat a bit more before you go.'

Rosanna began to stuff vegetables into her mouth, chewing feverishly. 'I didn't intend for you to break any records,' said her grandmother disapprovingly. 'It really isn't becoming for a young lady to fill her mouth so.'

Rosanna offered an apologetic smile, a green stalk protruding from her lips, then plunged back to her task, finishing in seconds. 'May I go now?'

'Don't you want any pudding?' asked Thomasin.

'No, thank you.'

'Well, I must say for someone who professed not to have an appetite you certainly made short shrift of that. It seems a bit pointless to call on the properties of fresh air now.'

Rosanna suppressed a scream. 'Oh, Nan, I'm beginning to agree with you that I shouldn't rush my food. I feel quite giddy.'

'For some reason, Rosanna, you seem intent on getting out into that garden.'

Patrick stepped to his grand-daughter's aid once more. 'Now, Tommy, ye know how Rosie hates to be cooped up. Run along child, I'm sure your Nan would hate ye to grog all over the dinner table.'

'D'you know, this house is becoming like a public restaurant,' replied Thomasin. 'I'd never've been allowed to leave the table at will like these youngsters seem to think is their right. And if I'd left all that on my plate it would've been waiting for me at suppertime, I can tell you.'

'Leave her be,' answered Patrick, pouring white sauce on his pudding. 'Ye know what she's like.'

'She's even more like it than ever today. If she'd been going anywhere else but the garden I'd swear there was a man involved.'

Up in her room Rosie stripped off her outer garments, then sat on the bed staring at her reflection from afar. The face that presented itself was that of some nervous animal wanting desperately to drink from the waterhole but aware that if it did some wild beast might come along and pounce on it. The hands in the mirror came up to cover her breasts. She ripped off her bodice, and flexed her chest muscles, thrusting her bosom outwards. Her teeth played nervously with her lip, then off came the rest of her clothes to bring her naked to the mirror. Was Tim doing the same? Of course he wasn't, that was stupid. – And neither should you be, she told herself, or you'll be too late to find out what he thinks of you. Hastily she donned clean underwear then tried on six outfits, flinging them all aside before deciding on a blue tartan dress that hugged her body, its grey sash showing off the slimness of her waist. Thrusting her feet into matching grey slippers she unpinned her hair, tugged a brush through its gleaming waves, then tried to rearrange it. The result was a failure. In desperation she rushed down to the kitchen to ask if Abigail would comb it up for her.

'I don't know why you want your hair doing in t'middle o'day,' tutted Abi. 'Where you thinking of going?'

'Just in the garden.'

'Just in t'garden an' you drag me from me work . . .'

'Oh, go on – I'll let you borrow my blue necklace for your next day off if you oblige me.'

Abigail surrendered and, following Rosie up to her

room, soon had the hair pinned into its required style. 'I don't know why you want to go to all this trouble,' she remarked when it was finished. 'Half an hour an' it'll look like you've been dragged through a hedge backwards.'

'Why should it?' demanded the girl sharply.

'"Cause you're just that sort o' person what never stays tidy, Miss Rosie,' retorted the maid into her face. 'I always said you ought to have been a lad.'

'Oh, yes, I see what you mean,' said Rosanna, relieved. – If only you knew how unlike a boy I am, she thought to herself.

When Abi departed Rosanna wrapped up against the cold then once again paused to stare at herself in the mirror. This was the last time she would look upon herself as a girl. When next she looked in that glass she would see a woman. Dabbing a little scent behind each ear she took a deep fortifying breath and went to her rendezvous.

'Don't stay out too long, muirneen,' warned her grandfather as she encountered him on her way to the garden. 'That wind'll take lumps outta ye.'

She went hot as her fingers closed on the key in her pocket, wondering would he notice its absence. She passed through the french windows, fully expecting with each step to hear someone shout: 'The game's up!' But the hundred miles to the bottom of the garden were attained with nary a whisper.

Fortunately the wall she needed to climb in order to escape was hidden from the house. There was no one to witness her ungainly ascent. She swore as her knee slipped and a hole appeared in her stocking, then dropped over to the other side. She was now in someone else's garden. After clambering over another wall she found herself on the public highway. It was bitterly cold. There were no cabs about. She must travel on foot.

She had run most of the way. Now with pumping heart and flushed face she arrived at their meeting place. Tim wasn't there, but then she was probably early. Going directly to the storehouse she inserted the key in the padlock, twisted it and let herself in.

The stove in the office was cold, but one of the men had prepared it for lighting on Monday morning. She found a match and lit it now, then sat back shivering, to wait. – He's not coming, I can feel it, I know. Stupid fool, of course he'll come. He said he would, didn't he? He won't. I felt it when he left me. I know I'll never see him again. Come, you're just saying that hoping it to be true because you don't want to . . . you-know-what. You'll be relieved if he doesn't come. Admit it. Oh, no! I want him, I do . . . but I know he won't come.

The door opened suddenly to reveal Tim's apprehensive face. 'Tim,' she said shyly, 'I thought I might've missed you. I wasn't sure what time it was,' then stepped up to him, pressed her warm cheek to his cold one and pulled away again.

'I didn't think you'd be here,' he confided. 'I thought they'd somehow find out an' stop ye.'

'They couldn't stop me. I'd still have come somehow. Have you got another job?' He told her a friend had got him fixed up. 'Good. Here, come by the stove, you look freezing.' So polite. She had expected them to fall into each other's arms and make spontaneous love, but here they were just talking, almost like strangers waiting for an omnibus. 'Let me warm you.' She took one of his hands between her own, loving the feel of him, sensing every whorl on his fingertips, every ingrained line, slipping one finger between two of his, moving it down to stroke the sensitive web of skin where the fingers forked.

Reaching up he took a pin from her hair, and another, draping it round her shoulders, working his fingers through it. He brought his eyelids slowly down over eyes suffused with longing, the lashes sweeping his cheeks, then opened them again. 'Oh, Rosie.' He reached for her and she came to him, touching her lips to his neck where the male smell made her dizzy, rubbling her nose behind the lobe of his ear.

'I've been thinkin' all week about this.' His voice was muffled by the tangle of her hair. 'Maybe . . . maybe it's not right.'

'You've changed your mind,' she accused with a sudden prickle of tears.

Seizing her hand he forced it to lay on the hardness that strained to sink itself into her. 'There! That's how much I've changed my mind. Is that somebody who doesn't want you?'

'Oh!' She attempted to pull her hand away.

'See! It's you who isn't ready for this, Rosie,' he said helplessly. 'I want ye, oh yes I want ye, but you've got to be aware of what we're doing, that if I should leave you with a baby . . . I'd not inflict that shame on ye.'

'We'd get married.'

'They wouldn't let us an' you know it. Rosie, don't. Please don't look at me like that else all my honourable notions are going to go clean out the window.'

'Tim,' she spoke earnestly into his face, 'I've thought about nothing else all week – since I met you. I want you. If I pulled away just now it was just because I didn't expect it to . . . well, to feel like that. Why is it hard?' Familiar with Nick's anatomy she knew this wasn't normal.

'That's because I'm burning for ye, Rosie.' It was painful even to talk. 'It has to be stiff so's we can do it.'

'Oh, I see. Tim . . . ,' a little laugh, 'I'm not sure what to do, are you?' In her discussions with her brother she had learned quite a lot, more than other girls her age she was sure, but that wasn't much help now.

He hesitated, then nodded.

'Oh, good. I mean, I know the main bit . . . oh, I feel so silly. But I do want you, Tim.' Without hesitation she replaced the hand that had shown such nervousness, making him close his eyes and swallow. 'There, that shows I do, doesn't it?' she whispered into his lips, then pressed her mouth to his. The cramp that she had experienced before in the pit of her belly came again as he ground his body into hers, hands searching. He broke away only to rip off his poor threadbare coat and throw it down for them to lie on.

'Shall I take this off?' she asked, pointing to her dress.

'It's cold . . . yes! take it off, I want to see you.'

379

Struggling with the buttons she did as he asked. 'I'm afraid I'm not much to look at.' The layers came off. She clutched her left upper arm with her right hand, the action serving to cover her breasts.

He reached out, but drew back at the last minute. 'Oh, you are. You are.' He began to take off his own clothes. Rosanna gazed in wonder at his body. It made her eyes burn. The feeling in her stomach grew more intense, spreading to the cleft of her thighs. She stood while he pressed a cold palm to her breast. 'Oh, sorry, sorry!' He felt her shiver. 'I should've warmed them.'

'I'm not cold.' Her legs buckled as his lips closed gently on a nipple. He caught her between the thighs. Ah, Jesus! Gently explored her. Tim, Tim, Tim. He pulled her down and lay on top of her, worked his way between her legs — then the most indescribable pain. 'Tim! Stop, please, stop.' But he held her more firmly to him, plunged, inflicting violent stabs of pain. Pain, no passion. His thrusting grew wilder. Oh, God, please stop. One final deep thrust, a tickling sensation deep inside her and it was over.

He flopped down with a great sigh and buried his face in her bare shoulder. It was better now he was still. She liked the feel of him inside her, the weight of his body on hers. But her disappointment was acute that it hadn't been at all like she had expected. Her silence must have transmitted this to him and he raised himself on his elbows to look down at her, his eyes shades darker than she had ever seen them. 'I hurt you.'

'Just a bit. No!' He had been about to slip out of her but she pulled him back. 'Stay there. I like it.' He put his head back on her shoulder and she stroked the back of his neck, fingering the fluff that grew from an untidy hairline.

'I'm sorry I hurt you. I was too eager. They say 'tis better the second time.'

'Was it your first time, too?'

'Yes.' His lips brushed her skin.

'Did it hurt you as well?'

He drew his head up to look at her again. He was

380

smiling. 'No, it was luscious.' He wriggled his bottom and snuggled his nose between her breasts.

The moment of disappointment past, she held him tightly, anticipating the next time. 'I do love you so.' Laughter. 'I can't stop saying it.'

For a while they lay there talking softly. But the time didn't last. 'Oh, Tim, I don't want to go. When will I see you again?'

'Can ye get away before next Sunday?' A shake of the head. 'Another dreaded seven days then.'

'I'll die.'

'Look, we can't meet here every time either,' he mouthed into her ear, sending shivers through her. 'Apart from the cold attacking my parts there's a chance we may be discovered.'

'Where else can we go?' She traced her fingers down his spine and back again. His buttocks contracted in delight.

'That's no way to get rid o' me,' he groaned, then, 'Did I say stop?' After a moment of thought, he said, 'We could go to Mr Dorgan's. He's not a man to throw a couple of lovers on the streets. I'd like you to meet him anyway, he's a good friend o' mine.'

'Is he a Fenian?' asked Rosanna.

His face was no longer soft. 'Ye heard then?' She nodded. 'You'll not tell?'

'What sort of sneak d'you take me for?' She could still feel his tenseness and sought to calm him. 'Tim, I would never give away your secrets, you know that. Won't you tell me about it?'

'About what?'

'Why can't you trust me?'

'Rosanna, it's not just a matter o' trust. I just don't think you should be involved . . .'

'I want to be involved! I want to know everything about you, everything you do. I want to share it, I love you.'

There was still a trace of reluctance. 'Ye must promise not to repeat anything about this.'

She crossed her heart. 'I swear.'

'Well . . . you'll maybe have heard there's been a

campaign to free Ireland from British rule for a long time now.'

'Oh, yes, we hear quite a lot about it at home.' She told him about her grandfather's attempts to influence the Irish vote some years back. 'But it didn't turn out very well. I think he gave up.'

'Your grandfather's like all the rest of those well-off; overweight from the platitudes fed to him by his English masters.' The words were not so fluent as when spoken by Dorgan but they made him sound knowledgeable in front of the girl.

'I'm sorry to disagree, Tim, but my grandfather cares for Ireland.'

The young man shrugged. ''S easy to care when all he has to do is shove a piece o' paper into a box . . . anyway, I'm not on about politics, Rosie, least not in that sense. There are some of us who feel the argument's gone on long enough. It's time for stronger persuasion. Slaves, that's what we've been for hundreds o' years, kept under the boot of one captor or the other. But I promise ye, Rosie, we'll not put up with another century of it.'

'I'm not really sure what you mean.'

'Read the papers, they'll tell you.'

'I'm not really interested in newspapers.'

'It's our duty to know what's going on, girl.'

She frowned, poked a finger in his chest. 'But, Tim, I thought you couldn't read?'

He looked like someone caught in a lie. 'Nor can I . . . but Mr Dorgan, he reads them out to me – even though they do give a distorted view. He's taught me such a lot, Rosie. More than anything he's shown me the need for us patriots to get together and do what the politicians have failed to do.'

She thought she knew all there was to know about Ireland but he talked to her of things she had never heard from her grandfather's lips. Such tales of abuse and persecution. 'Did you never hear of the Great Hunger?'

This time she could respond with confidence. 'Gramps

told us all about it when we were very tiny. I've never forgotten. It was so terrible.'

'I'll bet he never told you it was a devilish plot by the English to kill us all off, did he?' He nodded tersely when she offered no reply. 'I can see he never.'

'But surely all the English aren't like that, Tim,' argued Rosie. 'My grandmother is English. She'd hardly marry an Irishman if she felt that way, would she?'

'Ah, well now, there's times when passion by force overrules our principles,' said Tim, kissing her. 'Your grandfather probably felt the same way for her as I do for you.'

She smiled mischievously. 'I'll bet there's a little bit of English in you somewhere, too. You've hardly any accent.'

'Don't you say that.' His anger was quiet but very plain. 'Both my folk were Irish, my grandparents, my great-grandparents . . .'

'I didn't intend to upset you.' She was rather upset herself. 'One would think having English blood in one's veins was like some incurable disease.'

'Ah, now I'm the one doing the upsetting.' His face was kind again. 'I'd no meaning to. I think we'd best forget about Irish an' English and just concentrate on us.'

'No, it's good I know how you feel about things, about yourself, about me, even if you do get angry about it. I know if I was in your position I'd feel a sense of injustice, I'm sure.' The sigh she gave was so intense it lifted his body. 'Oh, I wish we were married, don't you?'

'Your parents would never consent.'

'Is that just your way of trying to wriggle out of it?' She smiled to show she was joking. 'When I'm twenty-one I won't need their consent.'

'That's a lot o' water to flow. You'll likely be bored with me when you reach that ripe old age.'

'Never! Don't you ever say things like that. What if we were to run away together right now?'

'Where to, might I ask?'

'Ireland!' came the cry. 'We'll go to Ireland. I could

383

sneak back to the house, collect my savings . . . oh, wouldn't it be wonderful?'

He rolled from side to side, holding her lovingly. 'That it would. But much as I adore you – an' I truly do, Rosie – I've other commitments. I can't go swanning off to Ireland and neither could you leave your grandfather, could ye? Truthfully.'

A rueful smile. 'No, I couldn't do that to Gramps – but it's nice to dream, isn't it? Oh, Tim, will we ever be together?'

'One day, if ye keep loving me.'

'And will we go to live in Ireland?'

'We will. But first we have to free her. I'll not live in a country in chains.'

'Could I help?' came the small plea.

'You? No, darlin'. It's tough strong men we need. Besides, I wouldn't put my Rosie in any danger.'

'Tim, how dangerous is it? You won't let yourself be hurt, will you?'

'Worry not, Timothy Rabb can take care of himself.'

'Tell me some more about Ireland, Tim.' She snuggled up to him. There was an icy draught swilling round her buttocks but she was loath to uncouple herself. 'Is it as beautiful as my grandfather says?'

'Ah, Rosie, there's no place on earth like it,' confirmed Tim with a dreamy glaze to his eyes. 'The grass is a dozen times greener than any to be seen over here. An' there's mountains an' lakes an' carpets of wild flowers, an' few big cities, just tiny villages dotted amongst the heather.'

He lyricised so vividly that she saw it all in her mind. Saw herself and Timothy in their little white cottage with a dozen babies all like him.

His body began to respond to his impassioned speech. She felt him grow inside her. It felt so strange. 'You love the place so much, don't you?' she said as he began to mouth her lips.

He stopped kissing her and a look of detachment clouded his eye. 'That I do. You asked me before if there was chance o' me being hurt. Well, that I can't say but I can tell ye this: if I thought it would free Ireland I'd gladly die for her.'

'Oh, Tim, please don't talk that way. Nothing is so important that you should have to die for it, and it makes me jealous to think that it's not me who inspires such sacrifice.'

'I feel the same way about you, Rosanna.'

'You'd die for me?'

'Ah-ha. In fact I'm dying for you right now.'

'Timothy Rabb, you old lecher!' She slapped him, then they rolled together on the crumpled coat, ignoring the hard grains of soil that clung to their skins, trying to make time eke out.

Typically the afternoon was over in a flash. Rosanna was forced to dress hurriedly, Tim in more leisurely fashion, grinning at her unladylike postures. 'They're going to wonder what you've been up to with your hair like that.'

'No, they won't. I always look this way when I come back from my outings.'

'Ah, an' have you always been up to the same thing as this afternoon?' he enquired roguishly.

'You devil!' She swiped at him. 'That's more your prerogative. I'll bet all the girls are after you.'

'I have to fight them off.'

She was finished dressing and waited for Tim to skip past before struggling with the padlock. It seemed to be thawing. But maybe that was just imagination. 'Are the girls in Ireland prettier than me?' The padlock clicked into place. 'Will I have much competition?'

'And how would I be knowing that?' replied Timothy. 'When I've never even been there.' With this strange remark he delivered a long, hard kiss and led her to the path home.

'Rosanna Feeney, what manner of mischief have you been up to?' asked Patrick as she slipped in by the french window hoping not to be noticed. 'D'ye realise how long ye've been out in that garden? We were thinking to send out a search party.'

'Sorry, Gramps.' She kept her face averted.

'Your Aunt Erin came out looking for ye. Searched high an' low she did.'

'I was sitting in the shed.'

'Can't I see that from the state o' ye? Sure, what would ye be wanting to spend your time in that dusty old place for? 'Tis full o' nothing but cobwebs.'

'Sometimes I just like to sit and think,' she answered, aware of Tim's scent clinging to her clothes. Could Grandfather smell it too? 'It was too cold in the garden so I went in there. I lost track of the time.' She began to edge towards the inner door.

He rose from his comfortable chair, smiling, and came to put an arm around her. 'Thinking, was it? I shouldn't do that too often – look what it's done to your hair.' He tugged at a loose strand.

A guilty hand went up. 'The wind did that. Abi would cry havoc if she could see it. It took her ages.' His arm pulled her closer. Surely he can tell, she thought.

If Patrick noticed the tenseness of her shoulder when he hugged her he merely put it down to her not being a little girl any more. It was hard to keep remembering that. When he released her she hurried to her room – what joy that Belle was away at school – threw down her hat and went to look in the mirror, touching her face and body as she searched for signs of change. She was posed thus when the door opened and her brother came in.

'Can no one in this house learn to knock?' she threw at him, whirling from the mirror. 'I could've been naked for all you knew.'

'I daresay if I'd encountered you an hour ago I would have witnessed that delightful state,' answered Nick, shutting the door and going to sit on her bed.

'And what construction am I to put on that cryptic little passage?'

He grabbed her wrist as she sailed past him and hauled her to stand between his open legs. 'Rosie, you know that nothing escapes the All-Seeing-One.'

'So you guessed.' Her lips were drawn together. 'And what do you intend to do – tell Grandfather?'

'Now why on earth would I want to tell the old man?' He shook her hands reassuringly. 'Did you enjoy it?'

She blushed, 'Nicholas, what a thing to ask,' and made an attempt to remove herself from his grasp.

He clung on. 'Did you?'

'What business is it of yours?' She gave in and wrinkled her nose. 'Not really,' a little laugh. 'But Tim says it'll be better next time.'

'Oh, Tim says, does he? I wonder if our Tim is as knowledgeable as he makes out.' She asked what he meant. 'Does he care enough about you to see you don't get pregnant?'

'Naturally he cares. As I care for him. We're going to be married when I'm of age.'

'Assuming that to be so, what happens in the meantime?'

A helpless shrug. 'There's nothing we can do to stop it happening, is there? Just keep our fingers crossed.'

'Better you applied that posture to your legs. Oh, Rosie-Posie you're so unworldly. Of course there's ways to stop it.'

'How come you know so much about it?' she demanded petulantly.

'I make it my business to know all the ins and outs of everything I enter into.' The metaphor caused a smile.

'Nick, you're in love too.' She had misread his expression.

'In love? Most definitely not.'

'Then . . .'

'I have someone I go to, yes, but I'm not in love with her, nor she with me. It's just a partnership of convenience.'

'That's terrible!'

'Is it more terrible than you pretending to Grandfather you're off for a walk in the garden and then sneaking off to copulate with one of his labourers?'

He was spoiling everything. 'You make it sound so sordid and it's not like that at all. I love Tim. I need him, and he loves me.'

'Of course he does, as I do, Rosie. That's why I don't want to see you get hurt. Let me help you. I could fetch you something that might be useful.'

'Useful for what?'

'To prevent you having a baby,' he sighed.

'I didn't know there were such things.' Where was the woman who had walked in here five minutes ago? Her brother seemed so much older; made her appear so ignorant and childish.

'Well, there are – though I can't vouch for their reliability. But they seem to have worked so far for us. I'll speak to Moira about it.'

'Is that your . . . mistress?' He nodded, amused at the term employed by his sister. But then he supposed that's what Moira was. 'I'd be embarrassed to think you were discussing that sort of thing with her.'

'Why? I'm discussing it with you, aren't I?'

'Well yes, but you and I have always talked about everything.' She looked at the hands that imprisoned hers; they seemed so large in comparison. She had never fully noticed her brother's maleness before. 'Do you and Moira use these things?'

'Yes, and so will you. Then you can sneak off and have your bit of fun without fear.'

'Fun?' Her voice rose.

'Rosie,' he spoke gently, kneading her fingers. 'You must realise that that is all it can ever be. Nan and Grandad will see to that. Father will listen to them and never give his consent for you to marry this fellow. He's not the right sort.'

She pulled away angrily. 'It doesn't matter what sort he is! I love him and whatever any of you say or think I'm going to damn well marry him.'

CHAPTER TWENTY-SIX

Mr Dorgan was a nice old man – well, at fifty-five he appeared old to Rosanna. For months now, they had been meeting under Dorgan's roof. At first there had been unease between the latter and Rosie: her English accent had made him wary and Rosanna for her part was embarrassed at the old man knowing what she and Tim were doing in the bedroom over his head. But now as the summer came upon them she performed the Sunday ritual without discomfort of any sort – the dash down the garden, the scaling of the wall . . . Her family, accustomed to her wandering ways, never missed her. It was only when Father and Mother paid their now monthly visits that she was forced to abandon her rendezvous and the week that followed would be torture.

But today was not her parents' day to visit. She looked both ways before approaching Dorgan's terraced house. Her vigilance was maintained until, without knocking, she opened the front door and slipped inside.

It was a very humble residence compared with her own. There was a passage from the front door, a front and back parlour and a scullery. Apart from the two bedrooms and a back yard that was the extent of Dorgan's abode. But all Rosanna cared about was that in one of those bedrooms she and Tim could be together.

'Hello, Mr Dorgan.' She unpinned her bonnet as she came in, then paused. 'Well, don't look so surprised – it is Sunday, you know.'

'So it is, colleen, so it is. I clean forgot.' The keen blue eyes that had raked her as she came upon him so unexpectedly softened and he pointed his pipe at a dingy armchair. 'Sit ye down. Tim's been but he just nipped out to do an errand for me. He'll not be long.' He fitted the pipe back in his mouth and watched as she seated herself, eyes crinkling in the puckish face; a face that radiated friendliness. She was a fine-looking girl. He often envied his young pal when he and she were up there together and himself down here on his own. He raised a hand to smooth back his thinning hair, once a raging fire now a pale sand. 'Well now, would ye be making us a cup o' tea while we wait for old Tim?'

'Oh yes, of course.' She swished her lemon skirts to the scullery, knowing where everything was kept. It was a different tale the first time Dorgan had asked this of her. To Rosanna tea came ready prepared in a cup. Faced with a kettle of cold water, a teapot and a caddy she was baffled. The first cup she had made had leaves floating on the surface, but now she had learnt to serve a passable brew.

'Where's Tim gone?' she called amid the clatter of cups.

'I told ye, he's gone on an errand for me.'

'Yes, but where exactly?'

'Ye ask a powerful lot o' questions, child.'

She emerged from the scullery with a kettle of water which she placed on the fire. Her face was turned away from him but he knew she was upset by his tone. 'I didn't mean to pry. I just thought I could go to meet him. We get so little time together.'

The face creased into a smile. 'Sure, I wasn't getting at ye. I think I've known ye long enough to tell if ye can be trusted. The boy's gone to collect a delivery from another friend o' mine. Ah, talk of the devil an' he'll appear.' The front door had opened.

Rosanna's serious visage turned to happiness as Tim came into the back parlour. She went straight to him and kissed him. 'Hello, you.'

'Hello, yourself.' He returned her kiss heartily, smiled into her eyes, then went across to the table in the centre of the room and placed his burden on it.

'Did you check if it's all there?' asked Dorgan.

'I did.' Tim rerolled a shirtsleeve which had fallen down. It was quite warm out there and his brow was glowing.

Rosanna reached up to push his mutinous hair from his eyes, wishing he and Mr Dorgan would get this over with.

While she wrapped a cloth around the handle of the kettle and lifted it from the fire Dorgan rose and approached the table. Taking hold of the bundle he began to unwrap it carefully. Tim's swift glance in Rosanna's direction did not pass unnoticed. 'You're not telling me ye don't trust your young lady, Tim?' He paused, watched her too.

'There's your tea,' said Rosanna, replacing the lid on the pot, 'I'll go fetch some cups in.' She was about to disappear into the scullery when Dorgan called her back.

'I think 'tis time our Rosie had a true picture of our aims if she's to join us, don't you, Tim?'

She whirled back ecstatically. She had always been shunted from the room whilst Tim and his mentor exchanged their secret words; this was so unexpected. Her face showed it. 'You're going to let me join you?'

Dorgan grinned affectionately at her childlike animation. 'I think you've been edged out long enough, don't you, Tim? An' her so good at making tea for the boys.' The young man returned his smile.

'If you're simply going to give me a job making tea then . . .'

'Tch, tch, so uppity.' Dorgan looked at Tim. 'I don't know whether she's ready for this now, son. 'Tis someone cool and calm we'll be wanting, we've enough hotheads . . .'

Rosanna jumped in alarmedly. 'I didn't mean . . .'

Tim came forward to embrace her. 'The old fella's having you on, aren't you, Mr Dorgan?'

'Am I now?'

'You are.' Tim kissed her fondly. 'You know Rosanna cares as much for Ireland as we do.'

'Do you, Rosie?'

'Oh, yes, Mr Dorgan.' It was said earnestly. Now! she told Belle from afar, now I can do something to please Gramps, something which you won't be able to spoil. 'I'll do anything, anything.'

'Ah well, I daresay we'll find something.' Dorgan's fingers completed the unwrapping, spreading the oilskin open to expose the contents. 'But today is just for looking.'

Rosanna's brow creased. She moved closer to the table and stared at the unfamiliar array. 'What is it?'

Dorgan laughed goodhumouredly. 'I don't suppose a young lady like yourself will have had much use for explosives before.'

Her lips parted. She stared at him. 'Explosives?'

'That's right. This little lot is going to help our cause, an' you're part of that cause now, Rosie. I know it's hardly necessary but I'm going to have to call on ye to swear an oath of secrecy. If you so much as utter one word we're all of us finished – an' that includes young Tim here.'

'I'll never breathe a word,' swore Rosanna, drawing a Cross upon her heart. 'I swear it on Our Lady's name. Thank you for trusting me, Mr Dorgan. You don't know what it means to me.' She reached her hand backwards to draw Timothy to her.

'Sure, I knew soon as ever I laid eyes on ye that here was a girl I could trust me life with. Phil, I said to meself, there's a young lady who's going to do as much for our cause as O'Donovan Rossa.'

'You honour me too much.' Her cheeks had reddened. 'I really don't see what help I could be – though I'd be willing to try, of course.'

'Ye'd be surprised. For one thing a respectable person like yourself would be allowed into any number o' places where the likes of us ruffians would be turned away. Oh yes, Rosie, you're going to be invaluable to us, isn't she, Tim?' He spotted the glint of desire in Tim's eye and laughed. 'Ah, God listen to the buffoon going on about causes when all the young lovers want is to be on their own. Go on then, off with yese while this poor old soul has to content himself with a cup o' tea.'

He busied himself with the teapot so as to detract from the girl's blushing cheeks. When the creak of the bed had told him it was safe he gathered up the bundle and carried it out into the yard. Stepping into the privy he bolted the door and reaching into the darkest corner prised three loose bricks from the wall. Inserting the oilskin bundle into the cavity, he replaced the bricks then pulled down his trousers and sat on the wooden seat. A sudden thought brought a chuckle to his lips: wasn't he always saying it'd take dynamite to shift his tight bowels?

As was customary when Belle had a school holiday Erin went to collect her from the college. Protests that she was almost an adult and could quite efficiently come on her own did not seem to register with the girl's mother. 'You are not an adult, you're a child, and how're ye going to manage your trunk?' she argued on their way to the station. 'How would you know if you were on the right train?'

'Mother, I'm hardly an idiot,' objected Belle. 'I can speak, you know. I could ask a porter. Why won't you trust me?'

'Of course I trust ye,' replied Erin lightly. 'It's other people I don't trust. What if, out of mischief, the porter was to direct ye to the wrong train?'

'And why would he want to do something as childish as that?'

'Because people aren't always nice to those they see as different.'

Belle did not disclose that she'd had plenty of experience of this at college. Whether it was done because of her deformity or that she was way out in front as far as school marks were concerned, she didn't know. Neither did she care. That they hated her was enough. She could not lay claim to one friend at that school. Not one. Oh, they weren't all mean to her, but she was cute enough to see that those who were nice were only being so because of her deformity, because they felt sorry for her, so it was all the same really. People were a perverse lot. She hated school. She detested its pupils, scorned its tutors.

'Besides,' Erin was saying, 'your whole argument is pointless. No respectable young lady goes about unchaperoned.'

'But . . .'

'Belle, would you like me to unpack this suitcase in the middle of the platform, take out a hairbrush and give ye a paddling?'

Belle gave in. It was hopeless trying to have a reasonable discussion with her mother. For all the woman boasted about Belle's forwardness she didn't credit her with an ounce of commonsense.

When they arrived home and had undergone the usual moist-eyed reunions with Grandfather and the others, Belle suddenly remembered the letter in her pocket and pulled it out. 'Sorry, Mother, I forgot to give you this.'

'Silly girl, it could be something important.' Erin took it and ripped it open. After apparently reading a few lines her eyes suddenly swam with moisture. She put a hand to her face and looked helplessly at her mother as Thomasin enquired concernedly what was wrong. 'Oh,' said Erin, unable to say more. Pressing her hand over her mouth she held out the letter. Patrick took it.

His face soon came alight. 'Why, ye soft pratie! I thought it was some disaster. Aw, Belle, congratulations!' He hugged her, passing the letter over her head to Thomasin. 'The child's only gone and passed all her examinations for university, that's all.'

Thomasin, without reading the letter, threw her arms around Belle and the hall became a mêlée of laughing congratulations. 'Come on, come on!' she beckoned. 'Don't stand out here. Patrick, get the glasses out.' She waved them on to the drawing room where toasts were made and Belle stood patiently until it all became too much of a bore. She asked if she might be excused. 'I feel awfully grubby from the train.'

'Oh, look at me,' said her mother, peering down at herself. 'Standing about drinking sherry and covered in soot. Come along, dear, let's call Abi and get you unpacked.' She made to collect the trunk from the hall but Nick went ahead. 'I'll get it.'

With Erin detained by her parents Belle went up with her cousins, Nick bearing the trunk on his shoulder, Rosanna at the rear.

'Well done, Belladonna,' he threw over his shoulder. 'May I presume you'll be collecting this fistful of degrees from London University, coz?' The residential college where Belle studied was affiliated to this establishment.

'I shall,' answered Belle as they took another flight. 'And that's as many questions on university as I'm going to answer. It's bad enough with Mother.'

'Shouldn't be such a brainbox then.' Nick's long legs stretched to four steps at a time, leaving the girls behind.

'Shall I help you unpack?' asked Rosanna as they caught up with Nick in their bedroom.

'My, I didn't foresee my intellectual achievements procuring such generosity,' jeered her cousin, then feeling in good spirits at being home decided to be a little kinder to her lesser-brained relative. 'It's all right. Abi will see to it. Now, everyone, please let me forget about school and tell me all that's been going on while I've been walled up in there.' At her Easter vacation she had been shocked to find that Tim was no longer working for her grandfather. She would miss him dreadfully but at least his absence meant that neither girl could have him so the rift between her and Rosie could be patched up. After all, it was no fun sharing a room with someone you detested. She had been rather surprised that Rosanna hadn't been more upset, having professed undying love for Tim. It just went to prove how fickle Rosie could be. For herself she intended to investigate Tim's whereabouts. If her cousin had forgotten him so quickly she definitely had not. 'And are you still helping Grandfather, Rosie?' She had thought perhaps that with Tim gone Rosanna's interest in the fruit and vegetable trade might have palled.

'Oh yes, I'm getting to be quite an expert book-keeper.'

'And you, Nick, have you been awarded any more promotion lately?'

'Grandmother's going to put me in charge of the Good-ramgate store,' he answered.

His sister looked at him intently. 'I haven't heard Nan mention that.'

'That's because she doesn't know yet,' replied Nick slyly. 'But she is.'

Belle laughed. 'Still the same old Nick. Oh, it's good to be home. If only I didn't have to go back.'

'Never mind,' said Rosanna amicably. 'We can have some good times while you are here. Would you like to come and help me one day at the storehouse? We could get round Gramps and slope off for a picnic.'

'I'd like that, Rosie,' replied Belle, smiling to herself. It was always like this at the start of the holiday; everyone all lovey-dovey. By the time it was over there would be blood splashing up the walls.

'And maybe you'd like to come to the store to see how I've improved the running of things,' offered Nick.

'He's really the man that sweeps the floor,' explained his sister scathingly. Belle laughed.

'You may mock.' Nick wagged a majestic finger. 'But one day I'm going to be running the show on my own and when I do I shan't allow riff-raff like you two in.'

Rosanna looked at Belle, then both said, 'Right!' and pounced on him, Belle sitting astride while Rosie pulled off his boots and tickled his feet until he cried for mercy. Then the three of them fell in a pile, laughing.

Rosanna had been itching to share her secret with someone other than her brother for ages – a female ear – but knew that Belle's was not the one to choose. A jealous Belle would be sure to give her away. Perversely the temptation was even stronger as the girls strolled arm in arm along the country lane on that hot summer's day, perhaps because she and Belle had exchanged fewer cross words than was usual during the time her cousin had been home. The sun filled Rosie with such feelings of kinship that she thought she would burst. How she kept rein on her tongue was a miracle.

Finding a pleasant spot Belle took the rug which had been folded over her arm and spread it on the grass. Rosanna deposited the hamper in the centre, pulled the cane pegs from their stays and opened the wicker lid.

'Ooh, good old Abi!' came her exclamation as she put aside a bowl of salad to lift out a ham and tomato flan, which was soon demolished, as was the parcel of sandwiches that came after it, the raspberry scones, two apples and several iced buns.

After eating they sat with their faces upturned, drinking in the sun, and talked until the neglected bowl of lettuce began to droop and turn brown at the edges.

'D'you think you'll ever marry, Belle?' mused Rosanna, her long hair flowing down behind to tickle the hands that supported her.

'What makes you ask that?' asked a startled Belle.

'Oh . . . nothing. Just wondering.'

Belle turned her face back to the sun. 'Maybe – if I can find the right man.' Tim came to mind. She smiled. 'Though I have a horrible feeling Mother has more in store for me than to waste myself on marriage.'

'How can it be wasting oneself if you love someone?'

'I didn't say I thought that, only that Mother sees it that way. What about you?'

It was so very tempting. 'Some day.'

The conversation faded as each dwelt privately on the matter, then all at once a figure stepped from nowhere, causing both young hearts to leap. Despite her handicap Belle was the first to spring up and fling her arms round his neck. 'Tim, how tremendous to see you! How did you know we were here?'

Tim kissed her cheek affectionately, observing Rosanna over the hunched shoulder. When the child had thrown herself at him Rosie had stepped back, her face uncharacteristically passive. 'I didn't.' Smiling, he disengaged her arms from his neck but held onto her hands. 'But it's nice to see you again, Belle. How's that school going down?'

'All right.' She made a face, then laughed ecstatically. 'Oh, but it's wonderful to see you! I feared I never would when I heard the bad news last time. I've been trying to discover where I might find you – and now you've found me. Won't you stay and share our picnic?' She tried to lead him to the rug. 'I think we could find a few crumbs at the bottom of the hamper.'

'That's kind of you but I daren't stay long.' He held back. 'I really came in the hope of passing a message to Rosie.'

Belle's smile levelled as Tim dropped her hands to approach his lover whom he kissed – much more tenderly than he had kissed her. 'Hello, colleen. How's the body?'

'The body's fine.' Her eyes engaged with his, and Belle, seeing that look, knew that everything Rosie had thrown at her that day was true: Tim had just been friendly to make Rosanna jealous. But Belle didn't give in that easily.

She stepped up to them, breaking their concentration. 'So!' she said, overly bright. 'What is this message? If it wouldn't be regarded as prying.'

Tim addressed himself to Rosanna. 'I came to see if ye could make it any earlier on Sunday, darlin'. I have a trip to make for our mutual friend at three.'

Rosanna chewed her cheek. 'I don't know if I can . . . Nan's very strict on matters of the lunch-table.'

Darling. He called her darling, thought the other girl bleakly. Yet still she persevered. Hooking her arm through his she said, 'I'm sure if Rosanna can't make it then I'll be able to oblige, Tim.' A resentful glance at her cousin. 'It was rather sneaky of her to corner you while I was away.'

The lovers exchanged pitying expressions.

'Or was the invitation confined to my cousin?' said Belle, dropping his arm.

'Belle . . .' began Tim.

'It was all true, wasn't it?' breathed the girl, her face a picture of betrayal. 'All the things she said about you, about you just being nice to me because you felt sorry for me.'

'No, it wasn't.'

'It's because I look like this, isn't it?'

'Don't talk stupid. You're a nice-looking girl.'

'I loved you . . .'

'Oh, Belle.' He tried to take hold of her hand but she

398

snatched it away. 'Belle, it had nothing to do with how ye look. In fact I think you're very beautiful. It's just that me an' Rosanna . . .'

'It's just that her body isn't twisted and mine is,' Belle threw at him.

'Belle, it was wrong of me to shower all that attention on ye and give the wrong impression.' His face held an apology. 'I was angry at Rosie and wanted to make her jealous.'

'And you used me!'

'It's true. I shouldn't've done an' I humbly beg your forgiveness if I hurt ye.'

'I'll never forgive you, never! Either of you.' She wheeled on Rosanna. 'Now I know why you didn't seem affected by Tim's dismissal; you were seeing him all the time, weren't you? While I was locked away in that dratted school you two were canoodling, laughing at me . . .'

'Belle, please don't tell Grandfather, he knows nothing about this,' begged Rosanna.

'And why shouldn't I tell him?'

'It would finish us, Belle,' answered Tim gravely.

'What do I care of that? Neither of you gave a jot for my feelings.'

'Belle, I've said I'm sorry. I didn't ever intend for ye to fall in love with me.'

'But I did!'

What could he say to give her comfort? In callow fashion he said the wrong thing. 'You're young yet, Belle. Give yourself time to grow up a little before talking of love. I'm not worth it, ye know. Some day you'll meet a nice young man . . .'

'No! I'll never love anyone else. You made me believe you loved me. I hate you. I hate you both. I'll never trust another man as long as I live!' She made to run away. Her heavy boot caught in a divot and nearly brought her down but she shook off their assistance. 'Leave me alone! I don't need you.'

'Belle, what're you going to do?' cried Rosanna fearfully.

Belle stopped then and trained a look of gleeful hatred

on her cousin. 'You think I'm going straight to Grandfather, don't you?'

Rosanna reached for Tim's hand. 'And are you?'

'You'll both just have to wait and see, won't you?' With
this Belle limped rapidly away down the track.

CHAPTER TWENTY-SEVEN

When Rosanna got back and saw her cousin standing
with her grandfather she feared the worst. But when she
nervously approached Patrick held out his free arm – the
other draped round Belle's shoulder – and gave a cheery
greeting.

'Ah, here she is!' He drew her into a squeeze. 'Wasn't
it too bad o' Belle to leave ye to pack up on your own.'

'Oh, I don't mind.' Rosanna snatched a glance at her
cousin's bitter face.

'Well, come on then, I think we'll go home early and
get us some lemonade.' He worked his dry mouth. 'I've
not enough spit to cover a flea.' Keeping his arms about
them he marched both along the path to where the carriage
waited. 'Ah good, Joseph's hitched the pony; no waiting.
Thank ye, Joseph,' he shouted as they approached. 'Ye
can tell the lads they can have an early hometime, too.
They've done a good day's work.'

'Thank ye, sir, that's very gentlemanly of ye.' Joseph
saluted.

'And how's your family keepin', Joseph?' Patrick took
charge of the reins.

'Oh, nicely, sir, thank ye. Oh, yes.'

'And our friend Molly?'

'Her too yes, sir, thank ye, sir. And your own, sir?'

'They're in excellent health, Joseph. Why, look at the
two fine specimens I have here as proof. What d'ye think
to them, eh?'

'Oh, they're as fine a pair o' young ladies as ever walked the streets, sir,' flattered Joseph, making Patrick roar with laughter. 'I always say to the wife: that Rosanna, I say, if ever an angel fell down from Heaven 'tis herself.' A smile from Rosanna. 'Why, 'tis a pleasure to see her smiling face every day. Makes the lads work that much harder. Ah, they all admire her greatly – an' if ye could see the way she turns the heads when she goes trotting by our house on her Sunday outing ye'd never believe it. Sure, they've never witnessed the like of her down our way. Oh, no.'

Rosanna's smile froze. She dare not look at her grandfather's face, awaiting his comment, but Joseph was still blarneying. 'An' could I be after askin' how Miss Belle's eddication is coming along, sir? I hear she's got herself a double dose o' brains.'

Yes, she must have yours, Joseph, thought Rosanna grimly as Patrick ended the conversation rather abruptly and helped his grand-daughters into the carriage, whence he whipped up the horse. No mention of the subject was made on the uncomfortable journey home, causing Rosanna to hope that perhaps Grandfather hadn't picked up that idiot's blunder. But directly they were in the house and Patrick ordered her to come alone to his study she knew this was it.

He spent a considerable time in lighting his pipe, forcing her to stew while he scrutinised her through the emerging clouds of tobacco smoke. Finally he sat down but did not offer her a seat. 'Well now, Rosanna, would ye care to tell me how come Joseph says he sees ye near his home on Sunday when you're meant to be takin' a walk in the garden?'

She nibbled at the skin on her lower lip.

'I expect the rigor mortis is affecting your tongue. Isn't your face as white as a corpse? Which leads me to thinkin' that this interview is making you uneasy. Take a sip o' that lemonade,' he gestured at the jug on a nearby table. 'It might help to grease your conscience – I assume ye've got one?'

She showed great reluctance to come near him, then her dry mouth got the better of her and she moved to pour a glass of the lemonade. He waited until she had consumed three-quarters of it before beginning again. 'Better? Then we'll try again. What were ye doing down Walmgate unaccompanied?'

She looked into her glass and whispered, 'I went to see a friend.'

'I'm sorry, I didn't catch that.'

She cleared her throat and said again, 'I went to see a friend.'

'A friend? Sure that's a most unlikely area to have your-self a friend if ye don't mind my saying so. An' what's this friend's name? I may know her – I assume it is a her.'

'Tim.' She looked up from the glass to see his reaction, then at his intent glare dropped her gaze.

'I believe Tim is a boy's name, is it not?'

She nodded, both hands clasped tightly round the glass.

'Would I make a guess as to his surname?'

There was no response.

'It wouldn't be Rabb, would it?'

At her nod his hands clamped down on the chair-arms and he pushed himself slowly upwards, pipe clenched in teeth. 'I thought there was more than a philanthropic interest when ye were asking me not to sack him,' he breathed. Then sharply: 'Come on now, let's be having it all!'

'What do you want to know?'

'Dammit, Rosanna, I said let's be hearing it all an' I mean all. I want to know how long this has been going on, where ye meet him, what you think you're bloody playing at.'

'I'm not playing! Tim and I love each other.' She put down the glass, using her freed hands to do her pleading.

'Oh, ye do, do ye?' he barked. 'An' d'ye know what sort o' man ye've pledged your love to? Didn't ye listen to anything I said when I fired him?'

'Grandfather, I know what you said about him, I recall every word but it's not true.'

'You're calling me a liar?'

'Oh, no, no! But Tim isn't what you think. He's not dangerous. He's sweet and he's . . .'

'Oh, aye – like aloes are sweet!'

' . . . he's gentle. I mean, you're always going on about how you love Ireland so much. Well, Tim feels that way, too. I thought you'd be glad that I'd chosen someone who's a patriot like yourself.'

'Patriot?' bellowed Patrick, obviously incensed at the comparison. 'Then the definition of the word must've changed since I learnt my letters.'

'Grandfather, that's most ungracious of you. They're kind and loyal . . .'

'They?'

She hesitated. 'The Brotherhood.'

He gave a groan and swiped at the air. 'Don't tell me he's managed to lure an intelligent girl like yourself into his skulduggery.'

'He didn't need to lure!' Rosanna matched his temper. 'I joined willingly because I feel as they do.'

'Then you're more of an eejit then ever I took ye for. Ye talk about patriotism and loyalty. Ye'll find more loyalty in the pigsty at feeding time. And the word is not patriotism but *power*, Rosie. Ye could read about these people any day in the paper if ye took the time, trying to force ordinary peace-loving folk into their dastardly organisation and when they decline beating the . . . living daylights out o' them.'

Rosie spoke energetically. 'But you of all people know how the newspapers distort things. Haven't I heard you say it myself? Depicting the Irish as drunken work-shy idlebacks, saying they are filthy . . .'

'And a host of choicer insults. Yes, I am aware of it, Rosanna. But in this instance the descriptions are fitting. I know most of the names that appear in print; they're out and out bullies with not one ounce o' patriotism between them, an' their fathers were bullies before them.'

'But Tim's not one of that kind!' cried Rosanna. 'You

403

could never accuse him of violence when he worked for you.'

'There's more than one sort o' violence, Rosanna,' responded Patrick. 'There's the physical sort and the spoken kind, the type that incites others to do the dirty work. Tim is obviously a speaker, but he's no less dangerous . . . that's why I'm forbidding you to see him ever again.'

She was furious. 'You can't forbid it! Tim and I love each other, you can't keep us apart!'

'Rosanna,' he tried to temper the tone of the argument. 'I know it'll be hard if, as ye say, ye love the fella . . .'

'I do! I do!'

With her intensity he had a terrible thought. 'He hasn't . . . taken your honour, has he?'

She blushed furiously and lied, 'Of course not – he wouldn't.'

'Well, thank God he has some decency. Look, ye must believe me when I say 'tis for your own good . . .'

'Oh, that's always the excuse people give when they don't approve of one's choice of marriage partner! You think Tim's not good enough for me because he's poor.'

'Not because he's poor,' insisted Patrick. 'Because he's bad.'

'No!'

'Yes! And ye can shove any idea o' marriage from your head. Rosie darlin', I've met his sort so many times. He's dangerous an' I won't have you consorting with him. I've been around a lot longer than you and . . .'

'Oh!' ejaculated Rosanna, flinging her arms up. 'Just because you've been around a lot longer doesn't mean in my book that you're wiser – it could just as easily indicate senility.'

'Rosanna Feeney!' He showed a face his grand-daughter had never seen before, the pale-blue eyes devoid of any warmth.

She was rightly afraid of this stranger and made immediate attempts at conciliation. 'Oh Gramps, I didn't mean that!' She flew at him, hurled herself into his arms.

'I love you, you know I do, more than anyone else in the world apart from Tim. Please, please say you forgive me. I couldn't bear it if you stayed angry with me.'

There was a period of tearful appeasement, after which Patrick kissed the top of her dark brown head and patted her kindly. 'Ah sure, I know it was only frustration speaking. Of course I forgive ye. How could I stay mad at my little Rosie for long?'

The light of hopeful expectancy came to her eye. 'Then you'll change your mind about Timothy?'

Solemnly, he put her from him and went to light a taper from the fire; his pipe had gone out, smothered no doubt by the heavy atmosphere. 'No, I'm afraid I'll not be swayed on that one, Rosie. I'm sorry for ye an' I wish I could let ye have this favour but 'tis far too important an issue.'

She drew on the ploy that had always worked when she was a child, coming to sit on his lap and tickle him under the chin. 'Ple-ease, Gramps,' she wheedled.

'No, Rosie. I refuse to budge this time. 'S no good wasting all that charm, the matter will be finished with after I say this one thing: I want your faithful oath that ye'll not try to see Timothy again.'

She was shattered. 'How can I promise such a thing? Don't you understand how we feel about each other?'

'Rosie, d'ye love your father and mother?'

'Oh, naturally I do but . . .'

'An' you know how much they love you. D'ye believe that your father would ever grant his consent for you to marry Tim?'

'He might do,' she said defensively.

'Rosanna, ye know very well that this silly old devil here is the only one who'll kow-tow to your flannel – usually, but not this time. Now, ye can go to your father if ye want an' ask him . . . but ye know what the answer will be, don't ye?'

She nodded her woe. 'Are you going to tell him and Mother?'

He shook his head. 'They have enough worries with four little girls without being burdened by the daft antics of their big one. Don't you see? They think you're an adult, Rosie, can be trusted to behave in an adult fashion, that's why they let ye stay here . . . Of course, if you were to disobey me an' continue to see this fella . . .'

The pipesmoke, always so sweet, suddenly provoked great irritation. She deserted his lap. 'Grandfather, you're taking advantage of my loyalty.'

'Your prime loyalty is to your family, Rosanna!' Then his voice caught. 'Please, please give him up before we all get hurt. I love ye so much I can't bear to see ye troubled like this an' I'd never go against him for any other reason than he's caught up with the wrong sort. They'll not love ye an' care for ye as we do, Rosie. Please, say it for me.'

She stared into his pleading face – such a dear face. Then, though they brought the vomit to her throat, she voiced the words that would put his mind at rest. 'All right, Gramps . . . I'll do it just for you,' and burst into tears.

'There, there.' He went to her, tried to ease the pain with his arms. 'I know how bad it hurts. Ye think ye'll never get over it, but ye will, believe me. Listen,' he pulled out his handkerchief to tend her runnelled face, 'what ye need is to get away from that little office o' yours where the memory of him will keep on dragging ye down an' make the wound harder to heal. How would ye like to take a holiday? You, me, Nick an' Belle – your Nan too if we can persuade her. Somewhere special where ye've never been. We could start in France an' work our way round . . .'

'Abroad?' Her breast shuddered with the aftermath of tears.

'Why not? Think I might kick me clogs with the exertion? There, I've managed to draw a smile from ye. Ah God, my poor wee colleen.' He held her comfortingly. 'I know it must be terrible for ye . . . but you'll see, we'll get out on them Swiss mountain tops an' dine in the poshest hotels, an' it'll make ye forget all about him.'

And Rosanna pressed her wet face into his shoulder, thinking how little her grandfather really knew her. For

the tears she shed were not because she must forget Tim
– but that she was going to have to deceive this dear man.

Nicholas sat in his own leather chair in his own counting
house, hands stroking the desk behind which he was
seated, a look of conceit on his face. The Goodramgate
store was a poor comparison to its sister in Parliament
Street but nevertheless had no rival in the thoroughfare
and he had sole charge of it, which was what he had been
gunning for all these weeks. Here he was boss, with three
assistants to bow and scrape – and he intended to make
full use of them. He was, at this moment, celebrating with
a cup of coffee made from his own beans, though not by
his own hand, which was a great step up in itself. The
reason for his self-congratulatory smile was that he was
awaiting the arrival of his grandmother, who was today
calling at closing time to inspect his first week's takings.
Anticipating praise, he was more than slightly disturbed
when her first words were in the fashion of a rebuke.

'I thought I might find you sat here on your backside.'
Thomasin swept into the office and threw her gloves on
the desk as he scrabbled to his feet. 'Can you tell me just
what is going on out there while you're drowning yourself
in coffee?'

'Sorry, Nan – is something wrong?' He straightened his
collar and tugged at his clothes as he noticed her eyes
moving over him.

'Come here.' She tugged him to the open door of his
lair and pointed. 'Do you see that girl there?'

'Yes.'

'Oh, good. I was beginning to fear you were losing your
sight. Then would you care to go over to where she is
standing – yes, right there – and look underneath the
counter.' Bemused, Nick stooped. 'Right down!' said his
grandmother. 'Hands and knees.'

'Nan . . .'

'Do it!'

Grimacing at his subservients' amusement he got down
on all fours.

407

'Now, tell me what you see.'

'Only a lot of dust.'

'Only, he says! What's it doing there, that's what I'd like to know?'

He rose, brushing the knees of his trousers. 'I don't know, Nan.'

'Well, I do.' She wagged a digit. 'That girl has just swept it there with a broom.' The culprit shrank into the white collar of her dress. 'Come here with me.' She grabbed him again and piloting him through the door dragged him along the street until they came to a similar store. 'See that? It's got everything going for it: prime situation, good frontage ... then tell me why the man who owns it has long gone home to his bed while we've just nicely finished being rushed off our feet?'

He doesn't have a bloody old dragon like you on his back, thought the young man tiredly, but of course said nothing.

'Don't worry, I'll tell you. For a start that window display – well, I can hardly credit it with the title, can I? A mound of green oranges and a few bruised bananas – always providing you can see it for the six-inch layer of muck that's clarting up his glass. Not very tempting, is it?'

She expected an answer. 'No, Nan,' he mumbled.

'No. Not very much there to coax a customer to his window, never mind through the door. Cleanliness and presentation are half the battle, Nick,' she told him as she led him back to her own store. 'If there's dirt on the window or someone sees one of the assistants brushing all the bits of bacon and spilt tea under the counter they're going to ask themselves what the quality of the goods is like or if the assistant has just been picking his nose before serving them. You do understand what I'm trying to say, don't you?' The latch was dropped as they went inside, the sign turned to 'closed'.

He nodded apologetically. 'I'm sorry, Nan, it won't happen again.'

'Another lesson learnt, Nick – and a lesson for you too,' she pointed at the culprit responsible for Nick's tongue-lashing. 'Everybody's allowed one mistake in my shop — and only one. If I catch you performing any more tricks like that you'll be looking for another position! Keep on top of them, Nick,' she told him as they retired to the counting house. 'Don't think that because you're in charge you can relax. If anything, management brings even harder work. Now, let's have a spez at your accounts.'

He handed them over. Any praise now would be an anti-climax. How could he have even expected it from this hard taskmaster? 'Your figures need a bit of seeing-to. Try to keep them in line, tens under tens, units under units. It makes it much simpler to add up — and look at all those crossings out, for pity's sake! It looks like a game of noughts and crosses.' She tapped the bottom of the page with a thumb. 'But, all in all, Nick, I'd say you'd not done a bad job for a learner. Not bad at all.' And this was as much praise as he was likely to receive.

'Next week I'll do better,' he promised.

'Not to worry, Nicholas.' She went to discharge the assistants and lock up for the night. 'I'll be getting rid of this place shortly.'

He felt as though he had been run down by an express train — and all on top of that public scourging. 'But Nan, you've given it to me!'

'Not given, Nick,' she corrected pleasantly. 'I simply wanted to see how you coped on your own, that's all, for future considerations.'

'But it's a grand little shop, Nan,' came his protest.

'Little being a word no longer in my vocabulary, Nicholas. Big, that's what we want and that's what we're going to get; the money from this shop will help see to that.' And with her next brief explanation Nick's short career in management took a retrograde step. 'I'll be bringing you back to the Parliament Street store — and the assistants, of course. There'll be no sackings.'

'When?' was all he could force himself to say.

'Pretty soon. Francis is doing a tour of the big northern cities. It was his idea to sell the Goodramgate store.'

Well, thank you, Francis, fumed Nick and when they

reached home, proclaimed he could not stomach any supper and went straight off to bed.

'What's up with the boy?' asked Patrick at bedtime, which was one of the few occasions he seemed to catch his wife alone. He had been wanting to pose the subject of the holiday all evening but couldn't offer a full explanation with Rosie present.

'Oh, he's a bit niggled 'cause I'm selling the Goodramgate shop and I've only just put him in charge.' She spoke to the mirror, pulling a brush through her hair. 'I think you've something to say, haven't you?' A smile for his expression. 'Well, I noticed you were a bit preoccupied at supper.' He told her of his plan. 'The Continent, eh? Taking up globe-trotting in your old age.'

Sitting on the bed to watch her he outlined his reason for wanting this holiday and his wife's face grew serious. She laid down the brush but did not turn, still addressing herself to his reflection. – It's as though she can't even bring herself to spend this short time with me face to face, thought Patrick. The mirror was just another obstacle she had placed between them. 'And d'you think a holiday will cure this infatuation?'

His eyes followed the brush which had started to move again. 'I can't say, but she knows how I feel and she's promised not to see him again. A month or so away may help to push him from her mind. It would also provide a good opportunity for you an' me to take a holiday.'

Yet again the brush stopped. 'Me leave the store for a month?'

'It'll hardly crumble to bits in your absence. What about Francis, can't he take care of it?'

'He can't be in two places at once. He's doing a bit of touring himself, though a bit less exotic than the sort you're proposing.' Finishing with the brush she began to plait her hair, and told him what she had told Nick, concluding with Francis's own words. 'In ten years' time there could be a *Penny & Co.* in every northern town.'

Patrick made no congratulatory noises, said simply and to her utter amazement, 'Then if not Francis, why not

410

leave Nicholas in charge?' As her mouth fell open he added, 'Aren't y'always saying what an innovator he is?'

'Well, he is . . . the lad's done very well at the Goodramgate shop. Oh, but I can't expect him to run two stores, Pat.' The three strands of hair worked rapidly through her fingers. 'And there's the warehouse, the factory . . .'

'Aye, go on,' he prompted, rising from the bed and looking intently at the glass. 'What other excuses can ye find so's ye don't have to be in your husband's company for a whole month?'

'It's not that I don't want to be with you . . .'

'No, just that your work is more vital. For Christ's sake, Tommy, anyone'd think you were married to that store from the amount o' time ye spend with me. An' if you're not there then you're out at some meeting with Francis.'

She fastened off the plait and primped distractedly at her hair. 'But you encouraged me to go. You hated sitting through dinner listening to all that talk about finance.'

''Tisn't so much that I mind ye going, Tommy, I'd just like ye to remember when you're battling to save some old relic from demolition that there's another old relic that needs ye, too.' Her detached expression crumpled in sympathy. 'It's not asking a great deal, is it, for you to spend just one month with your husband?'

In that moment she realised just how much he had been missing her. 'Well . . . I suppose Erin would be quite capable of running the factory for that time . . . and the warehouse manager is trustworthy . . . I'm not so sure about Nick – but then I could ask Francis to keep an eye on him.' A genuine smile. 'All right, Pat, you can take the thumbscrews off.'

CHAPTER TWENTY-EIGHT

So the holiday went ahead. With more than a few misgivings and despising her sentimentality, Thomasin left Nick in charge of financial matters with strict instructions to send a cablegram should anything – 'anything, you understand?' – be beyond his managerial capabilities. She gave him a list of addresses where they would be staying and the approximate times they would be found at these places.

'Go on your holiday, Nan,' he had said with that old-fashioned look. 'When you come back you won't know the place.'

'That's exactly what I'm afraid of,' had been her reply, but still she had packed her belongings alongside Patrick's and their two grand-daughters'. With Abigail in tow they had launched themselves at the Continent.

After a few days of wondering if Thomasin's worries would ever cease – 'I hope Nick remembered the quarterly accounts need doing. What if the staff have taken huff at his officiousness and walked out? You know how he can raise people's hackles' – the holiday settled into a mood of enjoyment that Patrick had not experienced for a long time. Apart from Rosanna's upset there had obviously been some discord between her and Belle too – but like their grandmother the girls appeared to perk up after a few days. Pat had not told Sonny of the true reason for this holiday, allowing his son to view it as just another example of Grandfather's spoiling. Thomasin had agreed it was best to keep it to themselves.

After enjoying a week in Belgium they moved to France and today they had taken an open landau to view the sights of Paris. The girls' excited comments on the ladies' fashion as they jogged down the Champs Elysées prompted Thomasin to laughter. 'Eh, Pat, do you remember those old poke bonnets we used to wear? Weren't they a sight when you think back?'

'Sure, I never wore a poke bonnet in me life,' announced her husband, bringing forth giggles from their grand-daughters. 'I always favoured the pork pie meself – if ye got sick o' wearing it ye could always eat it. God, will ye look at that!' He watched, awestruck, as a horseless carriage came chugging past at great speed. 'The things they think of . . . they'll be wanting to fly next.'

Thomasin, delighting him with a long-lost tenderness, laid her head on his shoulder recollectively. 'How things have changed since we married. The young'ns today don't know they're born with all these gadgets at their disposal. Still, I suppose we're all guilty of taking things for granted. We only had the telephone put in three years ago an' I never give a thought now to the marvellous brain that invented it.'

'An' these girls of ours will never know hardship.' He was loving the closeness of her, stroking her hand. 'The things we had to do when we were kids.'

'Ee, Ah say,' Thomasin's Yorkshire accent came rushing back with her memories. 'D'you remember t'old rush-lights? By, what a job it were to peel all t'rind away from the pith. Your fingers used to be red raw by the time you were done. An' if you happened to get your hands near that scalding mutton grease – by 'eck, you didn't half cuss!'

Patrick laughed aloud. 'Ye don't know how lucky y'are,' he informed the girls who, forgetting past quarrels for that split second, smiled at each other as their grandparents went on, 'An' do ye remember so and so . . . oh, an' what about those . . . yes, didn't we have a time that day!' Belle thought how good it was to see them holding hands like a pair of young lovers . . . though the sight conjured up images of Timothy. She turned to catch her cousin's reaction, but Rosie's eyes had glazed over – saw only a young man with unruly hair and a kind smile. She had tried desperately to get away, to tell Tim that it was just a holiday, but Patrick had stalled each move. After church on Sunday he had made every excuse to keep her in his sight, inviting her parents over from Leeds so that she would be unable to detach herself from the family gathering without appearing bad-mannered. During the time that the holiday was being arranged he had excused her from her bookwork as though this were some sort of favour, but she knew it was just to keep her imprisoned. Try as she might, she failed to get word to Tim.

Belle turned her eyes from her grieving cousin to look at the sights. She could not admit to feeling sorry for the girl. Though she had thought better of giving the game away herself she was grateful to Joseph for doing so. Knowing that Rosie had been denied him as well made her own hurt easier to bear. She shivered involuntarily as the carriage passed over a bridge. As ever, the mere knowledge that water was near sent shivers through her. It was a fear she felt she would never conquer.

After spending some time in France they moved on to Switzerland. Patrick felt marvellous and it wasn't just due to the clean country air. By some miracle he and Thomasin seemed to have recaptured their old relationship. They laughed, explored, reminisced, the years falling away. The blow came so sneakily . . . His guard down, he had no way to parry it. The family was enjoying a leisurely breakfast on their final morning in Switzerland, looking out over the most breathtaking panorama Pat had seen outside his homeland. A waiter stepped up to the table bearing a tray and directed himself at Thomasin. 'A cablegram, madame, for you if you please.'

The woman made him jump with her cry of dread. 'I knew it! I just knew he'd never cope.' She thrust the cablegram at her husband. 'Oh, you do it, Pat! I can't bear it.'

As the waiter left with a tip the Irishman opened it and read, '*Help Boadicea . . .* Boadicea?'

'Oh, it's from Francis.' She held out her hand for the cable. 'Yes, he always calls me that. Says I should have knife-blades attached to my skirts, the way I always carve through the council when they mention the word demolish.' She straightened the piece of paper to read it.

'Help Boadicea. Have found not one but two. Both prime sites. Excellent position. Leeds and Bradford. In a quandary. Please advise forthwith.' The hands holding the cablegram flopped to her lap. 'Well . . . what do I say?'

'Ye might as well ask the waiter as me. Sounds more like his lingo. What the devil's he on about?' Of course, it had had to happen. They couldn't spend an entire month without business creeping in like the insanitary cat.

'It's simple enough. I've got to choose which store I think we should buy. And how do I do that without seeing them?' She became deep in thought, eyes narrowed. 'I wonder when the auction is. It's all very well for Francis giving me half the story and expecting me to make a snap decision . . . Oh, it's no good, Pat.' Abruptly she began to gather her bits and pieces from the table. 'I shall have to go back.'

'Go back! But we've another week left.' With disbelieving face he watched her prepare to desert him.

'I'm sorry, dear, but I just can't sit here while there's important decisions to be made at home. Besides, Francis can't move either way without my signature.'

'But what's to become of us?' he demanded.

'I'll leave Abi to take care of you. There's no need to spoil everyone's holiday.' She clasped his hand. 'We've had three lovely weeks together. I've enjoyed every minute, but if I don't go we could lose out on a very big move. You do understand, don't you, love?'

'Aye,' he answered glumly, his spine losing its rigidity. 'I understand. You go ahead. We'll cope.'

Belle and Rosanna looked at each other as Thomasin left. Poor Grandfather. Then the glassiness took over Rosie's eye and she returned her unseeing gaze to the mountains.

The holiday seemed to go flat after this. When Thomasin had departed they went on to Germany but despite the magnificent scenery there was scant enjoyment for anybody except Abi, who had met with a nice German waiter named Gerhardt. Indeed, it was she who was the sorriest when the time came for them to leave and asked

Patrick if he might consider giving her the night off so that she could spend her last evening with her friend.

'You go ahead and enjoy yourself, Abi,' said her employer. 'The girls have decided to have an early night for their long journey tomorrow so they'll not be needing ye. Have a good time.' – You'll be the only one of us who is, he thought self-pityingly.

At eight-thirty Rosanna went off to bed leaving her cousin and her grandfather sitting on the balcony staring out into the purple evening. The heather-hued sky seemed to move in on Patrick, suffocating him. Not since home had he felt such depression. Despite his unwillingness for conversation he forced out a token sentence for his grand-daughter's sake. 'Soon be on your way to university, Belle.' His voice was soft, emerging on a cloud of cigar smoke, his favourite pipe inadvertently left at home – another comfort denied him.

'Don't feel you have to make words for my sake, Gramps,' replied Belle, taking a sip of her hot chocolate. 'I'm quite content just to sit here.'

He bestowed a smiling frown, as if not understanding. 'Sure, I'm not saying it 'cause I like the sound the air makes on me vocal cords. I've always been extremely inter-ested in your education, you know that.'

'Oh yes, I just meant . . .' she shrugged, smiled and took another sip.

He ignored the implication, wanting not to dwell on his troubles but to be taken out of them. 'I expect you're lookin' forward to it?' The lack of response caused another frown. She turned to meet the enquiring glance. 'You're *not* looking forward to it,' he corrected himself.

'I'll get by,' she smiled half-heartedly.

Her grandfather gave one of his special laughs. 'That's what I keep fortifying meself with; I'll get by.' The pretence was over. He half-hoped she would encourage him to talk about it, thought it might help, though God knew how.

'Grandmother's leaving made you very unhappy, didn't it?'

'Ah, the Irish aren't so good at hiding their emotions, Belle.' He drew long on the cigar; its tip glowed against the purple of the sky.

There was silence for a while, then she said – unexpectedly, for he had thought to hear a query on the rift between the aged lovers, 'Has life brought you what you hoped it would, Gramps?'

'Now that's a deep one,' his answer came on a long exhalation of smoke. 'Perhaps it brought me what I deserve.'

'I can't think you deserve unhappiness. You've always been so good to us – especially me.'

'Maybe, maybe . . . 'tis true I care deeply for those around me, but what have I actually done for the wider community – apart from that spell in 'eighty-three, which was hardly successful.'

'I imagine it made you wonder if those people were really worth the effort?'

'Aye, I admit it did. But then they can't help being the way they are, Belle, uncouth and apathetic though we may find them. There's times I thought I gave in far too easily, thought I might try again when Frank Lockwood got in, but then what would they say? Here's an old fella trying to buy his place in Heaven – God knows I was accused enough times during that election of rising to wealth on the backs of fellow Irishmen.'

'Hecklers,' said Belle firmly. 'They knew nothing whatsoever of your character.'

He patted her hand. 'I'm not sure I merit such loyalty, though it's awful glad of it I am at the moment. Ah, Belle, 'tis a rum life an' no mistake. Which of my friends would've thought thirty years ago that I'd be sitting here like the gentry looking out over a glorious scene like this when all we knew then was black, brown an' grey.'

'You seem to regard it as some sort of sin to be well-off and live in comfort, Grandfather.'

'It is if ye don't use your wealth and knowledge to profit others, Belle.'

'But apart from what you tried to do in 'eighty-three

you and Nan have given work to dozens of people,' she protested.

'Aye, but the problem goes deeper than that. I daresay ye'll remember when your mother took ye to see the place where she was born?'

'Will I ever forget it? If someone had told me that there were people who lived like that and more relevantly that my own grandparents started there I'd never have believed them.'

'An' 'tis still going on, Belle,' he answered wonderingly. 'Despite the surveys an' complaints about the filth an' squalor, the grand speeches we all made, people still have to live in those hovels. An' I'm doing nothing about it but talk.'

'Now listen, you did your best to persuade the Irish to use their vote.'

'Not hard enough, pet. Wrote them off without a fight.'

Another long silence in which Patrick's cigar burnt almost to his fingers, then Belle said experimentally, 'Gramps . . . when we get back to England, before I have to leave for university, would you take me there again?'

Surprise. 'Is once not enough for ye?'

'I'd like to see – no,' she corrected herself, 'like is hardly the word. But I feel I must see more, know the whole story.'

'To get the whole picture of how these people exist ye'll have to see more than their houses. They're lambasted from gutter to courtroom – not just the immigrants y'understand, though they come out the worse for it, but the poor in general.'

'Then you must take me there, too,' insisted Belle.

'Sure, I've never been near the place in . . .' He broke off suddenly.

'What's the matter, Gramps?' She noticed the strange look on his face. 'Are you unwell?'

'No, no . . . 'tis just that I was about to say I've never been near the place in me life – an' me tasting Her Majesty's justice at close quarters.'

She was astounded. 'You've been to prison?'

'There's no call for alarm, I only killed the five o' them.' He grinned, caught her hand and shook it. 'No, 'twas the Debtors' prison I was in.' He saw that she wanted more and reluctantly admitted to his stupidity. 'The simple matter was that I set meself up in a business I just wasn't ready for. Someone stole some goods that I'd purchased on credit an' without the goods I couldn't do the work an' without the work I couldn't pay for the goods. So the Law moved in an' we moved out; my wife an' kids to Grandmother Fenton's, me to one o' Her Majesty's hotels.'

She was staring at him. 'I never knew that.'

'It's hardly a thing ye tell your grandchildren.' He laughed ironically. 'There, an' I've just gone an' told ye. Ah well, now ye know it all.'

'I'm glad, it's very interesting.'

'Oh, very.' The laughter was sincere this time.

'Tell me some more about your life, Gramps.'

'More o' the sordid bits, ye mean,' he grinned, but soon found himself vacating his heart of the injustices, the hardships, the prejudice. When he had finished he said in amazement, 'Sure, I don't think I ever talked to anybody like this before – apart from your grandmother an' Father Kelly. Ye must be a witch.' She was a strange one was Belle. Looking back, Pat found that he could not envisage her as a child – only a miniature adult. It was the latter that had tempted him into saying all kinds of things he would never have dreamt of telling Rosie. The two were such opposites. Oh, he loved them equally, but for different reasons. 'Er, I trust you're not thinkin' to write a book?'

Her mouth turned up at the corners. 'My lips are sealed – on one condition.'

'There's always a proviso, isn't there?'

'That you take me to see these places you talked about, Gramps.'

'Belle,' he said carefully, 'I get this awful feeling there's more to this than just looking.'

'I hope I'm not so transparent when it comes to making excuses to Mother about why I can't go to university.'

'Oh, now wait . . .'

'Listen to me, Gramps. It was your own speeches all that time ago that helped to awaken me to these people.' This was only partly true. The current rejection she had suffered had made her re-examine her values, alter all the plans she had envisaged for the future. Not for her a husband and babies. When her mother had introduced her to that alien colony she had felt pity and revulsion but little else, no sense of obligation. But Tim's rebuff had caused her to think more deeply. There would be no man in her life now or ever, so the gap must be refilled with something of purpose. This holiday had lent her time to decide what that something might be. Patrick had helped in that direction, too. She would dedicate her life to helping those miserable wretches she had seen – educate and civilise them – and for this she would need her grandfather's support. 'I'm going to help them, Gramps. I haven't yet decided how but help them I will. Society's got to be made to change its mind.'

He was very uneasy. 'Belle, your mother would never forgive me if she thought it was me who'd turned you away from your education. You mustn't even contemplate giving it all up.'

'But this is important.'

'It is, but dammit you're a thousand times more important than any o' those people in that jungle. I'd drown the lot o' them if I thought you intended to waste your life on them. You must go to that university. If ye're truly intent on helping them, well . . . they'll still be there when ye get back. Oh, God,' he put a hand to his head. 'This bloody family o' mine . . . ye realise what this holiday was for, don't ye?'

'To get Rosie away from Tim,' she answered.

'Aye, I thought you might be in on that from the looks on both your faces.'

'I'm not in on anything.'

'Good! And listen, don't think I'm taking ye to see these

420

places so's ye can choose yourself a fancy-man like your cousin did . . .'

'Don't be ridiculous, Gramps. I'm not interested in men.'

'Thank God for that.' He asked if her mother knew about Tim and Rosie. Belle said not as far as she was aware. 'I'd be obliged if ye kept it to yourself. I told Rosie her father wouldn't get to hear of it.'

'He won't hear from me. You'll take me then?'

'If you promise – Jaze, I seem to be forever extracting promises; I hope to God they'll be kept . . .'

'They will by me,' she replied. 'You want me to promise I'll go to university?'

'I do.'

'Well, that's painless enough. I promise.'

'Must say that sounded most sincere.'

'All right, pass me that penknife and I'll write it in blood. Look, it's of no consequence to me if I go or not. If you'd like me to go then very well I'll go. All right? But I warn you it won't make the slightest difference to my eventual proposals.'

Patrick had much more to say on the subject but was foiled by Abigail's return. Instead of interrogating Belle he settled back into his chair. 'What a long face, Abi. Looks as if your last evening was a failure.'

'Oh no, sir, I had a wonderful evening,' she replied, still wan-looking. 'Really marvellous.'

'Sure, I'll have to have an evening like that meself some time; ye look as if ye really enjoyed it. Ah well.' He slapped his knee and taking a last puff at the cigar stubbed it out. 'I expect everyone will want to get to their beds. We've an early start tomorrow. Make sure ye get these lasses up in time.'

Abigail waited while Belle performed her goodnights and limped off to her room. 'Was there something ye wanted, Abi?' asked Patrick at her awkward stance.

'Well . . . yes, sir, I'd like to ask a favour if you can spare a minute.'

'Sure, I'm clean short o' favours, girl . . . Abi, I'm only

joshing ye, for God's sake don't cry.' The face had grown longer.

'Oh, I'm ever so sorry, sir . . .'

'Sounds bad. Come sit down, Abi. I'm not sleepy anyway.' – Jazers, if it isn't one o' them 'tis another, he thought despairingly.

'It's a very big favour, sir.' She remained standing.

'They always are. I can always say no, can't I?'

Urged on by his kind expression she finally plucked up courage. 'I want to get married, sir.'

'Sorry but I'm not available, colleen.'

Oh, he was outrageous at times was the master. 'I mean to Gerry, sir – that's the gentleman I've been seeing so much of.'

A sound of amusement. 'But, Abi, we've only been here a week.'

'I know, sir, but him an' me . . . well, we seemed to hit it off right away. I was dreading leavin' him, honest. Anyroad, tonight he asked if I'd stay an' marry him.'

'But . . .' He spread his hands. 'God, you're a fast one, Abi. Oh no, no, I didn't mean it like that.' Her face had reached proportions of misery hitherto unplumbed.

'You're not angry, are you, sir? I mean, if you really won't release me from me duties . . . I'd go back . . . only . . .'

'My dear child, I wouldn't dream o' dragging ye from the man ye love.' He rose to touch her cheek. 'If ye want to marry him then go ahead an' do it an' may ye both be very happy.'

'Oh, thank you, sir!' She flushed. 'I'm ever so relieved. I didn't know what you'd say. The thing is, you see I'm not getting no younger an' well . . . I never met anybody quite like Gerry. Only I'm not quite sure it'd be legal, like, me stayin' on here.'

'Oh, sure it wouldn't take much clearing with the authorities. I'd love to help you in that region but with going so early tomorrow . . .'

'Oh no, sir, I don't expect nothing like that. Me an' Gerry will sort it out.' Her expression became anxious again. 'D'you reckon the mistress'll be angry when I don't come back?'

'She'll miss your efficiency, I'm certain of that, but annoyed? Never. Mrs Feeney would say what I'm going to say now: congratulations, Abi, I'm very happy for ye. Here, will ye not sit down now you're no longer a servant? Take a drink with me to celebrate.'

'Oh, I couldn't, sir.'

'Rubbish.' He clinked a decanter and two glasses, handing one to her. 'Never insult a man by telling him ye won't drink with him.' She took it bashfully while he held up his own. 'Health an' long life to ye, Abi. May ye have a dozen children.'

She giggled. 'I don't know about that, sir. One would be very acceptable what with me gettin' so long in the tooth.'

'Nonsense. A mere slip of a girl. Now sit down. Go on!'

'Thank you, sir.' She worked her way through the drink whilst providing Patrick with snippets of information about her Intended. He was a grand man, the master. It was a crying shame he wasn't treated better at his time of life. She finally handed over the empty glass. 'Ooh, I don't know whether I should've had that. I've been drinking all night – just to celebrate o' course, you know, sir. Well, I'd best let you get off to your bed. Thank you once again for being so understandin'. I've enjoyed my years working for you an' the mistress, sir. I really shall miss you all. Oh dear, I'd best go before I start blubbering. I'll have the young ladies off to an early start tomorrow, sir, don't you worry. Er, I wonder would you mind sayin' goodbye to Mrs Howgego for me?' Patrick said naturally he would fulfil her request. 'And . . .' she didn't know whether it would be in order to say this to one's former employer, but decided she would anyhow. 'Don't you worry, sir.' This was delivered in confidential tones. 'Mrs Feeney'll find what she's looking for in the end – an' it'll be right under her nose. Goodbye, sir, an' God bless you.'

She moved swiftly from the room leaving a dumbstruck Patrick more depressed than ever.

CHAPTER TWENTY-NINE

'An' which one did ye decide on?' asked Patrick as his wife fussed over him and their grand-daughters on their Sunday return. Hearing them in the hall she had come out to welcome them.

'Both,' came the smug reply.

'God love us, the woman'll be buying up America next.'

'And I've got a buyer for the Goodramgate store.' She grinned and took his hat, enquiring where Abi was. When he explained she clicked her tongue at the inconvenience of it. 'Ah well, I suppose happiness comes before duty – just as well I hired another maid, wasn't it?' This had been done on her return from the Continent. 'I'll miss her, though.' She ushered them through to the drawing room where Patrick remarked on the absence of a welcoming party. 'Erin and Nick're upstairs. I'll shout them down in a minute – unless you want to go up and see your mother, Belle?' Not noticing Belle's disinclination she dragged Patrick to his favourite chair and went to pour him a whiskey. 'Nick did really well while I was away. By the time the new shops are ready I'll be able to put him in charge permanently. Oh, but you should've been at the auction, Pat! It was so nerve-racking. We'd just begin to think it was all in the bag when this fat old plodder would tap his nose and up the price would go. Thankfully we didn't reach our ceiling before he ran out of bids.' Patrick slipped a query in between her babble, asking when she was going to open. 'Oh, not for ages yet.' She passed him the whiskey. 'There's a load of restoration work to do – but they're both in spanking positions. Francis says ... oh, how I go on! Poor loves, I've not even asked how you enjoyed Germany.' She looked round. 'Where did Rosie go? I thought she followed us in.'

'She went up to her room,' provided Belle.

'I'll go up and see her in a minute,' said Thomasin.

'I shouldn't bother,' Patrick told her. He caught Thomasin's hesitancy. ''Tis all right, Belle knows about the young fella.'

Thomasin rolled her eyes. 'Poor little soul, still mooning over him, is she?'

'Well, it wasn't an easy crossing home but yes, I think 'tis more than mal de mer that's churning her up.'

'I can't help but think that a lot of this is my fault,' said his wife. 'If I'd realised how she was growing up and introduced her into the company of young men she wouldn't have had to find her own. Well, I'm going to remedy that. I know some lovely young chaps. I'll start inviting one or two round for tea.' She looked at her other grand-daughter. 'You never know, Belle, you might see something you fancy.'

Belle found her grandmother's forthrightness annoying sometimes. She rose. 'I think I'll take a leaf from Rosie's book and have a nap. It was a tiring journey.'

'Don't you want anything to eat?' asked Thomasin. 'Surely you must be famished.'

Belle said she couldn't stomach anything at present. 'Perhaps in an hour or so,' and moved to the door. Directly she grasped the handle someone turned it from the other side and the door opened in on her.

'I beg your pardon, miss.' The man bowed his head and stepped aside for Belle to make her exit.

Before the door divided her from the others she heard her grandmother explain, 'Pat, this is the new footman. John, this is your master, Mr Feeney. I thought you might welcome some assistance, Patrick. John could act as your valet.'

Belle was well able to imagine her grandfather's comment: 'Sure, I'm not having no fella help me off with my breeches', and smiled to herself as she climbed the stairs. Once at her destination she opened the door as gently as possible in order not to wake Rosie – not out of concern but because that would mean having to speak to her.

She needn't have put herself out; the bedroom was empty.

'All the time I was thinking, he'll swear I've walked out on him! He'll think I've stopped loving him!' Rosanna gripped two handfuls of her lover's shirt, chattering breathlessly into his face.

'I did,' admitted Tim, hands locked in the small of her back. 'I thought, she's finally got sick o' this rag-tag little bark an' found herself a toff.'

'Infidel!' The fists that clenched his shirt banged at his chest in indignation. 'I'll never grow tired of you, Tim.'

'I came to look for ye.'

'Where? To the fields?'

'And to the house.' He laughed at her dismay. 'I posed as a hawker. There was a wee kitchen maid answered the door. I got her talking. She told me the family had gone on holiday.'

'I had no chance to let you know. I've been going through agonies wondering if you'd still be here when I got back.' She smiled fondly as he said he would always be here. Then her face darkened. 'It wasn't just a holiday though . . . Grandfather found out about us.'

He was aghast. 'God, how? Oh . . . I suppose it was Belle.'

'It wasn't, actually. It was stupid old Joseph.'

'The crazy bugger.'

'Apparently he'd seen me coming here . . .'

'Here?!' interrupted Tim sharply, afraid of the wider consequences.

'No, I always made certain no one saw me coming in here. I meant he saw me down Walmgate. Anyway, he let slip to Gramps. He says I'm to stop seeing you, Tim. We had the most terrible row.'

'So, that's what the holiday was for, to get you away from the Fenian.'

She moved her head. 'He thought a month away from you would make me forget.'

'The old bastard,' breathed Tim without thinking.

'Oh, don't call him that, Tim.'

'Oh hell, Rosie, I didn't mean . . .' He cuddled her lovingly. 'Ye know I'd never inflict hurt on you purposely.'

'I know, I know.' She returned his hug. 'But don't call him any name. He's my grandfather and I love him and I know he's only doing what he thinks is right, even if it isn't.'

'So . . . are ye going to do as he asks?'

'Would I?' Such idiocy, her tone implied. 'I promised him I would, but I'm afraid I'm going to have to break it, much as it shames me. I'm promised to you, Timothy Rabb, and no one – not even Gramps – is going to keep us apart.' A sigh. 'We'll just have to be extra devious, that's all. There'll be no saying I'm going down the garden for a walk . . . And there's Joseph, I'll have to wear some sort of disguise so he doesn't spot me. Oh, we'll have to be a lot more careful if we're to keep seeing each other.'

They kissed long and passionately. 'Mmm,' he groaned into her mouth. 'Careful isn't a word I'd apply to meself right this minute.'

'We'll start being careful tomorrow,' came her murmur. Then, 'Where's Mr Dorgan gone?'

'You dare to think of another man when ye've got me so inflamed?' But his eyes laughed.

'I just meant that it was a lovely surprise to find you here alone.' Her mouth brushed from side to side. 'I expected to have to explain.'

'To him – why?'

'Because,' she caught one of his lips between hers, 'he may think I've run out of the Society – I'll bet he said that to you, didn't he?'

'Well – ow, Rosanna!' He retrieved his lower lip from her teeth and touched a finger to it. 'You've drawn blood!'

'Sorry.'

'Then why're ye laughing if you're sorry? Wee cat.'

Her tongue fluttered at his wounded flesh. 'I'm not looking forward to facing him. How long will he be?'

'He said he'd be back around four.'

She stole a glance at the clock. It was ten past two. 'Then I propose that we go upstairs and have a reintroductory sitting of the Brotherhood.'

'Sister,' he mouthed her eagerly, 'your motion is seconded and carried.'

The question had been postponed but now as the hour of Dorgan's return grew near it would have to be answered: how were they to keep meeting without her grandfather finding out?

'He doesn't know exactly where we've been meeting,' said Rosanna. 'I suppose he thinks it's at your house. So once we're here we're pretty safe. It's just getting here . . .'

'Well, don't worry about Joseph, I'll sort him out.'

'Oh, no! You know what a clown he is, whatever you say to him might make things worse. No, if I can just find an old shawl to wear and wrap it round my face, and an old dress – if you can put up with me like that?'

He cuddled her. 'Matters not to me what ye wear. The more pressing thing is how're ye going to convince your family that it's really over?'

'I'll have to look miserable – which won't be hard when I'm away from you the whole week.' He asked how she would get out of the house. 'Easy. I'll pretend I'm going to have a nap in my room then climb out of the window like I did today.'

'That's a bit risky.'

'No, I'm a good climber.'

'I don't doubt it but I didn't mean climbing out of the window, though God knows that's risky enough. No, I mean what if any of them should visit your room an' find you're not there?'

She groped for an answer, saying exasperatedly, 'Oh, I'll think of some excuse. Don't worry so much.'

'I'm as much worried for Mr Dorgan – we're putting him at risk too, ye know. If your grandfather should get

to know and follow you here it could bring attention to
Mr Dorgan. Much as he likes me I think he'd put the
Brotherhood before a love affair. We should find some-
where else to meet, just use this place as a last resort.'

For a time her face was crestfallen. Then it mirrored
her brainwave. 'You could come to Leeds! I could start
visiting Father and Mother more often – they're always
moaning about not seeing me. You can meet me somewhere round about – they have no idea about us, Gramps
didn't want to worry them.' She was delighted at her
cleverness.

He thought how lovely she looked in her glee. 'You're
sure ye can stand the danger?'

Rosie declared that she could – not even realising
herself that it was the danger which made this relationship
so exciting.

So realistic was Rosanna's misery when she was in her
grandfather's presence that he was convinced the romance
was well and truly over. He had pampered her a lot and
tried to keep her amused and though she wasn't exactly
euphoric she was now beginning to emerge from her
torpor. He had thought it sensible to allow her back to
her book-keeping which might serve to occupy her mind
– but he kept an eagle eye out for Rabb who might well
be lurking round the fields. However, that wasn't necessary
today. Rosanna had taken a train to visit her parents chap-
eroned by Helen the maid and wouldn't be back until this
evening. This had been partly at Sonny's suggestion – or
so both men had been led to believe, neither guessing that
it had been choreographed by Rosanna. It had begun with
a telephone call to her father 'just for a chat', during which
she had confided that her conscience was troubling her
over not seeing so much of him and Mother these days.

'I'd love to come, you know that. It's just that . . . well,
I'm worried about the way it would look to Gramps. He's
getting very possessive. Maybe if you were to grumble at
him, make it look as though it's your idea for me to come,
then he wouldn't mind so much.'

And poor Sonny had unwittingly provided her with the chance to get away, telephoning Patrick to say he would like to see his children this weekend. Similarly duped, Patrick had said, 'Why wait for the weekend?' Being in the company of her little sisters might be just the tonic to take her mind off Rabb – though he had not stated this to Sonny. 'Nick's at the store, but Rosie could come tomorrow. I'm sure Josie'll be delighted to spend a day shopping in Leeds.' Not to mention that it would lessen the strain on himself, give him a chance to unwind . . . though it appeared that wasn't going to last long.

'Gramps, I haven't much time before I leave for university,' Belle reminded him when there were just the two of them in the drawing room after breakfast.

Patrick smiled up from his book, 'I shall miss ye,' then retrained his eyes on the print.

'You've forgotten, haven't you?' At her accusing tone he looked up, perplexed. She clicked her tongue. 'You promised to take me to the slums. This will be our last chance.'

He sighed his incomprehension, then closed the book, though he did leave his thumb in to mark the place. 'You're not still going on about that, are ye? I thought maybe it was the magic of the night putting words in your mouth.' He knew how the beauty of a deep purple evening could carry one away.

'How else will I be able to help them if I don't go there?'

He resigned himself to finding a proper bookmark and laid the tome aside. 'Belle . . .'

She anticipated the excuse. 'You promised!'

'I know . . . but on reflection I don't think it's a very sensible idea, darlin'. 'Tis a rough hole to get cornered in. Some o' these people could be violent.'

'These people? How patronising you sound, Grandfather. They're your people. You lived with them, ate with them, slept with them, your first wife died with them.'

'I'd no mind to sound pompous an' it isn't that I'm afraid to go meself, just that I'd sooner you didn't see it.'

'I *have* seen it! And I want to see it again. I won't be put off. If you don't take me I shall go alone.'

He threw up his hands. 'What's a man to do in the face of such bullying? Have it your way – but don't be surprised if ye encounter a great deal of bad feeling.'

'I'm going to help them, so why should they be antagonistic?'

'Some folk don't like busybodies.' He glared at her pointedly. She only laughed, then asked if they could go to the courtroom first as a way of introduction to the problem. When he complained that her mother would take his skin for a new pair of boots if she knew about this, she exclaimed, 'That's what we can tell her if she asks where we've been – to have me measured for a new pair of boots! These are getting too small anyway, so it wouldn't have to be a lie.'

'Oh God, the things I get into . . . Away then, get your accoutrements while I fetch me swordstick an' write me will.'

To make their excuse plausible the two did indeed visit the shoemaker where Belle was measured for new footwear. Then Patrick directed the manservant to drive the carriage to St Helen's Square and soon after he and Belle were seated in the apartment of the Guildhall devoted to legal proceedings, waiting for the first case to approach the bench.

This involved two twelve-year-old boys accused of stealing lead from a church roof. Belle stared intently at the bowed heads of the transgressors. They looked so pitiable in their dirty, over-large trousers gathered by a belt at the waist and rolled up to the required leg length. After listening to their case the Lord Mayor asked their accompanying mothers what their response to the crime was.

'He's brought shame on a respectable household, yer worship,' declared one of them. 'I might tell you his father kicked seven kettles out of him when the policeman come. 'Course,' a derisory glance for her neighbour, 'it's t'other that led him to bad ways.'

431

The other woman set up an argument at which the magistrate wrinkled his nose in disgust. 'Kindly cease this disgraceful bickering! This is a court of law.' He asked the second woman if she had any explanation for her son's behaviour.

'None, yer honour,' she replied flatly. 'I'm at me wits' end with him. If I try to clout him he just holds me at arms' length an' laughs. Well, he's such a lump. How can I be expected to control him?'

'Have you no man?' The woman replied that she had not. 'Very well, I order that this boy receive six strokes of the birch, the other's father having already meted out retribution. And in future kindly try to keep your children in order. Next case!'

Belle was horrified at such violence and even more so at the indifferent manner in which it had been delivered. Yet the woman seemed pleased. She asked her grandfather why.

'Probably 'cause they didn't have to fork out a fine,' he hazarded, then placed a finger to his lips as the next case, an old pauper woman, entered the court.

Her clothes and skin were filthy. On her feet was a pair of men's boots, the battered uppers threatening to part company with the soles. As a token of the importance in which she held this court appearance she had perched upon her head a tiny, moth-eaten bonnet which looked as though she had sat on it for half an hour before feeling able to wear it. The female child who accompanied her wore no shoes and very few clothes; a grubby shift ripped in many places.

The Lord Mayor leaned forward curiously. 'Has this woman been before me on another occasion? I seem to know her face.'

Molly Flaherty widened her eyes – mere slits in the dirt-encrusted face – assuming a look of innocence. 'Who, me, yer Mayorship? Most definitely not. 'Tis all a terrible mistake. As abstemious a body as your own dear mother.' She smiled sweetly, hugging the child to her hip.

The magistrate harumphed and wagged his pen to indicate that the case proceed. The court heard that Mary Carmel Bridget Flaherty had been at the nucleus of a drunken affray which had begun in the King William and continued into the public highway where passers-by were jostled and insulted by the defendant. On the arrival of the police one of the rioters seized an officer by the nose while Flaherty exhorted the crowd to further violence. On being requested by an officer of the law to go home she had resorted to insulting language and was subsequently arrested.

'Flaherty, do you dispute any of the evidence the court has just heard?'

'I do, yer worship. 'Tis a wicked lie. I was only tryin' to break up the fight before any o' them good policemens got hurt.'

'Do you deny that you were the worse for drink?'

'Never touched a drop in me life.'

'Come, come, Flaherty, we have heard several witnesses to substantiate the case for the prosecution.'

'Well, ye see, yer Excellence,' Molly pulled a rag from her sleeve and used it to mop at her eyes. 'I've just lost me poor man an' I was seeking to drown me sorrows in a dram – ye know how ye do. Just a little one, y'understand? What with my circumstances I couldn't afford more than the one, yer honour. Then this big slob of a steam-roller picked a fight with one o' my lads. Twice Brendan's size he was, a giant. Well, I tried me best to stop it 'cause our Brendan has a very poor constitution, any excitation an' he'll be off quicker than . . .' She thought better of using the rude analogy. 'Ten children he has This is one of his girls here. I couldn't let him take a throttlin'. Then when that bruiser come,' she pointed accusingly at a police officer whose nose bore evidence of the fracas, 'everybody scattered an' left me to take the blame. Me, the essence of immaculate womanhood.'

The Lord Mayor asked if this was her first offence.

'First an' last, yer Mayorship. I'll never allow another drop past me lips.'

Patrick shook his head at his incorrigible old friend, and

it was at that point she spotted him. 'Oh, Pat, Pat! Look, yer honour, that gentleman there will vouch for me character, won't ye, Pat? God love ye.'

All eyes turned to Patrick who pulled embarrassedly at his chin on being asked to speak in his friend's defence when he knew the Prosecution likely told the truth. He sought for words that would sound convincing without actually making a liar of him. 'Well, sir, I've known the lady for some years an' can verify that, as she herself told the court, she lost her husband' – he thought it prudent not to mention that Jimmy Flaherty's demise had taken place twenty-three years ago – 'and that her circumstances are very unfortunate indeed.'

The Lord Mayor nodded sympathetically and conferred with his colleagues, all agreeing on a small fine. 'Well now, Mrs Flaherty, I am going to show leniency.'

'Oh, thank ye, sir. You're a beautiful man, so y'are.'

Before issuing the fine the Lord Mayor asked the attendant Chief Constable if anything was known about Mrs Flaherty. The senior officer obviously took great delight in his answer that Flaherty had sixty-five previous convictions for drunkenness, wiping the look of compassion from the magistrate's face.

'So, Flaherty, you sought to escape justice by feeding us a tissue of lies!' He wasted no further words. 'One month's imprisonment – and you, sir!' He pointed at Patrick. 'Think yourself fortunate you were not on oath otherwise you should find yourself facing a charge of perjury.'

Patrick rose amid the hilarity that had rippled through the ancient chamber at the police officer's information. 'I did not lie! What I told ye was the truth; she has no husband.'

'Sit down!' cried the Lord Mayor. 'Take that woman away. We shall hear no more of this.'

Molly struggled and cursed as two policemen escorted her from the courtroom, the child clinging to her skirts. 'Thank you very much, y'ould bugger, an' I hope your nose drops off.'

Patrick flashed a helpless look at his grand-daughter who patted his hand comfortingly. 'You couldn't help it, Gramps.'

'God, she's her own worst enemy is Molly,' he groaned. 'If it'd been a fine I coulda helped her . . .'

After the disturbance had died down the next case was brought before the bench: another young boy, who was eventually fined one shilling for knocking on doors and running away. Following this came a case of embezzlement and then one which really aroused Belle's interest.

'Phelan O'Connor, you are charged that in April of this year you did wilfully steal two loaves of bread, the property of Sidney Rydale, baker, of Fossgate. Do you wish to plead Guilty or Not Guilty?'

The dishevelled young man in the dock looked blankly at his accuser.

The Lord Mayor sighed. 'O'Connor, when you are addressed you will please answer. Guilty or Not Guilty?' O'Connor replied that he thought he was Guilty. 'Is that the way you wish to plead?' asked the Lord Mayor hopefully.

'I didn't steal it, yer honour,' answered the man.

'O'Connel, how old are you?'

'Er, I'm . . . forty-five, sir.' This was plainly ridiculous but the magistrate let it pass.

'Then you are obviously old enough to know the difference between right and wrong.'

'I am, sir. I didn't steal it, sir.'

'Then if that is so you must plead Not Guilty, do you understand?' He mouthed the words as to an idiot.

'Yes, sir. Not Guilty, sir.'

'Very well. Proceed.'

During the case it transpired that O'Connor had little command of English. Recently arrived from County Mayo he had come to join his family who lived in Bedern. It also became increasingly clear from his answers that the questions fired from all angles of the room were confusing him. Patrick, still nettled over the previous case, shook his head and muttered an aside to Belle. 'They're getting the lad all mixed up with their folderol language. He hardly knows what time o' day it is.'

This was borne out by the following exchange. 'You tell us that at the time of the theft, O'Casey, you were at work.'

'I was.' After a slight hesitation he had realised the man was speaking to him.

'And what time would that be?'

O'Connor faltered, then decided. 'Four of the clock, yer honour.'

'Would that be four p.m. or four a.m.?'

Pause. 'A.m., sir.'

'Are we to believe, O'Connor,' – miracle of miracles, thought Pat, he's hit on the right one, – 'that an Irishman starts his work at four o'clock in the morning?'

'I told ye he didn't know what time o' day it was,' hissed Patrick to his grand-daughter.

'So, your working day commences at four in the morning, Mr O'Connely. At what hour does work cease?'

Hesitation. 'Four of the clock sir.'

'Is that the afternoon or the morning?' came the light-hearted query.

'The mornin', sir.' There were giggles.

Patrick could stand this no longer. 'This boy doesn't understand what you're telling him!'

'Silence in the gallery!'

'He doesn't even know what he's accused of!' Patrick began to speak in Irish to O'Connor who smiled in eager recognition of his language and nodded rapidly.

The magistrate rapped for order. 'Sir, we have heard enough of you already! If you persist with your interruptions I shall have you ejected.'

'Your honour, I'm just attempting to help the boy,' entreated Patrick. 'He's only recently come from a place where little English is spoken . . .'

'Sit down! Sit down!'

Fuming, Patrick flopped into his seat muttering all the while to Belle. 'The poor wretch is getting himself in deeper an' deeper. All this lot want is a good laugh to round the morning off.'

'Is there nothing you can do, Grandfather?'

'Wait, let's see what happens.'

'Conroy,' the case for the Prosecution went on, 'a moment ago you told us your working day commenced at four o'clock in the morning and terminated at the same time. I understand that the Irish see little merit in work but surely that must be the shortest working day in the history of mankind.' More titters. 'And what is the nature of your employment, Conroy?'

'I don't know, sir.' The man's face burned with humiliation.

'Are you a labourer, a hawker . . . ?'

O'Connor thought. 'A hawker, sir.'

'And what do you sell?'

Confusion. 'Sure, I don't sell nuthin', sir.'

'Such is the manner of O'Connery's employment that he begins the day the same time as he finishes it and retails invisible goods. I trust when sentence is issued you will not offer to pay the fine with invisible money?' The court exploded with mirth.

'This is outrageous!' Patrick leapt up, his face suffused with colour. 'If the honourable gentleman wishes to amuse himself he should do as normal folk do which is visit a circus, not squeeze his sadistic humour from a poor unfortunate wretch who's been denied the means to defend himself. Why, ye can't even get the boy's bloody name right.'

Enacting his earlier warning to have Patrick ejected if he persisted, the Lord Mayor sent a posse into the affray. Grabbing an arm each they manhandled Patrick to the exit amid boos and catcalls, his worried grandchild hobbling after them.

'Are you hurt, Gramps?' Belle tended him solicitously where he had been deposited and was still recovering from the exertion.

Patrick ran his fingers through his hair and breathed

437

deeply. 'The devils! The varmints. If I were twenty years younger . . .'

An anxious Belle waited for him to recover his breath, which he did, if not his good humour. 'I wonder what sentence the poor devil got. I hope I didn't make it the heavier for him through trying to help.'

'I'm sure they wouldn't be that harsh.'

'You're surer than I am, then.' He sought her assistance in rising. 'My interfering didn't do much good, did it?'

'You tried.' She almost toppled over as the weight of him took her off-balance.

He leant against a wall. 'Trying's obviously not enough. God, the villains! All they wanted was a good laugh. I mean, ye'd think they'd get him somebody to speak on his behalf who understood him.'

'Did you discover what really happened?' asked Belle as he shouldered himself from the wall and set off.

Patrick shook his head. 'Ah, not really. From what I gathered he witnessed another fella pinch the bread an' when he saw the policeman arrive decided to run away himself. They caught him.'

'So he's going to be fined or imprisoned for something he didn't do?'

A shrug. 'That appears to be the way of it.'

They moved into the tunnel that would lead them back to St Helen's Square and were about halfway along it when Patrick's look of woe disappeared at the sight of the tiny weeping figure that Belle almost stumbled over. 'Isn't this the child that was with Molly?'

'Poor little mite.' Belle, not renowned for her soft heart, was touched by the pathetic sight and probably influenced also by what she had just seen in the Guildhall. She bent down beside the crying child. 'Don't distress yourself, dear, your grandmother will be all right, I'm sure.'

The girl, about six years old, looked up with red eyes, her nose encrusted with mucus. 'I don't know 'ow to get 'ome,' she sniffed. 'Vey chucked me out an' left me.'

'Well, that's nothing to cry about,' answered Belle cheerfully. 'My grandfather and I will escort you home.

438

Come,' she pulled herself into a standing position with the aid of the cold wall and the girl warily accepted her hand.

'Now then, my pet,' Patrick chucked her under the chin, 'where would you be living?'

'Wesley Place.' She made a sound like a grunting pig in an attempt to clear her nasal passages.

'Have y'ever been for a ride in a carriage? No? Well, you're going to now. Come on, let's take ye home to your daddy.' He took the child's other hand which was very cool from her sojourn in the tunnel.

'D'you know me daddy, sir?' asked the girl, now recognising Patrick as the man who had spoken in her grandmother's defence.

'I do, but I doubt he'll remember me. 'Twas a long time ago.' A very long time, he thought. God, I feel so bloody old.

Brendan Flaherty was not at home but Patrick related the situation to the girl's mother who bowed and scraped and thanked him for taking care of the child. 'Sure, she should never've been with her Gran in the first place,' a look of reproof for the child. 'Brendan wouldn't like it. She's a bad influence, he says. Still, 'tis hard to keep a body from her grandchildren isn't it, sir?'

'It is.' He nodded.

'Would ye be after staying for a cup o' tea, your lordship?'

He knew she could little afford it but also knew she would be grossly offended if he refused. 'That's most kind of ye, Mrs Flaherty. But please, the name's Patrick.' He followed her indoors with Belle.

The latter examined her surroundings. The room was about twelve feet square, the floor carpetless, the whole ambience one of deprivation. The walls were two-toned, the lower, darker portion being the tidemark from frequent flooding, but of course Belle didn't realise that; the thought would have sent her into hysterics. Six little faces, pinched with the sharpness of poverty, held the visitors with wide eyes as Patrick and Belle stood awaiting their tea – there were no chairs.

After taking their refreshment and leaving a present of money, Patrick and his grand-daughter left, Belle commenting on the state of the walls.

'The river's just at the end o' the street,' Patrick told her. 'I should think they're flooded pretty often. Ah, these poor devils have it worse than I ever had.'

He was about to climb into the carriage but Belle stopped him. 'Could we look round some more?' Her arm was pointing down the street.

'Nearer the river?' said Patrick, conversant with her dread of water; the times he had taken her to the park and seen her break into a panic at the sight of the ducks on the lake.

'Not too close. I just want to see what that woman down there is doing.' She gestured at a slumped figure at the lower end of the street, reclining against a house wall, clutching a swollen abdomen. 'She appears to be ill.'

Patrick, after a moment's inspection, recognised the signs of labour. 'Belle, get back in the carriage. Belle, I said don't go down there!' She had set off at a limp. 'Oh, damn and blast! John, wait here but be ready to come if I shout.' He set off after her.

Too late to shield her from the ragged skirt hauled up over flabby thighs Patrick tried to edge his grand-daughter away. 'Belle, 'tis no sight for a young lady.'

'But what's wrong with her?' Belle watched the woman's face change from grey to red as she strained involuntarily.

'Belle, will you do as you're told an' go back to the carriage! I'll help her.' Patrick stooped and laid a hand on the woman's shoulder. 'Woman, for Christ's sake you're showing everything ye've got!'

The woman panted, her face like greased parchment. 'I'm sorry if I offend your delicate senses. Ooogh!'

'Oh, Jazers.' Patrick clutched his forehead. – God, will somebody tell me what to do? At that moment the woman was overtaken by a huge contraction. Belle quaked as the distorted mouth emitted its agony.

Patrick caught hold of the woman in alarm. 'Let me be!' she yelled. Then people came running.

At the top of the slope John saw them pouring out of their houses, heard the anger in their voices and decided it would be more diplomatic to stay where he was.

'Hey, you leave her alone!' A man ran at Patrick. 'Grab him, he's kilt her!' John, descending from the carriage, hid behind a wall where he couldn't be summoned.

Patrick was now surrounded by a mob. The woman screamed and screamed. 'Oh, Mercy on us!' Rough hands grabbed the old man. 'I was trying to help her!' he protested. 'She must be got to a hospital.' But no one heeded. He was pushed back and forth, roughly handled. Belle stood in horror as they abused him. 'Grandfather!' Then, in her hoppity fashion she lurched to his aid, dragging at their clothes to haul them off.

Patrick had his hands up in a gesture of submission. 'Is no one going to help the woman?' But they continued to push him threateningly.

Then two females hustled the woman from the scene, disappearing into one of the hovels. Belle wound her fingers into the hair of one of the ruffians. He sucked in his breath and lashed out, knocking her against a wall.

Patrick had offered no violence until now but, enraged at his grand-daughter's ill-treatment, drew back his fist to make contact with the culprit's jaw. Down the fellow went.

The man's comrades set on him with true vigour then. Once a renowned fighter the old man was no match for this. They swore and bashed him from man to man; women too, shrieking foul-mouthed harridans. Belle, scrambling to her feet, balanced herself then drew back her surgical boot and directed it at the nearest leg. The owner wore no boots himself and the effect of the heavy thing colliding with his ankle bone brought him howling to his knees. Wasting no time Belle aimed the boot again and again, scratching and clawing like a wildcat, desperate to stop her grandfather's punishment, calling to him as she fought.

Patrick's knees gave way. He clutched at the wall. 'Run, Belle, run!' then crumpled, unconscious, to the pavement.

'Jesus, it's a madwoman we're dealing with!' Another of

441

the attackers cried out in anger as Belle once again put her boot to good use. But this time the strength of her swing knocked her off-balance. When she fell the men were on her. She felt their steely fingers clamp around her wrists and ankles. 'Let go of me!' Felt herself being tipped upside down, then transported down the street, her skirts trailing along the dusty ground. One of the women ripped off Belle's hat and stuck it on her own head to lead the procession.

She could feel the cool air through the fine cambric of her drawers and raged to think of herself in such a humiliating position. 'Put me down at once, you thugs!' She tried to bite one of the hands that bound her, failed, and allowed her head to fall back to see where she was being taken. Upside down the view was hard to focus upon at first. Everything was a jumble of grey and drab gyrating shapes – but then she heard it, lapping gently at its banks, and the horrible dawning hit her like a sledgehammer. She started to wriggle desperately, using all her strength to piston her arms and legs. With the frantic movement one of the men lost his grip and dropped the leg he carried. Grabbing the opportunity she lashed out, but it did no good for he caught her again, his fingers hurting cruelly. She craned her neck. The river came closer. She could hear it taunting her. Smelt it. Oh no, please no. 'No!' she screamed aloud, the anger giving way to pure terror as they reached the river bank.

Without preamble the men tossed her in to the accompanying yells of the women. Belle shrieked in fear as she hit the scum-coated water with a loud wallop.

'Let's see yer kick yer way out o' that!' The men on the bank guffawed, then turned their backs and began to make their way back up the street. The laughing women stayed to shout a few more insults, then left too.

That they had selected a shallow point to throw her in mattered not. The tremendous surge of panic that their departure brought completely incapacitated Belle. Through a veil of red lace she watched their heads disappear out of view. 'Don't leave me!' Her hands flailed through the thick green slime, trying to find something amongst the river's debris – old cans and coils of wire, splintered planks of wood, a dead dog with no eyes – to hold onto. All anger had gone. There was only fear – sheer, mind-numbing terror as her legs lashed out beneath the foul carpet, seeking a foothold, finding none.

'He-e-elp!' Her eyes held the look of the slaughter-house. 'Oh God, sa-ave me! Grandfather! Daddy!'

Then the words wouldn't come any more. Instead emerged animal-like utterances. Her head worked deliriously, arms shuddering, her whole being taken over by a vast hysterical paralysis as the water caressed her.

CHAPTER THIRTY

'She's takin' a swim wiv all her clothes on.' The little girl on the bank watched agog at Belle's pathetic flounderings. Finger in mouth she looked up at her companion, a boy of about ten or eleven, then back at the river.

'She's not swimmin', dummy,' he answered scathingly and stepping closer to the edge looked about him for some way to drag Belle out. 'She's drownin'.'

It appeared there was nothing else for it but to jump in which he did, landing close to Belle in a belly flop. 'Hold onto me, missus!' he commanded, but Belle needed no urging and lashed the water to reach him. 'Careful!' He deftly moved out of range, ducked behind her, grasped her round the neck and hauled her in.

The girl had run away. There was no one else on the bank to assist. Straining he pushed and hauled the half-drowned Belle from the water, then fell down, hawking and spitting. Even on terra firma the panic refused to subside. Belle sat there shivering, teeth chattering, her mad eyes fixed on the river. The boy recovered quickly and sat up to look at her. ''S all right, miss, yer safe now.'

Still she trembled, her fingers locked into the flesh of her upper arms. He glanced around and seeing the discarded bonnet lying nearby dusted it off and put it on her head, back to front, and tied the ribbon as best he could. Still Belle shivered deliriously. A movement further up the street caught the boy's eye. Patrick had regained consciousness.

"S that yer grandad, miss?' No response. The boy watched Patrick stagger down the street, holding his head as though it might drop off, his other hand bearing his crushed hat. At his arrival the child rose. 'They chucked her in, sir.'

'The scoundrels.' Patrick gingerly lowered himself and placed a hand on Belle's shoulder. She flinched noisily. 'Belle, 'tis me, Gramps.' She directed a whimpering face to his then with a cry fell against him, sobbing. 'There, there. You're safe, 'tis all right now. Ssh, now.' The clumsily-tied bonnet fell off again as he stroked her dripping hair. 'Oh, the villains,' he breathed. 'Damn them. Damn them to hell! I'd see them all rot before I lifted a finger to help again.'

When the two had regained some equilibrium the old man patted the girl's shaking back. 'Come, darlin', let's have ye on your feet else ye'll be taking a chill.' Once risen he studied the boy, noticing that he was dripping too. 'Have I you to thank for rescuing me grand-daughter?'

'Weren't nothin', sir.' The boy scuffed his foot on the ground.

'Sure, that's what that bloody John must've thought. Where was he when the fun started?'

Belle, still shaken but coherent now, said to the boy, 'It was a valiant act. You were incredibly brave and I owe you my life.'

He wriggled further at such praise. 'No, it were only shallow. You'd've got out on yer own probably.'

'I doubt it,' said Belle and shivered again. 'Oh, Grandfather, those dreadful, wicked people. How could I ever have contemplated helping them? They're beyond redemption. I hate them!'

It was no use, Patrick saw, arguing that they were not all as rough, for Belle had been badly scared. He spoke to the boy. 'That was an extremely plucky thing to do an' ye must let us show our appreciation. Where d'ye live so's we can escort ye an' give ye some reward for your soakin'?'

The boy looked alarmed. 'Oh, please, there's no need, sir. I can get 'ome on me own.'

'Nonsense. We must explain to your mother about your state. Come on.'

'Please, sir, you just go an' leave me. I'll be all right.'

'I'll do no such thing. That'd be fine reward for your bravery. What's your name?'

'Lol Kearney.'

'An' where d'ye live, Lol Kearney?'

The boy was forced to tell. 'Carmelite Street – but oh, please don't make me go!'

'Make ye go? Why, ye make it sound like the depths o' hell.'

'I'm not supposed to go in before dark,' explained Lol. 'Me Mam'll kill me if I do.'

'She surely won't be expecting ye to stand about the streets dripping wet.'

Lol said that he and his brothers and sisters were put out into the street first thing after breakfast with instructions from their mother that she didn't want to see any of them before dark.

Patrick laughed. 'Sure, that's just a mother's ploy for keeping her children from under her feet. I can assure ye, son, she'll not skelp ye for saving someone's life.'

'She would, sir.' Lol refused to budge.

'Grandfather, can't you see the child is petrified?' said Belle, still quaking herself. 'What manner of people are these? I must've been absolutely mad. It's not they that need our help but the children that need protecting from their parents. Come along, Lol.' A little of her character was returning and she grasped the cold hand.

He pulled against it. 'No, please, miss!'

'Don't worry, you aren't going home for a beating, you're coming with us, isn't he, Grandfather?' And Patrick

445

was left with little choice but to follow the dripping trail back to where John had miraculously reappeared atop the carriage. The manservant faked horror and asked if he should fetch a policeman.

'Bit late for that now, son, isn't it?' Patrick grimaced and climbed on board. Thank the Lord, he thought, that Erin was out at work. She'd lose her hair if she knew what they'd been up to this morning.

At their woeful entrance Mrs Howgego threw up her scrawny arms and pulled over a chair for the master to flop into. 'Look at your poor face! Here, I've just made some tea, I'll pour you a cup.' She was bursting with curiosity.

'Ah, God love ye, Cook, but 'tis something stronger I'm in need of.' He addressed a sheepish John. 'Go fetch me a drop o' brandy, will ye, boy.' Then he instructed Belle to run along and get changed immediately. 'An' take Gawping Gertie to help ye.' He referred to the little kitchen-maid whom Thomasin had hired while he had still been on the Continent. 'Mrs Howgego, could ye find something to wrap around this young fella?'

'I've a towel here, sir.' She whipped the warm, fluffy towel from the drying rail and shook it at the boy. 'Away then, get those wet things off else we'll have a corpse on our hands.'

Showing none of the embarrassment which a young gentleman might when requested to disrobe, Lol ripped off his two sopping garments and stepped forward to be engulfed in the warm towel. Never had he felt anything so soft against his skin. Cook rubbed at him briskly, muttering, 'Poor bairn's nobbut skin an' bone.'

Patrick heard. 'Well, ye'll no doubt be able to remedy that, Cook. It appears young Lol is going to honour our table for lunch.' He recalled what Lol had mentioned earlier about not being allowed in until dark. 'Maybe ye'd like to stay through supper an' all, Lol? Then we could take ye home in the carriage.'

'Wouldn't he be better down here, sir?' ventured Cook, knowing her mistress well.

Patrick could not say, as he would have liked to, 'The boy saved my grand-daughter's life, he deserves better'; no one in the house must know. He replied simply, 'Ah, sure if we fancy him up a mite he'll not disgrace your mistress's table,' leaving Cook to answer with a 'Very well, sir,' and Lol to beam his acceptance. 'That's a fine boy. Cook'll put some meat on your ribs before ye go home – ah! here's John with the elixir of life. Be a good fella an' inject some vigour into that tea, will ye? The boy's, too.'

'But it's your finest brandy, sir,' protested the manservant; then, under a withering scowl from his master, poured the neatest drop into Lol's cup. After Patrick had sufficiently recuperated he rose creakily. 'I'm off to see how my grand-daughter is now, but before I do I want all of yese to promise that not one word o' this will reach Mrs Teale. She's not to know about any wet clothes till I've had chance to explain to her, understand?' He aimed his demand especially at John, but all present nodded. 'You too, Lol.' Patrick bent his head to the boy's, speaking quietly. 'I'm sorry to have to keep silent on your bravery but Miss Belle's mother would have a fit if she found out what had happened to her. I like a peaceful life.'

With Lol's promise Patrick left him to the rough and ready care of Mrs Howgego. The latter took the opportunity to pump John for information while the boy's clothes were put through the mangle and set to steam by the fire. When John had told her about the fight she exclaimed, 'Lord! The things that Miss Belle gets the master into!' and placed a biscuit barrel on the table. 'There y'are, Lol. Take a couple to go with your tea.'

Lol peered inquisitively into the barrel and his face lit up. 'Cor, biscuits!' He dug in and came out with a handful, trying his best to conceal them as he moved away.

'Oy, Ally Sloper, I said a couple. A couple is two, not half a dozen.' His smile dimming, he released some of his haul into the barrel. 'There's a good lad,' said Cook. 'Lunch is only fifteen minutes away. You don't want to spoil your appetite, d'you?'

Lol, head down, crunched the remaining biscuits, examining his surroundings from the corner of each eye. He decided he did not like the manservant who was staring at him distastefully, and giving in to natural inclination he forked two fingers up against his nose.

'Why, you cheeky little bleeder!' John took two strides across the kitchen and caught Lol a hefty slap round the ear.

'John!' shouted Mrs Howgego as Lol, the towel slipping from his shoulders, danced naked to escape the manservant's punishing hands. 'Don't you dare lay another finger on that boy!'

'Did you see what he did?' demanded John angrily.

'I didn't!' yelled Lol. 'I were just rubbin' me nose.'

'Give us it here, I'll bloody-well rub it for yer!' responded John noisily.

'Will you get about your work an' leave the lad alone?' stormed Mrs Howgego. 'Look at the width of him. The sound o' your voice is nearly knocking him over. Use them saucepan lids o' yours to carry that tray o' silver back upstairs, instead o' laying into this poor mite.'

'Poor mite? Puh! Anyroad, who're you to give me orders?'

Mrs Howgego adopted the stance that had put flight to many a door-to-door hawker and grabbed a posser. 'I'll tell you who I am! I'm Cook, that's who I am, an' when I say jump you ruddy-well jump lest you want your parting altered.' She laid into him with the posser and continued to do so until he made for the stairs. 'An' don't you dare come back to my kitchen till you know your place!' she bellowed after him. 'Jumped up nowt,' she said to Lol and threw down the posser in order to wrap the discarded towel round his shoulders. 'Cover your decency. My knives have a nasty habit o' cutting off owt that dangles.'

Lol grinned and sat down again. 'Is he the butler that John, then?'

'Huh. Likes to reckon he is.'

'Don't like him – but I like you, missus.'

'Oh, do you? Well, we'll see how you like me when I

get you peelin' spuds for tonight's supper.' But the child-less cook was inordinately pleased at the compliment and reached for another titbit for the boy.

'What're these?' Lol examined the round green things that hung in a little cluster.

'Eh, haven't you ever seen grapes before?'

'No.' He poked them. 'What do I do with 'em?'

'You eat 'em, soft article. Listen, I can't leave you hanging round my kitchen half-naked. I'm off to see if there's any o' Master Nick's old clothes up in the attic.'

'Who's Master Nick?' Lol still rolled the grapes through his fingers.

'He's the master's grandson.' She moved to the stairs. 'Sit there an' don't touch a thing. You've seen what happens to them as misbehave.' She left him to ponder on the grapes.

Lol stood, the towel slipping off yet again, and wandered about the kitchen, prying into cupboards. Finally he popped a grape into his mouth. It tasted good till his teeth crunched on the pip and he made a face. His normal reaction was to spit it out, then, after staring at the pip on Cook's nice clean floor, he retrieved it and looked for somewhere else to put it. There was a bowl of slops standing on a shelf beneath the sink. As he devoured the grapes he spat the pips into it.

After this he strolled about the kitchen lifting lids and peeping into more cupboards, helping himself to any food he came across. There was a sudden shriek as the tiny kitchen-maid returned to her base and was faced with his nudity. She stood there, hand over mouth, staring at him.

'What's up – haven't y'ever seen one before?' He grasped his penis and jiggled it at her. Whence she screamed again and ran for the stairs, crashing into Cook as she returned with a pile of clothes.

'Right, where's that knife?' By the time Cook had thundered down the remaining stairs Lol had the towel wrapped safely round him again and was sitting cross-legged to protect his threatened manhood. 'By, I won't half give it you if I catch you frightening my staff again,' she warned. 'Vinnie, lock yourself in the larder while His Lordship tries these togs on.' She thrust a pile of Nick's clothes at Lol. 'Well away, get 'em on! I haven't time to see to you and get lunch ready.' She went off to put a soufflé in the oven. When she turned back he was attired in a sailor suit with a pair of black buckled shoes. 'Oh, well,' she nodded approvingly, 'the proper gent – let's hope you don't spoil the effect by wagging your appendage at the mistress over lunch.'

'Patrick, he can't possibly stay to dinner,' hissed Thomasin over her chicken and ham vol au vent. 'We've guests coming.'

'If they've anything about them they'll hardly object to a starving child's company,' replied Patrick, smiling reassuringly at Lol who was seated next to Belle at the opposite side of the table.

'But, our own grandchildren never dined with our guests when they were small – and just look at him.' Lol was working his heavy way through a third helping of pastry. 'It's as though an express train's hit the table.'

'Tommy, the lad's probably never seen so much food in his life. Ye can hardly blame him for taking what he can while he can.'

The meal continued in oppressive silence. Thomasin, watching the half-starved child gorge himself, felt disgusted both at him and herself, and at the parents who had allowed the child to deteriorate to such proportions. Even when she and Pat had been poor they had always ensured that their children were fed.

'I suppose you'll think I'm being selfish,' she said. Only his eyebrows moved; they were adequately expressive. 'You're right. I'm getting very hard in my old age.' She forced herself to smile at the boy. 'Well, Lol, and where do you live?' He told her, spitting crumbs over the table-cloth. 'And won't your mother be worried as to your whereabouts?' He shook his head.

'Didn't I tell ye?' said Pat. 'The kids get chucked out on a morning an' aren't allowed in before dark. I couldn't

450

eat dinner knowing he was wandering round the streets hungry.'

She eyed the sailor suit. 'Nicholas's clothes fit you quite well, Lol. You must take them with you when you go.' Thomasin had been acquainted with the reason for Lol being dressed thus. Pat, with assistance from Belle, had explained to her and Erin how they had seen Lol struggling in the Foss and had pulled him out. It was fortunate for them that Lol set little store by his bravery and did not mind his glory being purloined.

'I still can't understand how you came to be down Hungate,' said Erin to her daughter, introducing a very dangerous element to the conversation. 'It's nowhere near the shoemaker's.'

'Oh, didn't I mention it? I thought I did.' Belle dabbed at her mouth, gaining time. 'Well, while we were at the shoemaker's the man asked if we might allow John to deliver a parcel of boots to the area as it was very close to where we lived. It was most urgent, he said, and as he was very busy in the shop he didn't know when he'd be able to deliver them. Of course Grandfather said we would. It was hardly out of our way, was it?' She looked over at Patrick. – What liars we are, her eyes said. 'The street ran down to the river. We could see this person thrashing about in the water. Grandfather found a plank of wood and used it to pull Lol to the bank.'

'Well, I trust he was suitably grateful,' answered Erin, and to Lol, 'You are a very lucky young man. I hope you thanked my father?'

Lol glanced at Patrick. 'Oh, he did,' replied the latter hastily.

'Ye wouldn't've thought anyone down Hungate could've afforded to have a pair o' shoes handmade, would ye?' frowned Erin. 'What street did ye say it was?'

'Oh, I've forgotten. Mother, do we have to give you a step by step account of our movements?'

'And that's quite enough rudeness from you, young lady,' warned her mother. 'Don't imagine that just because you're going to university you're too big for a thrashing.'

University! Belle's heart flipped over. With this morning's excitement she ad completely forgotten. Oh, what she would give for a little of Lol's freedom. Then she looked at him and changed her mind. No, that was a stupid thing to think. How could she envy a child whose every bone showed through the material of the sailor suit, whose face was a mass of scabs and who crammed himself with food as if he thought every mouthful would be his last.

During the afternoon Belle found out all she could about Lol and what she heard added even further to her admiration of him. It was not simply a feeling born of compassion, for Lol's cheeky, matter-of-fact nature defied pity; this street-boy was obviously well able to take care of himself. No, it was when she had given him an apple and the boy had said, 'I like you, miss,' as though she had given him the world, that the wheels in her mind began to turn.

Came the evening and Lol, though still not totally at ease in these sumptuous climes, was showing signs that he could quite easily take to this life.

'I do hope he'll behave himself at dinner,' worried Thomasin. It was quite an important occasion. Among the guests would be a young man whom Thomasin hoped would take the place of Patrick's ex-labourer in Rosie's affections.

'I'll take care of him,' promised Belle. 'You'd like to sit beside me again, wouldn't you, Lol?'

'Yes, Aunt Belle.'

Aunt Belle, muttered Erin to herself, and shook her head. Lol behaved impeccably, the pounding he had given the table at lunchtime serving to put a brake on his voracious appetite. This evening his table manners – gleaned from watching the others – were much more acceptable. The guests, a Mr and Mrs Eyeington and son, were most taken with the story of Lol's reclamation from the drink and sympathised with his homelife.

'The poor child,' sighed Mrs Eyeington. 'One thanks God one's own offspring will never suffer such deprivation.' She inserted a sliver of lemon meringue between her lips and ate genteelly, until her teeth happened loudly on a grape pip. Similar sounds began to emanate from the other diners as each encountered the pip-laced meringue. Lol, blissfully unaware that his earlier action was the cause of such puzzlement, extricated a pip from his own mouth and wiped it on the tablecloth. It seemed as though everything he ate in this house was full of these unpalatable things.

Belle, trying to consume her own portion without incurring too much damage to her teeth, looked across at Rosanna, clad in the dress that Josie had bought her in Leeds – pale-green figured silk, trimmed with russet ribbon and cream lace, the square-cut neck revealing a sculptured clavicle. Belle couldn't help the comparison with her own outfit. She did not favour the modern fashion which only made her deformity more pronounced. Instead, she wore loose-fitting jackets over all her gowns. Her hair was never chignoned but worn free to cover the undulating spine. When left naturally straight it only emphasised the deviation, but with the aid of rags and crimping irons she and the maid had coaxed it into a bushy wildness that served its purpose well – though to others it made her appear very Bohemian. Mrs Eyeington, for instance, was most gratified that her son had been selected to partner the other grand-daughter and not this rather outlandish young woman. Belle, still watching Rosie make smiling conversation with her selected beau, could not help a twinge of anger. All that fuss her cousin had made over Tim when she had thought Belle wanted him and now look at her making sheep's eyes at another. Rosie caught the hostile look and it made her want to laugh. If Belle was convinced that she was interested in this young man then they all must be . . . she only hoped she hadn't made it too convincing for the young man.

Belle was wondering how often Rosie had been kissed, and hung briefly on the idea of what it would be like to have someone kiss her properly, but then just as soon dismissed the thought. She would never know – did not even care. Let Rosie have her romance, for Belle had decided this afternoon what course her own life would follow. The moment when Lol had said, 'I like you, miss,' that was when her plan had been forged. A plan to help all children like Lol, to save them from their poverty, their ignorance, their parents ... but first, that dratted university.

PART FOUR

1892

CHAPTER THIRTY-ONE

Belle's movement through London University was so socially unobtrusive that if it were not for her brilliant scholastic achievement – a first-class Honours degree in mathematics – it would have been hard to find one person who could remember her. True to her character she mingled rarely, preferring to lock herself away and study alone. None of her contemporaries would confess to liking her. Most, if asked, would have said, 'Belle who? Oh, you mean the crippled girl.' Yet it was undeniable that by the time she graduated Belle had made more of a mark on this university than any student for a long time.

University life made little impression on Belle. She simply viewed the period as biding time until she could embark on her more worthwhile project. Though she was now almost an adult, to Belle's great annoyance her mother still insisted on travelling all the way down to London in order to transport her daughter safely home. 'Really, Mother!' Belle tipped the porter who had put her trunk on board the train. 'It isn't necessary for you to come all this way just to go straight home again. I could quite safely see to myself.'

A young man in his twenties occupied the compartment they had selected. He smiled and stood at their entry. Erin nodded politely, Belle ignored him.

Erin seated herself by the window, facing homewards. 'Well, I don't suppose ye'll have to suffer the embarrassment for much longer if ye put the same amount of effort into getting your Master's degree as ye have to this one. I trust you've given some thought as to what use you're going to make of it?' She turned from the window to see that Belle had opened a magazine on her lap. 'Please don't be so ill-mannered as to do that while I'm speaking.'

The young woman sighed and closed the journal. 'I'm sorry, but do you think we could open the dialogue beyond the bounds of my education?' Erin's chastisement for her rudeness coincided with a jerking movement as the train's pistons started to propel it northwards. Soon it was emerging from King's Cross, though it did not leave the outer limits of London for some time.

Belle, her expression still pained, happened to catch the young man's bespectacled eye – he was hoping for this – as she turned back to her magazine. He smiled his sympathy. Disregarding him she went on to wonder what her mother would say when she broke the news that this was not merely a holiday: she had no intention of ever taking her Master's degree.

She allowed the printed word to permeate her reverie and, like her mother, settled down to the long journey ahead. During this time their travelling companion made attempts at conversation, introducing himself as Brian Dyson. Only Erin responded to his small talk, polite but cool. She had noticed his eyes moving in fanciful admiration over Belle's face and had no wish to encourage him. Belle had better things to do than to dally with empty young men.

Primarily Brian thought it was simply shyness that forbade the young woman from answering his queries, but when Erin fell asleep with the motion of the carriage and he tried to press his suit he was left in no doubt as to Belle's opinion of him. He leaned over with outstretched palm. 'Would you care for a peppermint, Miss . . . I'm sorry, I didn't catch your name.'

'Hardly surprising when it wasn't donated,' she replied, refusing the mint.

He shrugged inwardly, sat back and slipped a mint onto his tongue. 'Are you going all the way to Edinburgh?'

'No.' She continued to read.

'Is your destination a state secret? Perhaps you are on a mission of world importance?'

'I really don't see how it could concern you if I were.' She flicked at the corners of two pages to separate them.

'If you don't like me why don't you just come right out and say it instead of hiding behind a book?' replied Brian.

'Very well, I don't like you. Is that sufficient to still your tongue?'

Brian laughed his amazement, infuriating her. 'You know, you really are the most rude person . . .'

'Yes, I do know, having been told on numerous occasions by other interfering busybodies. Mr Dyson, did I ask for your company?' He mouthed a no. 'Then it is hardly surprising that your attempts to curry favour are met with rudeness, is it?'

She was such a pretty creature, thought Brian. What a shame her personality did not harmonise. He wondered how old she was. Belle finished the magazine and, not wishing to sit looking at the young man opposite for the rest of the journey, decided to employ one of the books that was stashed away in her portmanteau. Rising, she stretched her arm up to the luggage rack. So that's it, thought Brian as her bushy hair swished to one side. He briefly inspected her ill-shapen form before leaping to assist. That was why she was on her guard all the time.

'Thank you, I don't require your assistance.' Belle snatched the bag's handle and swung it down, forestalling him.

Brian formed his mouth into a knowing – but not mocking – smile at her independence and sat down again. 'I couldn't help overhearing,' he began again after a short interval. 'You've just graduated.' Belle rolled disdainful eyes from the book. More interruptions! 'Did you do well, may one ask?'

'That's a matter of opinion,' muttered Belle.

'Actually, I've not long graduated myself,' said Brian. 'At medical school, that is. I'm a fully-fledged doctor now. I'm off to join a practice in York.' It obviously gave him great pride.

'How wonderful,' murmured the young woman. 'If my mother happens to have an apoplexy when I tell her my news at least we shall have a member of the medical profession on hand.'

Brian's forehead wrinkled quizzically. 'It must be very startling news to have such a profound effect.' Belle was silent. 'But not for my ears, eh?' Brian smiled and fished another mint from his pocket. The whole compartment hummed of peppermints now. Belle's mouth felt like a redundant washleather. She wished she hadn't refused his previous offer. As if guessing her thoughts he proffered the mints again. When she hesitantly reached for one he drew back his hand a little. 'First you must tell me your name. Fair exchange, I think.'

'How tiresome,' she sighed. 'If you consider it a matter of life and death, which apparently you do, then I must tell you. It's Belle Teale.'

He permitted her to take a mint. 'Belle – that accounts for your propensity for a ding-dong.'

She made a sound of utter contempt. 'Would you mind taking your silly humour elsewhere?' and slapped the book down onto her lap. Of all the stupid individuals with whom she had to share a compartment . . .

'And where do you suggest I take it?' asked Brian mischievously, indicating their enclosure. 'Of course, I could always disembark at the next stop and travel the rest of the way on the roof.'

'That would be most agreeable,' snapped Belle tartly.

'I'm sure it would – for both of us. Oh, come on, girl, let yourself go. Here I am trying to make a long journey a bit more pleasant and all you can find to do is sneer.'

'I am not sneering, despite the fact that your humour is on a par with that supplied by the inmates of the nursery. I simply wish to be left alone to read my book in peace. Is that too much to ask?'

'My, my,' retorted Brian. 'What a mouthful.' Then sighed. 'Very well, I give up,' and settled back into his seat to stare at her, which was even more unwelcome than his conversation.

Belle's face grew hot under the close inspection and she was most thankful when the engine driver applied his brakes to enter another station, the sudden jerk waking her mother and obliging Brian to finally tear his eyes away.

Erin apologised for being such bad company, then asked Belle to fetch her a cup of tea from the wagon on the station. It was while Belle watched the tea-woman pour black brew into two cups that there was a sudden commotion to her right.

'You little bleeder!' A man in a checked suit took a swipe at a boy's head, knocking him clean off his feet.

Belle launched into an indignant attack. 'You lout! Leave him be.'

'Listen, this 'ere ruffian just spilt tea all down me front!' He dabbed at his clothes.

'And that was sufficient to warrant such violence?' Belle stabbed a finger at the groaning figure on the platform whose ear trickled red. 'The child spills your tea so you must spill his blood.' She helped the boy to his feet and pulling a handkerchief from her pocket tended his bleeding ear.

'That's the trouble wi' these modern women,' sneered the man to those who might be listening. 'Think they've got the right to poke their noses into other folk's business. I know what I'd do with her if she were mine.'

'When violence occurs to a child it is everyone's business,' rejoined Belle. 'You may have damaged him for life with your brutality.'

'Bleedin' hell,' muttered the man to the tea-stall woman as he sipped a replacement. 'You'd think it were Little Lord Fauntleroy instead of a scabby bloody guttersnipe.'

Belle peered into the child's dirty ear. 'I think we should have a doctor see to this.' Her travelling companion was going to have his uses after all. Paying for the tea she ordered the boy to follow, and returned to the train.

Brian, seeing her coming, opened the door, but just as she neared it someone barged past her, knocking one of the cups from its saucer and spilling hot tea down her green velvet outfit. 'I say, was there any need for that?' Brian glared at the man in the checked suit – the same one who had just hit the boy – who had seated himself unconcernedly in their compartment. He leapt out to help Belle.

'Don't concern yourself with that!' she snapped impolitely whilst glowering at the intruder. 'I want you to have a look at this boy's ear. That boorish lout has just dealt him a nasty blow.'

While Brian examined the boy's ear Belle handed the remaining cup to her mother who was watching the enactment worriedly. 'What d'you think?'

'Well, it's difficult to say,' murmured Brian, holding the greasy head on a slant, trying to shed light on the orifice. 'Not being able to give him a proper examination.'

'I thought you said you were a doctor.'

'I am, but this is hardly the place . . .'

'Nonsense, I've heard of doctors performing operations on kitchen tables. You have the instruments, don't you?' She gesticulated at the bag on the luggage rack.

'Yes, but even if I ascertained the damage there's little I could do,' protested Brian, annoyed at being forced into such a position.

'If you're worried about being paid,' snapped Belle, reaching for her purse.

'Oh, please don't talk rot.' Brian flicked his hand. 'The train is about to pull out at any moment. I can't possibly be expected to give a proper diagnosis and treatment in such a short time.'

'Then we'll have to take him with us,' said Belle.

Erin felt it her duty to intervene. Her wayward daughter was attracting too much attention. 'Belle, will ye drop this fanciful notion. 'Tis quite impossible to take the boy with us an' you know it. For one thing, what are his parents going to say when he doesn't return? And your grandparents don't want their home cluttering with strangers. Now stop embarrassing everyone an' get back in the carriage.'

After a short period of defiance Belle capitulated with bad grace. Taking one of the sovereigns which she had saved from her purse she handed it to the injured party. 'I'm sorry, it seems that no one here is willing to help you. Please take this to a proper doctor and he'll treat your ear.'

The intended insult was not lost on Brian. Nevertheless, on climbing back into the carriage, he addressed the man in the checked suit. 'Sir, I think you owe this lady an apology for spoiling her clothes.'

The other smiled brazenly, 'She don't mind, do you, dear? A drop o' tea's nothing to get steamed up about,' and went back to his paper.

Brian would have said more on the matter but Erin, not wanting another unsettling display, leapt in with a question and the young man took his seat. It was not simply the oaf who angered him but Belle's attempts to discredit, insinuating that he was not a qualified doctor. He refrained from further conversation with her, not offering to take the empty teacups back. These had to be left on the station as there was no time to return them.

The train moved off once more to embark on the most disagreeable portion of the journey. The man in the checked suit lit a cheap cigar and though Brian opened a window the smoke continued to annoy them. So did the man, who set up a string of ill-bred comments on each item he read in his newspaper, boring them all with his bigoted opinions. Luckily, when he realised that his narrative was ignored by the others, he fell asleep – though his somnolent presence was almost as obnoxious as his conscious one, loud snores accompanying the kitty-come-home of the wheels.

Belle was still reading. – What's in that book that's so interesting, thought Brian irritably, and why is she so damned rude? After a further fifty minutes the train pulled into another small station where, having paused just long enough for passengers to alight, it gave an enormous jerk and set off again. The man in the checked suit woke with a grunt and stared blearily about him.

'Oh, Christ, this is my stop!' Still befuddled he leapt from the moving train . . . only to find he had left his luggage on the rack. Pounding alongside the carriage he had just vacated he shouted to Brian, 'Hey, you! Throw my bag out the window, will you?'

'Certainly!' Brian rose, took hold of the Gladstone bag

and hurled it from the window . . . on the track side. He chuckled at the others as the cries of outrage were lost amid the clanking of the train wheels and the tooting of the whistle. 'That might teach him a few manners!' And for the first time on the journey Belle smiled.

When they arrived at York, sooty and crumpled, Brian ignored Belle's protests when he helped with their luggage. 'Don't worry, I won't throw it onto the track,' he vouched, coaxing a reluctant smile from her. Erin thanked him as he loaded the cases onto a porter's trolley and said it had been very nice travelling with him.

'I've enjoyed it too,' answered Brian, adding hurriedly before they walked away, 'Perhaps we could meet again some time?' He had been delighted to find them alighting at the same stop as himself.

'I'm sure that would be very nice,' replied Erin, but made no definite offer. Doctor Dyson was a very presentable young man, but those looks he had been giving Belle . . . it simply would not do.

And so she escaped him – but not forever. Brian felt sure they would meet again. York was a very small place.

Though her mother's letters had kept her up to date with all the family affairs, Belle didn't mind hearing them again from Nick who happened to be the only one in the house when they arrived. She showed surprise as his voice summoned her when she clomped past his bedroom door on the way to her own. When she pushed the door further open there he was in bed, looking very washed-out. 'Good Lord! I didn't think indispensable people like you were allowed to be ill – what's up?'

'Don't worry, it's not catching,' he told her wanly, motioning her to sit on the bed. 'I bought a pie for lunch yesterday – must've been manky; I've been up and down all night and all morning.' He levered himself up. 'Hey, what about this degree then?'

She censored the question to ask for his news; it might be more enlightening than Mother's. 'Well, let's see . . .' He squirmed his back into the mound of pillows. 'Nothing much to tell about Grandad, he's still digging the praties with Rosie his scribe.' Belle asked if Rosie had chosen a young man yet. 'No, she likes the variety.' Though Nick wasn't gulled like the others. It hadn't taken him long to discover that she was still seeing Timothy. His hopes that it was just a fling had been exploded by the duration of the affair – she was obviously intent on marrying Rabb. But Nick felt that part of the attraction was that Timothy was forbidden fruit; once his sister was legally able to marry the idea might just seem less exciting. For this reason he would not tell Belle or anyone. As long as Rosie didn't get pregnant – and she wouldn't, for he had kept her furnished with preventative means – then he couldn't see the harm in it. 'You know of course,' he went on, 'that I'm managing the York store now?' Belle nodded. Her mother had told her that now the Leeds and Bradford stores were in action Nan was travelling daily to look after the first while Francis had moved into digs in Bradford to manage that store. Neither would be permanent of course, it was far too tiring. Nick told Belle of his hopes that Nan would not overlook him when hiring someone to manage the Leeds store.

'Are there no bounds to your ambition? You've hardly been in charge of this shop for five minutes.'

'And you should see the improvements I've made, Belle! Just think of what I could bring to the Leeds store. Anyway, enough of me. I know you don't like to talk about it, but what about this Master's degree?'

'You're right! I don't want to talk about it.' She rose. 'I've had enough from Mother. I'm off for a wash, then I'm going to meet Gramps. See you later.' She left Nick with the impression that she wasn't keen to go back to university – but then what was she going to do instead? He and the rest of the family were to find that out quite soon.

Belle had been home but two days when she asked her grandfather if he would accompany her to Hungate again. He clapped a hand over his brow. 'Oh, God love us, I thought ye'd got that out o' your bloodstream by now. I'm an old man, Belle, I can't be doin' with all that rough stuff – an' your mother will go up in the air if she finds out.' Belle, stubborn as always, said she would go by herself if he wouldn't take her. 'I don't doubt it! What's your plan this time?'

'No plan. I just thought it might be nice if someone showed an interest in how Lol Kearney is getting on these days.'

'People don't "get on" in that sort of environment, Belle. They just muddle through.'

'All the more reason why we should go and cheer up his day.'

'I don't know why I bother to put up these token arguments! You an' Rosie are a pair. No wonder I'm getting to be all bent up – it comes from being twisted round so many little fingers.' Though Rosie did seem a bit easier to cope with these days and had evidently got over her flirtation with Rabb. Apparently she was quite keen on the young man who was courting her at the moment. Pat hoped he would last a bit longer than the others had done. He rang for John to fetch the carriage. 'I don't know how ye expect to find Lol in that warren. Ye don't even know his address – I trust ye're not suggesting we go knocking on every door?'

'I have accumulated some gumption since the last time,' said Belle, tugging on her gloves. 'We'll stay in the carriage. It's safer and we probably won't need to go knocking on doors, Lol will be out in the street.'

He was. Though it was a couple of years or so since they had seen him last they had no difficulty in recognising him. At fourteen, his height had barely increased, his weight – by the look of him – not at all. His arms and legs were like sticks of charcoal, his mouth still ringed with sores.

'Lol!' Belle beckoned him from the carriage. 'It's Miss Teale – Aunt Belle. Remember?'

He loped up, warily at first, then recognising them his face split into a grin. 'Oh, hello, miss, sir . . .' He didn't know what else to say.

Belle said it for him. 'How nice to see you again, Lol,' she uttered genuinely and reached her hand from the carriage to touch his face. 'Would you like to come for a ride with us?'

'To your house, yer mean?' To Lol there was no point in going for a ride if there was nothing at the terminus. At Peasholme Green he knew there would be food.

'If you like. Then perhaps you could stay to tea with us?'

Lol didn't need asking twice and when the carriage door was opened for him he jumped inside. The hood was up today, for the weather was none too warm. It was all dark and leathery inside.

'Are those your friends?' Belle pointed to a handful of other children who stood, awestruck, in the road. 'Perhaps they would like to come too?'

'Nah!' Lol waved his hand disparagingly. 'We don't want them with us.' He didn't want anyone spoiling his treat, nor sharing the food.

'That's selfish, Lol,' reproved Belle sternly and turned to her grandfather. 'Do you mind . . . ?'

'I don't know why ye bother to ask me,' sighed Patrick. 'Ye've every intention o' taking them whatever I say.'

Belle crooked a finger at the ragged children who came rushing over, clambering onto the wheels of the carriage and pressing excited noses to the shiny bodywork – a morning's work up the spout, groaned John to himself. 'Would you children like to join your friend and take a ride with us?' Like Lol the urchins needed no arm-twisting and piled into the carriage, kneeling and scrambling over the seats, one of them even having the temerity to plant herself on Patrick's lap.

'See, I told yer about my friends an' yer wouldn't believe me,' said Lol boastfully to the others.

'I'm not altogether sure this is a good idea, Belle.' Patrick struggled in discomfort as the fleshless bottom grated his femur. 'Their parents might get the idea they've been abducted.'

'I doubt they'll even notice they're missing,' replied

Belle. 'But don't worry, we'll just keep them long enough for Mrs Howgego to feed them up.'

'She's going to love you.'

Belle turned her attention to Lol as the carriage set in motion. 'How have things been with you since last we met? Are your parents still as hard on you?'

'Haven't got none now,' said Lol unconcernedly. 'They're both dead.'

'Good heavens! But what has become of your brothers and sisters and yourself?'

'A man took 'em away,' Lol informed her. 'Didn't catch me, though. I hid till he'd gone.'

'But where d'you live? Who takes care of you?'

'Don't need nobody to take care o' me,' said Lol disdainfully. 'Take care o' meself. I sleep at Mrs Dalton's on a night. S'just the same as before really.'

'But how d'ye live, son?' enquired Patrick over the lousy little head. Lol asked what he meant. 'Well, d'ye work or what?'

'Sometimes, if I feel like it.'

'An' what d'ye do for food?'

'By the look of him he only eats when he feels like it too,' commented Belle. 'Does this Mrs Dalton provide food?'

He shook his head. 'Too many kids of her own. But don't fuss about Lol – he won't starve.'

'I do worry though, Lol,' said Belle strongly. 'A boy of your age shouldn't have to fend for himself.'

'I'm almost a man,' came the indignant response.

'Man or not you need a proper home and regular meals, not just when you can cadge it.' She made to beseech her grandfather.

'Don't say it, Belle,' he warded her off. 'If there's something ye want to do, do it, but don't involve me for I know who your mother will blame when this gets out.'

Belle formed her lips into a smile. 'Thanks, Gramps. I'll tell Mother you had nothing to do with it.'

'Oh, I'm sure she'll believe ye.'

CHAPTER THIRTY-TWO

Mrs Howgego threw up her hands and declared that there would never be enough food in her pantry to feed this lot. But of course to children who doubtless ate little more than bread and scrape, the meal that she saw as a hastily put-together snack they regarded as a banquet.

'How long can they stay?' Belle asked her grandfather.

'As long as they're out o' the house before your Nan an' your mother get home life'll be a lot safer.'

Though she hated to let them go Belle obeyed his request. After the children had taken their fill and each been provided with an apple and an orange she piled them into the carriage. 'Well, children, have you enjoyed your treat?'

The chorused their assent. Only Lol was silent. But he wouldn't be soon. Belle smiled inwardly, imagining his gratitude when she told him. She wished she could help them all but it just wasn't possible at the moment. The carriage turned into Garden Place where Belle told John to pull up. Garden Place, she thought grimly, what a ridiculous name – not a flower in sight. John climbed down and held the horse's head. 'Show some manners and open the door for Miss Belle,' he ordered Lol.

'I can manage, John, thank you.' Belle alighted, lifting the children out one by one. 'Here we are, you can run along home now.' When they had dispersed she turned to Lol. 'Right, young man, back in you get.' He looked askance. 'Don't you want to come home with me, then?' she asked lightly. Such was the volume of his enthusiasm that the scab at the corner of his mouth split open and trickled blood. 'D'yer mean forever?'

She laughed. 'Yes, for as long as you want anyway.' It

had not occurred to her to consult her family over this. No one had voiced their objection to Lol on his last visit.

'Oh, miss!' He made to grab her, then thought better of it and jigged about on the spot, unable to contain himself.

'Come along then.' She prodded him into the carriage. 'Let's get home and pick out a room for you.'

A room of his own! Lol couldn't believe it. He crowed with delight and hurled himself into the carriage. Belle was about to climb in too when a woman accosted her, dragging one of the children whom Belle had just entertained.

'Are you the lady what give her these?' The woman flourished an apple and orange.

'Yes,' Belle smiled, anticipating gratitude. 'Your little girl had a lovely time, didn't you, dear?'

'Oh, did she? And what sort o' time do you think these children's mothers have had when they look in the street and have someone tell 'em a lady's driven away wi' their bairns? What if I were to come to your street an' drag all the children off? What would you think?'

Belle's lips parted in surprise. 'I would consider myself fortunate that someone had taken an interest in my children's welfare.'

'You think we aren't concerned with their welfare?' More women were wandering out of their houses with the noise. 'You think because we have to live on fifteen bob a week an' can't afford fancy clothes that we don't care what happens to our children?'

Belle was less sure of herself now; the woman was so hostile and a crowd was gathering. She felt the river closing over her head once more. 'I was simply trying to bring them a little happiness.'

'Happiness? And how happy will they be now you've given 'em a taste of how the rich folk live, then clear off an' leave 'em to their own devices? Tell me that. You come sailing in here in your shiny carriage patronising us with your wealth an' tellin' us we don't know how to care for our own children. I'd like to see you feed a family of seven on fifteen shillings a week.'

'I assumed they were neglected,' protested Belle.

The woman was furious. 'Does it take posh clothes an' a full pantry before a mother can show love?' She thrust her face into Belle's. 'I think you'd better go, lady, before I really lose my rag. Go on, get out of here.' She flung the fruit at the would-be philanthropist. 'An' take your charity with you.'

Belle climbed hurriedly into the carriage as the crowd of women closed in on her. The phaeton moved off to the accompaniment of dull thuds as the oranges bounced off the paintwork. Lol looked at her but said nothing. Belle too was silent, waiting until she was home to erupt.

'Of all the ingratitude!' She complained strenuously to her grandfather after relating all that had happened. 'And so contrary. Having the gall to complain about their circumstances, then throwing good food to waste.' She could still picture herself flinching in the carriage as the missiles made contact.

'Maybe they thought you were patronising them,' offered Patrick.

'Patronising? If I was it isn't just a failing of the better-off. I've discovered the lower classes can be patronising, too. They appear to think they have the monopoly on suffering; never spare a thought that one doesn't need to be poor to be able to understand the emotion.'

'Not self-pity from you?' responded her grandfather surprisedly.

'O-oh, I'm just so angry!'

'Ah, 'tis all my fault,' sighed Patrick, picking up the bonnet she had thrown to the floor and laying it on the table. 'I should never've allowed ye to take those children without their mothers' permission. Here, come sit down an' cool your temper in a glass o' lemonade.' He picked up the jug and poured two glasses, looking at Lol as he did so.

Belle caught his meaningful glance and, picking up one of the glasses, handed it to the boy. 'Here, Lol, take your

471

drink out in the garden. I'll be out to join you shortly.' When the child was out of earshot she turned to Patrick. 'I couldn't leave him there, Gramps. I just couldn't. And after all, we do owe him something; he did save my life.'

'What're ye trying to tell me, dear?' asked the man, reseating himself with a glass of whiskey.

'I've told him he can live with us,' she revealed, then went on hurriedly, 'I mean there's plenty of room, isn't there? It's not as if one extra mouth is going to break the bank.'

'It might when it's built like the Grand Canyon.' Patrick swilled his drink round the tumbler.

'Oh, you aren't angry, are you?' she asked in a pained manner.

'Sure, I don't see why that should worry ye when ye never thought to ask my opinion on the matter.'

'You are angry. Oh, Gramps, I'm sorry, I didn't think.'

'That's your trouble, Belle, ye don't think. Ye go storming into a situation like a bull in a field o' heifers, never give a thought to the consequences. That child's mother was right to chastise ye for what ye did. Just 'cause you live a comfortable life doesn't mean ye can take it upon yourself to label those less fortunate as neglectful of their children. Your grandmother and me were poor once but that didn't stop us from loving your mother, from doing the very best we could for her. Those folk can't show their love in the same way as we might now, by making sure their family has good food an' nice clothes, but make no mistake those children are loved whatever their outward appearance. If ye viewed every dirty child as neglected an' wanted to pull it off the street ye'd need a house the size o' ten Buckingham Palaces to hold them all – an' even that's probably an underestimate.'

Belle was forced to admit she had been wrong about the others. 'But Lol's a different case, Grandfather. You must see that. He has no one. Please, you aren't going to throw him out, are you?'

Patrick filtered the whiskey through his teeth. 'Ye know me better than that. I just wish ye hadn't dropped him into me lap without prior warning. I could've used the time to talk your grandmother around. Oh, God, will y'ever look at the child? He's not even housetrained.' He pointed to the garden where Lol was urinating quite openly.

Belle took no notice. 'But can he stay?' she pressed urgently.

'As far as I'm concerned, yes, he can stay,' allowed Patrick. 'But I can't speak for the others.'

'You're the head of the house, Grandfather,' flattered Belle slyly. 'The others will just have to do as you tell them.'

'Like you do, ye mean?' Patrick finished his drink. 'Now look, if I take this lad on I don't want to have any repeat performances of this afternoon.'

'Don't worry,' said Belle. 'I realise I was mistaken in my assessment of those people. Next time I'll make certain I only pick the most deserving cases.'

'Next time,' groaned Patrick, and quickly poured himself another drink.

The atmosphere at the table that evening was tense. It was difficult to speak frankly in the boy's presence without upsetting him, but they might just as well have done for Lol felt the waves of ill-feeling attacking him from all fronts. Apart from Thomasin's displeasure, Erin was most unhappy about her daughter's behaviour. 'I'm sorry Belle has put you in this position, Mother,' she said as the tense meal came to an end and Helen started to collect the plates. 'She'll be disciplined, of course.'

'Why?' demanded Belle.

Erin turned to her coolly. 'I did not address you, young lady. Please be quiet.'

Crossly, Belle grasped a peach and began to slice it. Lol stretched his hand out too, but was stopped by Thomasin's disapproving glare. His hand returned, empty, to his lap. Belle simply pushed the plate of sliced peach in front of him and countered her grandmother's stare with defiance.

Thomasin decided to be blunt. 'So what do you propose we do with your friend, Belle?'

'In what respect, Grandmother?'

'In the respect of work. If the boy's to live here he must contribute the same as everyone else.'

'Well, I had hoped to offer him a little education first, then later we could provide him with a job. I wouldn't't've foreseen any difficulty there with all your businesses.'

'Perhaps he could manage the Leeds store,' muttered Nick under his breath to Rosie, who grinned.

'Are you suggesting I take him into my employ?' Thomasin's voice was tight.

Belle matched it. 'It seems a sensible proposition.' Then she dropped the coolness. 'Please, Nan, don't be difficult. Lol's not asking much.'

'Lol, as I'm aware, isn't asking anything. He's being manipulated like the rest of us.'

'I'm sorry,' Belle had become aloof once more, 'it was rash of me to suppose that my fellow-feeling would be endorsed by the rest of this family. I must apologise to Lol for leading him to believe he would find charity here.'

'Stop it, Belle!' snapped Erin. 'Just cease. 'Tis you who're wrong here. Ye had no right to bring anyone into this house without consulting your grandparents. Ye've placed them in an impossible position. There are societies to deal with children like Lol. Ye oughtn't to assume so much responsibility at your age.'

'If there are societies then why aren't they doing anything about those children?' asked Belle hotly. 'That's the trouble with too many people, they think: oh, it's nothing to do with me, there's a *society* to prevent that sort of thing!'

Erin made a growl of annoyance and obviously found great difficulty in forming a reasonable response. Patrick entered the argument but kept his voice level. 'If there's any blame for this it shouldn't go to Belle alone. I let matters get out of hand. Lol,' he said kindly at the boy's downcast face, 'don't think all this is directed at you.'

Thomasin softened too. 'Mr Feeney's right, Lol, this isn't to be taken personally. It's just the manner in which our grand-daughter chose to act that's not to our liking.'

'So it was wrong of me to practise charity, was it?' said Belle relentlessly. 'Tell me, Nan, if I hadn't done this thing which you all seem to regard as a cardinal sin, would you – or any of you for that matter,' she cast her eyes round the table, 'ever have thought to do the same? Does anyone among you ever spare a thought for children like Lol?'

'Belle, I think ye've caused enough upset for one day,' replied Erin. 'Be silent or go to your room.'

'I will not be silent! It's too pressing a matter. There's thousands like Lol. All right, perhaps it was wrong of me to tell the boy he had a home without consulting anyone, but can you tell me in all honesty that if I had said to you, Mother, or you, Nan, will you give a home to a loveless, needy child, that you would have given your consent unreservedly? Can you? I think not. You're all too busy thinking about yourselves to worry about children like Lol. All except Grandfather. He's the only one besides me who seems to care.'

Patrick moved his head sorrowfully. 'No, no, Belle, ye do your mother and Nan a great injustice. They care, too.'

'Do they? I think you pay them too much credit, Grandfather,' she replied sullenly. 'There's Grandmother and Nick immersed in making money, Mother concerned only with my brain and Rosanna with her string of shallow-minded beaux. None of them gives a damn. If they can truly say they care about these children why isn't this house filled with such as Lol?'

Rosanna tutted and asked, 'May I be excused from listening to this slander?'

'Oh, go on, that's right!' shot Belle as her cousin was granted permission. 'Run away like you always do.'

Instead of being angry Thomasin appeared subdued. 'Well . . .' a false lightness, 'it's certainly an evening for enlightenment.' She crumpled her napkin.

'Belle,' Erin rose. 'Go to your room at once.'

'No,' Thomasin wearily motioned her to sit down. 'Since when was a child in this house punished for speaking the truth?'

'Truth? 'Tis downright impudence.' The skin of Erin's face was mottled.

'No, Erin, I've never shared the belief that young people should only speak when spoken to. If Belle has a valid opinion she has a right to a platform.'

'Oh, she has an opinion all right,' said Erin. 'A very high opinion of herself. And 'tis not just the rudeness I object to but the inaccuracy of her claim. Look at the people we help already through employing them. We can't be expected to carry everybody.'

'But *what about the children?*' cried Belle. 'Who is helping them?'

'All right, Belle.' Thomasin warded off another outburst. 'I think you've made your feelings plain. Let's have a bit of order and talk about this calmly. Now then,' she laced her fingers. 'Lol is welcome to stay with us if he so wishes. He can spend a few months learning his letters, then I'm sure we can find him a job somewhere.' Lol's face shone.

'Thank you, Nan,' replied Belle warmly. 'I'm glad you understand.' She swapped triumphant smiles with Patrick.

'Aye, well, I shan't be so understanding if it happens too many times.'

The atmosphere lightened as coffee was brought in. 'Well now,' said Thomasin after putting the delicate china to her lips. 'We appear to have sorted Lol's future but no mention has yet been made of yours, Belle. Have you decided what sphere you'd like to work in? It's a pity women aren't welcomed into politics, I'm sure you'd do much better than the men, the way you've just knocked us into shape.'

Belle wondered if this was the right time to launch her project, then decided, with a swift glance at her mother's now passive features, to go ahead. She had won both her grandfather and Nan to her side and they were the ones who really mattered, the ones whose word counted. 'I have decided, yes, Nan.' She lipped the coffee cup and cast apprehensive eyes before going on.

476

'Well?' smiled her eager mother. 'Are you going to let us in on the secret?'

'I've decided . . .' oh, God. 'I've decided to dedicate my life to helping children like Lol.' She put down the cup to face them bravely, waiting for her mother's outcry.

There was nothing, not a sound . . . no, that was not quite accurate; there was a collective chink of cups being dashed into saucers.

'Just what exactly will this entail?' asked Thomasin carefully.

Belle hesitated. She must word this correctly or she would lose them again. 'I did a tour of the house yesterday. By my calculations there are two rooms more than you need, even when you have four guests to stay. I'd like your permission to use those and the old schoolroom.'

'Do I interpret you correctly?' said Thomasin. 'You want to bring more children into my house?'

'Yes. I think we could squeeze four into each room quite nicely.'

'Quite nicely?' Erin had found her voice at last. 'What the hell are ye saying, child?'

Belle thumped the table. 'Mother, I do wish you'd stop calling me child!'

'An' what else are ye, might I ask?' Erin rose to her feet, eyes hard in the pale face. 'Playing your childish games . . .'

'Not games. This is a deeply serious attempt to alter society's views.'

'Ye surely don't think I've seen ye this far through university just to let ye throw it all up on a whim? Because that's all it is. I know you. You're only doing it as an act of rebellion. Ye'll be bored stiff with Lol an' his kind in a few weeks.'

'It's not a whim.' Belle regained her patience and tented her fingers. 'I shan't get bored. I've given this very serious thought. In fact I've already informed the university that I shan't be going back to take my Master's degree.'

'What! Belle, I'm not going to allow ye to waste your life!'

'I'm sad you feel that I'd be wasting my life on deprived children, Mother, but I've made up my mind.'

'No!' Erin hauled the girl to her feet. 'I won't sit by an' let ye throw it all away. Don't ye know how privileged ye are to be accepted at university at so young an age?'

Belle gave up the defensive and sprang into attack. 'Mother, I'm sick to death of hearing from everyone how privileged I am and how I'm not to throw it away. What is it for, if not for the good of others? Up until now I've allowed you to dictate my life because you're my mother and I love you. But I can't go on living out your fantasies for you. I'm not you, Mother, I'm me! *Me!*' She thrust a savage jab into her chest.

At Patrick's attempted intervention Erin turned on him. 'See what ye've done, Father? Where all your spoiling has landed us!'

'Don't you think I have a mind of my own?' yelled her daughter. 'Grandfather isn't to blame.'

'Isn't he?' cried Erin. 'Who was the one who started all this by fetching that boy into the house in the first place?'

'For God's sake leave the poor child out of this.'

'Don't you use the Lord's name in such a tone to me!'

'Then stop using Lol as a whipping boy,' returned Belle. 'If there's one person who's totally innocent in all this it's Lol whose only crime was that he saved my life.'

Erin scowled. 'But you told me . . .'

'I know what we told you! That was because we knew how you'd react if you heard I'd been thrown in the Foss by a gang of thugs.'

Erin snatched the table for support. 'Jesus God,' she whispered, then louder as she wheeled on Patrick, 'God! Is this true?'

Heavily Patrick nodded and enlarged on the theme: how he had taken Erin's daughter on a tour of the ghetto, how they had both been attacked and how Lol had pulled Belle from the river.

'And it might never've come to light,' breathed Erin disbelievingly. 'I might never have known just how little you value the safety of my daughter.' Two deep clefts appeared between her eyes. 'I should've seen the way this was going when ye started talking about wishing ye'd done more to help them, saying ye were too old to start now. Well, ye certainly found a way round that didn't ye, Father? Instead o' doing it yourself ye found a silly young girl to do your bidding. I should never've come to live here. I could've controlled her on my own. But what chance has a mother against a silly old fool who puts stupid notions into her head? Well, ye've done a grand job, Father. Ye've turned a daughter against her own mother and ruined all our lives.'

'Mother, try to see I'm not against you,' Belle pleaded. 'And it wasn't Grandfather who set the wheels in motion. Do you recall the time you took me to see the place where you were born?'

Erin let out a hysterical laugh. 'Oh, God, that's funny! That's great. Here I am blaming everybody for something that I brought about meself. Oh, Mother o'God, that's hilarious.'

'Mother, please.' Belle laid a hand on her arm.

Erin shook it off. 'Say you're wrong an' we'll forget all this bad feeling,' she asked abruptly.

Belle looked at her pityingly. 'I can't, Mother. I'm sorry but I've made up my mind. It's something I must do.'

Erin addressed her father again. 'I'm begging your forgiveness. I hope ye'll not bear ill-will for the things I said. I meant none of it.'

Patrick reached for her fingers though failed to make contact. ''Tis already forgotten.'

'Then please, please will ye try to talk some sense into her stubborn head an' tell her how she wrongs herself?'

Patrick looked at his grand-daughter. – Please don't let me down, her eyes were saying. 'Erin, muirnin . . .'

'Oh!' Erin spun from the table impatiently, then veered back. 'Mother, for pity's sake surely you're not going to play accessory to such a crime? This is your house as well as Father's. Tell them what fools they're being.'

'Belle, your mother has a point, you know,' said Thomasin. 'There must be other ways you can help those

479

less-fortunate while putting your education to good use at the same time.'

'But I intend to put it to good use,' replied Belle calmly. 'I don't just propose to fetch these urchins from the streets simply to put them in glass showcases. These children have brains too, but never have the good fortune to stretch them.' She held up her hand to stall her grandmother's interruption. 'I know you're about to acquaint me with the Education Act. Well, that is all very nice for those to whom it applies, but what of children like Lol who have no parents? Who's to care if he goes to school or not?'

'There aren't many such as Lol,' replied Thomasin.

'Aren't there? Have you found that out for yourself or did you read it in some book? And even if it were true, even if there were but a handful of children who had slipped the authority's net, would that make my job less important? Though, at this point, I have to confess I'm not so much interested in educating them as in caring for them. Who has the right to deny them that?'

Thomasin beseeched Erin with her hands. 'What else can I say?'

'You could forbid her to use your home for her purposes,' said the woman earnestly. 'You must.'

Thomasin fought with herself. She could sympathise with both sides of the argument. She persisted a little longer with her grand-daughter. 'Why don't you put a few more years on your back, love?'

'In the hope that I'll forget about it?' asked Belle. 'Sorry, Nan, I don't see any point in delaying the matter. In the interlude some of those children may die.'

'Eh, you're as stubborn as your mother,' breathed Thomasin. 'One of you'll have to give.'

'I think I should say that if I don't receive your permission,' said Belle, 'I shall find myself living accommodation amongst those whom I wish to help.'

'I think you're forgetting, madam, that you're still under age!' snapped Erin.

'I'm not so sure I like your tone either,' contributed Thomasin. 'It stinks of blackmail.'

'I didn't intend it to,' replied Belle. 'I just want you all to know that nothing is going to stop me from helping these children.'

'And just who d'ye think is going to support ye while y'indulge yourself?' barked Erin.

'I don't expect anyone to subsidise me, Mother. I shall find work that can be undertaken from home. While I was at university I had some sketches accepted by a women's journal, so I shall probably continue in that field – or maybe tuition.'

'You have been doing a lot of thinking!' retorted Erin.

'Erin, the child's obviously got strong feelings on this,' said Patrick, then, including Thomasin in his proposition, added, 'Don't ye think 'twould be better if she carried out her plan from here instead of having to live in some ghetto?'

Thomasin agreed. 'As much as I understand your feelings Erin, your father has it right. Belle isn't going to change her mind. What she proposes would be better done under our supervision.'

'It never occurs to either of ye to simply forbid it,' replied her daughter angrily, then to Belle, 'There are places, you know, where a young woman can be locked up until she comes to her senses.'

'If that's what you wish to do then I can't stop you,' answered Belle, looking directly into her mother's eyes. 'But could you do it knowing that it would make me hate you for the rest of my life?'

Erin's eyes were all whites, her lips fused into a bitter gash. There was a blur of movement and a sudden crack, followed by Erin's swift exit. Belle fended off the attempts of consolation from her grandparents and stood looking at the door through which her mother had departed, the imprint of Erin's hand spreading scarlet fingers across her cheek. It was the last contact the two would make for some time.

CHAPTER THIRTY-THREE

When the sobbing had ceased Erin pulled herself from the disarranged counterpane and moved to the window where she flopped onto a chair. Outside was brilliant sunshine, in here desolation. She stared sightlessly at the bark of the tree that grew near the window, her mind empty for the while, until a Red Admiral butterfly settled upon the craggy surface catching her attention as it spread its wings to the sun.

The colour came and went as the butterfly alternated the position of its wings, one second a splash of brightness, the next almost disappearing, its duller underside merging with the bark of the tree. It stayed for a long time basking in the sunshine. She watched it closely; following the pattern of its wings took her mind off her troubles. Suddenly there was another flash of colour and the butterfly was gone, snatched away to feed a hungry robin. Startled, she continued to gaze at the spot where the insect had been for some seconds, lips parted in protest.

Then she relaxed into despondency again. – Why should I be surprised? she asked herself dolefully. Isn't that the vein of my whole life? Everything I ever prized snatched away in the blink of an eye. Sam, the baby, and now Belle. She recalled that dreadful time when she had been left alone with a crippled toddler with nothing to look forward to, no future in sight, and then she had discovered Belle's talent and the sun had come from behind the cloud. It wasn't going to come out this time. However brightly it might shine out there, in her mind was an infinite eclipse. Full circle: her parents had striven so hard to be free of those dreaded courtyards and now their grand-daughter was intent on taking them back there.

She did not go down again that evening. The family,

knowing how this must have affected Erin, did not expect her to. But when she did not show herself at breakfast the following day Patrick asked the manservant if Mrs Teale had requested anything to be taken to her room.

'Not to my knowledge,' replied John. 'Cook was unaware that Mrs Teale was ill.' He knew quite well of course, as did all the other staff, that Erin's absence was not due to illness, yet must undergo this charade for propriety's sake. 'If you wish I could inform Mrs Howgego to send a tray up.' He enjoyed relaying orders to Cook.

Patrick declined the offer. 'Mrs Teale may wish to be left undisturbed. I'll call in an' see her meself after breakfast.'

But it was Belle who first encountered Erin when she had breakfasted and was taking Lol to the schoolroom. Erin came along the landing towards them. Belle tendered a wary smile and said, 'Good morning, Mother, I hope you . . .' Her voice petered out as Erin waltzed straight past without acknowledgement. She might not have been there. 'Mother?' Belle's eyes followed Erin to the staircase. 'Mother!'

'Ah, Helen,' said Erin on meeting with the maid. 'I'm afraid I overslept this morning. Will ye extend my apologies to Mrs Howgego an' ask if she'd be so kind as to pack a little something for me to take with me to work. I shan't have time for breakfast.'

'Very good, ma'am.' The maid bobbed and went to do as she was bidden. Still not acknowledging her daughter's proximity Erin proceeded on her way.

''Smy fault,' provided Lol as Belle, with disturbed expression, moved him along to the schoolroom. 'Yer shouldn't've brung me here.'

'Nonsense,' she replied. 'You couldn't continue to live as you had been doing. Mother will come round, you'll see.'

'Not while I'm here,' insisted Lol. 'She dun't like me.'

'That isn't the case. She's just angry at me.'

'Then why did she pretend I weren't there?'

'She's thinking to get back at me, that's all. People are like that. Come now, let's get on with some learning.'

'Aunt Belle?' started Lol, using the title which Belle had instructed him to use, even though he thought it silly as the girl wasn't much older than himself. 'I thought you didn't care for all this schoolin' lark.'

'I didn't particularly enjoy it, no,' answered Belle.

'Then why are you makin' me do all these lessons? Is it just so's yer can have someone to bully like yer ma bullied you?'

Belle cuffed his ear lightly. 'There comes a time in everyone's life when one is faced with tasks which one would rather not do but which must be done.'

'Ho, does one?' Lol pranced along in front of her, hand on hip.

Belle threatened retribution. 'And the first of those tasks is obviously to teach you how to act in the presence of a lady. Come here while I give you a drubbing.'

Lol ran off, laughing.

Predictably, the first lesson made little impression on Lol who was unused to sitting still for such long periods. He listened assiduously for some time until Belle's repetition of 'C A T. C A T.' became just too much and what concentration he had mustered lapsed into boredom. 'Can't we do summat else?' he finally burst out. 'I'm sick o' writin'.'

'But we've hardly done anything, Lol,' scoffed Belle. 'You surely didn't imagine you were going to be able to read and write without some effort? Come, just copy a few more letters.'

Lol complied, but it was not long before he started to fidget again. Belle gave in. 'I think that's enough for one morning. I'm sure I wouldn't want you to feel as I did about schooling. Let's go and ask John to bring the carriage round. I've an urge to scan the streets again. You can be a great help to me in that direction, Lol. You'll be able to point out all the children who are most in need.'

'Bring 'em back 'ere yer mean?' he said doubtfully.

'Of course, that's the whole idea.' She picked up his chagrin. 'Now what's the matter with you?'

'I thought it were gonna be just me livin' 'ere,' he muttered into his shirt-front.

'Don't be selfish, Lol. I should've thought that you above all people should understand why I'm doing this.'

'No, I don't. Why are yer?'

'That seems to me an unnecessary question, Lol. Just look around you. Is it fair that I should live like this and other people live as you've been doing for years?'

He shrugged. 'In't no right nor wrong about it. 'S just the way it is. Some folk are rich, some poor.'

'But didn't you ever feel bitter when you saw, say, a restaurant full of rich people stuffing themselves with goodies while you perhaps hadn't had a meal in days? Didn't you ever feel a twinge of injustice when you looked in a butcher's window and saw a juicy chop that you'd never be able to afford?'

Lol screwed up his nose and shook his head. 'No – I'd just pinch it.'

Belle sighed. 'Well, there'll be no call for any of that now. If you want something you only have to ask.'

'You mean if I wanted that gold clock over there I'd just have to ask an' you'd give it me?'

'That is not what I meant, Lol. You can't eat a clock. I meant that you'll never go hungry again, never be cold.' She reached for his hand. 'Never want for anything, least of all affection.'

'Yer mean, yer love me?'

This was stretching things a little; Belle was not one for sentiment. But she didn't want to hurt him. 'Well . . . I'm very fond of you.'

'Cor!' he beamed, then added, 'I love you an' all.' She made the mistake of asking why. 'Cos yer gimme things,' he told her.

'That's not love,' she informed him.

'Innit? Well, I still like yer any road. Nobody gimme half the things you 'ave.'

'Come on,' she smiled. 'Let's go see if anyone else is

485

in need of our assistance.' She led him down to the kitchen where she asked Cook for a basket to be filled with food from the larder.

'Well, I don't know as I should, Miss Belle,' said a wary Mrs Howgego. 'The mistress isn't here to give her consent.'

'If there's any comeback just say I ordered you to do it, Cook,' replied Belle and moving to the larder frustrated any other protest. 'Now, let's see . . . plenty of eggs. Put half a dozen of those in and one of those pies . . .'

'I can't let you have that, Miss Belle,' complained Mrs Howgego. 'That's for supper.'

'Oh well, put in a jar of raspberry preserve, there's plenty of that.' She pointed to the store of tea. 'Some of that,' the finger moved over the shelves. 'Some of that, a bit of that, and that bit of cheese. That should do.'

'Can I be allowed to ask what you want with all this?' enquired Cook.

'Call it a peace-offering,' replied Belle, hooking her arm through the handle of the basket.

Cook gave an exclamation as Belle and the boy left through the kitchen exit. 'That girl, I shall never weigh her up. She's as many sides to her character as facets to a diamond – and she's twice as capable of cutting through things. One minute she's behaving like Lady Manners, the next she's divvying all our belongings to the poor. Anyway, come on, Vinnie, don't just stand there gawpin', that table wants scrubbing.'

'You know, I think it'd be a better idea if we didn't take the carriage,' Belle told Lol as they crunched down the gravelled drive.

'I don't think any of it's a good idea,' answered Lol unhappily. 'At least with the carriage we'd be able to make a quick getaway. Wha' happens if they set on yer like yesterday?'

'Don't be such a pessimist, Lol. I'm sure they'll accept my apology quite graciously.'

486

'What's a pissimist?' He laughed aloud. 'Oh, I know, it's somebody who can't hit the pot.'

'Don't be vulgar, Lol. A pessimist is someone who always looks on the black side of everything.'

'Like your mam?'

She smiled sadly. 'You could say that.'

John was not at all pleased to be told his young mistress no longer needed the carriage after he had all but broken his neck getting it ready. Belle compromised. 'Very well, you can take us so far, then wait.'

The short journey was hardly worth his effort but he was glad to doze while Miss Belle and the ragamuffin went off about their business.

Despite Belle's claims about the acceptance of her apology she could not help the tremble of apprehension that jellied her legs. 'You'll have to show me the way,' she told her companion. 'Can you remember where we picked up those children yesterday?'

He led her there and at her further request took her to the door of the woman who had abused her the previous day. It was impossible for Belle to square her shoulders, but she showed her spirit by rapping briskly on the wood. Whilst waiting for it to be answered she swapped wondering glances with the boy.

'Oh, it's you, is it?' The woman's face hardened when she saw the identity of the callers. 'I thought it were doctor. What d'you want, then?'

'I've come to apologise,' said Belle without preface. 'My actions and words yesterday were thoughtless and inexcusable. This is small recompense, I know,' she held out the basket, 'but I hope you will accept it and not think too harshly of me. I was genuinely trying to help, however clumsily.'

The woman's face melted at the edges but was still suspicious as she reached for the basket to examine the contents. She did not speak.

'I know it's barely adequate to make up for the worry I must have caused you,' said Belle.

'No . . . no, it's very thoughtful,' answered the woman

dubiously, and stepped aside for them to enter. 'Will you take tea with us?'

'That's most forgiving.' Belle smiled in relief. Shadowed by Lol she stepped into the little house, which despite its spartan condition, was neat and clean.

'I'm sorry we're in such a mess, Miss ... ?' Belle provided her name. 'Miss Teale. Sit down an' I'll make a brew.'

Belle's gaze went to the child in the bed next to the fireplace. Ignoring the three other children who gaped at her she moved across to the bed. 'I was waiting for the doctor when you called,' explained the woman, then hastily added that her name was Shaw. 'She was took poorly in t'night.'

It was one of the children whom Belle had abducted yesterday. The young woman placed a hand to the glistening forehead. A pair of feverish eyes opened to observe her over the ragged blanket. 'She's very hot.'

'Aye, an' in such pain, too.' Mrs Shaw handed a cup of tea to Belle – but not to Lol whose class did not demand this courtesy – and the young woman thanked her. 'Been cryin' out with it all night. That's why I had to send for the . . .' She was interrupted by a knock at the door and someone inserted his head into the room.

'Mrs Shaw? I'm the doctor.' He opened the door wider and came in, starting as he came face to face with Belle. 'Miss Teale!'

'Doctor Dyson.' Belle did not register her own surprise so openly, as though it was as natural for him to be here as it was for her. She stepped aside for him to approach the bed. He too felt the child's head, then pulled down the covers to make a fuller examination.

'The boy who came for me told me she'd been crying with the pain, is that correct?'

Mrs Shaw said it was. 'Keeps drawing her legs up to her chest, Doctor.'

The child cried out as Brian placed his palm on the right side of her abdomen, where a slight swelling could be seen through the skin. Even though he was quick to remove his hand she continued to sob for her mammy who came rushing up to comfort her.

'How long has this persisted?' asked Brian.

'Since late yesterday, Doctor. She's been sick an' all. I thought maybe it was 'cause she hadn't . . . done her number two, but it seems too bad for that.'

Brian nodded grimly. 'I'd like to perform a more detailed examination. May I have some water, please?' A short time later he was unrolling his sleeves.

'Is it serious, Doctor?' asked the anxious mother.

'Pretty serious, I'm afraid, Mrs Shaw.' He rummaged in his bag. 'I'm going to give her something for the pain.' A short pause while he did this. 'Then I'll have to leave her for a while, as I have more calls to make, but I shall return as soon as I'm able.'

'Should I keep putting the hot water bottles round her, Doctor?'

'By all means . . . and prop up her shoulders a little; that may make her more comfortable.' He washed his hands.

'She is going to be all right, isn't she, Doctor?' asked a worried Mrs Shaw.

'I shall do my utmost to help her,' evaded Brian.

'I'm sure you will, Doctor. Would you like a cup of tea now?'

'No, thank you, Mrs Shaw. I'd sooner get on with my rounds.' He snapped his bag shut and made for the door.

'Just a minute, Doctor,' called Mrs Shaw, reaching for a pot on the mantel.

'Don't concern yourself over payment for the moment,' replied Brian. 'Just take care of her until I come back – and don't give her any food, just tiny sips of water if she asks for it.' He opened the door. Belle, completely taken aback by all this, was poised with empty cup in hands. 'Are you going my way, Miss Teale? Perhaps I could give you a ride?'

On another occasion Belle might have spurned such attention but the fact of meeting the young doctor in such insalubrious quarters had snared her interest. Putting an arm around Lol she thanked Mrs Shaw for the tea whilst handing back the cup, and made to leave. 'And I hope your little girl is soon well again. Would you think it an intrusion if I called to check on her progress tomorrow?'

'That's kind of you, miss,' answered the woman. 'An' I'm sorry I was so short with you the other day.'

'You were perfectly entitled to be,' forgave Belle. 'It was stupid of me. I hope the groceries go a little way to salving my wrongdoing.'

Mrs Shaw replied that they did and thanked her again. The young woman and her charge followed the doctor out.

Brian made as if to help her into the dogcart but she stood back. 'Thank you but I have my own carriage waiting up there. I followed you because I'm concerned to know more about the child in there.' Brian ran a finger down the side of his freckled nose, smiling. 'And what is your interest, Miss Teale? I must say, I was most surprised – delightedly so – to encounter you in such a district.'

'Your surprise can surely be no greater than my own. I'd expected you to hold your surgery in a much more genteel area.'

'I'm most flattered to hear I've been the subject of your mental exercise, Miss Teale,' he grinned. 'From our last meeting I would've imagined that when we parted I would be completely obliterated from your lovely brain.'

'What can be lovely about a brain?' responded Belle tiredly.

'Oh, to a medical man it is a wondrous thing. And as for my surgery it's just around the corner in Pavement.'

'Then I should imagine the majority of your patients are drawn from the slum areas,' guessed Belle. 'The dividends for such a practice must be limited.'

'If by dividends you refer to pecuniary gains then you're absolutely right,' conceded Brian. 'But I prefer to measure success in terms of effect rather than profit. Money was not a prime consideration when I decided to join the medical profession. My main interest is the welfare of my fellows and especially the sections of the community of which my colleagues seem sadly neglectful. That in itself I find strange. Supplied with the knowledge that it's from districts such as this that epidemics are spread, one would think the entire medical profession of York would centre its skills here, if only out of self-interest. With improved sanitary facilities there wouldn't be half the disease there is. And this isn't the worst street I've seen, by a long chalk. I persuaded a colleague of mine to show me round the other slum areas. My God, I've never witnessed anything like it. Some of those yards down Walmgate defy description.'

'I don't need a description, I've already seen them,' murmured Belle.

'You have?' frowned Brian. 'Forgive me for finding that so unlikely but it's extremely difficult to visualise a young lady of your standing in such circumstances.'

'It was my mother's idea, Doctor,' answered Belle with a smidgeon of defiance. 'She took me there in order to cure my holier-than-thou attitude.'

'Yet it didn't have the desired effect I fear,' teased Brian.

She bridled at first, then gave a dry laugh. 'If I've been unduly rude in the past I didn't intend to be.'

Brian smiled. 'Miss Teale, I deal with much ruder people than yourself. I recognise the symptoms of inclemency.'

She was immediately on her guard once more. 'Oh? Pray give me your diagnosis, Doctor.'

His expresssion was soft with understanding. 'I think, Miss Teale, that you have suffered much in the past due to your unfortunate spinal disability and have developed this aura of loftiness as a means of protection. It forbids people from making approaches to you.'

'Really? How very perspicacious of you. What a pity this aura of mine does not deter interfering medical men. Perhaps you could give me the information that I originally requested so that Lol and I may be on our way.'

Brian cursed himself for not recognising the depth of her sensitivity. 'I meant no insult. Only to sympathise.'

'The child, Doctor Dyson,' said Belle. 'Well, you

certainly didn't imagine that I stood to listen to your gossip purely from enjoyment?'

'Ah yes, the child,' sighed Brian, climbing into the small carriage.

'Well?' snapped Belle.

'She'll die,' said Brian bluntly.

Belle was shocked. 'If it's a question of money . . .'

'Why do you people have to bring everything down to the level of money?' rejoined the doctor testily, then calmed himself. 'I apologise . . . It's not you who angers me but the fact that there's a child in there who needs my help and all I can do is stuff her full of morphine.'

'You really mean she's going to die?' gasped Belle. 'But you told her mother . . .'

'What did I tell her?' he demanded. 'I said I'd do all I could to help her, which in effect is nothing.'

'But aren't you even going to send her to hospital?'

'What's the point? If she's going to die it might as well be at home.'

'But you must!'

'Dammit, the child has appendicitis! No surgeon I know would be willing to touch her. There's poison in her gut and no way to syphon it. She's going to die and I can't do a bloody thing about it.' He turned his anguished face from her, whipped the horse savagely and the dogcart jerked away, leaving a dumbfounded Belle on the pavement. Mother of God! She had taken that child yesterday and crammed its shrunken belly full of rich food, stuffed it to bursting point. What effect must that have had on a stomach that only ever saw gruel or bread?

'Where we off now?' She looked at Lol vaguely. 'Yer said yer wanted me to help yer find more kids like me.'

She only half-emerged from her stupor. 'I don't think we'll bother today, Lol.'

He squinted up at her. 'What's up? Yer've gone all pale.'

'I don't feel very well at all.' She reached out to him and he supported her.

'Soft article! Yer should've got a ride wi' the doc 'stead of havin' to find that John.'

'I'll be fine,' said Belle, then stopped to face him. 'Oh, Lol, you heard what the doctor said: she's got something wrong with her stomach and she's going to die.' At his incomprehension she said loudly, 'Don't you see? It's all that food she ate yesterday. It's damaged her insides.'

Lol scoffed. 'Don't be daft. It didn't do owt to me, did it? An' I trenched like a good'n.'

'Yes, but she's much smaller than you, Lol. Only a baby. Oh, what have I done?' They began to walk again, Belle worrying at her lip with shaking fingers. 'I've told Mrs Shaw I'll call tomorrow. How can I stand there looking at the child knowing it was me who caused her suffering?'

'She'll be all right,' replied the boy unconcernedly. 'Away, let's go 'ome an' get Mrs H. to serve us a plate of her cakes. I'm starvin'.'

Belle told no one else of her fears – not even her grandfather – it was too horrible. There she'd been, accusing them of neglecting their children, thinking that she was much more qualified to care for their needs, and how had she shown that proficiency? She had abducted those unfortunate children from their homes, filled one of them so full of food that its insides had burst, then taken it back to its mother who must now watch it die.

Lol grew impatient at her prolonged attack of guilt and sneaked off to play a practical joke on the maid. By the evening Belle's worry had expanded and, unassuaged by fitful sleep, the morning saw it achieve unbearable dimensions. Though she had no desire for breakfast she was forced to show herself at the table.

No one commented on her poor appetite, attributing it to the rift that had set in between her and Erin. After drinking half a cup of tea Belle could wait no longer for Lol to satiate his appetite and rose with the excuse that she would go and prepare his lessons for that day and he could join her when he had finished doing his impersonation of a pig.

'I've got me jobs to do first,' said Lol, munching. He had been designated a number of small tasks around the house such as cleaning the brass letter plate and bringing in the coal.

'That's fine,' replied Belle. 'Come when you've finished, then.' It would give her a chance to do what she must.

Instead of going to the schoolroom she went through the hall, picking up a cape on the way, and set off towards Hungate. It took great courage to set her knuckles at that door, but she must know one way or the other.

Her knock was answered by one of the children. 'Is your mother at home?' she asked. The child nodded. 'May I come in?' The child nodded again and stepped aside.

When she stepped into the room it was to face a dishevelled Brian who was in the motion of unrolling his shirt-sleeves. He gave her barely a glance. His crumpled clothes, untidy hair and circles of fatigue beneath his eyes signified that he had been here all night. Her automatic glance was for the bed by the fireplace. The blankets had been pulled over the child's face. Mrs Shaw, stricken with grief, rocked to and fro at the bedside. Brian finished straightening his hair and came towards Belle, speechlessly drawing her aside. But the girl resisted, unable to tear her eyes from the bed. He continued to press her to the door. 'There's nothing you can do here, Miss Teale'.

Wordlessly, Belle allowed herself to be led outside. Even on the pavement she found it hard to voice her distress. Finally she managed to force out the word, 'When?'

Wincing, Brian reached up to grasp the knotted muscles in his shoulder, kneading them. 'Fifteen minutes ago.' Glancing round he saw there was no carriage. 'Can I get you a cab?'

She shook her head dazedly. 'I only live at Peasholme Green . . . next to The Black Swan.' She had divulged what he had omitted to ask her yesterday. Somehow he would find the excuse to visit her. Despite his own weariness he noticed the whiteness of her face and wondered out loud at her involvement with this family.

'The day before yesterday,' she revealed mechanically, 'I came to this street, loaded half a dozen children – including that one in there – into my carriage and took

494

them back to the house for what I vainly considered to be a treat.' He frowned, his mind dulled by the night's exactment. 'I gave them carte blanche in the larder, Doctor Dyson; let them eat whatever took their fancy.'

'Of all the . . . !' Brian reared in anger. 'Do you realise what you've done?'

'Yes, I . . .'

'I've been forced to sit by that young child's bed watching that racked little face go through its death agony, and all because of your stupidity!'

'I only thought to inject a little happiness into her dreary life,' came Belle's weak protest.

'Did you indeed? Are you certain it was her welfare you had at heart, or was it merely an exercise in self-indulgence? God, the times I've seen it happen! You'd be amazed at the amount of people there are like you, Miss Teale. Oh, you surely didn't think you were unique? Oh no! There's an abundance of little rich girls like you playing at Lady Bountiful, wealthy housewives bored with their circle of friends so they seek out new toys and call it their charity work. Well frankly, Miss Teale, your sort makes me sick! I just hope you think your spree was worth the death of a child.'

With this he strode away up the street.

CHAPTER THIRTY-FOUR

When Patrick arrived home from his work on the evening of the same day Mrs Howgego sought his attention. He perched on one of the kitchen stools to remove his soil-encrusted boots; it was a habit born of old custom. Before the advent of servants Thomasin would never countenance the use of the front entrance in muddy footwear. Rosanna and he always parted company at the gate.

'Well now, Mrs Howgego, an' what can we be doing

for you? Jaze, that's better.' He brought one of his feet to rest on a knee while he massaged his toes.

'It's Miss Belle, sir,' said Cook. 'We've not seen her all day . . . well, I wouldn't normally think there was anything odd about that but young Lol here says she's shut herself in her room an' won't come out.'

Patrick turned his attention to the boy who was trying to comfort his insatiable appetite with a lump of sponge cake. 'What's all this, Lol?'

Lol champed as he spoke. 'I went up for me lessons this mornin' an' she weren't there. So I came down to 'elp Cook.'

'To see if there was owt he could scoff, he means,' pronounced Mrs Howgego, adding salt to a saucepan on the stove.

'Anyroad,' Lol continued, 'when I got chucked out o't'kitchen I went back to t'schoolroom an' she still weren't there so I tapped on her bedroom door.' Patrick asked if she was in there. 'Aye, but she didn't come out. Just shouted that she weren't feelin' too good an' lessons were cancelled for today an' for me to find summat useful to do.'

'So he came down here to fill his belly again,' snorted Cook. 'Well, when he told me Miss Belle was poorly I sent Helen – oh, that's another thing! She wants to hand her notice in . . . anyway I'll see the mistress about that. I sent Helen up to see if she wanted a tray but Miss Belle sent her away. She's been up there all day.'

'Have ye told Mrs Teale?' asked Patrick.

'She's not in yet, sir. You're the first to know.' Not that there'd be much point in telling her, thought Cook, who was aware of how things lay between mother and daughter.

'Very well, I'll go and see what I can do. Thanks for telling me, Mrs Howgego. Pass us me slippers will ye, Lol?' Lol jumped from his stool and transferred the slippers that sat on the hearth to the old man's hand. 'Thank ye, boyo.' Patrick slipped his feet into them, then went to find out what was amiss upstairs.

Midway up the staircase he met with Rosanna who was

in the act of flouncing down. 'Oh, good, Gramps. Look, can you do anything about Belle? She's locked herself in and I'd like to get into our room if it's possible. Honestly, I can't see why I should still have to share with her when we're hardly children any more.'

'First things first,' replied Patrick, breathing heavily as he took the rest of the stairs. 'You go down an' wait in the drawing room. I'll get no sense out of her if you're leppin' about on the landing.' If it isn't one it's the other, he thought as Rosanna descended. He reached Belle's room and tapped at the door, calling her name softly. There was no response and he was prepared to knock again when the door slowly opened a fraction. Speechlessly she let him in and wandered over to stand by the window, staring out.

'Cook said ye'd been up here all day,' Pat told her. 'She omitted to mention ye'd joined a silent order.' She flashed a brief look of apology, then went back to staring from the window. 'Well?' She looked at him again. 'Are ye going to volunteer the information or do I have to resort to torture?'

She sighed. 'I'm not ill, if that's what they told you.'

'Sure, I've been told nothing.' He moved to stand beside her at the window. 'Come on now, ye've never had secrets from your old grandfather.' Still she was unresponsive. He laid a gnarled hand on her shoulder and gripped it encouragingly.

The face that turned to his was devoid of moisture – Belle was not given to tears – but the expression it bore advertised the torment she was going through. 'It's not a secret you'll want to share, Gramps.'

'Tell me anyway.'

'I'm responsible for someone's death,' she blurted. 'A little child of four years.' She searched for the shock on his face but there was only puzzlement. 'Those children I brought home the day before yesterday; she was one of those. I sat there and watched her stuff herself with cakes and pastry and jelly and cream, laughed at the way her cheeks pouched as she and the others gorged themselves.' She looked at the floor. 'Then, when I went yesterday to apologise to the mother I found the child desperately ill. She died this morning.'

'But that doesn't mean to say you're responsible!' Patrick tried to reason with her.

'Yes, it does! Don't you see, Grandfather? It was due to all that unaccustomed richness that her insides couldn't cope. I'm responsible. I caused her death as surely as if I'd fed her poison.'

'Ye can't possibly know . . .'

'Would you accept a doctor's word?' she asked dully.

'He said you were to blame?' Patrick was aghast.

'In no uncertain terms. He made it very plain what he thought of people such as me, the "interferers" who go where we aren't wanted and cause nothing but distress.'

'Then he's talking out of his rear end,' expostulated her grandfather. 'My God, it'd be a poor show if everyone thought like that: mind your own business, it doesn't concern ye. Where would we be without the Shaftesburys, the Tukes and the Nightingales? They were all dubbed as interferers when they began.'

'I can hardly be compared to any of those.'

'Why not? Ye care, don't ye? They all had to start somewhere. One day folk will recognise the good you're attempting to do.'

'I don't think so.'

'Sure, you're not giving up? Where's all the fighting talk from the other night? There's people out there waiting for your help. Don't let this one unfortunate incident spoil your whole ambition.'

'Oh, I don't know,' sighed Belle. 'Perhaps the doctor was right. Maybe I am spurred by selfish motives.'

'Gob, he must be a terrible clever bloke this doctor fella,' exclaimed Patrick. 'He's succeeded where your own mother failed, an' God knows she put up a devilish fight. Come on, Belle, don't tell me the man's got the better of ye.'

She was thoughtful for a span. 'I'm going to have to think very carefully about it all, Gramps.'

'Well, at least y'are thinking. That's a good sign. Won't

ye come downstairs with your old grandpater an' have a spot o' crack till supper? Give your cousin a chance to get into her room.' He waited until she gave a tight smile, linked arms with him and the pair of them went down.

They had not been long in the drawing room, Patrick sipping whiskey, Belle a glass of orange juice, when the maid informed them that there was a visitor. 'A Doctor Dyson, sir.'

'Oh, dash,' said Belle. 'How do I get through the hall without bumping into him?'

'Let the fella drive ye from your own drawing room? I think not. Anyway, I want to see this hard man. Send him in, Helen.'

The doctor was shown in, hanging back when he saw Patrick. He had hoped to be allowed to see Miss Teale alone. 'Come in, Doctor,' invited Patrick unsmilingly as the maid took the visitor's coat away. 'I can see ye expected to find your target unguarded but there's a few words I'd like to put to ye.'

Brian came forward awkwardly. 'I think I may be able to guess what those words might be, sir, and let me say you would be well within your rights to voice them. However,' he glanced at Belle who had not acknowledged him, 'I hope that I may be permitted to offer vindication before you do so.'

'I'm a fair man, Doctor Dyson. Go ahead.' Patrick did not, as he would to any other guest, offer the man a drink.

Brian turned a penitent face to the young woman. 'Miss Teale, this morning I made certain accusations against yourself. It's no excuse to say that I had been without sleep for twenty-four hours and was lacking my normal sensibilities, it was unforgiveable and quite without justification. I can well imagine what torment my impulsive tirade must have put you through. I can only throw myself on your good nature and trust that you will employ the same charity as you showed Mrs Shaw and forgive me.'

'Then, my grand-daughter didn't cause the child's death?' asked Patrick, who felt in a way that he shared Belle's responsibility.

Brian shook his head. 'I'm afraid I allowed frustration to take control of my tongue. The child was ill with appendicitis, from which she might very well have suffered had she taken her usual meal of bread and butter.'

'You mean you allowed me to stew all day until you plucked up the decency to tell me the truth?' ejaculated Belle, looking at him for the first time.

'I share your disgust, Miss Teale.' Brian picked at his cuffs. 'It was wrong of me to blame you for my own inadequacies. Oh, I'd such big ideas! I was going to be a doctor and make the lame to walk, the blind to see . . . Such pomposity. It was anger at myself that gave rise to this morning's outburst. Unfortunately you happened to be in the way. I cannot apologise profusely enough.'

'Nothing you can say will make amends,' spat Belle.

Patrick intervened. 'Belle, the man's had the decency to humble himself, don't make him eat dirt. Here, doctor, come sit down. Will ye take a drink with me?'

Brian thanked him, then looked to Belle who remained sullen. 'I can see I've caused you great distress.'

'Yes, you have!' The blackness of her expression was half-concealed by the hand which propped up her chin.

'Now, Belle.' Patrick handed a drink to the doctor. When she looked at her grandfather he made a prompting motion with his mouth.

She sighed. 'Very well, I accept your explanation, Doctor, and your apology. I am greatly relieved to learn that I was not a contributor to the child's death. Now, if you will both excuse me . . .' She limped to the door.

Brian and Patrick rose, the former scurrying to open it for her. When he returned to his seat his shoulders sagged. 'I fear I've made a permanent enemy of your granddaughter, sir. That's the last thing I would have wished for.'

Patrick searched for his pipe and lit it. 'I wouldn't let one skirmish deter ye.'

'I isn't exactly the first.' Brian took off his spectacles to wipe them with a handkerchief and told Patrick of their meeting on the train. 'I must confess to finding your grand-daughter very attractive. Unfortunately the admiration was one-sided. The young lady's mother, too, discouraged me from further approach.'

'Don't take that too personally, Doctor Dyson.' Patrick puffed contentedly. 'My daughter would've viewed any man in a similar light. She had high hopes for Belle before all this came about an' wouldn't have wanted her wasted on marriage.'

Brian asked what 'all this' meant.

'The orphanage lark. The night before last Belle ups an' tells her mother that instead o' going back to university she's off to set up a home for waifs an' strays. There was merry hell. The girl's mother sent her to Coventry till she comes to her senses. They're both as stubborn as a waggonload o' donkeys.'

'So that was her purpose in visiting Hungate?'

'Aye, she was likely searching for recruits – till the wee girl died, that is. It kind o' put the kibosh on things.'

Brian cursed himself openly for a fool. 'If only I'd been aware. I thought she was just amusing herself.' He hooked his spectacles back round his ears.

'That's understandable.'

'No, it's not, it's foolish and short-sighted, as if I was the only one with the right to care.'

'Well, console yourself with this little theory o' mine: I think maybe there was an element of amusement in it for her at first – till she got chucked in the drink o' course.' Concisely he told Brian the facts. 'After that I think a little bit o' revenge crept into it. She wanted to get her own back by using the children. I may be quite wrong o' course, but anyway 'tis all different now. She seems quite serious about helping them. She was heartbroken about the little girl, ye know.'

'I can imagine, knowing what I felt like myself. Oh, you don't know how useless it made me feel.'

'There was no hope o' saving her?'

'I've sometimes seen them recover, but this was too far advanced. The only comfort I could perform was to sit and mop her brow until the poison in her gut put an end to it.' He brought his hands up to his face, rubbed it briskly, then combed his fingers through his hair.

'Ye look tired, son.' Patrick reached for the doctor's glass to refill it. 'Haven't ye caught up on the sleep ye lost last night?'

Brian gave a short humourless laugh. 'I'm afraid it was straight from the deathbed back to the surgery. There was a queue a mile long. If I'm lucky I'll have an early night and pray that no one decides to come into the world or go out of it until eight o'clock tomorrow morning.'

'Have ye nobody who could deputise?'

'I *am* the deputy.' Brian took the refilled glass gratefully. 'I'm a junior partner in the practice. I do what I'm told – usually.' He smiled, remembering the set-to he'd had with Dr Barley over payments from the poor.

'Well, 'tis sorry I am I can't take the weight off your shoulders,' said Pat. 'But at least I can offer ye dinner. Will ye stay?'

'Actually, my housekeeper will have something prepared . . .' Brian's voice trailed away as he pictured the plate of faggots and peas that awaited his return, then imagined what the meal would be like in this house. 'But perhaps she'll understand if I tell her I couldn't possibly refuse the offer.' He grinned and settled back to chat with his host until the rest of the family arrived home for their evening meal.

Belle was none too pleased to find Dr Dyson still there at dinner and, even more annoyingly, seated next to her at the table. She spread her napkin with barely a glance in his direction, though she knew he was looking at her all the time. After several attempts at conversation had failed, however, he turned his attention to Erin, seated at his right. 'This is an excellent meal, is it not, Mrs Teale?'

Erin replied that it was and carried on eating. Though the people on the opposite side of the table smiled and chatted Brian found it most disconcerting to be situated between two people who were not on speaking terms. Well, actually it appeared it was only Mrs Teale who wasn't on speaking terms. Brian considered this highly childish from a middle-aged woman, even accounting for the vast disappointment she must have experienced at her daughter throwing up an academic career. But for God's sake, the girl was doing something useful for society, wasn't she? Rashly he brought up the taboo subject.

'If I might say so, Mrs Teale, I think your daughter has undertaken a most commendable task.' No one actually dropped their cutlery but he was aware of the tension which followed his remark.

Erin laid down her knife. 'Would someone pass me the water jug, please?'

Brian was quick to provide it, supplementing his former comment with: 'There must be many children in the city who'd benefit from her scheme.'

Erin positioned her knife and fork on the plate with finality. 'If ye'll all excuse me I have a headache. I'll go lie down for a while.' She rose and left the room.

Brian looked embarrassedly at the gathering. 'I'm sorry. Often matters are better if they're aired. It seems not to be so in this case.'

Belle rose as abruptly as her mother had done. 'Doctor Dyson, you seem to have a talent for upsetting people.'

'It takes a lot of practice.' Brian didn't know what had made him say that. He stood up, too. 'I'm sorry but I was trying to make reparation for my aggression this morning. If your mother had stayed I would have tried to persuade her to see the wrong she's doing you.'

'Did I ask you to take sides?' she demanded. Brian said she hadn't. 'Then kindly don't presume to intrude on what is essentially a family matter. I don't need assistance from you, or from anyone. Please mind your own business.' She stormed out.

Brian looked lamely at his host. 'There are going to be a lot of leftovers.'

'We'll get a dog,' replied Patrick. 'Don't you worry about them two silly devils, son. I have it to put up with all the time.'

What a funny way you have of showing a girl you care

503

for her, Brian told himself, sitting down. Couldn't you just see the love in her eyes?

However, before dinner broke up, her sense of fairness overcoming her anger, Belle was back to apologise. Whilst the others retired to the drawing room for coffee she bade the doctor stay a moment. 'I can't allow you to leave thinking we're all termagants in this house,' she half-smiled.

'Not to worry, I had a few kind words from your grandmother.'

'Don't be fooled; she's the worst of the lot. Anyway, what I want to say is there's been enough childish behaviour from my mother without me acting the same, so . . .'

'No, you had every right to be angry,' Brian assured her. 'It was grossly impertinent of me to abuse your grandfather's hospitality by poking my nose in. That is, I regret to say, one of my greatest faults. But you see, the explanation I gave you was true; I was trying to make amends for this morning. I should hate for you to throw away your fine intentions on account of my hasty words.'

'Now that you've told me I wasn't responsible for the child's death there's no danger of that. As to my mother, well, it was very kind of you to try, Doctor Dyson, but I really don't require your help in that or any other quarter. So, after telling me you accept my apology would you care to join the others for coffee?'

He failed to stifle a yawn. 'Oh dear, I do beg your pardon. I really would love to extend my stay but if I don't catch up on my sleep I shall be a proper quack in the morning.'

Belle rang for the maid while Brian looked in on the others to proffer his thanks and to say goodnight. Then, the girl delighted him by accompanying him to the end of the drive.

'Tell me, how do you propose to start your venture, Miss Teale?' he asked as she crunched lopsidedly along the gravel path.

'I've already started. You met Lol at dinner; he's my

first child.' Brian tried not to smile, but it did sound funny the way she said it, her age being not that much more than the boy's. He asked where she had found Lol and Belle told him a similar story to that given by her grandfather earlier. She came to a halt when they reached the gate and confessed to not knowing where she would find her next recruit.

'Perhaps I could be of help there,' said Brian, then smiled. 'I know you said you didn't need assistance but it would make a change after all the aggravation I've caused you.' She was interested to know more. 'Well, I do practise in the poorer areas – although ironically you might find more candidates for adoption in the better-class households.' She made a dubious *moue*. 'I'm completely serious. Many people imagine that because a child is ragged and unwashed it means he is neglected. I've been in dozens of houses such as the Shaws' and found very few cases of wanton deprivation. You would be as likely to find it in what might be termed a privileged household – such as your own. It appears from the large number of offspring these people bring into the world that they are genuinely fond of children – as well they might be, some of them – but in many cases they are merely chattels.'

She was half-impressed, half-annoyed that he had said 'households such as your own'. 'I can assure you that neither I nor my cousins were ever starved of affection, Doctor.'

He hurried to correct the misunderstanding. 'I most certainly didn't mean to imply such a thing. I doubt that your grandparents are the sort of folk who'd allow their home to be used as an orphanage if they didn't like children.'

She smiled that infrequent smile; it completely altered her face; made her really beautiful. 'Without their help I should have found it very hard. But make no mistake – I wouldn't have let it stop me.'

He was quite sure she wouldn't. Her independence verged on the obsessive. Some people in her position might have become meek invalids, but her disability had

505

turned Belle into a firebrand. No one would dare to view such a strong-minded, accomplished person as a cripple. Another yawn distorted his face. He was forced to excuse himself again. 'I really must be going. I do hope that my blunder hasn't destroyed the chance of us being friends. I wonder, could I see you again?'

'Oh, we'll probably meet on our own separate courses,' she answered casually.

'I'd prefer something more definite than just a chance meeting.' – There it is again, he thought glumly, that defensive wall. I can't seem to get near her.

'I don't think . . .'

'As I've already said I can be of help to you – in fact I may have an idea already.' He saw her face perk up and went on, 'I have a patient who's dying. I seem to have nothing else lately, do I? Anyway, the woman has pulmonary bleeding. If she lasts another day it will be a miracle. I can do nothing for her medical condition but I could give her peace of mind – at least, you can. She has four children whose ages range from a mere babe to a six-year-old. She's desperately worried that she has no relatives with whom she can place them when she dies, and being a former inmate of the workhouse herself is greatly troubled at the thought of her children being taken there. If I could assure her that they'd be taken care of . . . adopted into a loving home, her final hours would be contented ones.'

'Then assure her and let her mind be at peace,' instructed Belle adamantly. 'I'll take them.'

'You may wish to discuss it first with your grandparents.'

'They're already conversant with my plans.'

'I reiterate that there is a young baby among them. Whoever takes charge of it would be in for many disturbed evenings, not to mention having to cope with the distress of the older ones.'

'I'm sure I shall manage,' said Belle. 'A few sleepless nights never hurt anyone. Oh well. . . .' she was forced to laugh at Brian's disgruntled look. 'I'm sorry, I'm sure you must be aching for your bed. I'll keep you gossiping no longer. Just send word when the . . . when you need my help and I shall make it my business to be there.'

'I shall tell my patient tomorrow. It'll be one less worry for her to bear. Well, it's goodnight then, Miss Teale, and please thank your grandparents for the excellent supper. I shall hope to see you again soon.'

After ten paces he turned to look back to see if she was watching his departure, but Belle was on her way back to the house. Still, he had made a start.

CHAPTER THIRTY-FIVE

It was another week before the woman succumbed to her illness and her spirit, at peace now, departed this world for the next. Brian arrived at the Feeney household one overcast morning accompanied by a nurse who carried the baby whilst Brian himself held the second youngest. Belle was in her room, making half-hearted sketches. She was on a tight schedule. The illustrations which she had been commissioned to do for a ladies' journal were barely started and were meant to be sent off tomorrow. She had come by this means of earning a little money whilst still at university. Overhearing a discussion between two fellow students about one of them having an article published in a magazine, she listened more intently and picking up the basic details of how to go about it had submitted a short story of her own. It had been accepted – not, primarily, for its literary content but because Belle had decorated the title sheet of her manuscript with exquisitely detailed portraits of her characters which had drawn the Editor's eye. Henceforth, he had commissioned her illustrations on a regular basis and also printed her stories. Occasionally she would write more serious articles on topical events and had had many published in newspapers, but for those she required concentration and that had been somewhat elusive since Dr Dyson had told her about the children. She could hardly summon enough to finish these simple paintings.

Today, though, she had determined to finish them in one fell swoop and swore that she would not come out of that room until they were done. Her paintbrush was in the act of sweeping round the outline of a lady's skirt when there was a tap on the door and the maid informed her that the hall was full of children. Spattering the half-finished picture with dots of paint as she flung the brush aside, Belle rushed down to welcome them.

'Good day, Miss Teale.' Brian's face was etched in dark lines. Death still affected him. He wondered if he would ever cease to become emotionally concerned with his patients. 'These are the children. They've been informed that they are to come and live with you. You'll understand of course if they're a bit weepy for a time.'

'It's natural when one has lost a parent, Doctor.' Belle limped forward to take the baby from the nurse, receiving also the information that it required changing. 'I'll see to it immediately.' The day after Brian had told her of the family she had gone out to buy baby clothes and other necessary items and had received very odd looks when it came to the purchase of a feeding bottle. She and Vinnie had enjoyed a good laugh about it on their way home. Passing the baby to the maid, who held it as awkwardly as she had done, she divested the doctor of his burden, asking if he and the nurse would care for some refreshment. 'I'm afraid I shan't be able to join you if I'm to see to the children, but I'm sure someone will make you at home.'

Brian was disappointed. He had hoped for a bit of time with Belle. 'No, we'd better go back to the surgery.' He looked at the nurse. 'There might be someone requiring treatment.'

Belle thanked him for bringing the children. 'Maybe you'd like to call for dinner on Friday to see how they're being looked after?'

The lines of fatigue dispersed with his smile. 'Why thank you, Miss Teale, that would be delightful – till

Friday then.' He donned his hat and ushered the nurse through the front doorway.

Belle looked round at her new charges and said cheerfully, 'Now first of all we must know your names for we can't call you "You there" or "Boy", can we?' The eldest provided their tags: Edward, Anna, Cicely and baby Lucy. 'What lovely names. I shall be known as Aunt Belle.' She made her voice more in keeping with the situation. 'I know it won't be like living with your real mother and the shock of her death must seem unbearable, but I hope you'll soon come to think of this as your home. I'll do my best to make you happy.'

The little boy started to cry, infecting his siblings right down to the baby. Happy! thought Vinnie dismally as she followed the procession upstairs bearing the squawling baby. Since Helen's departure she had borne the title maid-of-all-work . . . and had the terrible suspicion that she was about to add nursemaid to her capabilities.

Belle was pleased to report to Brian when he came to dinner that, after the initial strangeness, the children had settled down with little disruption to the household. The baby, though unburdened by the emotional difficulties of the others, was the most exacting in the physical sense, needing changing and feeding every couple of hours. In this she had the maid's help, though when Vinnie's complaints of overwork – 'I don't know why she should expect me to know all about babies just 'cause I'm a maid! S'all right for her, she doesn't get the mucky jobs to do!' – filtered up from the kitchen, Thomasin was forced to employ a proper nursemaid who took complete charge while Belle directed her energies at the others, Lol acting as helper. The latter had not viewed the idea of sharing Belle with four more children in a very healthy light and had felt no pity for their loss, but now he had come to accept their presence and was quite pleased to have underlings to boss about. The rest of the household, with the exception of Erin who showed no interest whatsoever, doted on the young boarders and they were always passed around for goodnight kisses before bedtime, sometimes even receiving one of Patrick's splendid tales. They were not, however, allowed to eat at the family table. Belle was told by her grandmother that this would only make things worse between her and Erin.

During the following months the number of Belle's foundlings grew to seven, comprising Lol – of whom Belle saw little now as he was in full employment at Thomasin's factory – the four children of the dead woman, another baby whose unmarried mother had died giving birth and a boy of eight, Cedric, who had been a street arab like Lol until swept into Dr Dyson's cart and spirited here. The authorities were agreeable to the arrangements as it lessened the burden on them; Patrick had deemed it best to advise them at the outset – though they were unaware of Belle's age and would probably not have sanctioned the orphanage if they had been. It was Patrick's name which was put forward as the founder.

The house began to groan in protest at the little feet which pounded up and down its halls, played vociferous games of hide and seek in its cupboards, slid down its polished balustrades and shrieked aloud their happiness in its rambling gardens. As yet there had been no complaints from her grandparents, but Belle recognised that young as she was it would soon be time to find a place of her own. The maids couldn't be relied upon to keep patience with the sticky fingermarks that appeared on the mahogany furniture five seconds after they had polished it – and Nick's bedroom turned upside down in the search for the darts he had confiscated when one of them had almost skewered him to the door. And even though Belle wasn't exactly the best of friends with Rosanna she knew she could not expect the girl to keep putting up with her stockings being used for swingball – Rosie was ratty enough these days, thought Belle, wondering over the reason. It couldn't be lack of male attention, for there was always some young man or other being invited for her. Thank God that she herself was spared that. It would be Rosie's twenty-first birthday very soon. Belle doubted there would be any announcements of betrothal — Rosie never seemed to stick with one of them for more than a month. Flighty creature.

The flighty creature stared blankly into the mirror of her dressing table, then leaned on her elbows and spoke to her reflection. 'Just be nice to him for a little while longer. It's not that hard is it? He is very pleasant.' No, he isn't, sulked her reflection. He grates on my nerves — they all do, thinking I'm really interested in them. Just a week, she begged herself. Just hold on for another week. You've managed perfectly for all this time, none of them but Nick has the slightest idea . . . just think of what a week will bring. You'll be twenty-one and nobody will be able to tell you what to do. Her thoughts strayed to Tim. He hated it, she knew; hated to think of his beloved in the company of all those young men. But he put up with it as she did for in another week or so none of this would matter.

What a slow week it was. Most of Sunday was spent in her parents' house as had become a regular occurrence over the past couple of years — most of it, but not all. While poor unsuspecting Father and Mother relaxed downstairs after Sunday lunch, Rosie would sneak from the house and pass a torrid couple of hours with Timothy in some field, or barn if it were cold. It was a far from satisfactory courtship, but it was better than not seeing him at all. Then, after a clinging kiss she would scamper back to her room, from where she would emerge looking tousled and Josie would laugh and say, 'I've never known Sunday lunch have the same effect on anybody as it has on you!'

When the day of her twenty-first birthday finally dawned, Rosie woke up and thought, today is the beginning of my real life. As most of their friends and family lived around York the party was held in the house on Peasholme Green. Sonny, Josie and the girls travelled over for the occasion. There was much amusement over Rosie's shouts of glee at her splendid gifts and also much speculation on whether she would eventually marry the young man with whom she danced most that evening. And for Rosie the best part of all was when it was over.

On the Saturday morning following her coming of age, Rosanna appeared at the breakfast table in a deep crimson dress and jacket, presented to her by her mother on her last visit to Leeds. This was its first airing and everyone commented on how magnificent she looked. Nick whistled. 'Blimey, what a stunner!'

'A real grown-up lady,' said Patrick, stirring his tea. 'And where are ye gadding off to this morning? Going shopping?'

She stopped eating to present a deadpan expression. 'Didn't Father tell you? I'm going over today instead of tomorrow.'

Her grandmother looked as surprised as Patrick. 'When was this arranged?'

'At my party,' answered Rosanna, resuming her meal and wishing that Nick would take that look from his eye. 'He was grumbling about having to go somewhere on Sunday and not being able to see me so I said I'd go today.' She had blessed Father for this perfect opportunity.

'Oh aye, I do remember him saying something about it,' nodded Patrick. 'Well, I hope the weather stays fine for your trip – taking Vinnie, are you?'

'Gramps, I am twenty-one now, you know.' She smiled at her grandmother. 'I hardly need a chaperone.'

Thomasin unwittingly came to her support. 'We'll need Vinnie here – I've got dinner guests tonight.'

'Well, be careful,' warned Patrick. 'What train are ye catching?'

Rosanna glanced at the clock as she scraped the last of the food from her bowl. 'I thought I'd get there nice and early. I feel a bit guilty about Mother and Father, hardly spending any time with them at my party.'

'Yes, I noticed you and Jeremy were enjoying yourselves,' smiled Thomasin slyly. 'Is he going to be the lucky man, I wonder?'

Rosanna winked at her grandfather. 'You'll have to wait

and see, won't she, Gramps?' To sounds of despair from her grandmother she began to rise. 'I'd better stir myself if I want to catch that train.'

Patrick told her to be careful of talking to strangers. 'And I'll telephone your father and ask him to meet you at that end.'

'Gramps, will you behave yourself! Father knows what time I'll be there, you don't imagine he'd allow me to stand about on the station, do you? He's as bad as you are. Stop fussing.' She came around the table to kiss him and Thomasin. Her grandparents shared a chuckle at the tight squeeze she gave them both, unaware that it was as much a gesture of guilt as affection. Passing Nick she dipped her head and kissed him too. 'Wish you were coming.'

'No, you don't.' But his eyes smiled fondly. 'Have a good time.'

'I will – and I'll ring you as soon as I get there, Gramps, just to put your mind at rest. Bye!' She sailed from the room.

Thomasin sighed. 'Still as harum-scarum as ever. God help the poor man who has to keep her in tow – eh, but didn't she look lovely, Pat?' Not just lovely – blooming. The thought seemed to trigger another, making her frown. She cast her mind back to reflect if the young couple had been left on their own during the time Jeremy had been paying court. They had, once or twice... but no, it couldn't be that. Jeremy was a respectable young chap. Still... it wouldn't harm to start discussing wedding plans.

Patrick was voicing his frustration. 'I worry my head loose about that child. I'll bet she goes and forgets to telephone me an' all.'

But Rosanna didn't forget. Later in the morning Patrick received the call to tell him she had arrived in Leeds and for him not to worry any more. At his objection she added, 'Oh get away with you! I know you've been sitting by that telephone all morning, chewing the end of your tie. I'm all in one piece, I promise, and I'll see you tomorrow evening.'

'Right – and love to everyone there!' he shouted before she hung up.

'He sends you his love,' Rosanna told Tim, before thanking the man in the office for the use of his telephone.

Tim grimaced. 'Why didn't you just tell him the same as ye told your parents? If he should telephone them . . .'

Rosie didn't seem concerned. 'Why should he do that? He thinks I'm already there. Besides, if I'd told him I'd missed the train he would be straight down to the station looking for me and then where would we be? It's much better if Father and Mother break the news to him. Once we've told them of course.' She wrapped impulsive arms round his neck and kissed him. 'Oh, I'm so happy! I only hope Mother and Father see that. I'm dreading having to tell them.' Pulling away, she noticed that Tim seemed uneasy and asked what was the matter.

He escorted her outside and hurried her to the cab that had been waiting for them in Blake Street, directing it to the railway station. 'I've something I have to tell you, Rosanna . . . a confession.' She stopped at the carriage door but he motioned for her to get in before divulging, 'Mr Dorgan says it might be wiser if we didn't break the news yet.'

'Oh Timothy!' She raged and flung herself away from him. 'I've waited four years for this!'

'And so have I, pet.' He put a gentle hand to her mouth, using the other to smooth the ridges of bad-temper from her brow. 'But as he says, there's not just us to consider. If there's trouble over this – and there will be – it could cause disaster for the Brotherhood.'

'I'm getting sick of the blasted Brotherhood!' spat Rosie, jogging up and down with the motion of the carriage.

'Now . . .' He wagged a finger.

'Oh, you know I didn't mean it – but I just feel so let down! I mean, what have we wasted time in there for?' She jabbed a finger at the building they had just left.

'Regretting it already, are ye?' came the soft query.

'Don't be silly,' she sulked. 'I just expected that after today we'd be together – why didn't you tell me earlier?'

'I thought as I'd wangled the day off we might as well go through with it.'

'Huh! What a way to regard our special day.'

He tried to embrace her. 'I only meant that I can't afford to be having too many days off, specially not at this time of year, or I'm likely to get finished altogether. Anyway . . . if I'd told ye before ye might not have wanted to go ahead with our plan.'

She laughed bitterly. 'What plan? It's ruined!'

His face denied this. 'No, this is still our special day. Just because no one else knows of it doesn't make it any less special. We've got most of what we wanted. I love ye, Rosie.'

She sighed and told him she loved him too. 'I *was* looking forward to showing you to my parents, you look so smart.' She stroked the jacket he had bought for the occasion. 'So, how much longer do we have to keep this secret?'

'Not long.' He soothed her with a kiss. 'I'm as eager as you to be away. I'm only sorry that it can't be this afternoon.'

'Why can't it?' she asked bluntly, sitting up.

'I told ye, because of the Brotherhood.'

'Yes, but whenever we tell them – next week, next year – there's still going to be trouble for the Brotherhood.'

'Rosie, trust me, it'll be as soon as I can possibly make it.' To evade further questions he covered her mouth with his.

The kiss redirected her mind to the more pressing issue. 'So . . . what are we going to do now?' she asked as the cab rumbled over Lendal Bridge.

'You'll go to your parents as planned.'

'Oh marvellous! And what will you be doing?'

'Mm, I may as well come to Leeds with you, I've nothing better to do.' Grinning, he chucked her indignant chin. 'While you go see your mam and dad I'll get myself a room – no barns today, eh? An' then I'll lay back and wait for you to come to me.'

'I may decide I don't want to come,' she pouted, then raised a laugh at his disgruntlement. 'Oh but, Tim!' She snuggled up to him as the cab rolled nearer the station. 'It's going to be murder having to come home and pretend everything's normal.'

'Rosie,' he took the point of her chin in his fingers, 'in your own words we've coped with this for four years – a wee while longer isn't going to destroy everything, is it? An' the day hasn't been entirely wasted surely?'

'Far from it.' She smiled forgivingly and responded to his kiss. Then, 'So,' she sighed, 'it looks like we'll be sticking to the old Sunday routine . . . oh, hell!' She broke free. 'I won't be able to meet you in Leeds next week, Father and Mother are going to visit friends in Nottingham. I doubt you'll be able to make it right down there even if I got myself invited.'

Tim didn't view this as an obstacle. 'Come to Mr Dorgan's if you can manage to get away. I'm sure he'll be pleased to see you.'

'I'm not sure I want to see him – keeping us dangling . . . he's quite ruined my day.'

Tim cuddled up to her and slipped a hand inside her jacket. 'Oh but, Rosie, think what a great old time we're going to have in unruining it when we get to Leeds.'

Over the years it had become relatively easy for Rosanna to respond without blushing whenever her grandparents enquired what she had been doing at her mother's and father's house and whether she had enjoyed herself. But this homecoming would be rather different – would her frustration over Mr Dorgan's dictate show through the façade and give the game away?

She need not have worried. During her spell of absence another situation had developed. Belle had reached a decision about her orphans – she would rent a house of her own. It was to Rosie's advantage that her cousin chose Sunday's evening meal to air her proposal, thereby diverting the questions from Rosie. The diners were waiting for coffee when Belle spoke of her plan. Everyone – except Erin, whose only reaction was an extra blink – turned to Belle in wonderment. Patrick was first to voice his opinion. ''Tis a big step, Belle, and you're very young. Even if you were a woman I'd not like to think of you living alone.'

'If by alone you mean without a man to protect me there's always Lol.' She saw the doubt and cracked a grin. 'I see! It's him you're really worried about, isn't it, Gramps? I've noticed how his eyes stray – well, don't worry, he doesn't think of *me* in that way.'

Thomasin shared a look of despair with Patrick at the worldliness of their grand-daughter. 'Even so, Belle, people will talk.'

'They've always had plenty to say where I'm concerned,' retorted Belle. 'And I don't give a hoot what they say about me.'

'Well, I do,' said Patrick firmly. 'Look, if it's only more room you need we could build an extension.'

'You could build it right out as far as Malton but I still wouldn't be able to constrain them to their own side of the house. They'd soon be annoying you all again – yes they do, I know they do,' she countered Patrick's disclaimer.

He grasped for a solution. 'What if Lol stays here, then?'

'You're determined I'm not going to be ravished, aren't you? Anyway, it would be very inconvenient for you, Nan, wouldn't it? You've never exactly welcomed his presence.'

'I daresay I could put up with him – and if we're speaking of convenience it would be harder for Lol to get to work if he came with you, Belle. Here he's got transport to the factory.'

'Even if Lol agreed to stay here then we're back to Grandfather's original worry,' Belle pointed out. 'I'd still be in the house without male support.'

'Ah, dear,' sighed Patrick. 'Your Nan and me would be much happier if ye continued to live here until ye married.

If we shuffle the kids around I'm sure we could find a few more nooks and crannies to shove 'em in.'

Belle glanced at her mother, whose face was taut. 'If I were to stay here till I got married then I'd be a very old lady indeed. I can't ever foresee myself attaining that state.'

Patrick's mouth twitched and he too looked at Erin. 'I seem to recall a certain Erin Feeney voicing those same words.' Erin barely responded, forcing him to turn back to his grand-daughter. 'Belle, you're a beautiful girl, ye know . . .'

'You misunderstand me,' she shook her head. 'It's not that I don't think anyone would marry me, but that I prefer to stay single. Dear Gramps, I do love you, but you men are so pompous, regarding a woman on her own as a helpless creature. I'm quite prepared for the hardships that living alone will entail.'

'Perhaps your mother . . .' began Patrick. At which point Erin said she'd finish her coffee upstairs. Rosie took the opportunity to leave, too. She was feeling rather queasy – must have eaten something that disagreed with her. Nick excused himself as well and shadowed her to the door. He had been anticipating some announcement from Rosie and wanted to know why there hadn't been one.

'I *was* going to say perhaps your mother might like to come an' live with ye,' said Patrick when the exodus had ceased. 'But I doubt I'd be popular with either party.'

Belle couldn't argue. 'I've no need to tell you that she's the real reason I have to get away. I don't mind arguments but this silence is driving me up the wall. God knows what it's doing to her.'

'If you cared for your mother as much as you seem to do your waifs then you'd see what it was doing to her, Belle,' censured Thomasin. 'And personally I can't see how it will help matters, you going to live somewhere else. But then I don't suppose that anything I say will convince you of how selfish you're being, so I won't waste my time. I think your mother deserves more of my attention than you do.' She left.

Patrick grimaced. 'I must say I feel for your mam as well, colleen.'

Belle tutted. 'You both seem to think I don't! It's partly because I do love her that I'm going away, so that she can feel comfortable in her own home. If the talk turns to me or the children she ups and leaves the table. I don't want it to get to the point where she has to take all her meals in her own room! I do love her, Gramps, but Mother's choice of life isn't mine – and after all, you know, it is Mother who's chosen not to speak to me, not the other way around, so I don't see how you and Nan can blame me.'

'I'm not blaming you, I just wish you'd hang on . . .' At her look of defiance he sighed. 'You always were an independent cat – even when you were a tot you'd never listen to anyone or let them help ye. All right, you go if go you must, but swear to me that if ever you're in need of anything you'll come home.'

She made this promise, knowing it would never have cause to be fulfilled.

Armed with a list of rentable properties, culled from the nightly presses over the week following the discussion, Belle set about the business of finding suitable accommodation. By Sunday she had still not seen anything that really fitted her requirements, so when Brian called after Sunday lunch to say he might have something she took up his offer. 'But I hope for your sake that this isn't another dump like the ones I've been seeing or I may just find a use for your scalpel.'

Leaving the children in her grandfather's care she departed on her mission. The house they were to view was in Barbican Road. It was as they drove in the direction of Walmgate Bar that Belle thought she spotted Rosanna. She was about to hail her cousin and had half-raised her hand in greeting, when the furtive manner in which the girl was acting and also the fashion of her dress made her drop the hand to her lap, frowning in confusion. The girl's shabby scarf obscured most of her face as she disappeared into a house, but the brief flash which Belle had caught had looked just like Rosanna. Brian caught Belle's puzzlement as the carriage rolled on and asked what ailed her.

She still frowned. 'Oh . . . nothing. I could've sworn that was Rosie back there.'

'What on earth would your pretty cousin be doing around these parts?'

Exactly, thought Belle. What on earth was Rosie playing at dressed like that – if it had been her, that is. But she smiled at Brian. 'My pretty cousin? So, you're an admirer too. Well, I'm sorry, Brian,' the months of familiarity had brought them to using each other's Christian name, 'but you'll have to take your turn, there's a very long queue.'

Brian returned the smile but it was a rather sad little effort. Doesn't she know how I feel about her? he thought. Then answered himself: no, she has no earthly idea. Then you're just going to have to tell her, old chap, aren't you?

'God, I don't know how I've lasted!' gasped Rosanna as their lips broke suction. Then she lowered her voice to a whisper. 'Have you asked him yet?'

'Asked him what?'

Rosanna spun as Dorgan rattled in with a tea tray. 'Oh, Mr Dorgan, Tim and I can't go on like this! It isn't fair of you to ask us to keep it a secret any longer. My grandparents keep inviting young men round and I just don't feel I can continue to entertain them.'

'Still trying to marry you off are they, Rosie?' Dorgan allowed her to take over serving the tea.

She made a face, dashing milk into each cup. 'It's like the Hydra-headed monster – you cut one off and two more appear. I think Nan's ordering them in bulk. The latest is very persistent.'

Tim laid his fingers over her mouth. 'I thought we'd agreed you wouldn't talk about them in front of me. I want to break their heads, every one.' As she put the teapot down he unbuttoned her coat and helped peel off her gloves and scarf, then watched as she stood warming herself by the fire.

'I'm not trying to make you jealous, I'm just attempting to show Mr Dorgan how unreasonable he's being.' She seated herself on the sofa close to Tim, wishing that Dorgan would go about his business and allow her and Tim to see to theirs.

Dorgan took up his cup. 'Ah well, it won't be for much longer.'

'That is what Tim said last Saturday!' volleyed Rosanna. 'And it's my opinion we've waited long enough. We've got the Lord Mayor and his family coming to dinner tomorrow and we all know at whose side the son will be seated – then he'll no doubt invite me to partner him to the banquet at the Mansion House on Wednesday. Nan's already been invited.'

Tim's anxiety seemed to be more pronounced. 'Ye'll say no of course?'

Taking this as just another example of jealousy she laughed and kissed him on the nose. 'Of course.'

'Don't,' said Dorgan.

The young couple both looked to him, Rosanna in confusion, Tim in dismay. Dorgan left his chair to cup Rosanna's face. 'Rosie, my cherub, as if your delightful presence in my house isn't enough you've brought the means to rid me of a massive problem.'

Tim was really concerned now and it wasn't just jealousy. 'Mr Dorgan, I don't think we should involve Rosie . . .'

'She's already involved, purely by association.'

Rosanna twisted her face from Dorgan's caress to frown at Tim. 'Involved in what?'

'Nothing that concerns you, Rosie,' said Tim hurriedly.

'Ah, leave the lass be,' cried Dorgan, then spoke directly at Rosanna again. 'Rosie, ye've always said how ye'd like to help the Brotherhood.'

'But how can my spending a boring evening at the Mansion House help our cause?' demanded Rosanna.

Dorgan spread his mouth in approval. 'Did ye hear that, Timothy? Our cause, says she. I like that, colleen.' His mouth retracted. 'You've no idea just how important this can be to us, Rosie . . . but before I tell ye what I want ye to do I need your agreement. I know it's a bit back to front, but I need to know you're fully with us.'

Rosanna, who had always craved something important to do for the freedom of Ireland, swore her allegiance readily, though Tim's reaction baffled her, for he seemed to be against her inclusion. Before she could ask him why, Dorgan produced a rolled-up document and spread it on the table, placing a cup at each of the top corners to anchor it down. 'Come an' look at this, Rosie.' As she leaned over his shoulder to study the paper he asked, 'D'ye know what it is?'

'It's some sort of plan.'

''Tis a plan of the Mansion House. This here,' he tapped an area of the document, 'is where they'll be doing all the dancing.'

'But you haven't said yet why you want me to go.'

'I want you to meet with Tim,' supplied Dorgan.

She turned swiftly on Tim in delight. 'You never said!'

'I'll be there as a waiter.' A glance at Dorgan.

Rosanna was mouthing her pleasure at this, envisioning cuddles by the backstairs, when Dorgan disclaimed the role of Cupid. 'He'll not be there for any fun and games, Rosie. He's going there to kill somebody.'

Shock displaced frivolity. The only word she could utter was, 'Who?'

'His name is Sir Frederick Milner,' answered Dorgan. 'You know him?'

'I know the name,' she replied hollowly, thinking of all the names her grandfather had called the man. 'Why him?'

'Well . . . doesn't really matter who it is, nor which party he belongs to, 'tis just to show the Government that we're sick of all these promises they've been makin' for years an' not keeping. Milner's as good a target as any, I don't like him.'

Rosanna could feel herself quaking and hoped it did not show. 'How is it to be done?'

'We've had the plan set up for some weeks, ever since we knew he'd be at this do . . . that's why I didn't want you and Tim to go letting out your little secret.' Rosanna understood now and glanced at Tim who hung his head, proving that he had known about it but hadn't wanted to tell her. Dorgan went on, 'Everything was fine, we'd got the layout of the place, an alternative escape route if the first was blocked . . . our one problem was how to get Tim inside with the gun in his pocket. There's bound to be strict security what with all these death threats flying around. I wish I could get me hands on the soft buggers who sent them – oh, excuse my language, Rosie. But if you're going to kill somebody ye hardly give them prior warning, ye just go out and kill them. If they only realised how they've messed things up for us . . . anyway, we had it in mind that Tim could hide the gun among all that food what'll be going into the place and retrieve it once he's inside, but it's far from satisfactory and I'm so grateful that you've provided us with the perfect solution.'

'You want me to take the gun to Tim?' she asked, white-faced.

'I do. They'll search the waiters an' the maids but they'll hardly search the guests, especially one so attractive as yourself.'

'But it's such a responsibility . . . wouldn't you rather undertake it yourself?'

'In other words, what part do I play in all this?' said Dorgan.

'I didn't mean to be disrespectful . . .'

'While you're handing the gun to our friend I'll be at my worship at the Minster.'

'But you don't worship at . . .' and then she understood. 'You're going to plant a bomb?' It came as a whisper. All of a sudden it had ceased to be the game it had been. He was asking far more of her than to pick up mysterious packages from his contacts. He was asking her to become involved in murder.

Dorgan had seen the dissension creep into her face. 'There's no backing out now, Rosie, ye gave your oath.'

She tossed her head then. 'I've no intention of backing

out. I'm for a free Ireland as much as you are . . . I'm just worried for Tim. I mean – what if he's caught?'

'Haven't I told ye the escape route's all fixed? There'll be that much confusion he'll be away before they've realised what's happened. And next week,' he grinned and took hold of her hands, 'the two of you will be sitting pretty in old Ireland. Isn't that what you've always wanted?'

Rosie gripped the old man's hands whilst gazing into Tim's eyes, and thought – oh yes, yes . . . but not this way.

CHAPTER THIRTY-SIX

Each had her own room now. Rosanna was never more glad of it. Listlessly she sat on the bed, staring down at the gun cuddled in her palm, ran trembling fingertips along the barrel, then rested the weapon in her lap.

Everyone had been delighted when she had told the Lord Mayor's son that, yes, she would accompany him to the ball. They had no inkling that she was not going there to enjoy herself but to help end someone's life. She was desperately afraid; more for Timothy than for herself. What if he didn't get away? What if something went wrong? And, if all went according to plan, what of the man who would die? Did he deserve to? Did his hostile words on the platform deserve to condemn him to death? Did his wife love him as much as she loved Tim?

All these questions she had asked herself over and over again since Sunday. The answer kept resounding through her brain: *Thou Shalt Not Kill*. But she had committed herself, sworn her allegiance to Ireland. She still passionately believed in that cause . . . if only it were not Tim who must pull the trigger. He was afraid too; she had sensed it when they had made frantic love that Sunday afternoon, felt it in his silence afterwards as they lay drenched in love-sweat. But she had no qualms that he would do it.

She felt the gun again, tested its weight, imagined herself in Tim's place. Would she be able to curl her finger round that trigger and squeeze? Each evening on her return from work she had come straight up here to her room; not to just wash off the dust of the storehouse but to check that the weapon was still in its hiding-place. It was a ritual now. She kept picking it up and laying it down, experiencing now the way her legs would turn to jelly on Wednesday when Milner was gunned down. Would they be able to read the guilt on her face?

The door opened – too suddenly for her to do anything about the gun. Reflex brought her swiftly to her feet. The gun fell from her lap and clattered to the floor. They both stared at it, Rosanna and her grandfather, seemingly hypnotised.

'I'm sorry, I forgot to knock,' said Patrick, sounding to his own ears idiotic. He took a slow step forward, bent down and carefully wrapped his hand around the gun. He said nothing, just stared from the weapon to his grand-daughter, bewilderment on his face.

'One of us is going to have to speak eventually, Rosanna.' His voice cracked the unbearable silence. 'I've no answer to this but you'd better have.'

She turned her back on him. 'What would you like me to say?'

'God dammit!' He realised he was waving a dangerous weapon and stilled his hand if not his voice. 'I expect you to tell me what my grand-daughter is doing with a gun in her room.'

'I'm sorry, I can't.'

Throwing the weapon on the bed he strode up to her and spun her round. 'You're damn-well going to!'

'I promised!' She tried to wrest herself from his grip.

'Promised who? Who, Rosanna, who?' He shook her.

'I won't tell you!'

The realisation sent a shadow across his face like the sun passing over a hillside. 'Mother o'Mercy, you're still

525

mixed up in that Fenian rubbish, aren't ye? You're seeing that bloody Rabb again!'

'Yes, I am!' she hurled back at him. 'And it's not rubbish. How can any Irishman call it that when we're fighting for you?'

He recoiled. 'Good Christ, they've really indoctrinated ye with their filth, haven't they!' Then duty overcame shock. 'Where is he hiding, Rosanna?'

'You expect me to tell you?'

'I'll find out.'

'Then do so. Why don't you ask Joseph? He's your spy, isn't he?'

'Joseph's no spy.'

'No, he's just stupid and ignorant!'

'We're not talkin' about Joseph. For God's sake, ye don't think I'm going to stand by while my grandchild consorts with a man o' violence, d'ye?'

'Why, you hypocrite, Grandfather! All those stories you told us about the old days. The fights you won.'

'That was just sport, lass.' He seemed amazed.

'Sport? Then which of you is the more violent, Grandfather? You, who fights for the pleasure of it or Timothy, who fights for a cause?'

'D'ye not think I want to see Ireland freed?'

'Then what are you doing about it?' she demanded.

'There are other ways to attain Home Rule besides violence, Rosie.'

'The ballot box,' she sneered.

'Aye, the bloody ballot box!'

'Bits of paper that might as well be ripped to shreds for what they're worth.'

'An' that's how your glorious cause will end up, Rosanna,' he said softly. 'In tatters. The British Government will crush ye an' rip ye to pieces an' scatter ye to the wind. What impression can a handful o' men, however dedicated they may think they are, make on the Government?'

'At least we'll have tried! Not given in like you did when

the vote didn't go the way you wanted it. Anyway, there are more of us than you think.'

Us. God damn them, they had really got to her. 'As many as in the British Army?'

'Numbers don't matter when you have . . .'

'Right on your side!' he finished for her. 'Oh Christ, Rosie, that's the oldest entry in the rebel's manual.'

There followed a bitter silence and Patrick's eyes once again fell on the gun. When he spoke his voice was less harsh. 'Don't ye understand, Rosie, they're using ye? However much you praise their cause, learn all the words o' their rebel songs, you'll never truly belong. These Fenians . . .'

'Not Fenians!' she corrected. 'The IRB.'

'IRB, FB, they still spell the same word – murder! An' there's one thing ye seem to have overlooked in all this patriotism, my girl. There's English blood running through your veins.'

She stared at him for agonising seconds, then collapsed into his arms. 'Oh, Gramps, I'm so afraid!' She sobbed into his chest, seeking comfort in his familiar feel and smell.

'Rosie, oh my Rosie, what have the devils done to ye?' He crushed her to him and stroked her hair.

'It was all so simple until Sunday,' she wept. 'And now I'm in such a mess.'

'You can tell me,' he said gruffly.

'I can't! I wish I could but I gave my word.'

'Rosanna,' he said firmly, holding her at arms' length, 'there's a gun lying on that bed. Guns are for shooting people. Now I must know how you are implicated in this. Are you the one who's supposed to use it?' She sniffed and shook her head. 'Is it Rabb?' She didn't answer. 'So it is. When is it going to happen?'

Still silence from her. Patrick's mind tried to fathom it out. It took a little time but he got there. ''Tis tomorrow, isn't it, at the Mansion House? Something's going to happen there? All those important people . . . ' Still she didn't betray them. His temper soared again. 'For God's

527

sake, Rosanna, your grandmother's going to be there! Don't you care about her? Tell me! Tell me!' He shook her again.

In a fit of weeping she gave in. 'I'm going to carry the gun in my bag. Once inside I pass it over to Tim. He's going to shoot Sir Frederick Milner . . .'

'Jesus!' The number of times he had wished the man dead and now . . .

'And that's not all . . . they're going to blow up the Minster, too. Oh Gramps, I'm so frightened. I don't want to do it. I only wanted to free Ireland. I didn't want to kill anyone.'

The bastards! Patrick cursed them as he tried to console his weeping grandchild. They weren't bothered who they used in their evil fight. 'Oh, Rosie, ye do get yourself mixed up in some things. Listen, ye realise we must put a stop to this?'

She nodded and sniffed, then stiffened. 'You're not going to the police?'

'Oh, I'd like to, believe me there's nothing I'd like more than to see that villain Rabb behind bars. But those varmints are clever. They've made sure that if anything should go wrong tomorrow night you're the one who's in possession of the gun. What am I going to say to the police when they ask me how I know about the plot? My granddaughter has the gun but don't worry, officer, she's only holding it for a friend? You're implicated as much as they are – more so, in fact. I'll not see my grand-daughter go to jail for a bunch o' murderin' villains.' He gripped his chin in concentration. 'The first thing is to get rid o' this blasted thing, then we can make some story up about how I overheard the men talking in a pub. Aye,' he seemed satisfied. 'That's it – but ye'll have to give me more details.'

'Listen, Grandfather, I've had an idea. We don't have to go to the police at all. I could simply pretend to be ill tomorrow evening and not turn up. Without the gun the plan wouldn't be able to go ahead.'

''Twould stop Milner's death, colleen, but the bombing'd probably still go ahead an' there'll be people worshipping there. I couldn't have that on my conscience. No, we have to put them away for good.'

'But Tim . . . I can't do that to him, Grandfather.'

'We're talking about murder, Rosie – an' surely 'tis better they catch him before he's carried out his dirty deed?'

'But they'll hang him whether he's done it or not!'

'Maybe not.'

'You know they will! Don't pretend that you're doing this to save his neck. All you're concerned about is getting him out of the way.'

'An' why not?' He was livid. 'D'ye think I like the idea of my grand-daughter going around with a potential killer? Holy Mother, he could have a string o' murders under his belt for all we know.'

'He hasn't. This will be his first time.'

'No it won't, because I'm going to see he never gets there.'

'Please, I beg you to at least let me go and warn him so he has a head start!'

'An' give him the opportunity to come back an' kill again when the fuss has died down? I don't think. Besides that, I don't want ye seeing the fella ever again – an' I mean it this time! I understand how strongly ye feel about the lad. Ye'd not've disobeyed me an' taken up with him again if ye didn't . . . how long has it been going on this time?'

She confessed quietly that it had never ended. 'I hated lying to you . . . but I just couldn't bear to be parted from him.'

'I really ought to be congratulating ye,' said Patrick tersely. 'Ye made a brilliant job of keeping it quiet. Can I ask how ye did it?' She dropped her eyes. 'Ah,' he gave a knowing nod, 'now I see why ye were so keen to visit your parents . . . what a silly old fool I must be.'

'I wasn't just using them as an excuse! I love seeing Father and Mother.'

'I'm pleased to hear that, Rosie. It might make it a little easier for your father to take this.' He stifled her objection. 'He's going to have to know this time. It's far too

529

serious . . . God knows the love affair was bad enough –
but this . . .' He became coaxing. 'Look, ye must see that
he's only using ye, Rosie my pet. He cares nothing for ye.'

'He does care for me! You don't know him like I do.
He's not really a killer, he's as frightened as I am. When
he's with me he's kind and gentle. He truly loves me.
Please, Grandfather, I'll never ask you for another thing
as long as I live, just give me ten minutes before you send
for the police.'

'I can't do it, Rosie. I'd be guilty of causing someone's
death. Ye don't imagine they'll stop here, d'ye?'

'But he'll think I've betrayed him!'

'An' what about me? Haven't ye been betraying me,
having us all thinking you were interested in them young
fellas when all the time ye were laughing behind our
backs!'

'Oh no, Gramps, I hated doing it!'

He flapped a hand. 'No matter! 'Tis done with. Now,
I want something positive to tell the police – where do
these people meet?'

'I'll tell you nothing,' she replied stubbornly.

'Then I'll just have to send them to Rabb's address. I
still have it written down somewhere.' He started to the
door. 'An' don't think ye can sneak out the minute I've
gone for I'm locking you in. Ye've shown me how much
ye can be trusted.'

She ran after him. 'You've no right!'

He spun on her. 'An' your lover has no right to snuff
out a human life! Forget him, Rosanna, 'tis all over now.
I'll make sure o' that, even if I have to chain you up for
the rest o' your days.'

'I can't forget him,' Rosanna said, more calmly than at
any point in the exchange. 'You see, Tim's not just my
lover, Grandfather, he's my husband. We were married
last week.'

She thought for one moment he was going to fall, and
put a hand out to steady him. 'I wanted to tell you before,
but Tim said . . .'

'Get your hands off me,' he warned and glared at her.

'You've connived, cheated and lied to me, an' ye were quite ready to commit murder if I hadn't stepped in . . . I doubt I'll ever be able to trust you again. God forgive you for your wickedness, Rosanna, for I never will.'

Despite her screams and the thumping on the door Patrick twisted the key, put it in his pocket with the gun, then went outside to toss the latter in the cesspit before informing the police. After the noisy display of protest Rosanna tucked her skirts around her waist and took the exit she had used many times before – the window.

Dorgan answered the frantic banging on his door and stepped aside as the breathless Rosanna pushed past him. 'Ye've got the wrong day, Rosie,' he said mildly and, relocking the door, followed her into the back room.

There were others there: Tim, a man she knew as Rory and another she hadn't met. She forestalled Tim's greeting. 'Listen . . . the police are coming!' She was panting heavily. 'I haven't time to explain. I've run all the way. I thought they might be here already.'

The meeting split up rapidly, Rory and the other man slipping through the back door while Tim hopped about and Dorgan pressed Rosie for an explanation.

'My grandfather knows all about tomorrow. Oh, Tim, Tim!' She clung to him. 'I'm sorry! I didn't betray you, he just walked in and saw the gun – and then I got so angry with him . . . I had to tell him we were married. I'm so sorry if I've ruined everything.'

'Calm down now, Rosie.' Dorgan patted her shoulder kindly. ''Tis nothing to get worked up about. If we all keep calm we'll do much better. Tell me now,' he pressed gentle hands to her face, 'does he know this address?'

She shook her head and gulped for breath. 'He knows yours though, Tim.'

Her eyes begged forgiveness. 'I didn't tell him. He had it in his files.'

'Er, was my name mentioned at all?' enquired Dorgan casually.

She foundered. 'I don't think so. Oh, God, I'm so sorry, I'm so confused, I can't really remember what I told him.'

The kind old face reassured her. 'Now, just sit you there an' get your breath back while I do a little thinking.' He turned to Tim. 'Go to the railway station, buy a ticket for Scarborough.' Tim questioned this and Dorgan elucidated. 'They'll alert the ports on the west coast, won't be expecting us to go this way. Just do it, boyo.' He saw Tim's frantic look at Rosanna. 'Don't worry, ye'll see her shortly. Well – ye didn't think I'd leave your pretty wife behind, did ye? 'Tis just that we'll be better going separately. The two o' yese together an' ye'd be spotted right away.'

Tim gave her as long a kiss as Dorgan would permit, then dashed towards the front passage.

'Back door!' said Dorgan sharply.

The young man swivelled in his step and went out the back way. When he had gone Dorgan seemed to lose all urgency, filling the kettle and going on to make a pot of tea. 'Sure we can't have ye leaving the house in such a state,' he explained. 'We'll have to get ye straight first. There's no panic if ye say ye didn't give them this address.'

'Oh, Mr Dorgan.' She began to cry again. 'I'm so, so sorry. Whatever must you think of me? I've betrayed you and you're being so kind about it.'

'Ah, you're young. 'Twas foolish of me to expect ye to bear such a burden. An' don't worry about Tim. We'll soon have the two o' yese together again.' He pottered collectedly about the room, lifting two cups and saucers down from the cupboard at the side of the fireplace and setting them near to the teapot. Rosanna, still anxious, perched on the edge of her chair while he stirred the pot. Did nothing excite the old man? Her thoughts went to Tim. Would he be apprehended at the station? Would she ever see him again?

Her hand reached up to her neck and tugged at the chain which held her wedding ring, pulling it out from under her bodice. The golden band was warm from her breasts. She did not transfer it to her finger immediately, but sat there gripping it, deep in thought.

'There we are, that's fine.' Dorgan tapped the spoon on the rim of the pot and replaced the lid. He looked around for the milk jug, tutted, and travelled through to the scullery to fetch it.

'Where will we go from Scarborough, Mr Dorgan?' she asked, watching the milk go into the cups.

'Why, to Ireland, colleen – though the long way round. That was the plan, was it not?'

'The plan that I messed up.'

'Ah, sure there'll be other opportunities,' he comforted. 'Don't go blaming yourself. Ye were afraid. I quite understand.' The tea poured, he handed her a cup. 'Settle back. We've got bags of time. I'll just collect a few things.'

While Rosanna drank her tea he took a revolver from a drawer, levelled it and shot her once through the temple.

He had been there before. It was a long time ago but a mortuary was a place you did not forget. He had sat in this corridor, in virtually the same seat, staring at the old man reflected in the tiled wall, attempting to shield his nostrils from the smell of death by breathing through his mouth. One tiny glimmer of optimism forced itself through the swathes of black despair: the last time he had sat here it had all been a terrible mistake; the body had not been that of his son. This was the thought that had kept him from breaking down completely these past hours since the police had informed him – it was all a terrible mistake.

He glanced at the reflection seated next to the old man. The face beneath the auburn hair was haggard. The grey eyes met briefly with Patrick's, then both pairs fell to watch their respective owner's hands gripping out their anxiety on each other. He had informed Sonny the moment he had realised she had gone. His son had arrived just in time to be told that the police had found a young woman's body in a known Republican house. He hadn't wanted Patrick to accompany him here, but the old man had insisted. He had to see for himself, otherwise he would never believe . . .

'This is my fault.' His voice came as a croak, forcing him to clear his throat. 'If I'd told you about the relationship at the beginning . . .' Sonny didn't want to hear it – didn't want to talk. He gave a dismissive gesture and his father fell silent. – Yes, *if* you'd told me, thought Sonny. But I wasn't important enough, was I? I was only a figurehead. You saw *yourself* as her father . . . Then guilt overcame selfishness – how his father must be suffering. He reached sideways and clamped a hand over one of Patrick's.

They were being called in. Patrick knew – he knew before ever that sheet was turned back that it was Rosanna. A moan escaped his lips as his eyes were magnetised to the neat hole in her temple. The attendant thought it a blessing that the bullet had lodged deep in her brain; there was no messy exit point to scalp her shiny brown hair. This tiny consideration mattered not to Patrick – all he saw was a little girl cuddled on his lap, rubbing her hand over his bristly face, a vital young woman with a gleam of defiance in her blue eye. His own eyes told him that his darling Rosie was dead, but his mind could not fathom it.

'Yes . . . that's my daughter,' said Sonny. Then, 'Oh, Father!' He broke down and wept as the cover was pulled over her face. 'The bastards! The bloody murdering bastards.' Crushing a handkerchief to his face to stifle the sobs, he escaped into the corridor then out into the fresh air.

Patrick's exit was slower. He looked down upon the shrouded figure for some seconds, still gripped by disbelief. Then he too resolved to find a fresher climate. The attendant, however, halted him.

'I don't like to add to your grief, sir, but we'll need some particulars. Perhaps if you could give me them so we could spare the other gentleman?'

Patrick nodded and slowly followed the man into an office. 'Could I have the young lady's full name, sir?' The attendant had seated himself behind a desk, pen poised over a form. 'Oh, please.' He waved the pen at the chair on the opposite side of the desk.

Patrick made use of it. 'Rosanna Feeney.' Her last words came tumbling back: 'Tim and I are married, Grandfather. We were married last week.' Well, he'd be damned if he'd soil her memory by giving her the name of her murderer. To Patrick she was still a Feeney.

The man asked her date of birth. That was another obstacle. Patrick couldn't be accurate. He gave the date on which she had always celebrated her birth since she had come to live with the family. 'Fifth of November, eighteen seventy-one.'

'And was she single, sir, or married?'

'Single,' answered Patrick without hesitation.

Well, that answers my worry whether I should tell him or not, decided the man as he scribbled on the form.

Patrick completed the remainder of the paper, then went out to join his son, oblivious that along with Rosanna had perished his first great-grandchild.

PART FIVE

1892–1900

CHAPTER THIRTY-SEVEN

As was his habit, Dickie examined his clothes for convicting testimony of the afternoon's dalliance. Satisfied that there were no rogue hairs he proceeded towards the house. His stealthy approach was useless. There was Mary at the door, ever vigilant. Gracing her with his crinkly smile he went to seek out his wife. It had just turned Christmas. The room he entered was still heavy with the scent of pine and other greenery. Dusty's face smiled up at him – then seeing the dog at his heels she gave a groan. 'Oh, not another one!' Dickie was always bringing her 'presents' like this, a kitten or some other waif. She felt it must be his way of making up for her childlessness but had never put it to him – they didn't talk much about that.

Dickie bowed to the dog. 'Bonzo, meet your mistress, Primrose Feeney!' Dusty set her mouth at the use of her real name which she hated. Her husband swung across the room. 'Come along an' little Primmy will give you a kiss.'

'Little Primmy will give him a kick – motheaten thing! What sort do you call that?'

'It's a lurker.'

She tutted. 'You mean a lurcher.'

'No, a lurker – watch this.' Dickie marched around the perimeter of the room. The dog clung to his heels like a limpet. 'See? Lurker! I know I promised not to bring any more but I couldn't get rid o' the bloody thing – tossed it a candy an' got a friend for life.' He collapsed into a seat beside her. ''S a good feeling.'

'Go give it to Mary and tell her to feed it! I don't want fleas all over me – oh, there's a couple of envelopes on the mantel from Sonny. I haven't opened them.'

He got to his feet and moved to pick up the letters, the

dog with him. 'Get away, Bonzo!' he issued gruffly as he almost tripped. 'Two, eh? Must have a conscience for forgetting my birthday.' Dickie had just reached that dreaded forty years – and had been happily surprised to find he didn't feel any different. 'I hope there's money in 'em.' He grinned, ripped the knot from his tie and, after pouring himself a drink, opened one of the letters.

Dusty had never seen her husband cry – not like this. Genuine sobs of grief assailed her as she sat there completely taken aback. Seconds passed before she could finally bring herself to utter, 'For God's sake, what is it?'

Both letters fell from his grasp as he put his hands up to hide his distress. The only tears Dickie had ever shed had been those of self-pity or cowardice. He had never felt so utterly devoured by grief. He gave a huge shuddering sigh. 'It's Rosanna . . . she's dead. She's been shot!' All of a sudden his big body looked decidedly shrunken, like a spider screwing itself into a ball.

With a cry of sympathy she flew to him, fell at his knees and clasping his wet, distorted face between her palms dotted it with soothing kisses. And though she had never known Rosie she wept, too. The dog, unnerved, scurried about the room, finally coming to rest under a table from whence it watched as the couple tried to comfort each other. After the flood of sorrow had abated, Dusty sniffed and said, 'I'm so bloody useless . . . If I could've given you a baby . . .'

'Oh, no, no . . . no.' He tightened his hold on her, pressed his hard cheek to hers. 'If there's anybody useless here it's me. What sort of father would I have made, I ask ye? All I ever did for Rosanna was to get her born . . . it's Sonny who's done the job for me. Oh Christ, what must he be going through?' He fixed his wife with despairing eyes. 'An' what the hell am I ever going to write? Will he even want to read it?'

'He's written to you, hasn't he?' She stroked and patted him. With her gentle words the dog sidled back to its former position at Dickie's feet. Dusty ignored it. 'He wants you to write.'

'You know me . . . always say the wrong bloody thing. I can't think of how to comfort him.'

'There was a time when you wouldn't have even thought about things like that. I'm sure you'll manage.' Her knees were hurting. She rose and transferred herself to his lap, both of them lying back in the chair contemplatively. 'Dickie . . .' she said finally, 'how would you feel about adopting a child?' She turned her face to his and saw that she had stunned him. 'It's not going to happen now for us, is it? I'm even more decrepit than you.'

'I don't mind . . .' he began.

'Yes you bloody do!' She came alive. 'Dickie, it's no good pretending any longer! You do mind! I mind!'

He studied her distraught features, then drew her back into his embrace. 'We'll think about it.'

'We'll think about it now!'

'I've just lost my daughter!'

'She wasn't your daughter! She was Sonny's daughter!' At his moan of pain she grabbed his face. 'We're going to talk about it, damn you! I want a child!'

'All right!' he barked. Then, 'All right . . .' His tone lowered and he kissed her. 'We'll see about it.'

'When?'

'Dusty, I can't think straight . . .'

'When?'

'My God, you're a wee terrier . . . ! All right, we'll go tomorrow.'

They both relaxed. After great pondering he heaved a long sigh. 'What sort d'you want?'

'Come on, Dickie,' she chided softly. 'Stop talking about it as though it's a dog. I know you want a child – don't you? I said, don't you?'

He accomplished a shaky smile, though the pain in his breast was still terrible. 'Aye, you bugger . . . I want a child . . . a son. But I don't know if the adoption society would consider an old reprobate like me.'

'You, who could charm the . . .' Dusty grasped for a simile. The knickers off a nun, Sonny would say. Dickie closed his eyes at the vision of his grieving brother. 'It doesn't have to be a baby. The Lord knows there must be plenty of older children whom nobody wants. We could have one or two.'

'Oh God, steady on, Dusty! I'm a poor old bugger of forty.' His downward glance caught the other unopened letter. Dusty noticed it too and reached for it, wondering what it bore. Dickie looked at the date on the front. It had obviously gone astray, having been posted long before the other. 'My birthday card,' he guessed – and it was, bringing the tears back to his eyes. He fought them this time, but not for long. Enclosed in the card was a photograph of the family taken on Rosanna's coming of age.

'Ah, Dusty,' he mopped his face and stared at the picture. 'The old fella must be absolutely crippled with misery over this, ye know. God, I wish . . . I wish to bloody hell it'd been me instead o' her.'

The old fella was slumped in a chair, staring out at the frost-furred garden. There was a glass of whiskey in his hand, the only thing that seemed real. Since Rosie's death he couldn't set his mind to anything. The pain of missing her was physical; it raked his mind, leaving it raw and suppurating. His liver-spotted hands gripped the arm of the chair as he stared at his memory of her. How on earth had she managed to get herself wed without any of them suspecting it? It must have been after her twenty-first birthday – probably when she had gone to visit Sonny for the weekend. He should have told Sonny about the liaison long ago. Poor Sonny . . . but his trial hadn't ended at the mortuary: because Rosanna had been shot in a Republican house her whole family automatically came under suspicion. There had been a visit from the Special Branch. Patrick hoped he had convinced them how he detested that scum as much as they did. He had offered total assistance . . . not that it would help Rosie now.

He couldn't understand how the rest of his family could go about their daily habits when he himself was still incapacitated weeks after the funeral. He knew that Thomasin was hurting as much as he was – they had cried bucketfuls together – but now she was back at the store and working as normal. Patrick still needed to cry and to talk about his dead grandchild, but everyone else seemed too busy getting on with their own lives. And then he had thought of Molly – she would listen to his sorrow, would cry with him. He had gone across the field to where Joseph was working and asked if it wouldn't be too much of an inconvenience to the man's wife if he called to have a jaw with his old pal. 'She'll not chew me head off, will she, Joe? I know us Feeneys are none too popular.'

'Why, I'm sure 'twould be fine enough, sir,' Joseph had answered. 'But sure, I thought somebody woulda tellt ye – Molly's been dead this past half year. She took one too many and got herself drowned.'

Deeply shocked, he had offered garbled condolences, then retreated, gone home, where he had remained ever since. Stephen Melrose was a good enough foreman and could run the business quite ably. He didn't need for Patrick to be there . . . come to that, who did need Patrick? His chest heaved. God, I'm seventy-three years old. Why didn't Ye take me, eh? Why did Ye take Rosie who was so young and vital, who meant so much to me, who made me laugh . . .

He was about to raise the glass, then, feeling eyes on him, rotated his head to find Belle standing in the doorway. 'Now how long have you been standing there spying on me?'

She smiled and limped her way carefully between the furniture, carrying a tray which bore a jug and glasses. Poor Grandfather, how badly Rosie's death had hit him. Nobody could seem to hold his attention for long. One minute he'd be listening and the next his eyes would mist over and you'd know he was thinking about Rosie. Belle could not say that she felt the same depth of bereavement, for she had never been close to her cousin, but she did feel sadness for her grandfather, left behind to grieve. She put the tray on the table. Small puffs of steam billowed from the jug. 'There'd be no need for spies if you left the whiskey bottle alone.'

'Ah, you're as bad as the rest.' Again he swilled his throat with whiskey.

'They're only concerned about you, Gramps.' She pushed an armchair next to his and sat to watch him.

'I know, darlin', I know.' The glass visited his lips again.

'You're not going to find her in there.'

'It numbs me a little,' he said tiredly.

'That's all right for a while . . . But sitting here dwelling on your sorrow in this fashion isn't going to bring her back.'

A spark. 'Christ! She hasn't been gone two months. Y'expect me to be laughing like a hyena?' The glass was depleted. He reached for the bottle. Quicker than he was, she whipped it away and went to pour two glasses of hot lemon and honey. 'I'm not havin' any o' that pitchwiss,' he told her as she handed him the warm glass.

She placed it on the table. 'It's that or nothing. You're not having the whiskey back. I won't be accomplice to your suicide.'

'God dammit – give me that whiskey!'

'No!' As he struggled to rise she went to retrieve the bottle, but instead of giving it to him she took the cork out and poured it into an aspidistra pot.

'You wee bitch!' His fingers clawed at the chair arms.

'And you're an old misery!' she flung back. And was horrified to see tears begin to roll down his face. She was at his side immediately. 'Gramps, I didn't mean it! I didn't mean to hurt you. I just wanted to bring some of your old fight back.'

He shook his head and pulled out a handkerchief to mop his face. ''S not you. Oh God, Belle, will it ever go away, this bloody awful pain?'

She sat on the chair arm and cradled his head, while he continued to weep. 'Gramps, you said yourself it's only been a few months. It'll go in time, I'm sure. I wish there was something I could do to help you.'

He blew his nose and screwed the handkerchief in his fist. 'There's nothing anybody can do. I feel so bloody alone.'

'You still have me, you know,' she said in a small voice.

He raised bloodshot eyes. 'But I don't, do I, Belle? You're going away, too.'

'I haven't found a house yet.' This was untrue, but the anguish in his old eyes had produced a rare pang of conscience. She would have to go back on her word. She couldn't leave him like this. 'Anyway, I'm sick of tramping round in the cold. I thought I'd wait until the weather got a bit kinder . . . that's if the children won't be too much?'

'Ah no, I like to hear their noise. It reminds me I'm still alive. God knows I need reminding sometimes.' He fumbled for one of her hands. 'I'd love nothing more than for you to stay, Belle, but I'd not interfere with your plans.'

'Just because I accused Mother of that doesn't mean I think the same of you.' She leaned over and hugged him. 'I'll stay for as long as you like – anyway, as everybody keeps trying to tell me, it'll put a few years on my back, won't it?'

For the moment the pain was lifted and he grunted his content. Then he said, 'Harking back to your previous sentiment there is one thing you can do to make me a little happier. Make it up with your mother. There's been enough heartbreak in this house.'

'I'd love to oblige, but she won't speak to me and I'm not about to throw the children out, which is what she would like.'

'Jaze, I don't know what's wrong with this family. It's composed of a load o' goats. You're as bad as any o' them. There's a grand young fella who can't take his eyes off ye . . .'

'You mean Brian?'

'Ye couldn't do much better than him for your husband.'

'Now, Gramps, I've told you I have no intention of marrying – even to suit you. And I think you're got the wrong idea about Brian – our friendship is based on mutual interest. He's as little plan of marrying as I have.'

'Open your eyes, Belle. The fella's in love with ye.'

Belle had the idea that her grandfather was right, but she wasn't going to admit it.

'Well . . . if that's true then I'm sorry but I can't return his emotions. I just feel that men can't be trusted.' She noted his expression. 'Oh, I don't include you in "men", Grandfather.'

She had managed to make him laugh, but it was a brittle sound. 'Ah God, that does wonders for my masterful image.'

A light tap. 'You know I meant no disrespect. Apart from you I've found no reason to rely on men. There was that business with Ti . . .' She pulled up swiftly, but too late. 'Oh, Gramps, I didn't mean to bring his name into it. How stupid I am.'

His old head moved wearily. 'Ye were right it seems not to trust Timothy.' He sighed. 'So, I must rely on Nick to provide me with great-grandchildren?'

'If it's natural ones you refer to, yes. Those upstairs are the only ones I can give you.'

'Ah well, they're grand wee bairns. I shall miss the sound of their chatter when ye finally go.'

'That won't be for a long time yet.'

'You're not just doing this for me? I should hate to feel like one o' your charity cases.'

'Pff! Who'd be charitable towards a grumpy old devil like you?' She found a tartan rug and tucked it round his knees, pressing the still warm drink into his hands. 'And if you think that my reason for staying is that I feel sorry for you then just you wait until this weather perks up and I'm dragging you round York to look for a house. I'm going to need your expert advice if I'm not to land myself with a load of dry rot.'

'Rot is the word,' he replied cynically. 'Ye've never needed anyone's advice – an' ye still haven't answered me about your mother. Please, Rosie . . .' Belle's heart went out to the poor old fellow – he was getting so confused. 'Put your independence aside for once and be the one to stuff the baccy in the pipe o' peace.'

'I'll try,' she sighed. 'But you know Mother doesn't smoke – and if I do this then I want something in return. You must stop this silly drinking.'

'Tut! Haven't I always been the hard-drinking man? I don't know why everyone's so concerned all of a sudden.'

'I wouldn't be so concerned if you were getting drunk for enjoyment, but you're not, are you?'

'Ah, don't worry, Belle. I always had a tendency to hit the bottle when things got rough . . . your mother will tell you that. It'll pass.'

'It will if you make the effort.'

He pondered, then nodded.

'Right! I'll talk to Mother when she comes in if it will make you happy.'

Patrick gripped her hand, saying sincerely, 'If anyone can make me happy, then it's you, my pet.' But my God, it's going to take some time, came his silent cry.

If Patrick had assumed that because the rest of the family had returned to their normal habits they had recovered from Rosie's death then he was very wrong. Thomasin grieved for her vivacious grandchild as much as he did, but she would not allow her sorrow to destroy her like it was destroying Patrick. Much as she sometimes felt as if she were in a trance she forced herself to carry on. It was the way it had been with Dickie. She couldn't sit still for one moment. As soon as she had eaten dinner she'd be out and away to some meeting or other. For to stay in that house would be fatal. But there were times when she was alone in her counting house when she would think of Rosie and her eyes would swim. The vision that came was not the one that gave Patrick nightmares, but that of the girl's stunning appearance the day she had gone to visit Sonny . . . the bloom on her face. Had Thomasin's suspicions been well-founded? Had she indeed been pregnant? She tried to convince herself otherwise, for to imagine thus only made things worse. And if Patrick had been told then he had made no mention.

She damned her husband's weakness. Why did it always have to be her who was the strong one? What would become of the family should she seek remedy in the whiskey bottle? Oh, it wasn't just the drinking that irritated her but his whole attitude – he didn't seem to consider that she or anyone else might be suffering as acutely as he was. He viewed Nick's lack of tears as coldness, but Thomasin didn't need tears as evidence of her grandson's hurt. Nick was flattened by this, though he managed to cope with it better than his grandfather. To help the lad over this terrible bereavement she had considered sending him to the Leeds store as manager, but felt it might be too great a burden. Besides, had she swapped places with him and returned to look after the York shop that would mean more time in her husband's company and in his miserable state he was the last companion she wanted. She decided to wait another few months. Maybe by the time he was twenty-one Nick would be ready for the responsibility. Twenty-one ... she hoped that the boy's coming of age would see Patrick's emergence from his depression.

For all Thomasin sensed Nick's hurt she had not the vaguest inkling of the guilt that partnered it. He held himself as much to blame for his sister's death as the person who had pulled the trigger, for only he had known she was meeting Rabb. He could have put a stop to it any time with one sentence to his grandfather, but in this one crucial instance his perceptive brain had miscalculated. Hear all, see all, say nowt: the one who knew everything about everybody had failed to see the danger his sister was in. At this moment he couldn't give a damn about the Leeds store or anything else. He could only imagine his pretty Rosanna cowering from the assassin's bullet ... and perhaps the biggest penalty to pay was that he was unable to share his guilt with anyone else – not even Moira, for she had left him as well, in search of someone who would offer her marriage.

For Sonny, too, the grief was overpowered by guilt. All these years Rosanna must have been meeting with her killer under his nose. Yes, his father was partly to blame for not telling him – but if he had been any kind of father he would have questioned her comings and goings instead of attributing them to her tinker blood. Thank God he had Josie and the girls to get him through this.

Erin was equally affected by Rosie's death, though her guilt took the form that might normally follow any bereavement. In the wake of the murder she had scourged herself for all the times she had blamed Rosanna for some childhood prank when Belle had been the real culprit. Oh, it was a futile, destructive practice to hark back so many years, but she couldn't help it. And being met by the sight of her inebriated father every evening when she came home from work didn't help matters. Here he was again tonight, slumped in his chair with a near-empty bottle on the table. Standing in the doorway, about to enter, Erin felt the temper boil up around her. How many times had she scolded and begged him to ease off this habit and here was the room stinking like a brewery. He must have been shut up in here all day for it to smell like this. She just could not bear to put up with such a depressive atmosphere this evening. Instead of waiting for the others to arrive for their supper she would ask for a tray to be sent up to her room.

'Are you going in, Mother?' Erin started as her daughter approached from behind, but made no move nor comment, just cast her eyes back on the drawing room scene. Belle strained to look over her shoulder, then groaned. 'Oh, Lord . . . I see he's found another bottle. I took one off him this morning and he seemed to be doing all right the last time I looked in. He must have decided to see if I kept my part of the bargain before embarking on his.' In explanation she added, 'I told him I'd offer you the pipe of peace.'

'Well, I trust you're not intending to light it in here? With these fumes the place would go up like a volcano.'

Well, that was a start, thought Belle. At least she's responding. 'He said if I made it up with you he'd make the effort to stop drinking.'

'Oh, so you're going to be the one who's to have the honour of saving him from himself where all of us less important folk have failed,' said Erin coldly. 'All right,

549

then, I'm listening. Are you going to tell me you're prepared to go back to university?'

'No, but . . .'

'Then you may as well go in there and top up his glass for him!' Erin brushed past her and continued up the stairs, ignoring Belle's plea for her to talk about this.

As angry at Patrick as at her mother, Belle pitched into the drawing room, delivering a vicious jab to Patrick and, when he woke, brandished the whiskey bottle at him. 'You didn't even give me the chance to put my side of the bargain to Mother before welching on your own, did you?'

'For God's sake, don't go waking a man like that . . .' Patrick moaned and screwed a hand round his sleepy face. 'What're ye spouting about?'

'This!' The bottle was thrust at him again. 'You said you'd dispense with it if I made it up with Mother.'

'An' did ye?' He began to come awake, stretching his old limbs.

'No – but that's no reason for you to renege! I humbled myself on your account.'

'I never asked you on my account!' retorted Patrick. 'I was thinking of you an' your mother – an' humble? Hah! That's hilarious.' Then he took time to study her angry face and expelled a sigh. 'Ah well . . . I suppose I wasn't showing very much faith in your bargaining power.'

She vibrated her lips. 'And you'd be right – Mother wouldn't listen unless it was to hear that I was going back to university. So! I'd better do as she suggests.' She tipped the whiskey bottle at his empty glass. He asked what she was doing. 'As Mother said, if I can't bring my half of the deal into practice then I can't expect you . . .'

She broke off as he pushed the bottle away before it had wet the glass. 'I'll try,' he said quietly.

Belle fully expected to see a bottle at Patrick's side when she looked in on him the following morning, but was delighted to see that there wasn't. Nor did she spot one at any time during the day whenever she popped her head round the door to check up on him. Towards the time when the others usually arrived home for supper she looked in one more time. He put down his book and fluttered his hands. 'Look – no glass.'

'Taken to drinking from the bottle, have you?' She smiled at his mock outrage.

'I'll have you know I haven't touched a drop since you laid the law down – not even my usual quota.' She asked what his usual quota was. 'Oh, two, three glasses on an evening.'

'Well, as you've been so good I'm going to let you have one glass.' She poured this out and handed it to him.

'Oh, Belle, I can just see the kindness and compassion oozing out o' ye.' But he accomplished a smile before sipping at her offering.

'That'll be your daily allowance from now on,' she instructed. 'And mind you adhere to it.'

While the winter months persisted it was a hard pledge for him to stick to – the days were so long. Thinking of Rosie made it difficult to sleep, especially with the recent news that her killer had escaped – probably to America. He rose very early. After breakfast he would fill in as much time as he could by reading the newspaper from back to front, then maybe take a walk before lunch. The presence of Belle's children helped to fill in a portion of the afternoon, but they could not be expected to keep company with an old man for more than an hour. Belle spent what time she could with him, but she had her own commitments. With little else to do but read, his 'evening whiskey' began earlier and earlier.

However, when the summer came Belle was grateful to see her grandfather return to his fields, relying more on work than whiskey to dull his pain. Even Nick's leaving to manage the Leeds store didn't set him back as she feared it might. By autumn the re-emergence of his self-respect led her to the decision of looking for a house again. It really had been a sacrifice having to stay for so long, the way her mother behaved towards her and the children.

Alas, Belle's plans were thwarted once again by the anniversary of Rosanna's death, when Patrick returned to the anaesthetising properties of the whiskey bottle. Thank goodness, she thought, that these bouts of drinking tended to ebb and flow. When her grandfather had his family around him – as at Christmas – he was able to behave perfectly sensibly. Only when Sonny and his tribe went back to Leeds and everyone else was at their respective occupations did his loneliness conquer his better judgment. Belle resolved to ensure that he did not spend another winter like the last, but was equally determined that this wasn't going to mean her staying for another year either. So, fifteen months after her original decision to rent a house she finally made the move.

Within a week she found a place large enough to meet her needs, with a rent she could afford. The latter was due to the house's neglected state; it seemed that the landlord preferred to take the same money year after year instead of putting any work into his property. However, Belle was to use this to her advantage. Who better to bring it into shape than her grandfather? And so, during those bleak months Patrick was given a reason to stay off the liquor, pointing brickwork, plastering, painting . . . It was a great shame, thought Belle, that the house had not been more dilapidated so that the repair work could have lasted until summer. But once she was settled in she would try to involve him somehow until he was able to get out to his fields again.

With the house ready for its new occupants she was today sorting all her belongings into packing cases ready for the move. It was in this pose that Brian came upon her when paying one of his frequent visits to the house in Peasholme Green.

'Oh, Brian, what a time you've chosen to socialise,' she bemoaned as he caught her with hair a-riot and dirt smudges on her face, her belongings spread all over the drawing room floor. 'Come in if you must, but don't expect me to break off and send for tea.' The sorting continued, book on that pile, picture on another.

'How odd, I could have sworn I saw "welcome" on that doormat, Belle.' Showing just how at home he felt here,

Brian walked straight to the bellrope, 'I'll ring for my own tea, thank you very much,' then sat down to watch her. 'Anyway, what makes you think I want to spend an afternoon in the company of a scruffy old scold?'

Used to his ways by now, she didn't need to see the grin to know·he was joking. 'Then why are you here?'

'I thought we might take a trip.'

'In this weather?' She indicated the window, though it was impossible to see through the layer of condensation, which of course spoke for itself. 'I've a thousand and one things to do. If you really want to make yourself welcome you can load these crates onto your carriage and transport them to the new house.' She selected a piece of crystal which had previously stood on her dressing table and wrapped it noisily in newspaper. There was a piece missing; Vinnie had initially been helping but after smashing the crystal had been banished.

'Delighted to help. We can do that when we go on our trip.'

The scrumpling of paper ceased. 'For goodness' sake, what trip?'

'Our trip to Walmgate. I've someone I'd like you to meet. We can do both jobs at the same time.' The house Belle had rented was in Lawrence Street, just outside Walmgate Bar.

She resumed her packing. 'And just who is this important personage?'

'She's a prostitute,' said Brian as Vinnie entered. 'I thought she might be a suitable candidate for your clan.'

– God love us, thought the little maid, the house is going to be turned into a knocking shop. She bobbed at Brian's order of tea. 'And some of those delightful cakes of Mrs Howgego's,' he added. 'The ones with the coconut on.' The maid departed.

Belle had ceased packing again to stare at him.

'Good Lord, I do believe my words have had an effect. Don't worry, Belle, she's really a very small prostitute.' His expression became grave and he made a move to help her pack, spreading out a sheet of newspaper on the carpet.

'It's not at all amusing, I don't know why I make a joke of everything.'

'Things don't hurt so much if you can joke about them, do they? What're the details?'

He folded the paper around an ornament until she stopped him. 'Leave that and tell me.'

'She was brought to my surgery last night, unconscious. A young fellow had found her lying in the street. Several people had stepped over her before he came to her aid. It transpired that she'd been beaten by a customer.'

'Goodness.' Belle gave up all idea of packing, sitting beside him on the carpet. 'Is she recovered?'

'In a fashion. I patched up her wounds, gave her a superficial examination and made her sleep on the couch for the night. It was in the morning, after she'd breakfasted with me – Mrs Whiteside almost died, I might add – that she confided the problem I'd overlooked.' He faltered. This was where it became slightly embarrassing.

Belle guessed. 'She's pregnant.'

'Would that she were, I could do something about that. No, it's much worse. She's diseased – do you know what sort of disease I mean, Belle?'

'I think so,' she replied carefully. 'I believe it's a risk of her profession?'

He was glad and slightly surprised that he did not have to explain. 'Where did you learn about such things?'

'There's a medical dictionary in Grandfather's library. I read it from cover to cover when I was six. Naturally none of it meant much then, but over the years things fell into place. I remember Gramps being awfully embarrassed when I asked why a certain "lady" kept approaching men while we stood waiting for Nan in town one day. Being a voracious reader of the newspaper I'd be forever asking him what certain words meant and noticed that his cheeks would go pink when the word prostitute was spoken from my infant lips.' She laughed. 'Well, when words have that effect it makes a subject extremely interesting. I decided to find out more and in time associated the disease with the profession – though of course I realise it isn't restricted to prostitution.' Another smile. 'I suppose nice girls aren't meant to talk about those kinds of things.'

'True – but then that wouldn't apply to you, Belle, would it?' He ducked at her swipe.

She became serious once again. 'What I can't understand is, if they know they risk this dreadful disease why do these women choose such a trade? I should like to ask this woman of yours.'

'She's not a woman, Belle. She's thirteen years old.'

'But that's illegal!'

'That doesn't seem to have counted for much,' said Brian. 'Anyway, when the man refused to pay after he'd taken his go she had taunted him about her disease and he'd gone crazy.'

'Where is she now?' demanded Belle, preparing to leave.

He hoisted himself from the carpet. 'She's at her mother's house in Walmgate.'

'Good Christ, she has a mother? What sort of woman would allow her child to lead such a life?'

'It appears it's a family business,' sighed Brian.

'And you permitted her to go back there?' yelled Belle, eyes flashing.

'I could hardly restrain her against her wishes,' he protested. 'But listen, I've told her all about you and she said she'd think about coming here.'

'You should've made her do more than think, Brian.'

'Ah well, I leave that sort of thing to you. You have a more persuasive manner than I.'

'Is there any chance of her infection spreading to the other children?'

'She has no open sores. The disease is in the early stages. I'm attempting to contain it with mercury. She'll be no problem to you. So, after we have our tea do you wish to take a ride to see her?'

'Tea? We're not waiting for any tea. Come along.' She hauled him after her. 'You must take me there at once.'

The young girl, whose name was May, needed rather more persuasion than might have been expected to leave her way of life. She had heard tales of the Refuge at Bishophill where once they got you in you couldn't get out again.

'But it wouldn't be like that if you were to come and live with me,' said Belle, appalled at the state of the house and its occupants. 'My home isn't a prison. You may come and inspect it first, if you wish. I'm sure you'll find it to your taste, and there'll be other children there for you to play with.'

'I'm not a kid,' replied the girl scornfully. Each item of her clothing was badly crumpled and all composed from the same piece of drab. The only bright thing about her was the pheasant plume she had stuck in her hatband: it added a certain defiance to the glint in her eye. She was about four feet ten in height and weighed, Belle would guess, maybe four stones. The boots on her feet, being obviously meant for a much bigger person, gave her a comic look; the lank bedraggled hair, pathos.

You certainly aren't a kid, Belle sighed to herself. My God, how many men have you had – at thirteen? And here's me who'll never know what it's like . . . For that instant she put herself in May's place, beneath all those male bodies. Then she said kindly, 'Of course you're not a kid, May. I meant only that you'd have company and could look after the little ones if you cared to.'

'I'd have to come an' have a look round first,' said the girl warily.

'Naturally,' conceded Belle. 'We are in rather an untidy state at the moment as I'm in the throes of moving. The new house is in Lawrence Street so you wouldn't be too far from home if you wished to visit your mother.' Though God forbid that the child would ever want to come back to this.

'Is he comin'?' May nodded at Brian.

'Doctor Dyson will accompany us,' said Belle. 'Do say you'll come. We'd love to have you.'

With the girl's agreement – her mother was blind drunk in the corner and anyway Belle saw no need to ask her permission – the three went outside to climb into the doctor's carriage, proceeding to the house in Lawrence

Street. After careful scrutiny of the room in which she would be sleeping, May said grudgingly, 'All right, I'll stop here.' And Belle had got herself another child.

Erin had intended to be out of the house and away to the factory before the move got underway, but sadly her timing was inefficient. It seemed that she had missed Belle's instruction to Mrs Howgego that those departing would need an early breakfast, for at the normal time this meal was taken the children were dashing up and down the landing bawling orders to those down below in the hall.

Erin heard her daughter's voice chastise them and the emphatic clomp of Belle's boot on the stairs. She waited until it grew fainter before slipping down to the dining room and taking her own breakfast. She felt her parents' searching look but kept her head well down over her meal, making no comment other than on the weather.

'Aye, 'tis a rare day for Belle to be doing her flitting,' remarked Patrick – just as his grand-daughter came in.

'We're about ready.' She was looking at her mother's stiff back.

Thomasin dabbed a napkin to her lips and began to rise. 'Oh, that was quick. You're well organised, Belle. Get your coat on, Patrick, I don't want you standing round in that climate.'

'I don't see *your* coat.' He pushed back his chair.

'Aye well, I'm not so fragile as you.' Thomasin cocked a wink at her grand-daughter.

'An' ye've got more meat on ye,' said her husband, receiving a tap.

'Aren't you coming, Erin?' Thomasin looked back at her daughter who was still seated. Belle waited, too.

'I can just as well say goodbye in here.' Erin didn't even turn.

The three people at the door swapped wearied looks. Patrick went on to make a prompting action with his head at Belle, who took a few steps towards the table. 'Goodbye then, Mother. You'll always be welcome, you know.'

'Goodbye.' No good luck or I'll miss you – just goodbye.

Once outside Thomasin kissed her grand-daughter. 'She will miss you, you know – and so will I.'

Belle returned the sentiment, but her fondest display was for her grandfather to whom she issued instructions that he was to come round this afternoon and occupy the children while she unpacked the cases. 'Somebody has to keep them in order and Brian's on duty.' Patrick said he'd love to come. 'An' I'll bring me shillelagh.' Erin, now upstairs, watched them from the window and saw her daughter drive away after the removal men. In a few more revolutions of the wheels Belle was gone.

CHAPTER THIRTY-EIGHT

For the rest of the year there was no verbal contact between Belle and Erin. On the isolated occasions when Belle had found the time to visit Peasholme Green her mother had kept well out of the way, so now Belle rarely bothered. One advantage this had was to lure Patrick out of his own house and along to hers where the lively company helped to keep his depression at bay – for as usual when the winter came upon them he was very low. Both he and Thomasin seemed tireless in their attempts to reconcile mother and daughter. With this in mind Belle was dreading the Christmas party that her grandmother had arranged, knowing that she would find herself seated next to her mother at the table. But when, on arrival, she took a crafty peep at the seating arrangements she was relieved to find that her grandmother had been unusually considerate; she and her charges were seated as far away from Erin as was possible. Only when the time came to eat and she caught the look on Thomasin's face did she understand – Mother had switched all the labels round herself.

The New Year was born into terrible coldness – both

in Erin's heart and in the elements. The tenth day of February, eighteen ninety-five, dawned to find the Ouse frozen over. Those lucky enough to have foreseen this event were ready equipped and able to spend the Sabbath skating up and down the petrified river. Belle, being too preoccupied with earning her living and the care of her brood to notice the worsening climate, had to wait until Monday to purchase several pairs of skates, so infuriating the clan.

'Ch, ch, ch!' she scolded the children now as they danced about excitely on her return from the shop. 'You'll all have a pair if you just have patience.' She dropped the skates in a heap and the children fell on them like wolves. 'Such savages. I hope they're all prepared, Sally?'

'Yes, miss,' replied the nursemaid. 'They've all got their chest protectors on.'

'Capital! Well, I'd better go and change myself or I'll be going the way of those skates.' The children were tugging and fighting over them. 'Stop that or we won't be going anywhere!'

Going upstairs, she changed her dress for one which was much shorter and would not brush the ice. Between this and her undergarments she wore a sheet of brown paper around her chest. It crackled when she moved but it would serve admirably to keep out the cold. Several layers of clothes later she went downstairs.

The eldest girl, May, had taken charge of the others. She was much changed from the dirty suspicious waif whom Belle and the doctor had rescued from a life of prostitution. Quite a pretty child, she was dressed in a plaid dress with white stockings, fur-trimmed coat and hat. Clothes for the children had been donated by various friends though some, like May's outfit, were new. Her own clothes had had to be burnt on entry to her new home. The girl was eager to be off, pushing the others into order. The two youngest, Lucy and Tom, were to be left in the nursemaid's charge.

Belle, straightening a child's bonnet, enquired if all were

wearing mittens. 'I don't want anybody complaining they're cold. And do any of you need to relieve yourselves? I'm not putting half a dozen pairs of skates on and then have someone say they want to go – Cedric, what about you?'

Cedric, at ten, was mortified to be asked such a personal question in front of others. 'I've already been.'

'You said that before our last outing,' riposted May. 'Then we all had to come 'ome early just so's you could have a pee.'

'May!' rebuked Belle.

'We-ell, he's always spoilin' it for us,' was May's petulant complaint.

'Nevertheless, that's no way for a lady to talk. Now Cedric, are you absolutely sure?'

'It wasn't just me,' objected the boy. 'Eddie wanted to go an' all.'

'Look, we don't wish to have an hour-long discussion on people's bodily habits,' said Belle. 'I shall ask one more time. Is there any of you who wants to go?' Her examination of each was met by a unified shake of head. 'Very well, but if we get there and any person says otherwise that person stays at home the next time. Understood?'

'Oh, please can we go now?' begged little Anna.

Belle arranged them to her satisfaction with May at the back of the queue and, each clutching a pair of ice skates, they set off. The river was a marvellous sight on this crisp February day. A vast ribbon of ice stretching far away to meet the brilliant blue of the sky, it seemed to sparkle with mirth at the way it had crept so sneakily through the night to encase the unsuspecting barges tethered along the quayside, rendering them unusable for who could guess how long. Vendors had taken advantage of the severe snap, rigging up their stalls on the hibernating river: hot-chestnut sellers, trays spread with fresh parkin, muffins that steamed on the nippy air. There were sleds and toboggans and hundreds of skaters.

'Oh, look,' said May, pointing to the man selling ice-skates. 'I bet he was here yesterday. We could've come, after all.'

'Yes, but look at the price,' replied Belle. 'Tuppence ha'penny more than I paid.'

May grumbled as she sat down to put on her skates. 'All that brass you've got an' yer worried about a few pence.'

'Your impression is sadly mistaken, May, but if I do have any money it's because I look after the pennies and don't throw them away. Now, did you come here to grouse or to skate?' May mumbled her answer. 'Then help the little ones on with their skates, or by the time we're ready the ice will be thawed.'

The skates in place, she watched the children totter onto the ice, then seated herself on a convenient box to observe. The temperature remained static but the sight of her charges having the time of their deprived lives was sufficient to ward off the cold. Shortly – inevitably – the children became peckish and clamoured for nourishment. Belle forked out for six portions of pie and peas which were attacked with verve and consumed so rapidly that little pockets of steam still hovered around the devourers' heads, even after the plates had been returned.

After lunch the children returned whooping to the ice, whereupon it was decided by May that they should all skate up to Poppleton. 'And I'm to sit here shivering while you glide off for a couple of hours, am I?' called Belle at May's proclamation.

'It's not cold,' shouted May. 'I'm sweatin' cobs.'

'Don't be uncouth, May, please,' scolded Belle. 'And there's no wonder you're hot, you're never still. I have to sit here and freeze while you lot have all the enjoyment.'

'We could buy a sledge an' drag you with us,' suggested May. 'Oh away, Aunt Belle. Look, everyone's off. We can't get lost – it's a straight road.'

'You think I'm bothered about you getting lost? I'll be glad to see the back of you. Oh, go on then, but – May! Wait until I've finished speaking, please.' May spun round on the ice, arms windmilling. 'Don't be hours, I have a pupil coming later this afternoon.' Apart from writing articles for women's journals Belle gave tuition in several musical instruments; also educational assistance to those who could afford to pay for the privilege. 'Make sure the little ones don't stray. Everyone hold hands. Stay in a chain.'

She stood to watch them go, the tiny ones wobbling dangerously as May hauled the chain after her. 'And come straight back! No sitting around on the ice or you'll get something nasty.' She pulled her collar up around her face and began to limp along the river bank. There was no point in loitering there for an hour or more, she might as well keep the circulation moving.

'Belle!' She turned to see Brian hurrying up. 'I thought it was you,' he panted, slowing to walk beside her.

'Well, I'm hardly to be mistaken for anyone else, am I?' she responded jocularly. 'And what is our illustrious doctor doing here when he should be treating the sick?'

'If you don't object I was just between calls when I spotted you from the bridge. I've a call to make up at Friargate. I may as well walk this way. On your own?' He looked at the frozen river for signs of the children.

'I've been deserted,' she told him. 'May's taken the others up to Poppleton. I hope it doesn't tire the little ones too much. She can be over-enthusiastic at times.' Her cheeks were bright pink, as was the tip of her nose. Brian thought how lovely she looked.

'How's she settling down?'

'Quite well, I'll never be able to make a lady of her of course,' she smiled. 'But she's very good with the others.'

'And is it safe for gentlemen to enter your house now?' At first May had treated every one of Belle's male visitors as prospective customers, apart from Patrick who to her was obviously past it. It had been highly embarrassing. Belle had been compelled to have a strict talk with her.

'Well, I can't say if it's safe for gentlemen yet but you'll certainly be all right.'

'Thank you so much.'

'Doesn't it look lovely?' Belle moved leisurely beside him in her up and down gait, eyes sparkling with the frost.

'Wonderful. I wish I didn't have to make the call. I'd

be on there with them. Why haven't you got your skates on?'

'With this?' Belle indicated her surgical boot.

'I'm sure with our ingenuity we could improvise.'

'Thank you very much, but I prefer to keep my feet on dry land.' The thought of all that water lurking beneath the ice produced an involuntary shiver.

'So what are you going to do while you wait for the clan to return?' he enquired. 'You can't keep parading up and down in this area. You'll be arrested.'

'Brian, I wish you wouldn't be so heavy-handed with the compliments.'

'Come with me,' he suggested.

'On your rounds?'

'Just to this call,' he pointed to the sidestreet. 'I've a child to see.'

Belle pondered for a moment, then said, 'All right – but I must be back here before the children else they'll wonder where I am.'

The house to which Brian took her had a freshly-painted frontage. The interior, too, was exceptionally neat and tidy. Yet there was a definite malaise that hit Belle immediately she entered. Looking at Brian she could tell he sensed it, too.

'Good afternoon, Doctor.' The woman who had let them in took Brian's hat and laid it on the hallstand. Her mouth curved upwards but the outer edges of the smile twitched nervously and the eyes seemed reluctant to meet his as she spoke. 'It's my son. He's upstairs. Had a bit of an accident.'

'What sort of accident?' Brian followed her upstairs with Belle taking up the rear.

'He pulled a hot iron on himself.'

'Good heavens, how did he manage to do that?' They had reached the bedroom. Brian stepped in and approached the bed where a pale face stared up at him, the covers pulled down to the owner's waist despite the formation of ice on the small window.

'Well, I'd been ironing, you see,' said the woman,

563

rubbing her arms either through cold or apprehension. 'I had another iron heating on the hob when Samuel, that's him, he sort of . . . oh, I don't know how he did it but he managed to knock the iron onto himself.'

On the sparrow-like chest stood a perfect imprint of the iron, lobster pink and puckered at the edges, obviously more uncomfortable than the intense cold of the room. The doctor bit back his exclamation and studied the wound more closely, assuring the wary child that he wasn't going to touch it. 'How did you come to do this, old chap, eh?'

'I knocked it off the hob by accident,' recited the boy, keeping a close eye on the position of Brian's hands. 'It hurts.'

'I'll bet it does,' murmured the doctor, then looked at Belle. 'Would you care to take a look?' He moved aside in order for her to step closer to the bed.

'That's dreadful.' Her forehead creased into a frown.

'It's even more dreadful when you know how the wound was inflicted,' said Brian, his eyes riveted to the mother's. Belle looked from one to the other as Brian asked the woman, 'Would you care to tell me what really happened?'

'But I told you,' the woman would not meet his stare. 'He pulled the iron on himself.'

'It's impossible to incur such a burn in that fashion. That wound was inflicted deliberately.'

'No!'

'The red-hot iron was placed flat on the boy's chest and held there.'

'No!' There was fear in the eyes. 'He'll swear, it was an accident.'

'Brian, what are you saying?' asked Belle.

'I should've thought that was patently obvious,' said the doctor angrily.

'God Almighty,' breathed the young woman.

'It was an accident,' insisted the patient's mother. 'You've no right to come in here saying things like that. I shall contact my lawyer and have you sued for slander.'

'Oh, do stop all this idiotic pretence,' snapped Brian. 'I

know and you know that this burn was inflicted purposely. The question is, by whom? Was it the boy's father?'

'No!'

Brian turned to the frightened boy. 'Was it your father who did this?' The head moved from side to side. 'Then who?'

'It was an accident. I did it myself.'

'No one is going to hurt you for telling the truth,' said Brian firmly. 'But you must tell us for your own good. Was it your father?'

'No . . .' Samuel agonised, then said, 'Mother did it – but she didn't mean to!' he cried as Brian turned on the woman, his face contorted with disgust.

'He doesn't know what he's saying,' defended the woman. 'He's delirious.'

'I'm going to report this matter to the SPCC,' decided Brian abruptly.

'What's that?'

'You know very well, I think!'

'I didn't do it deliberately!' The woman finally broke her pretence. 'He was just getting on my nerves, dancing about with no clothes on, like a savage, screaming and shouting. He looked just like his father. Something seemed to take over me. I just picked up the iron and pressed it to his chest . . . oh, God, he did scream. I couldn't believe what I'd done. When I saw that great big mark appearing on his skin I couldn't believe it was me who'd done it.' She put her face in her hands.

'It's all right, Mam.' The boy tried to leave his bed.

'Stay there,' commanded Brian firmly, but then more softly, 'Your mother will be recovered in a moment.' He turned a disbelieving face to Belle. Her own expression mirrored his feelings. How could the boy show such loyalty to one who had treated him so barbarously? 'What're we to do?'

'He can't stay here,' said Belle positively. 'She may do it again.'

'Oh no, ma'am, I wouldn't, honestly,' sobbed the woman. 'Please don't take him away, he's all I have. His father's dead and I've no other children. I swear I didn't mean to do it. Everything just got on top of me. Please, please don't report me.'

The doctor ran his hand over his hair, his expression communicating his indecision to Belle.

'I don't want to leave my mam,' said Sam pitifully. 'I love her. It wasn't her fault, it was my naughtiness made her do it. I promise I'll be good but don't take me away.'

'Well, I can't think that removing the boy is going to help him,' said Brian to Belle who nodded her agreement, though loathing what she had witnessed. 'Pining for his mother won't aid recovery.'

'I've a suggestion to make,' said Belle to both adults. 'What if Samuel were to come to me – just for a holiday of course, until he's better. It would give you time to put your affairs in order.' This to the woman. 'By rights we should report this. I find it totally unbelievable what you've done. It was a dreadfully severe punishment to inflict on a small boy however much he may have incited you. Terribly cruel. And if I thought that the boy would profit by my taking him away from you then believe me I shouldn't hesitate . . . but Samuel's obviously very attached to you, illustrating that this was probably an isolated event.'

'Oh, it was, it was! I'm devoted to the child. I don't know how I could've done it.'

'Well, you have done it,' replied Belle brutally. 'And he'll bear the scar for life. Don't for one moment look upon my decision as weakness or gullibility. I'm not easily fooled. But for Samuel's sake I'm willing to grant you the benefit of the doubt. He will come to me for three months until you've both had time to heal.'

'Well, I don't know . . .'

'I'm not giving you a choice,' retorted Belle. 'He comes with me now or else he goes to the cruelty people. If it's the latter you'll doubtless never set eyes on him again. This way you have a chance, though I'm positive you don't deserve it.'

It was agreed, though the mother did not like the plan at all. Samuel was wrapped up in blankets against the intense cold, though he cried out pitifully when his wound was chafed.

'I'm sorry, old chap,' said Brian, carrying him down the stairs. 'You won't be in discomfort for longer than we can help.'

'I'm not going for good, am I?' asked Samuel as his tearful mother waved goodbye and the trio marched up the slope towards Clifford Street to get a cab.

'Of course not. Didn't you hear me say so to your mother?' asked Belle.

'I thought you were maybe just saying that,' the boy replied.

'When you know me better you'll understand that what I say I mean and what I mean I say. This is simply a kind of holiday to give your mother a rest. She'll be able to visit you any time she likes.'

'Hey, what's that?' Brian scooped something out of the gutter and dropped it into Sam's blanketed arms. 'There you are, a friend to keep you company while you're away.'

Belle watched the small boy's fingers dig into the kitten's fur and rub it against his face. 'Brian, you can't do that, it might belong to someone.'

'You've got it the wrong way round,' corrected the doctor, scratching the kitten's head with a finger. 'Cats don't belong to people, people belong to cats. And that one's just adopted Sam. Look, they love each other already.'

'It's crawling with vermin,' she complained. 'It'll have to be loused before it sets foot in my home.'

'That's nothing different,' smiled Brian.

'No, you're right there.' Belle closely examined Sam's head. Fortunately this one seemed to be clean.

'Can I keep it?' asked Sam as they neared the thoroughfare.

'It's yours,' answered Brian. 'And he'll make you feel less homesick. He'll be away from home, too.'

Belle hailed a cab and allowed Brian to climb in with his burden. She closed the door after him.

'Aren't you coming?'

'No, I have to wait for the children. Sally will let you in and show you where to put him. I'll try not to be long but you know what they are. Might you still be there when we get back?'

'Possibly. I'll tend to the wound anyway and see him settled in.' The cab rolled away and Belle went back to the river.

When she returned with her brood ninety minutes later she found Samuel tucked into bed, a large square of lint covering his wound and Brian at his side, storybook in hand. 'What a bedside manner you have, Doctor. I hope that cat's not in here?' Brian told her it was in the yard being scrubbed. 'Good. And how will you like it here, Samuel?' she asked the patient. 'Have you been made comfortable?'

'Yes, thank you, ma'am,' he replied civilly.

'Call me Aunt Belle, the others do. You'll meet them shortly I imagine. They were all for coming up straight away when they heard about the new boy but I thought you might be feeling a bit strange and didn't want you to be overwhelmed. Are you hungry?'

'No, ma'am – I mean Aunt Belle.'

'I'm sure you are. Boys are always hungry. We've brought some fish and chips in with us.'

'My, we are getting degenerate,' exclaimed Brian.

'I had brought a portion for you,' she said loftily, 'but I can see your fastidious tastes would forbid you to consume such lowly fare.'

The book snapped shut. 'If that, in your own inimitable style, was an invitation to tea I should be delighted.'

She smiled at the boy. 'Excuse us Samuel, while we eat. I'll send Sally up with a tray for you.'

'Right.' Samuel lay back against the pillow.

'Hello, Doc,' shouted May at Brian's entry. 'Are you gonna stay an' have some o' these?' She was helping to divide the fish and chips.

'I most certainly am.' He made to steal a chip and she slapped him. 'Eh, none o' that, till you've had your hands washed. I don't know where they've been.'

'May, that's very rude,' reproved Belle.

'He's a doctor, in''e?' said May. 'Touchin' all them sick people. Anyroad you're allus telling us lot to get our hands washed.'

'Get the plates handed round and don't be so cheeky,' commanded Belle.

'No, she's absolutely right,' said Brian. 'May I?' He indicated the scullery and at Belle's nod went through to wash his hands.

'Is the kettle on, May?'

'Tea's made,' said the girl, providing everyone with a plateful of fish and chips then sitting down herself. 'I've just left it to mash.'

'Wait until the doctor comes back,' ordered Belle to the children who had started to tuck in.

'Blimey, they'll be cold if he doesn't hurry up,' said May. 'Oy, Doc!'

'May, be quiet.' Belle sat down and when Brian returned the meal commenced. 'If Great-grandma Fenton could see me now she'd have a fit,' she laughed. 'Fish and chips, indeed!'

'They're delicious,' said Brian.

'They are. They're also quick and convenient. I only hope we can get rid of the smell before my pupil comes.' She glanced at the clock. 'Oh, Lord, half an hour!' and tucked straight in.

After the meal had been consumed several plates of cakes were brought in. 'Put some aside for Samuel,' ordered Belle.

'Why's he got to stay in bed?' asked Cedric.

'I told you, because he has a nasty burn on his chest and he's a bit wobbly with shock,' said Belle. 'You can play with him later.'

'How'd he get the burn?' asked May with jam dribbling down her chin.

'Please don't speak with your mouth full, May.'

The girl swallowed. 'How'd he get the burn?'

'His mother did it – not on purpose, so you must not

imply to Sam that she did,' explained Belle. 'But because of a momentary lapse.'

'What's a momentary lapse?'

'She reached the end of her tether, as I'm going to do if you don't start behaving like a lady. Really, May, you do guzzle. One would think you came from a family of pigs.'

'I do.' May patted her stomach. 'Cor, full as a pregnant elephant.'

'I take it you've had enough?'

'Yes – thank you.'

'Brian?' Belle handed the plate of cakes to him.

'Oh, no thank you. Anything further and I'll be calling for a doctor. You don't believe in underfeeding, do you, Belle?'

There were two cakes left. Edward piped up, 'Please may I have another?'

'I really don't know where you put it all, Eddie,' chided Belle. 'You had better ask if anyone else wants one first. We may have to divide them.'

'May I have one?' asked the boy's sister.

'Of course, dear. Anyone else? You're sure? Then there's one each.'

Edward looked at the plate. One of the cakes was much smaller than the other. Reaching for the plate he surprised Belle by offering it to his sister.

'Why, you are a well-mannered young man, Eddie. I'm glad to see that someone takes notice.' This was for May's benefit.

Shortly May gave a cackle. 'There! That's how good-mannered he is. He knew he'd get an earful if he took the biggest an' his sister was too polite to take the big'n, that's why he let her choose first. Hah! D'you know, Doc, he's got more wrinkles than me grandad's prick, that'n. This after . . .'

'May! Leave the table at once,' commanded Belle in a shocked voice.

'What've I said?' The girl looked from an angry Belle to Brian who pretended to be blowing his nose.

'Go to your room this instant and do not come out until you've learned how to be a lady.'

May went sullenly to the door and slammed it behind her. 'I'm terribly sorry about that, Brian,' apologised Belle. 'She'll never change.'

'You wouldn't want her to, would you?' answered the doctor, having given way to his amusement.

'I suppose not.' Her bad temper collapsed into a smile of resignation. 'May is May. But I really can't have her coming out with such things. Imagine if I should invite my grandparents to tea. They'd wonder what sort of house I was keeping.' She lifted the teapot. 'More tea? No? Then I think we'll do the washing up. Cedric, open that window, there's a dear. Yes, I know it's cold but we don't want the smell of fish and chips sticking to the tapestries, do we?'

Brian stood. 'Well, I'll have to make a move if I'm to catch evening surgery.'

'Isn't it odd how when washing up is mentioned people start to exit?'

'Pile them up,' joked Brian. 'I'll do them tomorrow when I call.'

'Oh, we're to see you tomorrow then?'

'I've a patient upstairs, Miss Teale.'

'Ah yes, it was too much to hope that I would be the object of your visit.'

He paused at the door, smiling fondly at her. 'You'll always be the object of my visits, Belle.'

'Now, now, you know I don't allow sentimentality, Doctor.'

Brian laughed as he departed, 'I'll see you all tomorrow,' but felt more than a twinge of frustration. How long did they have to keep up this pretence, this insignificant banter as though neither of them cared . . . but then maybe it wasn't pretence on her part. Maybe it was just wishfulness that she cared as much as he did. In all the time he had known her she had never given any indication that his feelings were reciprocated. Indeed, if he so much as let the love in his eyes speak for him her caustic wit would come to the rescue.

There was no one else, he was certain – he had asked her once and had received a mouthful for his curiosity – so why would she not let him near her?

CHAPTER THIRTY-NINE

He called at the house every day, ostensibly to benefit his young patient, but Samuel's wound could have been adequately attended to by either Belle or the nursemaid, Sally. It provided a good excuse for him to have the pleasure of her company. Pleasure! That brought a smile. Not the word one might have selected when referring to Belle's company. She scolded, she gibed, she bullied – but the young doctor was ready to bear all this for the sake of one smile from that dear face.

Today, thought Brian, standing by her fireplace, it had the appearance of a pastel sketch as she hobbled in from the yard. Her features were muted by the cold, as if viewed through a wedding veil, soft pinks and creams. He was greeted by laughter as she and the maid bore between them a sheet that had just been removed from the washing line. It stood on its own, a rigid board of frozen linen, the laughing women merely holding a fingertip to its upper corners as they presented it for inspection.

'There you are, Ced, go put your sheet back on,' said Belle playfully.

Cedric's face dropped. He knocked on the sheet as at a door. 'But it's all frozen.'

'I know it's all frozen,' rebuked Belle, though not seriously. 'So are we, aren't we, Sally? It's bad enough having to wash once a week in this climate without some people making more.'

'I'm sorry.' Cedric hung his head. 'I'll try very hard tonight.'

Belle fingered his cheek in a rough caress. 'Good boy.'

There was further amusement as she and the nursemaid tried to fold the sheet. 'Come on, Brian, we need some tactical strength.'

The doctor gladly gave assistance and heaved exaggeratedly at the frozen sheet, the children joining in. When the creaking linen was folded Belle stood it like a birthday card in front of the fire. 'Well, we don't need a clotheshorse.'

'Eh, look at this!' May, who had been helping to get the washing in, came in from the scullery bearing a pair of frozen knickers. With a hand behind each leg she made them 'walk' across the floor.

Belle whipped them away from the girl and hurriedly secreted them from public view.

'She's only annoyed 'cause they're hers,' divulged May to a smiling doctor.

When everyone was ready to partake of a pot of tea and a plate of May's warm scones Brian enquired where the patient was. Belle's eyes toured her foster children. 'There's a question. Has anyone seen Samuel?'

'May brayed him an' he went off roarin',' submitted Eddie.

'Why don't you join the Secret Service?' muttered the girl, filling her mouth with scone.

'May, have I not warned you about being heavy-handed?' Belle showed her annoyance.

'He smashed one o' your pictures,' replied May.

'That doesn't give you leave to take over my responsibility . . .'

'You're always tellin' me to look after 'em, aren't yer?' came the protest.

'Don't interrupt, please. If it was my picture he broke, then it's my duty to chastise him, not yours. Which one did he break?'

'It were your favourite,' mumbled the other sullenly. 'I were gonna take it to get some new glass put in before yer noticed.'

'That was very thoughtful of you.' Belle was chastened.

'Well, yer needn't trouble yerself 'cause I'm not now,' retorted May.

573

Belle exchanged a look of helplessness with the doctor. 'So where did Sam go to?' No one seemed to know. Belle placed a saucer over her cup to keep the tea warm. 'I'd better go look. He could be miles away for all they care.'

'Shall I help?' offered Brian.

'No, you sit there and have one of May's scones, they're delicious.' She stole a peep at May to see if this token would gain forgiveness.

The girl mellowed. 'Well . . . they're not as good as Aunt Belle's,' she was telling the doctor as Belle went off in search of the boy.

Faced with the emptiness of all the other rooms Belle became slightly alarmed, but when Cedric said on her return, 'Maybe he's in the closet,' she nodded sagely and went out to the back yard.

Someone – probably Eddie, thought Belle crossly – too idle to use the proper convenience, had piddled in the yard. She swore as her feet skidded under her. Righting herself with the aid of the clothesprop she continued to the lavatory and knocked on the door. There was no answer. Lifting the latch she hauled on the tongued and grooved door.

'Samuel, why didn't you answer?' she asked at the appearance of the white face. 'I've been looking all over . . . what are you doing?' She followed his wide eyes to the ceramic bowl. 'Oh, you're not bunging it up, are you?' The children, fascinated by the newfangled water closet which Patrick had insisted on installing for her, often shoved items down it just to see them flushed away. Then she looked a little closer. 'Oh, Sam.'

In the six inches of water, its back end disappearing under the bend, the black and white kitten struggled for survival. Claws unsheathed, it scrabbled frantically at the porcelain, eyes filled with fear and incomprehension. Swiftly, Belle dipped into the lavatory bowl and seizing the half-drowned creature by its skinny neck plucked it to safety, summoning the boy to follow her to the house. Here she flicked a towel from the airer that hung over the range and wrapped the animal in it, rubbing briskly while the other children crowded round her.

'There we are, no damage done.' Belle finished rubbing and placed the fuzzy-headed kitten on the hearth where it ducked skittishly at the bright fire and ran under a chair. 'How the devil did it get in there, Sam?' she asked when she had told Brian the reason for the kitten's soggy state.

The boy seemed reluctant to answer.

'Why, you nasty little get, you shoved it down!' accused May, bringing Belle's wrath upon herself.

'May, I will not have such talk!' Belle then returned a puzzled glance to Sam, and suddenly realised that May was absolutely right. 'Why, Sam?' she breathed. 'It's such a wicked thing to do, especially to someone who's never done you any harm.'

Sam became agitated and pointed at May. 'I never did her no harm but she hit me. I hate her.'

'I hate you an' all!'

'May, shut up.' Belle took Sam into the privacy of the scullery, closing the door behind them. 'Sam, I don't understand you. You love that kitten. Why did you do it?'

'I don't know,' replied Sam, then at her doubtful expression, 'I don't!' He began to cry, sobbing into her shoulder.

'Sam, Sam.' Belle patted him, though not understanding his action, in sympathy with his torment. 'May was wrong to punish you . . .'

'I bust your picture,' he wept.

'I know. She told me.'

'I didn't mean to, it was an accident. I threw my boot at Eddie and hit the picture instead.'

Belle managed a smile. 'I suppose I should be grateful it wasn't Eddie's head that got broken.' Holding him from her she dried his eyes with her fingers. 'I thought you liked it here, Sam? You seemed to be getting on so well with the others.'

'They don't like me,' he sniffed and looked glazedly at the scullery window.

'Now that's a silly thing to say. I know they're tearaways but no one could accuse them of being unfriendly.'

'It's not their fault,' explained the boy. 'It's mine. Nobody likes me.'

She uttered a soft laugh. 'Now you are being silly. For one thing *I* like you – otherwise I'd never have brought you to stay with me, would I?'

'Then why does everybody keep hitting me?'

Belle struggled for an explanation, knowing that when Sam said 'everybody' what he really meant was 'mother'. 'Sam . . . sometimes when people get angry they lash out at others – even those they think a lot about. It's wrong and they shouldn't do it, but sometimes they get so frustrated they just can't hold back. Do you understand what I mean by frustrated?'

'You mean when things aren't going the way they should?'

'Something like that. That's when they take it out on the person who happens to be nearest to them, nearest in the literal sense and also closest to their affection.'

'But I'm not close to May's affection.'

'The reason May lashed out was from loyalty to me. She knew I loved that particular painting and that I'd be sad, so she did the first thing that came into her head. I'm sure she's sorry about it now.'

'Only because the cat nearly got drowned though,' replied Sam.

'Oh, Sam, how can I make you see . . . Look, what did you do the moment May struck you? You went out and took revenge on the person most dear to you.'

'It's not the same.'

'Yes, it is.'

'Nobody likes me.' The face was stubborn.

Belle sighed. 'Sam, if I didn't like you would I be here talking to you after what you did to that cat? It was a very cruel thing to do to a defenceless animal, even more so when it had placed its trust in you, but nevertheless I understand the reason you did it and I'm ready to forgive you. That's because I like you, Sam.'

'Why?'

Belle faltered. 'Because . . . underneath that hostility I think you're really a very nice boy who loves his mother and misses her very badly.'

Sam's expression showed this to be true. 'When can I see her?'

'Not long, Sam. We'll give her a few weeks' rest, then we'll invite her to visit you – I promise. Come, we'll join the others or they'll have eaten all the scones.' She led him back to the living room where the doctor was entertaining the other children. All faces turned to them.

'May, I believe you have something to say to Samuel,' Belle gave the cue. May presented a truculent brow and began to pile the plates one on top of the other. 'May, we're waiting.'

The noise of the pottery stopped. 'I'm sorry I clouted yer,' she told the boy grudgingly, then resumed her stacking.

'There you are, Sam,' said the woman brightly, nudging him into the circle. 'Now I think it's your turn for apologies, isn't it? Where's the kitten?'

Brian retrieved the animal from its hideaway and presented it to Sam. 'I'm sorry, Kit,' said the boy and held out his hand, but the kitten spat and dug its claws into Brian's tweed jacket.

'He's still a bit shaken,' comforted Belle, motioning for Brian to put the creature back where he had found it. 'He'll come round.'

'He doesn't like me now,' said the boy sadly.

'Don't suppose I would if I'd been up to me neck in the bog,' muttered May as she went to the scullery.

Belle felt one of her rare moments of despair, then overcame it. 'Right, no more slacking. It's time for lessons. All of you, go fetch your books while Doctor changes Sam's dressing.'

When this had been performed and Belle and he were alone, Brian noted her gloom. 'You've a mixed bag there, Belle.'

But she disagreed. 'On the contrary, the trouble is that

577

they're all the same, all seeking approval, vying for affection. My job is to get them to plumb those qualities in themselves which invoke friendship, make them see that they're worthy of it, whatever they've done. Sam is going to be more difficult than I'd anticipated. The poor child blames himself for his mother's weakness, thinks nobody could possibly like him.'

'I'm certain that if anyone can make him see the opposite is true then you can.' Brian polished his spectacles with his handkerchief before replacing them on his nose.

'I shall have a damned good try,' said Belle. 'I'm going to make this lot into decent, civilised, caring adults – even if I have to break every bone in their bodies.'

After a further series of minor ups and downs Samuel eventually integrated quite nicely with the family. A fortnight after his arrival, though not yet allowed into the rough and tumble of everyday life, he was able to join in the more sedate pastimes – few though these might be. Brian, on his way there yet again, grinned at the thought of May, then, as he invariably did, turned sombre as he thought what might become of her in later life due to the disease she had contracted at such tender years. He and Belle had made themselves responsible for her and must help to give her back a little of her childhood if that were possible.

However, 'I'm not a kid!' May was at that moment screeching at Belle. 'You've let me take the others skatin' nearly every day, why can't I go today?'

'Because, idiot,' replied Belle tightly, 'a thaw is on the way and you'll end up giving them swimming lessons. Besides, you've all been let off the hook far too often. It's time we got some schoolwork done. It was only because of the unusual circumstances of the Ouse being frozen over that I allowed the lapse. Anyway it's over now . . .'

'It was still rock 'ard yesterday,' argued May.

'Yesterday was yesterday. Now I've said you can't go and that's final.' Belle was sitting at her davenport trying to balance the household accounts.

'But . . .'

'May Flowers!' Belle threw down the pen and rose majestically. 'You – will – do – as – you – are – told. I may or may not allow you to use my painting equipment later, depending on how you behave now, but until then you will sit in your room and do the work I have set for you!' The action of raising her voice produced a bout of coughing. She had been a little under the weather for two days and having to deal with May did not help.

'I don't like it,' sulked May.

'Like it or not, you'll do it. Now go and leave me in peace.' Taking for granted that she would be obeyed Belle sat down again, still hacking into her handkerchief. May flounced out.

Belle was subjected to another interruption shortly afterwards when Brian arrived. 'Don't worry!' He held up protective palms to ward off the short-tempered outburst. 'No need for you to come running. I'll just see to the patient then be out of your hair.' Only when he had closed the door did he permit his disappointment to register in his expression.

Belle was halfway through totalling a column of figures when something distracted her again: a white handkerchief fluttering through the crack of the open door. 'Come in, Brian.' She downed the pen, head in hands.

'Sorry.' He crept in. 'Just to say all's well with Sam. How's that cough of yours?' She told him it was gone. 'Well, keep warm, won't you? I've a call to make down Friargate so I thought I'd look in on Sam's mother and see how the land lies and perhaps invite her to visit the boy . . . just thought I'd keep you informed.'

'How very kind,' said Belle unconvincingly.

'Right . . . I'll get out of your way then.'

'Goodbye, Brian.' Belle retrieved the pen, but paused before restarting on the column of figures, anticipating more disruptions. After listening with cocked ear for a few seconds she heard the front door close, smiled and attempted the task once more.

Thirty minutes later Belle, arriving at two figures which

balanced, felt sorry for the way she had been so short with both Brian and May and decided to make peace. The children, as usual at this time of day, were in the front parlour which served as a schoolroom. Each morning Belle would set a piece of work to suit each child's individual needs. This would not be undertaken until the afternoon, for the best part of the morning was taken up by formal lessons and perhaps a short outing afterwards to blow away the cobwebs. Today, each had been given a section of a book to read – most of them could read quite well now – and should by this time have completed a comprehension test which had been drawn up for them.

She closed the lid of the davenport and went to check on their progress. The room was devoid of humanity. Disquieted, she went to seek out the nursemaid. Upstairs she could hear the latest baby crying. The nursemaid was in the kitchen, putting down the coalbucket which she had just hauled in from the yard.

'Sally, have you any idea where the children might be?'

'No, miss, not since the doctor was here. I thought they were a bit quiet but I didn't like to tempt Providence by going to see why. Aren't they in the front parlour, then? Oh eh, have you heard His Lordship?' She rolled her eyes at the baby's yell. 'He won't go down, you know. If anyone asks what to buy me for Christmas tell them a mallet.'

'No, they're not in the schoolroom,' said Belle detachedly, then, 'I'll wager five pounds that little . . .' Going to the cupboard under the stairs she flung it open. All five pairs of skates were missing. 'That little . . . !'

'What's up, miss?'

'It's May!' Belle was furious. 'I told her she couldn't take the children skating today and she's deliberately disobeyed – and she's taken Sam, too. Right, well, just let her wait till I catch her. Where's my coat?'

'Eh, you oughtn't to go out with that bad chest o' yours,' said Sally, but found the coat and helped her on with it, watching her portentous departure. 'Well, I'd best go tend to Sir Tatton Sykes,' she said, and both women went their separate ways.

*

There was no longer the sharp bite to the air that had been present for the last fortnight. The thaw had started. It showed in the way Belle's hair frizzed from under her hat with the damp atmosphere, and by the hot flush that lit her face as she limped determinedly down Lawrence Street – though that may have been due more to anger than to cold. When she eventually reached the river her dress was sticking to her back, the scarf she had wrapped round her throat and mouth was damp with her breath and proving a great annoyance. She unwound it, seeking the children with a bad-tempered frown.

The stalls had gone – someone had sense, thought Belle – but a few rash skaters still glided down the river.

'May – get to me at once!' Belle had spotted them and roared her disapproval.

May waved, mouth laughing. 'I can't hear yer, Aunt Belle! Yer too far away. Look! Watch what I can do now.' She performed a less than perfect figure of eight on one leg.

'May Flowers, I demand that you come here instantly!'

'Aunt Belle's calling,' said Anna.

'I'm not deaf, clown,' replied May, through smiling teeth. 'But I'm damned if I'm going yet. She'll string me up when she catches me.' She continued to sail around the ice, imagining her audience's applause, while the little ones watched. Sam, not having any skates, was fed up anyway so made his way over to Belle and stood beside her wordlessly.

'We'd better go too,' decided Eddie. 'Aunt Belle looks mad.'

'Oh, all right,' snapped May, grabbing hold of him to keep her balance. 'Gor, doesn't she get worked up over nowt?' She took hold of a small hand and steered for Belle's gesticulating figure, propelling the wooden skates over the watery ice. The thing that narked most was that the woman had been right. It wasn't any good for skating now; too sloshy.

They were about twenty feet from the bank when the tragedy occurred. It was preceded by an ominous creaking which May's loud laughter obscured from the children's ears. Then, with a groan and a loud crack the ice before them disintegrated and all, with the exception of Cicely, plummeted into the water.

There were screams of horror from the victims. Also from Belle. Little Cicely stood petrified on the ice that had remained intact and watched her friends thrashing about amongst the floes.

Oh, God. Oh, God. For precious seconds Belle stood transfixed, gazing at the struggle, then suddenly came to life. 'May! Keep their heads above the water. If they go under they'll never . . .' – Oh Christ, you fool, she chastised herself. Don't frighten them. Keep them calm. She looked frantically about her. 'Help! Help, someone!' There was no one within shouting distance. Those who heard were on the ice themselves and, seeing the situation, kept well away, making their passage gingerly back to a safe part of the bank on the far side of the river.

Shouting to the lone survivor of the accident Belle said, 'Cicely, walk to me. Walk very carefully away from the hole. Cicely, do as you're told! That's right. Good girl. Now,' she moved along the bank, 'make your way over here. Come on, just a little further. A few more inches . . .' When the scared child reached the bank Belle leaned over and swung her onto firm ground, then looked around desperately to see if anyone had heeded her cries. Oh, damn, damn! Was everyone deaf? There was no other solution but to get down onto that ice.

Sitting on the embankment she lowered herself carefully onto the almost transparent surface. 'Oh, hurry, hurry, Aunt Belle! Save us!' Their pleas tore at her. 'I'm coming!' She got cautiously to her knees and let herself down until her body was horizontal, her face almost touching the ice – she felt the chill of it on her cheek and shuddered, but not with the cold, with nausea at what lay beneath those two glassy inches. – Don't think about it, don't! She steeled herself. You're on dry land. There's no water. You can do it. You can, damn you, stupid bitch! Go on! Mind screaming encouragement and abuse, she inched her leaden body forward towards the jagged hole. She must, for their sakes, she must go on. Go on, you blithering coward!

She was almost there. There was no pretending she was on dry land now. The water from their terrified splashing lashed across her face, covering her flesh with a thousand slugs that coated her with their slime. I can't let go, she thought. I can't let go of the ice. I must cling onto something.

Few would know what courage it took for her to release her grip on the ice and put out a trembling hand. It was snatched fiercely by the nearest child, Eddie. Then – how odd – the feel of that small hand in hers, the look of trusting relief in his eyes, made everything all right. The water receded. It wasn't there any more – at least it held no terror for her. She had something to hold onto. She would save them.

Carefully, her twisted spine shrieking under the effort, she dragged Eddie from the water to slither, seal-like, beside her. The fragile support groaned. 'Eddie,' she said. 'Eddie, listen carefully. Get back onto the bank . . . very slowly now . . . you can do it . . . that's a good boy.' Still prostrate, she craned her neck with difficulty to watch his inch-by-inch escape. As soon as he was near the bank she began to haul out the others. Arms reached up to grab at her coat. 'That's right, hold on to me. You'll soon be safe.' One by one she watched them slither to safety. She had done it. She had beaten the water. There was only May to go. Silly, stupid May. She clasped the girl's hands tightly but the water in May's skirts made her impossible to lift. 'Oh, May, you'll have to help me! You're far too heavy.'

'Belle! Hold on, I'm coming!' It was Brian. Coming down Friargate he had seen the tragedy that was taking place on the river and was already clambering down the bank.

Her gladness at seeing him turned to panic when she saw he was about to add his weight to the overloaded ice. 'Get back! You'll only make it worse. I don't need you. I can do it.' The words were no sooner out than the platform gave way. The water had won after all. Belle screamed as it seeped into her woollen skirts, biting into her skin. The section on which she lay floated temporarily, then submerged, taking her with it.

Brian leapt back onto the staith just in time and yelled to her to hang on. Then, seizing a pole that was used to haul in boats, he began to smash at the ice, to carve himself a channel so he could swim out to her. She couldn't understand what he was doing, kept shouting for him to stop, thought he was mad.

When the channel was wide enough he ripped off his boots and jacket and plunged into the water. 'Don't struggle, Belle! I'm going to take you back to the bank.' He manoeuvred around her.

'May!' she spluttered. 'May's gone under!'

'I'll come back for her.'

'No! You mustn't leave her! I can manage.'

'For Christ's sake stop trying to prove to the world you don't need anybody! Shut up. I'm taking you in now.' With his arm locked around her throat she had no choice but to go with him, her vision blurred by black treacle.

By now there were others on the bank who helped to drag the sodden young woman to safety and wrap the shivering children in blankets. Brian struck out again, risking his life by diving under in an effort to find May.

But poor May was gone.

CHAPTER FORTY

The telephone rang. Patrick crossed himself. 'Holy Mary, that dratted thing! Making me spill good whiskey.' He brushed the imaginary drops from his blue-serged knee.

Erin's eyes came up from the lace handkerchief she had been stitching. There was apprehension in them. 'T'would be a good thing if it did,' she murmured vaguely. Though this was the first one she had seen him take today she didn't want this to be the start of another winter binge.

He snorted. 'Ye might as well've gone to the factory if all you're going to do is lecture me. What's up with ye, anyway?' He was remarking on her strange manner.

She forced her eyes from the door to focus on the handkerchief, working her needle into delicate stitches. 'I've a feeling on me. I've not been able to concentrate for a week. Then this morning it was stronger.' She stopped sewing. ''Twas as if something was physically restraining me from leavin' the house. I just can't settle. I'd be better at work, but...' Her eyes met his.

Unlike her late husband who might have said, 'Eh, you and your feelings, Erin Teale,' Patrick, ingrained with Celtic superstition, took her words seriously. Looking into her disturbed eyes he began to absorb the fear that haunted them.

They were still looking at each other when the door opened and the manservant entered. Noiselessly closing the door he padded across the carpet to address Patrick. 'Doctor Dyson is on the telephone, sir. He wishes to speak with you.'

Patrick's eyes, which had broken contact with Erin's at the servant's entry, now adhered to hers again, then slowly he rose and followed John who held the door open for him. The telephone receiver was balanced on top of the main unit attached to the wall. Hesitantly Patrick's gnarled fingers gripped it and lifted it to his ear. He shouted into the box, 'Hello! This is Patrick Feeney.'

At the other end Brian moved his ear slightly away from the receiver. 'Mr Feeney, I don't wish to alarm you but I think you ought to know about Belle.'

'What's up?' cried Patrick immediately. 'What is it?'

'She's suffering from pneumonia, sir. I know I should've informed you much sooner but Belle wouldn't allow...'

'Pneumonia?!'

Brian's voice grew sombre. 'Yes... and it's getting worse. I'm very worried about her...'

'I'm coming now!' Patrick slammed down the receiver

and returned as swiftly as he could to the drawing room, cursing himself for not visiting Belle lately.

Erin, seeing the strain on his face, clutched the ruffle at her throat. 'It's Belle.'

'It is – but don't worry, we'll soon have her right.' He came quickly to her side. 'Brian's looking after her.'

'What's wrong?'

'Pneumonia.'

She clamped a hand to her mouth.

'It may not be as bad as it sounds. I said I'd go . . .'

'I'm coming with ye.' She came alive.

'Right, I'll get John to fetch the carriage . . .'

'No, there's not enough time,' said Erin flusteredly. 'We'll be quicker to get a cab the speed John works.'

Without a word to anyone they picked up their coats and hurried from the house. Luckily a cab happened to be dropping a passenger at The Black Swan as their eager footsteps pattered down the few steps from the front door. 'Hey!' Patrick stopped it from driving away and clutched Erin's arm. Droplets of mud polka-dotted Erin's skirts as her fast-moving feet took her to the carriage.

'Get in, Father.' She made to help him.

'I'm not infirm yet,' he said testily. 'You get in.'

She did as she was told and, with Patrick aboard, the cab pulled away. 'Lawrence Street!' shouted the old man to the cabbie. 'Quick as ye can.'

Slush spurted from the carriage wheels as it gathered motion and weaved in and out of the narrow streets. At one stage it almost knocked over a policeman and there were several minutes wasted while the cabbie earned a reprimand. It started moving again, Patrick and Erin rocking about inside, their faces stone-like with worry. The overcast sky blackened the interior of the cab, hiding their feelings. Neither spoke, but Erin found her father's hand and he gripped it supportively.

When they arrived Patrick tipped the cabbie for his inconvenience and followed Erin into the house.

'Where is she?' asked Erin immediately they came upon Brian.

'She's upstairs – but she's not herself, Mrs Teale!' The spectacles in his hand paused in mid-air as Erin ignored his warning and flew up the staircase. Donning his glasses he pursued her, signalling to Patrick. 'I hope she doesn't wake her. The poor girl's just nicely gone off after hours of insomnia.'

When they reached the bedroom Erin was kneeling by her daughter's bedside, smoothing the glistening brow. 'Belle, oh, Belle.'

Brian beseeched her to lower her voice, then allowed Patrick to move in beside his grand-daughter. 'She's in a critical period. That's why I rang . . .'

He inwardly collapsed as Belle seemed about to emerge from her precious sleep.

'But how long's she been like this?' demanded Erin. 'An' why have ye waited till now?'

''Tis not his fault,' soothed her father. 'Sure, ye know how independent Belle is.' He turned to Brian. 'What's being done for her?'

'All that can be. My senior partner's treating her. He's a fine doctor, Mrs Teale, he's doing absolutely everything – as we all are. It's just a matter of waiting.'

'For what?' Erin's eyes were fearful.

Brian shrugged helplessly. He had sat with her for the last two nights, listening to her wheezing breath, watching her get progressively worse and kicking himself for not recognising her illness earlier. The strain showed in the deep lines that ran from his nose to the corners of his mouth, the black circles beneath the eyes and the stubble on his chin.

Grim-faced, Patrick pulled up a chair for Erin, then found another for himself, positioning it on the other side of the bed. 'How'd she get like this, Bri?'

The young doctor perched on the end of the bed and stared at the clammy face on the pillow. 'It started innocently enough, might not have even come to this, but . . .' He decided to tell them the full tale. 'The children went ice-skating – Belle had warned them not to but they disobeyed her. When she found out she went after them.

The ice broke and the children fell in.' Both Patrick and his daughter made sounds of concern. 'I'd been doing my rounds which took me by the river. When I got to her she was stretched out on the ice pulling the children from the water. Honestly, Mrs Teale, she was marvellous . . . but then the ice beneath her gave way.' Erin gave another exclamation. 'I managed to get her out . . . but we lost one of the children – young May.'

Patrick crossed himself. 'I'll never understand God if I live to be a thousand. Why does it always have to be the young'ns?'

Brian said nothing of May yet, still referring to Belle. 'Well, you know what she's like, she wouldn't stay in bed, had to see to the children she said. It wouldn't have been so bad perhaps if she'd stayed in the house, but she was back and forth to the police station to ask if they'd found May's body . . . I said I'd see to everything, but would she listen?' He became angry. 'Really, Mrs Teale, you have the most awkward pig-headed daughter . . .' Rising from the bed he thrust his hands deep into his pockets and glared at Belle whose head now moved from side to side, muttering deliriously.

'Don't need . . . go 'way . . .'

'It's all right, dear.' Erin removed the cloth from her daughter's brow, dipped it into the bowl of water on the bedside table, wrung it out and mopped the fevered brow. 'Mother's here . . . don't talk, just rest an' get well.' She looked up at Brian. 'Isn't there anything else ye can do?'

He shook his head. 'I wanted to tell you before it got this bad, if only that her family should know what a heroine she'd been. But she wouldn't hear of it, said I wasn't to upset you about May.'

'How long will it last?'

'Well . . . she may be out of it by morning.' But which way out? Oh, God . . .

Patrick noted the man's fatigue. 'Why don't ye go home an' catch a few winks, Doctor? Me an' her mother will stay an' look after her.'

'No, I'm staying,' replied Brian firmly.

'Then take a nap in one o' the children's rooms,' begged Patrick. 'Ye'll be no good to Belle without all your faculties.'

The young man sighed. 'If I was in possession of those she wouldn't be lying here now. I should've forbidden her to go out in the condition she was in.'

'Like ye said yourself, she's an independent hussy.' Patrick rubbed a hand over his mouth, experiencing a sudden dryness. 'I don't suppose ye've a drop o' whiskey in the house, Bri?' There came an apology. 'Ah, never mind. You go on an' take that nap.'

'You'll wake me if you're at all concerned?'

'We will.'

Brian rubbed his hands over his face, then pulled a watch from his pocket. 'I should really be at evening surgery . . . but I'm not leaving her.' He turned wearily from the bed and went to the room next door where he flopped his head onto the pillow and allowed his consciousness to slip away.

Supported by endless cups of tea brought in by Sally, the old Irishman and his daughter played sentinel to the sick girl until it grew dark. 'I'll never forgive myself for this,' murmured Erin, voice almost inaudible. 'Never. If I'd allowed her to do as she pleased she might never've left home an' all this would not have happened.'

'Might's a fragile condition,' replied Patrick, entertaining the sudden thought that he hadn't had a drink for five hours and could do with one badly. 'Ye can't stop your children living their own lives for fear that they might get hurt. Ye could wrap them in cottonwool all their days an' wake up one morning to find they'd suffocated on the fluff. Ye just have to let them get on with it. Sam'd tell ye that if he was here.'

Erin wrung out the cloth once more and laid it across Belle's tossing head. 'I still think she's wasted it, ye know, Dad. She's so clever . . . she could've really made something of herself.' Her teeth clamped down on her lip and tears formed. 'Why does everything have to happen to my child?' She collapsed sobbing while Patrick leaned over the fretful girl on the bed to pat his daughter comfortingly.

'She'll come through, Erin lass, don't distress yourself.' But would she? Was he going to lose another precious grandchild? – I can't bear this, he shrivelled within himself. God, I wish I had a drink.

In time the woman sat up and, breathing deeply, wiped her eyes. 'I suppose we should send for the priest . . .' Her red eyes met Patrick's and she knew he shared the thought that was in her own head: Father Gilchrist was the last person on earth they wanted to see at this time. If only Liam were here.

Patrick rose creakily. 'I'll see if I can get hold o' the priest from St George's. Sure, 'tis nearer to home anyway.'

His exit was simultaneous with Brian's awakening. The doctor yawned, stretched, tasted his tongue and pulled a face. When his glued-up eyes finally came open he picked up the watch on the bedside table and squinted at it. With a groan he rolled off the bed, lifted his leg to straighten his trouser bottoms, then splashed some water on his face at the washstand. After mopping it dry he combed his hair with his fingers and went to check on Belle. Erin glanced up as the rumpled physician came in rubbing at his itchy eyes. 'No change?'

She shook her head.

He occupied Patrick's still-warm chair and, lifting the cloth, placed a hand to Belle's forehead, allowing his fingers to trail her cheek before pulling it back. 'Why don't you go down for a bit? Have something to eat.'

'I don't feel like anything. Anyway, I'd rather stay.'

'She's not going anywhere. Go on, just for five minutes. You may have to take over from me when I disintegrate again.'

'Well . . . I could do to stretch me legs.' Erin began to shove back the chair. 'Ye'll call me . . . ?' At Brian's nod she left the room and went downstairs.

The scene she came upon caused her to hang about uncertainly in the doorway. The children were grouped around the dancing fire, some with cups of cocoa, others with opened books on their laps. The little girls had rags in their hair, the boys were smoothed and curried. All were properly clad in their night attire, save one whose nightgown began at the waist, the redundant sleeves tied around his midriff to stop it falling down. Samuel wiped away a moustache of cocoa and feeling eyes upon him looked to the door. 'Who're you?'

Erin only half-emerged from her suspension. She managed to answer, 'I'm Mrs Teale,' but her eyes refused to leave the vivid scar that completely obscured the left breast.

'Samuel, don't be so rude,' rebuked Cicely, and to Erin, 'You must excuse him. He hasn't yet learnt his manners. I have, though.' Standing, she went to fetch a chair and manhandled it into the circle. 'Do please sit down.'

Sitting now, Erin found her eyes kept straying to the disfigured boy. 'You'll have to excuse his state of undress,' said Cicely. 'But, you see it's a bit sore if he wears anything up top. You live at Mr Feeney's house, don't you?' Erin nodded.

Sam wished the woman would stop staring at him. He played with his bare toes, hoping to distract her, and was thankful when Eddie asked, 'Would you like me to read to you?' He flourished a book. 'Aunt Belle usually reads us a bedtime story but she's ill at the moment.'

'I know,' said Erin softly. 'I'm Belle's mother.'

This generated great interest. 'Are you really? I didn't know Aunt Belle had a mother.' Erin flinched, but then how would they know when she had always avoided them during their time spent at Peasholme Green. 'You're not alike, are you?' The child was examining her for lumps.

At that point Sally came in and warned, 'Oy, don't you be pestering Mrs Teale. She's tired. She doesn't want to be harried by you lot.'

'It's all right,' said Erin, gratefully accepting the offer of cocoa from the nursemaid. 'Eddie, is it? Eddie was just going to read for me, weren't ye?' She held out her hand. 'What book d'ye have?'

'It's not a storybook. It's French.' Eddie clambered to

his bare feet and came to stand at her knee. 'I've been practising because I'm not very good. Aunt Belle says she's almost reached the end of her tether. Doctor Brian says perhaps if I practise very hard it'll make Aunt Belle get better. D'you think it will?'

Erin nodded to his earnest little face. 'I'm sure the doctor's right. Let me hear ye an' see how well ye've practised.' She glanced down once again at Sam who immediately dropped his face. – I must stop this, thought the woman, I'm embarrassing the poor child.

'Dans le jardin il y a un chat. Il est noir . . .' Eddie's finger traced each sentence as he recited in monotone.

'That was excellent,' praised Erin when he had finished. 'I'm sure your Aunt Belle will feel better straight away when she hears that.' God, they've even got me doing it now, she thought with a twinge on hearing her own lips bestow the title on her daughter. She sat with them for more than the five minutes she had originally allocated herself, holding conversation with each of them – apart from Sam, the person she wanted to know about most, but who volunteered no information except to say, when she finally asked him what he wanted to be when he grew up, 'I'd like to be a teacher.'

'That's very ambitious,' replied Erin with interest.

'Aunt Belle says I have it in me.'

'An' does Aunt Belle work ye very hard?'

He nodded. 'But her lessons are more interesting than at school. I wish I could keep having my lessons here when I go home.'

Erin showed surprise. 'Oh, ye aren't here for good, then?'

'No, I've two months and ten days to go.' That made it sound as if he had been marking it off like a prisoner serving a sentence, which was only slightly true. Samuel's time here was not unpleasant now that he had really got to know the residents, but he did miss his mother. This he told Erin, and: 'I'm only here to give her a rest, you see.'

Erin's incomprehension must have shown, for when

Samuel's head bowed under her scrutiny Cicely piped up, 'Sam's mother burnt his chest – but she didn't mean to. So he's come to stay with us for a little holiday, haven't you, Sam?' The other nodded. 'He's almost better now. Doctor Brian's been putting some special ointment on him. It's not half so bad as it was.'

Erin suddenly realised that her mouth had fallen open and made a conscious effort to hide her horror at the matter-of-fact explanation for the boy's terrible injury. 'An' ye'll be glad to go home?' she asked Sam tentatively.

'Of course.' Sam looked at her as if she was half-mad, then smiled cheerfully. 'Mother's coming to see me next week. I'll be able to show her how clever I'm getting.'

Anna pursed her lips, then called, 'Sally, you're going to need more stitches on the hat you're knitting for Sam.'

Eddie spoke. 'Do you think Aunt Belle knows it wasn't our fault? We didn't know she'd told May the ice was dangerous. I'm glad May drowned, it serves her right.'

Erin was shocked. 'Oh no, Eddie, ye must never say that, however much ye think a person might deserve it. May was obviously foolish but no one should have to die simply for being a fool. We all make fools of ourselves at some time in our lives, but not all of us have to pay for it so cruelly. Ye mustn't blame her for what happened. Your Aunt Belle would be very sad.' She finished her cocoa and rose.

Cicely, untangling her legs from her nightgown, ascended with her. 'Are you going to see Aunt Belle now?' When Erin nodded the girl ran over to a table, picked up a piece of paper and ran back to Erin. 'Would you mind very much taking her this? We're not allowed in to see her.'

Erin looked at the hand-made card. Cicely had drawn a picture of a bed with a person in it. The person had lots of curly hair and a big red smile. 'Is this Aunt Belle?' The child said it was. ''Tis very good. I'll bet she doesn't always have a big smile like this, does she?'

Cicely mulled this over. 'No . . . but I know it's there underneath.' She spotted the moisture in Erin's eyes and said in an alarmed voice, 'Aunt Belle's not going to die, is she?'

Erin blinked away the tears, angry both at herself and at the child for this suggestion. 'Of course not!' Her voice was brusque. 'How could she when there's so many of us praying for her to get better – ye have been praying, haven't ye?'

'Oh, yes!' clamoured the children, infected by Cicely's alarm. 'We say our prayers every night.'

'Good. Ye must keep on asking Our Lady to make Aunt Belle better.'

'Who's Our Lady?' frowned Eddie.

Erin looked at him for a moment, then said, 'Are none of ye Catholics?'

Eddie responded with another question. 'What's a Catholic?'

Erin sighed to herself. Belle never was one much for church. 'Never mind. Just you keep praying an' she'll get better.'

'God says she'll be better by tomorrow,' announced Sam.

'He never did,' scoffed Eddie.

'Yes, He did. He spoke to me.'

'Well, why didn't He speak to me then?'

'I don't know, do I? You'd better ask Him.'

Erin interceded. 'Well, if that's what God says then I think we can believe it, don't you? Just pray extra hard tonight . . .' She turned abruptly and went back upstairs.

'You're a liar, Sam Norton,' Anna stated firmly. 'God never spoke to you. Now if Aunt Belle does die you'll have made God a liar.'

The only thing different about the room on her return was that another lamp had been ignited. Erin's shadow preceded her as she tiptoed across to join the doctor and sat down, looking at Belle as she spoke. 'I've just met the children.'

Belle's delirious mutter intervened. 'Don't need . . . go . . . manage . . .'

594

'Ah, they're a grand crew, aren't they?' Brian held the patient's wrist to check on her pulse, then replaced it under the blanket.

'That little boy ... Sam ... they said his mother ... she couldn't possibly?'

'She did,' replied Brian gravely. 'With an iron.'

'God Almighty.'

'She was utterly repentant afterwards, of course.'

'I should think she was!' Erin fought to control her voice. 'She ought to be hanged. I wonder the child can find so much enthusiasm for her visit – an' I'm certainly surprised at you for allowing him to go back to her.'

'If I thought there was any danger he wouldn't be going back,' answered Brian. 'But I'm confident it was only a temporary madness. The woman's just lost her husband and Sam can be a handful. We all do things we're ashamed of at some time, Mrs Teale.'

His words had the effect of subduing Erin who merely nodded her understanding. A while later she asked about the other children and Brian provided each child's curriculum vitae, brief though it was. 'An' what about the child who died?'

'Poor May ... she'd been a prostitute for two years when Belle and I rescued her.' Erin's face crumpled. 'Her death wasn't such a tragedy as it might seem on the surface. She would've died anyway, if not quite so soon and definitely not so cleanly. She was diseased.'

Erin closed her eyes. – How could I ever have accused you of wasting your life? she asked her insensible daughter. Here's you with less than half my years done so much to make these children's lives bearable, an' what've I ever done but condemn? She began to pray. Oh, Merciful Mother, have pity on this wretched woman. I know I don't deserve another chance but please, oh please don't take her. She's all I have ...

Patrick returned with the priest. Brian, at first angry at this pessimism, controlled himself enough to allow the rites to be carried out while he kept well out of the way of what he saw as a lot of ineffective nonsense. Later he returned to sit with Erin and Belle while Patrick entertained the priest downstairs – though the old man too would rather have been up here.

'Does she know how ye feel about her?' asked Belle's mother after a long period of silence.

Brian looked startled.

She found the strength to smile. 'I may not have been on speaking terms with Belle for some time, Doctor, but I could never be accused of goin' round with my eyes shut.'

'I wish it were that obvious to her.' Brian relaxed and pulled up the covers that Belle's fretful jerking had shrugged off.

'Why don't ye tell her?' asked the woman softly.

'I've tried, but she makes a joke of everything. On the few occasions I've almost got close to her she became very uppity about it.'

'She's a funny child.' Erin moved her head from side to side. 'I've never been able to fathom how her mind works. I was never as close to her as she was to her father.'

'Water, water . . .' mumbled Belle, lashing her head about the pillow.

Brian tried to dribble a few drops between her lips but a hand came up to knock it away. 'Water . . . May!'

'Belle.' Erin leaned forward. ''Tis all right, there's no water, it's gone. Ssh.' She explained to Brian, 'She's always been terrified of water.'

'I had no idea,' he replied. 'She gave no indication of being afraid of anything.'

'She wouldn't – it would've been a sign of weakness. Oh yes, she's a funny one . . .'

'It must have taken great courage, then, for her to rescue those children.'

'It must. Let's hope God recognises that.'

'You're a funny one yourself, Mrs Teale, if I may say so. I was under the distinct impression that you were against any feeling I might have for Belle, yet . . . it appears now as if you might be glad of it.'

'It was nothing I had against you personally, Doctor,

just a private obsession. I've said and done a lot of silly things. I hope God will grant me time to put them to rights.'

The priest left, enabling Patrick to be where he wanted to be. The three grew weary as they stood guard through the long night. Though he was the oldest Patrick's was the only head not to loll at some point. He gazed at the beautiful young woman fighting for her life, relived that life in his mind: her birth; Sam's tragic death. Would things have been different if Sam had been there to guide her? Pat doubted it. She was a headstrong, self-opinionated, courageous girl and he loved her so. Ah, God, not another. Please, not another. He got to wondering what Thomasin's thoughts would be on finding him and Erin gone. They had left no word. That had been thoughtless. She had a right to know. – That's how much ye think of her, he told himself. Then argued, now ye know that's not so. 'Twas just a slip o' the mind. A slip of the mind that's robbed her of the knowledge that her grandchild might die.

Dawn came. Brian stirred, stretched and automatically felt Belle's forehead. He gave a long, drawn-out sigh which roused Erin immediately. She dared not ask.

The doctor closed his eyes, 'Her temperature's down,' then opened them to throw a tired smile at the others. At Patrick's alertness he turned to see Belle's eyelids fluttering.

'The water . . .' Her eyes came fully open and she looked dazedly at the three relieved faces. With the lifting of the mist relief flooded her own, producing a weak smile. 'It's all right,' she told them. 'The water's gone. I beat it.'

The tiredness which Patrick had valiantly suppressed all night now crept into every corner of his body. Crossing himself and giving thanks for Belle's deliverance he lifted himself from the chair and addressed himself softly to Erin. 'Your mother'll be worried. I'd better go. Will I tell her you're staying?'

'I'd like to stay, at least till she wakes up,' whispered

Erin. After her brief awakening Belle had drifted into a peaceful sleep. 'There's things I must say.'

Pat nodded. 'I'll go join Brian then. See you later.'

Brian was in the kitchen being breakfasted by Sally. Hearing of Belle's recovery had restored the children's normal ebullience and their chatter at the table was deafening. 'Keep it down,' ordered the doctor at Pat's entry. 'Aunt Belle needs all the sleep she can get.'

'I'm off, Bri,' Patrick informed him.

'Won't you have some breakfast, sir?' asked Sally, holding up the frying pan.

'It'll do me no good to eat if me throat's likely to be cut when I get home,' replied the old man. Then, 'No, thank ye, dear, I'll get along now. I might be back later, Brian, when I've had some rest.'

Patrick's first act on reaching home was to pour himself a drink. The glass had barely touched his lips when the door's opening brought an enraged Thomasin in to confront him. 'Where the hell have you been?' She marched into the room – one would think she was twenty years younger than me instead of only five, thought Patrick, retreating to a chair.

'Oh, ye noticed I was missing, then?'

'Don't play silly bloody games with me!' There was no need to act the lady with Pat. 'What happened to you and Erin?'

'Belle almost died,' he told her brutally, 'Me an' Erin spent the . . .'

'What!'

He felt instant remorse for causing the horror that had flashed across her face. 'Now don't worry, she's . . .'

'Don't worry? You blithely tell me my grand-daughter almost died and then say *don't worry!* I think I deserve an explanation.' He was reaching for the decanter again. 'Before you get too fuddled to speak, please!'

He regarded her insolently as he poured another drink, then decided that she had a right to be angry and modified his stance. 'Belle caught pneumonia. Apparently she'd had a bad cough for a couple o' days, then the children fell through the ice an' Belle fell in too, tryin' to save them . . . it's a long story. Anyway, it didn't do her condition much good. Doctor Dyson telephoned yesterday afternoon. By then she was in no fit state to object about him worrying us. Me and Erin went straight away.'

'And you never thought to leave word?'

He averted his guilty face. 'There was no time – we weren't thinking straight. When Erin heard, she all but dragged me out by the scruff. I thought afterwards we'd slipped up by not telling anybody but 'twas too late then.'

'How come Brian could find a telephone and you couldn't?'

He tutted at himself. ''Course, how stupid . . . Tommy, I'm sorry if we worried ye.'

'Worried?' It came out as a bitter laugh. 'There's neither sight nor sound of my husband and daughter all night . . . why the devil d'you think I'm still in the house at this time of morning?'

He glanced at the clock. 'Oh aye, ye'd best be off, your store might collapse without ye.'

Her lips tightened. 'Where's Erin, then?'

'She's stayed with her daughter – at least that's one good thing to come o' this.'

'And how is Belle now?'

'I wondered when ye'd get round to askin'.' His expression folded. 'Aw, Tommy, I don't know why I'm takin' it out on you. I was just so bloody frightened.'

'Oh, I can see that, Patrick.' She was eyeing his glass sourly. 'That, presumably, is why you visited the whiskey bottle before your wife.'

'How was I to know my wife was here! You're never here!'

'And is there any bloody wonder?' She remained just long enough to give him another scathing glare. Everything she felt about him was in that look. Patrick sagged beneath its contempt. To her he was no longer a man, a husband, just a silly old fool who drank too much. When she had gone he gave proof to her opinion by pouring another whiskey down into his empty stomach.

*

599

Some hours after Patrick had left, Belle opened her eyes to see her mother smiling down at her. 'Mother . . . I've had such an awful dream.' She offered no surprise at Erin's presence, but looked about the room. 'I thought there was someone else here before?'

'There was.' Erin smoothed the sheets which she and Sally had changed whilst Belle slept. 'Both the doctor and your grandfather went home for a bit of sleep. Your Nan called too. She's coming back after work.'

'How long have I been like this?' asked Belle.

'Days,' said her mother. 'Ye've been unconscious. Sit up, dear, so I can swap your nightgown, and put a fresh pillowslip on. We didn't want to disturb ye before.' Belle, allowing herself to be changed, asked if her mother had been there all along. 'No, just since the doctor told us about you yesterday afternoon. I'd like words with you on that one. Fancy not wanting us to know . . .' She settled her daughter back on the pillows.

'And you've been sitting here since then? Grandfather too?' An answering nod. 'Oh, you shouldn't have let him, Mother. I'll bet I know just what he was thinking. He must be worn out.' She gave a loud bark and winced.

'Not as much as Brian, I think. He's been here for the duration, worrying over you. That young man's very fond of ye.' Erin held a glass of lemon juice to Belle's lips.

Belle smiled. 'I'm very fond of him, too. He's a good friend.' She sipped gratefully; her windpipe felt as if it had been slashed.

'You're not fit to be let out on your own, ye know that?' scolded her mother crossly. Then, 'Belle . . . I'm sorry I was so . . .'

'There's no call for that.' Belle raised a weak hand which Erin clasped fiercely.

'Yes, there is! I didn't understand before, didn't even try. Not until I saw those children . . . God, 'tis so awkward to phrase.'

'I know exactly what you're trying to say and I'm sure that I've done more to be sorry about than you have. As long as you're here and speaking to me it doesn't matter what happened between us before. That's yesterday. Let's start this day afresh.'

Erin smiled her affection and was hugging her when Brian entered. 'Oh, sorry.' He made to go. 'I'll come back.'

'No, Brian.' Erin released her daughter and stood. 'I was just about to come down for a bite to eat. All of a sudden I could tackle an elephant sandwich.'

'I've just sent Sally out to shoot one,' Brian informed her seriously. 'Though you may have to stretch the bread.' He looked better for his trip home, having slept for a few hours before getting washed, shaved and changed.

Erin gave one last squeeze of Belle's limp hand and said she would come up later. 'Er, I trust you won't all sit guzzling and forget about the patient,' Belle called after her.

Erin laughed. 'Oh dear! We were all so relieved . . . I'll fetch something.'

'Nothing heavy,' croaked Belle. 'Elephant soup will do.' She dropped her head back on the pillow as Brian approached the bed.

'As your grandfather might say, you're a terrible woman, Miss Teale. You gave me an awful fright. I really thought you were going to die on me.'

'Pff,' said Belle.

'I mean it. You've been very ill – and it's all your own fault. I told you what would happen, but would you listen? You're so pig-headed, Belle.'

'I must say it sounds as though you'd have missed me. Anyway,' she gave him a dig in the ribs, 'I don't remember giving my permission for you to treat me.'

'I gave you to Doctor Barley.'

'Oh, in the slave trade now, are we? Well, it wouldn't have been so bad if I had snuffed it – my not being one of your patients, would it?'

'If you'd let me get close enough for a second I'd show you how much I would've missed you.'

'Oh no, don't start on that again, Bri,' she sighed painfully. 'I don't need it right now.'

'There you go again! I don't know why you think it's a

sin to need people . . . some sort of weakness. I'm not ashamed to admit I need you.'

'Brian . . .'

'Yes I do! And if you find it too nauseating to admit to need, what about want? Where on earth's the weakness in wanting someone? Belle, you've always gagged me when I've tried to get close before. I'm sorry that it has to be while you're imprisoned in your sickbed to ask you, but I have to take my chance while I can. I want you to marry me.'

'I know, I know.' She moved her head impatiently.

'Is that all you can say?' Brian looked amazed.

'You try saying more with a throat like sandpaper. Look, Brian . . .'

'I love you, Belle.'

'Listen . . .' She tried to put a hand to his mouth but he avoided it.

'I won't be . . .'

'Brian!' she yelled, then broke into a fit of coughing. He fed her with juice till she pushed his hand away. 'See what you've done to me? Please don't say any more, you're only making it worse for yourself, I owe you a great deal and I'll never be able to repay you, but . . .'

'You owe me nothing! I sat here because I love you.'

'Brian, shut up!' She pressed a hand to her chest and calmed herself before going on. 'You're a very dear friend – if you attempt to interrupt me once more I'll throttle you!' He allowed her to proceed. 'You are a very dear friend. Without you those children downstairs might not be here and neither would I. Despite what insults I've jokingly flung at you I like and respect you very much and I hope our friendship continues for many years. But friendship it can only be, Brian. Apart from the fact that I've no time for anyone but those children I just don't love you in that way.' She saw the hurt on his face and slammed her fist into the mattress. 'Oh, I told you to shut up, didn't I? I said you'd only end up hurting yourself. Look, it's not just you who I don't want to marry, I simply don't want marriage full stop.'

'But why?' He spread his hands. 'What's so horrible about wanting a husband and children?'

'What do I need with a husband? I already have a horde of children downstairs.'

'But not your own. You love children so much. Wouldn't you like one of . . .'

'Love?' Belle burst out laughing which brought more discomfort to her chest. 'I hate the little blighters! I'd be an abominable mother.'

He almost fell off the edge of the bed. Behind his spectacles his eyes were blank. 'But how can you say that and in the same breath talk of devoting your life to them?'

'You don't really know me at all, do you? Brian, you don't need to love children to see the injustices they suffer, the cruelties. Personally I'm always highly suspicious of people who keep professing, "Oh, I adore children!" They must be suffering some insecurity if they have to keep saying it; probably trying to convince themselves. Children can be revolting creatures – but they still have to be protected. I'm not saying I don't like them – naturally you can't help liking some of them – but I'd do the same for a dog.'

He stood abruptly and began to march to the door. How could he have misjudged her so?

'Bri!' She halted him. 'Don't go off in a huff. You're making me out to be ungrateful and I'm not. I still want your friendship . . .'

'How very kind!' he responded sarcastically. 'I'm so glad there's something I can give you.'

Despite her dreadful fatigue her temper matched his own. 'You know very well this isn't about what you can give me! It's what you want me to give you. I'm supposed to fall into your arms out of gratitude: "Oh, darling, you saved me! Marry me, marry me!" Well, I'm sorry, Brian, I am grateful, I truly am – but I can't give you something that isn't there.'

Tiredness overcame his offensive. 'This seems to be going all wrong, as usual. I never meant to get angry. I'm sorry for putting you through this when you're so ill. It's just that I want you so much, Belle.'

That was evident from the way he was looking at her. Belle had to admit to herself that it was very flattering, and she could not pretend that she lacked sexual feelings, for some nights they almost drove her mad. But if she gave rein to the latter she would simply be using him. 'Come back, Bri.' She held out her hand. Slowly he returned to the bed and clasped the outstretched fingers. 'We had a good arrangement, didn't we? Don't let's spoil it by one of us wanting more. You should know by now I'm not the romantic type.'

'Forget about the romance,' he told her. 'Plenty of marriages are based on friendship.' At her expression he said, 'All right, I'll shut up – for now. But there'll be other days.'

'If you want to be a martyr.' But the annoyance had gone. 'Now will you please go help Sally to catch that elephant? Otherwise I feel I will expire.'

CHAPTER FORTY-ONE

Patrick went to visit Belle regularly. After a few days he found her very much improved in body. Her temper was in fine fettle too; she had discovered that she wasn't going to be allowed out of bed for a month.

'Do you know what they've done, Grandfather?' she demanded as he pulled the customary chair up to her bedside. 'Brian and that nursemaid I was stupid enough to employ, they've taken my clothes away – hidden them!'

'An' well done to them too, I say,' replied Patrick, inciting greater annoyance. 'Well, would ye stay in bed voluntarily? Would ye? 'Twas only out of cocksuredness that ye got like this in the first place. Thought ye knew better than the expert.'

'So that's how you describe my heroism,' griped Belle, then twitched her lips to show she wasn't really cross with him. 'Oh, God, I think I'd go mad if it wasn't for your visits.' She eyed the brown paper package on his knee. 'And what have you brought me today?'

'I haven't brought ye anything.'

'Oh, thank you.'

'Thought I'd treat meself for a change.'

'I wasn't aware that whiskey came in square packets.' She knew from Erin that her illness had scared him into drinking again. Mother had gone back to the factory now the crisis was over, so there was no one at home to watch him.

Patrick cautioned her. His horny-nailed fingers picked at the string, then threw it onto her lap. 'You do it, your nails are longer than mine.'

Belle placed the object on her blanketed lap and teased at the knot until it slackened. She unravelled the paper. '*The Time Machine*. The things you read, Grandfather.' She leafed through it, sampling a few paragraphs, then passed it back.

Patrick gave a cursory ripple of the pages. 'I'm looking forward to getting me teeth into that.' There were few things he could apply that optimism to these days. 'If you're not nice to me I might just go home an' do so.'

'You're not meant to eat it, you're meant to read it.'

'Aye.' He became meditative, staring at a point on the wallpaper over her head. 'I wish I had one.'

'One what?'

'A time machine.'

'I could do with one of those myself,' said Belle, anticipating the day she was released from this prison. 'And where would you ask it to take you?'

That was a mistake. 'I'd ask it to turn back the clock to one hour before Rosanna was killed.' His hands tightened on the book, so hard she felt he was going to crush its spine. 'Because then I'd know to do anything in my power to stop her leaving the house. I could've saved her, Belle, if I'd handled it differently.'

'Gramps, it's no good going back . . .'

'I took it for just a passing fling, ye know. Thought she'd forget about him after a month's parting. I'd forgotten what it's like to be young an' passionate.'

'We can all find ways of reversing events with hindsight. Life just doesn't come that way.' She didn't tell him about seeing Rosanna going into that house in Walmgate.

'Seeing you lying there that night made it worse,' he rambled. 'Brought it all back . . . I thought I was going to lose you, too.'

'Well, you haven't,' she told him, shaking his hand. 'Wouldn't you rather the machine took you back to a happier time?'

He pondered for so long with eyes closed that she thought he'd fallen asleep, but eventually he answered, 'Eighteen sixty.'

'That was very definite. It must've been an exceptionally good year.'

'It was a hell of a year – diabolical. 'Twas the year your nan an' me almost split up.' She gave a little laugh of bafflement. Patrick stretched himself, then relaxed. 'No, I don't know what made me choose it, either. The date just came into me mind. Maybe because it was such a passionate time. It must be hard for you to contemplate me an' Nan as a couple o' hot-blooded youngsters, but we were once. Oh, yes . . .' His voice trailed away.

'I wish there was some way I could make it easier, Gramps,' she said earnestly.

'There is – get some whiskey in for next time I call. I can't stand these temperance houses.' But he was smiling again. He looked up as a visitor was admitted. 'God love us an' save us! They told me the drink would get to me eventually though I didn't know the hallucinations would be that dastardly.' He levered himself from the chair as Sonny came forward bearing a large bunch of flowers.

His son laid the blooms on the patient's lap and bent to kiss her. 'Somebody appeared to forget we have a tele-phone. I've only just heard about your drama. Josie and everyone send their love and hope you've got the old bilges working properly again.'

'I'd be better if some people would stop treating me like an invalid.' Belle sniffed the flowers. 'A dress would've been more appreciated than these.'

'Oh, don't mention it, Belle!' Sonny waved a hand. 'They only cost me a fortune.' He perched on the bed. 'Glad to hear you and your mother are on speaking terms again. In fact I expected to find her here looking after you.'

'And so you would have done, if I hadn't told her to sling her hook!' His niece smiled. 'But yes, it is nice to have her understand at last.'

Sonny nodded. 'And how's Father then?' During their telephone conversation his mother had mentioned that the old man was drinking rather heavily again. That was another reason for his visit.

'Oh, Father's quite well considering it takes a near-tragedy for him to get to see his son. I thought it was at Leeds you lived, not Timbuctoo. Josie well? And the girls?' Sonny said that all were fine. 'An' how's your mother keeping?' Sonny exchanged glances with Belle. 'Well, don't you see more of her than I do?'

'All right, no more buggering about,' replied his son. 'Maybe if you didn't drink so much she might be more inclined to talk to you.'

'Ah-ha!' said Patrick knowingly.

'I thought you'd got over that by now, Dad?' Sonny was reproving.

Patrick screwed up his face in disbelief. 'Got over Rosie? God, I'll never get over her – even if everybody else has.'

Sonny was famed for his even temperament but now he cracked. 'I didn't mean Rosie! For Christ's sake, you miserable old bugger, I miss her too, you know! Just because I don't go round with my face down to my boots or reach for the whiskey bottle every five seconds doesn't mean I don't feel her loss – Jesus, she was my daughter. Having four more doesn't make the loss easier to bear. I could still scream with the pain sometimes, but it won't bring her back and it only upsets those around you.'

Patrick was unmoved. 'And that's your way of telling me I'm getting everybody down with my long expression.'

'Yes! But I'm far more concerned about your drinking. If you're not careful you'll kill yourself!'

'An' who'd care?'

'Oh, Dad . . .' Sonny stopped ranting. 'What a bloody state you've got yourself into . . . We all care about you, you know that.'

'So why do I always seem to find meself on me own? Your mother's out all hours saving her ancient monuments, Nick's back with you at Leeds, Erin's at the factory, Belle's got her children – 'tis only 'cause she's trapped in her sickbed that I've anyone to listen to me grumbling.'

'Well, I'm listening.' Sonny placed a hand over his father's. 'I'll try and get over more often.'

'Oh, I don't want to force people into spending time with a grizzly old bugger who they'd rather avoid.'

'Oh, do stop it, Grandfather,' snapped Belle irritably. 'You're making me feel ill.'

He laughed then. 'Ah well, it's had some good effect then, it's served to keep you in that bed. Oh, I'm sorry if I've been getting on everyone's nerves, Son . . . I sound a right self-pitying devil, I know. It's just that when I'm on me own I get to thinking, an' when I get to thinking . . . I get to drinking.'

'I do know,' murmured Sonny. 'I can be in the middle of painting a picture when all of a sudden there she is . . .'

Patrick nodded. 'And Dickie.'

Sonny was dealt a sharp reminder. Yes, that's how it would be . . . Oh, how he would have loved to tell his father that there was no need for this double mourning, but he daren't.

He came alive and thrust a hand into his pocket, throwing a five-pound note onto Belle's coverlet. 'Right, we're taking bets! A fiver says you can't lay off the booze until Christmas.'

But Patrick wouldn't be provoked. 'Take it back, I'm damned if I'm going teetotal for anybody.'

Sonny distorted his mouth at this failure. 'Can you do anything with him?' he demanded of Belle.

She jabbed at her temple. 'What d'you think all these grey hairs are?'

'Eh, I don't know . . . Josie was just saying last night how nice it would be if the family could spend a week under the same roof and make a proper reunion of it – even when we do all get together these days it's never for more than a day or two. I told her she was being a bit optimistic.'

'That she was. Faith, your mother'd have kittens if ye suggested she spent a whole week in the company of her husband – hey, that's an idea! She could start selling them at the store, a new pet department.'

Sonny laughed. 'Eh, but if we held this reunion at Christmas when everybody's spent all their money she'd have no excuse to be rushed off her feet, would she? An' you're the one who's just been moaning about never having any company – wouldn't you enjoy it?'

'Oh aye, I think it's a fine idea.' Pat chuckled. 'It's a bugger, isn't it? Having to make advance appointments of nine months to see your wife.'

'It'll take me that long to save up enough brass to feed you all,' said Sonny. 'You'll come with your sprites, won't you, Belle?' She said she would.

'Listen,' his father promised, 'if you can get your mother to spend an entire week with her husband I'll not only regulate my drinking, I'll give you a gold medal.'

'So where's the gold medal?' enquired Sonny nine months later when his parents arrived in Leeds with their suitcases.

'What's the boy talking about?' Thomasin followed the butler and maid into the holly and mistletoe-laden hall.

'I promised our son a gold medal if he could get you away from the store,' declared Patrick. 'I said it'd be too much of a hardship for ye to spend a full week with your husband.'

'You poor, neglected soul.' But the rebuke was delivered without malice. Sonny had put such effort into this reunion that they all must try exceptionally hard not to fall out. She let the maid take her hat and coat, then stripped off her gloves. 'Brr! Point me to the fire, it's brass monkey weather out there.' This when they were out of earshot of the servants.

'That's exactly how Father feels, you know,' said Sonny, taking her into the drawing room while Patrick went upstairs for a brush-up.

'I thought I could hear something clanking.' Thomasin stood before the blaze rubbing her hands.

'I didn't mean like a brass monkey, thank you, Mother! You know very well what I mean. You've not spent an awful lot of time with him since we last met, have you?'

Her jocular smile fizzled out. Coming away from the fire she took a seat. 'I have tried . . . but I can't sit at home with him, Sonny, I just can't. We're like two bookends. He drives me mad with his tales of the old days and how good it was. It wasn't good, it was damned hard, you know that and so does he at heart. It's just his way of getting at me.' Sonny shrugged. 'Oh, I know what he means when he says "the old days". He refers to when we were young and gay – but he can't expect things to stay the same, can he? I mean, you just don't feel the same way about some-body when you get older – especially when they seem intent on pickling their liver for posterity.'

'No better, then?'

'Well . . . he's up and down really. Some days he doesn't touch more than a glass.'

'You know, something struck me the other day. We've contributed as much to his drinking habits as he has. Every time there was some upset it'd be "Here, get this down you, Dad". Just think back, Mam. We're not really within our rights to blame it all on him.' The expression on her face agreed this was a good point. 'Instead of condemning, we should be more positive – maybe if the drink's not on display he might be less inclined to reach for it.'

'I suppose I should've been the one to suggest that. I

really do care about him you know, Sonny. It's just that this weakness of his makes me so mad.'

Sonny was about to point out that his mother had her weaknesses too – for didn't she plunge herself into her work when she couldn't face life as it was? But she would not have appreciated this – work to her was a virtue, not a weakness – and anyway, at this juncture his thoughts were interrupted by Josie's entry with their daughters.

'Oh, you're even bonnier than ever!' Thomasin rose to kiss them all. 'And look at Elizabeth! What a young woman – we'll soon have to see about finding you a husband.'

Sonny smiled. Dear Mam, ever the matchmaker. If only she could do a little matchmaking for herself and Father. 'Where's my sister, by the way?'

'She's catching the train,' his mother told him. 'Says she'll be here this evening with Belle – they seem to be spending quite a bit of time together now. Bosom pals.'

'Yes, well I trust Belle hasn't acquired any more children lately, else we're going to have to stick labels on them all to remember whose are whose.'

'Oh, it's going to be lovely, all of us together,' enthused Thomasin. Then her smile frayed a little.

Sonny knew what was going through her mind – Oh, Mam, if only I could tell you that he's still alive.

Later, Sonny took his parents to see the neat row of cottages he had built for his mill-workers. After this they visited the workhouse with a Christmas tree and gifts of food. On their exit, Thomasin expressed a desire to visit the store. 'I promise I won't be long. I just want to see how Nick's coping,' so after dropping their son back at the house, she and Patrick were driven into town.

On the way, however, they passed a park and having no wish to compete with the Christmas crowds Patrick said he would take a walk round it while his wife conducted her business with Nick.

'I don't know if that's wise,' replied Thomasin as he alighted from the carriage. 'Have you got enough clothes on? I don't want to come back and find you frozen to a park bench.'

He assured her he would be fine as long as she didn't take all day about it and Thomasin, wishing him a happy walk, told John to drive on.

Briggate was packed with shoppers and traffic. There was barely room for Thomasin's carriage to park outside her own store. 'I hope you remembered to fetch the goose grease, John,' she told her driver as he helped her to the pavement. 'It's going to be a right squeeze getting in there.' He smiled and followed her to the door where a man in uniform saluted and asked Thomasin if she was keeping well. She inspected his appearance automatically. 'Very well, Stanley – and you?'

'Couldn't be better, ma'am.'

'That's the show.' Thomasin was about to go in when a shabbily-dressed woman blocked her entry. She was bearing the sorriest-looking fowl Thomasin had ever seen and when she had passed Thomasin remarked to the doorman, 'I hope she didn't buy that in my store.'

He smiled. 'I think she just wanted them to cook it for her, ma'am.'

'And they've turned her away?' Thomasin donned a concerned expression and addressed her manservant. 'Quickly, John – go ask that elderly lady if she'd mind stepping back to the store.' She watched as John detained the woman and led her back. 'Come into the warm, my dear,' she said kindly to the confused woman. 'I fear you may have been mistreated.' The doors were opened to her again and she passed through, coming to rest beside a large poster which read: *Provident cheques accepted*. She then asked the woman what had happened.

The other looked at her askance. 'I just came in to ask if they'd cook my Christmas bird 'cause I've no oven but they said no.'

'Were you offered any explanation?' The woman shook her head. 'Just told no?' Another movement of the head. 'I see. Well now, we shall have to do something about that, won't we?' It always delighted Thomasin when she had to fight her way into one of her stores but even this fact and the wooden cash containers that whizzed noisily around the overhead railway couldn't dispel her outrage. Asking the woman to take one of the chairs provided, she struggled through the crush to the counter and asked which of the assistants had dealt with the old woman.

At first everyone was too busy to notice who the personage was, but then: 'I did, madam,' spoke up a pristine-aproned young woman. 'She didn't buy the bird here so I told her I was sorry but she'd have to take it somewhere else to get it cooked.'

'On whose authority?' Thomasin watched the hands that packed the customer's basket; at least they were clean.

'Well, no one's actually, ma'am.' The girl blushed at Thomasin's tone. 'But we had another one asking last week and Mr Feeney told us we could only give the service to regular customers.'

'Well, I'm telling you now – and you can pass it on to the others when you get chance – that if anyone makes the request in future you are to fulfil it. Now, would you kindly go over there and offer your apologies to the lady and while you are there you will take her basket and fill it with as many groceries as can be fitted in while I go and speak to Mr Feeney.'

'Nan! How nice to see you. Father said you were coming over for Christmas.' Nick offered his own chair which she took. 'A Merry Christmas to you.'

'And a not-so-merry Christmas for some,' she replied cryptically, then explained about the customer.

'Nan, you've seen how busy we are down there,' he defended. 'We've barely enough room in the oven for regular customers' birds. We can't do everyone's.'

'If it were Lady Manning's bird you'd find room, though, wouldn't you? We're not just here to cater for the carriage trade, Nicholas. I can see I'm going to have to explain yet another area of commerce. That may look like just a shabby old woman to you, but she's capable of taking a good part of our business. On her way home she could meet three of her friends and tell them what bad treatment

613

they'll receive if they visit our store. They will go their separate ways and in turn meet three of their friends and so on and so on, until half of Leeds has come to hear what swines they are down at *Penny's* and how their food is rotten and how their staff are vampires – you know how distorted these tales become. However humble her appearance she has the power to destroy us. Always remember that and treat each person who comes through that door in a courteous manner.' She slapped his knee. 'Ticking-off over. Now, let's see those books.'

Nick grinned and placed a ledger in front of her, opening it at the current entry. She studied the figures then looked up at him, a congratulatory smile on her lips. 'Well, I can't say I'm surprised, Nick. I'd expected some sort of improvement, say, perhaps ten per cent, but a fifteen per cent rise in the takings is excellent. Well done.'

'So when am I to become a director?' replied Nick. *Penny's* had become a limited company that same year.

She closed the ledger. 'Double the fifteen per cent a year from today and we'll see about it.'

'Are you descended from Ghengis Khan, Grandmother?'

'Only on the distaff side – you didn't really expect to be made a director on such modest gains did you, Nick? Ah,' she interpreted his expression – it was hard not to, 'I can see you did.'

'It would've made a nice Christmas present, Nan,' he said reprovingly.

'I daresay it would – *if* I was called Mrs Santa Claus. Is that what I promised when I put you in here? No? Then it was rash of you to assume such rapid rewards, wasn't it?'

'I suppose it would also be rash of me to ask if you could lend me a tenner?'

'Now, Nicholas,' she rose stiffly, 'you know me too well for that. Neither a borrower nor a lender be. I don't know what you do with all your money. Now I'd better go and collect your grandfather or he'll be like a block of ice.'

'Oh, I almost forgot.' Nick reached for a newspaper and passed it to her after folding it into position.

'Am I mentioned in the Christmas Honours at last?'

'Bottom left-hand corner,' he tapped the page.

She scrutinised the advertisement for a moment, then let rip. 'Damn and blast! The incompetent fools.' A misprint had occurred. The price of turkey, instead of reading ten to fourteen shillings, was ten *for* fourteen shillings. She thrust the paper back at him. 'You'd better get onto them quickly before we get trampled to death in the rush. I believe in charity at Christmas but not to that extent. Tell them they can put it in again – correctly this time – or we don't pay.'

'What do we do in the meantime?'

'Well, how have you been coping?'

'I've nearly sent myself blue in the face trying to explain it's all an error but I've had a few rough spells. I managed to get rid of them – but of course we don't want them going home and meeting three of their friends . . .'

'Puh! They're just trying it on. Tell 'em if they know anywhere that sells turkeys ten for fourteen bob they're welcome to take their custom there and get me a crateful while they're at it.'

'Did you see my window display when you came in?'

'I did. Exceptional, Nicholas. You have your father's artistic flair.' And then she remembered he was not Sonny's true issue and that of course brought back memories of the boy's real father. But then thoughts of Dickie were always strongest at this time of year, the anniversary of his birth. She shook the visions from her mind and prepared to leave. 'Those labels you designed are quite eye-catching, aren't they? Well, I'm off. I'll see you at supper, I suppose?'

'S'pect so,' answered Nick dully.

Patrick had finished his tour of the park some time ago and was seated on a bench, staring out over the sparsely-populated gardens. His thoughts as usual were of his dead grand-daughter, but just lately he had found that added to these memories thoughts of his homeland had begun to creep in. Perhaps it was simply old age, but he found himself dwelling on Ireland more than ever these days.

Two women, travelling in opposite directions, met in front of the bench where he sat.

'Ee, hello, love, in't it cold?'

The second moved her shoulders rapidly under her shabby coat. 'By 'eck, aye. I's'll atta put some thicker drawers on, I think.' They cackled. Patrick might just as well have been invisible. The first enquired after the second's husband.

'He's no better, love. Doctor can't find owt wrong with him. He's had tubes stuck up right, left an' centre. Can't sleep neither, not just wi' t'pain, it's them noisy buggers next door.'

'Oh, them Jews?'

'Aye.' The other nodded, her expression tart. 'Ee an' the muck. Yer've never seen owt like it. She's never had her nets down since they moved in. Yer could use 'em as funeral drapes.'

'Aw, an' it used to be ever such a nice street, din't it, love?'

'Aye, it was before that lot moved in. An' they're tekkin all t'jobs, yer know. I don't know where they all come from. They're everywhere.' She used her forefinger to pick at a tooth. 'I'd move but they've brought price of our property right down. We'd get bugger-all for it.'

'Well, who'd want to move next door to them, eh? Summat should be done.'

'Well, what can yer do? Say owt to 'em an' yer get a load of foreign abuse. Eh,' a wistful sigh, 'I'd give owt to have them Irish folk back. That Mrs Casey what used to live over t'road, she used to be up at six every mornin' stonin' her step . . . an' such lovely bairns they had.'

'Oh aye, they're very clean-livin' folk are the Irish.' A distant bell chimed the hour. 'Eh, I'll have to be off, love. See you again an' 'ave a nice Christmas. Tara!'

They parted, leaving Patrick free to release his mirth. He was still chuckling when his wife arrived.

'By, something's tickled you.' She lowered herself onto the bench beside him.

'Oh, glory be to God.' He wiped away the moisture that was threatening to freeze into the creases around his eyes. ' "The clean-livin' Irish", she called us. It appears 'tis the turn o' the poor bloody Jews to carry Society's can. I wonder who'll get it next century?'

Poor old bugger, thought Thomasin sadly, he's failing. 'Come on, let's have you home where it's warm.'

Still laughing, Patrick permitted himself to be led back to the carriage and the pair of them returned to their son's home to await the night's celebration.

CHAPTER FORTY-TWO

Sonny and Josie went out in the late afternoon to collect some large Christmas presents for the children which had been hidden at a friend's house. Thomasin and Patrick were entertained by their grand-daughters the eldest of whom, Elizabeth, was now almost sixteen. She was nothing like Rosanna had been, but nevertheless a lovely girl and Patrick enjoyed the sensible conversation she provided whilst she and her sisters dressed the Christmas tree. Shortly though, the girls were ordered upstairs by their governess to tidy the appalling mess they had left in their rooms.

It was too much to expect, of course, that Thomasin could suffer his company on her own. Barely five minutes passed before she left to 'telephone Francis to see how the Bradford store is doing'. After half an hour she still had not returned. What else was there to do? He went to pour himself a drink.

Finding no decanters on the sideboard he tried the cupboard. It was locked. At first this didn't register. Then, as he was going back to his chair he suddenly realised –

it had been locked for his benefit. His face darkened. My God, they were making him out to be an alcoholic! Well, damn them, he wouldn't be treated like this. Striding across the room he yanked at a bell-pull.

Shortly the butler answered his summons. 'May I be of assistance, sir?'

'Do you happen to know where my wife is?'

'I believe Mrs Feeney went out some twenty minutes ago, sir.'

'Right, then would ye be after having the key to this cupboard?' Patrick banged on the wood.

'I would, sir. Shall I pour you some refreshment?'

Patrick nodded curtly. 'Whiskey, if ye please.' He watched the man unlock the cupboard and pour a small measure into a crystal tumbler. 'Ye can leave it out,' he added on seeing the bottle about to be locked away.

'I regret I have orders not to leave any liquor unsupervised, sir.'

Inside, Patrick seethed, but he forced his voice to be casual. 'An' why's that, I wonder?'

'The master doesn't like to leave temptation in the servants' way, sir.'

'In his father's way!' snarled Patrick and disposed of the mean measure in one gulp. 'Now just get that bloody bottle out an' less o' the flannel.' But the butler was an inflexible sort of man and would not budge. 'Sullivan,' said Patrick evenly, 'ye didn't know me in my younger days, did ye?'

'Unfortunately not, sir.'

'Unfortunately nothing! If ye had known me ye'd also know I had the reputation of having the biggest fists in York – I could still put them to good use if I felt like it, so would ye like to pass me that bottle or am I going to bunch ye?'

'Sir, if I disobey a direct order I'll be sacked . . .'

'If ye disobey my orders ye'll also be sacked – dropped into one, the neck tied up an' the whole nasty thing dropped into the cut. Look, you know an' I know that my son would believe Attila the Hun if he said he was a member of the Band of Hope – tell him a fairy picked the lock. Anyway, how will he know it's missing? I'm certainly not going to get you into trouble.'

'I'm sorry, sir, I really am.' The man backed to the door. 'But I've never lied to my employer and I don't intend to start.'

'Sullivan, come back here!' Patrick rose but the butler had already left the room. 'God dammit, I'll smash the bloody cupboard so I will!' He was on his way to do just that when the door opened again and thinking it was the butler he spun, primed for the attack. The little girl appraised his fighting stance solemnly. On seeing it was one of his grand-daughters Patrick controlled his temper immediately, smoothing away all signs of irritation with an embracing smile. 'Ah, back at last! Is your room all neat an' tidy now?' She said it was. 'Then come sit on my knee, sugar, an' I'll tell ye a story.' He placed his hands on his knees, bending to welcome her.

She ventured towards him. 'Do you know anything about mice, Grandfather?'

'A story about a mouse, eh?'

'No, about catching them.'

'Sure now, didn't I take my City and Guilds in the very subject. Come plant yourself here, my little Annie.'

'Amelia,' corrected the girl. Grandfather was always getting names wrong. She let him take her on his knee. 'I've lost my mouse.'

'Oh, we'll have it found in no time at all – where did ye last see it?'

'Oh, I know where it is. It's in the nursery, but it's gone behind a cupboard and won't come out because Miss Robinson is making such a din.'

'Cupboard is it? Sure, aren't cupboards being the very devil of it today? Ah, God love ye!' Patrick squeezed the little girl. 'Come on, let's go see what we can do.'

In the nursery he asked, 'Right then, where'd this varmint go?'

Amelia pointed, and Patrick applied his shoulder to the huge cupboard that travelled almost to the ceiling and was crammed with books. He started to heave.

'Don't hurt it, will you?' begged Amelia.

'Didn't I tell ye I'm an expert? Be ready to catch it when it runs out – oh God, look out!' The cupboard had started to rock. He tried to hold it but ended up having to leap forward and snatch his grand-daughter out of its way as it crashed to the floor, spilling books as it went. 'Jaze, that was close!' He mopped his brow, then looked up as the governess came running. 'I'm sorry to frighten ye, Miss . . .' he couldn't think of her name. ''Twas just this silly old eejit thinking he can move mountains.'

'I'll fetch Sullivan,' said the governess primly and within minutes the cupboard was being hauled back into place by the butler and another man.

Amelia bent down to pick something up. She clutched it to her bosom, stroking the tiny head.

'Ah God, that's a grand-lookin' creature,' observed Patrick, coming nearer. 'Is it a man or a woman?'

'It's not anything now.' She held out her palm, the blue eyes accusing. 'You killed it.'

'Ah, Amelia, I never woulda . . . 'twas an accident!'

'You're horrid.' Her glaring eyes compelled him to leave the nursery. Before the door slammed after him, however, he heard the child tell her governess, 'I hate that man.'

Nick's brain reflected the activity that was humming on the floor below his office. He must have that money for tonight, he must. He would impress nobody with the paltry amount he had in his possession at the moment, and it was essential that he impressed tonight. Had Nan been acquainted with the reason for his need she would probably have lent him the money – but Nick wanted to surprise her.

Whilst at the theatre not long ago he had locked eyes with a pretty creature in the box opposite. It wasn't just her smiling interest that held him; she was obviously from a wealthy family, for her swan-like neck was encircled with a shimmering white and green necklace – and it certainly wasn't glass. On making enquiries of a member of the theatre staff during the interval he had discovered that she was the Hon. Edith Waddington. The man with her was her father, a peer of the realm.

Since the split with Moira, Nick had been thinking that it might not be a bad idea to enter himself for the marriage stakes – and what better match than this little bloodstock filly? His ensuing machinations had brought him into the company of the peer, where his charming conversation had earned tonight's dinner engagement. If it went well the invitation would be returned – Nick would be invited to the peer's home where he would meet the daughter and things would progress from there ... at least they would if he could get his hands on enough to entertain the peer in the manner to which he was accustomed. It had been a bit impulsive to make the invitation before he was sure of the funds. He counted the money again as if half-expecting to have made a mistake, then sighed – he never made mistakes about cash. Damn. He couldn't sit at that table with this measly amount in his pocket. He could have borrowed it from the till, but didn't know when he would be able to put it back. Anyway, once one started dibbing into the till things could get out of hand. Should he postpone the engagement? No, he might not get another chance. Besides which, supper at home would hardly be the jovial affair it once might have been what with Father locking the drinks cabinet – Gramps put the miseries on everyone unless he'd had a few jars down him. ... My God! Nick laughed delightedly. Why didn't I think of it sooner? Checking the contents of his pocket one last time he left the office, grinning confidently.

On his arrival home he entered by the kitchen in order to get the information he needed from one of the maids. Discovering that all were out save the girls and old Mr Feeney, he marched determinedly to the drawing room.

Patrick was about to apply a piece of cutlery to the drinks cabinet when his grandson came in. 'Ah, God, I thought it might be your father!' The old man reviewed the cupboard again, then banged his fist on it in defeat. 'Don't suppose you have a key for this thing, d'ye?'

'Why?'

'Because I want to see what colour it is on the inside – why d'ye think, eejit?'

'You need a drink?' Nick came to stand beside the crouched man.

'I don't *need* it, but I'd like one if it wouldn't be like trying to squeeze charity out o' Father Gilchrist.'

'Unfortunately I don't have a key, Grandfather.' Patrick cursed. 'But,' Nick grinned and from the inside pocket of his coat brought out a bottle wrapped in tissue, 'I have brought you a present.'

'Ah faith, the man should be canonised.' Patrick held out his hand.

'I'll pour,' said Nick, going for glasses.

'I thought ye said 'twas a gift?'

'It is.'

'Then I'll use my gift the way I see fit.' Patrick snatched the bottle. '*I'll* pour. I want no fairy thimblefuls, thank ye very much. Where the hell are the glasses?'

'In the cupboard.' Nick laughed at Patrick's groan. 'Don't worry, I'll ring for a couple from the kitchen.' He pulled the rope.

'A couple – who said I was sharing it with you?'

'I was the one who came to the rescue.'

'So ye were, son. I was only joshing ye. Ye'll be welcome to keep me company.'

'Well, I'm really supposed to be at the store.' Nick seated himself in the easy chair opposite Patrick's. 'I only came to collect a few papers I forgot this morning and then I thought, I'll bet poor Gramps is sat there all on his own again, so I nipped into the off-licence on the corner and purchased that.'

'You're a good lad to think of your old grandfather.' Patrick looked at the door. Sullivan had entered and was looking most disapprovingly at the bottle. Pat threw him a look of triumph. 'Would ye be so good as to fetch us two glasses, my man?' Sullivan's lips seemed glued together. 'Er, could we be having them now?' asked the Irishman, 'or did ye think I meant next Christmas?' He winked at his grandson as the butler went to unlock the cupboard.

With the two glasses supplied and Sullivan gone, Patrick poured generous samples. 'Hey, Grandad, go easy!' Nick snatched a glass away before the whiskey reached the rim. 'I've to cash up yet.'

'Sláinte.' Patrick consumed the drink immediately, then poured another. After slaking his need he tossed a question to Nick. 'Can I ask why you haven't joined the conspiracy?'

'Sorry?' Nick hid behind the glass.

'The drink, boy, the drink. All of 'em on at me, nag, nag, nag – "You're drinking too much, Patrick, 'tisn't good for ye" . . . why not you?'

'Maybe I understand why you need it.'

'I've told you I *don't* need it.'

'Well . . .'

Patrick wrinkled his brow and flapped a hand. 'Aye . . . it could be true. I'm all right when I've plenty to occupy me, s'just when I get bored – an' then I come here an' find that my own son is treating me like an alcoholic . . .'

Nick dipped his finger into his glass, stirring at the liquor.

'It's over three years since Rosie went . . . and I still feel such pain.'

This was going down the wrong track; the whiskey was intended to put Grandfather in a more benevolent state of mind. 'D'you fancy going to the theatre next week, Gramps? I thought you and me might go up town, then have a bite to eat and a few jars.'

'Ah, it's good of you to try an' cheer me up, son . . . but I don't know if I can be bothered to drag me body out. I'm never in the mood to go far these days.'

'I wasn't trying to cheer you up, I wouldn't have minded going myself . . . still, never mind.'

'There must be a young lady who'd make better company.'

'Are you fishing, Grandfather?' smiled Nick.

'Well, I can't deny I'd like to see one o' my grandchildren married before I meet my Maker. Belle shows no inclination, though that doctor makes it pretty plain what his feelings are.'

'Well, as you know, the store is my sweetheart, Gramps. It would have to be an exceptional woman to displace her in my favour . . .'

'That bloody store! You're as bad as your grandmother. Invite me to spend Christmas with the family an' where are they all – out working for the bloody store!'

'We do have to earn a crust, Grandad.' Nick cursed the old man for changing the subject.

'Aye, I know, I know. I'm just being a grumpy old shit. I'm sorry, boy, don't think I don't appreciate you popping in to see me with this.' He picked up the bottle. ''Course I do, ye saved me life – well, ye saved your father's fine bit o' furniture anyway. D'ye know, do you know what that child said?'

'What child?' It was often hard to interpret the old man now; he hopped about from subject to subject like a frog with St Vitus' Dance. 'Annie . . . Amelia – oh, I don't know! The one with the blonde locks. She said, "I hate that man." She meant me – *me!*' He stabbed his chest in disbelief.

Nick tried to make light of the matter. 'She's always saying things like that about everybody. Yesterday it was Father when he wouldn't allow her to stay up half an hour later.'

''Twas a bit more serious than that,' confessed Patrick. 'I killed her mouse.'

'Oh . . .' Nick scratched his head, then dismissed the matter. 'Oh, well, she'll soon forget it. I'll buy her another. Don't take it to heart, Gramps.'

'She said it with such feeling.'

'She's a very dramatic child.' Nick stole a glance at the clock. He must not be here when Nan returned. Damn and blast. The whiskey on which he had spent his paltry funds had been meant to make the old man all jollified, not take one step nearer the grave. 'I suppose I'd better be getting back to the shop . . . some use I am in cheering folk up.'

'Oh, I'm fine, son. Don't worry about me. See y'at supper then?'

'Probably . . . actually,' Nick uttered a tight laugh, 'I had hoped to be dining out this evening, but with Father organising this reunion . . .'

Patrick brightened. 'A young lady, was it? Well, don't put her off just 'cause o' this reunion, son. I don't mind in the least.'

'No, it's all right, Gramps, the money I have wouldn't have provided her with much of a night out, anyway.'

'Sure, if money's your only hurdle stop fratching.' Patrick leaned on the chair arm and hoisting one buttock dug deep into his pocket, throwing a fistful of notes onto the table. 'Take what ye need an' be buggered this reunion. Never let it be said that Patrick Feeney put the dampers on a budding romance – an' your Nan would feel that way too, I'm certain.'

'Really, I couldn't . . . I don't want that much, Gramps.'

'Take it! What use are all them bits o' paper to me?'

'If you're sure . . .' Gently, Nick disentangled the crumpled notes and smoothed them lovingly. God, there must be about forty pounds here. The neatened pile totalled forty-five.

'Don't bother, just take the bloody lot. I'll get your Nan to print some more.'

'But if I take this you'll be left with nothing.'

'Take it, damn ye!'

'No,' said Nick firmly. 'I'll only take what I need.' He folded thirty pounds into his pocket – that should give the peer a good old do – and pressed the remaining fivers back into Patrick's hand. 'Thanks, Grandfather. I hope Father won't be mad at you for this.'

'If there's anybody going to be mad 'tis me – locking the drink away from his own father! Go on now, away to your store before Nan gets back an' gives ye a scalpin' for bringing me this – oh, an' I expect ye to bring this girl to see me before ye go fixing the date.'

'Don't fret, Gramps,' grinned Nick on his way out: 'I

will – oh, but don't say anything to Nan. I want it to be a surprise.'

Erin rolled up in the early evening, Vinnie travelling with her. Shortly afterwards Belle arrived, accompanied by Brian whose visit was to be fleeting as he was on call over Christmas. Belle's progeny – never shy – introduced themselves to Sonny's brood and were soon pelting about the hall and up the stairs until Belle called a halt. By the time unpacking was over the clock had worked its hands around to supper time. After everyone was seated at the table Thomasin eyed the vacant seat.

'I see Master Nicholas won't be joining us for supper.'

'By God, d'ye know who you just sounded like then?' ejaculated her husband with a broad grin. 'Your mother.'

'Strange,' said Thomasin, ignoring his observation, 'that Nick was asking me for money this afternoon which I refused. I wonder where he acquired his loan.'

Patrick reached nonchalantly for a bread roll.

'It really is quite thoughtless of him to do this when we're all together,' said Josie. 'John, you should've made sure he was here.'

'I wasn't to know, was I?' replied Sonny. 'I'm never privy to his arrangements. He seems to come and go as if this were an hotel. You say he was touting for money, Mother?' The soup came. He broke a bread roll onto his side plate.

'He was but he didn't get any. I presume he wanted it for this evening out.'

'I hope he hasn't been getting round you, Dad?' asked Sonny.

Patrick made no reply, pretending not to hear and spooning up his soup.

'You don't really need to ask, Sonny, do you?' said his mother frostily.

'All right, I gave it to him,' admitted Patrick. ''Tis no great sin, is it?'

'Here's Sonny trying to organise a family reunion and you paying members of the family to stay away.'

'If the lad would rather be somewhere else – an' I can't say I blame him – why should we force him to sit here with us?'

'Because that's what family reunions are supposed to be for,' snapped Thomasin.

'Oh, so that's why ye cleared off an' left me this afternoon.'

Sonny looked at his wife. He hoped they hadn't been brought together just to argue. 'Nick's doing quite well at the store, don't you think, Mother?'

'He's doing exceedingly well,' affirmed Thomasin. 'He'd show even more promise if he wasn't indulged by people who are old enough to have learnt the difference between good and bad manners.'

'I think she means me,' Patrick informed the others, scraping his bowl. He laid down the spoon and smacked his lips.

'I do hope this isn't going to carry on throughout the holiday,' said Belle. 'Because if it is I'm going home.' She turned to one of the children. 'Don't think that dawdling over your soup will keep you from an early night, young man. You can just as easily be sent to bed without tasting Cook's excellent dessert. I believe it's peach meringue, isn't it, Aunt Josie?'

'I don't see why we have to go to bed early,' objected Eddie.

'I've told you, it's been a long journey and you need to catch up on your sleep or you won't be able to come to the pantomime tomorrow.'

'I should've thought ye'd seen enough o' pantomimes,' ventured her grandfather, then put a hand over his mouth like a caught-out schoolboy under Thomasin's glare.

'Are we allowed to come?' asked one of Sonny's girls.

'Naturally,' replied Belle. 'The more the merrier. Grandfather can come and help me keep you all in tow.'

'I shan't come then,' said Amelia flatly.

Everyone stared at her. Whatever Patrick was to the adults children always warmed to him. 'Whyever not?' Belle asked.

'*He* killed my mouse,' Amelia informed her.

'Amelia, that's no way to refer to your grandfather,' rebuked Sonny. 'It was an accident.'

'No, it wasn't,' retorted the child. 'He was drunk.'

'Amelia Rose!' Josie took control. 'That's a very rude thing to say. You must say you're sorry to your grandfather.'

'I won't! He *was* drunk. Nanny said so. I heard her say it to Sullivan. He killed Benjamin.' She began to sob.

Everyone's eyes were on Patrick; some sympathetic, others – notably his wife's – accusing. 'Sure, I wasn't drunk, Tommy. I swear it. For God's sake wasn't the drink locked away? I'd never . . .' He did not finish. His wife had looked away in disgust.

'I'll just take Amelia upstairs for a while,' whispered Josie, excusing herself. 'Carry on, everyone. I won't be long.'

The meal was uncomfortably resumed, but without Patrick who had lost his appetite. The maid was about to place the main course in front of him when he rose, almost knocking the plate from her hands. 'Sorry, girl,' he muttered. Then to the others, 'If ye'll excuse me I'm not feeling so good . . .' He made for the door.

'Have one for me while you're there, Patrick.'

He checked at Thomasin's loud instruction, looked back at her, but there was no sparkle in her eye. In fact she wasn't even looking at him. A few minutes later the diners heard the front door slam.

Thomasin flopped back in her chair and raised her glass. 'Merry Christmas, everybody. It is Christmas, isn't it?'

Sonny was not the only one to notice that the glass never touched her lips.

'Did you know,' slurred Patrick, 'that I once struck a priest?' The public house in which he was sitting – or slumping – was the fifth he had visited that evening. In each of the other four he had managed to get himself thrown out before anyone had taken him up on his fighting stance: 'Get on with yer, owd lad, back to yer granny before yer turn up in tomorra's stew.' In this one there had already been some sort of fracas going on and he had tried to join in, until the barman hauled him out of the way of swinging police truncheons with, 'Away now, don't get involved in all this at your age. You don't know what you're at.'

'I do! Leave me be or I'll shred your bloody nose!'

'Eh.' The barman wagged a finger. 'Just behave yerself an' sit here while that little lot get sorted out.' Then the priest had come in and had sorted the matter in no time at all and now sat with a humiliated Patrick drinking his reward.

'Is that a fact?' he responded to Patrick's provocative statement. 'An' tell me, is this a habit with you? Am I to prepare some sort o' defence?'

Patrick swayed and patted the priest's arm to show he was safe. ''Twas just the one. Father Kelly was his name. Did ye know him by chance?'

'Kelly? That's an uncommon name.' The priest smiled and took a drink.

'Ye never heard of him? Faith, there's not a sinner in York that the man didn't help.' The priest reminded Patrick that he was in Leeds. 'Ah, sure I was forgetting. I wish I could forget about other things so easy.'

'You're from York, then?'

'I sometimes wonder where I am from.' A loud tap on the bar for another drink.

The priest asked what part of Ireland Patrick came from, sparking a lengthy piece of dialogue about what they both missed about the country, also about the famine. After several drinks the priest said he should go. 'I'll not be able to perform Midnight Mass should I take any more. Would you be walking my way?'

Patrick blinked and wobbled on his stool. 'No, I think I'll stay a little longer.'

'Won't they be worried about you at home?'

'Nup.' Patrick shouted at the barman to provide more whiskey. 'They know where I am.'

629

'Well . . . don't drink too much o' that stuff,' warned the priest.

'Jazers, is the bloody needle stuck?' bawled Patrick. 'That's all anybody seems to be able to say.'

The priest had a word with the barman on his way out. 'Keep an eye on the ould fella. He's well kettled. If he goes down he'll never get up. Goodnight, lads!' He hoisted his arm. 'Don't let's have the Law in again before twelve. I want no broken heads at Mass.'

Alone at his table Patrick began to sing, disjointedly at first, tapping the table with his glass, then, when the others picked up the rebel thread he came to full cry. They sang long and vociferously, taking it in turns to keep the old man's glass filled – a songbird was always popular – until the rousing words and the drink drove Patrick to picking another fight and he was slung out.

The street was deserted. Patrick wondered over this for a moment, then remembered it was Christmas Eve; most folk would be home with their families. Home – now where was that? He staggered, took a step backwards. 'Home is where the hearth is,' he proclaimed loudly, then looked both ways. 'But how do I bloody get there?' He used his finger like a metronome to decide which direction to take. 'Eeny meeny macker acker, aero domino, alley wacker, judy acker, om-pom-push! This way.' He headed to his left, weaving drunkenly about the pavement.

Unfortunately the route proved to be the wrong one as Patrick found out after two miles, when the buildings started to give way to open fields. Puffing and wheezing with the cold the old man flopped his buttocks onto a low wall and dropped his head to his chest. 'We're lost.' Stupefied, he hoisted himself and continued to walk in the same direction, telling himself he would come to Sonny's house eventually.

After a further two miles he came across a lighted barn towards which he attempted to steer his wayward feet. The barn was unoccupied. He leaned at the doorway and peered inside. The beam of the lantern fell on a pile of feathers and nearby a string of naked fowl which had, until a moment ago, been wearing them. Patrick's bleary eyes wavered onto another pile. This time potatoes. Suddenly the years slipped from his shoulders. It was the year of the famine when he had marched to York, creeping into the fields under darkness to steal potatoes for his hungry wife. A grin added its light to that of the lantern. Stumbling inside he approached the pile. Bending gingerly he took a potato in each hand and started to stuff them into his suit pockets till they bulged. 'That's no bloody good.' He searched around for a sack and, finding one, started to cram it with potatoes.

When it was almost full he gathered the top into his fists and with a grunt swung it up over his shoulder. The weight of the sack propelled him backwards and he collapsed on top of it roaring with mirth. Still hanging onto his burden he tried to rise – a dozen times – laughingly bemoaning his feeble efforts. Finally he gave up, closed his eyes and slept where he had fallen. When he woke – which felt like hours later but was actually a matter of minutes – a pitchfork was pricking his chest. 'Bugger me, said the abbot an' turned around to find a queue.' He blinked his eyes and pressed his jaw to his chest to stare down at the pitchfork.

'Stop where y'are, yer thievin' owd sod.' The farmer had returned from his late supper to tidy up after a long day's preparation for Christmas and instead had found the sleeping intruder. 'Constable's on his way.'

'Constable?' Patrick's eyebrows fused. 'Wha' for?'

'Well, not to paint thy bloody picture. Unless I'm mistekken you were about to make off wi' my spuds.'

'Spuds – where?'

'What's in that sack you're hanging onto – lumps of air?'

'Call them spuds?' Patrick tried to rise. 'Sure, they're nuthin' but bloody riddlers. I've seen bigger marbles. I'd never soil my hands with such insults.'

'Well, be that as it may they're *my* bloody marbles so talk yer way outta that one when the Law arrives.'

Patrick began to laugh. Oh, Christ, that was a turn-up;

the husband of the illustrious Mrs Feeney being done for theft.

The village constable arrived, none too pleased at being roused on Christmas Eve. 'Now then, sir,' – the clothes told him this was not the vagrant he had been led to expect – 'let's be having you on your feet, shall we?'

Patrick tried to rise. 'Yer'll need a crane,' said the farmer. 'Yon's kalied.'

'It might be better if you let go of the sack, sir.' The officer leant down and hooked a hand under Patrick's armpit, then looked at the farmer. 'Away George, give us a hand.'

Grumbling, the farmer lent assistance and the Irishman was hoisted unceremoniously to his feet.

'Now then, I think we'll begin with your name.' The police officer conjured up a notepad. Patrick tottered. The farmer caught him. 'Can you remember your name?'

'I can,' announced Patrick proudly as though this was some great achievement. 'Patrick Feeney.'

'And your address?'

Patrick collapsed. 'I'm buggered if I can remember.'

'A night in the cells, is it, sir?'

'No, no, I'm sorry I can't oblige 'cause I'm spendin' Christmas Eve with my son.'

'And what's your son's name?'

'John Feeney.'

The officer stopped writing and looked up from his pad. 'Would that be the mill owner, by any chance, sir?'

''Twould. John Feeney, mill owner. I'm married to Thomasin Feeney, shop owner, factory owner, Irishman owner . . .' A belch came to his throat. He allowed it to escape.

'Can one ask what you intended to do with these potatoes, sir?'

'Them piddlin' things in the sack?'

'That's right, sir.'

'Listen, there's no call to talk to me in that frame o' mind.' Patrick thumped his chest. 'I'm not a child. I'll have ye know my wife's a very important woman.'

The officer sighed and made a discreet aside to the farmer. 'What d'you want me to do with him, George? I don't think he were reckoning to steal 'em really, he's just had too much lotion. Anyway, it'd be a waste o' time prosecuting if you ask me. He's right when he says his wife's an important woman. You'd get no joy from court.'

The farmer waved a dismissive hand. 'Ah . . . do what tha likes wi' t'soft owd pisspot,' and went to unhook the lantern with which he lit their path from the barn to the road.

'I'd best take him home,' said the officer, trying to hang onto Patrick. 'If he collapses on t'road he'll perish in this weather. You wouldn't care to get cart out, would you?'

'Cart him 'ome when t'owd sod was gonna clean me out? Tha's gorra nerve.'

'Away George, it's only a couple o' mile down t'road.'

'I were just off to me bed.'

'Goodwill to all men, an' that? Or to phrase it another way, obstructing a law officer in the course of his duty.'

'Oh . . . sod it!' The farmer went off to hitch a pony and, bringing it round to the gate, helped to shove Patrick in the back of the trap. The Irishman sang loudly all the way home.

'There's a policeman in the hall, sir,' the butler informed Sonny, breaking up the contented family atmosphere late that evening.

'Oh, God, d'you think Father could've been hurt?' Sonny threw an alarmed look at his mother. 'I knew we should've gone looking for him.'

'Mr Feeney is with the policeman, sir,' Sullivan coolly divulged. 'And another . . . gentleman.'

'You'd better show them in, then,' replied his employer.

Every adult in the family was present to see Patrick's belittlement – or rather, Thomasin's, for the old man seemed to regard all this as a huge joke. Steered to a chair by the constable and the farmer, Patrick flopped heavily into it and observed the gathering with a stupid grin.

The police officer told Sonny what had happened. 'But, I'm happy to tell you that this gentleman,' he directed his

hand at the farmer, 'won't be pressing charges. Well . . .
people do sometimes have more than's good for them at
Christmas, don't they?'

'Some more than others,' said Thomasin, then stepped
forward and added, 'That's very charitable of you both,
especially considering the amount of trouble my husband
must've put you to, coming all this way in the cold. I'm
sure we're all very grateful. Sonny, can I take a liberty and
ask these gentlemen to take something warming before
they make their return?'

'If you hadn't asked I was going to,' returned her son.
'Gentlemen, what could we tempt you with?'

'A cup of summat hot wouldn't go amiss, sir, thank you.'

Sonny rang for Sullivan and ordered tea and hot mince
pies for the guests – much to Cook's displeasure as she
had thought her work over for the night. When the men
had supped their brandy-laced tea and had left, Thomasin
descended on her recalcitrant husband. 'I hope you're
proud of yourself, bringing this family's good name into
the gutter.'

'An' where did this family get its name from, might I
ask?' He thumbed his chest. 'From me, Patrick Feeney.
Only ye didn't seem to think it was such a good name
when it came to putting it over your store, eh?'

Thomasin threw up her hands in despair. 'Bloody
Christmas again! Without fail something always happens
to spoil everything. Is there owt else you'd like to confess
to apart from drunkenness and thievery?'

'Aye,' said Patrick. 'I've pissed meself.' And pulling off
his boots he tipped them upside down to dribble over the
carpet.

She gave a sound of disgust. 'You silly, stupid old devil.'
Then wearily to her son and the rest of her family, 'If
you'll forgive me I'm off to bed. Suddenly I don't feel in
very festive spirit.'

'Talking about festive spirits . . .' said Patrick hopefully.

His son signalled to Nick, who had not long been home
himself and was grateful to his grandfather for taking the
heat off his own situation, to help lift the old man. He

couldn't ask Sullivan to do it. It was bad enough the butler knowing about the police business without adding the rest. 'Come on, Dad, let's get you sorted out, shall we?'

Patrick grappled their shoulders as they half-carried him to the door. 'I'm sorry, Son. Ah, Jaze, I'm so sorry I spoilt it for yese.'

'It's Mother you should feel sorry for,' replied Sonny as they juggled with him on the stairs, trying to stop his feet from banging against each and every step. 'It can't be easy for her, watching you drink yourself to death.'

'You're right,' slurred Patrick. 'It can't. I'll give it up. I'll never touch another drop.'

CHAPTER FORTY-THREE

Whether it was his little grand-daughter's accusation of drunkenness that did it, or whether last night's over-indulgence had soured his palate, the family wasn't sure. They were only glad that Patrick abided by his promise. On Christmas Day sheepish apologies were made, allowing the rest of the holiday to be passed in agreeable form. With the purchase of another mouse he earned Amelia's forgiveness. Seeing him in sober form playing with the rowdy gang of children brought back some of the old affection from his wife, too. Yet Thomasin could not resist a little moan about his Christmas Eve performance to Francis when the holiday was over.

Now that the Bradford store was running smoothly Francis was living back in York. However, they were in Leeds at the moment where the board meetings were always held. This month's meeting had just broken up and the two were sharing a pot of coffee. 'If you could've seen him, Fran! It was so embarrassing having that policeman bring him home.'

'Ah, poor Patrick,' sighed her friend.

She was astounded. 'Poor who?'

'I know how tiresome it must have been for you, Thomasin, but if the poor chap's unhappy . . .'

'Oh yes, and we all know who's to blame! We all get unhappy with being old but we don't all turn into drunks.' She caught his reproachful look and said in more temperate vein, 'Anyway . . . I think he realises what a fool he's been; he hasn't touched a drop since we've been home. I've told him I don't expect him to give it up altogether – he's always been fond of a tipple – but just to keep it in reason, that's all.'

Francis nodded in sympathy, then proceeded to another subject, though still pertaining to the family. 'Dare I ask if you've come to a decision about Nicholas?' There had been discussion between himself and Thomasin about making Nick a director, though Thomasin felt the boy was not quite ready.

She showed her hesitancy. 'I'm just not convinced he's truly ready for it, Fran. He's shrewd, yes, but in a few areas he shows a definite lack of judgment.' She teased her mouth into a wry smile. 'I'm quite sure he thinks I don't know about the peer's daughter. Reckons he's going to surprise me.'

'Is it serious?'

'Not in the sense that Nick loves the girl, he's far too detached for that. But serious in that it could lead to marriage, certainly – and that *would* be serious.' Outside, ear pressed to the boardroom door, Nick depressed his brow. 'I've always taken Nick for a wiser bird and yet here he is thinking he's about to make some sort of brilliant move by cornering a peer's daughter when the fellow hasn't enough shekels to cover his family crest.' The eavesdropper clenched a fist at his own lack of perception.

'It's easy for anyone to be misled,' replied Francis with a mischievous twinkle. 'I seem to recall your own pleasure on gaining such an illustrious customer . . . until you tried to get your cash out of him.'

She laughed then. Yes, it was easy to be wise afterwards. The reason she knew so much about the peer's finances was that she was in possession of several of his unpaid bills. He was now barred from obtaining credit at any of her stores. There was nothing in writing, for Thomasin, however furious, had thought better than to humiliate the peer and had sufficed with a private warning herself. 'Aye, he must've thought he'd found a right prize in me. I have to admit I was taken in. I wonder who's giving him his free groceries now – let's hope it isn't my grandson. I should've warned Nick but I didn't think the old devil would be cheeky enough to try it on again. He must've been round all the shops in Yorkshire and now he's working his way back round.'

'You'd better tell Nick, then.'

'No, let him find out for himself. But let's hope he twigs before any engagements are announced. I'll be very disappointed if he doesn't. I've always been proud of Nick. But . . .' she clicked her tongue regretfully.

'So the directorship hangs fire?' asked Francis.

'For now.'

'I've a feeling you'll still be saying that when the boy's in his dotage – he is twenty-four this year, Thomasin.'

'Still young . . . All right, look, we'll leave it until his birthday. That gives him time to spring their trap – 'cause trap it is, Fran. I know these buggers, they don't mind mixing with us "trade people" if there's owt to be had. Don't misunderstand all this, I'm not averse to him marrying the right girl, in fact I think it would contribute a lot to his position in the firm. Now, if it had been a Miss Marks he'd found himself . . .' She smiled. There was a brief period of dialogue on the man called Marks who had made quite a name for himself among the Leeds tradefolk. Thomasin said she felt sure he was going places. 'Anyway, if it's over by his birthday we'll consider that directorship.'

It took Nicholas a much shorter period than this to end the fruitless relationship. Three hours after taking his ear from that door he was 'regretfully' cancelling his appointment at the peer's home, saying with tongue firmly in cheek that he was unavoidably pressed to attend his grandmother's bankruptcy hearing. And the peer's daughter ceased to exist for him.

With the directorship uppermost in his mind, Nick set out to remedy the previous slip-up by moving to a different fishing hole further downriver – trade people, that's what Nan had said. Well, this area should be easy enough to infiltrate. All he had to do was tour the high street, pick out the most profitable businesses, narrow the list down to the ones who had eligible daughters and stick in a pin – simple.

However, when he had finished his compilation the list was shorter than he had imagined – so few of the larger store owners had female offspring of a marriageable age. Undaunted, he confined his efforts to the ones who did, using his position as manager of *Penny's* to initiate the proceedings. First he 'bumped into' the store owners, got chatting about business and after becoming friendly got himself invited into their homes. From then on it should have been simply a matter of selecting the most attractive girl but, alas, it didn't quite work like that. The first family turned out to be Quakers and would hardly smile upon his grandfather's penchant. The daughter belonging to the second family was far too ugly to contemplate marrying even for money. So, it looked as though it would have to be the third.

Winifred Cordwell was a very pretty girl. She met Nick's other criterion too – she was nothing like his hard-headed grandmother. He would have preferred her business to be just that bit bigger, but needs must; the directorship was the thing that mattered most. He began to call more regularly at the Cordwell home. By the crucial deadline of his twenty-fourth birthday the family were treating him as one of their own.

'Are you thinking of having a birthday party, Nick?' asked his grandmother during one of her visits to the Leeds store.

'Nobody's mentioned anything, Nan.'

'Well, if you leave it to your father there won't be one.'

She grabbed a piece of paper. 'Come on, it's ages since we've had a good do, let's see who we can invite.'

'Don't you think we'd better ask Father and Mother before we fill their house with people?'

'Oh, tickle! If they don't like it we'll hold it at my house. Now then, might there be anybody special you'd like to invite?' She hoped it wouldn't be who she thought it was – Nick was still keeping regular appointments with somebody.

He turned away so she wouldn't see his smile – she was so obvious. 'As a matter of fact, yes, there is.' He sauntered about, hands in pockets. 'I've been meaning to bring her home to meet the family.'

Thomasin veiled her disappointment by keeping her eyes fixed to the list under her pen. 'You've known her some time, then?'

'Mm, not really.'

'But you must consider her important if you want to bring her home?'

'Oh yes, she's important.'

'And is your Nan going to be privy to the young lady's name?'

'Oh, how slipshod of me! Yes, Nan, it's Miss Marks.' His lips twitched as her eyes came up swiftly from the desk. 'Sorry, just my little joke.' He smiled inwardly at her narrowed eyes.

'Have you been . . .' she began suspiciously.

'Been what, Nan?'

'Never mind.' She was still perusing him through slitted apertures.

'Actually,' he wandered back to stand near her, 'joking apart, her family is in business. They have a footwear store on Boar Lane – *Cordwell's*.'

'I know it,' she said instantly. 'They get a good bit of trade. The window display could do with a touch more flair, though – but I daresay you'll be able to give them a few pointers when you unite the two families.' She smiled her congratulations. 'Well done, Nick, a fine choice. It'd be a nice idea if the engagement were to be announced on your birthday, wouldn't it?'

He laughed. 'You're pushing it a bit, Nan! I haven't asked her father's permission yet.'

'Hah! The man'd be crackers if he turned you down! Get him asked as soon as you like, then we can have a double celebration – there may be an extra bit of something for you this year, too.'

If Nick had taken this to mean that his directorship was to be presented at the party then he was to be badly let down. Announcements flowed: Nick was to be engaged to Miss Winifred Cordwell; Sonny announced that Josie was expecting her fifth child when everyone had thought her past all that; Patrick announced that this champagne was like gnat's piss though luckily no one heard him – but no mention, no hint even, was made about the directorship.

Winifred noticed his preoccupation. 'Nicholas, that's the third time I've asked you! I'm beginning to wonder why I came to this party.'

He turned to her effusively and kissed her cheek. 'Oh sorry, Win, I'm not very good company tonight.'

Her good features were hidden beneath a sulk. 'No, you're not. One would never guess that we've just become engaged – what's wrong with you?'

'Well, I was kind of expecting . . .' he began dully, then spotted his grandmother coming straight towards him, a secretive smile on her lips.

'Expecting what?' asked Winnie as he broke into a grin and squared his shoulders.

'I hope I'm not interrupting you two lovebirds,' said Thomasin, taking Nick's arm and steering him aside. 'I won't keep him two seconds, Winifred. Erin, dear! Come and keep Winifred company for a moment.' She led Nick over to a quiet corner where they sat down.

Over Erin's shoulder Winifred watched her fiancé's changing expression and wondered what was transpiring, while at the same time making polite nods to Erin's conversation.

When Nick returned to take his aunt's place his mien

was one of bad humour. 'Nick, what's happened? What has your grandmother said to make you like this?' Winifred snatched a drink from a passing tray and pressed it into his hand.

'You and my grandfather should get on well.' He smiled tightly and downed her offering. 'Nan was just giving me her birthday present – a cheque for two thousand pounds.'

'How generous!' Winifred's gloved hand stroked the breast of his jacket.

'Yes, wasn't it?'

The hand withdrew. 'Nicholas, I'm sorry but I don't understand your grumpiness and if you don't tell me I'm going to walk right out of here for good!' She felt it was something she had done – Nick often made her feel like this. But she worshipped him.

Instantly he became more affable, 'Oh, I'm sorry I've been such a bore this evening,' and put his arm around her. 'It's nothing to do with you – and you're right, two thousand is a very generous gift . . . it's just that I was expecting a rather different reward.' He told her then about his hopes for a directorship, the tests his grandmother had set him. 'How long does she intend to wait, Win? She asked for a thirty per cent increase and I gave her it. Still she holds out. It's not fair, the work I've put in. I'm beginning to think she's just using me.'

'I don't suppose one of the stipulations for this directorship could have been to find yourself a wife?' She smiled at the pink flush that crept into his cheeks. 'No, I rather thought my father's balance sheets interested you more than I did. You're a fine one to talk about using folk.'

He had not credited her with a brain but now, looking her in the eye, he realised that though Win might be pliable she was in no way stupid. 'Win . . . I'm not just marrying you for your background – I do care about you.' He felt a surge of genuine affection.

She studied his face, then laid her head against his shoulder. 'Perhaps you'll get your directorship next year. Perhaps,' she became contemplative, 'this two thousand pounds isn't just a reward, but another of her tests – the final one?'

Yes, that would be just like his grandmother. She was waiting to see what he did with the money. 'Win,' he said, squeezing her, 'you're a gem.' And he meant it.

There were two other events that year – unfortunately for Win neither of them was a wedding – Belle's coming of age and the birth of Josie's son, Patrick John, on the last day of the year. It looked to Winifred as though the engagement was to be a long one; a year after the announcement there was still no hint of wedding bells. Nick was far too busy putting his grandmother's gift to best use to devote any time to matrimony. It infuriated him that he couldn't come up with anything spectacular. Win, loving him as she did, saw that the only way to bring the date nearer was not to nag but to be patient and sympathetic.

Sadly, the only celebration that took place in eighteen ninety-seven was the Queen's Diamond Jubilee when Nick's grandmother threw a party at York – two, actually. The one held during the afternoon was mainly for the benefit of the children and the servants who, for the event and with the aid of staff from two other households, had made a huge pie twenty-five feet long, full of apples and mincemeat and other fruit which, even after the hundred guests had been dealt a hefty slice, was still not half-consumed.

Patrick sat on one of the wrought-iron chairs on the terrace, smiling as Belle's young charges hared about the garden waving Union Jacks and blowing whistles. She'd done a good job with them, had the lass. Like Lol, Cedric was employed at the factory now. Young Sam, now back at home with his mother, had been reunited with them for this celebratory affair – his mother with him. According to Belle he was a near-genius. She was continuing to give him lessons free of charge, not wishing to put to waste the amount he had learnt while in her care. Patrick waved to his little ginger-haired grandson whom he had been holding until a moment ago when Josie had repossessed him. His birth had cheered Patrick up no end, though he was still prone to occasional bouts of depression when the weather kept him indoors.

Fortunately, the weather was behaving itself today. Because there were so many guests the party was being held outside. His eyes searched the crowded lawn for his wife. Among the white dresses and frilled parasols he spotted her talking to Francis who leaned on a cane, nodding attentively – Ah, Fran, you're a lucky old chap, came the dispirited thought after watching them awhile. She must've been talking to ye for all of ten minutes. I'm lucky if I get ten seconds – an' me so good at laying off the juice. Almost eighteen months it had been since that Christmas night when he had humiliated her and he had kept his promise never to have more than a nightcap.

Lifting his glass he swilled his mouth with lemonade, washing it noisily through what teeth he had left – No, you're right, he told himself suddenly – why should ye bother? All this effort ye've made to stay sober, poisoning yourself with this muck an' all ye get to see is her backside.

'More lemonade, sir?' Vinnie and the others had been given the afternoon off – the eating arrangements were of a help-yourself variety – but feeling naked up here among the upstairs folk she had armed herself with a tray to hide behind.

'God love ye, no.' Patrick made a face, then looked at her properly. 'Why, Vinnie, 'tis a picture you look if I might make so bold.' Her hair was glossed back and fashioned into a teapot handle. Only a fringe of curls invaded the now blushing face. The girl had a fine figure too, thought Patrick, unaware that this close scrutiny was the reason for her blush, funny how he'd never noticed before. Maybe it was the pinny that always hid her charms, for the mauve dress she wore now was, to say the least, well-filled.

'Are you sure you won't have owt, sir?' begged Vinnie.

Patrick suddenly noticed what his stare had done to her

complexion and apologised, deepening her blush. 'Well, if you don't want anything, sir . . .' she began to turn away.

He caught one of her huge sleeves. 'Come an' sit with me, Vinnie.'

'Sir.' She indicated the tray.

'Sure, I thought ye'd all been given the afternoon off.'

'We have, but . . .'

'Then put the bloody tray down an' come sit by me.' The fact that he wouldn't let go of her sleeve forced her to comply, but under protest.

'I shouldn't be sitting here with you, sir.'

'I've not got leprosy, ye know.'

'I meant the mistress wouldn't like it.'

'Herself is off talking to whoever takes her fancy, why shouldn't I? 'Tisn't fair that everyone here should be enjoying themselves an' not me. I mean, look at them, Vinnie. Can ye show me one man here who hasn't got himself a woman to talk to. Can ye?' She shook her head. 'No, only Soft Old Mick here. So you can be my partner, Vinnie.' After a drawn-out silence he prompted her. 'Well, come on girl, talk to me.'

Vinnie appeared how she felt – nervous. 'What should I say, sir?'

'Say anything – what d'ye think to this party for instance?'

'Oh, it's lovely, sir. I've right enjoyed meself.'

'Enjoyed yourself, among this lot? Come on, Vinnie, you can do better than that. Tell me what ye really think of my wife's friends. Faith, will ye look at them. I've never seen so many stiff little fingers in all me life. There's a bloody forest of 'em out there, all supping their lemonade an' sayin', "Oh, Thomasin, how wonderful y'are an' what a marvellous gown you're wearing an' what simply beautiful parties ye give . . . " They're all on the bloody take, ye know, Vinnie. Haven't got two farthings to rub together. They come to us for a free binge, then go home calling us from pigs to dogs. Everybody gets free booze 'cept Yours Truly.'

644

'Oh, I think I see Mrs Howgego waving for me, sir,' stammered Vinnie and shot out of the chair.

He sighed. 'I'm sorry, Vinnie. I didn't mean to use you as my sounding board. I just get so bloody mad when I see your mistress being all polite and refined to these two-faced leeches.' He saw her discomfort. 'Ah, go on with ye, Vinnie. I'd not want to waste your time listening to a silly old fool like me.'

There was concern. 'Oh, no, sir . . . I don't think you're silly. I think . . . I think you're very nice.'

'Thank ye, dear.' But the compliment had fallen flat. He watched her scurry across the terrace to where Cook was applying her mouth to another slice of pie. Even the bloody servants didn't want to know, he thought bitterly. Then curling his lip at the glass of lemonade he placed it firmly on the table and went into the house.

'I didn't know where to put meself, Cook,' Vinnie was whispering excitedly. 'Fancy him saying a thing like that to me – an' that weren't all.'

Cook brushed the flakes of pastry from her lap. 'This is where I'm meant to prick up my ears, is it?'

'Mrs Howgego, his eyes were all over me. Honestly, if there hadn't been a garden full o' people I don't know how I'd've kept his hands off. The old devil. You'd think he'd be past all that, wouldn't you?'

'You're a daft cat, you are. He's lonely, that's all. I mean, is there any wonder with the missus flitting about all over the place? She's hardly ever at home.'

'That weren't loneliness I saw in them eyes, Mrs Howgego,' said Vinnie definitely.

'You wouldn't know a cross-eyed kipper if it hit you in the face. I tell you he's lonely. Least you could've done was to lend the poor old gentleman your ear – 'cause he is a gent despite your fanciful spoutings. He's never said a wrong word to me in all the time I've been here, nor you neither, I'll warrant. No. Nor anybody else in this house, upstairs or down, lest they deserved it.'

'But he shouldn't've said what he did about them lot

though, should he, Cook?' said Vinnie, angling for forgiveness. 'I mean, it's not done.'

'I'll 'llow you're right, Vinnie.' Cook inclined her greying
head. 'But you see he's not himself.'

'Who is he then?' giggled Vinnie, then at Cook's sharp
expression said: 'Sorry.'

'See, the master isn't really one o' them,' Mrs Howgego
gestured to the gathering on the lawn. 'And much as her
ladyship reckons she is – she in't. But, whereas she doesn't
mind 'em looking down their noses at her long as she gets
their business – skin like an elephant she has – the master,
he feels it. Mindst, some of it's his own fault for the way
he treats them – one or two of them are very nice people.
No, the master can be a bit of a snob himself, but the
other way round, if you understand me. He looks down
on the posh folk.' She craned her neck around Vinnie,
eyes in the direction of Patrick's chair. 'See he's gone.'

Vinnie glanced over her shoulder. 'I'll bet he's gone to
raid the drinks cabinet.'

'You want to watch your tongue, my lass. You'll be
tripping over it.'

Vinnie grinned. 'Eh, he isn't half funny when he's
slewed, in't he, Cook?'

'I'm sure the mistress thinks so,' said the other ironically. 'Eh, up, she's looking for him; seen his empty chair.'

'I don't know what she sees in that old stick,' murmured
Vinnie, studying Francis. 'The master's a much better-
looking bloke. Eh, Cook, I wonder if they . . .'

'Don't you dare say it, my lass,' interjected Cook. 'It's
wicked of you even to think it. Anyroad,' she stretched
her back, 'I think I'll allow you to fetch me another piece
o' that pie.'

'What, another? How many's that you've had?'

'If it were thirty-six it'd still be none o' your business,
an' somebody's got to eat it otherwise we'll be celebrating
Her Majesty's next Jubilee with it. Silly bloody idea it was
to bake it anyway. But 'course, the mistress has to impress.
Go on now, an' I'll have a glass o' that red stuff them lot
are drinking. Never mind the lemonade – I'm on holiday.'

At Vinnie's departure Cook turned her eyes once again to Patrick's seat and, finding him reappeared, nodded and smiled deferentially.

Patrick held his glass aloft and smiled back, the half-bottle of whiskey stacked neatly in his stomach. Whilst Cook and the maid had been talking he had found time to nip over to The Black Swan and join festivities there. The juice of the barley helped to make him a wee bit more charitable towards his wife's abominable friends. Thomasin, seeing him back in his chair, smiled relievedly and winked, unaware that 'the problem' had returned.

At five o'clock the dismembered pie was barrowed off to the larder along with the other remains of the afternoon party and everyone retired to change into their evening wear for the continuation of the festivities which were to take place outside the home. Thomasin had hired a ball-room and made catering arrangements, the latter in order that the servants could enjoy their time off to the full. It was, after all, only once in sixty years that a Queen celebrated a Diamond Jubilee. She was extremely satisfied with the way the celebrations had gone and Patrick was behaving impeccably.

She hadn't really believed her husband when he made that Christmas promise of abstention, but she was pleasantly surprised when he kept to it. She knew that as a certainty – because of the marks on the decanter and the close inventory she had made of the wine cellar. If Pat was getting the stuff from anywhere outside then he was carrying it remarkably well.

It wasn't the fact of his actual drinking that upset her but that it made him so garrulous, and when Patrick's tongue ran away with him he usually ended up being humiliated. But looking at him now she decided that if the hired staff followed instructions and performed a detour round him with their trays the evening should remain unsullied.

A liveried footman was admitting other guests. Thomasin rolled her eyes to herself. Trust Belle to wear something like that. You'd think it was a funeral, not a party. But the dress which had at first appeared uninspiring was transformed as Belle limped into the light of the crystal chandelier. The taffeta was of the darkest green and with the aid of illumination took on the sheen of abalone. Little rainbow puddles nestled in its dark folds, like oil on water. Its wearer's shoulders, as usual robed in her luxuriant hair, stiffened as many eyes alighted upon her. At the defensive expression Thomasin sighed, bewailing the girl's self-doubt. What a shame she was blind to the admiration in the brown eyes of the man accompanying her. The woman glided across the ballroom to welcome them. 'Belle, how splendid you look. Doesn't she, Brian?'

'I've never seen her look lovelier,' he replied warmly.

'You'll have to be careful,' Thomasin warned him. 'I've noticed a lot of eyes turning when she came in. You should snap her up while you can.'

'Now Nan, don't embarrass the doctor,' said Belle.

'On the contrary,' replied Brian. 'I'm not at all embarrassed. And, Mrs Feeney, I would be delighted to snap up your grandchild *if* she'd consent.'

Belle tutted. 'I'm off to sit with Gramps. Come and join me when you know which side your bread's buttered.'

'She's a funny girl.' Thomasin wafted her face with a black-feathered fan. 'You'd think she'd bite your hand off, wouldn't you?'

Brian watched Patrick's face light up as his granddaughter reached him. 'She doesn't look upon me as a very good catch. I can't say I blame her.'

'Oh, come on now, Brian. You're in an excellent profession, you're good-looking – yes, you are, don't be modest. I don't know what's wrong with the girl. The Lord knows she won't get many chances of matrimony – and certainly not a better one.'

'I think you underestimate your grand-daughter,' he answered warily.

'Oh, I wasn't lying when I said she looked gorgeous. But you know how people are, Brian. Anyone a bit out of the ordinary . . . they're not exactly queueing up to court her, are they?'

Brian watched the dead hummingbird on Thomasin's fan. The increased rapidity of her hand caused it to appear as if hovering, the minute purple wings outstretched in flight. 'I really must defend my sex, Mrs Feeney. We men aren't all the shallow creatures you depict, and I find the manner in which you regard my affection for Belle as slightly offensive. I'm not some sort of noble hero who wants to marry her out of pity . . .' He shook his head, lost for words. The fan stopped, suspending the humming bird in mid-flight, rendering it merely a pathetic, dead jewel.

'Well, I hardly think I deserved that!' gasped Thomasin.

'Yes, you did.' Brian's indignation mustered the words he had been seeking. 'I know it might be neither the time nor place to say it but since the opportunity has arisen I feel I mustn't waste it. You talk about Belle being grateful – well, tell me, why should she be? Look at her, Mrs Feeney,' he gestured at Belle who was laughing with Patrick. 'The girl is absolutely enchanting. She's no cause to be grateful that a fuddy-duddy old spec-eye wants to make her his wife.'

'Brian, I've admitted she's got the best looks in the family . . .'

' . . . unless, of course, it's because she's deformed,' sprang in Brian. 'Why does it affect you so, Mrs Feeney? Oh yes, it does. I noticed when I said the word. It couldn't be because you think her deformity reflects on your status, could it?'

The voice was cold. 'Doctor Dyson, as this is meant to be a celebration I'll overlook that remark, but should you make such an insinuation again . . .'

'Mrs Feeney, I beg your pardon but you were the one to make insinuations. You haven't the courage to come right out with it and say that Belle should be grateful to me because no one else will marry a crippled girl. Well, that's absolutely ridiculous. She's as much chance of marrying as the next person if she so chooses. Is that how you've always looked upon her – as your crippled grand-daughter? Not just your grand-daughter nor your pretty grand-daughter but your *deformed* grand-daughter.'

Thomasin was used to controlling her voice. 'You are offensive, Doctor, and I think you should apologise.'

'No, I think you should, Mrs Feeney. It's high time you made reparation to Belle for the shabby way you've always treated her.'

'How long have you known my grand-daughter, Doctor Dyson?' asked the elderly woman frigidly.

'About five years.'

'Such a long time. I'm faintly surprised that you feel qualified to comment on what is essentially a family matter.'

'I think I know her better than you.'

'A family matter, Doctor, which does not concern outsiders. Now, you are welcome to stay as a guest of my grand-daughter if you wish, but let me make it clear that I will listen to no more defamatory statements! I love Belle.'

'Of course you do!' he said sincerely. 'I wouldn't dream of questioning that. But you *pity* her – and you pity yourself because of her.'

'I'll say goodnight, Doctor,' said Thomasin shortly. 'I trust our paths won't cross again this evening.' She moved away, wondering angrily what she had done to bring that down on herself.

Brian watched the false smile she had donned for the benefit of the other guests – Why have you got such a big mouth, Dyson? he asked himself, then went to join Belle and her grandfather. Always trying to build bridges with dynamite.

'Ah, now here's the fella that'll tell us!' cried Patrick. 'Sit down, boyo, an' cast your eyes on that woman in the pink frock.'

'Gramps,' chivvied Belle. 'Stop getting Brian embroiled in your wickedness.'

'D'ye see who I mean? Now tell me – are they or are they not her own?'

Brian's mouth quivered. 'I take it you are referring to her teeth, Mr Feeney?'

'Tee . . . sure as hell I am! Her bosoms, man!' Belle was convulsed and struggled to silence him, but Patrick evaded the hand that searched to cover his mouth. 'She's got those bloody concertina things shoved down her bodice. Look! Ye can see one o' them's half-folded up. It's given in. God, the things women do for attention.'

'Gramps, you swore to Nan you'd never touch another drop,' scolded a blushing Belle.

'An' what makes ye think I've been at the sauce?' demanded the old man.

'Because I know you wouldn't dream of embarrassing us like this if you were sober. Tsk. Nan'll be mad as anything – as I am myself. Where did you get it?'

'Ye mean how did I manage to collar one o' those flunkeys who've been blatantly avoiding me with their trays,' replied her grandfather. 'I didn't, I brung me own.' He caressed his pocket.

Belle became serious. Something must have upset him, for him to start drinking again. She voiced that concern.

'I'm not upset. Do I look upset? No, I'm enjoying meself. I just didn't see why I should be the only one to toast the Queen's Jubilee in lemonade – disgusting stuff.' He quietened. 'Ye won't tell your Nan, will ye?'

'I may do if I think it's for your own good.' She punched him laughingly. 'Of course I won't – as long as you promise to water it down a bit, Gramps. Brian, will you tell him how bad it is for him?'

'She's right, you know.'

'Ah, go 'way with ye both,' scoffed Patrick. 'Stop pontificating an' take this wench onto the dance floor.'

'You know I never dance,' Belle stated firmly.

'Then 'tis about time ye did.'

'I heartily agree,' said Brian, springing to his feet and trying to drag her from the chair.

'Brian, don't be silly.'

'This is what I have to put up with all the time,' said

Brian to the older man. ' "Brian, don't be silly. Brian, don't do this, Brian don't do that, be a good boy".'

She laughed at his affected simper. 'Don't be a clown.'

'See? I don't know why I bother to keep asking her to marry me. She'd treat me like a dog if we were wed.'

'I know the feeling,' remarked Patrick, but not sorrowfully. 'An' I don't know why ye keep bothering to ask her – tell her, man! There's too much o' this pandering to females nowadays. Ye say to her – right, we're getting married next week – an' she'll just have to go along with it.'

'Yet another one who doesn't know her,' muttered the doctor ruefully, catching Thomasin's stern examination. As he met her eye she turned away.

'What's that?' Patrick cupped his ear.

'I said I'm going to take your advice.' Brian refused to let go of Belle and dragged her to her feet. 'I shall start by demanding that she have this dance with me – and then who knows.' He hoped Belle could interpret the question in his eyes and looked for an answering gleam in hers. But sadly through the warmth he gauged her response: it was still no.

Thomasin couldn't seem to take her eyes off Belle for the rest of the evening – How could he say that? she asked herself over and over. I don't treat her like that, I don't. Once or twice, other members of her family asked if she was feeling all right for she didn't appear to be enjoying the party, which was highly unusual for Thomasin.

'D'ye think Mother's ill?' Erin muttered to Sonny as they waltzed past Thomasin's chair. 'She's looking very vague.'

Sonny followed his mother's eyes and assumed her to be staring at her husband who was sitting with Belle and the doctor. 'No, she's just worried about Dad. He's had one or two, I think. Still, it is a party.'

'Aye . . . let's just hope he doesn't extend the party into next week,' smiled Erin.

'Have you ever thought of getting married again, our lass?' her brother asked unexpectedly.

After laughing at the change of subject she mused, 'Once or twice . . . but no one could replace Sam – and I'm very happy as things are.'

'Good.' He pulled her into his body and performed an exaggerated step bringing forth laughter to endorse her statement.

At the end of the evening Thomasin and Patrick shook hands with their guests and saw them to their carriages. Thomasin was still in a state of mild agitation over Brian's words. He knew this, which was why he was very apprehensive on taking his leave of her.

'Goodnight, Doctor Dyson.' Thomasin extended a cool hand.

'Doctor Dyson?' said Belle. 'Sounds like you've been crossed off the Christmas list, Bri – what've you been doing to her?'

Thomasin broke the awkward handshake and turned to her grand-daughter who leaned forward to accept a peck on the cheek. Expecting this, Belle was taken literally off-balance to receive an impulsive and crushing embrace. She wobbled, then laughed her surprise as Thomasin showed reluctance to let her go. Thomasin pressed her cheek to the young woman's and patted her back. 'You look really beautiful, Belle,' she murmured into her ear, arms still wrapped tightly around her. 'I am proud of you, love.'

Belle was still marvelling over this unsolicited show of affection as she and Brian walked to their carriage. 'What on earth have you said to her, Bri?'

'Nothing,' he lied. 'The only exchange we had was the usual one I have with members of your family – when are you and I getting married?'

Belle groaned. 'I don't know why they're all so intent on seeing me married off. It can't simply be to get rid of me – I've already left home. People are funny, aren't they? You'd think they'd be pleased that I'm happy as I am.'

'It's not so much you they're concerned about, but me. They see the way I look at you.'

'Well, I trust you won't allow them to think it's me who's keeping you dangling,' said Belle firmly.

'Oh, they're well aware how you feel about losing your independence, Belle,' came Brian's reply.

She smiled as they reached the carriage. 'Yes, that's what they all think of me, isn't it? That I'm terrified of marriage because it would make me look weak, having to depend on some man – plus my deformity. It might have been that way once – that, and my distrust of men – but not any more. I've grown up enough to realise that none of us can be totally independent – and I do find you *very* trustworthy, Brian.' A fond grin. 'But I still won't marry you, simply because it would be too deceitful.'

There was a finality about her words that robbed Brian of the hope he had carried for five years. Yet still he doggedly refused to let go. He watched her climb into the carriage, saying despairingly, 'Well . . . if you don't mind, I'll continue to deceive myself for a while longer.' He climbed up beside her and gave a huge sigh. 'Oh, Belle . . . I wish that just for tonight you could be a man, so you'd know how hard these five years of celibacy have been for me.'

'If I were a man you'd hardly be asking me to marry you.' Her voice was as flippant as ever, but Belle had turned thoughtful. 'Anyway,' she challenged as he picked up the reins, 'if you're talking about sex, I would have thought that you were modern enough to know that women have those urges too.'

There was something in the way she had said that. Brian made no move to set the horse in motion, but turned to look at her. 'And what do you do to ease them?'

She smiled and averted her face. 'That's a bit personal, Doctor – and risky; I could ask you what you do about yours.'

He was still looking at her. 'There'd be nothing to tell.' He sat there staring at her with the reins in his hands, then gave a little laugh as he finally whipped up the horse. 'You were right that time you said I didn't really know you . . .'

'Don't feel too bad about it,' she said to the night sky, 'nobody does.'

'All these years I've been proposing marriage, doing the honourable thing – maybe if I'd simply asked you to share my bed . . .'

She turned to look at him now, saw the expression in his eyes. 'I don't want to mislead you, Brian. There's been no drastic change. I still only see you as my friend and I can't offer you a torrid love affair.'

Brian felt a thrill in the pit of his stomach, but managed to keep his voice even and his eyes on the horse. 'I've told you, I'll do without the romance.'

She put a hand on his arm and said earnestly, 'But wouldn't you feel I was using you?'

'I've been waiting five years for you to use me, Belle.'

She gave an embarrassed chuckle. 'Well . . . let's just see what happens when we get home, shall we?' And they both fell silent to reflect.

Thomasin gave a final wave as their carriage turned out of the drive, then took Patrick's arm. 'Away, let's get you home to bed.'

'What about me nightcap?'

'I think you've already had it, haven't you?' Standing next to him she had smelt the whiskey.

'Sorry . . .' He looked guilty. 'I did behave meself though, didn't I?'

She smiled a pardon and nodded.

'So will ye stop marking the bottles an' trust me to do me own regulating?'

'If you think you can manage it.'

'Listen.' He put his face down to hers and murmured sensuously, 'When we get home I'll show ye I can manage all sorts o' things.'

She laughed and flirted with him like a young girl as they took to their own carriage.

CHAPTER FORTY-FOUR

'Come here, Win.' Nick beckoned his fiancée over to the sofa.

'You come here if you want me – and I'm beginning to wonder about that!' Three years after their meeting and still he hadn't named the day, always too obsessed with finding some way to impress his grandmother. The two thousand pounds sat in the bank – earning interest, true, but otherwise unproductive.

'Aw, Win.' He bowed to her wish and came over to where she stood. 'You know how much I want you!'

'I know how much you want that directorship. I'm just not sure where I stand in relation to that.' She nibbled her lip. 'I love you, Nicholas . . . but maybe it might be as well if we called the engagement off.'

'Eh, don't make threats you don't mean,' he scolded.

She spun away from him. 'You're so damned sure of yourself, aren't you! Well, I'm not going to be put off forever. I've helped you as much as I can to get the position you want but I'm not prepared to wait another year. And if you really loved me you wouldn't expect it.' She took a deep breath. 'Directorship or no, you set a wedding date for no later than the end of this year . . . or it's over.'

He gazed into her face. She meant it. Slowly, he got down on his knees and took hold of her fingertips, face deadly serious. 'Win . . . I realise I've been totally selfish in making you wait. So, I'd better do it properly, hadn't I?' He kissed her fingers, then inhaled. 'Will you do me the honour of being my bride this year?'

Her lips parted in astonishment at his surrender and once again she was the pliable creature he was used to. 'Oh, Nick . . .'

'I couldn't lose you, could I?' he whispered earnestly.

'We'll set the date right now – would October be soon enough?'

'Oh, yes!' She clasped his hands to her breast, touched that for once he had put her before his work. 'I didn't mean to bully you – and I'll do my utmost to help you get round your grandmother.'

'Oh, you needn't trouble yourself about that, Win!' His air changed to one of gaiety. 'It's all in the bag.' At her vacant stare he grinned devilishly. 'I was going to name the day anyway – that's what I wanted to do when I said "come here".'

'You . . . !' She gave him a hefty shove with her knee and he fell away from her, laughing. 'Miserable villain!' But she was amused. 'How have you managed to do it, then?'

He pulled himself to his feet and put his arms round her. 'Well, it's not quite completed yet . . . but come October you'll be married to a director.' His eyes sparkled as he ground his body into hers. 'I don't suppose you want to practise being a wife . . . ?'

She stopped his hands from wandering too far. 'You've made me wait, you can do the same. Can I tell my parents?'

He kissed her nose. 'Just keep it under your hat for a wee bit longer – I have to work on my grandparents first.'

A few days after his pact with Winnie, Nick made a trip to York to see his grandfather and asked if Patrick would lend him the pasture land which he owned on Malton Road. 'Just for a short time – I'd pay rent, naturally.'

'Be buggered the money.' Patrick waved aside any question of rent. 'Why would I want to charge my grandson for what'll belong to him in a year or two – sooner, quite probably.'

'Ah, you'll last a good while yet, Grandad.'

'I will if it's flattery that's keeping me alive.'

'It is yours and not Nan's, isn't it?' asked Nick with a hint of anxiety.

'It is, though I don't see as that matters. But tell me,

657

what does a young buck like yourself want with pastureland?'

'Horses,' came the succinct reply. 'I'm going to buy some.'

'For racing? Sure, I hope they have more luck than the stumers I put me dollars on.'

Nick shook his head. 'Not for racing, no – you'll keep quiet about this for a while?'

'Oh, if it's a secret better not tell me.'

'It'll only be one for a few months,' said Nick assuredly. 'It's a kind of surprise for Nan. Can I have it, then?'

'Well, now.' Patrick placed his right hand below his ribs and winced but Nick failed to see the look of discomfort. 'I think you're about to be disappointed – I already rented it to a Mr Kettlewell yesterday.' Pat was barely aware of what he did or did not own these days. When Kettlewell had approached him the Irishman had accepted his first offer with no haggling. 'Truth, if I'd known ye wanted it, Nick . . .'

This didn't deter the young man's eagerness. 'If I can get him to change his mind would I be able to have it then – what's he want it for, by the way?'

'Sheep, I think. Sure, ye can have it, boyo . . . How's that Win o' yours? Are we going to see a wedding this year?' At Nick's secretive wink he smiled and pressed a finger to his lips. After a further period of conversation Nick left. Before reaching into his pocket the old man made quite sure the door was closed, then pulled out a bottle, uncorked it and downed a long swig, grimacing afterwards. He then went back to his modest ration of whiskey.

'Hosses!' exploded Thomasin to Francis after another board meeting at Leeds. 'I gave him two thousand pounds so's he can show me what he's worth and he wastes it on a bunch of nags.'

'Frankly, I can't see Nick as a horsey person, Thomasin.' Francis tried to soothe her.

'You're right, he isn't! If you could see the motley selection that's filling up my fields . . . hundreds o' the blessed things. What the devil is he up to?'

'Why not ask him?'

'He'll know I've been keeping tabs on him.'

'No, he won't. Just say you were passing the field and couldn't help noticing et cetera, et cetera.'

'Well, there's nowt so sure as I won't rest till I know what he's up to. But I think you can say that's his director-ship up the spout, Fran. Anyway,' she straightened the blotter on her desk and picked up a pen, 'let's have him in.'

Francis's slow passage to the door gave Nick time to scuttle away to a less-conspicuous position. When the elderly man emerged he was at the far side of the office looking extremely immersed in figurework. 'Nick, would you mind stepping in a moment?' Francis crooked a finger and the young man, straightening his tie as he went, moved into his grandmother's office.

'Sit down, Nicholas.' Thomasin leaned her elbows on the desk and studied him over laced fingers.

'Is there anything wrong, Nan?' he asked uncertainly.

'Would there be?'

'No, I can't think so.'

She stared deep into those artless eyes, saying finally, 'No, of course you're right, Nick. Francis and I are very pleased with the way you help us run things, aren't we, Fran?'

'Thank you.' Nick looked at Francis.

'How is Winifred?'

'Oh, admirable, Nan.'

'Good, good. Well, don't leave it too long before you set the date, will you? I'd like to see a great-grandson before I go.' Nick merely smiled. 'Well, have you?' she said annoyedly.

'Have I what, Nan?'

A sigh. 'Set a date for the wedding yet? You're not going to keep her waiting another year?'

'Well . . . Win and I thought October, but we'll see how things go.'

'What things?'

'Oh . . . just things.' – She's wondering how to introduce the subject of horses into weddings, he thought gleefully.

'I suppose you'll use the money I gave you to buy a house, eh?'

'Well, actually that's one of the reasons we're waiting, Nan. The money's tied up at the moment.'

'Tied up?'

'Mmm.' He wasn't going to put her out of her misery just yet. The calculating old slave-mistress had made him wait long enough, heaven knew.

It was left to her. 'It wouldn't be anything to do with what I saw on my land up Malton Road on my way home from the Scarborough shop last night?'

'Did it have four legs, a tail and go neigh?' he enquired maddeningly.

Her palm came down on the desk, ending this farce. 'What on earth possessed you to waste good brass on a mangy bunch of nags?'

'Mangy? I thought that's what dogs suffered from.'

'Winded, then, knock-kneed, saggy-backed, scraggy-haired, anything you like!'

'Actually, they happen to be very well-bred.'

'You are the most insufferable boy sometimes . . . all right, we'll not quibble about their parentage, but it's still a despicable waste.'

'Nan,' reproached Nick, 'I thought an astute woman like yourself would have been quick to spot the investment value.'

'Nicholas!' Thomasin's patience had been through the sieve once too often. 'Had the money been used to purchase shares in my company I could have seen the investment value, yes, but not when it's gone to buy a load of fleabitten candidates for the glue factory. Now of course, if you were to explain to me . . .'

'All right, Nan.' Nick crossed one leg over the other and folded his hands on his lap. 'But let me ask you a question first. Leaving out weapons and food, what would you say is the most important thing to an army?'

'I don't quite get the gist of this but I would guess from your tone that the answer is horses.'

'Correct. And in a war situation horses tend to vanish by the hundred in puffs of smoke, is that not so?'

'So who are we supposed to be fighting?'

'The Boers.'

Thomasin laughed outright. 'Not again!' Francis, too, smiled his dubiety.

'Not yet,' replied Nick, unabashed. 'But there's going to be trouble shortly.'

'It'll be nobbut a skirmish,' scoffed his grandmother. 'Over in no time. Our lads would squash 'em flat, then you'd be left with an awful lot of dog food on your hands. You've been reading too many newspapers, my lad.'

'Well, I'm not surprised you can't read between the lines, Nan, you're far too busy scouting for your stocks and shares. I predict it'll break out September or October time. At which point,' he added confidently, 'I shall sell my horses at a huge profit – might even sell them a couple of hundred head of cattle while I'm at it.'

'Hmm, and you thought you'd just deposit them in one of my fields, did you?'

'Your fields, Nan? I understood the land was in Grandfather's name – at least that's what he told me.'

'And of course your grandfather being easier to manipulate than I am you just . . .' she made a rolling motion with her hands. 'So how much rent is he charging you?'

'Nothing. I thought it rather generous of him.'

'Oh, I agree . . . especially when I seem to remember him mentioning that he'd already rented it to someone else. You presumably had to buy that someone off?'

'Not at all,' said Nick. 'In fact he was quite glad when I pointed out the unsuitability of the land for sheep. Much too boggy.' It had cost only a negligible amount to acquire a few sheep with foot-rot and to have them stationed on the land when Farmer Kettlewell came to inspect it. Damming off a dyke before a heavy shower had aided his deception, leaving the ground very marshy. Kettlewell had been grateful – if slightly puzzled – to find out just what he had been about to pay good money for.

Thomasin concluded this talk with a condescending smile. 'Well, Nicholas, I'm sure you've been extremely clever and if there is a war you can count on double profits: I'll match whatever you receive from the army.'

'If you throw in a directorship,' he answered cutely, 'I'll make it a deal.'

She laughed. 'Done – but I hope you like your bacon on the wing.'

In the October of that same year, 1899, war was declared on the Boers. Nick acquired his huge profit, doubled by his grandmother, a wife – and a directorship of *Penny and Co. Ltd.*

In ten days' time a new century would be born. Nineteen hundred – just to say it evoked such anticipation, such visions of progress. Patrick supposed he should be excited too, privileged to be alive in such an era, especially with a great-grandson on the way, but he wasn't. There would be the inevitable celebration parties. Thomasin, naturally, would be among the party-givers and Patrick dreaded the thought of all those people trampling his privacy. However much he complained about lack of company, there were times when he would prefer just to be left alone. There were things he would rather not share . . . He jumped guiltily as the door handle clicked and shoved the bottle from which he had been partaking under a cushion. This would be Vinnie to ask if he wanted some tea.

He was wrong about the visitor's identity – it was his son. 'Oh, 'tis you.'

'And a merry Christmas to you too, Dad.' Sonny, beginning to look like the middle-aged man he was, flopped down on the sofa. 'I thought you'd be busy putting all the decorations up.'

Patrick gave a snort.

'What was that – bah, humbug?'

662

'We-ell, I'm sick o' hearing about bloody Christmas,' moaned his father. 'There's your mother rushing about with fistfuls of invitations...'

Sonny interrupted with a curse and put a thoughtful hand to his chin. 'I'd hoped to get in before she arranged anything. Josie and me were going to ask you all to our place.'

'Oh God, don't bugger her arrangements up, she's bad enough as it is.'

Sonny mused for a while. 'Ah well, never mind. You can come over and spend the New Year with us – see in the new century.' At Patrick's grunt he added, 'Well, I didn't expect you to writhe with delight but you could at least smile about it – you're always grumbling about being left on your own ... I can't seem to win with you. You're getting to be a right grumpy old sod.'

Patrick bared his teeth in an artificial smile. 'There! How's that for ye?' He got up and made for the door.

'Eh, I came over especially to see you!' Sonny let out an exasperated sigh at the lack of response. When the door had closed he leapt up and reached behind the cushion where his father had secreted the bottle. *Saville's Liver and Stomach Mixture*, read the label. Sonny clicked his tongue, half-amused – though it was no laughing matter. At least if Father was boozing openly they could tell how much he had consumed. He wondered how long it had been going on this time. Mother couldn't know – she had never mentioned it. Putting the bottle into his pocket he travelled down to the kitchen, intending to pour the whiskey down the sink.

However, before doing so he put his nose to the bottle. The unexpected aroma made him sniff again. Not whiskey then. So why had Father hidden it away? Sonny pondered over this for a spell, then, instead of emptying its contents, pressed the cork back in and carried it back to the drawing room, where it was replaced behind the cushion. Nothing in there to harm the old man.

Despite Patrick's lack of enthusiasm he was inevitably

railroaded into participating in the New Year festivities at Sonny's home. He, Thomasin, Francis and Erin arrived on the afternoon of the final day of the old century, along with Nick and Winifred. Belle had opted to stay at home with her children. There had been three new additions just recently and she felt the visit might unsettle them. Brian would be there to see in the New Year with her.

'That young man must have more patience than I have,' opined Erin over dinner when the conversation got around to Belle. 'It's pathetic really, the way he hangs round her like a dog waiting for a pat and a "good boy". She'll never marry him.'

'Unfortunately I have to agree,' said her mother. 'What she finds so fearsome about marriage I don't know.' Her own words caused her to snatch a look at Patrick, but he hadn't been listening. Despite her impatience a wave of regret and compassion went out to him. He had, after all, been a fine man once, and look at him now. He'd grown even more introverted lately, but at least he wasn't drinking beyond his usual measure now. While she was watching him his right hand strayed up to his ribs, and for a brief flash his face contorted. Her brow furrowed.

'So is Mother, aren't you?'

'Sorry, what?' She tore her eyes away to look at Josie. 'Sorry dear, I was woolgathering.'

'I was just saying how you're looking forward to being a great-grandmother.'

'What? I still can't believe it.' She glanced back at her husband. The expression of pain seemed to be over. He sat impassively, staring at his plate. 'In here,' she tapped her head, 'I'm only twenty. It's a pity other folk have to keep reminding me I'm seventy-four. Still, I find it thrilling to think of a new generation to mark the new century; very fitting. Pat's pleased too, aren't you, dear?'

The vacant eyes toured the table. Thomasin repeated the question and the old light came into them briefly. 'Ah yes, Nick's boy's wonderful.'

'We don't know if he's going to be a boy.' Nick laughed fondly at his wife and felt for her hand under the table.

'No . . . well . . . whatever. 'Tis gonna be a grand year for the young'ns.'

'A great year for the old'ns too if I have any say in the matter.' Sonny mopped his chin with a napkin. 'I've a special New Year's gift for you and Mother. Come on, you'll need your coats, it's outside.'

'John, they haven't finished eating yet,' protested his wife, grasping her small son's hands to wipe them.

'Oh, rats, they can fill up with Christmas cake if they're still hungry. I can't wait a moment longer to see their faces. Actually, it was a Christmas present,' he explained to his mother as the maid brought their coats and everyone drifted from the dining room. 'But as you'd already organised a party of your own it had to wait. It was too big to stick a stamp on. Anyway, it's probably more fitting as a New Year present.'

'Y'know, I always prefer New Year to Christmas. Always have. Even more so these days. It's becoming so commercialised, don't you think? Not like when you were children.' Thomasin appeared blind to the fact that she herself was a chief contributor to this commercialism.

'Come on, Dad,' Sonny threw over his shoulder, 'Stand here beside Mam while I bring it round.'

'Brr, I hope it doesn't take long,' shivered Thomasin. They were now all clustered on the front step, faces expectant. 'I can't imagine what it can . . . s'truth!'

The delayed Christmas present had just chugged round the corner of the house with Sonny at the wheel. He steered the gleaming automobile around the row of terracotta urns, face beaming, and pulled up in front of the startled crowd, honking the horn. 'Well, what d' you think? What? Just a sec, I can't hear you.' He turned off the engine and jumped out, striding around the motor car proudly. 'Isn't she a spanker?'

Thomasin was involved in effusive thanks, touching the gift admiringly, when Sonny whispered, 'Look at Father.'

Patrick was making his slow way to the vehicle, his face alight for the first time in months – no, years, marvelled Sonny; he hadn't seen him look like that since . . . since before Rosie died. His father was searching for a way into the vehicle. Sonny jumped to his aid and opened the door, helping the old man onto the back seat, his mother beside him. Patrick's hands felt the seat beneath him. Everything about it smelt new: leather, oil, polish. His son was telling the others, 'You lot'll have to stand and watch, I'm afraid.' He made a lunge with the starting handle. 'Us three are off for a ride.' The engine sprang directly to life and he jumped into the driving seat. 'Oh, wait a minute!' Rooting under his seat he found a driving helmet and goggles which he thrust at his father. 'You'd better look the part. Hold tightly now, we're off.' The horn hooted again. Patrick gave an exclamation and clung to the edge of the seat as the car chugged out of the drive and onto the road.

'Careful now, Son. Not too fast. Sonny, take it easy!'

But he enjoyed every minute of the journey as the car throbbed along city streets and country lanes, waving at people, Sonny hooting the horn. They went first to visit Sonny's millworkers in their neat little cottage homes where they took tea, and best wishes for the coming year were exchanged between employer and employee. On the way back Sonny was forced to stop the car when Patrick suddenly doubled over in pain, his mother shouting her alarm.

"S all right,' the old man waved away their attentions. 'I've just eaten too much hot pastry. Come on now, Sonny,' he took a deep breath, 'get this thing started again. Can it go any faster?'

'You old daredevil,' laughed Sonny above the noisy rotation of the responsive engine. 'D'you realise how fast we've been going? Fourteen miles per hour. But just for you I'll put my foot down and see what we can get out of her.'

'God Almighty,' said Patrick as they hurtled down the lane. ''Tis almost fast enough to fly.'

'I don't know about flying,' shouted Thomasin, holding onto her hat, 'but I think it might be fast enough to get us arrested. Sonny, slow down, will you? My ears are nearly dropping off with the cold.' Nevertheless, she had to agree with her son later that the gift had injected new life into her husband. She hadn't seen him this happy for a long time, and for that she, too, was happy. Everyone was pleased to see that Patrick's apparent well-being continued for most of the year 1900. It was best labelled 'apparent' because it was such a flimsy thing. At times it would be greatly in evidence, as when Nick and Win's first son, John Richard Feeney, was born. There were, however, times when Patrick retreated into his old depression, though to the family these seemed fewer. He could be more easily coaxed out of himself, was less grumpy. Today, for instance, he had allowed Belle and her doctor friend to take him to a moving picture show that had set up in Parliament Street, an invitation that might have been turned down only a year ago. That car had certainly proved its worth.

'Would you like some sweets to eat while you're watching, Gramps?' Belle asked before they paid for their seats. She arranged the children in order. 'Eddie, stop pushing!'

'Jaze, ye'd think I was one of her bairns the way she talks to me,' said Patrick amazedly to the doctor, who laughed.

'She treats me like that, too. Eddie, do as Aunt Belle tells you!'

An' she talks about not wanting to be tied down by marriage, thought Patrick, watching the two sort out their problems. They're as much like an old married couple as I know.

The tickets were purchased and everyone edged into the booth. It was very dim, despite the use of artificial illumination. When everyone had ceased shuffling and coughing the proprietor of the travelling show made an announcement as to the splendid content of the moving pictures they were about to see. All the lights were blown out, at which the children screamed. Lucy went further and burst into noisy tears.

'Please, Lucy, if you don't shut up they'll throw us all out and that would spoil it for the others, wouldn't it?'

667

Belle sat the child on her lap. Lucy brought her anxiety under control, only to yell once again when the projector flashed into life. The light from the moving picture flickered over ecstatic faces. There were oohs! of delight and aaghs! of terror. Patrick sat bewitched, mouth open, completely mesmerised, until a hostile-looking gang of workmen started to march purposefully towards him. Leaping up he adopted his old fighting stance, ready to take on every one of them to protect his family. Laughingly Belle pulled him back into his seat as the workmen dissolved into a frame of a steam engine.

'God, that's the cleverest thing I saw in years,' he told Belle animatedly when they came out of the booth, all squinting at the bright afternoon. 'They ought to have it here regular. Ye should go over to the store an' tell your grandmother what she's missing.'

'Why don't you go?' asked Belle. 'Take her to see it. I'm sure you could stand a repeat showing.'

'Ah no, I've somebody to see.'

'Who?'

'No one you know. Anyways,' he began to move away, 'thanks for inviting me, Belle, You too, Bri. I really enjoyed it.'

'Hey, wait a moment, Gramps. We were going to take you home for tea.'

'Buy some pork pies instead,' shouted her grandfather huskily. 'They'll taste better.'

'Well, at least he's showing a spark of his old humour,' said Belle to the doctor.

Brian nodded thoughtfully, then, after they had walked for a while, said, 'How long has he been having these pains?' She asked what pains. 'I saw his face screw up in discomfort once or twice while he was with us.'

She shrugged. 'Well, I'm sure if there's anything wrong he'll tell us.'

'Just look at that,' complained old Mrs Howgego to Vinnie, dustbin lid in hand. 'I don't know where they're all coming from.'

Vinnie stared at the pile of bottles in the dustbin. 'I'd say the master, but they're not whiskey bottles.'

The withered cook slammed down the lid. 'Don't you be so unkind. Poor old lad. You know very well he only has the one a day now. No . . . I had a look at the labels. They're all medicine bottles – and at the number of 'em I'd say someone in this house is very poorly.'

'Hello, Patrick!' Francis paused to hail the Irishman with his cane but the grind of carriage wheels blocked the greeting. There was a large hold-up of traffic down the narrow High Ousegate. When it had cleared Francis looked across the road to call Patrick once more, but the Irishman had vanished into thin air. Farthingale looked up and down both sides of the street, then hoisted his shoulders. Patrick must have gone into that bookshop. He walked on, leaning heavily on his cane.

Above the bookshop was an office where Patrick was now seated, waiting for his turn. Whilst doing so he read the back to front gold lettering on the window: *R.BROWN PHYSICIAN*.

CHAPTER FORTY-FIVE

A bullet hit the wall behind him. He knew it was a bullet for he had been shot at once before . . . besides which, it took the skin off his neck prior to embedding itself in the brickwork. If he needed any more proof that the act had been intentional he had it on the scrap of paper in his pocket – '*My darling Dickie, I have to warn you that my husband has found out about us . . .* ' Not waiting for the sniper to take better aim, he ran.

It was unfortunate that his assailant was in possession of four wheels. While Dickie's legs tore hell for leather down the deserted sidestreet the cuckolded husband took potshots from the back seat of his automobile. Dickie wheeled round a corner, gasping for breath. He had only run twenty-five yards and already his thigh muscles were screaming their protest. A crowd – he needed a crowd to hide in. His tortured legs staggered back to the main street, the car still chugging alongside, its rear occupant shouting obscenities, his bullets zinging into the sidewalk – Dusty, I swear, *I swear* if I get out of this I'll never look at another woman.

Oh, lovely people! Dickie reached the main street and slipped into the drift of shoppers, hoping this would deter the trigger-happy pursuer. The motor car was forced to halt at the junction, giving him a chance to put a gap between them. But soon it was moving again. He must find somewhere to hide.

The driver of the automobile scoured the crowded street, then flung over his shoulder, 'I can't see him, Mr Stone – he musta gone into one o' those stores.'

The man in the rear seat shoved the gun inside his jacket and threw open the door. 'He did – that one.' He gestured towards a fabric store. 'You wait here in case there's another exit.' Dodging the traffic, Stone made straight for the target.

The girl assistant smiled as he approached the counter and said she wouldn't keep him a moment, she was just serving this lady. He asked if a man had come through here. 'Oh, yes!' Her expression showed disapproval. 'He went out the back – I told him it's against regulations but he totally ignored me.'

Stone ignored the regulations too, going to the back of the shop and opening a door. The rear of this shop backed onto a meatpacking company. Stone looked around but there were no live bodies, only a row of dead ones strung on hooks. Then something whirred in his brain – the customer who was being served back there had been particularly tall for a woman . . . and she had seemed reluctant for Stone to see her face. A knowing look replaced the one of hostility. Rushing back into the store he pulled out the gun and without hesitation rammed it into the tall woman's back. 'Turn around – very slowly.'

The assistant let out a shriek. Stone told her to shut up and once more urged the tall woman to revolve. She did . . . her face waxen in terror. Stone balked. 'Oh, pardon me, ma'am! I thought you were the man I was after . . .' She had begun to add her screams to those of the assistant, piercing his eardrums and his trance. He began to move backwards, muttering awkward apologies. Realising that he was still pointing the gun he stuck it away in a hurry and rushed out onto the footwalk. The women's screams alerted a police officer who now strode over to investigate. Stone ran to his car and ordered the driver to move off as quick as he liked.

Had he bothered to look more closely at the row of carcases behind the fabric store he would have found another. Dickie unbent his legs, swung his feet to the ground and loosed his grip on the steel hook. The knees of his light-coloured trousers were gory from pressing them against the beast's ribcage. Peeping round the huge side of beef he let out the breath he had been holding and put a hand up to feel his wounded neck. It stung . . . but not as much as if it had caught him between the eyes. Bringing out a handkerchief to remove the sheen from his brow he made rueful examination of his clothes. – That's it, Dust. That's the last one. This was just too bloody close. His heart was still beating at an abnormal pace. He stood awhile for it to settle, then made for the door of the fabric shop, pausing once to dip into a bin and extract a meaty bone.

The women were still jabbering hysterically to the police officer who was trying to calm them. All looked up as Dickie sauntered casually past. He bestowed his charming smile and held up the bone. 'Just popped in to get a little treat for the dog.'

With this he raised his hat and before the police officer could accost him had vanished into the crowd.

The Irishman studied the ticket in his hand for a long

time, indecision wrenching him this way and that. He desperately needed to use that scrap of card, but there were still things keeping him here. Thomasin? No . . . not really. She was low on the list. What he and Thomasin once had was gone. Oh, sometimes when she laughed he would see, behind that aged mask of materialism, the bright, vivacious creature she had been in her youth, and he would feel that old surge of affection. But he was kidding himself, he knew, if he imagined she felt the same. It was Thomasin's avid interest in business and saving historical monuments that kept her alive, kept her young and made him old.

Only a little higher on the list were his son and daughter, for they had their own sons and daughters, and though they might try to involve Patrick in their lives he realised it was made out of filial obligation and Christ, he didn't want to be pitied by his own children.

Belle didn't pity him. On the imaginary list she was queen, the thing which anchored him to this barren existence. How could he make that final break, put a channel of grey water between them? Yet he had to go. He must.

The solution was to be provided in the final moments of nineteen-hundred.

'Have you heard of Emily Hobhouse, Gramps?' was the casual utterance that was to mark the parting.

Belle and he were in the drawing room of Patrick's home. Brian was here, too. The children, as usual when they came to visit, were playing hide and seek in the big house. Patrick could hear their distant laughter. He liked to see her children and it was easier for Belle to call on him these days, his aches and pains being what they were. Though of course he had made other excuses for his stay-at-home behaviour.

Concentration brought more lines to the old face. 'Ah,' he said eventually. 'That'd be the one they call "that bloody woman"?'

Brian smiled. Despite this there was a serious fold to his brow, Patrick noticed.

'That's her.' Belle leafed blithely through a magazine

as she spoke. 'I went to one of her lectures last week down in London. She was very interesting.'

'Was she indeed?' Patrick sensed the air of hesitancy behind that chatter.

'Yes. Well anyway, she was telling us about the deep distress of the Boer women and children, how they're suffering very badly over there – I don't know if you've heard of it?'

'Oh, I don't get to read the papers very much now with these eyes o' mine.'

. She broke off her main theme. 'Yes, Brian said he'd seen you screwing them up as if you're in pain. Is that what's giving you bother?'

His alarm was well-concealed. 'Aye, but 'tis nothing to trouble yourself over, ye know, 'tis just me age.'

'You'll have to get yourself some specs,' prescribed Brian. 'Don't be a martyr. I'm sure they'd suit you. I'm as blind as a bat without mine.'

'Aye, I'm sure they'd make me feel like a new woman. Now ye were saying, Belle, about South Africa.'

'Oh yes, terrible suffering going on by all accounts, isn't there, Bri?' She went back to the magazine. 'She's marvellous, Emily Hobhouse. Some people might just rant and rave but Emily is going right to the scene of the crime as it were, so she can see conditions at first hand.' At last the magazine was deposited in her lap and she faced him. 'I'm beating about the bush . . .'

'I felt the draught,' said Pat. ''Tis not like you.'

'I'm going with her, Gramps.'

'To Africa?' The sinews stood out on his bony hands as they gripped the chair arm more tightly. 'Does your mother know?'

'Not yet. I decided to tell you first. I knew you'd be apprehensive at me going all that way but it's very important to me, Gramps.' She leaned forward intently. 'There are children that need help. It's my duty to go.'

'Before ye go rushing off,' said her grandfather quietly, 'what about your own kids?'

'Yes, they do pose a bit of a problem . . . I'm going to

surprise both of you now and admit I made a big mistake – oh, not in taking them in,' she hastened as their lips parted. 'But I realise that instead of keeping them with me I should've found families for them, a mother and a father. It's too late for Eddie and his sisters, they've been with me too long, but those I took in more recently, well, I'm going to see if I can find anyone who's willing to take all three of them. Apart from the fact of them needing a mother and father, I just can't keep them all – the house will burst. Placing the babies is no trouble, but the older ones . . . well, it'll have to be someone special, a couple who're desperate for children – anyway, that'll all have to wait until I get back. It's not for long, you understand, I'll probably be back just after the New Year. Sally's promised to look after them, but the thing is . . . she can't really cope alone. I need to hire some help for her, and well, if I'm over there I won't be able to sell any articles. No articles, no income . . .'

'Glory be to God!' despite himself Patrick laughed out loud. 'D'you realise this is the first time in your life you ever actually asked me for anything – asked anyone, I shouldn't wonder. Brian, get an earful o' this.'

'He's going too,' she provided.

'Is he, begod?' A speculative glance for the doctor. 'Then there's hope I'll see ye married yet. Who can say what those red-hot Transvaal nights will do to a girl?' Suddenly, with a jolt, Patrick realised what it was that made them appear the old married couple. They knew each other – *Knew*, as in Biblical terms. He could not say what had made him guess. Maybe it was the look that had passed between them when he had made his last statement, or that aura of intimacy that always seemed to emanate from them – the things he and Tommy used to have. The thought spawned a sudden and unwarranted anger, which just as quickly died. She was, after all, twenty-five years old, and Brian was a good man. The smile that followed brimmed with understanding. It made the feeling of emptiness all the more difficult to understand.

'Oh, I'm glad to see you like this again,' she gripped his hand, then, on further impulse, hugged him. 'I've been so worried about you.' Brian deliberately remained on the outside of the conversation; it was between the two of them.

'Worry no more, I'm fine. An' go ahead, hire as much help as ye need. I'll provide the spondulicks.'

'It'll only be temporary, mind, and I'll pay you back.'

'Oh, Christ, don't spoil it!' Brian joined Patrick's laughter as the old man slapped her thigh.

She hugged him again. 'All right, have it your way – but don't go thinking that just because you've given me a few bob I'll come back married.'

A wink for Brian, 'We'll wait an' see,' and a loving pat for her.

The mood changed. 'Please don't expect too much.'

'I'll try not to.'

She held her head to one side. 'Oy-oy, the noise has stopped. That means they're up to no good. I'd better just go check.' She wagged a finger at the men before she left. 'Don't be talking about me while I'm gone.'

Nevertheless they did. 'Ye'll take good care of her in Africa, Brian?'

The answer came with a warm smile. 'My pleasure.'

'Dare I hope she's got it wrong? Might ye come back as Mr and Mrs?'

Unlike previous occasions Brian was unable to give hope. 'No,' he said bluntly. 'She'll never marry: me or anybody. I know that now. But then I'm content to leave it the way it is if Belle's happy.' Perhaps content was not quite the right word, reflected Brian, for he would have much preferred that Belle loved him as he did her and would bear him a child . . . but if that wasn't going to happen, he would make do with what she was willing to give.

'Ah well,' Patrick nodded understandingly. 'Ye'll be careful, I trust? I wouldn't see her hurt. She's very dear to me, that child.'

'Me too.' And then Brian looked into the old man's

eyes: Patrick wasn't simply concerned about them going to Africa – somehow he knew about the intimacy of the relationship. How? Had the giveaway come from Brian? If so, Belle would kill him for upsetting her grandfather. That was the main reason she had forbidden Brian to move in with her; not because of what others might say, but that the old man would not have understood such modern behaviour. Brian felt she was wrong in this belief – at this moment, more than ever, he felt that Pat should know how happy she was with her role. I mean, Brian told himself worriedly, what if he thinks I'm using her? With this thought, he studied Pat's face. The latter was benign, causing him to rethink. Maybe Pat hadn't guessed at all – maybe it was just Brian being neurotic after having to keep quiet about it for three years. Nevertheless, he offered a comforting sentence. 'I won't hurt her, sir.'

'How long shall the pair of ye be away?' Patrick pointed to his pipe-rack and Brian went to select one, passing it to the old man along with his tobacco bowl. 'I ask because things might've changed when ye get back.'

Brian was puzzled. 'In what way?'

Patrick dodged the question. 'I don't want her comin' back alone. Ye must be with her – d'ye understand?'

'No . . .' Brian's questioning 'Sir?' was left unanswered at the rumbustious entry of Belle and the children.

'I'm sorry, Gramps, they've been causing havoc in your kitchen again.' It was obvious Belle was ready to leave. 'Mrs Howgego was about to use the wooden spoon on Eddie when I got there.'

'It wasn't my fault,' said the boy, who was growing rather large for a wooden spoon to have any effect on him.

'Oh no, it wouldn't be. Now go along – quietly, mind – and get your coats. We're going.'

Patrick puffed contentedly. 'Will ye send me a postcard?'

'I will.' His grand-daughter stooped to kiss him, and found nothing strange in the fact that he clung onto her; she was after all going a long way. 'And I shall send instructions on my homecoming. I shall expect you there with your Union Jack to meet me at the docks. Come along now, Brian,' she pulled away briskly. 'You have a surgery to see to, haven't you?'

Brian rose from his chair, still puzzling over the old man's warning, but it was apparent this wasn't to be enlarged upon in front of Belle. He went for his coat, like Belle not bothering to ring for the maid.

'Come along, say goodbye to Gramps,' Belle called the children together.

He patted cheeks and ruffled heads as they crowded about him, but his main attention was for Belle. This was the last time he would look upon that beloved face; he wanted to savour it.

'Right, we really must be off, Gramps.' Belle apologetically herded the children out.

'Take care of her, Brian,' called Pat as they left.

'Yes! See you as soon as we get back.' The door slammed.

She had made his decision for him. When Belle left for South Africa Patrick would make for home.

'Have y'ever been to Ireland, Fran?' asked Patrick during their after-dinner discussion. Francis dined regularly with them and Patrick, realising a long time ago that the man had no designs on his wife, had come to welcome this.

'No, I never have.' Francis watched the smoke from Pat's cigar float up over the Irishman's head and disperse before it reached the electric light. He recalled the man's childlike pleasure – as at the motor car – when Thomasin had had electricity installed a couple of weeks ago, rushing about from room to room, switching the lights on and off.

'Ye should. 'Tis a picturesque country.' Patrick tapped the ash from his cigar. 'Matter o' fact, I'm thinking o' taking a holiday there meself.'

Francis smiled. 'I should be interested to see you persuade your good lady to leave her work, but I'd applaud you if you could. She's working far too hard for a woman of her years. I tell her that's what we've got Nick for, to give her a hard-earned rest, but she pooh-poohs the suggestion.'

677

'Actually, I was thinking to make it a solo trip,' replied Patrick, drawing slight surprise from the other. 'As ye say, ye'd need the devil's own luck to get her to leave her work. Anyway, I doubt she'd want to come.'

'Would you like me to have a go at her?'

'No, no . . . don't do that, Francis.' Patrick regarded him carefully. There was something behind that look, but Francis was damned if he could read it. Was he meant to? 'I always said I'd go back, ye know, an' I never yet did. Fifty-three years it's taken me. How's that for indecision?'

'Is that how long you've lived in York?' The Irishman lowered his head. 'It's a long time.'

'It is. It is.' Patrick lifted a decanter. 'Would ye care for another?'

Francis refused. 'When were you thinking to go?'

'Oh, next week maybe.'

'Good Lord, next week? But it's Christmas.'

'Sure, don't I know?' – Bloody Christmas again, Thomasin would say when he'd gone, he always does it to me.

'Wouldn't it be better to wait till it's warmer?'

'It may not get warmer for me, Fran.' Again, that look. They were interrupted by Erin. 'Sorry to disturb you, gentlemen. I left my knitting in here, I think – ah, there it is!' She was making a little jacket for one of Belle's children.

'I've cast off for you,' supplied Patrick.

Erin smiled at Francis who said, 'What do you think of your father taking his holiday in this weather – mad, isn't he?' Looking at Patrick he knew straight away that he had spoken out of place.

Erin paused in her exit. 'It's the first I've heard of it – where would you be gadding off to?'

'Oh um, I just thought I'd have a week or so in the old country . . .'

Her face lit up. 'At last! Oh, I'm going with you!' She spoke headily to Francis. 'He's been promising to do this for years.'

'What about the factory?' asked her father.

'Blow the factory! I'm not Mother, you know. I'm entitled to a holiday.'

'Oh well . . . I'd be a bit of a burden to ye, Erin, me being so slow. Ye'd be better going with Belle in the summer. 'Twould be a grand trip – mother and daughter.'

She laughed. 'You won't be a burden! I'm not exactly in the first flush of youth. And even if I did manage to get Belle to go with me what use would it be without you to show us where you were born? Francis is right though, it is a bit cold. Why don't you wait till summer an' we'll all go as a . . .'

'No, Erin. I've already got my ticket, I don't want to waste it.'

'All right then, awkward, I'll go buy . . .'

'Erin, I do not want company!' Patrick looked away at the expression he had created. 'I'm sorry . . . I didn't mean to speak like that, it's just this damned indigestion making me irritable.'

'Oh, go on your bloody own if you want to! I'm sorry I asked!' Erin swept out. As if it wasn't bad enough, Belle worrying her by going to Africa, he had to desert her, too.

Francis apologised as Patrick covered his face in despair. 'Ah no, don't worry, Fran. I would've had it to come anyway.'

'Is there any particular reason why you have to go on your own, Pat?' asked Francis, searching the Irishman's troubled features.

Patrick did not answer. But after a short period of silence he said, 'I know you'll take care of Tommy for me, Fran.' And it was at this point that Farthingale understood the reason for the winces of pain, the impromptu 'holiday'.

'Oh, Patrick.' He reached out a concerned hand, as atrophied by age as Patrick's own.

'No, don't say anything,' came the quietly-delivered order. 'An' don't tell Tommy.'

'She has a right . . .'

'No. I don't want her to feel beholden, her or any of them. Just tell me I can rely on you to see to things here.'

'You can, of course you can, Pat.' Francis pulled his

hand back, somewhat distraught. 'I think I will have that brandy, if you don't mind.'

'I wonder if Father's there yet.' Up until ten-thirty on this chilly morning Sonny had been working on a new fabric design in his study, but now he had deserted his drawing board and sat drinking coffee with his wife, watching their little red-haired son play with a jar of coloured pencils. He was not so averse to being interrupted from his work these days, realising what fun he had missed when Nick was this age. 'I hope he's all right – I mean, he is eighty. Mother doesn't seem to realise that. I wish she'd told me before he'd gone – maybe I could've persuaded him to let me go with him.'

Josie held out a biscuit to the little boy who came to sit on her lap. 'There's nothing to stop you going after him.'

'Aye . . . that's an idea. I don't like to think of him all on his own, grumpy though he might be.' Sonny began to filter through the pile of mail that had arrived with the coffee and, selecting the one he recognised as being from his brother, read that first.

Dear Son,

Well, here we are again at that dreaded time of the year. When I was a kid November always seemed to be the time to look forward to Christmas and my birthday. Funny how when you're young you can't wait to gain another year then when you get to our age you tend to try and forget birthdays. Christmas isn't much fun when you get older either, is it? I suppose it still holds pleasure for you, what with you having youngsters. The adoption societies here haven't been any sweeter towards us, I'm afraid. Dusty's getting very depressed about it. We've tried dozens of places but they don't want to know – apparently I'm not respectable enough. Personally, I couldn't give a toss about adoption, what do I want with kids? But I hate to see what it's doing to Dusty. Christ, they won't even let us have one that nobody else wants. It's killing her, Son. I'm going to have to get her away from this big empty house for a long holiday before she goes really crazy. But I'll come to that in a minute.

Delighted to hear about Nick's boy! My little brother a grandad, eh? You poor old sod. At least that's one thing I don't have to worry about. I was privileged to read that he's named after me – or was that just coincidence? Thanks for the photograph of him. Dusty says to tell you he's a handsome baby – well, he would be with a name like that. Sad to hear that the old fella is failing. At least he's keeping off the juice. Maybe the old bastard needs some sort of shock to get him back into his old form. Now, that's where we come to the holiday, Son. Well, it's a bit more than a holiday. I'm in a spot of bother. I won't go into details, but there was this woman . . .

'Aye, there would be,' murmured Sonny, bringing his wife's eyes round to quiz him.

Just a platonic relationship you understand. Well, how was I to know she was married to one of the biggest bastards in New York? Anyway, to cut a long story short, he's going to cut something of mine short if he catches up with me, so you can see why I need somewhere to lay low for a while. At first I thought a month or so in Florida might suffice. Then I got to thinking . . .

Oh, Lord. There was always trouble when Dickie got to thinking.

As I said, Dusty is very depressed about this adoption lark. Part of it's her age, of course. It mightn't be so bad if she had some other family here but she's only got me and I'm not much comfort, am I? She's never felt totally at home here like I have. Even though she's got no close relatives in England she still looks upon it as home. We've always said, of course, that we could never come back because of being wanted by the law. But that was twenty-five years ago, Son, I can't see anything coming of it now, can you? And you said in your last letter about Dad needing a jolt to bring him back to his old self . . .

Sonny made a noise like a bullock on the rampage, startling his son who almost jumped from Josie's lap. 'He can't!'

'John, do you have to shout like that?' Josie tried to soothe the child but Sonny wasn't listening.

I know we agreed to keep me 'dead' but I'm getting to the stage where I might soon be permanently dead and I feel I just have to see you all again, even if it's only for you to tell me to bugger off. It's your letters, you see, Son. They just make me want to share it all. I must be getting old or something. As I said, it'll only be for a holiday. America's home. It's no good writing to tell me not to come – I've made my mind up. I knew what you'd say so I set sail shortly after posting this letter. Our ship docks on the thirtieth of December, so this year I'll be wishing you a Happy New Year in person. Pave the way for me, will you? I'm really excited now at the prospect of seeing you.

Much love
Darby and Joan.

'He's coming home! Josie, this is going to kill Dad off altogether!' Sonny's stomach was churning. 'I'll have to intercept him before he leaves that blasted ship and tell him he can't come! What port would a ship from New York dock at – Southampton?'

'I've no idea,' breathed Josie, rocking back and forth in an effort to calm the weeping boy.

'Neither have I. I'll have to make enquiries. Damn the little sod!'

'John, will you please stop swearing!'

'Sorry – but what will this do to Mam and Dad, Jos?'

'It's not just Mam and Dad! How's Nick going to feel? And Erin. What if you can't intercept Dickie before he gets here? If your paths cross and he comes to York while you're waiting at the docks . . .'

Sonny moaned. 'Forty-eight and he's still causing as much trouble as he did at fourteen! There's no way out – I'll have to tell them.' She asked when. 'There's no point in sitting here nursing it until he arrives on the doorstep, is there? But I can't get over to York before this evening . . . I don't suppose you fancy a ride with me, do you?'

She had managed to settle the child and nodded supportively. 'And Nick?'

Sonny heaved a sigh. 'I wish he still lived under the same roof. I could do without having to break this news twice.'

Later that day, Sonny called at the Leeds store, only to be told that his son had gone home early. It was just as well, thought Sonny as he drove over to Nick's house.

'Are we expecting you?' A tousled-looking Nick met his father in the drawing room to where Sonny had been shown by a maid. His father replied in the negative. 'Thank God – I thought I was going the same way as Grandad.' He hooked his braces over his shoulders and finished buttoning his shirt. 'Excuse the state.'

Weighed down by his problem, Sonny hadn't really noticed. 'I should be the one to apologise for barging in like this but I've got to go over to York and I wanted you to know first.'

'Well, it's very kind of you to tell me, Father . . .'

'Not about going to bloody York, you fool – where's Win?'

'Upstairs. She's er, indisposed.' Nick wore an impish expression.

All of a sudden the man understood the reason for his son's disarray.

'Oh, sorry . . . I hope I haven't spoilt anything?'

'Fait accompli,' grinned Nick and rubbed his groin. 'It's just that the afternoon seems to be the only time that child of ours sleeps. Would you like some coffee?'

Sonny shook his head. 'I haven't time . . . Nick, I know it's a bit late in the day to tell you about your real father.'

Nick sprawled into a chair, one of his legs draped over the arm. Presented in this devil-may-care pose he gave a strong reminder of Dickie, though he was as fair as Dickie was dark. 'I seem to remember you explained all that when I was a kid.'

Sonny stared up at the light fitting. 'Not all of it . . . there's something I've been keeping from you.'

Nick saw how difficult it was for his father to phrase this and out of kindness formed the words for him. 'You mean that he didn't really die in that fire.'

Shock paled Sonny's face and his eyes descended like ton weights. 'You've been reading my bloody letters!'

Nick made pained objection. 'What sort of thing is that to accuse your son of?' Then he gave a relenting chuckle. 'Aye, well . . . maybe I did have a peek – just a little one, mind.' He lit a cigar, offering one to his father who refused with a sharp exclamation.

'By God! If I were my father and you were me you'd find yourself on that carpet spitting teeth! Thank your guardian angel I'm a forgiving soul . . .' He reverted to his sombre state, trying to eject the next sentence. 'Did . . .'

'Rosie didn't know,' Nick reassured him.

'Good . . . good.' Sonny nodded gratefully, then looked into his son's face. 'So . . . this is all a bit of an anticlimax, isn't it? You know, Nick, life must be very boring for you – no one ever seems able to surprise you.'

Nick smiled, thinking of Win's hidden passion. 'Oh, I wouldn't say that.' He took a drag of the cigar, blowing the smoke up to the ceiling.

'How would you feel about seeing your real father?' asked Sonny.

'I thought I'd made that plain years ago: I regard *you* as my real father. Though I must admit,' he leaned forward to tap his cigar against an ashtray, 'I would like to meet your brother some time, if only to see if he lives up to his image as a member of the Hellfire Club.'

'Ah, I think you might find him a bit tame these days.' Sonny accomplished a smile. 'I'm certain he'd like to meet you, too. He's always been interested in your progress – course you'll know that.' His face was accusing now.

Nick merely laughed as Sonny went on, 'Aye, I think Dickie'd be proud to see how you've turned out . . . that's obviously one of the reasons why he's coming to visit us.' He laughed aloud at the rapid change in his son's visage. 'Oh, God, I've done it! I've finally managed to surprise him!' Abruptly, he strode to the door.

Nick's dumbfounded face pursued him. 'Eh, hang on! When's he coming?'

Sonny swivelled and pointed. 'Just for badness I'm going to keep you in suspense. I may decide to grant you more details when I've been and told your Nan – eh, and *don't* go reading any more of my letters!'

Thomasin expressed her delight at this unexpected visit from her son and his wife. 'I thought it was Francis! He's taking me and Erin to the theatre. Oh, come and sit down – where's little carrot-top?' When told that he had been left at home she said, 'Aw, meanies! What're you two doing here, then – not that it isn't nice to see you, of course.'

Sonny looked at his wife, but was given a reprieve by Francis's entry. Greetings were exchanged and all sat down to partake of a sherry for the play did not start for another hour. Sonny just didn't know where to begin. The conversation centred mainly on his little son, his grandson and Patrick's trip to Ireland.

'I had begun to think he was improving till he sprang this on me,' said Thomasin. 'What a time to choose for a holiday, leaving me to prepare for Christmas alone, all the gifts, the party to arrange . . .'

'Come on, Thomasin, you've done it for years.' Francis seemed a bit impatient. 'You thrive on it.'

'Aye, so I do,' she granted. 'But it's still inconsiderate of him!'

Erin agreed. 'Grumpy old devil. He can take my daughter all over the Continent but when I ask for a little trip to see his birthplace it's too much trouble.'

Francis held back his retort to ask Thomasin, 'Didn't anything other than the time of year he chose for his holiday strike you as odd?'

'Patrick's been behaving oddly for a long time.' She sighed. 'It's an awful thing to say of someone you love but I think he's going senile. It's hopeless trying to hold a conversation with him.' Francis objected. 'Well, you must have more patience than I have, Fran. It was Rosie's death that did it, you know. That's what started it off. You'd think after all this time he'd be able to perform rationally in company even if he is still grieving in private. All of us have to, don't we?'

She looked at Sonny who gave a melancholy nod. 'I still miss her, you know.'

'You always will,' said his mother softly. 'The pain might lessen but it never goes away.' She gave a little sound of amusement. 'Dickie would've been forty-eight this Christmas – it's hard to imagine, isn't it? I can't picture him with greying hair – come to that, I could never picture your father with greying hair. Eh, he was the loveliest man I ever set eyes on . . .' Her face softened as she travelled back in time – made love to Pat again, bore his babies. 'Do you realise that the year after next we'll be celebrating our Golden Wedding? Fifty years and never a cross word!' She chuckled. 'If we both last that long of course.'

'Mother . . .'

'Thomasin . . .'

Sonny and Francis laughed as their voices emerged simultaneously. The latter waved Sonny to go ahead. 'Oh no, it was nothing really . . .' Sonny glanced at his wife who urged him with her eyes: get it over with! 'Oh, I was just going to say d'you remember when Dickie disappeared for those three years, Mam, and we all thought he was dead?'

She rolled her eyes and laughed. 'Will I ever forget? My God, I thought I was seeing a ghost when I met up with him at that auction. By, he was a fly devil! I can laugh at it now but I was as mad as anything at the time – and not just because he'd got the financial betterment of me, neither. To think he kept us believing he was dead all that time . . .' She moved her head, as if still disbelieving it. 'And there he was, bold as brass.'

'Three years,' murmured Sonny, playing with his fingers. 'I wonder how you'd've felt if it had been twenty-five.'

Her face showed she thought this a peculiar hypothesis.

'I don't think even our Dickie could've managed to hide himself for that long.'

'No, I don't suppose he could . . . But can you imagine what it would be like to see him suddenly walk through that door? I mean, d'you think you'd recognise him?'

'I'd know him at a hundred and three,' vouched his mother. 'Little devil.' She looked at the clock and smacked the arm of her chair. 'Away, isn't it time we were moving, Fran? Sonny, d'you two want to come?'

Josie grimaced at her husband and hissed, 'John, for pity's sake get it over and tell her!'

Thomasin viewed her daughter-in-law with raised eyebrows. She had never known Josie so forceful. 'Tell her what?'

Sonny's chest heaved, his grey eyes begged for mercy. 'Before I tell you, will you promise to forgive me?'

His mother looked perplexed, then, mulling over his previous odd comments about Dickie, said slowly, 'This has something to do with your brother, doesn't it?' At his relieved nod she pulled herself out of the chair and took a step forward. 'Well, come on – what have you found?' As he was tardy in replying she tried to guess. 'Are you saying you've discovered another of his illegitimate children somewhere? Is that why you asked if I'd recognise him – because the child looks so much like him?'

'Not so much like him, Mam . . .' replied Sonny. Then after a long hesitation, '*Is* him. He didn't die in that fire. That was one of Peggy's men-friends . . . Dickie's been living in America for over twenty-five years.'

Thomasin staggered. Her lower jaw fell almost to her chest and she sought for assistance – but too late. She fainted. Francis and Sonny lifted her to the sofa and spread her on it. 'Erin, get the sal volatile!' cried Sonny, then saw that his sister was in no fit state to do this. 'Oh, I knew I shouldn't've told her! Josie, you – oh, thanks!' His wife had found the smelling salts which were duly put under Thomasin's nose. She came round, peering at them all blearily at first, then, remembering, she burst into tears, Erin too.

Francis had poured out two brandies which he handed to the women. After they had sipped them and recovered a little Thomasin stared at her son. 'I told him it'd do this to you!' he exclaimed. 'But he gave me no option, I'm sorry, Mam.'

'You mean ... you've been in touch with him?' Her chest was rising and falling very noticeably. Her eyes were like marbles, searching his face. 'I don't believe ... I must be ... Oh, Christ!' She took another mouthful of brandy, screwed up her face and started to cry into Erin's shoulder again.

Erin dashed a handkerchief to her face, then glared at her brother. 'What did you have to tell her for after all this time?'

Thomasin broke off sobbing to grab her daughter's arm. 'Did you know about this, too?'

'No! Of course not – look at the state of me.' She held up trembling fingers. 'God, my heart ...'

'And were you in on this right from the start?' Thomasin demanded wetly of her son.

He told her he had only made the discovery fourteen years after the fire. 'We thought it best to keep it to ourselves, not knowing how badly it would affect you or Dad.'

'Your Dad!' Thomasin grasped him. 'Wait till he comes back and hears this ... Sonny, I could strangle you! And you, Josie. We had a right to know! You've robbed us of twenty-five years of our son's life!' Another period of weeping followed. Her entire body seemed in the grip of some tingling palsy. She still found it totally incredible. 'Oh God, this hanky is drenched, give me yours, Francis.' After blowing her nose and wiping her swollen eyes she asked fearfully, 'What's he doing now, then? Where is he?' Her heart was still thudding as if trying to break out of her chest.

Sonny looked uneasy. 'Well, at this moment ... he's probably three-quarters of the way across the Atlantic.'

Both Thomasin and Erin gasped and clutched each other. 'You mean he's coming home?'

'For a holiday. He set sail shortly after he'd written to say he was coming so I had no chance to stop him.'

'The little . . .' Thomasin set her mouth at a determined angle. 'Does he really imagine he can come waltzing in here after twenty-five – no, it's twenty bloody six years! Wait till I tell your father – he'll kill him!'

Francis rejoined the discussion. 'Thomasin, why don't you take a trip and break the news to him?'

Thomasin was thoughtful for a minute, then wrinkled her nose. 'No, he should be back before Dickie arrives.'

Erin sighed. 'Let's hope this doesn't start him drinking again.'

'Yes – and trust him to be away when something like this happens! Sonny, are you certain it is Dickie? I mean . . .'

'Thomasin!' Everybody looked at Francis who regarded each one with indignation and pity. 'I'm sorry, but I really can't sit here and allow you all to talk of Patrick in this fashion . . . I promised I wouldn't tell, but I feel it most urgent that Patrick be told the news of his son right away.'

'What are you talking about, wouldn't tell?' quizzed Thomasin.

'Oh, Thomasin.' Francis beheld her sorrowfully. 'They say that those closest to a person are the last to know . . . Patrick hasn't gone to Ireland for a holiday. He's going home to die.'

CHAPTER FORTY-SIX

Nothing had changed. At this time last year he had been about to take an exciting step into the twentieth century, with telephones, electricity, motor cars; standing here he felt as though he had taken fifty steps backward, a hundred – two hundred even. There was nothing here to indicate progress. Everything was the same as he had left it over fifty years ago, apart from the pile of rubble on which he was now standing. This was once a home – his home – with a father and a mother and a little boy who would play among the lazybeds and make pratie men with chips of stone for eyes and twigs for limbs. Strangely, among that dereliction, the hearth was still intact, with the metal crane that had held the cooking pot reaching out to him like some famine-racked arm, beseeching. But there was no fire. 'If the fire dies, the house dies' was the old quotation. It was true. The house had died over fifty years ago when Pat had walked out of it to seek a new life – any life – on foreign soil.

To the right of the hearth was where Richard Feeney would sit. Patrick saw him now – felt him so strongly – with the old harp between his knees and the briar pipe protruding from his grizzled face. The other side of the fireplace was unoccupied. Patrick's mother had died when he was very young; he had no vision of her. But other memories came easily: himself on the rushes in front of the glowing peat fire; the animals that shared the one-roomed cottage and whose body-heat helped to keep him warm on howling winter nights; child Mary, his first wife who had only lasted two years in England . . .

His memories terminated agonizingly in a spasm that caused him to clutch his hands to his stomach, eyes disappearing in wrinkles, robbed for the moment of breath. Then remembering where he was, he lifted his face to roar his agony aloud, confident in his solitude that no loved-ones would come running – 'Grandfather, what is it?' Here he didn't have to hide it, bellowing outrage at the sky.

The spasm passed and tentatively he straightened, blinking. What would they say when he did not return? That was bad of him, not to tell anyone. Francis had got the hint, he thought. Who else could he tell it to? Liam was dead, Tommy estranged and who in his right mind would say to his beloved grandchildren, 'I'm dying'?

A movement caught his eye and he focused upon it; an Irish slide car bumping its way across the springy heather and making up the slope towards him. When it eventually came alongside, its pony's nostrils flaring red with the strain of uphill travel, its driver's face questioned. Patrick simply stared back at him.

"'Tis a grand class of a day.' It was delivered in Irish. The young man made no move to dismount, gazing from this vantage point at the fine view.

'It is.' Patrick slipped back easily into his native tongue, lifted his eyes to the clear sky; no sign here that it was Christmas.

'I heard your cry, it carried on the wind. Can I be after helping ye?'

'I didn't mean for anyone to hear it,' said the old man. 'There's no way ye can help – but thank ye all the same.' There was something familiar about the cut of the young man's jaw. 'Would I be knowing you, young fella?'

'The name's Fin Brady. I live down there aways.' A gesture was flung downhill.

'Patrick Feeney.' The old man held out his hand, but before the other could clasp it withdrew into another spasm.

Fin jumped down solicitously but Patrick shoved away his efforts. 'I'll be . . . all right in a second . . . just give me room.' When it passed he looked to the concerned face but did not speak, finding neither the breath nor the words.

'You're in need of a doctor,' advised Fin unnecessarily.

'Too late for doctors, son,' grunted Patrick, still suffering discomfort.

Fin looked away to the crumbling cottage. 'I used to live there,' Pat told him.

'You'd be the Patrick Feeney that married Mary McCarthy an' went to England?'

Patrick was only slightly surprised. The young man would probably have heard of Pat's great-grandfather, too. In a small community like this there was no need for history books. Before each child reached adulthood he could quote all the kings of Ireland, the victories, the defeats and even lesser accomplishments: the genealogy of each family was passed down by word of mouth, father

691

to son, mother to daughter. 'I would,' he answered. 'An' you'd be the son of Sean or . . . ?'

'Paedar Brady,' supplied Fin. 'Sean's son.'

'Aye, 'twould be,' nodded Pat. 'Ye've a definite look of your grandad.'

'Away, get on the cart,' ordered Fin. 'If ye stand here much longer the wind'll chamfer your ears.'

'Where we going?' asked Pat as he perched his buttocks on the edge of the cart.

'Home,' replied Fin matter-of-factly. 'They'll want to welcome ye back.'

Patrick smiled as the cart began to move. 'Ye know I was never on too good terms with your grandad.'

The youth shrugged. 'He was a terrier for a scrap so I hear, but then he'll hardly be picking up the cudgels today. He's been under the sod for the last thirty years.'

Patrick nodded sorrowfully. 'He survived the Hunger then.' – Well, he would, came the private thought. He'd suck the bones o' the dead would old Sean before he went under himself, the scoundrel.

When they reached Fin's home Patrick was given a rapturous greeting by the entire family, though he had never met any one of these generations. Out came the jug of poteen, plates of honey cakes and freshly-baked potato bread. The fire was replenished with peat, and flutes and fiddles produced. Fin was sent out to summon the rest of the village to celebrate Pat's homecoming.

The old man sat with a contented smile, tapping his foot to the whining fiddle, while the boys swung their girls off their feet, red petticoats swirled and the poteen helped to erode Pat's liver just a wee bit more. Fin's mother, Roisin, asked Patrick where he would be living now.

'That's a question I've asked meself,' smiled Pat. Though more pertinently, how *long* would he be living?

'Ah, sure stop worrying,' said Roisin above the lowing of the cow as it rolled its eyes at the wild music. 'Ye'll stop with us.'

'I'd not impose . . .' he began, but was silenced.

'A fine family we'd be to throw a ceilidh for your homecoming then sling y'out on your ear. Are y'enjoying yourself?'

'Ah, great,' he cocked his head. 'Just like the old days.'

'Then ye'll stop?' Though she eyed his clothes apprehensively and announced that it would not be what he was used to by the look of him. Patrick thanked her and said it would be more than fine. Having found himself a haven he was able to sit back and enjoy the party which carried on until the early hours. And if anyone noticed that the old man occasionally bent over and for the briefest instant his face clouded with pain, then they kept it to themselves.

Dawn broke to find the weary revellers staggering off to their homes while the Brady family prepared to stretch out on the floor for a few hours' sleep. A straw-filled palliasse was placed in the warmest corner for Patrick while the Bradys collectively employed a thick bed of rushes and, covered by a communal blanket, were soon snoring.

Despite his weariness, despite the fact that he had been dealt the choicest bed, the warmest corner, despite the poteen, he could not sleep. The pain was a contributor but not the only one. The other was that a half-revolution of his head showed him what he was leaving behind; the Brady family huddled in sour-breathed togetherness; father, mother, son, grandson . . . He wondered where Belle was now, imagined her trudging across the veldt, tending those stricken children. There was a lightning flash of Nick, holding his baby son out to be cuddled by a proud great-grandfather. Sonny, too, with his baby son and his troupe of girls. What lay in store for them? And what of Erin? She must be missing Belle, too. What about those children in his grand-daughter's care? What future for them? More than these children huddled beneath the patched blanket. The young Bradys' rise to adulthood would be a mirror-image of their parents': you were born, baptised, if you were lucky schooled by the priest, got married, had sons of your own, dug your lazybeds, harvested your praties, year in year out . . . then you died.

At least he had the certainty of knowing his own descendants would not live that rut.

'Why have you come back if you feel that way?' a voice – Thomasin's – asked him. 'Because I don't belong there. I never belonged there. If I'd been here I'd've been quite content to live my life working praties and taking my fun like this family does. You never understood that; that I'm just a simple man. Oh, you made a play of it when we were first wed, saying all you wanted was me and my babies, but time brought out the real Thomasin. You're happy with what your wealth has brought you – an' I don't blame ye, I don't really. Sure, wouldn't I rather be lying on my own featherbed than this lumpy old palliasse?

The pain came again, so badly this time that a tempest boiled up in his brow, raging around the sockets of his eyes. It lasted longer, too. When it passed he flicked away the moisture and tried to recount where he had left off . . . Thomasin, ah yes, Tommy. She'd be there now, alone in that bed. Would she be sleeping, or were her memories keeping her awake, too?

Grey light came seeping over the windowsill. It would be impossible to sleep now. Besides, the pain was becoming chronic. He needed to scream and he couldn't do that here. Holding his breath he staggered to his feet and pulled on his warm topcoat. Briefly he gazed down on the sleeping Bradys, experiencing a pang at the child with its thumb in its mouth, the lock of black hair over pale brow.

The cold hit him like a block of cold steel. Closing the door swiftly so as not to let in too much draught he pulled up his collar and rammed his hat further on, then set off towards the hill. He must again search out the pile of rubble that had been his home.

Once there, he sat down, back against the hearth, and tried to light his pipe. The wind kept snatching at the match-flames, playing games with him. Huddling into the neck of his coat he finally managed to outwit it, smoke from the triumphant effort whisked away the moment he lifted his head. Before long a flask of whiskey had joined the tobacco as comforter. He shuddered at the burn it inflicted but punished his insides a deal further till the pain started to give in. Then he leaned back, simply looking.

How long it took him to realise that this was no longer home he could not say, nor what had caused the revelation. Perhaps it was because the sky was not so blue today; in wintry hue it balanced heavily atop the mountain, hiding its summit. Unlit by sunshine, the granite landmark seemed not indigo but grey and slightly menacing, footed by unattractive swathes of brown and crumbling heather. Everything seemed lifeless. The sharp December wind dug its claws into his hat, whisking it away, way up over the valley and down the other side. Not content with this it returned to tease the sparse slivers of hair from his brow, tweaked at his nose, his ears, infiltrated his warm coat and hectored his bones.

He shuddered and rose. Revisited by pain he shrieked aloud. The wind roared down the hillside seizing his scream and forcing it back down his throat as if to say: I don't want your pain! This country has pain enough; take it back, take it home! He made one last examination of the ruined cottage before returning to the village. The Bradys still slept. Only the cow greeted him, flicking her tail as he slipped into the warmth. Scorning the palliasse he sat beside the fire to relight his pipe and remained there for a time, staring into the radiant peat.

Singly, the Bradys came to life, bickering and elbowing while they climbed into their clothes, the after-effects of the poteen souring their tempers.

What the hell am I doing here? Patrick demanded of himself suddenly. Sitting here with a roomful of strangers, waiting to die. What eejit wouldn't rather spend his last days with his loved ones? Or at least, where their memories are strongest. Why, for over fifty years, have I thought of this as home, pining my heart out for something that I already had?

He waited till the buttermilk that Roisin had brought was settled on his tormented innards in a soothing blanket before telling them.

They couldn't understand, he could see that, though

they made noises of absolution, saying he must go where he was most at home, despite thinking he was mad for wanting to be in England. He thanked them for their hospitality and gladly accepted the lift to the nearest town where he caught a connection to Dublin.

It was here, as he waited at the quayside for the steam packet to Liverpool, that he came face to face with Timothy Rabb.

Tim apologised for obstructing the elderly gentleman and was preparing to step aside when a hand clamped his arm, dislodging his haversack and bringing puzzled eyes to the old fellow's face. Patrick saw the flash of fear – rejoiced in it – then there was a tilt of the head in recognition. 'Mr Feeney.'

'Mr Rabb.' The reply was grimly ironic. Tim's appearance had matured since their last meeting – oh, but Patrick knew him. 'I did hear you were in America.'

Tim didn't answer. He had indeed been in America until recently, when Mr Dorgan had said it was safe for them to come home. Nothing was said for fifteen seconds or so while the two sized each other up, then Timothy asked, 'And how is Miss Rosanna keeping?'

The hand left his arm, only to be joined with another as it closed round Timothy's throat, the unexpectedness of it hurling him backwards and taking Patrick, too. The old man fell heavily atop him. No word came from Patrick, only a strength he had thought to have been bled with his youth. It seethed down his arms and into the fingers that were locked round the back of Rabb's neck, into the thumbs that squeezed the protruding Adam's apple, pressing, kneading the life from that treacherous throat.

To be realistic it was only the shock that kept Tim at this disadvantage, but that was of no consequence; he was still on the losing end. Gasping, face crimson, he attempted to struggle out of the murderous grip, his legs lashing out at the encumbrance on top of him. This was madness. This was an old man! Stars had suddenly appeared in the sky, the trapped blood thumped viciously in the sinews of neck and temple as he heaved and writhed in desperation and fear, bucking his whole body to remove the dreadful weight.

The world was going black when miraculously he felt the pressure suddenly give and, taking rapid advantage, thrust the weight from him, rolled over and struggled to his feet. He steadied himself on a capstan, waiting for another onslaught, gasping down at Patrick and clutching his bruised throat. The old man remained on the ground, shouting and cussing for all he was worth. A number of seamen had gathered to watch the strange incident. They waited for the fight to resume but, as Timothy staggered up to the groaning man, hauled him to his feet and straightened his clothes, they trickled away.

'Take your filthy hands off me, Rabb!' Patrick wrenched himself free. 'Christ, if it wasn't for this bloody stomach o' mine you'd be dead!'

Rabb was angry too, shaking Patrick by the lapels. 'You silly old bastard! What reason have you got to kill me? Ye got what ye wanted, didn't ye? Ye got Rosanna.'

'Got her?' roared Patrick. 'Aye, with a fucking hole in her head. An' by Christ if I had a bloody gun now . . .'

Timothy never heard the rest. The flush that Patrick's near-strangulation had brought about drained completely away.

' . . . that's how you're gonna free Ireland? By shooting children? Damn you all to hell!'

'You're telling me Rosie's dead? She's dead?' The taut fingers slackened their hold, slithered lifelessly down the old man's chest.

'You oughta know, Rabb, you did it!' Pat lunged for him again but this time Timothy was prepared and held his aged oppressor at bay.

'No! No, I tell ye! I loved Rosanna.'

'Aye, loved her so much ye didn't want anyone else to have her!' Pat fought to get at him. Damn these old man's limbs.

'If anyone's guilty o' that 'tis you! She was supposed to follow, come to Ireland. But you caught up with her and

697

stopped her. I waited,' his face bore his anguish, 'thought she might escape . . . but she never came.'

'Who gave you that shit?' sneered the old man.

Detachment vanished. The young man's hands gripped him persuasively. 'Look, I know it's true. Dorgan was there. He told me how you had to drag her screaming . . .' He broke off suddenly, reliving the experience. The doubt that had crept into his expression at the old man's scornful rejection now turned to awareness. 'Oh, f . . . oh, Mother o' bloody Christ!' He began to pace and hold his head, moaning.

'Rabb!' Patrick grabbed him determinedly, having come to understanding at the same time as the young man. 'D'ye know where to find him?'

Tim stopped pacing, wild eyes locking with Patrick's as he mouthed, 'I *know*.'

Grim-faced he broke away and made in the direction of the town. Pat collected his tortured senses and started to shadow as quickly as his age would allow.

'Fuck off, old man, I'll do this on my own.'

'Rabb! Rabb!' Patrick clutched his side as he broke into a crouching trot. 'Ye'll give me this. At least let me share it with ye. God blast your eyes, stop, I say!' He could hardly find the breath to fling one last sentence but fling it he did. 'You're to blame as much as he is. You introduced her to her murderer!'

The brake worked. Timothy, hate in his eyes, waited for the old man to catch up, but offered no explanations, no plea of vindication.

'What will ye do?' panted Feeney. 'Not kill him. There's been enough o' that . . .'

'Sure, I thought you wanted to share the experience with me?' said Rabb derisively.

'I did . . . I do want to see him dead . . . but not by your hand or mine. We have to go to the police.'

Rabb didn't even credit this with an answer. At least, not with words. But his response was graphic enough. Before moving on he grasped a stevedore's hook that someone had left on top of a barrel and dropped it into his pocket.

Patrick, elbow pressed into his right side, pounded after the younger man. The cancer dug in its teeth and spread a little further. If he had ever felt death as a tangible presence he felt it now. Every nerve, every cell shrieked with extinction. But first he had to see this man. The man who killed Rosanna. Rabb's legs seemed tireless, striding out purposefully along the cobbled streets and alleys. Though they had distanced themselves from the quay the distinctive smell trickled after them: fish crates, tar, mussel shells . . . Another alleyway – for God's sake make it this one, came Patrick's desperate thought, as it had each time their feet had turned. Street after street after street . . . Oh, Jesus, the bloody pain. He had lost all sense of direction; knew only that his feet were taking him to meet Rosanna's murderer. Houses flashed by his peripheral vision, chintz curtains, peeling whitewash, chalk on brick, '*Sile loves Danny*'. On and on and on.

The smell of fish was replaced by baking bread, warm, homely smells. Such paradox to herald a murderer. Rabb suddenly stopped before a modest terraced dwelling and without a word to his companion rapped on the door. Imperceptibly the bedroom curtains moved. Dorgan tried to discern the identity of his visitor. A snatch of curly head told him it was Rabb. He did not recognise the other.

A short period elapsed before he answered the door, angelic face a-beam. 'Why Timothy, what a pleasure it is, an' so long!' He was given little opportunity to say anything else. Timothy gripped the feeble old man and propelled him back down the passage, while Patrick, breath rasping, closed the door and hobbled after them.

Without preface, 'You callous bastard!' spat Tim into Dorgan's bemused face. 'Giving me all them lies about Feeney dragging her back – you killed her!' He threw the old man into a chair and paced the room, hands clasped to the sides of his head.

'Killed who, for God's sake?' Dorgan remained in the

position he had fallen, expression one of amiable bewilderment. 'Tim, what's got into ye?'

'My wife, damn your filthy black soul!' Tim visibly shook with rage.

'Rosanna?'

'How many fucking wives did I have? Yes, Rosanna!'

Dorgan attempted to pull himself straight in the chair, affecting smiling reproach. 'Oh now, Tim . . .'

'Don't lie!' Tim started towards him again and Dorgan shrank in the chair. 'I've a witness here.' He jabbed at Patrick who stood wordlessly.

Dorgan's eyes moved to the other occupant of the room, who swayed slightly. 'An' who might this be?'

'Ye know who I am,' growled Patrick. All the revulsion, the screaming agony of bereavement that had been with him at the viewing of that pathetic body came welling back. It bubbled up inside him, surging right into his finger-ends.

Dorgan turned to the younger man again. 'Tim, if he said I killed her then he's lying. She was fine when I . . .'

'He thought I killed her!' roared Timothy, banging his chest, the whites of his eyes reddened with blood. Then pitiably, 'Why, why did ye do it?' Even now he could give his old hero the benefit of the doubt. The things they'd shared together, the joint patriotism.

'I didn't. Believe me. I'd never dream o' such a thing. I thought the world of her, ye know that. Ah, Tim, y'always were a fine one for a tale. Can ye not see he's after taking ye for a fool?'

Tim did not hear him, his next words emerging on a sob. 'She came to help us escape. If it wasn't for Rosanna you'd be six foot under an' covered with lime . . . and you killed her.' He had never loved another woman since Rosie.

'Tim, ye surely don't believe it? Can't ye see the man's just trying to split up the Brotherhood? He'd say anything.' But the panic and fear in those eyes told it.

'Stop lying!' Tim's rage took his hand to his pocket. It pulled out the stevedore's hook, lifted it to strike.

Dorgan had seen the death-threat seconds before it was enacted. He pulled the minute gun – such an innocuous-looking thing, thought Patrick – from the pocket of his trousers. Simultaneous to Patrick's shout he levelled it and shot his compatriot through the chest.

Surprise came to Rabb's face as the velocity of the weapon suspended him in mid-air for a second. Then he crashed forward, the hook still gripped in his upraised hand. On impact the gun went off again. Patrick ducked involuntarily, then scrambled behind a settle, waiting for Dorgan to get up from that chair and finish him off.

After some moments the crevassed face slowly emerged round the edge of the settle. Half-lying with his head on the arm of the chair, left arm trailing to the carpet was Tim. Dorgan's left hand was rested on the other man's head as if in a gesture of affection. His other hand, Patrick saw, was empty now, hanging rag-like over the arm of the chair, the gun lying inches beneath the trailing fingers.

Patrick heaved his body out of his crouch and gazed in horror at the hook still gripped in Timothy's right hand, the majority of it disappearing into Dorgan's belly. When Dorgan blinked he jumped, having believed him to be dead. His eyes went once again to the gun. Stooping, he picked it up and toted it, staring into Dorgan's pallid face. His nostrils flared. He pictured Rosanna lying on that mortuary slab with the neat hole in her temple. With trembling hand he brought up the gun and pointed it at her killer's brow, forced his finger to touch the trigger. Momentarily he closed his eyes and roared at the pain which engulfed him for the millionth time. When he opened them Dorgan's bloodless face was observing him mockingly. Through mutual agony the old Fenian voiced his contempt. 'Go on, why don't ye?' Saliva, bloody-hued, drooled from the wounded man's chin as he uttered his scorn.

Whether or not Patrick would have been able to pull the trigger he would never know. As his trembling hands strove to keep the gun level Dorgan gave a bubbling sigh and expired. The gun remained in place for an age, until the film over his enemy's eyes spoke for itself. Slowly he lowered the weapon, placing it on the table.

A large fire danced in the grate. Patrick's weary eyes toured his surroundings, cosy until the intrusion of violence; now a tomb. He left the house the same way he had entered it. The sky was still grey – yet he felt as though he had stepped out into brilliant sunshine. For a while he didn't understand it . . . and then he realised, the pain was gone. It was as if he had passed some sort of test in there: God was smiling upon him. And in that moment he knew that he was going to make it home. Gaining his bearings, he set off, slow but resolute, not really sure if he was going in the right direction, knowing only that he must get back to the docks.

Again, God smiled: the welcome rumble of carriage-wheels brought Patrick's hand aloft and he climbed into the cab gratefully. 'The docks! An' please go as quickly as ye can or I'll miss my boat.' – And I can't miss it. I can't.

The bumping of the carriage as it sped over the cobbles jarred an exclamation from him – not for his pain but for his foolishness. Why had he ever left her? Houses whizzed by, children's laughter bringing memories, the smell of bread – please go faster! – of Grogan's porter house, of . . . yes! there it was, the smell of fish-crates, tar, the noise of the sea. We're there! I'm coming, Tommy, I'm coming!

'Sorry, sir, I did me best.' The cabbie offered profuse regrets as he and Patrick watched the smoke from the steam-packet curl above the horizon. 'But sure, ye know they're quite regular. There'll be another in no time at all.'

Patrick's eyes were still on the horizon. God, it seemed, had stopped smiling.

'There's a little place serves tea round the corner,' said the cabbie. 'Let me take ye. Sure, ye'll be half-frozen to death if ye wait here.'

'That's all right,' said Patrick wearily and sought for payment. 'I'll just go enquire when the next boat sails . . .'

This he did, then, fearing he might miss this trip too, found himself a seat on a pile of someone's luggage and stared out across the choppy waters. 'I don't know why you're so miserable,' he could hear her tell him. 'Haven't you got what you wanted – to die in Ireland?' Die? You can cut that out! he told her forcefully. Who said I was going to die – I'm going to get home if it kills me.

Still, the pain was absent. That was good. Without its interference he could sit here and think about them all to his heart's content: Tommy, with that tiny head pillowed on her breast, fluffy black hair, the smell of warm skin, round blue eyes peeping from a lace bonnet, the flash of auburn across a white pillowslip . . .

Amid the hoot of sirens another steam-packet docked. Patrick felt a wave of intense happiness: on its return it would be taking him home. Through the haze of memories he watched the thick ropes being secured to the capstans, the noisy lowering of the gangway, people awaiting loved ones. In dribs and drabs, rushes and embraces, the passengers disembarked. Portmanteaux, cases, trunks were seized and hefted onto strong shoulders, crates trussed up in a rope sling were lowered from boat to quay. Cratefuls of memories . . .

An elderly woman came slowly down the wooden ramp, stirring recognition. Instinctively, Patrick unbent his spine. The woman trod the gangway gingerly, looking about her as she gripped the rail.

But the Irishman's eyes did not see an old lady. He was looking beyond the years to the vibrant, red-haired girl in the green dress, the girl who faltered with the unexpectedness of seeing him there, then held up her face in gladness as she made straight towards him. She reached the place where he was still sitting – stood before him. 'Did you really imagine I'd sit by and let you out on your own among all these fallen women?' She gestured at a prostitute who was touting for custom.

He smiled ruefully. 'I doubt I could raise the energy, nor anything else – not that I'd dream of trying, naturally.'

She gazed at him for a while longer. Then a hand

came up to cup his cheek – a cheek that was smooth and handsome. 'You soft old chump.' She spoke gruffly, but her eyes glistened and a gentle thumb caressed the creases of pain and age from the face she loved.

Then just as abruptly she dropped her hand to cup his elbow, forcing him to rise. 'Away then, I can't be lozzocking here all day, I've got an important visitor coming . . . it's somebody I think you might want a few words with.'

And with this she linked her arm through his, her smile – that old Tommy smile – lending him all the strength he needed, to carry him home.